D1378057

READER'S DIGEST

CONDENSED BOOKS

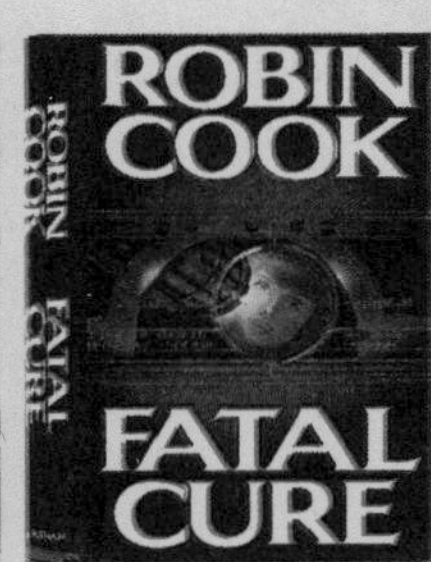

DE MARCO'S, NANTUCKET
by Carolyn Bucha

READER'S DIGEST CONDENSED BOOKS

VOLUME 4 1994

THE READER'S DIGEST ASSOCIATION, INC.
Pleasantville, New York

Reader's Digest Condensed Books are published every two to three months at Pleasantville, N.Y.

The condensations in this volume have been created by The Reader's Digest Association, Inc., by special arrangement with the publishers, authors, or holders of copyrights.

With the exception of actual personages identified as such, the characters and incidents in the fictional selections in this volume are entirely the products of the authors' imaginations and have no relation to any person or event in real life.

FIRST EDITION: Volume 214

Library of Congress Catalog Card Number: 50-12721
Printed in the United States of America

CONTENTS

FATAL CURE 7
by Robin Cook
PUBLISHED BY G. P. PUTNAM'S SONS

THE WRONG HOUSE 189
by Carol McD. Wallace
PUBLISHED BY ST. MARTIN'S PRESS

RED INK 337
by Greg Dinallo
PUBLISHED BY POCKET BOOKS
A DIVISION OF SIMON & SCHUSTER

HAVING OUR SAY 491
The Delany Sisters' First 100 Years
by Sarah and A. Elizabeth Delany
with Amy Hill Hearth
PUBLISHED BY KODANSHA AMERICA

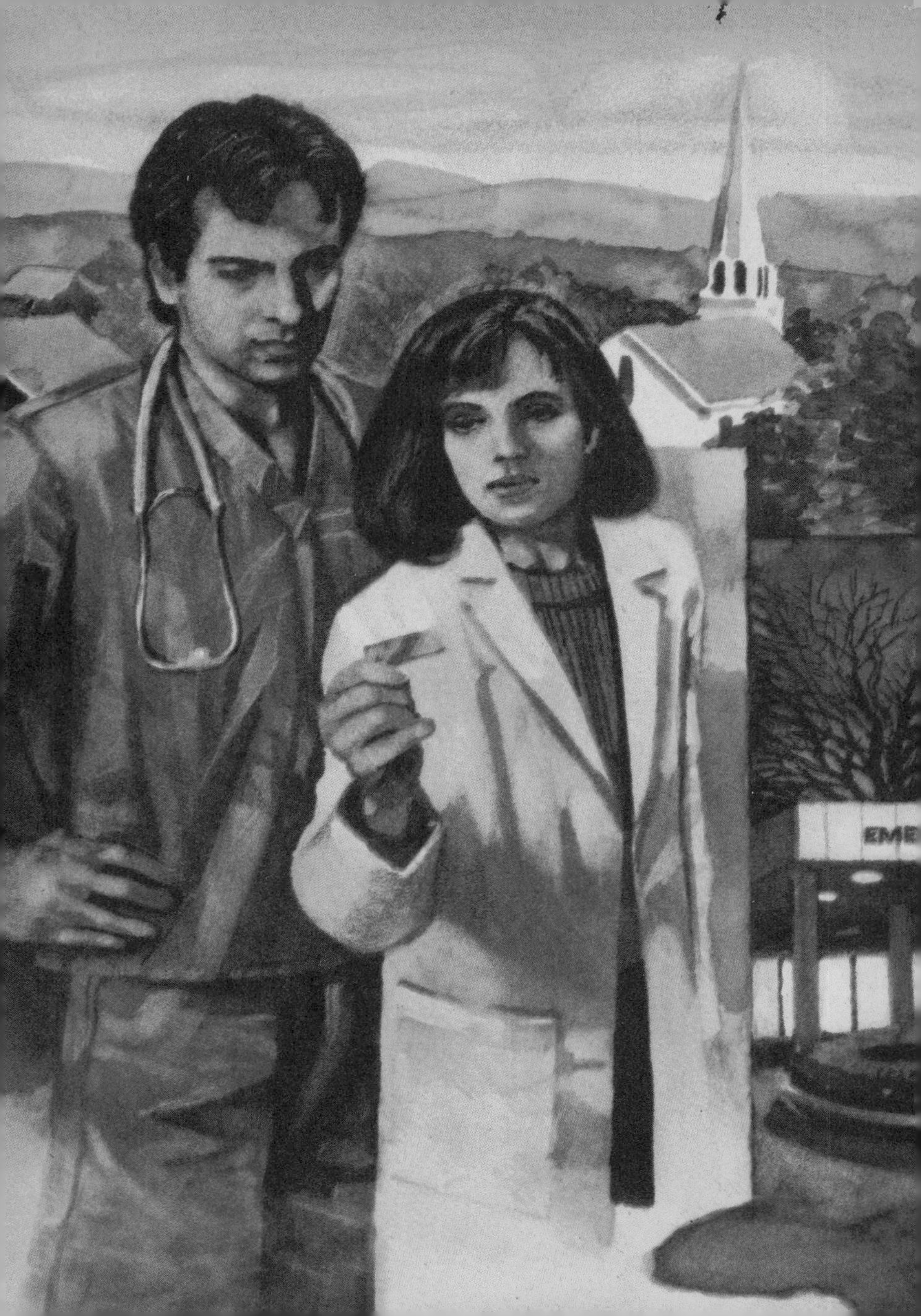

FATAL CURE

Robin Cook

A small hospital in a quiet New England town—just the place you'd expect to find good old-fashioned medical care, down-home values, and the up-to-date version of a country doctor.

It's the last place you'd expect to find what young physicians David and Angela Wilson did. They'd come for the simple lifestyle, to give their daughter, Nikki, a fighting chance against life-threatening cystic fibrosis. And to be good doctors.

But for some unexplained reason patients at Bartlet Community Hospital are dying at an alarming rate. And not from the illnesses they've been admitted for.

Prologue

FEBRUARY 17 was a fateful day for Sam Flemming.

Sam considered himself an extremely lucky person. As a broker for one of the major Wall Street firms, he'd become wealthy by the age of forty-six. Then, like a gambler who knew when to quit, Sam had taken his earnings and fled north from the concrete canyons of New York to idyllic Bartlet, Vermont. There he'd begun to do what he'd always wanted to do—paint.

Part of Sam's good fortune had always been his health; yet at half past four on February 17 something strange began to happen. Numerous water molecules within many of his cells began to split apart into two fragments: a hydrogen atom and a highly reactive, viciously destructive hydroxyl free radical.

As these molecular events transpired, Sam's cellular defenses were activated. But on this particular day those defenses could not stem the sudden, overwhelming tide. The hydroxyl free radicals began to nibble away at the core of Sam Flemming's body. Before long the cell membranes of the affected cells began to leak. Protein enzymes were cleaved and inactivated. Even many DNA molecules were assaulted, and specific genes were damaged.

In his bed at Bartlet Community Hospital, Sam remained unaware of the high-stakes molecular battle within his cells. What he did notice was an elevation of his temperature, some digestive rumblings, and the beginnings of chest congestion.

Later that afternoon Sam's surgeon, Dr. Randall Portland, noted

Sam's fever with alarm. After listening to Sam's chest, he tried to tell Sam that a touch of pneumonia was interfering with his recovery from the operation to repair his broken hip. But by then Sam had become apathetic and mildly disoriented.

The prescribed antibiotic failed to stop the developing infection. Sam never even recovered enough to appreciate the irony that he'd survived two muggings in New York City, a commuter-plane crash in Westchester County, and a bad four-vehicle accident on the New Jersey Turnpike, only to die from complications arising from a fall on a patch of ice in front of Staley's Hardware Store on Main Street, Bartlet, Vermont.

1

Thursday, March 18

STANDING before Bartlet Community Hospital's most important employees, Harold Traynor paused long enough to relish the moment. He'd just called the meeting to order. The assembled group—all heads of departments—had obediently fallen silent. All eyes were riveted on him. Traynor's dedication to his office as chairman of the hospital board was a point of pride.

"Thank you all for coming out on this snowy evening. I've called this meeting to impress upon you how seriously the hospital board is taking the unfortunate assault on nurse Prudence Huntington in the lower parking lot last week."

Patrick Swegler, the head of hospital security, avoided Traynor's accusatory glance. The attack had been the third such episode in the last year, and Swegler felt understandably responsible.

"These attacks must be stopped," Traynor went on. "Consequently, the executive board has proposed the construction of a multistoried parking facility in the lower parking lot—attached to the main building and with appropriate lighting and surveillance cameras."

Traynor gave Helen Beaton, president of the hospital, a nod. Beaton lifted a cloth from the conference table to reveal a detailed architectural model of the proposed addition.

Amid exclamations of approval Traynor stepped around the table to position himself next to the model. The conference table was often a repository for medical paraphernalia under consideration for purchase. Traynor reached over to remove a rack of funnel-shaped test tubes and scanned his audience. All eyes were glued to the model. The room was aglow with enthusiasm. Only sullen Werner Van Slyke, the head of engineering and maintenance, remained impassive.

Before Traynor could speak again, the door to the conference room burst open. Standing in the doorway was Dennis Hodges, a vigorous, if stocky, seventy-year-old with rough-hewn features and weathered skin. His dark green wool coat and red plaid hunter's cap were dusted with snow. In his hand he was clutching a sheaf of papers. There was no doubt he was angry. He also smelled of alcohol. His dark, gun-barrellike eyes strafed the gathering, then trained in on Traynor.

"I want to talk to you about my former patients, Traynor. You too, Beaton," Hodges said, throwing her a quick, disgusted look. "I don't know what kind of hospital you think you've been running here, but I can tell you I don't like it one bit."

Irritation quickly overtook Traynor's shock. "Dr. Hodges, I think it's quite apparent we're having a meeting here—"

"I don't care what the devil you people are doing," Hodges snapped. "Whatever it is, it pales in respect to what you and the board have been up to with my patients."

"Dr. Hodges," Traynor said with obvious anger. "I'll be happy to meet with you tomorrow to talk about your grievances. Now, if you will kindly leave and let us get on with our business . . ."

"I ain't waiting," Hodges insisted. "This is important."

"Hold on," Traynor said. "The fact of the matter is, we are here talking about the rape attempt that occurred last week. I'm sure you're not suggesting that one rape and two attempted rapes by a man in a ski mask are not important."

"Not as important as what's on my mind. Besides, the rape problem is obviously an in-house affair."

"Just one second!" Traynor demanded. "Are you implying that you know the identity of the rapist?"

"Let's put it this way," Hodges said. "I have my suspicions. But right now I'm interested in these patients." For emphasis he slammed the papers he'd been holding onto the table.

"All right, all right," Traynor sighed. He picked up Hodges' papers, thrust them into the man's hand, then escorted him from the room.

"We've got to talk, Harold," Hodges said once they were in the hall. "This is serious stuff."

"I'm sure it is," Traynor said, trying to sound sincere. Hodges had been the hospital administrator back when Traynor was still in grammar school. In thirty years Hodges built Bartlet Community Hospital from a small rural hospital to the sprawling institution it was when Traynor became board chairman three years before. "Look, we'll talk at lunch. If what you want to discuss concerns policy, which I assume it does, it would be best to have the vice-chairman and the chief of the professional staff there. Don't you agree?"

"I suppose," Hodges admitted reluctantly. "I still feel responsible for what goes on around here. And if it hadn't been for me, you wouldn't have been named to the board, much less elected chairman. I'm worried you've let the power go to your head."

"Oh, come on!" Traynor said. "What do you mean, power? This job is nothing but one headache after another."

"You're running a hundred-million-dollar entity, and it's the largest employer in this part of the state. That means power. I'm afraid you moneymen are forgetting the hospital's mission."

"Oh, bull!" Traynor snapped. "You old docs have to wake up to a new reality. It's not easy running a hospital in the current environment of cost cutting, managed care, and government intervention. Times have changed. Washington is mandating it."

Hodges laughed derisively. "Washington sure isn't mandating what you and your cohorts are doing."

Traynor took a deep breath. "Listen, Dennis, I've got to get back into the conference room. Go home. Relax. We'll get together tomorrow and go over whatever's on your mind. Okay?"

"I am a bit tuckered," Hodges admitted. "Tomorrow for lunch? Promise? No excuses?"

"Absolutely," Traynor said as he gave Hodges a prodding pat on the back. "At the inn at twelve sharp."

With relief Traynor watched his old mentor trudge toward the hospital lobby with his distinctive lumbering gait. Turning back toward the conference room, Traynor marveled at the man's uncanny flair for causing turmoil. Unfortunately, Hodges was going beyond being a nuisance. He was becoming a virtual albatross.

HODGES TRUDGED STRAIGHT UP Main Street in the middle of the road. Two inches of powdery new snow blanketed the town as still more flakes fell. Passing the town green with its deserted, snow-covered gazebo, he stopped to gaze at the mullioned windows of the Iron Horse Inn. It only took a moment for Hodges to decide he could use another drink. After all, now that his wife, Clara, spent more time with her family in Boston than she did with him in Bartlet, it wasn't as if she'd be waiting up for him.

Hodges stomped the snow from his rubber-soled work boots, hung his coat and hat on a peg, and went down a short hallway to the bar. The room was constructed of unfinished pine. A huge fieldstone fireplace with a roaring fire dominated one wall.

Hodges scanned the chamber. From his point of view the cast of characters assembled was unsavory. He saw Barton Sherwood, president of the Green Mountain National Bank and vice-chairman of the hospital's board of directors. Sherwood, a neighbor with whom Hodges had a bitter land dispute, was sitting in a booth with Ned Banks, the obnoxious owner of the New England Coat Hanger Company. At another table Dr. Delbert Cantor was sitting with Dr. Paul Darnell. Cantor, a radiologist, and Darnell, a pathologist, had both suffered when Hodges had arranged for the hospital to take over those departments five years earlier. They both hated his guts.

At the bar stood John MacKenzie, another local Hodges would just as soon avoid. John owned the Mobil station out near the interstate, and the last time he'd worked on Hodges' car, the problem had not been fixed. Hodges had had to drive all the way to the dealership in Rutland to get it repaired. Consequently, he'd never paid John.

For a moment Hodges teetered on the threshold of the bar, trying to decide if a drink was worth crossing paths with any of these people. Finally, ignoring everyone, he went to the far end of the bar and climbed up on an empty stool. The heat from the fire warmed his back. A tumbler appeared in front of him, and Carleton Harris, the overweight bartender, poured him a glass of Dewar's without ice.

"I think you'll want to find another seat," Carleton advised.

"Why's that?" Hodges asked.

Carleton nodded at a half-empty highball glass on the bar two stools away. "I'm afraid our fearless chief of police, Mr. Wayne Robertson, has stopped in for a snort. He's in the men's room."

"Damn, it's six of one, half a dozen of the other," Hodges murmured to himself. He decided to stay where he was.

Before he could take a drink, Hodges felt a slap on his back. "Well, if it isn't the quack!"

Swinging around, Hodges glared into the inebriated face of Wayne Robertson. Robertson was forty-two and heavyset, half muscle and half fat. He was still in uniform, gun and all.

"Wayne, you're drunk," Hodges said. "Why don't you go home and sleep it off." He turned back to the bar and sipped his drink.

"There's nothing to go home to, thanks to you."

Hodges slowly turned around again and looked at Robertson. Robertson's eyes were red, almost as red as his fat cheeks. His blond hair was clipped short in a '50s-style butch.

"Wayne," Hodges began, "we're not going over this again. Your wife, rest her soul, was not my patient. You're drunk. Go home."

"You were running the freakin' hospital," Robertson snarled. Reaching out, he grabbed Hodges' shirt at the collar and tried to lift him off the barstool.

Carleton Harris came around the bar with a swiftness that belied his bulk, and insinuated himself between the two men. "Okay, you two," he said. "Off to your own corners. We don't allow sparring at the Iron Horse."

Taking his drink, Hodges walked to the other end of the bar.

"Carleton, you shouldn't interfere," Dr. Cantor called out. "If Robertson blew old Hodges away, half the town would cheer."

"Not you too," Carleton said as he deftly mixed drinks.

There was a sudden commotion at the door. Traynor and the rest of the attendees at the hospital meeting trooped into the bar. Grabbing his whisky, Hodges followed Traynor to Sherwood's table.

"How about talking now?" Hodges suggested.

"For Pete's sake, Hodges," Traynor blurted out. "How many times do I have to tell you? We'll talk tomorrow!"

"What does he want to talk about?" Sherwood asked.

"Something about a few of his old patients," Traynor said.

"What's going on?" Dr. Cantor asked, leaving his table to join the fray.

"Dr. Hodges isn't happy with the way we are running the hospital," Traynor said. "We're to hear about it at lunch tomorrow."

"Some gratitude!" Dr. Cantor said. "Here we are donating our time pro bono to keep the hospital afloat, and what do we get in return? Nothing but criticism."

"Pro bono?" Hodges sneered. "None of you fool me. Your involvement isn't charity. Traynor, you've come to use the place to support your newly discovered grandiosity. Sherwood, your interest is purely financial, since the hospital is the bank's largest customer. And Cantor, all you're interested in is the imaging center, that joint venture I allowed in a moment of insanity."

"I'm not interested in opening this old battle," Dr. Cantor said.

"Nor am I," Hodges agreed. "But the point is, you people are concerned with financial gain, not the good of your patients."

"You're no one to talk," Traynor snapped. "You ran the hospital like a personal fiefdom. Who's been taking care of that house of yours all these years? The hospital grounds crew. Werner Van Slyke. You know that old expression, People in glass houses . . . ?"

Hodges started to say something but stopped himself. Instead, he stalked from the room in a fit of frustrated anger, grabbed his coat and hat, and plunged out into the snowy night. He headed south out of town on his long walk home, furious at himself for allowing a perk he had never asked for to derail momentarily his indignation about patient care.

Hodges turned into his unplowed driveway and took a shortcut into the lower meadow. Beyond the frog pond his empty house loomed out of the snowy darkness. Rounding the building, he entered the side door of the clapboard addition that connected the house with the barn. In the mudroom he removed his coat and hat, and hung them up. Fumbling in his coat pocket, he pulled out the papers he'd been carrying.

After placing the papers on the kitchen table, Hodges headed for the family room to pour himself a drink. Insistent knocking at his door stopped him midway across the dining room. He went back through the kitchen and into the mudroom. Using his shirtsleeve, he wiped away the condensation on one of the door's panes of glass. He could just make out the figure outside.

"What now?" Hodges muttered as he unlatched the door. He pulled it wide open and said, "Considering everything, it's a bit strange for you to come visiting, especially at this hour."

Hodges stared at his visitor, who said nothing.

"Oh, what the heck," Hodges said with a shrug. "Whatever you want, come in." He let go of the door and headed toward the kitchen. When he reached the single step up to the kitchen level, he started to turn to make sure the door was closed tight against the weather. Out of the corner of his eye he saw something speeding toward his head. By reflex, he ducked.

A flat metal rod glanced off the side of his head, but not before cutting deeply into his scalp. The force of the blow carried the rod to the top of his shoulder, where it fractured his collarbone, and sent him hurtling into the kitchen.

Hodges collided with the kitchen table. His hands clutched the edges, keeping him on his feet. Blood spurted in tiny pulsating jets from the open scalp wound onto his papers. Hodges turned in time to see his attacker closing in on him with arm raised. In a gloved hand he clutched a rod that looked like a short, flat crowbar.

As the weapon started down for a second blow, Hodges reached up and grabbed the exposed forearm. Still, the metal cut into Hodges' scalp. Fresh blood squirted from severed arteries. Hodges desperately dug his fingernails into the assailant's arm. For a few moments the two figures struggled against each other, smashing into walls, upsetting chairs, and breaking dishes. Blood spattered indiscriminately. The attacker pulled free. Once again the steel rod rose up before smashing down onto Hodges' raised forearm. Bones snapped like twigs under the impact.

Again the metal bar was raised above the now hapless Hodges and brought down hard. This time its arc was unhindered, and the weapon impacted directly onto the top of Hodges' unprotected head, crushing his skull and driving deeply into his brain.

2

Saturday, April 24

"WE'RE coming to a river up ahead," David Wilson said to his daughter, Nikki, sitting in the passenger seat next to him. "Do you know what its name is?"

Nikki pushed a wisp of honey hair to the side. "The only rivers I know," she said, "are the Mississippi, the Nile, and the Amazon.

Since none of them are here in New England, I have to say I don't know."

Neither David nor his wife, Angela, could suppress a giggle. Both were thinking the same thought, and they had spoken of it often: Nikki frequently sounded more mature than expected for her chronological age of eight. They realized their daughter was growing up faster than she might otherwise have because of her health problems.

"Come on, you guys," Nikki protested. "But I don't care if you laugh or not, because I can find the name of the river myself." She took a map from the glove compartment.

"We're on Highway 89," David said.

"I know," Nikki said with annoyance. "I don't want any help."

She twisted the map on its side so she could read the lettering. "Here it is," she said triumphantly. "It's the Connecticut River."

"Right you are," David said. "And it forms the boundary between what and what?"

"It separates Vermont from New Hampshire."

"Right again," David said. "And here it is."

They were all quiet as their blue, eleven-year-old Volvo sped over the span. At the other side of the bridge the highway gradually swung back toward the northwest. An hour and fifteen minutes later they passed a sign reading WELCOME TO BARTLET.

David let up on the accelerator, and the car slowed. They were on a wide avenue aptly called Main Street. It was lined with large oaks. Behind the trees were white clapboard homes. The architecture was a potpourri of colonial and Victorian.

"So far it looks storybookish," Angela said.

"Some of these New England towns look like they belong in Disney World," David said.

After a short drive, the homes gave way to commercial and civic buildings, which were constructed mostly of brick. Engraved stone plaques announced late-nineteenth-century construction dates. At the heart of the town they discovered a number of imposing gray granite buildings, especially the Green Mountain National Bank with its crenellated clock tower.

They came to the town green. Crocuses, hyacinths, and daffodils dotted the park and circled the gingerbread central gazebo.

"We've got some time before our interviews," Angela said. "Why don't we drive around a little more, then have lunch?"

"Sounds good to me." David continued along Main Street. They passed the library, which was constructed of gray granite but looked like an Italian villa. Just beyond it was the elementary school, an appealing turn-of-the-century, three-story brick building.

"Would that be where I'd go to school if we come here to live?" Nikki asked.

"Probably," David said.

"It's pretty," Nikki said noncommittally.

David parked, and they got out and strolled up Main Street.

"It's amazing, isn't it: no litter, no graffiti, and no homeless people," Angela said. "It's like a different country."

David stopped outside of Staley's Hardware Store. "I'm going to run in and ask where we should eat."

Angela nodded. She and Nikki were looking into the window of the neighboring shoe store.

David was back in a flash. "The word is that the diner down the street is best for a quick lunch."

"Well, that settles that," Angela said.

All three had hamburgers the old-fashioned way—with toasted buns, raw onion, and lots of ketchup.

On the way back to the car they passed a woman with a golden retriever puppy on a leash. "Oh, how cute!" Nikki exclaimed. She walked sideways to keep the puppy in sight. "If we come to live here, may I have a dog?"

David and Angela exchanged glances. Both were touched. Nikki's modest request after all the medical problems she'd been through melted their hearts.

"Of course you may have a dog," Angela said.

"Then I want to come here," Nikki said with conviction. "Can we?"

Angela wrestled with her answer. She didn't know what to say. "Whether we come here or not is a difficult decision," she said finally. "There are many things we have to consider."

"Like what?" Nikki asked.

"Like whether they want me and your father," Angela said, relieved to have come up with a simple explanation, as the three got back in the car.

Bartlet Community Hospital was larger and more imposing than David or Angela had expected, even though they knew it was a referral center for a significant portion of the state.

Despite a sign that clearly said PARKING IN THE REAR, David pulled to the curb in the turnout before the front entrance. "This is truly beautiful," he said. "I never thought I would say that about a hospital."

"What a view," Angela said.

The hospital was midway up a hill just north of the town. It faced south, and its façade was bathed in bright sunlight. Just below them, at the base of the hill, they could see the whole town. The Methodist church's steeple was especially prominent. In the distance the Green Mountains provided a scalloped border to the horizon.

Angela tapped David's arm. "We'd better get inside," she said. "My interview is in ten minutes."

David drove around to the back of the hospital. They found a visitor slot next to the rear entrance in the lower parking lot.

Appropriately placed signs made finding the administrative offices easy, and a secretary directed them to the medical director's office. Angela knocked on the jamb of the open door. Michael Caldwell looked up from his desk, then rose to greet her.

"Come in!" Caldwell said with enthusiasm. "Please. All of you." He quickly got more chairs. After brief introductions he was back behind his desk, with Angela's folder in front of him.

"I've been over your application, and I have to tell you I am impressed," he said. "From your letters of recommendation I have the feeling that the department of pathology at the Boston City Hospital thinks you have been one of their brightest residents."

Angela smiled. "I've tried to do my best."

"We would like to have you here at Bartlet Community Hospital. It's as simple as that. But perhaps you have questions for me."

"David has also applied for a job in Bartlet," Angela said. "It's with one of the major health maintenance organizations in the area—Comprehensive Medical Vermont."

"CMV," Caldwell said. "It's the only HMO in the area."

"I indicated in my letter that my availability is contingent on his acceptance," Angela said. "And vice versa."

"I took the liberty of contacting them," Caldwell said. "CMV's office is right here in our professional building. Of course I cannot speak for them officially, but it is my understanding there is no problem whatsoever."

"I'm to meet with Mr. Kelley, their regional manager, as soon as we're through here," David said.

"Perfect," Caldwell said. "So, Dr. Wilson, the hospital would like to offer you a position as associate pathologist. Your first year's compensation will be eighty-two thousand dollars."

Angela looked David's way. Eighty-two thousand dollars sounded like a fortune after so many years of burdensome debt and meager income. David flashed her a conspiratorial smile.

"I also have some information in response to your query letter," Caldwell said. He hesitated, then added, "Perhaps this is something we should talk about privately."

"It's not necessary," Angela said. "I assume you are referring to Nikki's cystic fibrosis. She's an active participant in her care, so there are no secrets."

"Very well," Caldwell said. "I found out that there is a patient with that condition here in Bartlet—Caroline Helmsford. She's nine years old. I've arranged for you to meet her doctor, Dr. Bertrand Pilsner. He's one of CMV's pediatricians. I confess I didn't read up on the condition when I made the inquiries. Perhaps there is something I should know in order to be of more assistance."

Angela looked at Nikki. "Why don't you explain to Mr. Caldwell what cystic fibrosis is."

"Cystic fibrosis is an inherited condition," Nikki said in a serious and practiced tone. "The main problem is with the respiratory system. The mucus in the lungs is thicker than in the lungs of normal people. The lungs have difficulty clearing the thicker mucus, which leads to congestion and infection. Chronic bronchitis and pneumonia are the big worries."

"Very interesting," Caldwell said. "Maybe you should be a doctor when you grow up."

"I intend to study respiratory medicine," Nikki said.

Caldwell got up and gestured toward the door. "How about if I take you doctors and doctor-to-be over to the medical office building to meet Dr. Pilsner."

It was only a short walk from the hospital's old central building to the newer professional building. Dr. Pilsner was in the middle of his afternoon office hours but graciously took time to meet the Wilsons. His thick white beard made him look a bit like Kriss Kringle. "We've got a great respiratory therapist here," he told them. "And the hospital is well equipped for respiratory care. On top of that, Bartlet—with its low pollution and clean, crisp air—would be a healthy environment for your daughter."

Caldwell escorted the Wilsons to CMV's regional headquarters. The three of them barely had time to pick up magazines in the waiting area before Charles Kelley emerged from his office.

A big man who towered eight inches over David, Kelley was dressed in a meticulously tailored suit. His face was tan, and his sandy-colored hair had pure blond streaks. His manner was more like a high-powered salesman than a health-care administrator.

Like Caldwell, Kelley invited the whole Wilson family into his office. He was also equally complimentary.

"Frankly, David," Kelley said, "we need you as part of our team. We're pleased that you've taken an internal-medicine residency, especially at a place like the Boston City Hospital. You'll be an enormous addition to our primary-care–gatekeeper crew. Your compensation will be forty-one thousand the first year."

David nodded. He knew he'd be in for some teasing from Angela, even though they'd known all along that her earnings would be significantly larger than his. On the other hand, they hadn't expected hers would be double his.

"CMV is expanding rapidly in this area of Vermont, especially in Bartlet itself," Kelley boasted. "We've signed up the coat hanger mill, the college, the computer software company, as well as all the state and municipal employees. Why don't I show you your prospective office. It will give you a better feeling for our operation and what it will be like working here."

To David's mind the waiting room to his office was dreamlike. The view south over the Green Mountains was so picture-perfect, it looked like a painting.

"You'll share this suite with Dr. Randall Portland, an orthopedic surgeon," Kelley explained. "Let me see if he's available to say hello."

Kelley walked over and tapped on what David thought was a mirror. It slid open. Behind it was a receptionist. Kelley spoke to her before the mirrored partition slid closed.

"He'll be out in a second," Kelley said, rejoining the Wilsons. He then explained the layout of the office. Opening a door on the west side of the waiting room, he gave them a tour of empty, newly redecorated examining rooms. He also took them into the room that would be David's private office. It had the same fabulous view as the waiting room.

"Hello, everybody," a voice called out. The Wilsons turned from gaping out the window to see a youthful but strained-appearing man stride into the room. It was Dr. Randall Portland. Kelley introduced them all, even Nikki, who shook hands.

"Call me Randy," Dr. Portland said as he shook David's hand. "I hope you come to Bartlet."

David smiled. He sensed the man was sizing him up.

"Well, it's nice to meet you folks. I'm afraid I have to get back to work," Randy said.

"He's a busy man," Kelley said after Dr. Portland left. "Well, what do you say?"

"I'd say we're impressed," David said. He looked at Angela.

"We'll have to give it all a lot of thought," Angela said.

After leaving Charles Kelley, the Wilsons returned to Caldwell's office. He insisted on taking David and Angela on a quick tour of the hospital. Nikki was left in the hospital day-care center. The first stop was the pathology laboratory, where Angela would be doing most of her work. It was truly state-of-the-art. Caldwell took them in to meet the department chairman, Dr. Benjamin Wadley, a distinguished-looking silver-haired gentleman in his fifties, who reminded Angela of her father.

Next on the tour was the emergency room, followed by the imaging center. David was particularly impressed with the new MRI machine. Last they toured the new radiotherapy building, which boasted one of the newest linear accelerators.

"I don't know what to say," David admitted when the tour was over.

"We'd heard the hospital was well equipped," Angela said, "but this is far better than we'd imagined."

"We're understandably proud of it," Caldwell said as he led them back into his office. "We had to upgrade significantly to land the CMV contract. We were competing with the Valley Hospital and the Mary Sackler Hospital for survival. Luckily, we won."

"But all this equipment costs a fortune," David said.

"That's an understatement," Caldwell agreed. "It's not easy running a hospital in this era of government-mandated competition. Revenues are down; costs are going up. It's hard just to stay in business." He handed David a manila envelope. "Here's a packet of information about the hospital. Maybe it will help convince you to come up here and accept our job offers."

"What about housing?" Angela asked as an afterthought.

"I'm glad you asked," Caldwell said. "Go down to the Green Mountain National Bank to see Barton Sherwood, vice-chairman of the hospital board. He's also president of the bank. He'll give you an idea how much the town supports the hospital."

After rescuing a reluctant Nikki from the day-care center, where she'd been enjoying herself, the Wilsons drove back to the town green and walked to the bank. Typical of everyone who'd received them in Bartlet, Barton Sherwood saw them immediately.

"Your job applications were favorably discussed at the last executive board meeting," Barton Sherwood told them as he leaned back in his chair and hooked his thumbs in his vest pockets. He was a slight man, nearing sixty, with thinning hair and a pencil-line mustache. "To encourage you to join the Bartlet family, I want you to know that Green Mountain National Bank is prepared to offer both first and second mortgages so that you'll be able to buy a house."

David and Angela were stunned. Never in their wildest imaginations had they thought they would ever be able to buy a house the first year out of their residencies. They had very little cash and a mountain of tuition debt—over a hundred and fifty thousand dollars. Sherwood went on to give them the specifics, but neither of them could focus on the details. It wasn't until they were back in their car that they dared to speak.

"I can't believe this," David said.

"It's almost too good to be true," Angela agreed.

"Does this mean we're coming to Bartlet?" Nikki asked.

"We'll see," Angela said.

Since David had driven up from Boston, Angela offered to drive home. As she drove, David perused Caldwell's information packet.

"This is interesting," David said. "There's a clip from the local paper about the signing of the contract between the hospital and CMV. It says the hospital board finally agreed to CMV's demand to provide hospitalization for an unspecified monthly capitation fee."

"What's capitation?" Nikki asked.

David swung around. "Say that CMV pays Bartlet Hospital a thousand dollars each month for each person in the health plan. Then if anybody has to be hospitalized during the month for whatever reason, CMV doesn't have to pay any more. So if no one gets sick for the month, the hospital makes out like a bandit. But what if everybody gets sick and has to go to the hospital? What do you think will happen then?"

"If everybody got sick, the hospital would go broke," Nikki said.

David smiled with satisfaction and gave Angela a poke in the ribs. "That's my daughter," he said triumphantly.

3

Monday, May 3

HAROLD Traynor fingered the mahogany-and-inlaid-gold gavel he'd bought for himself at Shreve Crump & Low in Boston. In front of him was the lectern that he had had built for the Bartlet Community Hospital conference room. The model of the proposed parking garage dominated the conference table. He checked his watch. It was exactly six p.m. Striking the gavel sharply, he called out, "I would like herewith to call to order the executive committee of the Bartlet Community Hospital." Traynor was dressed in his best pin-striped suit. On his feet were freshly polished elevator shoes. He was only five feet seven and felt cheated as far as stature was concerned. His dark receding hair was carefully combed over his apical bald spot.

Traynor spent a great deal of time and effort preparing for hospital board meetings. That day he'd gone directly home to shower and change clothes after a trip to Montpelier, without stopping at his office. Harold Traynor was an attorney specializing in estate planning and tax work. He also had business interests in a number of local commercial ventures.

Seated before him were Barton Sherwood, vice-chairman; Helen Beaton, president and C.E.O. of the hospital; Michael Caldwell, vice president and medical director of the hospital; Richard Arnsworth, treasurer; Clyde Robeson, secretary; and Dr. Delbert Cantor, current chief of staff.

As soon as the minutes of the last meeting had been approved, Traynor cleared his throat in preparation for reading his scrupulously prepared monthly chairman's report. He looked at each member of his executive committee in turn, making sure they were all attentive.

"We face significant challenges here at the Bartlet Community Hospital," Traynor began. "We're going to have to work even harder than we have in the past if the hospital is to survive. However, even in these dark times there is occasional light. As some of you have undoubtedly heard, an esteemed client of mine, Sam Flemming, passed away in February of pneumonia coming on after hip surgery. While I very much regret Mr. Flemming's untimely passing, I am pleased to announce officially that Mr. Flemming had generously designated the hospital as the sole beneficiary of a three-million-dollar insurance policy."

A murmur of approval spread through the people present.

Traynor lifted his hand for silence. "This charitable gesture couldn't have come at a better time. It will pull us out of the red and push us into the black, although not for long. The bad news for the month is that our sinking fund for our major bond issues is short of its projected goals."

Traynor looked directly at Sherwood, whose mustache twitched nervously. Then he went on. "The problem is to keep any outside examiners from getting wind of the shortfall. We can't afford to have our bond rating change. Consequently, we will be forced to put off floating a bond issue for the parking garage until the sinking fund is restored. As a temporary measure I have instructed our C.E.O., Helen Beaton, to have lighting installed in the parking lot."

Traynor glanced around the room. "My last item concerns Dr. Dennis Hodges," he said. "As you all know, Dr. Hodges disappeared last March. No clues as to his whereabouts have surfaced. If Dr. Hodges met with foul play, there has been no evidence of it, although Chief of Police Robertson allowed that the longer Dr.

Hodges is missing, the more likely it is that he is no longer living. I wanted the executive committee to know that Dr. Hodges' estranged wife, Mrs. Hodges, has decided to sell her home and to sever her connections with Bartlet. I only raise this matter now because I think that in the near future the board might wish to erect a memorial befitting Dr. Hodges' considerable contributions to Bartlet Community Hospital."

Having finished, Traynor gathered up his notes and formally turned the meeting over to Helen Beaton so that she could give her monthly president's report. Beaton pushed her chair back from the table. She was in her mid-thirties with reddish brown hair cut short. Her face was wide, not unlike Traynor's. She wore a businesslike mauve suit accented with a silk scarf.

"I've spoken to several civic groups this month," she said. "My topic on each occasion was the financial plight of the hospital. I made it very clear that if the hospital were to close, every business and every merchant would be hurt. After all, the hospital is the largest employer in this part of the state."

Beaton paused as she consulted her notes. "Now for the bad news," she said, referring to several large graphs illustrating the information she was about to relay. She held the graphs at chest height as she spoke. "Admissions for April were twelve percent over forecast. Our daily census was up eight percent over March, and our average length of stay was up six percent. Obviously, these are serious trends."

"Health care is becoming a nightmare," Sherwood said.

"Tell that to your representative in Washington," Beaton said.

"Let's not digress," Traynor said.

Beaton continued. "Two areas of underutilization are the neonatal intensive care unit and the linear accelerator. I discussed this situation with CMV, since our fixed costs for maintaining these units are so high."

"That reminds me," Traynor said. "What is the status of the old cobalt-sixty machine that the linear accelerator replaced?"

"The machine is being sold to a government hospital in Paraguay," Beaton answered. "We're waiting for the funds."

"I don't want to get involved in any bureaucratic snafu with that machine," Traynor warned.

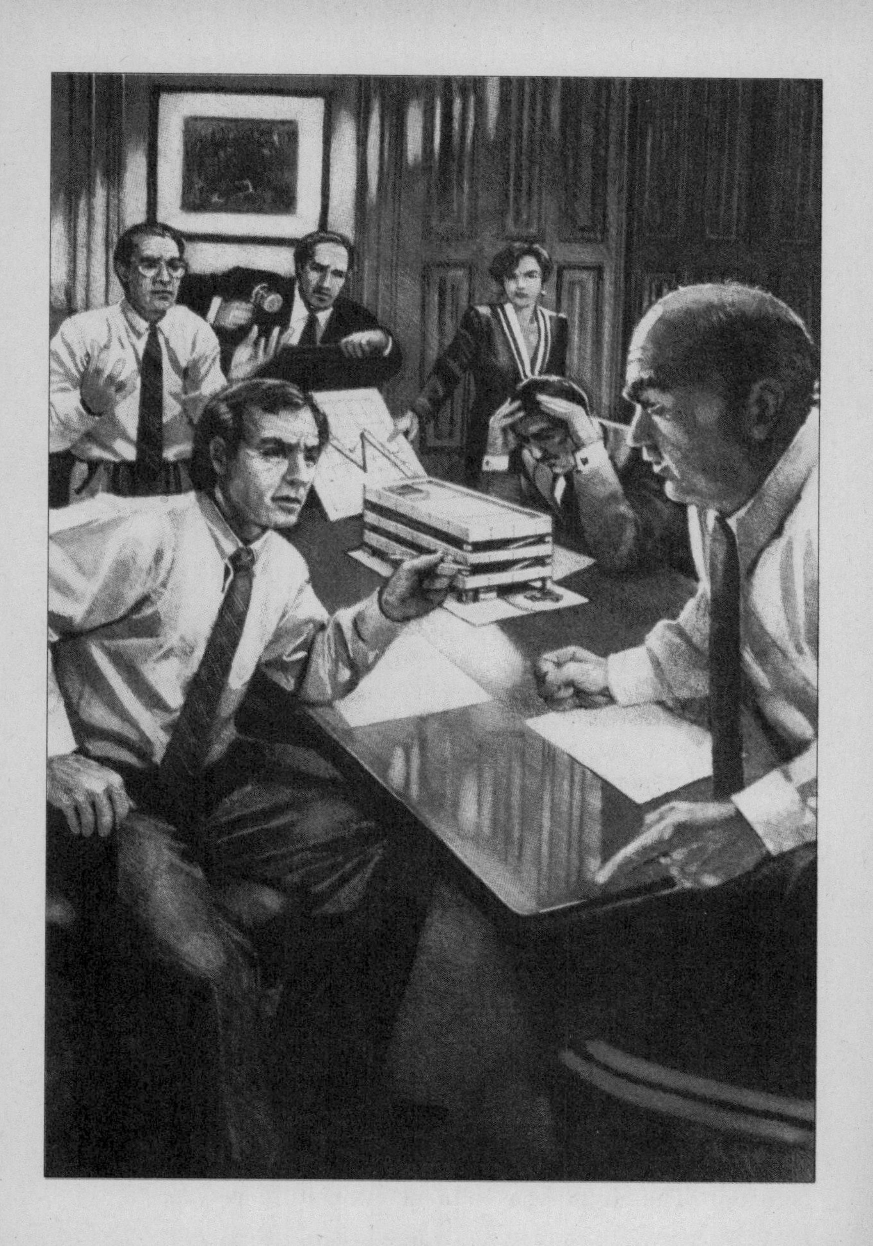

Beaton nodded. "I'm afraid I have some additional bad news. Last night, just before midnight, there was another attempted assault in the parking lot."

"Why wasn't I informed about this?" Traynor cried.

"I tried to call you this morning as soon as I heard," Beaton explained, "but you weren't in. I left a message for you to call back, but you never did."

"I was in Montpelier all day," Traynor said. "Beaton, this has to stop. It's a P.R. nightmare. I hate to imagine what CMV thinks."

"We need that garage," Beaton said.

"The garage has to wait until we can float a bond issue," Traynor said. "I want that lighting done quickly. Understand?"

"I've talked to Werner Van Slyke," Beaton said. "I'll follow up on it so that it's done ASAP."

Traynor sat down heavily and blew through pursed lips. He picked up the current meeting's agenda, glanced at it, then called Richard Arnsworth, the treasurer, to give his report.

Arnsworth got to his feet. He was a bespectacled, precise accountant type who referred everyone to the balance sheet each had received in his information packet that morning. "What's immediately obvious," Arnsworth said, "is that monthly expenses still significantly outstrip the monthly capitation payments from CMV. As a result, the hospital's cash position has deteriorated. Consequently, I recommend switching from one hundred and eighty days' investing to thirty days'."

"It's already been taken care of," Sherwood announced.

When Arnsworth took his seat, Traynor asked for a motion to approve the treasurer's report. It was immediately seconded, and carried with no opposition.

Dr. Cantor gave his medical staff report; then Traynor asked if there was any new business. When no one moved, he asked for a motion to adjourn. Dr. Cantor so moved. After a resounding chorus of yeas, Traynor struck the gavel and ended the meeting.

Traynor and Beaton slowly gathered up their papers. Everyone else trooped out of the room, heading for the Iron Horse Inn.

"I thought it was a good meeting," Traynor said.

"I agree," Beaton said. "But I'm worried about the financial situation. The hospital has to break even, at the very least."

"Do you think there's any chance we could renegotiate the contract with CMV?"

Beaton laughed scornfully. "Not a chance."

"I don't know what else to do," Traynor said. "We're losing money despite our drastic-utilization-measures plan."

"Caldwell and I have come up with an idea that might help," Beaton said. "Like all HMOs when they are dealing with their own hospitals, CMV has an economic incentive for their doctors to limit hospitalization—something the public has no idea about."

"You mean like actual payments to the doctors?"

"Exactly. It's a bonus bribe. The more each doctor cuts his hospitalization rates, the bigger the bonus. It's very effective. Caldwell and I believe we can fashion a similar economic incentive here."

"Sounds great," Traynor said with enthusiasm. "Let's pursue it."

"I'll arrange a meeting with Charles Kelley to discuss it," Beaton said as she got her coat.

They passed out of the hospital into the lower parking area. They arrived at their cars, which were parked side by side. Traynor glanced around in the darkness, up toward the copse of trees that separated the lower lot from the upper.

"We need those lights," he said. "It's like asking for trouble."

"I'll get right on it," Beaton promised.

"What a pain," Traynor said. "Now we've got to worry about a rapist. What are the details about last night's episode?"

"This time it wasn't a nurse," Beaton said. "It was one of the volunteers—Marjorie Kleber, the teacher."

"How about the rapist?"

"Same description: about six feet, wearing a ski mask. Ms. Kleber said he had handcuffs."

"How'd she get away?" Traynor asked.

"It was lucky," Beaton said. "The night watchman just happened along while making his rounds."

"I wonder if Hodges really did know the rapist's identity."

"Do you think his disappearance could have had anything to do with his suspicions?" Beaton asked.

Traynor shrugged. "I hadn't thought of that. I suppose it's possible. He wasn't one to keep his opinion to himself. See you down at the Iron Horse."

4

Thursday, May 20

ANGELA got bogged down in rush-hour Boston traffic, and when she finally reached the school, Nikki was sitting forlornly on the front steps. It was not a pretty area. The school was awash with graffiti and surrounded by a sea of concrete. Except for some sixth graders shooting baskets beyond a high chain-link fence, there were no grammar school–age children in sight. Listless teenagers in ridiculously oversized clothing loitered alongside the building, and across the street was the cardboard shanty of a homeless person.

"I'm sorry I was late," Angela said as Nikki climbed into the car and plugged in her seat belt.

"It's all right," Nikki said, "but I was a little scared. There was a big problem in school. The police were here and everything."

"What happened?"

"One of the sixth-grade boys had a gun in the playground," Nikki said calmly. "He shot it and got arrested. Nobody was hurt."

"Why did he have a gun?"

"He's been selling drugs."

"I see," Angela said, trying to maintain her composure. "How did you hear about this?"

"I was there," Nikki said, suppressing a yawn.

Angela's grip on the steering wheel involuntarily tightened. Public school had been David's idea. Up until this episode Angela had been reasonably satisfied. But now she was appalled. It was frightening to realize that Nikki viewed this as an ordinary event.

AFTER putting groceries in the refrigerator, Angela and Nikki attended to Nikki's respiratory physiotherapy. The routine started with Angela's listening with her stethoscope to make sure Nikki didn't need a bronchodilating drug. Then, by using a large beanbag chair, Nikki would assume nine different positions that utilized gravity to help drain specific areas of her lungs. While Nikki held each position, Angela tapped sharply over the lung area with a cupped hand. In twenty minutes they were finished.

A half hour later David came home. He was exhausted, having

been up the entire previous night with a number of sick patients.

"What a day!" he said, stepping into the tiny kitchen and pulling a beer out of the refrigerator. "We had two AIDS patients come in through the ER. On top of that, there were two cardiac arrests."

"If you're looking for sympathy, you're talking to the wrong person," Angela said as she put pasta on to boil. "You are also in my way. My day has been stressful too. I had to leave unfinished work in order to pick Nikki up from school. And on top of that, she has some disturbing news."

David moved out of the kitchen and squeezed into one of the dining-area chairs. Nikki told him about her day.

"Are you still as supportive of public school when you hear about guns and drugs in the sixth grade?" Angela asked.

"Public schools have to be supported," David said. "I went to public school."

"Times have changed," Angela snapped. "I'm not willing to be idealistic when it comes to my daughter's safety."

Once dinner was ready, they ate their spaghetti and salads in strained silence. Angela sighed loudly several times. She was on the verge of tears. David fumed. After working as hard as he had for thirty-six hours, he did not think he deserved this kind of treatment.

Angela suddenly scraped back her chair, picked up her dish, and dropped it into the sink. It broke. Both David and Nikki jumped.

"Angela," David said. "You're being overly emotional. Let's talk about picking Nikki up. There has to be another solution."

Angela wiped a few wayward tears from her eyes. She resisted the temptation to lash back at David and tell him that his conception of himself as the rational, agreeable partner was hardly reality.

"You know," she said, "the real problem is that we have been avoiding making a decision about what to do come July first. It's less than a month and a half away."

"Okay," David said with resignation. "Let me get my lists." He started to get up. Angela restrained him.

"We hardly need your lists. We have three choices, now that New York's responded: we can go there, and I'll start a fellowship in forensics and you in respiratory medicine; we can stay here in Boston, where I'll do forensics and you'll go to the Harvard School of Public Health; or we can go to Bartlet."

David tried to think. He was numb from fatigue. "It's a little scary leaving academia," he said finally.

"I couldn't agree more," Angela said. "But quality of life has to become an issue at some point. The reality is that if we stay here in Boston, we'll probably have to stay in this apartment. We have too much debt to do anything else."

"It would be about the same in New York," David said.

"I agree," Angela said. "Another thing that we have to consider is Nikki's condition. There's a lot of pollution here and in New York. And I'm getting pretty tired of all the crime here in the city."

"Are you saying you want to go to Bartlet?" David asked.

"No," Angela said. "But I have to admit, when I hear about guns and drugs in the sixth grade, Bartlet sounds better and better."

"I wonder if it's as heavenly as we remember," David asked.

"There's one way to find out," Angela said.

"Let's go back!" Nikki cried.

"Today's Thursday," David said. "How about Saturday?"

"Sounds good to me," Angela said.

"Yippee!" Nikki said.

5

Friday, May 21

TRAYNOR was on his way through the outer office en route to the Iron Horse for lunch when his secretary, Collette, called him back to take a call from an important client, Tom Baringer.

"You'll never guess where I am," Tom said. "In the emergency room, waiting for Dr. Portland to put me back together."

"What happened?" Traynor asked.

"Something stupid. I was cleaning leaves out of my gutters when the ladder fell over. I broke my hip. Obviously, I won't make the meeting we had scheduled for this afternoon."

"Of course. Was there something you wanted to discuss?"

"It can wait," Tom said. "But listen, how about giving the powers that be here a call. I figure I deserve some V.I.P. attention."

"You got it," Traynor said. "I'll see to it personally. I'm just on my way out to have lunch with Helen Beaton, the hospital's C.E.O."

Traynor was first to arrive for his luncheon meeting. After ordering a dry martini, he scanned the beam-ceilinged room. As usual of late, he'd been given the best table in the house, one in a cozy bay with a particularly dramatic view of the Roaring River, which raced past the rear of the inn.

Helen Beaton and Barton Sherwood arrived together. "Sorry we're late," Sherwood said, pulling back Beaton's chair.

Beaton and Sherwood were served their usual drinks, and they all ordered their meals. As soon as the waiter left them, Beaton spoke. "I have some good news. I met with Charles Kelley this morning, and he has no problem with our idea of instituting a bonus program for the CMV doctors. His only concern is whether it would cost CMV anything, which it won't."

"Wonderful," Traynor said.

"Now all we need is the start-up capital," Beaton said. "So I met with Barton, and I think we have it solved. We thought a vacation in the Bahamas could function as a grand prize. It could be awarded to the doctor with the lowest hospitalization percentage for the year."

"That's perfect," Traynor said. "This whole idea is sounding better and better."

"We'd better get it up and running ASAP," Beaton said. "So far the May figures are worse than April's. Admissions are higher and money loss correspondingly greater."

"It's just one crisis after another," Traynor complained.

"I have some good news," Sherwood said. "The hospital sinking fund is back to its projected level with the infusion of the cash from the insurance bequest. Do you want me to go ahead with the bond issue for the parking garage?"

"No," Traynor answered. "Unfortunately, we can't. We have to go back to the board of selectmen for another vote. Their approval was contingent on starting the project immediately."

After the coffee had been served, Traynor remembered the call from Tom Baringer. He relayed the information on to Beaton.

"I'm already aware of Mr. Baringer's admission," Beaton said. "Caldwell's taking care to make sure that he gets proper V.I.P. treatment."

After they had finished their lunch, they walked out into the bright late spring sunshine.

"What's the status on lighting the parking lots?" Traynor asked.

"It's all done," Beaton said. "We decided to restrict the lighting to the lower lot. The upper is used only during the day, and by doing only the lower, we saved a considerable amount of money."

"Sounds reasonable," Traynor said.

After exchanging farewells and good wishes for the weekend, the three returned to their respective jobs.

Back at the hospital, Beaton went directly to room 204, where she expected to find Tom Baringer. She intended to make sure he was comfortable. He wasn't there. Instead, Beaton was surprised to discover a patient by the name of Alice Nottingham. Beaton descended to the first floor and marched into Caldwell's office.

"Where's Baringer?" she asked curtly.

"Room 204," Caldwell said.

"Unless Mr. Baringer has had a sex change operation and is going by the name of Alice, he's not in 204."

Caldwell quickly got to his feet. "Something's gone wrong." He pushed past Beaton, hurried across the hall to Janice Sperling in admissions, and asked what had happened to Tom Baringer.

"I put him in 209," Janice said.

"I told you to put him in 204," Caldwell said.

"I know," Janice admitted. "But since we talked, 209 came available. It's a larger room. You said Mr. Baringer was a special patient. I thought he'd like 209 better."

"Room 204 has a better view, plus it has the new orthopedic bed," Caldwell said. "The man has a broken hip. Either change rooms or change beds."

6

Saturday, May 22

DAVID had set the alarm for five forty-five as if it were a normal workday. By six fifteen he was on his way to the hospital. By nine he was finished with his rounds and on his way home.

"Okay, you guys," he called as he entered the apartment. "Let's get this show on the road."

Nikki appeared in her doorway. "That's not fair, Daddy. We've been waiting for you."

"Just kidding." David gave Nikki a playful tickle.

Soon they were off. Before long, urban sprawl gave way to tree-dotted suburbia, followed by long stretches of forest. The farther north they went, the prettier the surroundings became. When they reached Bartlet, David slowed to a crawl. Like eager tourists they drank in the sights.

"It's even more picturesque than I remembered," Angela said.

"There's that same puppy!" Nikki cried. She pointed across the street. "Can we stop?"

David pulled into an empty parking slot. "You're right," he said. "I recognize the lady."

Nikki opened the car door and got out.

"Just a second," Angela called. She jumped out of the car and took Nikki's hand to cross the street. David followed.

"Hello," the woman said when Nikki approached. The puppy caught sight of Nikki and strained at its leash. As Nikki bent down, the dog licked her face. Nikki laughed with surprise.

"I don't know if you'd be interested, but Mr. Staley's retriever just had puppies a few weeks ago," the woman said. "They're right over in the hardware store across the street."

"Can we go see them?" Nikki pleaded.

"Why not," David said. He thanked the woman.

Recrossing the street, the Wilsons entered the hardware store. Near the front, in a makeshift playpen, was Mr. Staley's dog, Molly, suckling five floppy puppies. Mr. Staley stood nearby.

"They're adorable," Nikki cried. "Can I pet them?"

"Sure, you can," Mr. Staley said. "In fact, they're for sale." Nikki reached into the pen and gently stroked one of the puppies. "Pick him up if you like. He's the brute of the litter."

Nikki scooped the puppy up in her arms. The tiny dog snuggled against her cheek and licked her nose. "I love him," she said. "I wish we could get him. Can we? I'll take care of him."

David felt an unexpected surge of tears that he had to forcibly suppress. He looked at Angela. Their eyes met in a moment of complete understanding. Considering all that Nikki had been through with her cystic fibrosis, it wasn't much to ask for.

"Good-bye, crime and pollution," David said. He looked down at Nikki. "Okay. You can have the dog. We're moving to Bartlet."

Nikki's face lit up. She hugged the puppy to her chest as it licked her face. David turned to Mr. Staley and settled on a price.

"I figure they will be ready to leave the mother in four weeks or so," Mr. Staley said.

"That will be perfect," David said. "We'll be coming up here at the end of next month."

With some difficulty Nikki was separated from her puppy, and the Wilsons went to the Iron Horse Inn to celebrate over lunch.

They sat at a cloth-covered table with a view of the river. David and Angela each ordered a glass of white wine. Nikki had a cranberry juice. They touched their glasses.

"I'd like to toast our arrival in the Garden of Eden," David said.

"And the beginning of paying back our debt," Angela said.

"Hear, hear," David said, and they drank.

"Can you believe it?" Angela asked. "Our combined income will be over one hundred and twenty thousand dollars."

David sang a few bars of the song "We're in the Money."

"I think I'll call my dog Rusty," Nikki said.

"That's a wonderful name," David said.

"What do you think about me earning twice what you do?" Angela teased.

David was prepared. "You'll be earning it in your dark dreary lab," he teased back. "I'll be seeing real, live, appreciative people."

"Won't it challenge your delicate masculinity?" Angela asked.

"Not in the slightest," David said. "Also it's nice to know that if we ever get divorced, I'll get alimony."

Angela lunged across the table to give David a poke in the ribs.

After lunch they decided to go straight to the hospital. They presented themselves to Caldwell's secretary and were ushered in right away.

"That's fantastic," Caldwell said when they informed him of their decision. "Does CMV know yet?" he asked.

"Not yet," David said.

"Come on," Caldwell said, "let's go give them the good news."

Charles Kelley was equally pleased. After congratulating David, he asked when he thought he'd be ready to start seeing patients.

"July first," David said without hesitation. "With our debt, the sooner we start working, the better we'll feel."

David asked if they could go back to the office he'd be assigned. Kelley was happy to oblige.

David paused outside the waiting-room door, fantasizing how his name would look in the slot under Dr. Randall Portland's. David opened the door and stepped over the threshold. A figure dressed in surgical scrubs leaped off the waiting-room couch.

"What is the meaning of this?" the man angrily demanded.

It took David a moment to recognize Dr. Portland. He had changed since David had seen him. He'd lost considerable weight; his eyes seemed sunken, and his cheeks were pale and gaunt.

Kelley pushed his way to the front and reintroduced David, explaining why they were there. Dr. Portland's anger waned. Like a balloon losing its air, he collapsed back onto the couch.

"Sorry to have bothered you," David said.

"I was just getting a bit of sleep," Dr. Portland explained. His voice was flat. He sounded as exhausted as he looked. "I did a case this morning, and I felt tired."

"Tom Baringer?" Caldwell asked.

Dr. Portland nodded. "The operation went fine. Now we have to keep our fingers crossed for the post-op course."

David apologized again, then herded everyone, including himself, out of the office.

"Sorry about that," Kelley said.

"What's wrong with him?" David asked. "He doesn't look well."

"I thought he looked depressed," Angela said.

"He's busy," Kelley admitted. "I'm sure he's just overworked. So, now that you're coming, is there anything we can do to help?"

"We'll have to go look at a few houses," Angela said. "Who do you suggest we call?"

"Dorothy Weymouth," Caldwell said. "She's far and away the best Realtor in town. Come back to my office and use my phone."

A half hour later the whole family was in Dorothy Weymouth's office, in the building across the street from the diner. She was a huge, pleasant woman attired in a shapeless, tentlike dress.

"I have to tell you, I'm impressed," Dorothy said. Her voice was surprisingly high-pitched for such a large woman. "Barton Sherwood called to tell me the bank is eager to help you. Now, it doesn't happen often that the president of the bank calls before I've even met the client." Dorothy began putting photos of properties out on her desk. "Here's a particularly charming property that's just come on the market. It's a beauty."

Angela caught her breath. She picked up the photo. "I do like this one." She handed the picture to David. It was a brick, early Federal–style home with double bow windows. Below a large Palladian window, there was a pedimented portico with fluted white columns.

"That's one of the oldest brick homes in the area," Dorothy said. "It was built around 1820. The property used to be a dairy farm."

"It's gorgeous," Angela said wistfully. "But I'm sure we could never afford it."

"You could according to what Barton Sherwood told me," Dorothy said. "The owner, Clara Hodges, is very eager to sell. I'm sure we could get you a good deal. Anyway, it's worth a look. Let's pick four or five others and go see them."

Cleverly orchestrating the order of the visits, Dorothy left the Hodges house for last. It was located about two miles south of the town center, on the crest of a small hill. The nearest house was an eighth of a mile down the road. When they pulled into the driveway, Nikki noticed the frog pond and was immediately sold.

Dorothy pulled to a halt between the house and the pond. From there they had a view of the structure with its connected barn. David and Angela were both awed by the home's noble and imposing character.

"Are you sure Mr. Sherwood thinks we can afford this?" David asked.

"Absolutely," Dorothy said. "Come on, let's see the interior."

In a state of near hypnosis they followed Dorothy around the inside of the house. She continued her steady stream of Realtor chatter, saying things like "This room has so much promise" and "With just a little creativity, this room would be so cozy." Problems such as dry-rotted window sashes she minimized. Good points, like the many fireplaces and the beautiful cornice work, she lauded with an uninterrupted flow of superlatives.

David insisted on seeing everything. They even descended the granite steps into the basement, which seemed exceptionally musty.

"There seems to be a strange smell," he said. "Is there a water problem down here?"

"Not that I've heard of," Dorothy said.

"There's no floor," David said.

"It's a packed-earth floor," Dorothy explained. "It's common in older homes like this." She showed them the root cellar and proudly pointed out the huge old furnace. "This used to burn coal," she explained, "but it was converted to oil."

David nodded, though he didn't know much about furnaces no matter what they burned.

Before they left the basement, Dorothy opened a door, revealing a second flight of granite steps, which led up to a hatchlike door. "These stairs go out to the backyard," Dorothy explained. "That's why the firewood is here." She pointed to several cords of firewood neatly stacked against the wall.

The Wilsons had Dorothy drop them off at the Green Mountain National Bank. They were nervous and excited at the same time. Barton Sherwood saw them almost immediately.

"We found a house we like," David said. "It's owned by Clara Hodges. The asking price is two hundred and fifty thousand dollars."

"It's a great old house," Sherwood said. "I know it well. And the location is fabulous. As far as the price is concerned, it's a steal."

"So the bank would be willing to underwrite our purchase at that price?" Angela questioned. It seemed too good to be true.

"Of course, you'll offer less," Sherwood said. "I'd suggest an initial offer of one hundred and ninety thousand. But the bank will be willing to back the purchase up to the asking price."

Fifteen minutes later David, Angela, and Nikki stepped back out into the warm Vermont sunshine. "Well?" David asked.

"I can't imagine finding something we'd like better," Angela said. "Let's do it."

Back in Dorothy's office, they told the pleased Realtor their decision. A few minutes later Dorothy had Clara Hodges on the phone, and although it was a bit unconventional, a deal was concluded orally at a price of two hundred and ten thousand dollars.

By the end of the day, after a bit of shuttling back and forth between Dorothy's office and the bank, all the appropriate papers were filled out and a closing date was set. After one more visit to the hardware store so Nikki could pet Rusty one last time and say good-bye, the Wilsons got on the road for the drive back to Boston.

Angela drove. Neither David nor Nikki dozed. They were all keyed up from what they'd accomplished and full of dreams about their new life that was imminently to begin.

"What did you think about Dr. Portland?" David asked after a period of silence.

"What do you mean?" said Angela.

"The man was hardly friendly," David said.

"I think we woke him up."

"Most people wouldn't act that irritable. Besides, he looked like death warmed over. He's changed so drastically in a month."

"I thought he sounded and looked depressed."

David shrugged. "Something about him makes me uncomfortable. I hope sharing an office with him doesn't become a sore spot."

7

Monday, May 24

TOM Baringer didn't look good, and Traynor didn't want to get too close lest he catch some awful illness. Tom's face was gray, and his breathing was labored. A plastic tube snaked from behind his head, feeding oxygen into his nose. His eyes were closed with tape, and ointment oozed out between his eyelids.

"Tom," Traynor called softly. When there was no response, he called louder. But Tom did not move.

"He's beyond responding."

Traynor jumped, and the blood drained from his own face. Except for Tom, he'd thought he was alone.

"His pneumonia is not responding to treatment," the stranger said angrily. Cloaked in shadows, he sat in a corner of the room. "He's dying like the others."

"Who are you?" Traynor asked. He wiped his forehead, where perspiration had instantly appeared.

The man got to his feet. "I'm Mr. Baringer's doctor, Randy Portland." He advanced to the side of the bed and lifted the sheet so that Traynor could see Tom Baringer's tightly sutured wound. "The hip has been repaired. No problem whatsoever. But unfortunately, it's been a fatal cure. There's no way Mr. Baringer will walk out of here." Portland dropped the sheet and defiantly raised his eyes to Traynor's. "There's something wrong with this hospital," he said. "I'm not going to take all the blame."

Traynor was stunned. He could understand how doctors might become emotionally involved in their patients' conditions, but Portland seemed unhinged. Traynor slipped out of the room and quickly walked to Beaton's office. Charles Kelley was there.

"Do you both know Dr. Portland?" Traynor asked.

They nodded. Kelley spoke. "He's one of ours. He's an orthopedic surgeon."

"I just had a very unnerving encounter with him," Traynor said. "I popped in to see my client, Tom Baringer, who's very sick, and Dr. Portland was sitting in the corner of Tom's room. When he spoke, he acted strangely. He said something about not taking all the blame and that there was something wrong with the hospital."

"I think he's been under strain from overwork," Kelley said. "We're short at least one orthopedic surgeon. Unfortunately, our recruiting efforts have been unsuccessful so far. I'll have a talk with him. Maybe he needs a little time off."

"Well, so much for that," Traynor said, composing himself.

"By the way," Kelley said, flashing one of his winning smiles, "my superiors are very upset about that negative ruling from Montpelier on the certificate of need for open-heart surgery. CMV had expected the open-heart program to be up and running by now. It was part of the contract."

"It was part of the contract provided we got the certificate," Traynor corrected. "But we didn't. So let's look at what has been done. We've updated the MRI, built the neonatal ICU, and replaced the old cobalt-sixty machine with a linear accelerator. I think we have been showing remarkably good faith, and we've been doing all this while the hospital has been losing money."

"Whether the hospital loses money or not is not CMV's concern," Kelley said. "Especially since it's probably due to minor management inefficiencies."

"The problem is, the current capitation rate is too low," Traynor said bluntly. "Hospitalization from CMV is running more than ten percent above projections. We can't support such an overrun for long. We need to renegotiate the capitation rate. It's that simple."

"The capitation rate doesn't get renegotiated until the contract term is over," Kelley said amicably, getting to his feet. "What do you take us for? You offered the present rate. You signed the contract. But I don't mean to imply that I'm not willing to work together with you. This should be a dynamic relationship. After all, we have the same goal—the health of the community." With that, Kelley smiled again as if to show off his perfectly straight white teeth, shook hands with Beaton and Traynor, and left the room.

"I didn't appreciate his impudent suggestion of incompetent management," Traynor said. "I don't like his cocky attitude. It's unfortunate we have to deal with him."

"Our bargaining position is even weaker than I thought," Beaton said.

The buzz of the intercom surprised them. "Some bad news," Beaton said once she hung up. "Tom Baringer has died."

8

Wednesday, June 30

THIS was the day David and Angela would leave Boston for their new home and careers in Bartlet, Vermont.

"Are you excited?" David asked Nikki.

"I'm excited to see Rusty," Nikki announced.

They'd rented a U-Haul truck to help make the move. Once they were finally packed, Angela got into their Volvo station wagon and David got into the U-Haul. For the first half of the trip, Nikki elected to ride with her dad.

Just south of the New Hampshire border, they stopped for lunch. Eager to arrive at their new home, they ate quickly.

"I feel wonderful about leaving the frantic, crime-filled city behind," Angela said as they left the restaurant and approached their vehicles. "At this point I don't care if I ever go back."

"I don't know," David joked. "I'll miss hearing sirens, gunshots, and cries for help. Country life is going to be so boring."

Both Nikki and Angela pummeled him in mock anger.

For the rest of the trip Nikki joined Angela in the station wagon.

As they drove north, the weather improved. In Boston it had

been hot, muggy, and hazy. By the time they crossed into Vermont, it was still warm, but clear and much less humid.

Bartlet appeared serene in the early summer heat. Flower-filled window boxes adorned almost every sill. Slowing down, the Wilsons' two-vehicle caravan crept through the lazy town. Few people were on the streets. It was as if everyone were napping.

"Can we stop and get Rusty?" Nikki asked as they neared Staley's Hardware Store.

"Let's get a bit settled first," Angela said. "We'll have to build something to keep him in until he gets housebroken."

David and Angela pulled into their driveway and parked. Now that the house was officially theirs, they felt even more awed than they had on their initial visit.

David climbed out of the truck, his eyes glued to the house. "The place is lovely," he said. "But it needs more attention than I realized."

Angela walked over to David and followed his line of sight. Some of the decorative dentil work had fallen from the cornice. "I'm not worried," she said. "That's why I married someone who is handy around the house."

David laughed. "I can see it'll take some effort to make a believer out of you."

With a key they had been sent in the mail, the Wilsons opened the front door and stepped inside to tour their new home. They had forgotten its enormity in contrast to their Boston apartment. Aside from a few pieces of furniture they'd agreed Clara would leave behind—a stool, a kitchen table—the place was bare.

In the center hall, just before the grand staircase, an imposing chandelier hung. There was a family room and dining room to the left and a huge living room to the right. The hall led to a spacious country kitchen, which stretched across the back of the house. Beyond the kitchen was the two-story clapboard addition that connected the house to the barn. It had a mudroom, several storerooms, and a back staircase leading up to the second level.

Returning to the grand staircase, the Wilsons climbed up to the second story. There were two bedrooms with connecting baths on each side and a master suite over the kitchen area. They walked into the room Nikki wanted, which faced the frog pond.

"Okay, you guys," Angela commanded. "Time to unload."

Returning to the vehicles, they began to bring their belongings into the house. The couch, the bedding, and the heavy boxes of books made it quite a struggle. When they had finished, David and Angela stood beneath the archway leading into the living room.

"It would be funny if it wasn't so pathetic," Angela said. Their threadbare couch, two armchairs, and coffee table looked as if they had been rescued from a garage sale.

"Understated elegance," David said. "Minimalist decor."

"What about Rusty?" Nikki asked.

"Let's go get him," David said. "You want to come, Angela?"

"No, thanks," Angela said. "I'll stay and get more organized."

While David and Nikki went to town, Angela unpacked a few of the boxes in the kitchen—including their pots, pans, dishes, and flatware. She also figured out how to work the stove and got the refrigerator running.

Nikki returned, carrying the adorable puppy with its wrinkled face and floppy ears. He'd grown considerably since they'd seen him last. While she and David fashioned a pen for him in the mudroom, Angela made dinner for Nikki. Nikki wasn't happy about eating before her parents, but she was too tired to complain. After she'd eaten and done some postural drainage, she and Rusty, both exhausted, were put to bed.

"I have a little surprise for you," Angela said as she and David descended from Nikki's room. She took him by the hand and led him into the kitchen. Opening the refrigerator, she pulled out a bottle of chardonnay.

"Wow!" David exclaimed, inspecting the label. "This isn't our usual cheap stuff."

"Hardly," Angela said. Reaching back into the refrigerator, she took out a dish with two thick veal chops.

"I have the feeling we're in for a feast," David said.

"You'd better believe it," Angela said. "Plus salad, artichokes, and wild rice."

David cooked the meat on an outdoor barbecue built into the side of the terrace off the family room. By the time he came in, Angela had the rest of the food on the table in the dining room.

Night had descended softly, filling the house with shadow. In the darkness the glow from the two candles that formed the centerpiece on the table illuminated only the immediate area. The disarray of the rest of the house was hidden.

They sat at opposite ends of the table. They didn't speak. Both of them were moved by the romantic atmosphere, realizing that romance had been missing from their lives over the last years; the demands of their respective residencies and Nikki's ongoing health problems had taken precedence.

Long after they'd finished eating, they continued to sit and stare at each other while a symphony of sounds of a Vermont summer night drifted in through the open windows. The candles flickered sensuously as the clean, cool air wafted across the room and caressed their faces. It was a magical moment they both wanted to savor.

Mutual desire drove them from the dining room into the dark living room. They fell onto the couch, their lips meeting as they enveloped each other in a warm embrace.

MORNING brought mass confusion. With the dog barking to be fed and Nikki whining that she couldn't find her favorite jeans, Angela felt her patience was at an end.

"Calm down, dear," David said. "Getting upset isn't going to solve anything. I'll go get the baby-sitter."

"I'm not a baby," Nikki whined.

"Oh, save me," Angela said, her face raised to the ceiling.

David went off to fetch Alice Doherty, Dorothy Weymouth's older sister, who turned out to be a godsend. She looked quite grandmotherly, with an engaging manner and surprising energy for a woman of seventy-nine. She also had the compassion and patience a chronically ill, willful child like Nikki required.

"Don't you two worry about a thing," Alice called to David and Angela as they went out the back door. Nikki was holding Rusty, and she waved the dog's paw to say good-bye.

"I want to ride my bike," David announced, once he and Angela got outside.

"Are you serious?" Angela asked.

"Absolutely," David said.

"Suit yourself," Angela said as she climbed into the Volvo and started the engine. She waved once to David as she descended the long drive and turned right toward town.

Although Angela was confident of her professional capabilities, she still felt nervous about starting her first real job. Mustering her courage, she reported to the clinical lab. As soon as Dr. Wadley saw her, he leaped up from his desk and even gave her a hug.

"Welcome to the team," he said with a warm smile. "I've been anticipating this day for weeks."

Angela was again aware of how much the man reminded her of her father. She was charmed by his demonstrative welcome. It was reassuring to feel so wanted on her first day.

"Let me show you your office," Wadley said, rubbing his hands together. His green eyes shone with childlike excitement. He pushed open a connecting door from his own office into another, which looked recently decorated. The room was entirely white: the walls, the desk, everything. "Like it?" he asked.

"It's wonderful," Angela said.

Wadley pointed back toward the connecting door. "That will always be open," he said. "Literally and figuratively."

"Wonderful," Angela said.

"Now I want to introduce you to the staff," Wadley said. He took a long, crisp, professional white coat from a hook and put it on.

For the next fifteen minutes Angela met more people than she could hope to remember. After circling the lab, they stopped at a windowless office next to the microbiology section. It belonged to Dr. Paul Darnell, Angela's fellow pathologist, a short man with rumpled clothing. Darnell seemed agreeable but plain and retiring.

After the tour was over, Wadley escorted Angela back to his office, where he explained her duties and responsibilities. "I'm going to try to make you one of the best pathologists in the country," he said with a true mentor's enthusiasm.

DAVID had enjoyed his bicycle ride immensely. The clean, crisp morning air had been delicious,. and he'd caught a glimpse of several deer across a dew-laden field just after crossing the Roaring River. Arriving at the professional building, he discovered he was too early.

"My word, you are eager!" Kelley said when he spotted David perusing magazines in the CMV waiting area. "Come on in."

David followed Kelley into his office, where Kelley had him fill out a few routine forms. Then he accompanied David to his new office. As David stopped to admire his nameplate on the outside of the door, he was surprised to see the name Dr. Kevin Yansen in the slot above his.

"Is this the same suite?" David asked.

"Same one," Kelley said. He knocked on the mirror, and after it slid open, he introduced David to the receptionist he would be sharing with Dr. Yansen.

Over his shoulder Kelley told the receptionist to send Dr. Yansen in to meet Dr. Wilson when he appeared between patients. He then led David into what had been Dr. Portland's office. The walls had been painted a light gray, and new gray-green carpet had been installed.

"What do you think?" Kelley asked, beaming.

"I think it's fine," David said. "Where did Dr. Portland go?"

Before Kelley could respond, Dr. Yansen appeared and whisked into the room with his hand outstretched. He introduced himself and told David to call him Kevin, then slapped him on the back. "Welcome. Good to have you join the squad," he said.

"Are you an orthopedist?" David asked as he looked at his new suitemate. He was a squarely built man with an aggressive-looking face and thick glasses. He was four inches shorter than David, and standing next to Kelley, he appeared diminutive.

Kevin laughed scornfully. "Hardly! I'm at the opposite end of the operative spectrum. I'm an ophthalmologist."

"Where's Dr. Portland?" David asked again.

"Dr. Portland is no longer with us," Kevin said.

"I'm afraid Dr. Portland committed suicide," Kelley said.

"Right here in this room," Kevin said. "Sitting there at that desk." He pointed at the desk. "Shot himself through the forehead. That's why the walls had to be painted and the carpet changed."

David's mouth went bone-dry. He gazed at the blank wall behind the desk. "How awful," he said.

"A real tragedy," Dr. Yansen said with a nod.

"He didn't look good the last time I saw him," David said. "Was he ill?"

"Depressed," Kelley said.

David sighed. "Boy, you never know!"

Kevin wished David well and headed back to one of the examining rooms. Kelley introduced David to Susan Beardslee, the nurse he'd be working with. Susan was in her mid-twenties, with dark hair cut short to frame her face.

"Your first patient is in the examining room," she said cheerfully. She handed him the chart. "When you need me, just buzz."

"I think this is where I leave," Kelley said. "Good luck, David. If there are any problems, just holler."

David flipped open the cover of the chart and read the name: "Marjorie Kleber, age thirty-nine." The complaint was chest pain. He read the diagnostic summary: "Breast cancer treated with surgery, chemotherapy, and radiation, after diagnosis at age thirty-five." At the time, the cancer had spread to the lymph nodes.

David was mildly unnerved. A patient with breast cancer that had metastasized, or spread from the breast to other areas of the body, was a serious case with which to begin his medical career. Happily, Marjorie had been doing well.

David knocked on the door, entered, and introduced himself. Marjorie was sitting on the examining table, dressed in an examining gown. She looked up with large, sad, intelligent eyes.

"Thank you for coming to Bartlet," she said. "You'll never know how much I have prayed for someone like you to come here."

"I—I'm happy to be here," David stammered.

"Prior to your coming, I've had to wait up to four weeks to be seen. That's the way it's been since my school's health-care coverage was switched to CMV. And every time it's been a different doctor. Now I'm told you'll be my doctor. It's so reassuring."

"I'm honored to be your doctor," David said.

"Last winter I had the flu so bad, I thought it was pneumonia. Luckily, by the time I was seen, I was over the worst of it."

"Maybe you should have gone to the emergency room."

"I wish I could have," Marjorie said. "But we're not allowed. I did go once, the winter before last, but CMV refused to pay because it turned out to be the flu. Unless my problem is life threatening, I have to come here to the office."

"But that's absurd," David said. "How can you know in advance if your problem is life threatening?"

Marjorie shrugged. "That's the same question I asked, but they didn't have an answer. They just reiterated the rule. Anyway, I'm glad you're here. If I have a problem, I'll call you."

"Please do," David said. "Now let's start talking about your health. Who is following you in regard to your cancer?"

"You are," Marjorie said.

"You don't have an oncologist?" David asked.

"CMV doesn't have one. I'm to see you routinely and Dr. Mieslich, the oncologist, when you think it is necessary. Dr. Mieslich is not a CMV physician. I can't see him unless you order it."

For the next fifteen minutes David applied himself to the process of working up Marjorie's chest pain. While listening to her chest, he asked her what she did at the school.

"I'm a third-grade teacher," Marjorie said proudly.

"My daughter is to start the third grade in the fall," David said.

"How wonderful. She'll be in my class. My husband, Lloyd, and I have two children: a boy in high school and a girl in sixth grade."

David began an EKG. Half an hour later he felt confident enough to reassure Marjorie that her chest pain was not at all serious. She thanked him once again for coming to Bartlet.

Taking the file from its holder on the second examining-room door, David perused his next patient's chart. The diagnostic summary read, "Leukemia treated with massive chemotherapy for three and a half years." David inwardly groaned; it was another difficult case. Stepping into the room, David introduced himself. The patient's name was John Tarlow. After a short conversation it was clear to David that John's complaint of insomnia was an understandable reaction to a death in the family. David gave him a prescription for some sleeping medication that he was certain would help.

After he was through with John, David searched for Susan. He found her in the tiny lab used for simple, routine tests. "Are there a lot of oncology patients in the practice?" he asked hesitantly. Susan assured him that there were only a few such patients. When his next case concerned diabetes, he felt reassured.

David's morning passed quickly and happily. The patients had been a delight. They'd all been affable, attentive to what David had to say, and, in contrast to the patients he'd dealt with during his residency, eager to follow his recommendations.

David met Angela for lunch at the coffee shop. Over sandwiches, they discussed their morning. David told Angela about the patients he'd seen. She was particularly touched to hear about Marjorie Kleber's reaction to his arrival.

"She's a teacher," David added. "In fact, she teaches the third grade, so she'll be Nikki's teacher."

"What a coincidence," Angela said. "What's she like?"

"She seems warm, giving, and intelligent," David said. "I'd guess she's a marvelous teacher. The problem is, she's had cancer."

"Oh, dear," Angela said.

"But she's been doing fine," David said. "I don't think she's had any recurrence yet, but I haven't gone over her chart in detail. Did you hear about Dr. Portland?"

Angela shook her head.

"He committed suicide in the office that I'm now using."

"That's terrible," Angela said. "The poor man."

"On a lighter note," David said, "Charles Kelley told me that there's a bonus plan to reward me for keeping hospitalization at a minimum. I can even win a trip to the Bahamas. Can you believe it? I personally find it insulting."

"I've heard of that kind of ploy," Angela said. "Health maintenance organizations use it to reduce costs." She shook her head in disbelief. "Well, on a lighter note of my own, Dr. Wadley's invited us to his home for dinner tonight. I can call a sitter."

"Do you want to go?" David asked.

"He's being so generous. I don't want to appear ungrateful."

"Then let's go," David said.

"WELCOME," Wadley said, opening the door to greet the Wilsons.

The house was immaculate. Every detail had been attended to. Antique furniture stood on thick Oriental carpets. Nineteenth-century pastoral paintings adorned the walls.

Gertrude Wadley and her courtly husband were significantly different people, lending credence to the saying Opposites attract. She was a retiring, mousy woman who had little to say, as if she'd been submerged by her husband's personality. It was Wadley who dominated the evening. He pontificated on a number of subjects. And he clearly doted on Angela.

"One thing is for sure," David said as they drove home. "Dr. Wadley's thrilled with you. Of course, I can't blame him."

Angela snuggled up to her husband.

DAYS melted into weeks and weeks into months as summer advanced. The sweet white corn grew chest-high across the road from the Wilson's house and could be heard rustling in the evening breeze. Plump tomatoes ripened to a deep red in the garden by the terrace. Crab apples the size of golf balls began to drop from the tree next to the barn. Cicadas buzzed in the mid-August heat.

David's and Angela's work continued to be stimulating and rewarding as they settled into their jobs. Each day brought some new experience that they enthusiastically shared with each other as they lingered over quiet suppers. David discovered that he had several more oncology patients in his practice, and he saw them on a regular basis. Mary Ann Schiller, Sandra Hascher, and Jonathan Eakins had a lot of medical problems, which he hardly found surprising considering the amount of treatment they'd undergone.

Rusty's appetite was a source of wonder as he grew quickly and with great exuberance. Yet he maintained the same adorable quality he'd had as a puppy. Everyone found it impossible to pass him without offering a pat on the head or a scratch behind a golden ear.

Nikki flourished in the new environment. Her respiratory status remained normal, and her lungs stayed clear. She also made new friends. She was closest to Caroline Helmsford, a petite child a year older than Nikki who also suffered from cystic fibrosis. Having so many experiences in common, they formed a strong bond.

Nikki also befriended Dr. Yansen's boy, Arni, who happened to be exactly Nikki's age. Arni was like his father: short, squarely built, and aggressive. He and Nikki hit it off and spent hours in and out of the barn, never at a loss for things to do.

As much as they loved their work, the Wilsons delighted in their weekends. Saturday and Sunday afternoons David and Angela devoted to work on the house. While Angela busied herself with curtains and stripping old furniture, David tackled outdoor projects like fixing the porch or replacing the drainpipes. David proved even less handy than Angela had feared. He was forever running off to Staley's Hardware Store for more advice.

9

Monday, September 6

TRAYNOR pulled his Mercedes off the road and bumped across the field to the line of cars parked near a split-rail fence. He was headed for the eighth annual hospital Labor Day picnic. Festivities had begun at nine, starting with field-day races for the children.

Traynor parked and got out, and as he trudged back along the fence, he saw Beaton, who waved and started to come to meet him. She was with Wayne Robertson, the chief of police, and Traynor immediately suspected something was wrong.

"I've got some bad news," Beaton said without preamble. "I'm afraid there was another assault on a nurse last night. The woman was raped."

"You're not serious!" Traynor snarled. "Was it the same guy?"

"We believe so," Robertson said. "Same description. Also the same ski mask. This time the weapon was a gun rather than a knife, but he still had the handcuffs. The assault occurred in the upper lot, where there are no lights."

"Who knows about this rape?" Traynor asked.

"Not very many people," Beaton said. "I took it upon myself to contact George O'Donald at the Bartlet *Sun,* and he's agreed to keep it out of the paper. So we might get a break."

"I'd like to keep it away from CMV if possible," Traynor said. "The selectmen are convinced that the new garage is a bad idea. Maybe this rape, as bad as it is, could be the catalyst we need to get it to pass." He turned to Robertson. "Can't the police do anything?" he asked.

"Short of putting a deputy up there on a nightly basis," Robertson said, "there's not much we can do."

"What about the hospital security?" Traynor asked. "What does Swegler say?" He leaned against the fence, feeling a little weak.

"There wasn't much he could have done," Beaton said. "The nurse had done a double shift, and she did not call security before she left—as we'd repeatedly instructed nurses to do whenever they leave late. To make matters worse, she'd parked in the upper lot when she'd come to work for the day shift."

"That does it!" Traynor said. "Tell Werner Van Slyke that I want that upper lot lit just like the lower. In fact, tell him to light it up like a ball field." He turned back to Robertson. "And why haven't you been able to find this rapist, anyway? Considering the size of the town and the number of rapes, all presumably by the same person, I'd think you'd have at least one suspect."

"We're working on it," Robertson said.

"Would you like to head over to the food tent?" Beaton asked.

"I'm not hungry," Traynor said. "Let's circulate."

"The bonus program is working well," Beaton said. "CMV admissions are down four percent over last August. That's not a lot, but it's in the right direction."

"It's warming to hear some good news once in a while," Traynor said. "But we can't relax. In July and August a good portion of the hospital census was paying patients. Now the tourists will be going home."

"I think we should reactivate our strict utilization control," Beaton said. "It's our only hope of holding out until the current capitation contract runs out."

They walked down by the lake and watched the volleyball game for a while. Then they strolled toward the softball diamond. A game was in the process of being organized.

"There's Dr. Wadley," Beaton said. She waved, and Wadley waved back. Next to him was a young, attractive woman with dark brown hair, dressed in shorts. She was wearing a baseball cap turned jauntily to the side.

"Who is that woman with him?" Traynor asked.

"She's our newest pathologist," Beaton said. "Angela Wilson." She watched Wadley shepherd Angela to her position at second base. "There's been quite a change in old Doc Wadley. Angela Wilson has evoked the suppressed teacher in him. She's given him a new lease on life. He's been on cloud nine since she got here."

Traynor watched Angela Wilson field a practice ground ball and lithely throw it to first base. He couldn't attribute Wadley's interest purely to a mentor's enthusiasm. Angela Wilson didn't look like a doctor, at least not any doctor Traynor had ever met. She looked like a Dallas Cowboys cheerleader.

10

Monday, October 18

EVEN though David and Angela had spent four years in Boston during their residencies, they hadn't truly experienced the full glory of a New England fall. In Bartlet it was breathtaking. Each day the splendiferous color of the leaves became more intense. The crisp air made waking up in the morning a pleasure, and each evening a crackling fire kept the nighttime chill at bay.

Nikki loved school. Marjorie Kleber did become her teacher, and she was superb. Although Nikki had always been a good student, she now became an excellent one. At night she was full of stories about all she had learned in class.

The magnificent weather continued well into October, preserving the peak foliage long after what the Bartlet natives said was usual. Then one weekend of gusty wind and cold rain drove the leaves from the trees. The Wilsons had been touring around New Hampshire with the Yansens. By the time they returned home, the temperature had plummeted into the thirties and Nikki had a sore throat.

Nikki did not have a good night, nor did her parents. By the wee hours of morning it was clear that she was becoming progressively more congested. Well before dawn Angela listened to Nikki's chest with her stethoscope. She heard rales and rhonchi—sounds that meant Nikki's breathing tubes were becoming clogged with mucus.

Before eight a.m. David and Angela called their respective offices to explain that they would be late. Bundling Nikki in multiple layers of clothing, they took her to see Dr. Pilsner. Angela told him how the congestion had not responded to the usual postural drainage. Dr. Pilsner listened to Nikki's chest.

"Definitely clogged up," he said, removing the stethoscope from his ears. "We'll have her back to normal in a wink, but I think we'd better admit her. I want to start intravenous antibiotics and some intensive respiratory therapy."

"Whatever it takes," David said. He stroked Nikki's hair.

In a few minutes they were on their way upstairs. Janice Sperling from admissions led them to room 204 and opened the door.

"Excuse me," Janice said with confusion. Room 204 was already occupied; there was a patient in the bed.

"Mrs. Kleber," Nikki said with surprise.

"Marjorie?" David asked. "What on earth are you doing here?"

"Just my luck," Marjorie said. "The one weekend you go away, I have trouble. But your covering doctor was very kind."

"I'm so sorry to bother you," Janice said to Marjorie. "I can't understand why the computer gave me room 204."

"No trouble," Marjorie said. "I like the company."

David told Marjorie he'd be back shortly. The Wilsons followed Janice to the nurses' station, where she phoned admissions.

"I want to apologize for the mix-up," Janice said after the call. "We'll put Nikki in room 212."

Within minutes of Nikki's arrival in room 212 a team of nurses and technicians appeared and attended to her. Antibiotics were started, and the respiratory therapist was paged.

When everything was under control, David returned directly to Marjorie's room. She appeared tiny in the large orthopedic bed. David thought that Nikki would have been dwarfed.

"Okay," he said, feigning anger. "What's the story here?"

"It started on Friday afternoon," Marjorie said. "I didn't feel well at all. By Saturday my right leg started to hurt. When I called your office, Dr. Markham saw me right away. He said I had phlebitis and that I had to go into the hospital."

David examined Marjorie and confirmed the diagnosis. "We don't like to take chances with phlebitis. Inflammation of veins goes hand in hand with blood clots. But it's looking good."

"It feels twenty times better than it did," Marjorie said.

Before leaving, David asked the head nurse, Janet Colburn, why Marjorie was in an orthopedic bed.

"No reason," Janet said. "It just happened to be in there. At the moment, it's not needed elsewhere. She's better off, believe me. The electronic controls never break down—something I can't say about our regular beds."

Finally David headed over to the professional building to start seeing his patients. He was almost an hour late. Susan had tried to juggle the patients' appointments and cancel those that she could, but there were still a number waiting. David launched into work with gusto. By midmorning he was caught up, and took a brief time-out to return some phone calls. The first person he tried was Charles Kelley.

"Neal Harper's in my office," Kelley said. "He's from CMV utilization in Burlington. We have something to go over with you."

"In the middle of my office hours?"

"This won't take long," Kelley said.

At the CMV offices, the receptionist told David to go right in. Kelley got up from behind his desk, appearing tall and tan as usual. But his manner was different. He was serious, almost dour—a far cry from his usual ebullient self. He introduced Neal Harper, a thin, precise man with pale skin and a small amount of acne. To David he appeared the apotheosis of the bureaucrat who'd been forever locked in his office filling out his forms.

They all sat down. Kelley picked up a pencil and played with it with both hands. "The statistics are in for your first quarter," he said in a somber tone. "And they are not good."

David looked anxiously back and forth between the two men.

"Your productivity is not satisfactory," Kelley continued. "You are in the lowest percentile in the whole CMV organization according to the number of patient visits per hour. To make matters worse, you are in the highest percentile in ordering lab tests. As far as ordering consults outside the CMV community, you're completely off the graph. And that's not all. Too many of your patients have been seen in the hospital emergency room."

"That's understandable," David said. "I'm fully booked out for two weeks plus. When someone calls with an acute problem needing immediate attention, I send them to the ER."

"Wrong!" Kelley snapped. "You don't send patients to the ER. You see them in your office, provided they're not about to croak."

"But if I take time out to deal with emergencies, I can't see my scheduled patients."

"Then so be it," Kelley said. "Or make the so-called emergency patients wait. It's your call, but don't use the ER."

"Then what's the ER for?" David asked.

"Don't try to play smart guy with me, Dr. Wilson," Kelley said. "You know full well what the ER is for. It's for life-and-death emergencies. All this is pretty simple. Let me spell it out for you. You must seriously increase your productivity, you must lower your use of lab tests drastically, you must reduce—or better yet stop—using consults outside the CMV family, and you must keep your patients out of the ER. That's all there is to it. Understand?"

David stumbled out of the CMV office. He was flabbergasted. He'd prided himself on always keeping the patient's needs to the fore. Kelley's tirade was unnerving, to say the least.

"You'd better get hopping," Susan said the instant David reached his office suite. "You're getting behind again."

MIDMORNING, Angela ducked out of the lab and went to check on Nikki. She was pleased to find her doing as well as she was. The fact that she wasn't running a fever was particularly encouraging. There was also a definite decrease in Nikki's congestion.

"When can I go home?" Nikki asked.

"You just got here," Angela said, tousling Nikki's hair. "But if you continue to improve the way you've been going, I'm sure Dr. Pilsner won't want to keep you long."

Entering her office, Angela hung up her white coat in preparation to read a series of hematology slides. Just before she sat down, she peeked into Wadley's office. He was sitting at a double-headed teaching microscope. He caught sight of her and waved for her to come over.

"This is something I want you to see," he said.

Angela stepped over to the scope and sat opposite her mentor. Their knees almost touched beneath the table. She put her eyes to the eyepiece and peered in. Immediately she recognized the specimen as a sample of breast tissue.

"The patient is only twenty-two years old," Wadley said. "We have to make a diagnosis, and we have to be right. So take your time." To make his point, he reached under the table and grasped Angela's thigh just above the knee. "Don't be too impulsive about your impression. Look carefully at all the ducts."

Angela's trained eye began to scan the slide, but her concentration faltered. Wadley's hand had remained on her thigh. Its weight made her feel acutely uncomfortable throughout a long explanation about why the biopsy had to be considered positive for cancer.

Finally Angela got up. She knew she was trembling. She bit her tongue and turned back toward her office.

"I'll be ready to review those hematology slides as soon as you are through with them," Wadley called after her.

Closing the connecting door, Angela went over to her desk and sank into her chair. Near tears, she cradled her face in her hands. Going over the previous months, she recalled all the episodes when Wadley offered to stay late to go over slides and all the times he appeared when she had a few free moments. If she ever went to the coffee shop, he appeared and always took the seat next to her. And as far as touching was concerned, now that she thought about it, he never passed up an opportunity.

All at once the mentorlike effort and affection Wadley had been expending had a different, less generous connotation. Even the recent talk of attending a pathology meeting in Miami next month made her uneasy.

Angela wondered if she was overreacting. After all, David was forever accusing her of being overly dramatic. Angrily she shook her head. Deep down she knew she wasn't. Wadley's behavior was inappropriate. The question was what she could do to put an end to his unwanted familiarity. After all, he was her boss.

AT THE end of his office hours David walked over to the hospital to check on Marjorie Kleber and a few other patients. Determining that all were doing well, he stopped to see Nikki.

His daughter was feeling fine—thanks to a judicious combination of antibiotics, mucolytic agents, bronchodilators, hydration, and physical therapy. She was leaning back against a pile of pillows with a TV remote in her hand. She was watching a game show, a pastime frowned upon at home.

"Well, well," David said. "If it isn't a true woman of leisure."

"Come on, Dad," Nikki said, "I haven't watched much TV. Mrs. Kleber came to my room, and I even did some schoolwork."

"That's terrible," David said with improvised dismay. "How's the breathing?"

"Good," Nikki said. "A little tight, but definitely better."

Angela appeared at the doorway. "Looks like I'm just in time for a family reunion," she said. She came in and gave both Nikki and David a hug. With Angela sitting on one side of the bed and David on the other, they talked with Nikki for half an hour.

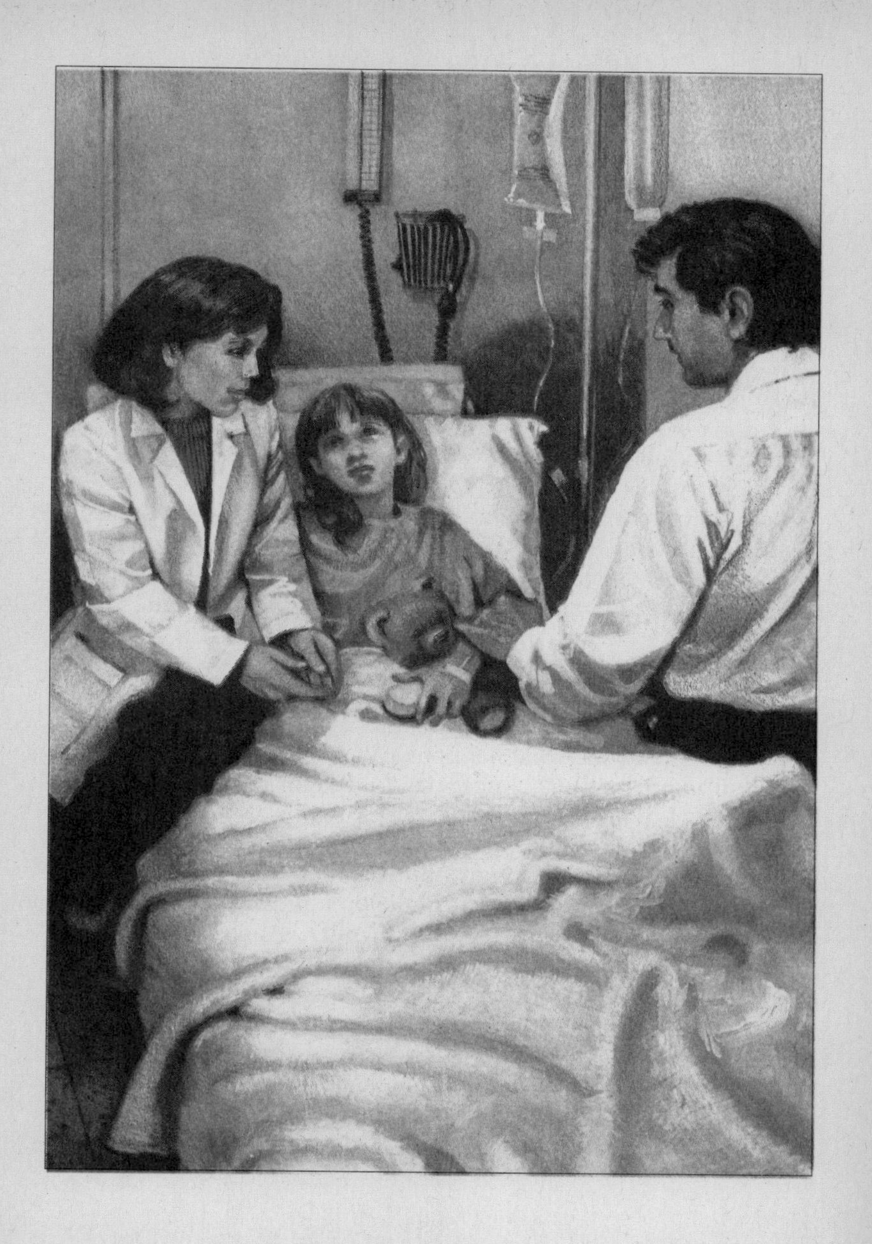

"I want to go home," Nikki whined when they got up to go.

"I'm sure you do," Angela said. "And we want you home, but we have to follow Dr. Pilsner's orders. We'll talk to him in the morning."

DINNER was a stifled affair without Nikki's presence. They ate at the kitchen table as the rain pelted the windows. Finally Angela found the strength to describe what had happened with Wadley. By the time she was finished, David was gaping in astonishment.

"That bastard!" he said, slamming his palm down onto the table. "There were a couple of times it passed through my mind he was acting a bit too enamored. I convinced myself I was being ridiculously jealous. But it sounds like my intuition was right."

"I don't know for sure," Angela said. "Which is partly why I hesitated to tell you. I don't want us to jump to conclusions."

"I'm sorry this happened," David said. "If you'd like, I'll get in the car, drive to his house, and punch him in the nose."

Angela smiled. "Thanks for the support."

"I had a bad day too," David finally admitted, and then told her about his utilization review with Kelley and the CMV man.

"What nerve to talk to you like that," Angela said. "Everyone knows that doctor-patient relationships are the cornerstone of good medical care. What are you going to do?"

"I don't know. I'll try to compromise somehow. I'll just take it a day at a time and see what happens. What about you?"

"I don't know either," Angela said. "I keep thinking that I was wrong, that I'm just overreacting."

"It's possible, I suppose," David said gently. "All along, Wadley's been a touchy-feely kind of guy. Since you never said anything up to this point, maybe he doesn't think you mind being touched."

"Are you saying I brought this on myself?" Angela demanded.

David reached across the table and grasped her arm. "Calm down. I'm on your side. I don't think for a second you're to blame."

Angela's sudden anger abated. There was the possibility that she had been unknowingly encouraging Wadley. After all, she'd wanted to please the man, as any student might, especially since she felt a debt to him for all the time and effort he'd expended on her behalf.

"I'm sorry," Angela said. "I'm just stressed out."

"Me too," David said. "Let's go to bed."

11

Tuesday, October 19

IT WAS still raining in the morning. However, Nikki was in high spirits and doing marvelously. Even her color had returned.

"I want to go home," she said.

"We haven't talked with Dr. Pilsner," David said. "But we will, sometime this morning. Be patient."

After the visit with Nikki, David went to the nurses' station to pick up Marjorie's chart. He'd been considering discharging her until he walked into her room. Her lethargic response to his greeting told him something was wrong.

"Marjorie, what's the matter?" David asked as his pulse quickened. He touched the back of his hand to her forehead and guessed she had a fever. She responded to his questions with barely intelligible mumbling. She acted drugged, although not in any apparent pain.

Marjorie's breathing was mildly labored. Listening to her chest, David heard faint sounds of congestion. Next he checked the area of phlebitis and found it was all but resolved. With mounting anxiety he examined the rest of his patient. Finding nothing, he hurried to the nurses' station and ordered a barrage of stat laboratory tests.

The first thing to come back from the lab was her blood count, but it only added to David's puzzlement. Her white cell level was in the lower percentile of normal. The low count seemed contradictory to her clinical state, which suggested developing pneumonia.

David debated what to do. More lab tests came back, but they were all normal. David thought about calling in some consults, but after his utilization review he was reluctant. The consults who might have been helpful were not part of CMV.

David consulted the *Physicians' Desk Reference*. Since a gram-negative bacteria might have appeared as a superinfection, he looked up an antibiotic that was specific for such an eventuality. When he found one, he felt confident it would take care of the problem.

IT WAS Angela's turn to handle the day's surgical frozen sections. She always found the task nerve-racking, since she knew that while she worked, the patient remained under anesthesia awaiting her verdict whether the biopsy was cancerous or benign.

The frozen sections were done in a small lab within the operating suite. Angela worked with intense concentration, studying the patterns of cells in the specimen under the microscope.

She did not hear the door silently open behind her. She was unaware that anyone was in the room until he spoke.

"Well, honey, how's it going?"

Angela's head shot up as adrenaline coursed through her body. With her pulse pounding in her temples, she looked up into Wadley's smiling face.

"Any problems?" Wadley asked.

"No," Angela said sharply.

"Let me take a look," Wadley said, motioning toward the microscope. "What's the case?"

Angela gave Wadley her seat. Succinctly she gave the history. He glanced at the slide, then stood up. For a moment they talked about the slide in pathological jargon. It was apparent they agreed the growth was benign.

"I want to see you later in my office." Wadley winked.

Ignoring the wink, Angela turned away. She was about to sit down when she felt Wadley's hand brush across her buttocks. "Don't work too hard, honey," he called, and slipped out the door.

The episode had happened so fast that Angela had not been able to respond. But she now knew for certain that the thigh-touching the day before had not been an innocent oversight.

For a few minutes Angela sat in the tiny lab and trembled with indignation and confusion. She wondered what was encouraging this sudden boldness. She couldn't just idly sit by and allow it to go on. That would be an open invitation. She decided she had two possibilities. She could confront Wadley directly, or she could go to Dr. Cantor, the chief of staff.

The raucous buzz of static coming over the intercom shocked Angela back to reality. The static preceded the voice of the head nurse. "Dr. Wilson," she said. "They are waiting on the biopsy results down in OR three."

DAVID found it difficult to concentrate on his patients' problems that morning. Not only was he still upset about his review, but now he had Marjorie Kleber's worsening condition to worry about.

Midmorning, David saw another of his frequent visitors, John Tarlow, the leukemia patient. John was feeling poorly. Following a meal of raw shellfish the night before, he'd developed severe G.I. problems with both vomiting and diarrhea. He was dehydrated, and in acute discomfort with colicky abdominal pain.

David hospitalized him immediately and ordered a number of tests to try to determine the cause of his symptoms.

JUST before eleven in the morning Traynor was told the bad news by his secretary, Collette. The final vote on the hospital parking garage, which Traynor had managed to get on the agenda once more, had been thumbs-down. "I can't believe it!" Traynor raged, and paced the area in front of his desk.

Unable to work, Traynor grabbed his raincoat and stormed out. Climbing into his car, he drove up to the hospital. If there was to be no parking garage, he would at least inspect the lighting. He didn't want to risk any more rapes in the hospital parking lot.

Traynor found Werner Van Slyke in his windowless cubbyhole that served as the engineering/maintenance department's office. Traynor had never been particularly comfortable around Van Slyke. Van Slyke was too much of a loner, and Traynor also found him physically intimidating—he was several inches taller than Traynor and significantly huskier, with the kind of bulky muscles that suggested weight lifting was a hobby.

"I want to see the lighting in the parking lots," Traynor said. "I want to make sure it's adequate."

Van Slyke pulled on a yellow slicker and walked out of the office. Outside the hospital, he pointed to each of the lights in the lower lot without comment.

As Traynor tagged along through the copse of evergreen trees and climbed the wooden steps that separated the lots, he wondered what Van Slyke did when he wasn't working. He realized he never saw him walking around the town or shopping in the shops. Uncomfortable with the continued silence, he cleared his throat. "Everything okay at home?" he asked.

"Fine," Van Slyke said.

"House okay? No problems?"

"Nope." Van Slyke began pointing out the lights in the upper lot.

There seemed to be plenty. Traynor made a note to swing up with his car some evening to see how light it was after dark.

They started back toward the hospital. Traynor looked over at Van Slyke's wet profile and found it hard to believe they were related. Yet they were. Van Slyke was Traynor's only nephew.

When they reached the stand of trees, Traynor stopped. "How come there are no lights on this path?"

"No one said anything about lights on the path," Van Slyke said.

"I think one or two would be nice," Traynor said.

Van Slyke barely nodded.

"Thanks for the tour," Traynor said in parting. He was relieved to make his escape. He felt guilty for feeling so estranged from his own kin, but the man was such an enigma. Traynor had to admit that his sister hadn't exactly been a paragon of normalcy. Her name was Sunny, yet her disposition had been anything but—she'd suffered from depression. Traynor still didn't understand why Sunny had married Dr. Van Slyke, knowing he was a drunk. Her suicide had been the final blow. In any case, given Werner Van Slyke's parentage, it was hardly a surprise that he was strange. Yet with his naval machinist's training he'd been helpful and reliable. Traynor was glad he'd suggested that the hospital hire him.

COMING out of one of his examining rooms, David was surprised to find that the basket on the other room's door was empty.

"No charts?" he asked.

"You're ahead of yourself," Susan explained. "Take a break."

David took advantage of the opportunity to dash over to the hospital and tell Nikki that Dr. Pilsner had called and said she could go home in the afternoon. Then he stopped in to see Marjorie, hoping her condition had improved. He was shocked. She was practically comatose.

Panic-stricken, David listened to Marjorie's chest. There was more congestion than earlier, but still not enough to explain her clinical state. Rushing to the nurses' station, he demanded to know why he hadn't been called.

"Called on what?" Janet Colburn, the head nurse, asked.

"Marjorie Kleber," David yelled while he wrote orders for more stat blood work and a portable chest X ray.

Janet told him that one of the LPNs had been in Marjorie's room less than half an hour previously and had reported no change.

"That's impossible," David snapped as he grabbed the phone. Earlier he'd been reluctant to call in consults. Now he was frantic to get them to come in as soon as possible. He called the oncologist, Dr. Clark Mieslich, and an infectious disease specialist, Dr. Martin Hasselbaum. Neither of them was a CMV doctor. David also called a CMV neurologist. When they arrived, they reviewed the situation before descending en masse on Marjorie. Having examined her closely, they withdrew to the nurses' station to confer.

As they discussed possible causes, Marjorie's heart suddenly slowed and then stopped. The monitor displayed an eerie flat line. The resuscitation team arrived and shocked her in hopes of restarting her heart, but there was no response. They quickly shocked her again. When that didn't work, they tried closed-chest cardiac massage frenetically for thirty minutes. But nothing worked. Gradually discouragement set in, and finally, by general consensus, Marjorie Kleber was declared dead.

David was devastated.

"It's too bad," Dr. Mieslich said. "She was such a terrific person."

"I'd say she did pretty well, considering the history in the chart," the neurologist said.

"Wait," David said. "You think she died of her cancer?"

"Obviously," Dr. Mieslich said. "She had disseminated cancer when I first saw her. She was one sick lady."

"But there wasn't any clinical evidence of tumor," David said. "This fatal episode seemed to suggest some sort of immune-system malfunction. How can you relate that to her cancer?"

"Her tumor wasn't apparent, that's true," Dr. Mieslich said. "But if we were to open her up, my guess is we'd find cancer all over. She had extensive metastases when she was originally diagnosed."

David nodded and thanked the consults for coming in. They all thanked him for the referral, then went their separate ways. His sadness and sense of guilt at Marjorie's passing was even more acute than he'd feared. He'd come to know her too well.

"Excuse me," Janet Colburn said softly. "Lloyd Kleber, Marjorie's husband, is here. He'd like to talk to you." She directed David to the patients' lounge.

Lloyd Kleber was staring out the window at the rain. David guessed he was in his mid-forties. His eyes were red from crying. "Thank you for taking care of Marjorie," he said. "She really appreciated your concern for her."

David nodded. He tried to say things that reflected his compassion. Finally he ventured to ask for permission to do an autopsy. He knew it was a lot to ask, but he wanted desperately to understand Marjorie's swift deterioration.

"If it could help others," Mr. Kleber said, "I'm sure Marjorie would want it done."

David walked over to the lab and found Angela in her office. She was pleased to see him, then noticed his strained expression.

"What's wrong?" she asked anxiously.

David told her, stopping a few times to compose himself.

"I'm so sorry," Angela said. She put her arms around him and gave him a reassuring hug.

"Mr. Kleber agreed to an autopsy," David said. "I'm glad because I haven't the slightest idea why she died. The consults all think it was her cancer. I'd like to confirm it. Could you see that it gets done?"

"Sure," Angela said. "But please don't get too depressed over this. It wasn't your fault."

"Let's see what the autopsy shows," David said.

David returned to his office to see patients. He'd only managed to see four when Susan waylaid him between examining rooms.

"Charles Kelley is in your private office," she said.

David stepped across the hall into his office. Kelley was impatiently pacing. His face was hard and angry.

"I find your behavior particularly galling," he said, towering over David.

"What are you talking about?" David asked.

"Just yesterday I spoke with you about utilization. I thought it was pretty clear and that you understood. Then today you irresponsibly ordered two non-CMV consults to see a hopelessly terminal patient. You obviously have no comprehension of the major problem facing medicine today: unnecessary and wasteful expense."

David struggled to keep himself under control. "Just a minute. Tell me how you know the consults were unnecessary."

"It's obvious," Kelley said with a supercilious wave of his head. "The patient's course wasn't altered. She was dying, and she proceeded to die. Money and other resources should not be thrown away for the sake of hopeless heroics."

David stared into Kelley's blue eyes. He was dumbfounded.

RELUCTANTLY Angela went to Wadley's office.

"What can I do for you, honey?" Wadley smiled.

Wincing at being addressed as honey, Angela swallowed her pride and asked about the procedure for arranging an autopsy.

"We don't do autopsies," Wadley said. "It costs too much to do autopsies, and the contract with CMV doesn't include them."

"What if the family requests it?" Angela asked.

"If they want to shell out eighteen hundred and ninety dollars, then we'll accommodate them. Otherwise we don't do it."

Angela nodded, then left. She walked over to the professional building and went into David's office. She was appalled by the number of patients waiting to be seen. She caught David as he shuttled between examining rooms. He was clearly frazzled.

"I can't do an autopsy on Marjorie Kleber."

"Why not?" David asked.

Angela told him what Wadley had said.

David shook his head with frustration. "My opinion of this place is going downhill fast," he said. He then told Angela about Kelley's opinion of his handling of the Kleber case.

Angela didn't know what to say. Kelley was beginning to sound dangerously uninformed. "Hang in there," she said. "I'll take Nikki home and come pick you up when you're done. We'll talk later."

Angela went back to the lab, finishing up for the day, collected Nikki, and drove home. Nikki was ecstatic to get out of the hospital. She and Rusty had an exuberant reunion.

David called at seven fifteen. With Nikki ensconced in front of the TV, Angela returned to the hospital to get him. She drove slowly. It was raining so hard the wipers had to struggle to keep the windshield clear.

"What a night," David said as he jumped into the car.

"What a day," Angela said as she started down the hill toward town. "Especially for you. How are you holding up?"

"I'm managing," David said. "It was a help to be so busy. But now I have to face reality—what am I going to tell Nikki?"

"You'll just have to tell her the truth, though that's easier said than done." Angela sighed. "I had another minor run-in with Wadley today."

"What?" David said. "What did he do now?"

"He called me honey a few times," Angela said. "And he brushed his hand across my backside. I really have to do something. I just wish I knew what."

"I think you should talk to Dr. Cantor," David said.

When they pulled into their driveway, Angela came to a stop as close as possible to the door to the mudroom. They both prepared to run for shelter. "When is this going to stop?" David complained. "It's been raining for three days straight."

Once they were inside, David decided to make a fire to cheer up the house. Descending into the basement to get some wood, he noticed that moisture was seeping through the grout between the granite foundation blocks. Along with the moisture was the damp, musty odor he'd smelled before.

After dinner David joined Nikki in front of the TV. Finally, during a commercial break, he put his arm around his daughter.

"I have to tell you something," he said gently.

"What?" Nikki asked. She was contentedly petting Rusty, who was curled up on the couch next to her.

"Your teacher, Marjorie Kleber, died today," David said. "It makes me very sad, especially since I was her doctor. I'm sure it upsets you too."

"No, it doesn't," Nikki said quickly. She looked down at Rusty, pretending to be concerned about a knot behind his ear, then looked at the television as if she were interested in the commercial.

"It's okay to be sad," David said. He started to talk about missing people you cared about when Nikki suddenly threw herself at him, enveloping him in a flood of tears.

David patted her back and continued to reassure her.

Angela appeared at the doorway. Seeing David holding their sobbing child, she came over, sat down, and put her arms around both David and Nikki. Together the three held on to each other, rocking gently as the rain beat against the windows.

12

Wednesday, October 20

DESPITE Nikki's protests, David and Angela insisted that she stay home from school another day. Alice Doherty arrived exactly at the time she promised. David and Angela were thankful to have someone so reliable.

As Angela and David climbed into their Volvo, David complained that he'd not been able to ride his bike all week. It wasn't raining hard, but a heavy mist rose out of the saturated earth.

They got to the hospital at seven thirty. While Angela headed for the lab, David went up to the patients' floor. When he entered John Tarlow's room, he was surprised to find drop cloths, stepladders, and an empty bed. Continuing on, he inquired at the nurses' station.

"Mr. Tarlow has been moved to 206," Janet Colburn said.

"How come?" David asked.

"They wanted to paint the room," Janet said. "Admitting told us to transfer the patient to 206."

"I think that's inconsiderate," David complained.

"Well, don't blame us," Janet said. "Talk to maintenance."

Feeling irritated for his patient's sake, David marched down to the maintenance/engineering office. Bent over a desk was a man close to David's age, dressed in rumpled green work clothes.

"One of my patients was moved from his room," David said. "I want to know why."

Van Slyke looked up. "If you are talking about room 216, it's being painted. We have a schedule."

"Schedule or no schedule," David said, "I hardly think patients should be inconvenienced."

"Talk to Beaton if you have a problem," Van Slyke said.

Taken aback by Van Slyke's insolence, David was seriously considering taking his advice, until he returned to the patients' floor and walked into John Tarlow's new room. Suddenly David was presented with a more pressing problem—John's condition was worse.

John's diarrhea and vomiting had returned with a vengeance. On top of that, he was dull and apathetic. David could not understand these symptoms, since John had been on IVs since his admission and was clearly not dehydrated.

Hurrying to the nurses' station, David pulled John's chart from the rack. He desperately pored over the data that had returned overnight from the lab. As a result of the run-in with Kelley, he was reluctant to request consults, since the two he wanted—oncology and infectious disease—were not CMV doctors.

David closed his eyes and rubbed his temples. He did not feel he was making much progress. Unfortunately, a key piece of information was lacking: the results of the stool cultures plated the day before. David still didn't know if he was dealing with a bacteria or not. On the positive side John was running no fever. David asked for John's temperature to be taken every hour and ordered that he be called if it rose above normal.

ENTERING the office, Angela immediately noticed the connecting door from her office into Wadley's was ajar. As silently as possible she moved over to the door and began to close it.

"Angela!" Wadley called out, making Angela flinch. She hadn't realized how tense she was. "Come in here. I want to show you something fascinating."

Angela sighed and reluctantly opened the door. Wadley was sitting at his desk in front of his regular microscope.

"Come on," he called again, "take a gander at this slide."

Warily Angela advanced into the room. Several feet away she hesitated. As if sensing her reluctance, Wadley gave himself a little push, and his chair rolled back from the desk. Angela stepped up to the microscope and leaned over to adjust the eyepieces.

Before she could look in, Wadley lunged forward and pulled her onto his lap. "Gotcha!" he cried.

Angela shrieked and struggled to get away. The unexpected forcefulness of the contact shocked her. She'd been concerned about his touching her subtly, not manhandling her.

"Let me go!" Angela demanded angrily, trying to unlock his fingers and break his grip. He was chuckling.

"I've got good news. The trip is all set. We're going to the pathology meeting in Miami in November."

"Wonderful," Angela said with as much sarcasm as she could muster. "Now let me go."

Wadley released her, and she sprang from his lap. "It's going to be fantastic," he said. "We'll be staying on the beach. I got us rooms in the Fontainbleau."

Angela was beside herself with anger. Biting her tongue to keep herself from exploding, she dashed into her office. Mortified and demeaned, she slammed the connecting door, grabbed her coat, and stalked out.

"THIS is not easy for me," Angela began. "It was hard for me to come here, but I don't know what else to do. I'm being sexually harassed by Dr. Wadley."

Dr. Cantor leaned forward at his desk. Angela was encouraged that he was interested, but then she noticed his smirk.

"How long has this been going on?" Cantor asked.

"Probably the whole time I've been here," Angela said.

"Probably?" he questioned with raised eyebrows. "You mean you're not sure?"

"It wasn't apparent initially," Angela explained. "At first I just thought he was acting like a particularly enthusiastic mentor, almost parental. He always took advantage of opportunities to be close to me and touch me seemingly innocently. He also insisted on confiding in me about personal family issues."

"This behavior you are describing can all be within the framework of friendship and the role of the mentor," Cantor said.

"I agree," Angela said. "That's why I allowed it to go on. The problem is that it has progressed."

"You mean it has changed?" Cantor asked.

"Most definitely," Angela said. "Quite recently." She then described the hand-on-the-thigh incident, feeling embarrassed as she did so. She mentioned the hand brushing her backside and Wadley's sudden use of the appellation honey.

"I personally don't see anything wrong with the word honey," Cantor said. "I use it all the time with my girls here."

Angela could only stare at the man. Clearly, she couldn't begin to expect a fair hearing from a doctor whose views on women were probably more archaic than Wadley's. Nonetheless she described Wadley's pulling her onto his lap to announce their trip to Miami.

"I don't know what to say about all this," Cantor said. "Has Dr. Wadley ever implied that your job depends on sexual favors?"

Inwardly Angela groaned. "No," she said. "Dr. Wadley has never intimated anything like that. But I find his unwanted familiarity extremely upsetting. It makes working very difficult."

"Maybe you're overreacting. Wadley is just an expressive guy. You yourself said he's enthusiastic." When Cantor saw the look on Angela's face, he added, "Well, it's a possibility."

Angela stood up. She forced herself to thank him for his time.

"Not at all," Cantor said. "Keep me informed, young lady. Meanwhile, I promise I'll talk with Dr. Wadley."

As Angela returned to her office, she couldn't help but feel that turning to Cantor wasn't going to help matters any. If anything, it was only going to make the situation worse.

WHEN David entered John Tarlow's room late in the afternoon, John was as listless as he'd been that morning, perhaps even a degree more so. When pressed, he could still say his name, but as to the month or the year, he had no clue.

Back at the nurses' station David went over the laboratory and diagnostic results that he had available, most of which were normal. The preliminary stool culture was negative for pathological bacteria.

"Please call me if Mr. Tarlow's temperature goes up or his G.I. symptoms get worse," he told the nurses before he left.

David and Angela met in the hospital lobby. Together they ran for their car. The weather was getting worse. Not only was it still raining, but it had gotten much colder.

When they arrived home, Nikki was happy to see them. She'd been bored most of the day until Caroline stopped over.

While Angela started dinner, David drove Caroline home. When he returned, Nikki met him at the door with a complaint. "It feels cold in the family room," she said.

David walked into the room and patted the radiator. It was blisteringly hot. "Where did you feel cold?" he asked.

"Sitting on the couch," Nikki said. "Come over and try it."

David followed his daughter and sat down next to her. Immediately he could feel a cool draft on the back of his neck. "You're right," he said. "We need to put up the storm windows. Come on, I'll show you what they are. We'll get firewood at the same time."

"I don't like it down here," Nikki said as they descended the cellar stairs. "It's scary."

"Now, don't be like your mother," David teased her.

Leaning against the back of the granite staircase was a stack of storm windows. As David moved one away from the others so Nikki could inspect it, he noticed something for the first time. He reached over the windows and ran his hand over the wall. "These cinder blocks are different from the rest of the basement and don't appear to be that old. I wonder why they're here."

"What are you talking about?" Nikki asked.

David showed her that the staircase was made of granite. Then he took her back beneath the stairs and showed her the cinder blocks. He explained that they must be covering some kind of triangular storage space.

"What's in it?" Nikki asked.

He shrugged. "Why don't we take a peek. Maybe it's a treasure."

David got out the sledgehammer that was used to split the firewood and brought it over. After having Nikki avert her eyes, he knocked out a portion of a cinder block near the top of the wall, creating a small hole. A musty odor wafted out.

"Run up and get a flashlight," he said.

While Nikki was gone, David used the sledgehammer to enlarge the hole. With a final blow, a whole cinder block came loose, and David lifted it out. By then Nikki was back with the flashlight. David took it and peered in. His heart jumped in his chest.

"What did you see?" Nikki asked. She didn't like the look on her father's face.

"I think you'd better get your mother," David said.

By the time Angela came down the stairs, David had a whole course of the cinder blocks dismantled.

"What's going on?" Angela demanded.

"Take a look," David said, handing her the flashlight.

"My God!" Angela said. Her voice echoed in the small space.

"What is it?" Nikki asked. "I want to see too."

Angela pulled her head out and looked at David. "It's a body," she said. "And it's obviously been in there for some time."

"A person?" Nikki asked with disbelief. "Can I see?"

Angela and David both nearly shouted, "No."

"Let's go build that fire," David said. He took Nikki to the woodpile, handed her a log, and picked up an armload himself.

While Angela phoned the town police, David and Nikki worked on the fire. Nikki was full of questions that David couldn't answer.

Half an hour later a police cruiser pulled up to the house. Two policemen had responded to Angela's call.

"My name's Wayne Robertson," the shorter of the pair said. He was dressed in mufti, with a quilted cotton vest over a plaid flannel shirt. On his head was a Boston Red Sox baseball cap. "I'm chief of police, and this is one of my deputies, Sherwin Morris."

Sherwin touched the brim of his hat. He was dressed in uniform.

Angela and David led the way. Only Nikki remained upstairs. Robertson took the flashlight and poked his head into the hole.

"Well, I'll be!" he said. "It's the quack." He faced the Wilsons. "Sorry this has happened to you folks, but I recognize the victim despite the fact that he looks a little worse for wear. His name is Dr. Dennis Hodges. This was his house."

Angela's eyes met David's, and she stifled a shiver. Gooseflesh had appeared on the back of her neck.

"What we have to do is knock the rest of this wall down so we can remove the body," Robertson continued.

"What about calling the medical examiner?" Angela asked.

Robertson regarded Angela for a few moments. He didn't like anyone telling him how to do his job, especially a woman. The only problem was that she was right. "Where's the phone?" he said.

"In the kitchen," Angela said.

Nikki had to be pried from the phone. She'd been back and forth between Arni Yansen and Caroline with the exciting news about finding a body in the basement.

Once the medical examiner had been called, Robertson and Morris set to work removing the cinder block wall. David brought down an extension cord and a floor lamp to help them see what they were doing.

"That pile of stuff in the corner looks like empty cement bags," Robertson said. He was using the beam of the flashlight as a pointer. "And there's the trowel. Heck, he's got everything in there with him. Maybe it was a suicide."

David and Angela looked at each other with the same thought:

Robertson was either the world's worst detective or a devotee of crude humor.

"I wonder what those papers are," Robertson said, directing the light at scattered sheets of paper in the makeshift tomb. And look at that." A tool that was partially concealed under the body resembled a flat crowbar.

"What is it?" David asked.

"A pry bar," Robertson said. "It's used mostly for demolition."

Nikki called down the stairs to say that the medical examiner had arrived. Angela went up to meet him. Dr. Tracy Cornish was a thin man of medium height, with wire-rimmed spectacles. He carried a large, old-fashioned black leather doctor's bag.

Angela introduced herself and led Dr. Cornish down to the tomb. He stood and stared at the scene for a few minutes. "Interesting," he said finally. "The body is in a particularly good state of preservation. How long has he been missing?"

"About eight months," Robertson said.

"Shows what a cool place will do," Dr. Cornish said.

The first thing he did was take a number of photos, including extreme close-ups. Then he donned rubber gloves and began removing objects from the tomb, placing them in plastic evidence bags. When he got to the papers, everyone crowded around to look.

"They're medical records from the hospital," David said.

"I'll bet these stains are all blood," Dr. Cornish said, pointing to large brown areas on the papers. He put all the papers into a plastic bag, which he then sealed and labeled.

Dr. Cornish turned his attention to the body. Searching the pockets, he found a wallet with bills and credit cards inside.

"Well, it wasn't a robbery," Robertson said.

Dr. Cornish then removed Hodges' watch, which was still running. The time was correct.

"What about bagging the hands?" Angela suggested.

Dr. Cornish thought for a moment. "Good idea," he said. He got paper bags from his kit and secured them over Hodges' hands. That done, he and Morris got the body into a body bag.

Fifteen minutes later the Wilsons watched as the police cruiser and the medical examiner's van descended their driveway and disappeared into the night. "Anyone hungry?" Angela asked.

Both Nikki and David groaned.

"I'm not either," Angela admitted. "What a night."

After Nikki's respiratory treatment, they all went to bed. Though not an antidote, sleep seemed to be the best alternative. Although Nikki and David were sleepy, Angela wasn't, and as she lay in bed, she became acutely aware of all the sounds the house made. She had never realized how noisy it was, particularly on a windy, rainy night. From deep in the basement she heard the oil burner kick on. There was even an intermittent, very low-pitched whine from wind coming down the master-bedroom flue.

A sudden series of thumps made Angela sit upright.

"What's that?" she whispered nervously, giving David a shove.

"What's what?" David asked, only half awake.

Angela told him to listen. "There. That banging."

"That's the shutters hitting against the house," David said. "Goodness sake, calm down."

Angela lay back against the pillow, but her eyes were wide open. "I don't like what has been happening around here," she said.

David audibly moaned.

"Really. I can't believe so much has changed in so few days. I was worried this was going to happen."

"You mean finding Hodges' body?" David asked.

"I'm talking about everything. The change in the weather, Wadley's harassing me, Marjorie's death, Kelley's harassing you, and now a body in our basement."

"We're just being efficient," David said. "We're getting all the bad stuff out of the way at one time."

"I'm being serious, and—" Angela began to say, but she was interrupted by a scream from Nikki.

In a flash both David and Angela were out of bed and running down the hall into Nikki's room. She was sitting in bed with a dazed look on her face from a horrible nightmare.

David and Angela did their best to comfort her. In the end they invited her to come sleep with them in their bed. Nikki agreed, and they all marched back to the master bedroom. Climbing into bed, they settled down. Unfortunately, David ended up sleeping on the very edge because inviting Nikki also meant inviting Rusty. But David would have slept on a bed of nails for Nikki's sake.

13

Thursday, October 21

THE weather was not much better the next morning. The rain had stopped, but there was no break in the heavy cloud cover. While Nikki was doing her postural drainage, the state's attorney's office called. An assistant from the office arrived within the hour to look at the crime scene. A pleasant woman with fiery red hair, she was dressed conservatively in a dark blue suit.

"Sorry to bother you so early," the woman said. She introduced herself as Elaine Sullivan.

"No trouble at all," David said, holding the door open for her.

David led her down the cellar steps. She took out a camera and snapped a few pictures. Then she bent down and stuck a fingernail into the dirt of the tomb's floor. Angela came down the stairs and looked over David's shoulder.

"I think I'll recommend that the state police crime-scene investigators be called," Elaine said. "I hope it won't be a bother."

"Do we have to be here when they come?" David asked.

"That's up to you," Elaine said. "An investigator may want to talk with you at some point. They'll be here soon, probably this morning."

"I'll arrange for Alice to come," Angela said. David nodded.

Shortly after Elaine had left, the Wilsons were off themselves. As they took Nikki to school, she couldn't talk about anything besides the body. They dropped her off and started for the hospital.

"I'm concerned about how my patient will be this morning," David said. "Even though I haven't gotten any calls, I'm worried."

"And I'm worried about facing Wadley," Angela said.

With a kiss for luck, they headed for their respective days.

David went directly to check on John Tarlow. Stepping into the room, he immediately noticed that John's breathing was labored—not a good sign. David pulled out his stethoscope and gave John's shoulder a shake. John barely responded.

Panic gripped David. Rapidly examining his patient, he immediately discovered that John was developing extensive pneumonia.

David raced down to the nurses' station, barking orders for John to be transferred to the ICU immediately. "Why haven't I been called?" he snapped. "Mr. Tarlow has developed pneumonia."

"He was sleeping comfortably the last time we took his temperature," the nurse said.

David grabbed the chart and flipped it open to the temperature graph. The temperature had edged up a little, but not the way David would have expected, having heard the man's chest.

With commendable efficiency John Tarlow was transferred into the ICU. David called the oncologist, Dr. Clark Mieslich, and the infectious disease specialist, Dr. Martin Hasselbaum, to ask them to come in immediately.

The lab responded quickly to lab work requested for the ICU, and David was soon looking at John's results. His white count, which had been low, was even lower, indicating that his system was overwhelmed by the developing pneumonia. It was the kind of response one might expect from a patient undergoing chemotherapy, but John hadn't been on chemo for months.

The consults arrived in short order to examine the patient.

"What do you make of the low white count?" David asked.

"I can't say," Dr. Mieslich admitted. "I suppose it is related to his leukemia. Besides, it's academic. I'm afraid he's moribund."

David couldn't believe he was about to lose a second patient in his brief Bartlet career. He turned to Dr. Hasselbaum.

Dr. Hasselbaum was equally pessimistic. He pointed to the fact that John's blood pressure was low and that his kidneys were failing. "It doesn't look good. If we treat, we'll have to treat massively. I have access to some experimental agents created to help combat this type of endotoxin shock. These drugs are expensive."

"A man's life hangs in the balance," David said.

An hour and fifteen minutes later the treatment had been instituted. David hurried to his office. Every seat in the waiting room was occupied. Patients were standing in the hall. Everyone was upset, even the receptionist.

David took a deep breath and plunged into his appointments. In addition to his scheduled patients, a number of semiemergencies had to be squeezed in as well. David felt compelled to hospitalize Mary Ann Schiller, who had a severe case of sinusitis, and Jonathan Eakins, with a disturbing cardiac arrhythmia. Two night-shift nurses from the second floor had flulike syndromes: general malaise, low-grade fever, low white counts—as well as nausea, vomiting, and diarrhea. David sent them home for bed rest and symptomatic therapy.

When he had a minute, he asked his nurse, Susan, if a flu was going around the hospital. "Not that I've heard," Susan said.

MIDMORNING, Angela phoned the chief medical examiner, Dr. Walter Dunsmore, in Burlington. She explained that she was a pathologist at the Bartlet Community Hospital and went on to describe her interest in the Hodges case.

Dr. Dunsmore promptly invited her to come to Burlington someday to see their facility. "In fact, why don't you come up and assist at Hodges' autopsy? It's scheduled for late this morning."

"That's very generous," Angela said. "Unfortunately, I'm not sure what my chief would say about my taking the time."

"I've known Ben Wadley for years," Dr. Dunsmore said. "I'll give him a call and clear it with him."

"I'm not sure that would be a good idea," Angela said, and was about to protest further when she realized that Dr. Dunsmore had hung up. She had no idea what Wadley's reaction would be.

Angela learned sooner than she expected. The phone rang.

"I'm caught up here in the OR," Wadley said. "The chief medical examiner called. Tells me he wants you to assist with an autopsy."

"I just spoke with him. I wasn't sure how you'd feel about it." It was obvious to Angela from Wadley's cheerfulness that Cantor had not yet spoken with him.

"I think it's a great idea," Wadley said. "It never hurts to stay on the medical examiner's good side. I encourage you to go."

"Thank you," Angela said. "I will."

Grabbing her coat, Angela left the hospital and headed home to change clothes. As she approached the house, she was surprised to see a state police van parked in front of her house. Evidently the crime-scene investigators were still there.

Angela explained her mission to Alice and went down to the basement. Three technicians had the area around the back of the stairs blocked off with crime-scene tape and brightly illuminated with floodlights. One man was using advanced techniques to lift fingerprints from the stone. He introduced himself as Quillan Reilly. Another man was carefully sifting through dirt. The third was using a handheld instrument called a Lumalight, looking for fibers and latent prints.

"Would you mind if we came back this evening when it's dark to use luminol on the walls upstairs?" Quillan asked.

"What's luminol?" Angela asked.

"It's used to search for bloodstains," he explained.

"Well, if you think it might be helpful," Angela said.

Ten minutes later Angela was on her way. In Burlington, she found the medical examiner's office without difficulty.

"We're waiting for you," Dr. Dunsmore said as Angela was ushered into his modern and sparsely furnished office. He made her feel instantly at ease. He even asked her to call him Walt.

In minutes Angela was dressed in a surgical scrub suit. Outside the autopsy room, as she donned a mask, a hood, and goggles, she felt a rush of excitement. The autopsy room had always been an arena of discovery for her.

Dennis Hodges was laid out on the autopsy table. X rays had been taken, and were already on the view box.

First they looked at the X rays. The penetrating fracture at the top of the forehead was certainly a mortal wound. There was also a linear fracture in the back of the head. In addition, there were fractures of the left clavicle, the left ulna, and the left radius.

"There's no doubt it was a homicide," Walt said. "Looks like the poor old guy put up quite a fight."

Angela described the pry bar that was found with the body. Using a ruler to measure the penetrating fracture and examining the wound itself, they determined that the pry bar could have been the murder weapon.

Then they turned their attention to the bagged hands. Walt carefully slipped the hands out of their covers and used a magnifying glass to examine the nails. "There is some foreign material under some of them. We'll have to wait for the microscopic," he said as he removed the material to specimen jars.

The autopsy itself went quickly. There was plenty of pathology to make things interesting. Hodges had significant arteriosclerosis, a small cancer of the lung, and advanced cirrhosis of the liver.

"I'd guess he liked his bourbon," Walt said.

After the autopsy was completed, Angela thanked Walt and

asked to be kept informed about the case. On the way back to Bartlet she felt in a better mood than she had for days. She was glad that Wadley had let her go.

No sooner had Angela hung up her coat in her office than the connecting door to Wadley's office banged open. Angela jumped. Wadley stormed into the room, crowding her against her desk.

"I'd like an explanation," he snarled. "Why did you go to Cantor with this preposterous story? Sexual harassment! That's absurd."

Angela shrank back, afraid he might hit her.

"Why didn't you say something to me?" Wadley screamed. "After all the effort I've lavished on you, this is the reward I get."

"I'm sorry that we've reached this point," Angela said.

"That's it?" Wadley yelled. "You've besmirched my reputation and that's all you can say? This is slander, woman, and I'll tell you something. I might take you to court." Wadley spun on his heels, strode into his office, and slammed the door.

SUSAN poked her head into the examining room and told David that the ICU was on the line. Fearing the worst, he picked up the phone. The ICU nurse said that Mr. Tarlow had just gone into cardiac arrest and the resuscitation team was working on him.

David broke out in a cold sweat. He dashed over to the ICU, but he was too late. By the time he arrived, it was over. The attending physician had already declared John Tarlow dead. "The man's lungs were full, his kidneys shot, and he had no blood pressure," the doctor said.

David went over to the main desk and sat down. He began to wonder if he was suited to be a doctor. Tarlow's relatives came, and David accepted their kind words, feeling like an impostor. He hadn't done anything for John. He didn't even know why he'd died.

Even though he'd now been informed about the hospital autopsy policy, David asked the family if they would allow one. They said they'd consider it.

Leaving the ICU area, David had enough presence of mind to check on Mary Ann Schiller and Jonathan Eakins. Unfortunately, David discovered something that gave him pause. Mary Ann had been put in room 206—the room that John Tarlow had so recently vacated. He had half a mind to have her moved, but what would he say to admissions—he never wanted one of his patients in room 206 again? That was clearly ridiculous.

David checked her IV. She was already getting her antibiotic. After promising he'd be back later, David went into Jonathan's room. He too was comfortable and relaxed. Jonathan said that the cardiologist was expected imminently.

When he returned to his office, Susan greeted David with word that Charles Kelley had called. "He wants to see you immediately."

"How many patients are we behind?" David asked.

"Plenty," Susan said. "So try not to be too long."

Feeling as if he were carrying the world on his shoulders, David dragged himself over to the CMV office.

"I don't know what to do, David," Kelley said. "The very day after I talk to you about avoiding unnecessary consults, you do it again with another terminal patient. What am I going to do with you? The costs of medical care have to be considered. You know there's a crisis in this country."

David nodded. That much was true.

"Then why is this so hard for you?" Kelley asked. "Helen Beaton called me moments ago complaining about the enormously expensive biotechnology drugs that you ordered for this sad, dying patient. Talk about heroics! The man had leukemia for years. Don't you understand? This is wasting money and resources."

Kelley sighed and shook his head. "Helen Beaton also complained about your autopsy request," he said in a tired voice. "Autopsies are not part of the contract with CMV. You were informed of that. David, you have to help me or . . ." Kelley paused.

"Or what?" David said.

"I like you, David," Kelley said. "But I have people above me I have to answer to. I hope you can appreciate that."

More confused and dejected than he could remember being, David stumbled back to his office. He was confronted by a waiting room full of unhappy patients angrily glancing at their watches and noisily flipping through magazines.

DINNER at the Wilson home was a tense affair. No one spoke. Everyone was agitated. It was as if their Shangri-la had gone the way of the weather.

After dinner David told everyone that it was time to cheer up. In an attempt to improve the atmosphere, he offered to build a cozy fire. But when he descended to the basement, he suffered the shock of seeing yellow crime-scene tape around his own stairs. It brought back the gruesome image of Hodges' body.

David gathered the wood quickly and dashed back upstairs. Building the fire, he began to talk enthusiastically about the upcoming winter. Just when Angela and Nikki were getting in the spirit, headlight beams traversed the wall of the family room.

David went to the window. "It's a state police van," he said. "What on earth could they want?"

"I totally forgot," Angela said. "The crime-scene people asked if they could come by when it was dark to look for bloodstains."

The technicians were the same three men who had been there that morning. Angela was impressed with the length of their workday. She introduced Quillan to David.

"How does this test work?" David asked.

"The luminol reacts with any residual iron from the blood," Quillan said. "When it does, it fluoresces."

The technicians started in the mudroom, setting up a camera on a tripod. Then they turned out all the lights and sprayed luminol on the walls.

"Here's a little," Quillan said in the darkness. David and Angela leaned into the room. Along the wall was a faint, spotty, eerie fluorescence.

"Not enough for a picture," one of the other technicians said.

The technicians moved into the kitchen and continued about their business. David, Angela, and Nikki hovered at the doorway. Portions of the wall near the mudroom began to fluoresce.

"It's faint, but we got a lot here," Quillan said.

"My God," Angela whispered. "My kitchen."

The Wilsons could see vague outlines of the men as they approached the kitchen table, which had been left behind by Clara Hodges. All at once its legs began to glow in a ghostly fashion.

"My guess is this is the murder site," one of the technicians said. "Right here by the table." The camera clicked loudly.

After the crime-scene investigators had left, the Wilsons returned to the family room even more depressed than they had been earlier. Angela sat on the hearth with her back to the fire and looked at David and Nikki, who had collapsed on the couch. Suddenly she broke the gloomy silence.

"Maybe we should move," she said.

"Wait one second," David said. "I know you're upset. But we're not going to allow ourselves to become hysterical."

"I'm hardly hysterical," Angela shot back.

"Suggesting that we move because of an unfortunate event which occurred almost a year ago is hardly rational," David said.

"It happened in this house," Angela said.

"This house happens to be mortgaged to the roof. We can't just walk away because of an emotional upset."

"Then I want the locks changed. A murderer's been in here."

"Okay," David said. "We'll change the locks."

TRAYNOR was in a rotten mood as he pulled up to the Iron Horse Inn. The weather seemed to fit his temperament: the rain had returned to monsoonlike intensity. Even his umbrella proved uncooperative; it wouldn't open. He cursed, and made a run for the inn's door.

Beaton, Caldwell, and Sherwood were sitting in a booth when he arrived. Cantor got there just after him. As the two men sat down, Carleton, the bartender, came by and took their orders.

"Thank you all for coming out in this inclement weather," Traynor said. "But I'm afraid that recent events mandated an emergency session."

"Oh, Harold," Cantor said, "get on with it."

"As you all know by now, Hodges' body turned up in rather unpleasant circumstances."

"The story has attracted media attention," Beaton said. "It made the front page of the Boston *Globe*."

"I'm concerned about this publicity's potentially negative effect on the hospital," Traynor said. "The macabre aspects of Hodges' death may attract still more media. Thanks largely to Helen Beaton, we've been able to keep word of our ski-masked rapist out of the headlines. But big-city reporters are bound to stumble across that brewing scandal if they're in town. Between that and Hodges we could be in for a slew of bad press."

"I've heard from Burlington that Hodges' death is definitely being ruled a homicide," Cantor said.

"Of course it will be ruled a homicide," Traynor snapped. "The man's body was entombed behind a wall of cinder blocks."

"I don't see how Hodges' death is the hospital's problem," Sherwood said. "It's not like we killed him."

"Hodges' name is intimately associated with Bartlet," Traynor said. "Lots of people know he wasn't happy with the way we were running things."

"The less the hospital says, the better," Sherwood said.

"I disagree," Beaton said. "I think we should issue a statement regretting his death and underlining the great debt owed him. The statement should include condolences to his family."

"Ignoring his death would seem peculiar," Cantor said.

"I agree," Caldwell said.

Sherwood shrugged. "I'll go along."

"Has anyone spoken to Robertson?" Traynor asked.

"I have," Beaton said. "He doesn't have any suspects. Braggart that he is, he surely would have let on if he had."

Sherwood laughed. "Heck, he could be a suspect himself."

"So could you," Cantor said to Sherwood.

"And so could you, Cantor," Sherwood said.

14

Friday, October 22

ANGELA was relieved to find that Wadley wasn't around when she arrived at the lab the following morning. Quickly she immersed herself in her work, but no sooner had she started than Dr. Dunsmore, the chief medical examiner, was on the phone.

"I have some interesting news," Walt said. "The material that we teased from beneath Dr. Hodges' fingernails was skin. I've already run a DNA screen. It's not Hodges' skin. I'd bet a thousand dollars it belongs to his assailant. It could prove to be critical evidence if a suspect is charged."

"Congratulations," Angela said. She thanked him for keeping her informed.

"I almost forgot," Walt added. "I found some black carbon particles embedded in the skin. It looks as if the killer scraped up against a hearth or a wood stove during the struggle."

Angela explained about the luminol test the night before. "The blood spatter wasn't anywhere near a fireplace or the stove. Maybe the killer picked up the carbon earlier, someplace else."

"I doubt it," Walt said. "There was no inflammation. The carbon had to be picked up contemporaneous to the struggle."

"It's a mystery," Angela said. "We're obviously missing some crucial piece of information."

THE day had dawned bright and clear; and after having been denied the opportunity to ride his bike for an entire week, David thoroughly enjoyed the trip from his home to the hospital. Entering the hospital, he felt better than he had for several days. The first patient he visited was Mary Ann Schiller.

Unfortunately, Mary Ann was not bright and cheerful. David had to wake her up, and while he was examining her, she fell back asleep. Beginning to feel a little concerned, David woke her up again, but while he was concentrating on her breath sounds, she fell asleep again. He looked at her peaceful face; it was in sharp contrast to his state of mind. Her drowsiness was alarming him.

David went to the nurses' station to go over Mary Ann's chart. His apprehension grew when he read the nurses' notes and learned that G.I. symptoms had appeared during the night. Mary Ann had suffered from nausea, vomiting, and diarrhea. David wasn't sure how to proceed. He went on to Jonathan Eakins, who was in an expansive mood. He was feeling chipper, and reported that his cardiac monitor had been beeping as regularly as a metronome.

The rest of David's hospital patients were all doing as well as Jonathan. David was able to move from one to the other swiftly, even discharging a few. With his rounds finished, he headed to his office, happy to be early. Knowing that his productivity was being monitored, he tried to keep each visit short. When two second-floor nurses asked to be seen as semiemergencies, he was able to take them the moment they came in the door. Both had flulike symptoms identical to the two previous nurses, and David treated them the same way.

David finished his morning patients before noon and dictated some letters before meeting Angela in the hospital lobby.

"With the weather as nice as it is, what do you say we go into town and have lunch at the diner?" David suggested.

"Let's get takeout," Angela said. "I want to stop by the police station and find out about the Hodges investigation."

"I don't think that's a good idea."

"Why not?"

"Intuition, I guess. To tell the truth, I didn't get the impression they were that interested in investigating the case."

"That's why I want to go," Angela said. "I want to be sure they know that we're interested. Come on, humor me."

They got tuna sandwiches to go and ate them on the steps of the gazebo in the center of the town green. After their meal they walked over to the police station—a plain, two-story brick structure on the green, directly across from the library.

The officer at the front desk directed David and Angela down a creaky wooden corridor to Wayne Robertson's office. Robertson invited them in and hastily took newspapers and Dunkin' Donuts bags off two chairs. When they were seated, he leaned his expansive backside against his metal desk, crossed his arms, and smiled. He was wearing reflective aviator-style sunglasses.

"What can I do for you folks?" he asked.

"We're here to offer our cooperation," Angela said.

"Well now, we appreciate that," Robertson said, smiling widely. "Without community support, we couldn't do our job."

"We want to see the Hodges murder case solved," Angela said. "We want to see the killer behind bars."

"Well, you're certainly not alone," Robertson said, his smile plastered on his face. "We want to see it solved as well."

"Living in a house where there's been a murder is very distressing," Angela said. "Particularly if the murderer's still on the streets. I'm sure you understand."

"Absolutely," Robertson said.

"What exactly are the police doing?" Angela asked.

The smile faded from Robertson's face. "We're working on it. Not much right now, but back when Hodges disappeared, we were working day and night."

"I'm surprised there hasn't been a resurgence of interest now that there's a corpse," Angela said testily. "The medical examiner has ruled the case a homicide. We've got a killer walking around this town, and I want something done."

"Well, we certainly don't want to disappoint you folks," Robertson said with a touch of sarcasm. "What exactly would you like done?"

David started to say something, but Angela shushed him. "You have the murder weapon," she said, "so test it for fingerprints. Find out where it was purchased. We shouldn't have to tell you how to carry out an investigation."

"The spoor is a little cold after eight months," Robertson said, "and frankly, I don't take kindly to your coming in here and telling me how to do my job."

"The basics ought to be done on this case," Angela said.

"They were," Robertson said. "Eight months ago."

"And what did you learn?" Angela demanded.

"Lots of things," Robertson snapped. "We learned there was no break-in or robbery. But there was a bit of a struggle."

"A bit of a struggle?" Angela echoed. "Police investigators have proved that the killer bashed the doctor with a pry bar, spattering blood all over the walls. Dr. Hodges had multiple skull fractures, a fractured clavicle, and a broken arm." Angela threw her hands in the air. "I don't believe this. The medical examiner suspects that the victim had skin from his attacker under his fingernails. That's the kind of struggle it was. All we need is a suspect. Forensics can do the rest."

"Thank you for the timely tip," Robertson said. "Now if you'll excuse me, I have work to do."

Robertson stepped over to the door and held it open. David practically had to yank Angela from the office. It was all he could do to keep her from saying more on her way out.

Back at his desk, Robertson picked up the phone and pressed one of the automatic dial buttons. "Sorry to bother you," he said deferentially, "but I think we might have a problem."

"DON'T you dare paint me as an hysterical female," Angela said as she got into the car.

"As deplorable as Hodges' death was," David said, "it doesn't involve us. It's a problem that should be left up to the authorities."

"What?" Angela cried. "The man was beaten to death in our kitchen. We're involved whether you want to admit it or not."

When they reached the hospital, the only parking space available was far from the entrance. They got out and started walking.

"We already have plenty to worry about," David said. "It's not as if we don't have enough problems at the moment."

"Then maybe we should hire somebody to do the investigating for us," Angela said.

"You can't be serious," David said, coming to a halt. "We don't have the money to throw away on such nonsense."

"I don't think it's nonsense," Angela said. "I think the issue is one of basic social responsibility."

"You're too much," David said. He leaned over and gave her a peck on the cheek. "We'll talk later. For now, calm down." With a wave he strode off toward the professional building.

In the lab, Angela went to look for her fellow pathologist, Paul Darnell. She found him hunched over stacks of petri dishes.

"You've lived in Bartlet all your life," Angela said. "Would you mind if I asked you a few questions?"

"Not at all."

"What was Dennis Hodges like?"

"He was a feisty old codger few people miss. He had a penchant for making enemies."

"I just had a conversation with Wayne Robertson," Angela said. "I got the distinct impression that he's dragging his feet about investigating who killed Hodges."

"I'm not surprised," Paul said. "There's not a lot of pressure to solve the case. On top of that, Robertson could have done it himself. He always had it in for Hodges. Robertson blamed his wife's death on Hodges."

"Hodges was Mrs. Robertson's physician?" Angela asked.

"No. By then Hodges was running the hospital full time. But as director, he allowed Dr. Werner Van Slyke to practice, even though everybody knew Van Slyke had a drinking problem. Van Slyke bungled Robertson's wife's appendicitis case while under the influence. Robertson blamed Hodges. It wasn't rational, but hate usually isn't. Now, Hodges was friends with Harold Traynor, whose sister was married to Van Slyke, and when Hodges finally denied Van Slyke privileges—"

"All right," Angela said, holding up her hand. "You're overwhelming me. I had no idea the town was quite this byzantine."

"It's a small town," Paul said.

"Hodges' murderer is still walking around," Angela said. "Presumably a man capable of extreme violence." She shivered. "I don't like it," she said. "This man was in my home."

Paul shrugged. "I understand how you feel. But I don't know what you can do about it. If you want to, talk to Barton Sherwood. As president of the bank, he knows everyone. He knew Hodges particularly well, since he's been on the hospital board forever."

Angela went back to her office and called Barton Sherwood. She came right to the point, describing how uncomfortable she felt about Hodges' murderer being on the loose. She told Sherwood she hoped he would be willing to help.

"Help?" Sherwood questioned.

"The local police don't seem to care about solving the case," Angela said. "With your stature in the town a word from you would go a long way in getting them to do something."

Sherwood was clearly flattered. "Thank you for your vote of confidence, but I truly don't think you have anything to worry about. Hodges was not the victim of senseless, random violence."

"Do you know who killed him?" Angela asked.

"Heavens no," Sherwood said nervously. "I didn't mean to imply that. It's just that Dr. Hodges was an unpopular man who'd hurt a number of people. So no one cares much whether someone is arrested or not."

"I care," Angela said. "The murder took place in my house. Besides, there's no place for vigilante justice in this day and age."

Following Angela's call, Sherwood came to the conclusion that it was best for him to do nothing other than pass on the information. He picked up the phone again.

"Something has happened I thought you should know about," he said when the connection went through. "I just had a call from the newest member of the hospital's professional staff. . . ."

DAVID finished with his last office patient for the day, then hurried over to the hospital to make his late afternoon rounds. Fearing what he'd find, he left Mary Ann Schiller for last. As he'd intuitively suspected, she'd taken a turn for the worse.

Her low-grade fever had gradually climbed during the afternoon, while she was on antibiotics. As David tried to talk to her, he found her apathetic. She was disoriented with respect to time and place, although she still knew her name.

David rolled her on her side and listened to her chest. When he did so, he panicked. She was developing massive pneumonia. It was like John Tarlow all over again.

David raced to the nurses' station, where he ordered a stat blood count as well as a portable chest film. Going over Mary Ann's chart, he found that the notes for the day suggested she had been doing fine. The blood count came back showing very little white blood cell response to the developing pneumonia, a situation again reminiscent of Tarlow and Kleber. The portable chest film confirmed extensive pneumonia in both lungs.

At a loss, David called Dr. Mieslich, but the oncologist could offer little help. He did confirm that the last time he had seen Mary Ann, there had been no evidence of her cancer.

While David was on the phone, a nurse yelled that Mary Ann was convulsing. David slammed down the phone and raced to the bedside. Mary Ann was indeed in the throes of a grand mal seizure. Fortunately, David was able to control it quickly with intravenous medication. Nevertheless, in its wake, Mary Ann remained comatose.

Returning to the nurses' station, David put in a stat call to the CMV neurologist, who said he'd be over as soon as he could.

David sent Mary Ann to the imaging center for an MRI, then called the oncologist back and asked for a formal consult. He also called Dr. Hasselbaum, the infectious disease specialist. David worried about Kelley's reaction, but he couldn't allow concern about Kelley to influence his decision making in light of the grand mal seizure. The gravity of Mary Ann's condition was apparent.

As soon as David was alerted that the MRI study was available, he dashed over to the imaging center. He met the neurologist in the viewing room as the first images were being processed. When the study was complete, David was shocked that there was no sign of a metastatic tumor. He would have sworn such a tumor was responsible for the seizure.

Dr. Hasselbaum confirmed David's diagnosis of extensive pneumonia. He also demonstrated that the bacteria involved was a gram-negative-type organism similar, but not identical, to the bacteria that had caused Kleber's and Tarlow's pneumonia. Worse still, he suggested that Mary Ann was already in septic shock.

From the imaging center David sent Mary Ann to the ICU, where he insisted on the most aggressive therapy available. By then her breathing was so labored she needed a respirator.

When everything that could be done for Mary Ann had been done, David stopped in again to see Jonathan Eakins. Thankfully, Jonathan was doing marvelously.

"I only have one complaint," Jonathan said. "This bed has a mind of its own. Sometimes when I press the button, nothing happens. Neither the head nor the foot rises."

David mentioned the problem to the evening head nurse, Dora Maxfield. "Not his too," Dora said. "I'll have maintenance take care of it right away."

AFTER dinner Nikki excused herself to watch her half-hour allotment of television. David and Angela lingered at the table. She related her conversations with Paul Darnell and Barton Sherwood.

"I'm not happy about your asking questions about Dennis Hodges," David said. "Did it occur to you that you might wind up questioning the killer himself?"

Angela admitted she hadn't thought of that. "You seem distracted," she said, changing the subject. "What's wrong?"

"Another one of my patients is in the ICU fighting for her life. It's another disaster. Frankly, I'm worried she'll die just like Kleber and Tarlow. Maybe I don't know what I'm doing. Maybe I shouldn't even be a doctor."

Angela came around the table to put an arm around David. "I don't want to hear any talk like that," she said. "You're a wonderful doctor. I wish I could help."

"Thank you," David said. "I know you mean it. Unfortunately, there's nothing you can do directly except understand why I can't get so worked up about Hodges' death."

"I can't just let it go," Angela said.

"But it could be dangerous," David said. "Whoever killed Hodges isn't likely to be thrilled by your poking around. Who knows what such a person might do? Look what he did to Hodges."

Angela stared at him. Potential danger to her family was her motivation for wanting Hodges' murder solved. She hadn't considered that her investigation could put them in even greater jeopardy. Yet all she had to do was close her eyes and see the luminol glow in her kitchen or remember the horrid fractures on the X rays in the autopsy room to know that David had a point: a person capable of that kind of violence was not someone who should be provoked.

15

Saturday, October 23

DAVID'S early morning arrival surprised the ICU nurses. Mary Ann's condition had not changed dramatically, although she had developed moderately severe diarrhea. David reviewed her case again from the beginning, but did not have any new ideas. He made his rounds to see his other hospitalized patients and headed home.

When he got there, Angela and Nikki were just finishing breakfast. While Angela tended to Nikki's respiratory treatment, David put the first-floor storm windows up. With that accomplished, David and Nikki rode off on their bikes into town on a shopping mission.

Left alone, Angela began to feel a little edgy. She noticed every creak the empty house made. Before long she was locking the doors and even the windows. Ending up in the kitchen, Angela could not suppress her imagination from coating the walls with blood.

"I can't live like this," Angela said aloud, realizing how paranoid she was becoming. "But what am I going to do?"

Walking over to the phone directory, she looked up private investigators, but didn't find any entries. Then she looked up detectives. One—a Phil Calhoun—was in Rutland, which was only a short drive away.

Before she had time to reconsider, Angela dialed the number. A man with a husky, slow, and deliberate voice answered. She pictured a powerfully built man on the other end of the wire, with broad shoulders, dark hair, maybe even a mustache.

Angela stammered that she wanted to investigate a murder.

"Sounds interesting," Calhoun said. "You want me to come there, or do you want to come here?"

Angela didn't want David finding out what she was up to—not just yet. "I'll come to you," she said.

"I'll be waiting," Calhoun said after he gave her directions.

CALHOUN'S office was also his home. Angela had no trouble finding it. In the driveway she noticed his Ford pickup truck had a rifle rack in the back of the cab and a sticker on the back bumper that read THIS VEHICLE CLIMBED MOUNT WASHINGTON.

Phil Calhoun invited her into his living room and offered her a seat on a threadbare sofa. He was far from her romantic image of a private investigator. Although he was a big man, he was overweight—and in his early sixties, she guessed. His face was a little doughy, but his gray eyes were bright. He was wearing a wool checkered hunting shirt and a cap with ROSCOE ELECTRIC emblazoned above the visor.

"Mind if I smoke?" Calhoun asked, holding up a box of Antonio y Cleopatra cigars.

"It's your house," Angela said.

Calhoun leaned back in his chair. "Now, about this murder."

Angela gave a capsule summary of the whole affair.

"Sounds interesting," Calhoun said. "I'll be delighted to take the case on an hourly basis. Now about me: I'm a retired state police officer and a widower. That's about it. Any questions?"

Angela studied Calhoun as he casually smoked. "Have you ever been involved in a murder investigation?"

"Not as a civilian," Calhoun said.

"What type of cases do you usually handle?"

"Marital problems, shoplifting—that sort of thing."

"Do you think you could handle a case like this?"

"No question. I grew up in a small Vermont town. I'm familiar with Bartlet. Heck, I even know some of the people who live there. I'm the right man for the job because I can ask questions without sticking out like a sore thumb."

Angela drove home wondering if she'd done the right thing in hiring Phil Calhoun. She also wondered when she'd tell David.

THAT afternoon Phil Calhoun parked his truck by the Bartlet library and walked across the green to the police station.

"Wayne around?" he asked the duty officer.

The duty officer merely pointed down the hall.

Calhoun walked down and knocked on the open door. Robertson looked up and smiled. Inviting Phil to take a load off his feet, he tipped back his chair and accepted an Antonio y Cleopatra.

"Working late on a Saturday," Calhoun said. "Must be a lot going on here in Bartlet."

"Lousy paperwork gets worse every year," Robertson said.

Calhoun nodded. "I read that old Doc Hodges turned up," he said.

"Caused a little stir, but it's already died down." Robertson's face became red as he aired his litany against Hodges.

"Much action on the case?" Calhoun asked casually.

"Nah," Robertson said. "Nobody cares much, not even his wife. After the medical examiner called the state's attorney, a state police lieutenant called me. I told him it wasn't worth his time and that we'd handle it. The state police have more pressing cases to attend to. Same with us. Besides, it's been eight months. The trail's stone-cold."

"What are you guys working on these days?"

"A series of attacks up in the hospital parking lot."

"Any luck snagging the perpetrator?" Calhoun asked.

"Not yet," Robertson said.

After leaving the police station, Calhoun wandered down Main Street and stopped in the bookstore. The proprietor, Jane Weincoop, had been a friend of Calhoun's wife. After a bit of chitchat Calhoun steered the conversation to Dennis Hodges.

"I understand he wasn't a popular man," he said. "Who all had it in for him?"

Half an hour later Calhoun stepped back out into the fading sunlight, clutching a list of over twenty people who had disliked Hodges. The list included the president of the bank, the chief of police, a handful of merchants, and a half-dozen doctors.

Calhoun stopped into Harrison's Pharmacy. The pharmacist, Harley Strombell, was the brother of one of his fellow troopers.

Harley wasn't fooled at all about the nature of Calhoun's inquiries, but he promised to be discreet. He even added his own name to Calhoun's list, as well as those of Harold Traynor and Helen Beaton, the hospital's C.E.O.

Calhoun left the pharmacy and crossed the street. He headed for the Iron Horse Inn.

"I HAVE A CONFESSION TO make," Angela said suddenly.

"What are you talking about?" David asked distractedly as he got into bed. Mary Ann Schiller was no better. He had been to the hospital to check on her.

"I did something today I should have spoken to you about before I did it," Angela said. As she slipped under the covers, she told David about going to Rutland and hiring Phil Calhoun.

David looked away. Angela knew he was angry.

"I was hoping you were going to be reasonable about this," he said. "Hiring a private investigator is going a little overboard. It's throwing money away."

"It's not throwing money away if it is important to me," Angela said. "And it should be important to you if you expect me to continue living in this house."

David sighed and turned out his bedside light. Hardly was it out than they heard several loud thumps, followed by the sound of Rusty's barking at the top of the stairs.

Angela got out of bed. David did the same. They grabbed their robes and stepped into the hall. David turned on the hall light. Rusty went downstairs and barked ferociously at the front door. David followed him. Angela stood at the top of the stairs.

David unlocked the front door and, holding Rusty's collar, stepped out onto the porch. The dark sky was strewn with stars. A quarter-moon provided enough light to see all the way down to the road, but there wasn't anything unusual to be seen.

"Come on, Rusty," David urged as he turned around. As he approached the door, he saw a typed note taped to the frame. He pulled it off. It read, "Mind your own business. Forget Hodges."

Closing the door and locking it, David climbed the stairs and handed the note to Angela.

"I'll take this to the police," she said.

"For all we know, it could have come from the police," David replied. He climbed back into bed, and Angela did the same.

The jangle of the telephone made them both jump. David answered it. Angela turned on the light and watched her husband. His face fell as he listened. Then he hung up the phone.

"Mary Ann Schiller had another seizure and died," he said. He raised a hand to his face and covered his eyes. Angela moved over

and put her arms around him. She could tell he was crying silently.

"I wonder if this ever gets easier," he said. He wiped his eyes, then began to get dressed.

AT THE hospital, David met Mary Ann's husband, Donald, for the first time. David commiserated with him, telling him what he wanted to hear: she hadn't suffered. But David had to confess his confusion as to the cause of her seizures. Then on the spur of the moment he went against Kelley's orders and asked Donald if he would permit an autopsy.

"I don't know," Donald said.

"Why don't you think about it overnight?" David suggested.

Leaving the ICU, David wandered over to the dimly lit second-floor nurses' station. As he was perusing Jonathan Eakins' chart, a night nurse told him that Mr. Eakins was awake, watching TV. David walked down and poked his head in.

"Is that ticker of yours staying nice and regular?" he asked.

"Like clockwork," Jonathan said. "When do I get to go home?"

"Probably today," David said. "I see they changed your bed."

"They couldn't fix the old one. Thanks for giving them a nudge."

"No problem," David said. "See you tomorrow."

David was surprised to see a light on in the family room when he got home. By the time he'd parked, Angela was at the door.

"Are you all right?" she asked as she locked the door behind him.

"I've been better," David said. "Why are you still up?"

"There was no way I would sleep without you here. Not after that note on our door. And I've been thinking. If you have to go out in the middle of the night like this, I want to have a gun here."

"We'll have no guns in our house. You know the statistics as well as I do about guns in houses where there are children."

"I'll take responsibility for making sure Nikki is well acquainted with the gun and its potential."

David headed for the stairs. "I don't have the energy or the emotional strength to argue with you."

"Good," Angela said as she caught up with him.

Upstairs, David decided to take a shower. When he came to bed, Angela was reading. She was wide awake.

"Last night you said that you wished you could help me," David said. "Do you remember?"
"Of course I remember," Angela said.
"You might get your wish," David said. "I asked Donald Schiller if he'd permit an autopsy. He said he'd think about it."
"Unfortunately, it's not up to him. The hospital doesn't do autopsies on CMV patients."
"But you could do it on your own."
Angela considered the suggestion. "Maybe I could," she said. "Tomorrow is Sunday and the lab is closed."
"Exactly," David said. "If you could find some specific reason why she died, it would make me feel a whole lot better."

16

Sunday, October 24

DAVID and Angela took Mary Ann's body from the morgue to the lab and rolled it into the autopsy room.
"Why don't you go see your patients?" Angela suggested.
"You sure you can manage?" David asked.
Angela nodded. "I'll page you when I'm done."
At the door David turned. "Remember the possibility of an unknown viral disease. And I want a full toxicological workup."
"You've got it," Angela said agreeably. "Now get out of here."
David fully intended to discharge Jonathan Eakins, especially after he'd been told by the nursing staff that there'd been no abnormal heartbeats. But that was before he went into Jonathan's room. Instead of experiencing Jonathan's usual cheerfulness, David found the man depressed. Jonathan said he felt terrible.
David felt a rush of adrenaline shoot through his body. Afraid to hear the answer, he asked Jonathan what was wrong.
"Everything," Jonathan said. His face was slack, and a string of drool hung from his mouth. "I started having cramps, nausea, and diarrhea. I've no appetite, and I have to keep swallowing."
"What do you mean you have to keep swallowing?"
"My mouth keeps filling up with saliva," Jonathan said.
David desperately tried to think. Salivation was a symptom of mercury poisoning. "Did you eat anything strange last night?"

"No," Jonathan said.

David was panicky. Except for the salivation, Jonathan's symptoms reminded him of those Marjorie, John, and Mary Ann had experienced prior to their rapid deterioration and deaths.

David listened to Jonathan's chest. Both lungs were perfectly clear. He returned to the nurses' station and took Jonathan's chart from the rack. Jonathan's temperature that morning had been one hundred degrees. It was borderline.

Impulsively David reached for the phone. He already knew the response he could expect from Kelley, but he didn't care. He called Dr. Mieslich and Dr. Hasselbaum, asking them to come in immediately. While he waited for them, he ordered a barrage of tests.

The infectious disease specialist was first to arrive. He went in to see the patient. Dr. Mieslich came in next, bringing his records of Jonathan's treatment when he had been his patient. The three men had just begun to discuss the case at the nurses' station when David became aware that the consults were looking over his shoulder. He turned to see Kelley looming above him.

"Dr. Wilson," Kelley said. "May I have a word with you?"

"I'm too busy right now." David turned back to his consults.

"I'm afraid I must insist," Kelley said.

"All right," David said. "Lead on, Mr. Kelley."

Kelley walked across the corridor and stepped into the patients' lounge. After David entered, Kelley closed the door.

"I presume you know Ms. Helen Beaton, the hospital C.E.O.," Kelley said, "and Mr. Michael Caldwell, the medical director." He gestured toward both people, who were sitting on the couch.

"Yes, of course." David glanced anxiously around him.

"You probably wonder how we've responded so quickly to your handling of Jonathan Eakins," Kelley said. "We were alerted by the floor nurses, according to previous instructions. As I've told you, you are using far too many consults outside the CMV family."

"And far too many laboratory tests," Beaton said.

"Too many diagnostic tests as well," Caldwell said.

David stared at the three administrators in disbelief. It was like the Inquisition, and not one of his inquisitors was a physician.

"We want to remind you that you are dealing with a patient who has been treated for metastatic prostate cancer," Kelley said.

"You have a history of excessive use of resources on three previous patients who were clearly terminal," Caldwell said.

David struggled with his emotions. Since he'd already been questioning his own competence, he was vulnerable to the administrators' criticism. "My allegiance is to the patient," he said meekly. "Not to an organization or an institution."

"We can appreciate your philosophy," Beaton said. "But we have an allegiance to the entire community of patients. Everything cannot be done for everybody. Judgment is needed in the rational use of limited resources."

There was a pause. David wasn't sure what to say. "My worry in these particular cases is that I'm seeing an unknown infectious disease. If that is the case, it would be disastrous not to diagnose it."

"We have an independent infectious disease consult here," Kelley said. "Let's ask him his opinion."

Kelley went out and returned with both Dr. Hasselbaum and Dr. Mieslich. Dr. Hasselbaum was asked if he thought that David's three deceased patients and Mr. Eakins might have been afflicted by an unknown infectious disease.

"I sincerely doubt it," Dr. Hasselbaum said. "There's no evidence whatsoever. All three of the deceased patients had pneumonia, and in each case the agent was a recognized pathogen."

"You both have seen the long list of diagnostic tests ordered by Dr. Wilson," Kelley said. "Are these tests crucial at this time?"

Dr. Mieslich and Dr. Hasselbaum exchanged glances. Dr. Hasselbaum was first to speak. "If it were my case, I'd hold off and see what happened. The patient could be normal by morning."

"I agree," Dr. Mieslich said.

"Well then," Kelley said. "What do you say, Dr. Wilson?"

The meeting broke up amid smiles, handshakes, and apparent amity. But David felt confused and humiliated. He walked back to the nurses' station and canceled most of the orders he had written for Jonathan.

When David got back to the autopsy room, Angela was just cleaning up. David noticed that she wasn't eager to talk about her findings. He practically had to grill her for answers.

"I didn't find much," Angela admitted.

"Nothing in the brain?" David asked.

"It was clean grossly. We'll see what the microscopic shows."
"Any tumor?"
"I think there was a tiny bit in the abdomen," Angela said.
"So nothing jumped out at you as a cause of death?" David asked.
"She did have pneumonia. I'm sorry I didn't find more."

17
Monday, October 25

DESPITE the possibility of rain, David rode his bike to work. After dropping Nikki off at school, Angela drove on to the lab. She had her coat on its hanger before she noticed Wadley. He'd been standing motionless near the connecting door.

"Good morning," Angela said, trying to sound cheerful.

"It has been brought to my attention that you did an autopsy here in the lab," Wadley said angrily.

"It's true," Angela admitted. "But I did it on my own time."

"You were specifically told no autopsies."

"I was specifically told they were not paid for by CMV."

Wadley's cold eyes bored into Angela. "Then allow me to clear up a misunderstanding. No autopsies are to be done in this department unless I approve them. Furthermore, I've ordered the techs not to process the slides, the cultures, or the toxicological samples." With that, he returned to his office and slammed the door.

As soon as she had composed herself, Angela carefully packed the cultures and the toxicological samples she had taken from Mary Ann and sent them to the department where she'd trained in Boston. She had enough friends there to get them processed. The tissue specimens she kept, planning on doing the slides herself.

DAVID made the rounds of his patients, leaving Jonathan for last. When he walked into his room, the bed was empty.

David went to the nurses' station, where Janet Colburn told him that Mr. Eakins had been transferred to the ICU.

David was dumbfounded.

"During the night Mr. Eakins developed difficulty breathing and lapsed into a coma," Janet added.

"Why wasn't I called?" David demanded.

"We had a specific order not to call you."

"Issued by whom?"

"By Michael Caldwell. The medical director of the hospital."

Beside himself with fury, David left to find his patient. He discovered that Jonathan was in a coma and on a respirator. David listened to his chest. Jonathan was developing pneumonia.

David had picked up the phone to call Helen Beaton when the ICU coordinator tapped him on the shoulder and handed him another phone. It was Charles Kelley.

"The nurses told me you'd come into the ICU," Kelley said. "I wanted to inform you that the Eakins case has been transferred to another CMV physician."

"You can't do that," David said angrily.

"Hold on, Dr. Wilson. CMV certainly can transfer a patient, and I have done so. We feel that you are too emotionally involved. We decided it was better for everyone if you were taken off."

David stumbled out of the ICU. It was still too early to go to his office. Instead, he went to medical records and pulled the charts on Marjorie, John, and Mary Ann. He read all his entries, all the nurses' notes, and looked at all the laboratory values and the results of diagnostic tests. The pager on his belt interrupted. Looking at the display, he recognized the screen number: it was the emergency room. Replacing the charts, David hurried downstairs.

He examined and admitted the semicomatose patient, who had diabetes. As David walked past one of the other examining stalls, he did a double take. Looking in, he saw Caroline Helmsford, Nikki's friend. Dr. Pilsner was at her side.

David slipped in alongside Caroline. She looked up at him with pleading eyes. Covering the lower part of her face was a clear plastic mask providing oxygen. Her breathing was labored.

Dr. Pilsner was listening to her chest. When he finished, he took David aside. "Poor thing is having a hard time," he said. "She's congested and running a high fever."

"Will you admit her?" David asked.

"Absolutely. You know we can't take any chances."

David nodded. He did know. He looked back at Caroline struggling to breathe. She looked so tiny on the big gurney and so vulnerable. The sight made him worry about Nikki.

"You've got a call from the chief medical examiner," one of the secretaries told Angela. Angela picked up the phone.

"Hope I'm not disturbing you," Walt said. "Got a couple of updates on the Hodges autopsy. Still interested?"

"Absolutely," Angela said.

"First of all, the man had significant alcohol in his ocular fluid. We also got confirmation that the DNA of the skin under his nails was different from his own. So it's undoubtedly his killer's."

"What about those carbon particles in the skin?" Angela asked.

"I've changed my mind about it being contemporary with the struggle," Walt said. "I realized the particles were in the dermis, not the epidermis. It must have been some old injury, like having your arm stabbed with a pencil back in grammar school."

"I've got one like that in the palm of my right hand," Angela said.

"I haven't done much on the case, because there's no pressure from the state's attorney or the state police. I'm swamped with cases."

"I understand," Angela said. "But I'm still interested. So if there are any more developments, please let me know."

After she hung up, Angela's thoughts remained on the Hodges affair, making her remember how vulnerable she'd felt when David had left in the night to go to the hospital. It was time for her lunch break, and she grabbed her coat and went out to the car. She'd told David that she wanted to get a gun, and she'd meant it.

There were no sporting goods stores in Bartlet, but Staley's Hardware Store carried a line of firearms. It took Angela less than fifteen minutes to select a pump-action 12-gauge shotgun. Mr. Staley was more than happy to show her how to load and unload the rifle. He was particularly careful to show her the safety and encouraged her to read the brochure that came with the firearm.

On the walk back to the car Angela felt self-conscious about her package even though she'd insisted that Mr. Staley wrap it in manila paper; the object within was still quite recognizable. In her other hand she had a bag containing a box of shells.

Angela put the rifle in the trunk of the car. Heading around to the driver's-side door, she looked across the green at the police station, and hesitated. Ever since her confrontation with Robertson she'd felt guilty. She also knew it was foolhardy to make an enemy of the chief of police, despite the fact that he was such a dolt.

She walked to the police station, where Robertson agreed to see her almost immediately.

"I hope I'm not bothering you," Angela said, sitting down. "I don't want to take much of your time. But something did turn up this morning." She told Robertson about the possibility of Hodges' killer having a deposit of carbon from a pencil somewhere under his skin.

She extended her right palm and pointed to a small stain beneath the skin. "Something like this. I got it in the third grade."

"Oh, I see." Robertson nodded his head, smiling wryly.

"Just thought I'd pass it along," Angela said. "The medical examiner also said that the skin under Hodges' fingernails was definitely his killer's. He has a DNA fingerprint."

"Trouble is, supersophisticated DNA malarkey is not much help without a suspect," Robertson said. He stood up as Angela got up to go. "Thanks for coming by."

Robertson watched through his window as Angela got into her car. As she drove off, he picked up his phone and pressed one of the automatic dialers. "You're not going to believe this, but she's still at it. She's like a dog with a bone."

At the hospital, all the parking slots reserved for the professional staff were occupied. Angela had to zigzag back and forth looking for a vacant spot. She finally located one, way up in the far corner of the upper lot. It took almost five minutes to walk to the hospital.

"This isn't my day," Angela said as she entered the building.

COLLETTE, Traynor's secretary, came into the room and placed a business card on the desk blotter in front of him. Traynor picked up the card. It read PHIL CALHOUN, PRIVATE INVESTIGATION, SATISFACTION GUARANTEED.

Traynor whispered, "Who the hell is Phil Calhoun?"

Collette shrugged. "I've never seen him before, but he says he knows you. Anyway, he's waiting outside."

Traynor peered into the outer office to get a glimpse of the P.I. he supposedly knew. Flipping through one of the hospital quarterly reports was a big man in a checkered shirt. Inviting him in, Traynor scoured his memory, but he still drew a blank. The two men shook hands and sat down.

It wasn't until Calhoun mentioned that he'd been a state policeman that it came to Traynor. "I remember," he said. "You used to be friends with Harley Strombell's brother."

Calhoun nodded and complimented Traynor on his memory.

"Never forget a face," Traynor boasted.

"I wanted to ask you a few questions about Dr. Hodges," Calhoun said, getting to the point.

Traynor nervously fingered the gavel he used for hospital board meetings. "Have you been retained?" he asked.

"You might say so," Calhoun said.

"By whom?"

"I'm not at liberty to say. As a lawyer, I'm sure you understand."

"If you expect me to be cooperative," Traynor said, "then you'll have to be a bit more open yourself."

Calhoun took his time, then spoke. "The family is interested in finding out who was responsible for the doctor's brutal murder."

"Okay. That's understandable. What do you want to ask me?"

"I understand you saw Hodges the night he disappeared."

"Hodges burst in on a meeting we were having at the hospital."

"I understand he was angry."

"Hodges was angry all the time," Traynor said. "He was chronically unhappy with the way we managed the hospital."

"I understand when Dr. Hodges burst into your hospital meeting, he had some hospital charts with him."

"Parts of charts," Traynor corrected. "But I didn't get a look at them. They undoubtedly concerned some of his former patients."

"I understand you ran into him a second time that night."

"Unfortunately. At the inn we go to. That night Hodges was there, drinking as usual and belligerent."

"And he had unpleasant words with Robertson and Sherwood?"

"Who have you been talking with?" Traynor asked.

"Just a handful of townsfolk," Calhoun said. "What about you? I've heard you weren't fond of Dr. Hodges either. I heard it was something personal. Something about your sister."

"It's no secret," Traynor said. "My sister, Sunny, committed suicide after Hodges pulled her husband's hospital privileges."

"So you blamed Hodges?" Calhoun asked.

"More then than now."

"One last question. Do you know who killed Dr. Hodges?"

Traynor laughed. "I haven't the slightest idea, and I don't care. The only thing I care about is the effect his death might have on the hospital. If you find out who did it, do me a favor. Let me know."

"YOU'VE got one more patient," Susan said as she handed David the chart. "A nurse from the second floor, Beverly Hopkins."

David took the chart and pushed into the examining room. "What's the problem?" he asked with a smile.

Beverly was sitting on the examining table. "I'm sorry to bother you, Dr. Wilson," she said. "I think it's the flu."

"No problem," David said. "What are your symptoms?"

The symptoms were similar to those of the other four nurses: general malaise, mild G.I. complaints, and low-grade fever. David agreed with Beverly's assessment. He sent her home for bed rest, telling her to drink plenty of fluids and take aspirin as needed.

After finishing up at the office, David headed over to the hospital to see his patients. As he walked over, he began to mull over the fact that the only people he'd seen with the flu so far were nurses.

David stopped in his tracks. He wondered if it was a coincidence that all five nurses were from the second floor, the same floor where all his mortally ill patients had been. What if nurses who were generally healthy got a mild illness when exposed to some mysterious disease, but patients who'd had chemotherapy and had mildly compromised immune systems got a fatal illness?

What about an environmental poison? David wondered, remembering Jonathan's symptom of excessive salivation. Even so, the idea seemed farfetched. How would the poison be spread? If it were airborne, then many more people would have come down with symptoms. But he decided to reserve judgment until he received the toxicology results on Mary Ann.

When he was finished with his rounds, David went down to search the lab for Angela. He found her in the chemistry area.

"Are you finished already?" Angela asked.

"For a change," David said.

"I had a little surprise when I got in here this morning," she said. "Wadley hit the ceiling about my doing the autopsy."

"I'm sorry," David said.

"He's refused to allow the specimens to be processed. But no need to worry. I sent the toxicology and cultures to Boston. I'm going to do the slides. In fact, I'll stay tonight to do them. Will you make dinner for you and Nikki?"

David told her he'd be happy to. He was relieved to get out of the hospital at long last and ride his bike home.

After sending Alice home, David enjoyed some time with Nikki. The two of them worked in the yard until dark. Then while Nikki did her homework, David made a dinner of steak and salad.

After the meal he broke the news about Caroline.

"Is she real sick?" Nikki asked.

"She looked very uncomfortable when I saw her."

"I want to go visit her tomorrow."

"I'm sure you do," David said. "But I think we better wait until we know for sure what Caroline has. Okay?"

Nikki nodded, but she wasn't happy. To be on the safe side, David insisted Nikki do her postural drainage.

After Nikki went to bed, David began to peruse the infectious disease section of one of his medical textbooks. Before he knew it, he woke up with his heavy book open on his lap. Checking the clock over the fireplace, he was surprised to see it was after eleven. Angela still wasn't home. Feeling mildly anxious, he called the hospital. The operator put him through to the lab.

"What's going on?" he asked when he heard Angela's voice.

"It's just taking me longer than I thought," Angela said. "The staining takes time. I should have called you, but I'm almost finished. I'll be home within the hour."

"I'll be waiting," David said.

IT WAS more than an hour by the time Angela was finally finished. Loading a selection of slides into a metal briefcase, she said good night to the night-shift techs, then headed out to the parking lot.

There were a few cars belonging to the night-shift personnel, but they soon fell behind as Angela trudged through the lower lot. She was entirely alone; the evening shift had long since departed. Approaching the path to the upper lot, she began to feel uneasy. She was unaccustomed to being out at such an hour, and had certainly expected to see someone. Then she thought she heard something behind her. When she turned, she saw nothing.

The lighting in the lower lot was more than adequate. But as Angela entered the path leading up to the upper lot, she had to pause to allow her eyes to adjust to the darkness. There were no lights along the path, and evergreen trees on both sides formed a dense archway.

Angela moved into the tunnel of trees, starting up a run of stairs constructed of railroad ties. She heard the rustling of wind high in the pine trees. She felt frightened and tense.

At the top of the stairs the path angled to the left. She had only another fifty feet to go.

Angela had just about calmed herself when a man leaped out of the shadows. He was brandishing a club over his head; his face was covered by a dark ski mask.

Staggering back, Angela tripped and fell. The man flung himself at her. Angela screamed and rolled to the side. She could hear the thump of the club as it sliced into the soft ground where she had been only seconds before.

Angela scrambled to her feet. The man grabbed her with a gloved hand as he began to raise his club again. Angela swung her briefcase up into the man's crotch with all the strength she could muster. The man's grip on her arm released as he cried out in pain.

Angela ran for the upper lot. Empowered by terror, she ran as she'd never run before, her flying feet crunching on the asphalt. She heard the man behind her, but she didn't dare look. She ran to the Volvo with one thought in mind: the shotgun.

Dropping the briefcase to the pavement, Angela fumbled with her keys. Once she got the trunk open, she yanked the manila paper from the shotgun. Snatching up a bag of shells, she hastily dumped them into the trunk. Picking up a single shell, she jammed it into the gun and pumped it into the firing chamber.

Angela whirled about, holding the gun at waist level, but no one was there. The lot was completely deserted. The man hadn't given chase. What she heard had been the echo of her own footfalls.

"CAN'T you do a little better than that?" Robertson asked. " 'Sorta tall.' Is that it? That's hardly a description. How are we supposed to find this guy if you can't describe him better than that?"

"It was dark," Angela said. "And it happened so quickly. Besides, he was wearing a ski mask."

"What were you doing out there in the trees after midnight, anyway? All you nurses were warned."

"I'm not a nurse," Angela said. "I'm a doctor."

"Well, you should have known better," Robertson said.

"Are you implying that this attack was somehow my fault?"

He ignored her question. "What kind of club was he holding?"

"I have no idea. I told you it was dark. May I use the phone?"

Angela called David. When he answered, she could tell he'd been asleep. "What time is it?" he asked. Then after a glance at the clock he answered his own question. "Holy smokes, it's after one. What are you doing?"

"I'll tell you when I get home," Angela said.

Ten minutes later Angela was hugging David at their door. David was alarmed not just by the late hour but also by the sight of his wife with a briefcase in one hand and a shotgun in the other. But he didn't ask about the gun. For the moment he just hugged Angela.

"I'd like to stay calm," she said evenly, walking into the family room. "Would you mind getting me a glass of wine?"

David complied immediately. Angela sat on the couch sipping the wine. She held the glass with both hands.

In a controlled voice Angela began to tell David about the attempted assault. But she didn't get far. Her emotions boiled over into tears. For five minutes she couldn't speak. Eventually she regained her composure and continued. She reached for the briefcase and handed it to David. She wiped the tears from her eyes.

"All this effort and the slides didn't show much at all," she said. "There was no tumor in the brain."

"No sign of a systemic infectious disease?" David asked.

Angela shook her head. "I brought the slides home in case you wanted to look at them yourself," she said.

"I see you got a shotgun," David commented.

"It's loaded too," Angela warned, "so be careful. And don't worry. I'll go over it with Nikki tomorrow."

A crash and the sound of breaking glass made them both sit bolt upright. Rusty started barking from Nikki's room; then he came bounding down the stairs. David picked up the shotgun, led the way to the living room, and flipped on the light. Four panes of the bay window were smashed, along with their frames. Attached to a brick on the floor was a copy of the note they'd received Saturday night.

"I'm calling the police," Angela said. "This is too much."

While they waited for the police, David sat Angela down.

"Did you talk about Hodges with anyone today?" he asked.

"His name came up when I talked with Robertson," Angela said. "I stopped at the station on my way back from buying the shotgun."

"Angela," David pleaded. "We have to stop messing with this Hodges stuff. It's not worth it. A note on the door is one thing; a brick through the window is something else entirely. Please, let's let it go, for Nikki's sake if not our own."

"All right," Angela said reluctantly. "I'll try."

"Thank goodness," David said.

Headlight beams played against the wall as a police cruiser pulled up the driveway.

"At least it's not Robertson," Angela said when they could see the approaching officer.

The policeman introduced himself as Bill Morrison. It was clear he wasn't terribly interested in investigating the incident. He asked only enough questions to fill out the requisite form. When he was ready to leave, Angela asked him if he was planning on taking the brick.

"Hadn't planned on it," Bill said.

"What about fingerprints?" Angela asked.

Bill's face registered confusion. "Fingerprints?" he asked. "I don't know if we'd send something like this to the state police."

"Just in case, let me get you a bag," Angela said. She disappeared into the kitchen and returned with a plastic bag. Turning it inside out, she picked up the brick and handed the bag to Bill.

"There," she said, "now you people are prepared if you happen to decide you want to try to solve a crime."

18

Tuesday, October 26

NEITHER David nor Angela slept well. Both were overwrought, but while Angela had trouble falling asleep, David woke well before dawn. He was appalled to see the time: five a.m. He tiptoed out of the bedroom, careful not to disturb Angela.

David was on his bike by five thirty and at the hospital before six.

Several of his patients were still asleep, and he didn't disturb them. On his way to see Caroline he passed the ICU. Steeling himself, he went in to check on Jonathan Eakins.

"Jonathan Eakins died about three this morning," the head nurse said. "It was a very quick downhill course. Nothing we did seemed to help."

David swallowed hard. He nodded, turned, and left the unit. Even though he'd known in his heart that Jonathan would die, the reality of it was hard to take. David still had a hard time absorbing the staggering fact: he had now lost four patients in a little over a week.

On a brighter note David discovered that Caroline had responded well to her treatment of IV antibiotics and intensive respiratory therapy. Her fever was gone, her color was pink, and her blue eyes sparkled. She smiled broadly the instant David appeared.

"Nikki wants to come to visit you," David said.

"Cool," Caroline said. "When?"

"Probably this afternoon," David said. "I'll call her."

DAVID decided to take this early morning opportunity to get through some of the never-ending reams of paperwork he was forced to process in connection with his practice. As he laid the first form on his desk, the phone rang. The caller was a patient named Sandra Hascher, with a history of melanoma.

Sandra told him she'd been having trouble with an abscessed tooth. "I'm sorry to bother you with this," she continued, "but my temperature is one hundred and three."

"Come right over," David said. "I'll see you immediately."

The abscess was impressive. The whole side of Sandra's face was distorted by the swelling. In addition, the lymph nodes beneath her jaw were almost golf-ball size.

"You've got to come into the hospital," David said.

"I can't," Sandra said. "I've got so much to do. And my ten-year-old is home with the chicken pox."

"You'll just have to make arrangements," David said. "If the infection gets into your nervous system, we're in deep trouble. You need continuous antibiotics. This is no joke."

"All right," Sandra said. "You have me convinced."

As Angela dressed that morning, she regretted her promise to David to try to forget about Hodges. She wondered about Phil Calhoun. She hadn't heard a word from him, and decided to give him a call. But all she got was his answering machine.

Downstairs, Angela found Nikki in the family room reading one of her schoolbooks. Nikki coughed a deep, productive cough.

"Okay," Angela said. "Upstairs for postural drainage."

After breakfast Angela spent a half hour going over the shotgun with Nikki, allowing her to pump it, pull the trigger, and even load and unload it. They went outside behind the barn, and each fired a shell. Returning to the house, Angela told Nikki that she wasn't to touch the gun. Nikki told her not to worry; she didn't want anything to do with it.

Since the weather was warm and sunny, Nikki wanted to ride her bike to school. Shortly after she started off toward town, Angela left for work. After parking in the reserved area, Angela couldn't resist the temptation to examine the spot where she'd been attacked. She retraced her steps into the stand of trees and found her own footprints in the muddy earth, then the spot where she'd fallen and the deep cut left in the earth by the man's club.

The cleft was about four inches deep. Angela put her fingers in it and shuddered.

Suddenly Angela realized something she hadn't focused on before: the man had not hesitated. If she had not rolled out of the way, she would have been struck. The man hadn't been trying to rape her; he'd wanted to hurt her, maybe kill her.

Against her better judgment Angela put in a call to Robertson.

"Nah. I don't buy it," Robertson said. "This guy is a rapist, not a murderer. He's had opportunity to kill in the past, but he didn't."

Angela wasn't about to argue the issue with Robertson. She thanked him for his time and hung up.

"I'll have a little more coffee," Traynor said to the waitress. As was their habit, Traynor, Sherwood, Beaton, and Caldwell were having a breakfast meeting in advance of the monthly hospital executive board meeting. They were seated at Traynor's favorite table at the Iron Horse Inn.

"We get one crisis under control and then have to face another,"

Traynor said. "It's never-ending. What's the story about a doctor being assaulted last night?"

"It was just after midnight," Caldwell said. "It was the new female pathologist, Angela Wilson. She'd been working late."

"Where in the parking lot did it take place?" Traynor asked.

"In the pathway between the lots," Caldwell said.

"Have lights been put in there?" Traynor asked.

Caldwell looked at Beaton.

"I don't know," Beaton admitted. "You ordered lights to be put there, but whether it got done or not, I'm not sure."

"They'd better be," Traynor said. "There's no way the parking garage can even get on the ballot now until spring."

"I checked with the Bartlet *Sun,*" Beaton said. "They have agreed to keep the rape attempt out of the paper."

"At least they're on our side," Traynor said.

"I think their loyalty is inspired by the ads we run," Beaton said.

Traynor looked around the table. "Anything else?"

"I had a curious visit yesterday afternoon," Sherwood said. "The caller was a P.I. by the name of Phil Calhoun. He asked a lot of questions about Hodges."

"He came to see me too," Traynor said.

"Who do you think retained him?" Sherwood asked.

"I asked him," Traynor said. "He implied that the family had. I assumed he meant Clara, so I called her. She said she didn't know anything about Phil Calhoun. Next I called Wayne Robertson. Calhoun had already been to see him. Wayne thought that the most likely candidate is Angela Wilson."

"That makes sense," Sherwood said. "She was very upset about Hodges' body being discovered in her house."

"That's a curious coincidence," Beaton said. "She's certainly having her troubles: first finding a body in her house and then experiencing a rape attempt."

"Maybe the rape attempt will dampen her interest in Hodges," Traynor said.

"What if Calhoun figures out who killed Hodges?" Caldwell asked.

"That could be a problem," Traynor said. "But it's been over eight months. The trail must be pretty cool by now."

After seeing off his last patient for the day, David stepped across the hall to his private office. Nikki was sitting at his desk leafing through one of his medical journals. "Are you ready?" she asked.

"Let's go."

It took them only a few minutes to cover the short distance to the hospital and up a flight of stairs. When they stepped into Caroline's room, her face lit up with joy.

"Look what I can do," she said. She reached up, grabbed an overhead bar, and pulled herself off the bed, angling her feet up in the air.

David clapped. Caroline was in a large orthopedic bed with an overhead frame. David assumed they'd put her in it for its entertainment value, since the child was obviously enjoying it.

"I'm going to check on my patients," David said. "I won't be long—and no terrorizing the nurses. Promise?"

"Promise," Nikki said; then she giggled with Caroline.

David's patients were doing well. When David examined Sandra, the abscess was the same size, but the symptomatic improvement was encouraging. Two other patients were doing so well he told them they could go home.

"Sorry I haven't been in touch," Phil Calhoun said. "I've been busy, but now I'd like to have a chat. Why don't I come over?"

Angela covered the phone with her hand. "It's the private investigator," she said to David. "He wants to come over."

"I thought you were letting the Hodges affair go."

"I have," Angela said. "But I have to pay him anyway. We should at least hear what he's learned."

David sighed with resignation. "Whatever," he said. They were sitting in the family room. Dinner was long since over; Nikki was up in her room doing her homework.

A quarter of an hour later Phil Calhoun came through the door. To David he appeared anything but professional in a red baseball cap and a flannel shirt.

"Pleasure," Calhoun said when they shook hands.

They sat in the living room on the shabby old furniture that they'd brought from Boston. The huge room had a cheap dance-hall feel with such meager, pitiful furnishings. The plastic bag David had taped to the window didn't help.

"I wanted to give you folks an update on my investigation," Calhoun said. "It's proceeding well."

"Who have you spoken with?" David asked.

"Just a couple so far," Calhoun said. "I've talked to a few of the higher-ups with the hospital—the chairman of the board, Traynor; and the vice-chairman, Sherwood. Both had reasons to hold a grudge against Hodges. And Dr. Cantor's on the list." Calhoun went on to explain the Traynor–Hodges–Van Slyke triangle, concluding with the suicide of Traynor's sister.

"What a terrible story," Angela said.

"Werner Van Slyke is related to Traynor?" David questioned with surprise. "Now, that smacks of nepotism. But have you come up with a suspect or narrowed the list down?"

"No, not yet." Calhoun took out a cigar.

"I think the important question now is whether Mr. Calhoun believes the case is solvable," Angela said.

"I think it is," Calhoun said. "You have to know something about small New England towns. I know these people; I understand the dynamics. In other words, I'm sure that some people know who the killer is. The problem is getting somebody to talk."

"I thought New Englanders were closemouthed," Angela said.

"Generally true," Calhoun said. "But some of the best town gossips happen to be friends of mine. Now I just have to start eliminating suspects. But before I begin, I have to ask you a question: Do you want me to continue?"

"No," David said.

"Wait a minute," Angela said. "You've told us that the case is definitely solvable. How long do you think it will take?"

Calhoun lifted his cap and scratched his scalp. "I'd say a week."

"That's a lot of money," David said.

"I think it's worth it," Angela said.

"Angela," David pleaded, rolling his eyes in exasperation.

"Come on, David," Angela said, "support me in this."

David hesitated, then thought of a compromise. "Okay," he said. "I'll make a deal. One week, then it's over—no matter what."

"All right," Angela said. "It's a deal." She turned to Calhoun. "What's the next move?"

"There are two major goals," Calhoun said. "One is to reconstruct Dr. Hodges' last day. The second is to get copies of the medical papers that were found with him."

"They're in the custody of the state police in Burlington," Angela said. "Having been on the force, can't you get copies easily?"

"Unfortunately, no. The state police tend to be very guarded when it comes to evidence in their custody. You'll have to do it."

"That's not part of the deal," David said. "I don't want her talking to anyone. Not with bricks coming through our window." They told Calhoun about the window, the threatening notes, and the police's response.

"There'll be no danger," Calhoun insisted.

"Why me?" Angela asked.

"Because you're both a physician and an employee of the hospital," Calhoun said. "They'll make you copies in a flash. Judges' and doctors' requests are always honored."

"I guess visiting the state police headquarters couldn't be very dangerous," Angela said. "It's not as if I'm participating in the investigation. But it will have to be on my lunch hour."

"I'll come pick you up at noon tomorrow in front of the hospital," Calhoun said. He stood up.

Angela offered to walk Calhoun to his truck. "There's something else I wanted to tell you," she said as they approached his vehicle. She told him about her assault and explained her new theory.

"Hmm," Calhoun said. "This is more interesting than I thought. You'd better be doubly sure to leave the sleuthing to me."

"I intend to," Angela said.

"I've been careful about not letting it be known that you've retained me," Calhoun said. "Maybe tomorrow I should pick you up at the library. No sense taking chances."

19

Wednesday, October 27

To David's and Angela's dismay, Nikki awoke with congestion and a deep, productive cough. Both were fearful that she might be coming down with the same illness that had briefly afflicted Caroline. Despite extra attention to her morning respiratory therapy, she failed to improve. David and Angela decided she shouldn't go to school. They called Alice, who agreed to come over for the day.

Already tense from events at home, David was edgy as he started his rounds. With so many recent deaths he was wary of seeing his patients. But his worries were groundless. Everyone was doing fine.

"Your swelling is down," David told Sandra as he tenderly palpated the side of her face. "But I think we have to keep you until we're one hundred percent sure this infection is under control."

"Oh, all right," Sandra said, feigning irritation. "But if I have to stay, could you do me a favor?"

"Of course."

"The electric controls of my bed stopped working."

"I'll go out and ask about it right away," David promised.

Returning to the nurses' station, David complained about the bed situation. "There's really nothing that can be done?" he asked.

"That's what maintenance told us," Janet Colburn said. "And frankly, we don't have another bed to spare at the moment."

David couldn't believe that he had to see Van Slyke over another maintenance detail. He found him in his windowless office.

"I have a patient upstairs who was told her bed couldn't be repaired," David said after a cursory knock. "What's the story?"

"The hospital bought the wrong beds," Van Slyke said. "They're a maintenance nightmare. You fix them, they break again."

"I want it fixed," David said.

"We'll do it when we get around to it," Van Slyke said. "Don't bother me. I have more important work to do."

"Why are you so rude?" David demanded.

"Look who's talking," Van Slyke said. "You're yelling at me, not vice versa. If you have a problem, go tell it to administration."

"I'll do that," David said. He turned around and climbed up the stairs, intending to go directly to Helen Beaton. But when he got to the lobby, he saw Dr. Pilsner heading for the main stairs.

David approached him, described Nikki's congestion, and started to ask whether Nikki should start some oral antibiotics. But he stopped in midsentence. He noticed that Dr. Pilsner was agitated; he was hardly listening to what David was saying.

"Is something wrong?" David asked.

"I'm sorry," Dr. Pilsner said. "I'm distracted. Caroline took an unexpected turn for the worse during the night."

"What happened?" David asked.

"Come and see for yourself," Dr. Pilsner said. "She's in the ICU. It started with a seizure—of all things. Then pneumonia developed rapidly. I'm afraid she's now in septic shock. We're having to maintain her blood pressure. I'm afraid I'm going to lose her."

They went into the ICU. Caroline was on a respirator and was covered with wires and intravenous lines. Monitors recorded her pulse and blood pressure. David shuddered as he looked down at the stricken child. In his mind's eye he saw Nikki in Caroline's place, and the image terrorized him.

As David walked out with Dr. Pilsner, he discussed Nikki's condition with him. Dr. Pilsner agreed that oral antibiotics were indicated. He suggested the type and dosage.

Before seeing his office patients, David called Angela to tell her about Nikki's antibiotics. Then he told her about Caroline.

Angela was dumbstruck. "You think she's going to die?" Angela asked.

"That's Dr. Pilsner's feeling," David said.

"Oh, God," Angela said. "Can you get the antibiotics and take them home over your lunch hour?"

"You're still going to Burlington?" David asked.

"Of course," Angela said.

"Have a good trip," David said, and hung up before he could say something he might regret. Angela's priorities irked him. While he was worrying himself sick about Caroline and Nikki, she was still obsessed with the Hodges affair.

HELEN Beaton would not answer Calhoun's questions, because Calhoun would not tell her who hired him. Descending to the basement, he found his next interviewee in the hospital shop replacing motors in several hospital beds.

"Werner Van Slyke?" Calhoun questioned.

"Yeah," Van Slyke said in a monotone.

"Name's Calhoun. Mind if I have a chat with you?"

"What about?"

"Dr. Dennis Hodges," Calhoun said.

"If you don't mind my working," Van Slyke said. He turned his attention back to the motors.

Calhoun retired to the workbench and sat on a stool. "I understand you knew Hodges pretty well."

"He was like a father to me," Van Slyke said.

"No kidding," Calhoun said.

"If it hadn't been for Hodges, I never would have gone to college. He'd given me a job working around his house. We used to talk a lot. I had a lot of trouble with my own father."

"That right?" Calhoun asked. "How come?"

"He got drunk most every night. He used to beat me—and my mother, she got beat herself."

"Did you and your mother team up against your father?"

"Of course not," Van Slyke said. "She always defended him. What are you asking all these questions for, anyway?"

"I'm interested in Hodges' death," Calhoun said.

"After all this time?" Van Slyke asked.

"Why not? Wouldn't you like to find out who killed him?"

"What would I do if I found out? Kill the murderer?" Van Slyke laughed. "I've had enough of this chat. I've got work to do."

After leaving engineering, Calhoun made his way around to the front of the hospital and walked over to the imaging center. Handing one of his cards to the receptionist, he asked to speak with Dr. Cantor.

"What do you mean, you want to discuss Dennis Hodges?" Cantor demanded once Calhoun was seated. "Why should I want to talk about that no-good?"

"Obviously, to bring his murderer to justice," Calhoun said.

"I think justice has already been served. Whoever rid us of that pest should be given a medal. He didn't care about physicians," Cantor said. "He had one priority and that was this hospital. He took over and put a bunch of us out to pasture. All of us wanted to throttle him."

"Could you give me names?" Calhoun asked.

"Sure. It's no secret," Cantor said. He then counted off on his fingers five doctors, including himself.

"And you are the only one of this group who's still around."

"I'm the only one still in radiology," Cantor said. "Paul Darnell's still here too. He's in pathology."

Suddenly Calhoun drew out his pocket watch. "My word," he

said. He stood up. "I'm sorry, but I have to break off this chat. I'm afraid I have another appointment."

Calhoun rushed from the room, then drove down to the library to meet Angela.

CALHOUN did all the talking at state police headquarters. The policeman in charge of the evidence could not have been nicer or more accommodating.

"While you're at it," Calhoun said to him, "how about making two sets of copies." He winked at Angela.

"No problem," the officer said. He handled the originals with gloved hands.

Ten minutes later Angela and Calhoun were back in his truck.

"That was a breeze," Angela said. She slid the copies out of their envelope and began looking through them.

"What are they?" Calhoun asked, looking over Angela's shoulder.

"They're copies of the admissions sheets on eight patients."

"Anything unique about them?"

"Not that I can tell. There doesn't seem to be any common element. Different ages, different sexes, and different diagnoses. There's a fractured hip, pneumonia, sinusitis, chest pain, abdominal pain, phlebitis, stroke, and kidney stone. I don't know what I expected, but this looks pretty ordinary."

The drive back to Bartlet seemed even faster than the drive had been to Burlington. But it was almost one thirty when Calhoun dropped Angela off at the library so she could get her own car.

Back in her office, Angela was donning her white lab coat when Wadley opened the connecting door without bothering to knock. "I've been looking for you for almost twenty minutes," he said irritably.

"I used my lunch hour to run an errand," Angela said.

"You've been gone longer than an hour," Wadley said. "I don't like my pathologists disappearing in the middle of the day."

"I was not gone long," Angela said. "I'm fully aware of my responsibilities and carry them out to the letter."

"I'm concerned about you," Wadley said. "I should remind you that you are still on probationary status. I can assure you that if you prove to be unreliable, you will be terminated."

After the last office patient had been seen, David reluctantly headed over to the hospital. Before making his afternoon rounds, he went to check on Caroline. The child was doing poorly and was clearly moribund. David found Dr. Pilsner sitting at the ICU desk in a hopeless vigil. The man was despondent.

Leaving the ICU, David started seeing his own patients. When he went into Sandra's room, he was appalled. Early that morning she'd been bright and aware. Now she was apathetic to her surroundings and was drooling. Her temperature, which had fallen, had crept back up over one hundred degrees.

When David tried to talk to her, she was vague. He pored over Sandra's chart, checked the IV fluids she'd had, then went over all the laboratory tests. He was desperate for some clue to explain her mental status, but there was none. The only possibility that came to his mind was early meningitis, so he went ahead with a lumbar puncture. The result was normal. He felt lost. All he could do was hope.

Climbing on his bike, David cycled home. He felt great concern for Caroline and Sandra, but he soon realized he couldn't wallow in self-pity. Nikki's congestion had increased, and her temperature had reached one hundred degrees.

David phoned the ICU and got Dr. Pilsner on the line. He said he felt obliged to let him know the oral antibiotic wasn't helping.

"Let's up it," Dr. Pilsner said in a tired voice. "And I think we'd better use a mucolytic agent and a bronchodilator with her respiratory therapy."

Angela got home at seven o'clock. She checked on Nikki, who was doing better after a respiratory therapy session with David, then went to take a shower. David followed her into the bathroom. "Caroline is no better," he said.

"The Helmsfords must be heartsick," Angela said. "I hope to heaven Nikki doesn't come down with whatever Caroline got."

David didn't answer.

"When I got back from Burlington," Angela said, "Wadley threatened to terminate me."

"No!" David said. He was aghast. "That would be a disaster."

"Don't worry," Angela said. "He's just blowing off steam. There's no way he could terminate me so soon after I complained about his sexual harassment. For that reason alone I'm glad I went to Cantor. The conversation officially established my complaint."

Around nine David called the hospital. He spoke at length with the head nurse, who kept insisting that Sandra's condition had not changed. She did admit, however, that she'd not eaten her dinner.

20

Thursday, October 28

DAVID looked at the alarm clock. It was quarter to five in the morning. He lay back on the pillow and shuddered through a wave of nausea. On the heels of the nausea came cramps, followed by a bout of diarrhea.

Feeling horrid, David limped to the bathroom and took a healthy dose of over-the-counter diarrhea medication. Next he stuck a thermometer in his mouth. As he searched for aspirin, he realized that he had to keep swallowing, just as Jonathan Eakins had.

David stared at his reflection in the mirror. What if he had caught the mysterious illness that had been killing his patients? They had the same symptoms I'm manifesting now, he thought. With trembling fingers he took out the thermometer. It read one hundred degrees. "Calm down," he ordered himself harshly. There was no reason to jump to hysterical conclusions. His symptoms were flulike, similar to those of the nurses he'd seen. He took two aspirins and washed them down with a glass of water. Almost immediately he got another cramp. He held on to the countertop until it passed, then went back to bed. By the time the alarm sounded, he was already feeling better.

"I think I'm coming down with something," David said to Angela. He told her about the flu symptoms. "Anyway, it's better than it was."

"Have you seen Nikki?" Angela asked.

"Not yet," David said.

They went to Nikki's room. She was a little more congested, despite the oral antibiotics. While Angela made breakfast, David called Dr. Pilsner and told him about Nikki's status.

"I think I should see her right away," Dr. Pilsner said. "Why don't I meet you in the emergency room in half an hour."

"We'll be there," David said. He was about to hang up when he thought to inquire about Caroline.

"She died this morning," Dr. Pilsner said. "Her blood pressure could no longer be maintained. At least she didn't suffer."

The news hit David hard. With heavy heart he went into the kitchen and told Angela. She looked as though she might burst into tears.

"Dr. Pilsner wants to see Nikki in the ER right away," David said. "I think we better go."

They bundled Nikki up and went out to the car. Nikki coughed most of the way to the hospital. Dr. Pilsner was waiting for them and immediately examined Nikki. When he had finished, he drew David and Angela aside.

"I want her in the hospital immediately," he said. "I don't want to take any chances after what happened."

"I'll stay with Nikki," Angela said to David. "You do your rounds."

"All right," David said. "Page me if there's any problem." Promising Nikki that he'd be by to see her all through the day, he got several aspirins from an ER nurse, then headed upstairs.

"How is Mrs. Hascher?" David asked Janet Colburn.

"Nothing much said at report," Janet said. "I don't think any of us have been in there yet this morning."

David looked at Sandra's chart. There had been no spikes of fever. Entering her room, he found her still asleep. He glanced at the swelling on her jaw. It appeared unchanged. He gave her shoulder a gentle shake, calling her name softly. When she didn't respond, he shook her more vigorously.

Finally she stirred, lifting a trembling hand to her face. She could barely open her eyes. David shook her yet again. She tried to speak, but all that came out was disconnected jabber.

Trying to remain calm, David drew some blood and sent it off for stat lab work. Then he devoted himself to a careful examination, concentrating on Sandra's lungs and nervous system.

When David returned to the nurses' station, he was handed Sandra's laboratory values. They were all normal, ruling out infection as an explanation for her current clinical state. That said, the sound of her lungs suggested incipient pneumonia.

Once again David was presented with the same trio of symptoms affecting the central nervous system, the G.I. system, and the blood or immune system. He was seeing a complex, but he had no idea what the underlying factor could be.

David agonized over what to do next. The life of a thirty-four-year-old woman hung in the balance. He was afraid to call any consults; and he was even reluctant to order further tests, since nothing had proved to be of any value with the other patients. He was at a loss.

"We have a seizure in room 216," one of the nurses shouted from down the hall. David went running. Room 216 was Sandra's room.

Sandra was in the throes of a full-blown grand mal seizure. Her body arched back as her limbs contracted on the bed. David barked orders for a tranquilizer. In an instant it was slapped into his hand. He injected it into Sandra's IV. Within minutes the convulsions stopped, leaving Sandra's body spent and comatose.

David stared down at his patient's now peaceful face. He felt as if he were being mocked for his intellectual impotence. While he had been indecisively sitting at the desk puzzling over what to do, the seizure had taken over Sandra's body in a dramatic gesture.

David erupted in a whirlwind of activity. He pulled out all the diagnostic stops—ordering consults, lab tests, X rays, even an MRI of the skull. Sandra was transferred to the ICU within half an hour. David helped push her down the hall. Once she was moved off the gurney, he started for the ICU desk to write new orders, but he stopped short of his goal. In a bed directly across from the central desk was Nikki.

David was stunned. He'd never expected to see Nikki in the ICU. Her presence there terrified him. What could it mean?

David felt a hand on his shoulder. He turned to see Dr. Pilsner. "I can see you're upset about Nikki being in here," he said. "Calm down. There are some fabulously skilled nurses here who are accustomed to taking care of patients with respiratory problems."

"Are you sure it's necessary?" David asked nervously. He knew how tough the ICU environment was on a patient's psyche.

"It's for her benefit," Dr. Pilsner said. "It's purely precautionary. I'll be moving her out of here just as soon as I can."

Before writing Sandra's orders, David went over to talk with Nikki. She was far less concerned about the ICU than he was.

The unit clerk tapped his arm. "There's a Mr. Kelley out in the patient lounge to see you," he said.

David felt his stomach tighten. He knew why Kelley was there. He wrote the orders first, then went out to meet Kelley.

"I'm disappointed," Kelley said as David approached. "The utilization coordinator called me a few minutes ago—"

"Just a minute!" David snapped. "I've got a sick patient in the ICU and I don't have time to waste with you. Stay out of my way." He glared up into Kelley's face, then spun around and started out of the room.

"Just a minute, Dr. Wilson," Kelley called. "Not so fast."

David whirled around and stormed back. Without warning he reached out and grabbed Kelley by the front of his shirt and roughly pushed him back. Kelley collapsed into the club chair behind him. David shook a clenched fist in his face.

"Get the hell out of here," David snarled. "If you don't, I don't take responsibility for the consequences. It's as simple as that."

Kelley swallowed, but he didn't move. As David marched out of the lounge, Kelley called out, "I'll be talking with my superiors."

David turned back. "You do that," he said. Then he continued into the ICU. His heart was pounding.

"Dr. Wilson," the unit clerk called out. "I have Dr. Mieslich on the phone. He's returning your call."

"I'M INVESTIGATING Dr. Dennis Hodges' murder," Calhoun said. "I understand you worked for him for some time."

"Over thirty years," Madeline Gannon said.

"Pleasant work?" Calhoun asked.

"It had its ups and downs. He was a headstrong man who could be cranky one minute and generous the next. But I was devastated when they found his body."

"Do you know who killed him?" Calhoun asked.

"I haven't the slightest idea," Madeline said. "To be perfectly honest, I don't think that a single one of the people Dr. Hodges regularly infuriated would have actually done the man harm. In the same way, Dr. Hodges would never have carried out any of the threats he voiced so frequently."

"Who did he threaten?" Calhoun asked.

Madeline laughed as she poured some coffee and handed a cup to Calhoun. "Just about everybody associated with the new administration at the hospital. The police chief, the head of the local bank, the Mobil station owner. The list goes on and on."

"Why was Hodges so angry with the hospital administration?"

"Mostly on behalf of his patients. Rather, his former patients. They started coming back to him, complaining about their health care under CMV. They wanted him to be their doctor again, but their health care had to come through CMV."

"Sounds like Hodges should have been angry at CMV."

"The day Dr. Hodges disappeared, he was really upset by the death of one of his former patients. In fact, several of his former patients had recently died. He used to yell and scream that CMV physicians couldn't keep his patients alive. He felt they were incompetent and that the hospital was abetting their incompetence."

"Can you remember the name of the patient Hodges was upset about the day he disappeared?" Calhoun asked.

"It was Clark Davenport," Madeline said. "No doubt in my mind."

Calhoun fished out his set of the copies he'd obtained in Burlington. "Here it is. Clark Davenport, fractured hip."

"Yup. He's the one," Madeline said. "The poor man fell off a ladder trying to get a kitten out of a tree."

"Look at these other names," Calhoun said. He handed the papers to Madeline. "Any of them mean anything to you?"

Madeline took the papers and shuffled through them. "I can remember each and every one," she said. "In fact, these are the patients Dr. Hodges was irritated about. They had all died."

"Hmm," Calhoun said as he took the papers back. "I knew they had to be related somehow."

"Dr. Hodges was also upset at the hospital people because of the attacks in the parking lot," Madeline added.

"Why was that?"

"He felt they should have been doing more than they were. He was convinced that the rapist was part of the hospital community."

"Did he have anybody specific in mind?"

"He indicated that he did. But he didn't tell me who. I do know that he planned to discuss the problem with Wayne Robertson. In fact, he'd planned to go see Robertson the day he disappeared."

"Did he see him?" Calhoun asked.

"No," Madeline said. "That same day he learned that Clark Davenport had died. Instead of seeing Robertson, he had me make a lunch date for him with Dr. Holster, the radiotherapist."

"Why was Hodges so eager to see Dr. Holster?"

"Dr. Holster had recently finished treating Clark Davenport."

"You've been wonderfully cooperative and most gracious," Calhoun said. "I'm appreciative of both your coffee and your excellent memory."

Madeline Gannon blushed.

ANGELA was leafing through a laboratory journal just prior to her lunch break when the chief medical examiner called.

"Something extraordinary has happened," Walt said. "Would you be able to jump in your car and come up here right now?"

"Can you give me an idea of what this is about?"

"I'd rather show you. It's really unique."

Angela was intrigued. "I'd love to come. But I'm worried about Dr. Wadley. We've not been on the best of terms."

"Oh, forget Wadley. I'll give him a call. This is important."

"You're making it hard to refuse," Angela said.

She grabbed her coat. On her way out she glanced into Wadley's office. He wasn't there. The secretaries told her that he'd gone to the Iron Horse Inn for lunch and wouldn't be back until two.

Angela asked Paul Darnell to cover for her in case there was an emergency. She told him that she'd gotten a request from the chief medical examiner to come to see something extraordinary.

Angela made it to Burlington in record time. "Wow!" Walt said when she appeared at his office door. "That was fast."

"To tell you the truth," Angela said, "I haven't much time."

"We won't need much time," Walt said. He led her to a microscope set up on a workbench. "First, look at this."

Angela adjusted the eyepieces and looked in. She saw a specimen of skin. Then she saw black dots in the dermis. "This must be the skin from under Hodges' nails," she said.

"Precisely," Walt said. "See the carbon?"

"I do," Angela said.

"All right. Take a look at this." Angela lifted her eyes and accepted a photograph from Walt. "This is a photomicrograph I obtained with a scanning electron microscope," he explained. "Notice that the dots don't look like carbon any longer."

Angela studied the photo. What Walt was saying was true.

"Now look at these readings from an atomic spectrophotometer." Walt handed her a printout. "The granules aren't carbon."

"What are they?" Angela asked.

"They're a mixture of chromium, cobalt, cadmium, and mercury," Walt said triumphantly.

"That's wonderful, Walt," Angela said. "But what does it mean?"

"I was just as perplexed as you," Walt said, "until I suddenly had an epiphany. These pigments are used for tattooing."

Angela immediately shared Walt's excitement. With the power of forensics they'd made a discovery: the killer had a tattoo. She couldn't wait to tell David and Calhoun.

Returning to Bartlet, Angela ran into Paul Darnell. He'd been waiting for her. "I got some bad news," he said. "Wadley knows you left town and he's not happy about it."

"How could he know?" Angela asked. Darnell was the only person she'd told.

"I think he was spying on you," Darnell said. "He came in to see me fifteen minutes after you left."

"I thought he'd gone out for lunch."

"That's what he told everybody. Obviously, he hadn't. He asked me if you had left Bartlet. I couldn't lie. I had to tell him."

No sooner had Angela returned to her office than a secretary appeared to let her know that Dr. Wadley wanted to see her. She found him sitting at his desk. He stared at her with cold eyes.

"I was told you wanted to see me," she said.

"I did indeed," Wadley said. "I wanted to inform you that you are fired. I would appreciate it if you would pack up your belongings and leave. Your continued presence is bad for morale."

"If you're upset because I was gone at my lunch hour, you should know that I drove to Burlington to visit the chief medical examiner. I've only been gone for a little over an hour."

"I'm not interested in excuses," Wadley said. "I warned you just yesterday about this very same thing. You chose to ignore my warnings. You've demonstrated yourself to be unreliable, disobedient, and ungrateful."

"Ungrateful!" Angela exploded. "Ungrateful for what? For your sniveling advances? For not wanting to rush off to Miami for a weekend of sun and fun with you? You can fire me, Dr. Wadley, but I can sue you and the hospital for sexual harassment."

Angela stormed out of Wadley's office, beside herself with rage. As she passed through the outer office, the secretaries scattered quickly. She went to her office, packed her things into a canvas tote bag, and walked out. She didn't talk to anyone for fear of losing her composure. She didn't want to give Wadley the satisfaction of making her cry; so she went directly to her car and drove aimlessly toward town.

Just as she was passing the library, she spotted Calhoun's inimitable truck in the parking lot. Angela parked her car. Checking the library, she found him reading in a quiet alcove.

"Mr. Calhoun?" Angela whispered.

Calhoun looked up. "How convenient," he said with a smile. "I've got some news."

"I'm afraid I've got some news as well," Angela said. "How about meeting me up at the house."

Angela went home and put some water on to boil. While she was getting out cups and saucers, Calhoun's truck came up the drive. She called out that the door was unlocked when he knocked.

"Coffee or tea?" she asked as he came into the kitchen.

"Whatever you're having," Calhoun said.

Angela busied herself getting the tea and the honey.

"You're off kinda early," Calhoun said.

Because she'd been reining in her emotions ever since she'd fled Wadley's office, Angela's response to Calhoun's innocent comment was overwhelming. She covered her face and sobbed. At a loss for what to do, Calhoun stood helpless. When she'd finally stopped crying, he told her that she better tell him what happened.

"I think I'll have some wine instead of tea," Angela said.

"I'll have a beer," Calhoun said.

Sitting at the kitchen table, Angela told Calhoun about getting fired. She explained how dire the consequences could be for her family. Calhoun turned out to be a good listener, and he made

Angela feel better. When Angela had talked herself out, Calhoun told her that he'd made some progress in the investigation.

Angela dried her eyes with a dish towel. "Tell me."

"First of all, I discovered how the eight patients whose admission summaries Hodges was carrying around are related," he said. "All of them were former patients of his who had been shifted to CMV and had subsequently died. Apparently each death came as a surprise to Hodges. That's why he was so furious."

"Does this help us find out who killed him?" Angela asked.

"Probably not. But it's a piece to the puzzle. I also discovered another one: Hodges believed he knew the identity of the parking lot rapist. What's more, he thought the perp was connected to the hospital."

"I see where you are going," Angela said. "If the rapist knew Hodges suspected him, then he might have killed Hodges. The rapist and Hodges' murderer could be the same person."

"Exactly," Calhoun said. "The same person who tried to kill you the other night."

Angela shuddered. "Don't remind me," she said. Then she added, "I learned something about our murder suspect today, something that could make finding him a bit easier: he has a tattoo." She told Calhoun what Walter Dunsmore had found.

"Hell's bells," Calhoun said. "I love it."

AFTER seeing his last office patient, David started off to the hospital. He'd been back and forth all day checking on Nikki and Sandra, so he expected no surprises.

When he entered the ICU, Nikki saw him immediately and beamed. She was doing remarkably well. She'd responded to the IV antibiotics and to the ministrations of the respiratory therapist. David was happy to learn that she was scheduled to be transferred out of the ICU the following morning.

Sandra's condition was just the opposite. She'd never awakened from her coma, and the consults had been no help.

David sat at the desk in the ICU and leafed through Sandra's chart. The MRI of her skull had been normal: no tumor and certainly no brain abscess. David looked at the laboratory tests he'd ordered. Some were sophisticated searches of the body fluids for viral remnants, using state-of-the-art biotechnological techniques.

While David was agonizing over Sandra, Charles Kelley came into the unit and approached the desk. "I hope I'm not disturbing you," Kelley said. "But I have a bit of news. As of this moment you're fired. You're no longer employed by CMV."

David's mouth fell open. "Is this decision final, or is it pending a hearing?"

Kelley was already on his way down the hall.

"It's final, my friend." With that, he was gone.

IT WASN'T until Angela and David were seated in the family room watching the evening news that David nervously cleared his throat.

"I'm embarrassed to tell you I was fired this afternoon," he said. David saw the shock registered in Angela's face. He averted his eyes. "I'm sorry. I know it'll be difficult for us."

"David," Angela said, grabbing his arm. "I was fired too."

David looked at Angela. "You were?"

She nodded.

He pulled her close. When they leaned back to look at each other again, they didn't know whether to laugh or cry.

"What a mess," David said at last.

"What a coincidence," Angela added, and also filled David in on Walt's latest discovery and her impromptu meeting with Calhoun.

"He thinks the tattoo will help find the murderer," Angela said.

"That's nice," David said. But his thoughts were already elsewhere. He was wondering what he and Angela would do to support themselves in the immediate future.

"And remember those admission summaries? Calhoun figured out how they're related," Angela said. "They'd all died, and apparently all the deaths came as a surprise to Hodges."

"What do you mean?" David asked, suddenly interested.

"I guess he didn't expect them to die," Angela said. "He had treated them before they transferred to CMV. Calhoun was told that Hodges blamed CMV and the hospital for their deaths."

"Do you have any of the histories on these patients?"

"Just the admission diagnoses. Why?"

"Having patients die unexpectedly is something I can relate to."

There was a pause in the conversation.

"What are we going to do?" Angela asked finally.

"I don't know," David said. "I'm sure we'll have to move, but what happens to the mortgages? I wonder if we'll have to declare bankruptcy. We'll have to talk to a lawyer."

"I'll sue for sexual harassment, if not wrongful dismissal," Angela said. "There's no way I'll let Wadley get off scot-free."

"I don't know," David said. "Maybe we should just get on with our lives. I don't want to get bogged down in a legal morass."

Later they called the ICU. Nikki was continuing to do well. She was still without a fever.

"We might have lost our jobs," David said, "but as long as Nikki is okay, we'll manage."

21

Friday, October 29

NEITHER David nor Angela slept well. David woke before dawn. Although he was exhausted, he didn't feel ill, the way he had the previous morning. Going down to the family room to ponder their financial situation, he made a list of things to do and people to call.

Angela appeared at the doorway in her robe. She'd been crying. David explained what he was doing, but she wasn't impressed.

"So what are we going to do?" Angela asked.

"First, let's go to the hospital and check on Nikki," David said.

"Okay," Angela said. "I want to talk with Helen Beaton."

NIKKI was fine, and eager to get out of the unit. Dr. Pilsner confirmed that she was going to a regular room.

"When do you think she'll be coming home?" David asked.

"As well as she's doing, she'll be home in just a few days," Dr. Pilsner said. "I want to make certain she doesn't suffer a relapse."

"Would you call Caroline and have her get my schoolbooks?" Nikki asked David.

"I'll take care of it," David promised, purposefully evasive. He still hadn't told his daughter about Caroline's death.

David couldn't help but notice that Sandra's bed in the ICU was now occupied by an elderly man. Mustering his courage, he went to the unit clerk and asked about her.

"Sandra Hascher died this morning about three," the clerk said. He spoke as if he were giving a weather report.

David's heart went out to Sandra's family. Now he had lost five patients in two weeks. Maybe CMV had been wise to fire him.

David walked over to administration to wait for Angela. Hardly had he sat down when Angela came storming out of Helen Beaton's office. She was livid. He had to run to catch up with her.

"It was terrible," Angela said. "She's upholding Wadley's decision. When I explained that sexual harassment was at the bottom of the whole affair, she denied that any had taken place."

"How could she deny it when you'd spoken with Dr. Cantor?" David asked.

"She said that Dr. Wadley said there had been no sexual harassment. In fact, he told Beaton that if there had been any impropriety, it was that I'd tried to seduce him!"

"A familiar ploy of the sexual harasser," David said. "Blame the victim." He shook his head. "What a sleazebag!"

"Beaton said she believed him," Angela said. "She told me he was a man of impeccable integrity. Then she accused me of having made up the story to try to get back at him for spurning my advances."

When they arrived home, they collapsed into chairs in the family room. They were too depressed and confused to do anything.

The sound of tires crunching on gravel broke the heavy silence. Calhoun pulled up to the back door. Angela let him in.

"I brought some fresh doughnuts to celebrate the first day of your vacation," Calhoun said. He passed by Angela and dumped his parcel on the kitchen table. "With a little coffee we'll be in business."

David appeared at the doorway.

"Uh-oh," Calhoun said. He looked from David to Angela.

"It's okay," said David. "I'm on vacation too."

"No kidding," Calhoun said.

Calhoun's presence was like an elixir. The coffee helped as well.

"Now," he said, rubbing his hands. "The problem has been reduced to finding someone with a damaged tattoo who didn't like Hodges. That shouldn't be so hard in a small town."

"There's a catch," David said. "Since we are both unemployed, I don't think we can afford to employ you."

"Hold on a second," Calhoun said. "Let's not be too rash here.

I've got an idea. I'll work for nothing. How's that? Besides, we might be catching ourselves a rapist in the process."

"That's very generous of you," David said. He started to say more, but Calhoun interrupted him.

"I've already begun the next phase of inquiry," he said. "I found out that several of the town's policemen, including Robertson, have tattoos. So I had a casual chat with Robertson. He was more than happy to show me his. It's on his chest—a bald eagle holding a banner that reads IN GOD WE TRUST. Unfortunately, the tattoo was in fine shape. But I used the opportunity to ask about Hodges' last day. Robertson confirmed that Hodges planned on seeing him, then canceled. So I think we're on to something. Clara Hodges may be the key. They were estranged at the time of the doc's death, but they still spoke frequently. Anyway, I called Clara this morning. She's expecting us." He looked at Angela.

"I thought she'd moved to Boston," David said.

"She did," Calhoun said. "All three of us could drive down."

"I still think Angela and I should drop this whole thing. If you want to continue, that's your business."

"Let's do it, David," Angela said. "Let's go. This town has pushed us around the same way it's pushed Hodges' death under the carpet. I want to know what's behind it all. Then we can leave here with our heads held high. If Calhoun thinks this visit to Clara Hodges might do the trick, let's try it."

David hesitated. Angela's pleas were hard to resist. Underneath his veneer of calm and reason, he was just as angry as she was.

"All right," he said. "Let's go. But we'll see Nikki first."

THEY had to take Calhoun's truck so he could smoke, but it did mean they could pull right up to the front door of the hospital. Calhoun waited while David and Angela ran inside.

Nikki was much happier now that she was out of the ICU. Her only complaint was that she'd been transferred to one of the old hospital beds, and as usual the controls didn't work. The foot would rise but not the head.

"Did you tell the nurses?" David asked.

"Yeah," Nikki said. "But they haven't told me when it will be fixed. I can't watch the TV with my head flat."

David found Janet Colburn and alerted her about Nikki's bed. Back in Nikki's room David assured his daughter that if her bed wasn't fixed by that evening, he'd do it himself. Angela had already informed her that she and David were going to Boston but would come see her as soon as they were back that afternoon.

Returning to the front of the hospital, Angela and David piled into Calhoun's truck. Soon they were on their way south on the interstate. David found the trip uncomfortable for more reasons than the truck's poor suspension. Even though Calhoun cracked his window, cigar smoke swirled around inside the cab. By the time they got to Clara Hodges' Back Bay address in Boston, David's eyes were watering.

Clara Hodges was a big-boned, solid woman with deep-set eyes and an intimidating scowl. She invited them into her parlor, decorated with heavy Victorian furnishings, and offered them tea. Only a meager amount of daylight penetrated the thick velvet drapes.

"I'm upset this ugly business has surfaced," Clara said. "I'd just about adjusted to Dennis' disappearance when I learned that he'd been murdered."

"Do you have any suspicions about who killed your husband?" Calhoun asked.

"I'm afraid there are a lot of candidates," Clara said. "I suppose any one of a dozen people could have gotten angry enough to do him in, yet I can't imagine any one of them actually beating him."

"I understand that he thought he knew the identity of the ski-masked rapist," Calhoun said. "Did he ever mention any names?"

"The only thing he said was that the rapist was someone connected to the hospital," Clara said.

"An employee of the hospital?" Calhoun asked.

"He didn't elaborate," Clara said. "But then he decided to go to that abominable Wayne Robertson with his suspicions."

"Was that the day he disappeared?" Calhoun asked.

"That's right," Clara said. "But in the end Dennis didn't see Robertson. He got all upset over one of his former patients dying. He said he was going to have lunch with Dr. Holster instead."

"Why was Dr. Hodges so upset about this patient?" Calhoun asked.

"They were acquaintances," Clara said. "Dennis had diagnosed Clark Davenport's cancer, which Dr. Holster had successfully treated. Dennis had felt confident that they'd caught the cancer early enough. But then Clark's employer switched to CMV, and the next thing Dennis knew, Clark was dead."

"What did Clark die of?" David asked suddenly, his voice urgent.

"I'm not sure I ever knew," Clara said. "But it wasn't his cancer."

"Did your husband have any other patients with cancer or other serious diseases?" David asked.

"Oh, yes," Clara said. "He had a number. And it was their deaths that upset him so. He became convinced that some of the CMV doctors were incompetent."

David fumbled with the copies of the admission sheets obtained from Burlington as he handed them to Clara. "Look at these names," he said. "Do you recognize any?"

"I'll have to get my reading glasses," Clara said. She stood up and left the room.

"Something is beginning to dawn on me," David said. "And I don't like it one bit."

Before Angela could ask David to explain, Clara returned with her reading glasses. She picked up the papers and quickly glanced through them. "I recognize all these people," she said. "I'd heard their names a hundred times, and I'd met most of them."

"I was told all of them died," Calhoun said. "Is that true?"

"That's right," Clara said. "Just like Clark Davenport. These are the people whose deaths had particularly upset Dennis."

"Were their deaths all unexpected?" Calhoun asked.

"Yes and no," Clara said. "As you can see from these papers, most of the people were hospitalized for problems that usually aren't fatal. But they all had battled terminal illnesses like cancer, so in that sense their deaths weren't totally unexpected."

David reached out and took the papers back. "Let me be sure I understand," he said. "These admission summary sheets are the admissions during which these people died."

"I believe so," Clara said. "It's been a while, but Dennis carried on so. It's hard to forget."

David stood up and walked over to the window. Pulling back the drapes, he stared out over the Charles River.

"I want to ask a few questions about the rapist," Calhoun said. "Did Dr. Hodges ever allude to whether or not he had a tattoo?"

"A tattoo?" Clara said. "No. He never mentioned a tattoo."

With a swiftness that took everyone by surprise, David returned from the window. "We have to leave," he said. "Immediately."

"David?" Angela said, astonished. "What's the matter?"

"We've got to get back to Bartlet," he said. His urgency had grown to near panic. "Come on!" he yelled.

Angela and Calhoun gave a hurried good-bye to Clara Hodges before running after David. By the time they got out to the truck, David was already behind the wheel.

"Give me the keys," he ordered.

Calhoun shrugged, handed David the keys, and followed Angela in. Before the door was closed behind them, David hit the gas.

For the first portion of the trip no one spoke. David concentrated on driving. Angela and Calhoun were still shocked by the sudden, awkward departure. They were also intimidated by the rapidity with which they were overtaking other motorists.

"This truck has never gone this fast," Calhoun said.

"David, what has come over you?" Angela asked.

"I had a flash of insight while we were talking to Clara Hodges," he said. "It concerns Hodges' patients with potentially terminal illnesses dying unexpectedly."

"What about them?" Angela asked.

"I think some disturbed individual at Bartlet Community Hospital has taken it upon himself to deliver some sort of misguided euthanasia. Hearing about Hodges' patients made me realize that all five of my recent deaths had battled terminal illnesses. I don't know why I didn't think of it before. How could I have been so dense? And the same is true with Caroline."

"Who's Caroline?" Calhoun asked.

"She was a friend of our daughter," Angela explained. "She had cystic fibrosis, which is a potentially terminal illness. She died yesterday." Angela's eyes went wide. "Oh, no. Nikki!" she cried.

"What's going on?" Calhoun said. "I'm missing something here."

"You know Nikki is in the hospital," Angela said anxiously. "She has cystic fibrosis, just like Caroline had."

"Uh-oh," Calhoun said. "I'm getting the picture. You're worried about your daughter being targeted by this euthanasia fiend."

"You got it," David said. "It answers a lot of questions. It even makes me think of Dr. Portland. Didn't Portland say he wasn't going to take all the blame for his patient deaths and that there was something wrong with the hospital?"

Angela nodded. "He committed suicide," she explained to Calhoun.

"If someone is performing euthanasia," David said, "it would have to be someone with access to the patients and someone with a sophisticated knowledge of medicine."

"That would limit it to a doctor or a nurse," Angela said.

"Or a lab tech," David suggested.

"I think you people are jumping the gun," Calhoun said. "I think we should slow down."

"Not while my daughter is at risk," David said.

"Do you think Hodges came to the same conclusion?" Angela asked.

"I think so," David said. "Maybe that's why he was killed."

"I still think it was the rapist," Calhoun said.

When they finally reached the hospital, David pulled right up to the front door. He jumped out, with Angela close at his heels.

To their supreme relief they discovered Nikki perfectly happy watching TV. David snatched her up in his arms and hugged her.

"You're coming home," David said.

"When?" Nikki asked.

"Right now," Angela said.

A nurse passing in the hall saw Angela detaching the IV. "What's going on here?" she asked.

"My daughter is going home," David said.

"There are no orders for that," the nurse said.

"I'm giving the order right this minute," David said.

ONCE they got home, David and Angela set Nikki up in the family room and restarted her IV to continue her antibiotics. Calhoun participated as best he could. Following Nikki's request, he brought wood upstairs from the basement and made a fire. But it wasn't his nature to stay silent. Before long he got into an argument with David over the motive for Hodges' murder.

"Hodges ranted about knowing who the rapist was the very day he got knocked off!" Calhoun exclaimed. "How's that for cause and effect? I'm sure the rapist and the murderer are one and the same."

"But Hodges was beaten to death holding the names of his patients," David said. "That couldn't have been a coincidence."

"What if it is the same person?" Angela suggested. "What if the rapist is behind the patient deaths and Hodges' murder?"

The idea shocked David and Calhoun into silence.

"It's possible," David said at last.

"I suppose," Calhoun said. "Anyway, I'm going after the tattoo clue. That's the key."

"I'm going to medical records," David said.

"Okay," Calhoun said. "I'll go do my thing; you go do yours."

After Calhoun left, David got the shotgun and proceeded to load it with as many shells as it would hold. He leaned it against the newel-post in the front hall.

"Have you changed your mind about the gun?" Angela asked.

"Let's just say I'm glad it's here," David said. "Don't let anyone in while I'm gone. And keep all the doors locked."

When David arrived at the hospital, the day shift was being replaced by the evening shift. No one paid the slightest attention to him as he made his way to medical records.

Sitting down at a terminal, David set out the admission summaries. He called up each patient's name and read the history. All eight were terminally ill. During each hospital stay the symptoms were similar to those experienced by David's patients—neurological symptoms, gastrointestinal symptoms, and symptoms dealing with the blood or immune system. In each case except for one, death resulted from overwhelming pneumonia, sepsis, and shock.

Putting Hodges' papers away, David began using the hospital computer to calculate yearly death rates as a percentage of admissions. He quickly discovered that the death rate had changed two years before, when it had gone from an average of 2.8 percent up to 6.7 percent. The last year, the death rate was up to 8.1 percent.

David then narrowed the death rate to those patients with a diagnosis of cancer, whether the cancer was attributed as the cause of death or not. They showed the same sudden increase in death rate.

The increased percentage of deaths seemed to back up David's theory of an "angel of mercy" at work. David was about to leave when he thought of asking the computer to search through all medical histories on all admissions for the words tattoo or dyschromia, the medical word for aberrant pigmentation.

It took almost a minute, but finally a list blazed on the screen. Twenty people who had been treated at the hospital had a mention of a tattoo in their records. Using the computer to match name and employment, David discovered that five of the patients with tattoos worked in the hospital: Clyde Devonshire, an R.N. in the emergency room; Joe Forbs from security; Claudette Maurice from dietary; Werner Van Slyke from engineering/maintenance; and Peter Ullhof, a lab technician.

Printing out a copy of this information, David went on his way.

HORTENSE Marshall, one of the health-information professionals, had been alerted to David's activities by a security program she'd placed in the hospital computer. As soon as he'd departed from records, she placed a call to Helen Beaton.

"Dr. David Wilson was in medical records," Hortense said. "He called up information concerning hospital death rates."

"Did he talk with you?" Beaton asked.

"No. He used a terminal. He didn't speak with anyone."

"How did you know he was accessing data on death rates?"

"After you advised me to report anyone requesting that kind of data, I had the computer programmed to signal me if someone tried to access the information on their own."

"Excellent," Beaton said. "I like your initiative. Would you let me know if Dr. Wilson comes back?"

"Most certainly," Hortense said.

BY THE time David returned home, Nikki had begun to feel worse. By early evening she was suffering from nausea and increased salivation—the same symptoms David had experienced Wednesday night. By six thirty she was lethargic after several bouts of diarrhea, and David was sick with worry. He was terrified that whatever had killed his patients had already been given to her.

Calhoun arrived at exactly seven.

"I got nine more people with tattoos," he said.

"I got twenty," David said, trying to sound upbeat.

When they combined the lists and threw out the duplicates, they had twenty-five names.

"What do we do now?" Angela asked.

"First, we run a background computer check on each person," Calhoun said. "Second, I start interviewing them. We need to find out where each person's tattoo is located and whether they mind showing it off. That tattoo must be the worse for wear and tear, and located someplace where it could have been scratched in a struggle. I'd say the forearm, maybe the wrist."

"How do we run a background check?" Angela asked.

"All we need is the social security number and the birth date," Calhoun said. "We should be able to get those through the hospital. The rest is easy. With a computer and a modem, it's staggering what can be obtained from the hundreds of data banks that exist. Financial history, criminal records, job history, consumer purchasing history, phone use, personal ads. It's like a fishing trip. But interesting stuff turns up. And with twenty-five people with tattoos, it will be very interesting, believe me."

"Did you do this when you were a state policeman?" Angela asked.

"All the time," Calhoun said. "Whenever we had a bunch of suspects—and we always got some dirt. And in this case, if David is right and the killer is committing euthanasia, I guarantee we'll come across lots of weird stuff. We'll need to get hold of some computer jock to help us tap into the data banks."

"I have an old boyfriend at M.I.T.," Angela said. "He's a computer genius. His name is Robert Scali."

"So why have I never heard of this guy?" David asked.

"I haven't told you every little detail of my life," Angela said. "I dated him briefly in college. We've kept in touch over the years."

"I can't believe I'm hearing this," David said.

"I think Mr. Scali would do fine," Calhoun said. "Any chance of getting a description of the tattoos from medical records?"

"I think so," David said. "Most physicians would probably note them in a physical examination."

"It sure would help prioritize our list," Calhoun said.

The three organized their efforts for the following day.

"I'll start interviewing tattooed hospital workers," Calhoun said.

"I'll go to records," David said. "I'll get the social security numbers and birth dates and see about descriptions of the tattoos."

"I'll stay with Nikki," Angela said. "Then when David's gotten the social security numbers, I'll take a run into Cambridge."

"What's the matter with sending them by fax?" David asked.

"I can't ask a favor by just firing off a fax," Angela said.

"What about that Dr. Holster, the radiotherapist?" Calhoun said.

"I forgot about him," David said. "I can talk with him tomorrow, when I finish at medical records."

"When should we talk again?" Angela asked.

"As soon as we have something to talk about," Calhoun said. "And both of you should get some sleep. I can tell you need it."

22

Saturday, October 30

ALTHOUGH Nikki suffered from abdominal cramps and diarrhea throughout the night, by morning she was better. She still wasn't back to one hundred percent, but she was clearly on the mend. David was vastly relieved.

"Can I go to school on Monday?" Nikki asked.

"It's possible," Angela said.

"I don't want to get too far behind," Nikki said. "Can Caroline come over and bring my schoolbooks?"

Angela glanced at David, who was petting Rusty on Nikki's bed, and a wordless communication flashed between them. "Nikki, there's something we have to tell you about Caroline," Angela said gently. "We're terribly sorry, but she passed away."

"You mean she died?" Nikki asked.

"I'm afraid so," Angela said.

"Oh," Nikki said simply.

At first Nikki seemed hardly concerned, but it took even less time than it had with Marjorie for her façade to crumble.

"Am I going to die too?" Nikki sobbed.

"No," Angela said. "You're doing wonderfully. Caroline had a high fever. You have no fever at all."

Angela and David did what they could to console Nikki, and her anguish tormented them. Once they had calmed her fears, David set out for the hospital. Arriving, he went immediately to medical records and set about matching social security numbers and birth dates to the list of names he and Calhoun had compiled.

With that out of the way, David began to call up each medical record for descriptions of the tattoos. He hadn't gotten far when someone tapped him on the shoulder. He turned around to face Helen Beaton. Behind her was Joe Forbs from security.

"Would you mind telling me what you are doing?" Beaton asked.

"I—I'm just using the computer," David stammered.

"You are no longer employed by CMV," Beaton said.

"That's true," David said. "But—"

"Since that's the case, you no longer have rights to hospital computer access."

David knew it was pointless to protest. He calmly gathered up his papers, hoping Beaton wouldn't strip him of these documents. Joe Forbs escorted him to the door.

Undaunted, David proceeded to the radiotherapy unit, which was housed in its own ultramodern building. Dr. Holster was only about ten years older than David, but his hair was almost white. Although he was busy that morning, he was hospitable.

"So, what can I do for you, Dr. Wilson?" Dr. Holster said.

"I was hoping to ask you some questions about Dr. Hodges," David said.

Dr. Holster shrugged. "Ask away."

"I understand that Dr. Hodges visited you the day he disappeared," David said.

"We had lunch, to be precise," Dr. Holster said.

"I know that Dr. Hodges wanted to see you concerning a patient by the name of Clark Davenport."

"That's correct," Dr. Holster said. "Unfortunately, Mr. Davenport had just died. I'd treated him for prostate cancer, with what we thought was great success. Both Dr. Hodges and myself were surprised and saddened by his passing."

"Mr. Davenport died in septic shock after a series of grand mal seizures," David said. "I don't think it was related to his cancer. His MRI was normal. Of course, there was no autopsy, so we don't know for sure. Did Dr. Hodges mention anything about Mr. Davenport's hospital course that he thought was unexpected?"

"Only his death," Dr. Holster said.

"Did anything else come up during your lunch?"

"Not really. Not that I can recall. When we were done eating, I showed Dennis the new linear accelerator he'd been responsible for us having received. He was truly impressed. The old cobalt-sixty unit couldn't be aimed as accurately. As the cobalt source is about four inches in length, the gamma rays come out in every direction and are difficult to collimate."

"I see," David said, although he wasn't quite sure he did. Physics had never been his forte. He suppressed a yawn.

"Dr. Hodges was quite interested when I gave him the tour," Dr. Holster said. "His face lit up. He even wanted to see the old machine. How about you? Want to run over there?"

"I think I'll pass," David said.

AFTER sleeping late, Calhoun didn't get back to Bartlet until midmorning. As he drove into town, he decided to attack the list of hospital workers with tattoos alphabetically. That put Clyde Devonshire first.

Devonshire lived above a convenience store. Calhoun made his way up the stairs to the man's door and rang the bell. When there was no answer, he rang again. When there was still no response, he tried the door. It opened in.

"Hello!" Calhoun called out. With no compunction whatsoever he stepped over the threshold and closed the door behind him.

The apartment was cheaply furnished but neat. On the coffee table in the living room Calhoun found a stack of newspaper clippings on Jack Kevorkian, the notorious "suicide" doctor.

Calhoun smiled. He thought that assisted suicide and euthanasia shared some areas of commonality and that David might like to have a chat with Clyde Devonshire.

Calhoun pushed open the bedroom door. Going over to the bureau, he scanned the articles on top. Opening the closet, he found himself staring at a collection of bondage paraphernalia, mostly items in black leather with stainless steel rivets and chains. On a shelf were stacks of accompanying magazines and videotapes.

As Calhoun closed the door, he wondered what the background computer search would uncover on this weirdo. Moving through

the rest of the apartment, he searched for photos. He was hoping to find one with Clyde displaying his tattoos.

Calhoun was about to return to the living room and go through the desk when he heard a door slam below, followed by footfalls on the stairs. He considered making a run for it but, instead, went to the front door and pulled it open. "Clyde Devonshire?" he asked sharply.

"Yeah," Clyde said. "What is going on here?"

"My name is Phil Calhoun," Calhoun said. He extended a business card. "I've been waiting for you. Come on in."

Clyde took the card. "You're an investigator?" he asked.

"That's right," Calhoun said. "I've been sitting here waiting for you to get home so I could ask you some questions."

"Well, you sure scared me," Clyde admitted. "Sit down. Can I offer you anything?" He then headed into the kitchen. "I've got coffee, pop, or—"

"Have any beer?" Calhoun asked.

"Sure," Clyde called. He came back into the living room carrying two beers. He handed one to Calhoun. "What kind of questions did you want to ask me?"

"Did you know Dr. Hodges?" Calhoun asked.

Clyde gave a short, scornful laugh. "Why on earth would you be investigating that detestable figure out of ancient history?"

"Sounds like you didn't think much of him."

"He was mean," Clyde said. "He thought we nurses were low-life forms who were supposed to do all the dirty work and not question doctors' orders."

"Do you know who killed Dr. Hodges?" Calhoun asked.

"It wasn't me, if that's what you're thinking," Clyde said. "But if you find out, let me know. I'd love to buy the man a beer."

"Do you have a tattoo?" Calhoun asked.

"I sure do," Clyde said. "I have a number of them."

"Where?" Calhoun asked.

"You want to see them?" Grinning from ear to ear, Clyde took off his shirt and assumed several poses as if he were a bodybuilder. He had a chain tattooed around each wrist, a dragon on his right upper arm, and a pair of crossed swords on his pectorals.

"Do you ski?" Calhoun asked.

"Occasionally," Clyde said.

"Do you own a ski mask?"

"Everybody who skis in New England has a ski mask," Clyde said. "Unless they're masochists."

Calhoun stood up. "Thanks for the beer," he said. "I've got to be on my way."

Calhoun descended the stairs, went outside, and climbed into his truck. He was glad to get out of Clyde Devonshire's apartment. The man was definitely bizarre, but could he have killed Hodges? Somehow Calhoun didn't think so. Yet he was eager to see what the computer check would bring up on Clyde.

Calhoun checked his list. The next name was Joe Forbs. The address wasn't far from Madeline Gannon's.

At Forbs' house, a thin, nervous woman with gray-streaked hair opened the door a crack when Calhoun knocked. Calhoun introduced himself and produced his card. She was not impressed.

"Mrs. Forbs?" Calhoun asked. "Is Joe Forbs at home?"

"No," Mrs. Forbs said. "You'll have to come back later."

"What time?"

"I don't know. It's a different time each day."

Mrs. Forbs shut the door. Calhoun heard a series of locks secured. He had the distinct impression she thought he was a bill collector.

Climbing back into the truck, Calhoun sighed. It was time to move on to the next name on the list: Claudette Maurice.

Calhoun pulled up across the street from Maurice's house. It was a tiny home that looked like a dollhouse. He went up to the front door and knocked. There was no response.

Calhoun went to the nearest neighbor. He got his answer quickly. Claudette Maurice was on vacation. She'd gone to Hawaii.

Now he was only one for three. Calhoun looked at the next name: Werner Van Slyke. He debated skipping Van Slyke, since he'd talked to him already—but he didn't know about Van Slyke's tattoo then.

Van Slyke lived on a quiet lane where the buildings were set far back from the street. Calhoun pulled to a stop behind a row of cars parked across from Van Slyke's home. The house was run down and badly in need of paint. Dilapidated shutters hung at odd angles from their windows. Set way back from the house was a barn. The place gave Calhoun the creeps.

Calhoun lit himself an Antonio y Cleopatra and eyed the house.

There was no sign of life around the building and no vehicle in the driveway. Calhoun doubted anyone was home. He climbed out of the truck and walked across the street.

Calhoun pressed the doorbell several times, but heard nothing. Leaving the front stoop, he circled the house, trying to see into the windows. It wasn't easy, since the windows were filthy. He went back and tried the front door. It was unlocked.

To be absolutely certain no one was home, Calhoun knocked loudly. To his shock, the door opened. Calhoun looked up. Van Slyke was eyeing him suspiciously.

"What do you want?" Van Slyke asked.

"Sorry to bother you," Calhoun said. "I just happened to be in the area, and I thought I'd stop by. I have a few more questions. What do you say? Is it an inconvenient time?"

"I suppose now's all right," Van Slyke said after a pause.

ARMED with the social security numbers and birth dates, Angela met Robert Scali at one of the numerous small Indian restaurants in Cambridge. As she entered, he got up from a table.

Angela kissed him on the cheek, then got down to business. She handed Robert her list.

"So you want background checks on these people?" he said, eyeing the sheet. "What is it you specifically want?"

"I want to find out everything I can," Angela said. She gave Robert a thumbnail sketch of the events in Bartlet. She started with Hodges' body being discovered in their basement, then went on to the tattoo, and finished up with the theory of misguided euthanasia.

"My goodness," he said. "You're shooting holes in my romantic image of the peaceful country life." He looked at the list. "Twenty-five names will yield a lot of data. Did you come in a U-Haul?"

"We're particularly interested in these five," Angela said. She pointed to the names of the people who worked in the hospital.

"The quickest information to get will be financial," Robert said. "There are quite a few databases we can tap with ease. So we'll soon have information on credit cards, bank accounts, money transfers, and debt. From then on, it gets more difficult."

"What would the next step be?"

"I suppose social security. Hacking into their data banks is trickier, but I do have a friend here at M.I.T. who is conveniently working on database security for various government agencies."

"Do you think he'd help?" Angela asked.

"Peter Fong? Of course, if I ask him. Come on, let's go."

PETER's office was hidden away at the rear of the fourth floor of a stuccoed building in the middle of the M.I.T. campus. It looked like an electronics laboratory—filled with computers, cathode-ray tubes, tape machines, and other electronic paraphernalia.

Robert handed Peter the list and told him what they wanted. Peter scratched his head and pondered the request.

"I agree social security would be the best place to start," Peter said. "But an FBI database search would also be a good idea. I've been working with a colleague in Washington who's on-line with both organizations."

Peter used a word processor to type out what he wanted, then slipped it into his fax. Within minutes data was pouring into his hard-disk drive. Peter pulled some material up onto his screen.

Angela looked over his shoulder and scanned a portion of the social security record on Joe Forbs, indicating the recent jobs he'd held, along with his payments into the social security pool.

Peter activated his laser printer. It began spewing forth page after page of data. Angela walked over and picked up a sheet. It was the social security file on Werner Van Slyke.

"Interesting," she said. "He was in the navy. That's probably where he got his tattoo."

The criminal records began coming in on another printer. The most significant discovery was that Clyde Devonshire had been arrested and convicted of rape six years earlier in Norfolk, Virginia, and had served two years in the state penitentiary.

"He works in the ER at the hospital," Angela said. "I wonder if anyone knew of his record."

Robert went to the other printer and rummaged through the data until he found Clyde Devonshire's information. "He was in the navy too," he called over. "In fact, the dates seem to indicate that he was in the navy when he was arrested for rape."

Angela stepped over to Robert to look over his shoulder.

"Look at this," he said. "There are a number of gaps in the social security history after Mr. Devonshire got out of prison. Such gaps suggest that he either did more time or was using aliases."

Half an hour later Angela and Robert headed for Robert's office.

"Let's get some financial information," Robert said, sitting down at one of his terminals. As his printers snapped into operation, pages flew into the collection trays with surprising rapidity. "I'll try to get more tonight, when there's less traffic."

"I'm overwhelmed," Angela admitted. "I never thought such reams of personal information could be obtained with such ease. Thank you so much." She tried to pick up her two boxes of material.

"I think I'd better give you a hand with all that," Robert said.

Once the material was stored in the trunk, Angela gave Robert a hug. "Thanks again," she said. "It's been good to see you."

Robert waved as Angela drove away. She watched him recede in her rearview mirror. It had been nice to see him. Now she was looking forward to showing all this material to David and Calhoun.

"I'm home," Angela shouted as she entered through the back door. She found David in the family room. "How's Nikki?"

"She's fine," David said. "She's napping. She's still terribly upset about Caroline. But physically she's doing great. How did you do?"

"You won't believe it," Angela said. "Come on."

Angela dragged David into the kitchen and showed him the boxes. He took out a few pages to look at them. "You're right," he said. "I don't believe it. This will take hours to go through."

"It's a good thing we're unemployed," Angela said. "At least we have plenty of time."

After dinner, while Nikki watched television, David and Angela began the chore of going through the computer data.

"This will take us days," David complained.

"Maybe we should concentrate on just those with connections to the hospital," Angela said. "There are only five."

"Good idea," he said.

Like Angela, David found the criminal information the most provocative. He was particularly taken by the news that Clyde Devonshire had not only served time for rape but had also been arrested in Michigan for loitering outside Jack Kevorkian's house. David wondered if Devonshire could be their "angel of mercy."

"This is interesting," Angela said, looking through the social security material. "All five of these people served in the military, including Claudette Maurice. Maybe that's why they all have tattoos."

After helping Nikki do her respiratory therapy, they put her to bed. Then they brought the printouts into the family room.

"I expected Calhoun to have called by now," Angela said. "I was looking forward to getting his opinion on some of this."

"Calhoun's an independent sort," David said. "He said he'd call when he had something to tell us."

"Well, I'm going to give him a call," Angela said. But she only got his answering machine, and didn't leave a message.

David was going over the social security data. All at once Angela reached over and took a paper that he was about to put on Van Slyke's pile.

"Look at this," she said, pointing to an entry. "Van Slyke was in the navy for twenty-one months. Isn't that unusual? I thought the shortest stint was three years. Let's look at Devonshire's record." She leafed through his pile. "He was in for four and a half years."

"Will you listen to this!" David exclaimed. "Joe Forbs has declared personal bankruptcy three times. With that kind of history how can he get a credit card? But he has. Amazing."

By eleven o'clock David was struggling to keep his eyes open. "I'm afraid I have to go to bed," he said. He tossed the papers he had in his hand onto the table.

"I was hoping you'd say that," Angela said. "I'm bushed too."

They went upstairs arm in arm, feeling satisfied they'd accomplished so much. But they might not have slept so soundly had they any inkling of the firestorm their handiwork had ignited.

23

Sunday, October 31

HALLOWEEN dawned clear and crisp, with frost on the grimacing pumpkins perched on porches and windowsills. Nikki awoke feeling entirely normal physically, and with the festive atmosphere of the holiday, even her spirits were much improved. Angela had made it a point earlier in the week to stock candies and fruits for possible trick-or-treaters.

After breakfast Nikki began to agitate to be allowed to go trick-or-treating herself. But Angela was not enthusiastic. She was concerned about letting Nikki out into the cold so soon after she'd gotten over her latest bout of congestion. As a compromise she sent David into town to buy a pumpkin and started Nikki making Halloween decorations out of colored construction paper. With Nikki occupied, Angela called Robert Scali in Cambridge.

"I'm glad you called," he said. "I've got some more data."

"I appreciate your efforts," Angela said. "But I've another request. Can you get me military service records?"

"Now you're pushing it," he said. "I doubt I could get anything classified unless Peter's colleague is on-line with the Pentagon."

"I understand," Angela said.

"Let me call Peter and ask," Robert said. "I'll call you back."

Nikki had cut out a big orange moon and was now cutting out a silhouetted witch on a broomstick. David returned with an enormous pumpkin. Nikki was thrilled, and soon she and David were absorbed in carving the pumpkin into a jack-o'-lantern. Angela helped until the phone rang. It was Robert calling back.

"Bad news," he said. "Peter can't help with Pentagon stuff. But I got some basic info I'll send with this financial material."

"In the meantime," Angela said, "can you tell me why Van Slyke was in the navy for only twenty-one months?"

There was a pause. Angela could hear Robert shuffling papers. "Here it is," he said finally. "Van Slyke got a medical discharge."

"Does it say for what?" Angela asked.

"I'm afraid not," Robert said. "But there is some interesting stuff here. It says that Van Slyke went to submarine school in New London, Connecticut, then on to nuclear-power school." There was more shuffling of paper. Then he added, "My gosh, isn't this a coincidence. Clyde Devonshire got a medical discharge too, having done hard time for rape."

"That does sound interesting," Angela said.

After thanking Robert for his efforts, Angela hung up. Returning to the kitchen, where David and Nikki were putting the finishing touches on the jack-o'-lantern, Angela told David what she'd just learned. "I wish we could find the reasons for these medical discharges," she said.

"I bet I know how we could," David said. "Get someone in the VA system to pull it out of their data banks."

"Do you have any suggestions who we could ask?"

"I have a doctor friend at the VA in Boston," David said.

"Do you think he would mind doing us a favor?" Angela asked.

"It's a she," David said. "She's an ophthalmologist. Her name is Nicole Lungstrom."

"I've never heard you mention her before," Angela said. Two could play at this jealousy game.

"We went to high school together," David said. "We're friends."

"Honest?" Angela asked.

"Honest," David said.

"You think that if you call out of the blue, she'll help us?"

"I doubt it," David said. "If we want to take advantage of her status with the VA, then I should go down there today. There's no way I can ask her to violate confidentiality rules over the telephone. I'll call first to make sure she's available; then I'll go. I can even stop at M.I.T. and pick up that material you want from Robert."

While Angela cleaned up the mess from the gutting of the pumpkin, David went into the family room and called Nicole Lungstrom. Angela could hear bits and pieces of the conversation even though she tried not to. It bothered her that David sounded so cheerful. A few minutes later he came back into the kitchen.

"It's all arranged," he said. "She's expecting me today."

After Nikki lit a candle in the pumpkin, David carried it out onto the front porch. He let her decide where she wanted it.

"It looks cool," Nikki said, once it was in place.

While David went upstairs to get ready, Angela gave Robert a call and said David would be stopping by. Then she tried to call Calhoun. Once more she got his answering machine.

David came down wearing his blue blazer and gray slacks. He looked quite handsome.

"Do you have to get so dressed up?" Angela asked.

"I'm going to the VA hospital," David said. "I'm not going in jeans and a sweatshirt."

"I tried to call Calhoun again," Angela said. "Still no answer. That man must have come in late and gone out early. He's really involved in this investigation."

"Did you leave a message?" David asked.

"No," Angela said. "I hate answering machines. Besides, he must know we want to hear from him."

"I think you should leave a message," David said.

After Angela watched David pull down their drive, she gave her full attention to Nikki. More than anything, she wanted her daughter to enjoy the day.

Robert Scali seemed like a genuinely nice guy. David shook hands with him. "I want to thank you for your help," David said.

"That's what friends are for," Robert said, handing over another box of information. "There's something new on the financial side. In the last year Werner Van Slyke opened several new bank accounts in Boston and Albany. There's less than ten thousand in each."

"That's still a lot of money for a man running a maintenance department at a community hospital," David said.

"This day and age it probably means the fellow is running a little drug ring," Robert said with a laugh.

David thanked Robert again for his help. "Let me know when you guys next come to town," Robert said. "There's a great restaurant nearby, Anago Bistro. It will be my treat."

"Will do," David said as he waved good-bye.

It took twenty minutes to get to the VA hospital. David had Nicole paged, then waited in the lobby. She took him to the doctors' lounge. Once they were seated, he told her the story of his and Angela's disastrous sojourn in Bartlet. He then told her what he wanted.

"Will this be just between us?" Nicole asked.

"Word of honor," David said. "Except for Angela, of course."

Nicole pondered the situation. "Okay," she said. "If someone is killing patients, then I think the ends justify the means."

David handed Nicole the short list of people: Devonshire, Van Slyke, Forbs, Ullhof, and Maurice. "We know all five of these people were in the military," he said. "And all five have tattoos."

Using the social security numbers and birth dates, Nicole obtained the military I.D. numbers on each person. She then began calling up the records. There was an immediate surprise. Both Forbs and Ullhof had also been given medical discharges. Only Maurice had been mustered out normally.

Both Forbs' and Ullhof's discharge diagnoses were pedestrian. Van Slyke's and Devonshire's were not so innocuous. Van Slyke's was the most complicated. He had been discharged with a psychiatric diagnosis of schizoaffective disorder with mania and strong paranoid ideation under stress.

"I'm not sure I understand all of that," David said.

"I gather the translation is that the guy is schizophrenic with a large component of mania," Nicole said, scrolling through the material. "But for all his mental trouble, look at all the schooling he went through—even nuclear-power school. I hear that's quite rigorous."

"Wait," David said. He read aloud a passage that described an incident where Van Slyke had had a psychiatric break while on patrol on a submarine. At the time, he'd been working as a nuclear-trained machinist's mate for the engineering department.

> "During the first half of the patrol the patient exhibited elevated mood which led to poor judgment and feelings of hostility, belligerence, and ultimately to paranoid thoughts of being ridiculed by the rest of the crew and being affected by computers and radiation. His paranoia reached a climax when he attacked the captain and had to be restrained."

"Good grief," Nicole said.

"He's not quite as wacko as this makes him sound. I've spoken to him. He's not sociable or friendly, but he does his job."

"I'd say he was a time bomb," Nicole said. "There's more." She read aloud.

> "Van Slyke has a history of being a loner type. He was raised by an aggressive, alcoholic father and a fearful and compliant mother. The patient has demonstrated the tendency to idealize certain authority figures but then turn against them with minor provocation, whether real or fancied."

Nicole looked at David. "I certainly wouldn't want to be his boss."

Moving on to Devonshire, they found less material, but it was more significant. Clyde Devonshire had been treated for sexually transmitted diseases on several occasions. He'd also had a bout of hepatitis B. Finally, he'd tested positive for HIV.

"This might be really important," David said. "The fact that

Clyde Devonshire has a potentially terminal illness himself could be the key. Could I get copies of these records?"

"That might take some time," Nicole said. "I'll have to get a key to get access to a printer."

"I'll wait," David said. "But I'd like to use the phone first."

WHILE Nikki hovered by the door waiting for trick-or-treaters, Angela tried Calhoun one more time. Again she got his answering machine. That afternoon she'd left a message, as David suggested, but Calhoun had never called back. Angela began to worry. Looking out the window at the gathering gloom, she also began to worry about David. Although he'd called many hours ago to say he'd be late, she thought he should have been home by now.

Angela was thinking about starting dinner when the doorbell chimed. Nikki had already gone upstairs to take her bath, so Angela headed for the front door. As she passed the table in the front hall, she picked up a glass bowl filled with chocolates. Through the sidelight she caught a glimpse of a reptile-headed man.

Angela unlocked the door, opened it, and began to say something about how great a costume it was when she noticed that the man was not accompanied by a child.

Before Angela could react, the man lunged inside, grabbing her around the neck in a headlock. His gloved hand slapped over her mouth, suppressing a scream. Angela dropped the bowl of chocolates to the foyer floor, where it shattered into pieces.

"Shut up or I'll kill you," the man said in a raspy half whisper. He gave Angela's head a fearful shake. "Where's your husband?"

Angela couldn't respond. She was beginning to feel dizzy, as if she might black out.

"I'm going to let you go," the man snarled. "If you scream, I'll shoot you. Understand?" He gave Angela's head another shake, bringing tears of pain.

As promised, the man let her go. Her heart was racing. She knew that Nikki was upstairs in the bathtub. Rusty, unfortunately, was out in the barn. He'd been a nuisance with the trick-or-treaters.

Angela looked at her attacker. His reptile mask was grotesque. A red forked tongue hung limply from a mouth lined with jagged teeth. She noticed the man had a pistol in his hand.

"My husband is not at home," Angela managed to say at last. Her voice was hoarse. The headlock had compressed her throat.

"What about your sick kid?" the man demanded.

"She's out trick-or-treating with friends," Angela said.

"When will your husband be back?" the man asked.

Angela hesitated. The man grabbed her arm and gave it a tug. His thumbnail bit into her flesh. "I asked a question," he snarled.

"Soon," Angela managed.

"Good," the man said. "We'll wait. Meanwhile, let's take a look around the house and make sure you're not lying to me."

NIKKI was not in the bathtub. She'd been out for some time. When the door chimes sounded, she'd rushed to finish dressing and had just gotten to the head of the stairs when the glass bowl shattered, stopping her in her tracks. Helplessly she'd watched as her mother began to struggle with a man wearing a serpent mask.

After the initial shock Nikki ran to the master bedroom and picked up the telephone. But there was no dial tone. Rushing back down the hall, she peeked over the stairs just in time to see her mother and the man disappear into the family room.

Advancing to the head of the stairs, Nikki looked down. The shotgun was leaning against the back of the newel-post.

Nikki had to jump back out of sight when her mother and the reptile man reappeared from the family room. Nikki forced herself to peek over the edge of the stairs again. She saw her mother and the man vanish down the central corridor toward the kitchen.

Nikki inched forward and again peered down at the shotgun. Starting down the steps, she got only halfway before she heard her mother and the man coming back. Panicked, Nikki raced back up the stairs and along the hall. She stopped. To her horror her mother and the man started up the stairs.

Nikki dashed into the master bedroom and ducked into one of the walk-in closets. In the back of the closet was a door leading to a short hall connecting with the barn. Several storerooms ran off it. At the end a narrow staircase led down to the mudroom.

Nikki raced down these stairs, then through the kitchen and along the first-floor corridor to the foyer. She snatched up the shotgun. She checked to see if there was a shell in the magazine just as her mother had taught her. There was. She released the safety.

Nikki's elation quickly changed to confusion. Her mother had explained that the gun sprayed pellets in a wide arc. It would hit just about everything it was pointed at. The problem was her mom. Nikki didn't want to hit her.

She had little time to ponder her dilemma. Her mother appeared in the foyer, stumbling down the last few stairs. Apparently she'd been pushed. Right behind her was the reptile man. He gave her mother another cruel shove that sent her flying through the archway into the living room. In his right hand was a pistol.

The man started after her mother. He was about twenty feet away from Nikki, who was holding the shotgun at her waist. She had her left hand around the barrel and her right hand around the stock. Her finger was on the trigger.

The intruder turned briefly to face Nikki, then did a double take. He started to raise his gun in her direction. Nikki closed her eyes and pulled the trigger.

The sound of the blast was horrendous in the narrow hallway. The recoil knocked Nikki over backward, yet she stubbornly held on to the shotgun. Regaining her balance enough to sit up, she used all her strength to cock the gun. Her ears were ringing so much, she couldn't hear the click the shotgun made as a fresh shell was rammed into position and the spent cartridge ejected.

Angela suddenly appeared out of the smoky haze. She took the shotgun from Nikki, who was only too glad to give it up. From the family room they heard the sound of a door banging open, then stillness.

"Are you all right?" Angela whispered to Nikki.

"I think so," Nikki said.

Angela helped Nikki to her feet. Slowly they inched past the archway, catching sight of the damage caused by Nikki's shotgun blast. The charge had carried away another four panes of glass from the living room's bay window, the same window damaged by the brick.

Next they rounded the base of the stairs. As they approached the family room, Angela kept the shotgun trained ahead. One of the French doors leading to the terrace hung open, gently swinging back and forth with the evening breeze.

With Nikki clutching one of Angela's belt loops, they advanced toward the door. Angela closed it and locked it. Still gripping the gun, she bent down and hugged Nikki with all her might.

"You're a hero," she said.

"I didn't mean to hit the window," Nikki said.

"The window doesn't matter," Angela said. "You did splendidly." She went over to the phone. Surprised to find it dead, she shuddered. The intruder had gone to the trouble of cutting their lines first. Had it not been for Nikki, Angela hated to think what might have happened.

"We have to make sure the man is not still here," Angela said. "Come on, let's search the house."

Together they went through the dining room into the kitchen. They checked the mudroom, the two small storage rooms, and returned to the foyer. While Angela was debating whether to check upstairs, the door chimes rang. Both she and Nikki jumped.

Looking out the sidelights on either side of the door, Angela and Nikki saw a group of children dressed as witches and ghosts standing on their stoop.

David pulled into the driveway. He was surprised to see that every light in the house was on. Then he saw a group of teenagers leap from the porch, dash across the lawn, and disappear into the trees lining the property.

David got out of the car and went up to his front door. It was plastered with raw eggs. The place was a mess. Tomatoes had been thrown against the front of the house.

Not until he discovered the broken glass and scattered candy did David become truly worried. Almost immediately Angela and Nikki appeared at the top of the stairs. Angela was holding the shotgun. Nikki started to cry and ran down into David's arms.

"He had a gun," Nikki managed to tell him through choking sobs.

"Who had a gun?" David asked. "What's happened?"

"We had a visitor," Angela said, coming down the stairs.

"Who?" David demanded.

"I don't know," Angela said. "He was wearing a Halloween mask. He had a handgun." She told him exactly what had happened.

"I never should have left you alone here," David said. "I'm sorry. Did you call the police?"

"Our phone line was cut. All we've done since the man bolted is huddle upstairs."

"Where's Rusty?" David asked.

"In the barn. He got so hyper with the trick-or-treaters."

"I'll get my portable phone from the car, and I'll get Rusty while I'm at it," David said.

Angela and Nikki were waiting for him when he returned. He drew them to him and sat them both down on the family-room couch. As soon as they had calmed down, David used his portable phone to call the police.

"I should have anticipated Nikki and I would be in danger," Angela said. She then conceded that the rape attempt in the hospital parking lot had possibly been an attempt on her life. She said that she'd told Calhoun about it and he tended to agree with her.

"Why didn't you tell me this?" David demanded.

"I should have," Angela admitted. "I'm sorry."

"If nothing else, we're learning that we shouldn't hold secrets from each other," David said. "Have you heard from Calhoun yet?"

"No," Angela said. "I even left a message, as you suggested."

It took the police almost three quarters of an hour to arrive. Robertson came in full uniform, accompanied by a deputy. Robertson glanced at the refuse on the porch and took in the broken window. "You people having a minor problem?" he asked.

"Not minor," Angela said. "Major." She then described what had happened from the moment the masked man appeared.

Robertson obviously had little patience for Angela's story. "Now, are you sure this was a real gun?" he asked. "Maybe it was just a toy gun, part of a costume." He winked at his deputy.

"Just one minute," David said, breaking into the conversation. "I'm getting the distinct impression that you're not taking this seriously. This man had a gun. There was violence here."

"Don't you yell at me," Robertson said. "Your wife here has already admitted that your daughter blew out the window, not the purported intruder."

"Get out of my house!" David raged.

"I'll be happy to," Robertson said.

David slammed the door. "Well, we no longer have any illusions about the local police. We can't expect any help from them."

Angela hugged herself and fought off tears. "What a mess," she said. David stepped over and comforted her.

"Are you hungry?" he asked.

Angela shrugged. "Not really. But I was about to start dinner before all this happened. I'll put something together."

David called the phone company and reported that their house phone was out of order. The repairman arrived while they were eating, and quickly determined that the line had been cut where it entered the house.

After dinner David boarded up a portion of the bay window. Then he made sure all the doors and windows were locked. After Nikki went to sleep, he and Angela retired to the family room to go over the material he'd brought back from Boston.

"You know what I think," Angela said as David opened the envelope that contained the medical records. "I think the man who came in here tonight is the same person who's behind the euthanasia and Hodges' murder."

"I agree with you," David said. "And I think our best candidate is Clyde Devonshire. Read this."

David handed Devonshire's medical record to Angela. She quickly scanned it. "Oh, my," she said. "He's HIV-positive."

David nodded. "I think we have a serious suspect here, especially when you combine his HIV status with other facts like his having been arrested outside Jack Kevorkian's house. His interest in assisted suicides could extend to euthanasia. He's a trained nurse, so he has the medical expertise, and if that isn't enough, he has a history of rape. He might be the ski-masked rapist."

Angela nodded, but she was troubled. "It's completely circumstantial," she said. "Would you know Devonshire by sight?"

"No," David admitted.

"I wonder if I'd be able to identify him by his height or the sound of his voice," Angela said. "I doubt it."

"Well, let's move on," David said. "The next best candidate is Van Slyke. Take a look." He handed the record to Angela.

"Good grief," Angela said as she came to the end. "It's an interesting psychiatric history. But I don't think he's the one. Just because he's mentally ill doesn't mean he's a criminal. If Van Slyke had an extensive criminal history of violent behavior, that would be different. Besides, he doesn't have a sophisticated knowledge of medicine."

"I agree," David said. "But look at this material from Robert." He handed Angela the listing of Van Slyke's bank accounts.

"Where on earth is he getting this money?" Angela asked.

David shrugged. "Robert suggested that Van Slyke was dealing drugs. It's possible. If it's not drugs, it would be ominous."

"Why?" Angela asked.

"Let's suppose Van Slyke is the one killing these people. If he's not selling drugs, he could be getting paid for each death."

"What an awful idea. But who would pay him and why?"

"It's probably some misguided mercy killer," David said. "All the victims had potentially fatal illnesses."

"I think we're getting too speculative," Angela said. "Most of this information probably isn't related." She tossed the papers onto the coffee table. "I'm exhausted. Maybe after a good night's sleep something will come to us."

24

Monday, November 1

IN THE morning David and Angela tried phoning Calhoun again but got the answering machine with the same message. They talked about calling the state police to report him missing, but couldn't make up their minds. They admitted they didn't know Calhoun that well, that his behavior was eccentric, and that they were probably jumping to conclusions.

"The one thing I do know," Angela said, "I don't want to spend another night in this house. Maybe we should just pack everything up and leave this town to its own devices and secrets."

"If we're thinking of that, I'd better call Sherwood," David said.

"Do it," Angela said. "I'm serious."

David phoned the bank to make an appointment to see the president. The first opening available was that afternoon at three o'clock. David took what he could get.

"Where should we spend the night?" Angela asked.

David sighed. "I suppose I could call my parents."

David made the call to Amherst, New Hampshire, and asked

his mother if they could come for a few days. She was delighted.

Angela tried to call Calhoun again, still with no luck. While she began packing, David got out the phone book and looked up the addresses of the five tattooed hospital workers. He told Angela that he wanted to cruise by just to check out their homes.

"I don't want you going anywhere," Angela said sternly.

"Why not?" David asked. He was surprised at her response.

"For one thing, I don't want to be here by myself. Second, I don't want you snooping around the house of a potential killer. Why don't you give us a hand packing the car?"

It was almost noon before they were ready. After they made sure all the doors to the house were locked, they climbed into the Volvo. Rusty hopped in beside Nikki.

David's mother, Jeannie Wilson, welcomed them warmly. David's father, Albert, was off for a day's fishing trip and wouldn't be back until that evening.

After they carried everything into the house, Angela collapsed on the quilted bed in the guest room. "I'm exhausted," she said.

"Why don't you rest?" David said. "There's no need for both of us to go back to talk with Sherwood."

"You wouldn't mind?" Angela asked.

"Not in the least," David said. He pulled the edge of the quilt down and encouraged Angela to slide under it. As he closed the door, he heard her advise him to drive carefully.

David told his mother and Nikki that Angela was napping. He suggested that Nikki do the same, but she was already involved in making cookies with her grandmother. Explaining that he had an appointment in Bartlet, David went out to the Volvo.

David arrived back in town with three quarters of an hour to spare. He stopped alongside the road to pull out the list of tattooed hospital employees' addresses. The closest one was Devonshire's.

David was surprised to find a convenience store at the address listed for Devonshire. He parked in front of the building, got out, and went into the store. While paying for a carton of orange juice, he asked one of the two clerks if he knew Clyde Devonshire.

"Sure do," the man said. "He lives upstairs."

"I was told he had a tattoo," David said.

The man laughed. "Clyde's got a bunch of tattoos. He has tattooed chains around both wrists, a tattoo on his upper arm, and more on his chest."

David thanked the clerk and left the store. At least he'd found out Clyde had tattoos where they could be damaged in a struggle. And he still had twenty minutes before his meeting with Sherwood: time for one more address.

In just a few minutes David turned onto Van Slyke's lane. He slowed down to check the numbers on the mailboxes. Suddenly David jammed on the brakes. He'd come abreast of a green truck that looked a lot like Calhoun's.

Backing up, David parked behind the truck. It had a sticker on the back bumper that read THIS VEHICLE CLIMBED MOUNT WASHINGTON. It had to be Calhoun's.

David got out and peered into the truck's cab. A moldy cup of coffee sat on the open glove compartment door. The ashtray was overflowing with cigar butts. The truck was definitely Calhoun's.

David looked across the street. There was no mailbox in front of the house, but he could see the address on the riser of the porch stairs. It was 66 Apple Tree Lane—Van Slyke's address.

David crossed the street for a closer look. The house was badly in need of paint and repair. It hardly looked lived in except for the indentation of tire tracks in the gravel of the driveway. After checking that no one was observing him from the street, he walked to the door and tried it. It opened with a simple turn of the knob. He pushed it open slowly; the rusty hinges groaned.

David peered inside. What furniture he could see was covered with dust and cobwebs. He called out to determine if anybody was home. No one answered. He called out again.

Making a tour of the first floor, he moved quickly from one dirty room to the next until he got to the kitchen. There he stopped. On the table, in an ashtray, was the butt of an Antonio y Cleopatra cigar. Just beyond, an open door led down to the cellar.

David approached the doorway and looked down into utter darkness. He tried a light switch. An anemic glow filtered up the stairs.

Taking a deep breath, David started down. He stopped midway and let his eyes sweep around the basement. It was cluttered with old furniture, boxes, and a hodgepodge of tools and junk. The floor was dirt, although near the furnace there was a slab of concrete.

David continued down the stairs, then went over to the concrete. Bending down, he examined it closely. The slab was still dark with dampness. He put his hand on it to be sure. David shuddered. He straightened up and ran for the stairs. As far as he was concerned, he'd seen enough to go to the police. Reaching the top of the stairs, David stopped in his tracks. He heard the sound of car tires in gravel. A car had pulled in beside the house.

For a second David froze. He heard the car door open, then slam shut. Panicking, he pulled the door to the cellar shut and descended the stairs. At the rear of the basement were several doors. The first one had an open hasp. As quietly as possible he pulled it open. Beyond was a root cellar illuminated by a single low-watt bulb.

Hearing footsteps above, David quickly went to the second door. He gave the knob a tug, but the door wouldn't budge. He exerted more strength. At last it creaked open. Beyond was a flight of concrete steps leading up to angled hatchlike doors. David closed the door to the basement, scrambled up the dark stairs, and crouched just beneath the doors. He was able to raise them half an inch, but no more; they were padlocked from outside.

David tried to keep calm. His pulse was hammering in his temples. He knew he was trapped. The next thing he heard was the cellar door crashing open, followed by heavy footfalls on the steps.

David squatted in the darkness and held his breath.

The footfalls drew nearer, then the door to his hideaway was yanked open. David found himself staring into the frenzied face of Werner Van Slyke.

Van Slyke appeared to be in a worse panic than David. His unblinking eyes bulged from their sockets. His pupils were so dilated he seemed to have no irises. Drops of perspiration beaded on his forehead. His whole body was trembling. In his right hand he clutched a pistol, which he pointed at David's face.

Without a word Van Slyke reached out, grabbed David by his jacket, and rudely yanked him into the cellar. David sprawled headfirst onto the dirt floor, crashing into a stack of cardboard boxes.

"Get up!" Van Slyke screamed. His voice echoed in the cellar.

David warily got to his feet.

Van Slyke was shaking convulsively. "Get into the root cellar."

"Calm down," David said, speaking for the first time.

Van Slyke indiscriminately fired the gun. Bullets whizzed by David's head and ricocheted around the basement until they embedded themselves in an overhead joist, the stairs, a wooden door. David leaped into the root cellar and cowered against the far wall.

Van Slyke shut the heavy door with such force, plaster rained down on top of David's head. Then he heard the sound of the hasp being closed over its staple and a padlock being applied.

After a few minutes of silence David looked around his cell. The only light source was the single bulb. On one wall were bins filled with fruit that appeared mummified. On the other wall shelves lined with jars of preserves reached to the ceiling.

David moved to the door and put his ear to it. He heard nothing. Looking more closely at the door, he saw fresh scratch marks across it, as if someone had been trying desperately to claw his way out. David leaned against the door and pushed. It didn't budge. Then the light went out, plunging him into absolute darkness.

SHERWOOD buzzed his secretary and asked what time it was.

"Three fifteen," Sharon said.

"That's what I thought. If David Wilson shows up, tell him he'll have to reschedule." He lifted his phone and dialed Harold Traynor.

"It's been a good day," Traynor said. "I've just heard this afternoon from the board of selectmen. They've caved in. They'll back the parking garage after all."

Sherwood smiled. "Should I put together the bond issue?"

"Absolutely," Traynor said. "Beaton tells me the balance sheet looks a lot better. October wasn't nearly as bad as predicted."

"Nothing but good news this month," Sherwood said.

"Well, I wouldn't go that far," Traynor said. "Beaton also told me that Van Slyke never showed up."

"He didn't phone?" Sherwood questioned.

"No. I suppose I'll have to ride over after the executive meeting. Trouble is, I hate to go in that house. It depresses me."

JUST as unexpectedly as the overhead light had gone out, it went on again. In the distance David could hear Van Slyke's footfalls coming back down the cellar stairs. After that, he heard the clatter of things being dropped onto the dirt floor.

On two more trips up and down, Van Slyke dropped something particularly heavy. Suddenly David heard the lock on the door open. He braced himself as the door was yanked ajar.

David sucked in a breath of air at the sight of Van Slyke. He appeared even more agitated than he had earlier. His dark unruly hair stood straight out from his head as if he'd been jolted with a bolt of electricity. His pupils were still dilated, and his face was now covered with perspiration. He'd removed his green work shirt and was clad in a dirty T-shirt, which he hadn't tucked into his trousers.

Van Slyke was powerfully built, and David quickly ruled out the possibility of trying to overpower the man. He noticed that on his right forearm Van Slyke had a tattoo of an American flag held by a bald eagle. A thin scar about five inches long marred the design.

"Out!" Van Slyke yelled, waving his gun recklessly.

David stepped quickly out of the root cellar. Van Slyke angrily motioned for him to continue on toward the furnace.

"Stop," Van Slyke commanded after David had moved some twenty feet. He pointed down toward the ground. Next to David's feet were a pick and shovel. Nearby was the slab of concrete.

"Dig!" Van Slyke yelled. "Right where you are standing."

Afraid of hesitating a second, David bent down and lifted the pick. He considered using it as a weapon, but Van Slyke stepped back out of reach. He kept the gun raised, and although it was shaking, it was still pointing in David's direction.

David noticed bags of cement and sand on the floor. He swung the pick. To his surprise it dug a mere two inches into the densely packed earthen floor. There was no doubt in his mind what Van Slyke had in mind for him. He was having him dig his own grave. He wondered if Calhoun had been put through the same ordeal.

David knew his only hope was to get Van Slyke talking. "How much should I dig?" he asked as he traded the pick for the shovel.

"I want a big hole," Van Slyke said. "Like the hole of a doughnut. I want my mother to give me the whole doughnut."

Psychiatry hadn't been David's forte in medical school, yet even he recognized that what he was hearing was called clanging, or loosening of associations, a symptom of acute schizophrenia.

"Did your mother give you a lot of doughnuts?" David asked. He was at a loss for words, but desperate to keep Van Slyke talking.

Van Slyke looked at David as if he were surprised he was there. "My mother committed suicide," he said. "She killed herself." Van Slyke then laughed wildly. "Dig faster!" he yelled.

David dug more quickly. "Are you hearing voices?" he asked, trying another approach. He dug with the shovel several more times. When Van Slyke didn't answer, David looked over at him. Van Slyke's eyes narrowed; his trembling became more apparent.

David stopped digging. "What are the voices saying?" he asked.

"Nothing," Van Slyke shouted.

"Are these voices like the ones you heard in the navy?"

Van Slyke's shoulders sagged. "How did you know about the navy?" he asked. "And how did you know about the voices?"

"I know a lot about you," David said. "I want to help you. I'm not like the others. I'm a doctor."

Van Slyke didn't speak. He simply glared at David.

"Are you upset about the patients?" David asked.

Van Slyke's breath went out of him as if he'd been punched. "What patients?" he demanded.

David swallowed again. His mouth was dry. He knew he was taking risks. "The patients that you've been helping to die."

"They were going to die anyway," Van Slyke shouted.

David felt a shiver rush down his spine.

"I didn't kill them," Van Slyke blurted out. "They killed them. They pushed the button, not me. It was the radio waves."

David nodded and tried to smile compassionately despite his anxiety. "Are the radio waves telling you what to do?" he asked.

Van Slyke looked at David as if David were deranged. "Of course not," he said with scorn. "How did you know about the navy?"

"I told you, I know a lot about you. And I want to help you. I want to know who 'they' are. Do you mean the voices that you hear?"

"Shut up and dig," Van Slyke said. With that, he aimed the gun just to David's left and pulled the trigger. The slug thumped into the root-cellar door.

David quickly resumed his digging. Van Slyke terrified him. But after a few more shovelfuls, he took the risk of resuming talking.

"I know you are being paid for what you've been doing," David said. "I even know you've been putting money in banks in Albany and Boston. Who's been paying you? Who is it, Werner?"

Van Slyke responded by moaning. David looked up from digging in time to see him grimacing and holding his head with both hands, covering his ears as if shielding them from painful sounds.

"Are the voices getting louder?" David asked.

Van Slyke nodded. His eyes darted wildly around the room.

"Who is it? Who is speaking to you?" David asked.

"It's the computers and the radiation, just like in the navy."

"But you're not in the navy. You are in Bartlet, Vermont, in your own basement. There are no computers or radiation."

"How do you know so much?" Van Slyke demanded again. His fear was again changing to anger.

"I want to help," David said. "I know you killed Dr. Hodges."

Van Slyke's mouth dropped open. David wondered if he had gone too far. He only hoped Van Slyke's rage wouldn't be directed at him. "Did they pay you to kill Dr. Hodges?" he asked.

Van Slyke laughed scornfully. "That shows how much you know," he said. "They didn't have anything to do with Hodges. I did it because Hodges had turned against me, saying I was attacking women in the parking lot. But I wasn't. He said he'd tell everybody I was doing it unless I left the hospital. But I showed him."

Van Slyke's face went blank again. He rubbed his eyes, then stared at David as if surprised to find him standing before him with a shovel. Van Slyke raised his gun, aiming it directly at David's eyes.

"I told you to dig," he snarled.

David rushed to comply. Even then he fully expected to be shot. His current approach was not working. He was stressing Van Slyke, but not enough or perhaps not in the right ways.

"I've already talked to the person who is paying you," David said after a few minutes of frantic digging. "That's one of the reasons I know so much. He's told me everything."

"No," Van Slyke shouted.

"Oh, yes," David said. "He also told me that if Phil Calhoun got suspicious, you'd have to take the blame for everything."

"How did you know about Phil Calhoun?"

"I told you I know what's happening. The whole affair is about to destruct. And your sponsor doesn't care about you. You are nothing to him. He wants you to be hurt. They want you to suffer."

"Shut up!" Van Slyke screamed.

"The person who is using you has told lots of people about you. And they have all had a good laugh over the fact that Van Slyke will be blamed for everything."

"Shut up!" Van Slyke lunged at David, ramming the barrel of the gun against his forehead. David froze as he peered at the gun cross-eyed. He let go of the shovel, and it fell to the floor.

"Get back in the root cellar!" Van Slyke screamed. He backed David in, slammed the heavy door in his face, and locked it.

David could hear Van Slyke running through the basement, crashing into objects. He heard the cellar door slam shut. Then the lights went out. Very faintly he heard a car engine start, then quickly fade. Then there was only silence and the pounding of his own heart.

David felt tears well up in his eyes. He'd certainly managed to evoke the man's psychotic paranoia, but the result was not what he'd hoped. He'd wanted to befriend Van Slyke, get him to talk about his problems and free himself in the process. Instead, he was still imprisoned, and he'd released a madman into the town. His only solace was that Angela and Nikki were safely in Amherst.

Struggling to control his emotions, David tried to think rationally about his predicament, wondering if there was any chance of escape. But as he thought of the solid stone walls encircling him, he had an acute rush of claustrophobia. Sobbing, he vainly attacked the stout wooden door, hurtling his shoulder against it, crying for someone to let him out.

At length David managed to stop his self-destructive batterings. Then he stopped crying. He thought about the Volvo and Calhoun's truck. They were his only hope.

With fear and resignation he sank to a sitting position on the dirt floor to wait for Van Slyke's return.

25

Monday, November 1: Later That Day

ANGELA slept much longer than she'd planned. When she awoke around four thirty, she was surprised to hear that David had neither returned nor called. As the time crept toward five, her concern grew with each passing minute. Finally she picked up the phone and called Green Mountain National Bank. But she only got a recording that told her the bank's hours were nine to four thirty.

Next Angela tried their home in Bartlet. But after letting the phone ring ten times, she gave up. She wondered if David had decided to play sleuth after all. The possibility only made her more concerned. She went to her mother-in-law and asked if she could borrow the Cherokee.

"Of course," Jeannie answered. "Where are you going?"

"Back to Bartlet," Angela said. "I left some things in the house."

"I want to go too," Nikki said.

"I think you'd better stay here," Angela said.

"No," Nikki said. "I'm coming."

"Nikki, I want you to stay here," Angela said.

"I'm scared to stay here by myself," Nikki said. She broke into tears. In the end Angela gave in.

By the time Angela and Nikki entered Bartlet, it was still light out, but some of the cars already had their headlights on. Angela only had a sketchy plan of what to do, and it mostly involved hunting for the Volvo. The first location she wanted to search was the bank, and as she neared it, she saw Barton Sherwood and Harold Traynor walking toward the town green. Angela pulled over to the curb and jumped out.

"Excuse me," she said. "I'm sorry to bother you. I'm looking for my husband."

"I have no idea where he is," Sherwood said irritably. "He missed our appointment this afternoon. He didn't even phone."

"I'm sorry," Angela said. She dashed back to the car, convinced now that something bad had happened.

"Where's Daddy?" Nikki questioned.

"I wish I knew," Angela said. She made a rapid U-turn that sent the car's wheels screeching. "Everything will be all right."

Angela sped to their house, hoping to see the Volvo parked near the back door. But as she pulled into the driveway, she was immediately disappointed. She jerked to a stop next to the house.

"Stay in the car," she told Nikki. "I'll just be a second."

Taking a quick run through the house, Angela snatched up the shotgun and checked the magazine. There were four shells in it. She went into the kitchen, took out the phone directory, and wrote down the addresses of Devonshire, Forbs, Maurice, Van Slyke, and

Ullhof. Carrying the list and the shotgun, she returned to the car.

The first address turned out to be a convenience store. Angela pulled in to park, and Nikki looked at her mother.

"What are we doing here?" she asked.

"I'm not sure," Angela said. "Keep an eye out for the Volvo."

"It's not here," Nikki said.

"I realize that, dear." Angela put the car in gear and headed for the next address. It was Forbs' residence. She slowed as they came to the house. The lights inside were on, but there was no Volvo. Disappointed, she gunned the engine and they sped away. She was gripping the steering wheel so hard, her fingers had gone numb.

A few minutes later, when she turned onto Van Slyke's street, Angela spotted the Volvo instantly. So did Nikki. Angela pulled directly behind the car, turned off the ignition, and jumped out.

As she approached the car, she saw Calhoun's truck in front of it. She looked in both vehicles. In Calhoun's truck she noticed a moldy cup of coffee. She looked across the street at Van Slyke's house. There were no lights on, which fanned her growing alarm.

Running back to the car, Angela got the shotgun. Nikki started to get out, but Angela yelled at her to stay where she was. Angela's tone let Nikki know there was to be no arguing.

Carrying the shotgun, Angela climbed the porch steps. Something was seriously wrong; there was no doubt about it.

She tried ringing the doorbell, but it clearly didn't work. Failing that, she banged on the door. When there was no response, she tried the door. It was unlocked. Cautiously she stepped inside.

Then as loudly as she could, she yelled David's name.

DAVID heard Angela's yell. He straightened up. He'd been slouched against a bin filled with desiccated apples. The sound had been so faint that at first he questioned if it had been real. He thought he might have been hallucinating. But he heard it again.

This time David knew it was real, and he knew it was Angela. He leaped to his feet in the utter darkness and screamed Angela's name. But the sound died in the confined, insulated space with its dirt floor. David moved blindly ahead until he hit against the door. Then he tried yelling again, but he could tell it would be in vain unless Angela was in the basement.

Groping along the shelves, David seized a jar of preserves and pounded the door with it. But the sound was hardly as loud as he'd hoped. Changing tactics, he hurled the jar of preserves against the ceiling, covering his head with his hands. Climbing the shelving, he pounded the ceiling with his fists. But the shelf he was standing on gave way and collapsed to the floor, David along with it.

ANGELA felt frantic and discouraged. She'd rapidly toured the first floor of the filthy house, turning on what lights she could, but found no evidence of either David or Calhoun. Except for a cigar butt in the kitchen that could have been Calhoun's. When she reached the second floor, she yelled David's name several times, but after each shout there was nothing but silence.

Angela was about to head back downstairs when she noticed something on a small console table. It was a rubber Halloween mask fashioned to look like a reptile—the mask the intruder had worn!

Trembling, Angela started down the stairs. At the base of the stairs she thought she heard pounding from the direction of the kitchen. She hurried into the room. The noise was definitely louder. Bending down, she put her ear to the floor. Then she heard the knocking distinctly.

She yelled David's name. With her ear to the floor she could just barely hear him answer. She scrambled to the cellar stairs.

She found the light and headed down, still clutching the shotgun. She yelled his name again. Tears sprang to her eyes when she heard his reply. Weaving her way through the clutter, Angela followed the sound of his voice to the padlocked door.

Angela shouted to David that she'd get him out. Leaning the shotgun against the wall, she scanned the basement for an appropriate tool. Her eyes soon came to rest on the pick.

Swinging the tool in a short arc, she hit the lock several times, but with no result. Trying a different approach, she inserted the end of the pick beneath the hasp and used it as a pry bar. Pushing with all her might, she snapped the hasp out of the door.

David rushed out and embraced her.

"Thank God you came," he said. "Van Slyke is the one behind all this. He killed the patients and he killed Hodges. He's in a psychotic panic and he's armed. We've got to get out of here."

Angela snatched up the shotgun. Together they hurried to the stairs. Before they started up, David put a hand on Angela's arm. He pointed to the cement slab. "I'm afraid Calhoun is under there," he said.

Angela gasped. David gave her a nudge up the stairs.

As David and Angela reached the kitchen, headlight beams suddenly filled the room, playing across their horrified faces.

"Oh, no," David whispered. "He's back."

Angela thrust the shotgun into David's hands. He gripped it with sweaty palms. They heard the car door close, then heavy footsteps in the gravel of the driveway. David motioned for Angela to step back through the cellar door. He followed and partially closed the door.

For a few terrifying minutes there was no sound whatsoever. David and Angela held their breath. Then to their surprise they heard the footsteps recede.

"Where did he go?" Angela whispered.

"I wish I knew," David said.

The house was eerily silent. Finally David pushed the door open and stepped back into the kitchen.

"Let's get out of here," Angela whispered. "I'm afraid if I'm in here too long, Nikki will get out of the car."

"What!" David whispered. "Nikki's here?"

Quietly they opened the door. It was completely dark. Van Slyke's car was twenty feet away, but he was nowhere to be seen.

David sprinted to Van Slyke's car, keeping the shotgun ready. He looked in the passenger-side window, but Van Slyke wasn't there. David waved for Angela to join him.

"Where did you park?" he asked her.

"Right in back of you," Angela said.

David led, with Angela behind him. As they reached the street, their worst fears were realized. In the light of a streetlamp they could see Van Slyke's silhouette in the driver's seat of David's mother's Cherokee. Nikki was next to him.

"Oh, no," Angela said. "Do you think he has a gun?"

"I know he has a gun," David snapped.

"Maybe we should get help," Angela suggested.

"It would take too long," David said. "We'll have to handle this ourselves. We've got to get Nikki far enough away so that we can use the shotgun if we have to."

For a few harrowing moments they simply stared at the car.

"Let me have the keys," David said. "He might have locked the doors."

"They're in the car," Angela said.

"Oh, no!" David exclaimed. "He could just drive off with Nikki. This is getting worse and worse. But have you noticed? The whole time we've been here, Van Slyke hasn't moved. Last time I saw him, he couldn't hold still."

"It's almost as if they're having a conversation," Angela said.

"If he isn't watching, we could slip behind the car. You could go to one side and I to the other. We'll open the front doors, you pull Nikki free, and I'll aim the shotgun at Van Slyke."

Angela groaned. "Don't you think that's taking a lot of chances?"

"Tell me a better idea. We have to get her out of there."

After crossing the street a good distance back from the Cherokee, David and Angela approached the car from behind. "Okay," David whispered. "Are you ready?"

Angela gripped his arm. "Wait," she said. "I think we should both go to her door. You open the door; I'll pull her out."

David thought for a moment. "Okay," he whispered. "When I give the signal, we do it."

Slowly he rounded the car and started crawling along its right side, holding the gun up against his chest. When he came abreast of the rear door, he turned to make sure Angela was behind him. She was. But before he could give Angela the signal, Nikki's door opened and she leaned out and looked back.

"What are you guys doing?" Nikki asked.

David leaped forward and pulled the door completely open. Nikki tumbled from the car. Angela grabbed her, dragging her onto the grass. Nikki cried out in shock and pain.

David trained the gun on Van Slyke. He was fully prepared to pull the trigger if need be. But Van Slyke didn't so much as move. He merely looked at David; his expression was completely blank.

David warily moved a little closer. Van Slyke remained seated calmly, his hands in his lap. He did not seem to be the agitated psychotic that he'd been less than an hour earlier.

"What's happening?" Nikki cried. "Why did you pull me so hard? You hurt my leg."

"I was worried," Angela said. "The man you've been sitting with is the same man who was wearing the reptile mask last night."

"He couldn't be." Nikki wiped her tears away. "Mr. Van Slyke told me he was supposed to talk with me until you came back. He was telling me about when he was my age—how wonderful it had been."

David was intently watching Van Slyke, who continued to stare at him blankly. Keeping the shotgun aimed, David stepped around and opened the driver's-side door. Van Slyke didn't move.

"Where's the gun?" David demanded.

"Gun run done fun," Van Slyke said.

David grabbed him by the arm and pulled him out of the car, then frisked him for weapons. "What did you do with the gun?"

"I don't need it anymore," Van Slyke said.

David peered into Van Slyke's calm face. His pupils were no longer dilated. The transformation was remarkable.

"What's going on, Van Slyke?" David asked.

"On?" Van Slyke said. "On top. Put it on top."

"Van Slyke," David shouted. "What's happened to you? Where have you been? Are you still hearing voices?"

"No more voices," Van Slyke said. "I made them stop."

"What do you mean?" David asked.

"I took care of them. They won't use me as a dupe."

"Who do you mean by they?"

"The board," Van Slyke said. "The whole board."

"What does he mean by the board?" Angela asked. She and Nikki had come around the front of the car.

"Board sword ford cord." Van Slyke smiled.

"Do you mean the hospital board?" David asked.

"Yes," Van Slyke said.

"Okay. Everything is going to be all right," David said, trying to calm himself. "Did you shoot someone?"

Van Slyke laughed. "No, I didn't shoot anyone. All I did was put the source on the conference-room table."

"What does he mean by the source?" Angela asked.

"I have no idea," David said.

"Source force course horse," Van Slyke said, still chuckling.

Feeling frustrated, David grabbed Van Slyke by the front of his shirt and shook him, asking him what he'd done.

"I put the source and the force on the table right next to the model of the parking garage," Van Slyke said. "I'm glad I did. I'm not a dupe for anybody. The problem is, I burned myself."

"Where?" David asked.

"My hands." Van Slyke held them up so David could look at them. "I'm tired," he said. "I want to go see my parents."

David absently waved him off, his thoughts suddenly elsewhere. Van Slyke walked across to his yard. Angela stared at David. "What are you doing?" she asked. "Shouldn't we call the police?"

David stared after Van Slyke while his mind began pulling everything together: his patients, the symptoms, and the deaths.

"Get in the car," David said.

"What is it?" Angela didn't like the tone of David's voice.

"Just get in the car," David shouted. "Hurry!" He climbed into the driver's seat and started the Cherokee.

Angela put Nikki into the back seat and climbed in next to David. Before she could close her door, David was backing up. Then he made a quick U-turn and accelerated up the street.

"Where are we going?" Angela asked.

"To the hospital," David said.

"Why the hospital?" Angela asked.

"It's suddenly making sense to me. I think I might know what Van Slyke was talking about when he referred to the source."

"I thought that was just schizophrenic babble."

"He may have been babbling," David said, "but I don't think he was talking nonsense when he said source. Not when he was talking about putting it on a conference table that had a model of a parking garage on it. That's too specific."

"Well, what do you think he was referring to?"

"I think it has to do with radiation," David said. "I think that's what Van Slyke was talking about when he said he'd burned his hands. Van Slyke's training in the navy involved nuclear propulsion. And nuclear reactors mean radiation."

"But people can't just go out and get radioactive material."

"There's an old radiotherapy unit in the basement of the hospital," David said. "It's a cobalt-sixty machine. It has a source."

"I don't like the sound of this," Angela said.

"I don't like it either," David said. "And think about my patients' symptoms. They could have been from radiation, especially if the patients had been subjected to overwhelming doses."

"I never thought about radiation when I did Mary Ann Schiller's autopsy," Angela admitted. "Radiation isn't something you consider unless there is a history of exposure."

"That's my point exactly," David said. "Even the nurses with flulike symptoms could have been suffering from a low level of radiation. And even Nikki."

"Even Nikki what?" Nikki asked from the back seat. She'd not been paying attention until she'd heard her name.

Angela turned around. "We were just saying that you had flulike symptoms just like the nurses."

"And Daddy too," Nikki said.

They pulled into the hospital lot, parked, and went to the lobby. Nikki discovered a TV and was content for the moment. She promised not to leave.

Angela and David went to the radiotherapy center. It took them about fifteen minutes to find a Geiger counter. Back in the main hospital building, they found Ronnie, one of the janitors David vaguely knew. David neglected to mention that he'd been fired from CMV. It took a few minutes to find the key to the old radiotherapy unit in the basement. The machine looked like an X-ray unit with a table attached. David put the Geiger counter on the table and turned it on. The needle barely moved on the gauge. David positioned the Geiger counter by the treatment arm, where he thought the source should reside. There was still no reading.

"Uh-oh," Angela said. "David, look at this." She pointed up to an access panel in the arm that was loosely attached by four nob screws. David unscrewed them, discovering a circular metal plate secured with eight lug bolts. All eight were loose. Removing them, he lifted the heavy metal covering and peered down a long cylindrical cavity. It looked like the hollow barrel of a huge gun.

He stuck the Geiger counter into the muzzle of the treatment arm. There was no reading above background. "The source is not in there. It's gone."

"What are we going to do?" Angela asked.

"Let's get lead aprons from radiology," David said. "Then we'll do what we can."

They headed straight for the imaging center. The X-ray technician was suspicious of David's request, but he wasn't used to contradicting doctors. He gave David, Angela, and Ronnie nine lead aprons as well as one pair of lead gloves. Weighed down with their burden, they made their way back to the hospital.

"All right," David said once they reached the door of the conference room. "Put everything right here."

David tried the Geiger counter again. Immediately the needle pegged to the right. "We couldn't get any better evidence than that," David said. He thanked Ronnie and sent him on his way.

David pulled on the lead gloves and picked up three aprons. Angela picked up four. David opened the door and went into the conference room, with Angela close behind. Traynor, interrupted in midsentence, glared at David. Those in attendance—Sherwood, Beaton, Cantor, Caldwell, Arnsworth, and Robeson—all began to murmur. Traynor banged his gavel.

Scanning the cluttered conference table, David spotted the source instantly, a cylinder whose diameter matched the size of the bore he'd examined only minutes ago. It was standing upright next to a model of a parking garage.

David started for the cylinder, clutching a lead apron in both hands. "What do you think you're doing?" Caldwell demanded.

"I'm trying to save all of you if it isn't too late," David said.

"What are you talking about?" Traynor demanded.

David nodded toward the cylinder. "I'm afraid you have been having your meeting around a cobalt-sixty source."

Cantor leaped to his feet. "I saw that thing," he cried. "I wondered what it was." Saying no more, he turned and fled the room.

David snatched up the brass cylinder in his lead gloves, then rolled it in one of his lead aprons. He wrapped that apron in another and that one in another still. He proceeded to do the same with the aprons Angela was carrying, while she stepped out to get the others.

"I don't believe you," Traynor said, breaking a shocked silence. But his voice lacked conviction.

"This is not the time for debate," David said. "Everyone better get out of here. You've all been exposed to a serious amount of radiation. I advise you to call your doctors."

Traynor and the others exchanged nervous glances. Panic soon broke out, as first a few and then the remaining board members, including Traynor, ran from the room.

Turning the Geiger counter on, David was dismayed to see that it registered a significant amount of radiation. "Let's get out of here," he said. "That's about all we can do. I think I know how the patients were irradiated." He led Angela to the patients' rooms.

Half an hour later they collected Nikki and took the Cherokee back to Van Slyke's so that David could get the Volvo. As David started it up, he looked at Calhoun's truck in front of him and sadly shook his head.

As soon as they got on the main road, David picked up his cellular phone and called the state police. He explained that he wanted to report a very serious plot that included murder and deadly radiation at the Bartlet Community Hospital.

Epilogue

Four Months Later

DAVID knew he was late as he pulled up to a modest house on Glenwood Avenue in Leonia, New Jersey. He jumped out of the car and ran up the front steps.

"Do you know what time it is?" Angela asked, following him into their bedroom. "You were supposed to be home at one. It's two."

"I'm sorry," David said as he quickly changed his clothes. "I had a patient who needed extra time. Where's Nikki?"

"She's out on the sun porch," Angela said. "She went out there over an hour ago to watch the *60 Minutes* crew set up."

David slipped on a dress shirt and did up the buttons.

"I'm sorry," Angela said. "I'm anxious about this TV thing."

"I'm nervous too," David said as he tied his tie and put on a jacket. Angela checked herself in the mirror. When they both felt they were ready, they walked out to the sun porch, blinking under the bright lights.

Ed Bradley quickly put them at ease. He began the interview casually by asking them what they were currently doing.

"I'm taking a fellowship in forensic pathology," Angela said.

"I'm working with a large medical group at Columbia Presbyterian Medical Center," David said.

"I understand you had a difficult experience in Bartlet, Vermont," Bradley said. "How did it start?"

David and Angela looked at each other.

"My part of it started when a number of my patients began to die unexpectedly," David said. "They were patients with histories of serious illnesses like cancer."

"It started for me when I began to be sexually harassed by my immediate superior," Angela said. "Then we discovered the body of a homicide victim entombed under our cellar steps—Dr. Dennis Hodges, the hospital administrator for a number of years."

With his usual clever questioning, Ed Bradley pulled out the whole sordid story. "Were these unexpected patient deaths instances of euthanasia?" he asked.

"That's what we thought initially," David said. "But these people were actually being murdered not through some misguided gesture of mercy but to improve the hospital's bottom line. Patients with potentially terminal illness often use hospital facilities intensively. That translates to high costs. So to eliminate those expenses, the patients themselves were eliminated. The hospital was losing money, and they had to do something to stem the red ink. This was their solution."

"Why was the hospital losing money?" Bradley asked.

"The hospital had been forced to capitate," David explained. "That means furnish hospitalization for the major HMO in the area for a fixed fee per subscriber per month. Unfortunately, the hospital had estimated utilization at too low a cost. The money coming in was much less than the money going out."

"Why did the hospital agree to capitate?" Bradley asked.

"It had to do with the new competition in medicine," David said. "The hospital had to capitate if it wanted to compete for the HMO's business. It didn't have any choice."

Bradley nodded as he consulted his notes. Then he looked back at David and Angela. "The new administrator of Bartlet Community Hospital says that your allegations are, in his words, pure rubbish."

"We've heard that," David said.

"The same administrator went on to say that if any patients had been murdered, it would have been the work of a single deranged individual. But you don't buy it?"

"No, we don't."

"How did the patients die?" Bradley asked.

"From full-body radiation," Angela said. "The patients received overwhelming doses of gamma rays from a cobalt-sixty source."

"How was this radiation administered?" Bradley asked.

"An orthopedic bed was fitted with a heavily lead-shielded box," Angela said. "It was mounted under the bed and contained the source. The box had a remotely controlled window that was operated by a garage door opener with radio waves. Whenever the port was open, the patient was irradiated through the bed."

"And both of you saw this bed?" Bradley asked.

David and Angela nodded.

"After we found the source and shielded it as best we could," David explained, "I tried to figure out how my patients had been irradiated. I remembered that many of them had been in hospital beds that malfunctioned. They'd wound up being transferred to an orthopedic bed. So we went looking for a special orthopedic bed. We found it in the maintenance shop."

"And now you contend this bed was destroyed," Bradley said.

"The bed was never seen again after that night," Angela said.

"How could that have happened?" Bradley asked.

"The people responsible for its use got rid of it," David said.

"And you believe the hospital executive committee was responsible?" Bradley said.

"At least some of them," David said. "Certainly the chairman of the board, the administrator, and the chief of the medical staff."

"Regrettably, none of these people can defend themselves," Ed Bradley said. "I understand that all of them died of severe radiation sickness despite some heroic measures to save them."

"Unfortunately," David admitted.

"Can you substantiate these allegations?" Bradley asked.

"Werner Van Slyke essentially confessed to us both," David said.

"Werner Van Slyke is the man you believe was the worker bee behind this operation," Bradley said.

"That's correct," David said. "He'd had nuclear training in the navy, so he knew something about handling radioactive materials."

"This is the same Werner Van Slyke who is schizophrenic and is now hospitalized with severe radiation sickness, who refuses to talk with anyone, and who is expected to die."

"He's the one," David admitted.

"What I'm hearing is that neither of you have any hard evidence," Bradley said.

"I suppose that's true," David said reluctantly.

"With the kind of accusations you've made, why do you think there have been no criminal charges?" Ed Bradley asked.

Angela and David looked at each other. Finally David spoke. "Basically, we think there are two reasons. First, everybody is afraid of this affair. If it all came out, it would probably shut the hospital, and that would be disastrous for the community. Secondly, the guilty, in a sense, have been punished. Van Slyke took care of that when he put the cobalt-sixty cylinder on the conference table."

"That might explain why there hasn't been any local response," Bradley said. "But what about the state's attorney?"

"This episode cuts to the quick of the direction of health-care reform," Angela said. "If this story were to get out, people might begin to reevaluate their thinking on the route we seem to be taking. Our experience may be an extreme example of medical bureaucrats run amok, yet it happened. It could happen again."

"What about the series of attempted rapes in the hospital parking lot?" Bradley asked. "Were they part of this plot?"

"No, they weren't," Angela said. "At one point we thought they were. So did the private detective who lost his life investigating this with us. But we were wrong. DNA testing has proved that Clyde Devonshire, an emergency-room nurse, was responsible for the two rapes."

"Have you learned from this experience?" Bradley asked.

David and Angela said yes simultaneously.

"I've learned," David said, "that it is dangerous to allow financial and business people to interfere in the doctor-patient relationship."

"It should be the patient's needs that determine the level and type of treatment," Angela said.

"Sam Flemming and Tom Baringer died in Bartlet Community

Hospital with the exact same symptom complex as your patients," Bradley said. "They were patients of Dr. Portland."

"Then we wouldn't know anything about them," David said. "Dr. Portland killed himself shortly before we moved to town."

"What I wanted to ask," Bradley said, "is whether you believe that these two people could have died from radiation sickness as you allege your patients did."

"I suppose if the symptoms were the same in type, degree, and time frame, then I would say yes," David said.

"That's interesting," Bradley said. "Neither one of them had any medical problem other than the acute problem they'd been admitted with. But both had taken out multimillion-dollar insurance policies, with the hospital as the sole beneficiary. Would either of you care to comment?"

"If they had been irradiated, then the motive was even more directly economic than in the other cases," David said. "And it would certainly make our case that much more convincing."

"If the bodies were exhumed," Bradley asked, "could it be determined unequivocally whether they had died of radiation?"

"I don't believe so," Angela said. "The best anyone could say would be that the remains were consistent with radiation exposure."

"One last question," Bradley said. "Are you happy now?"

"We're certainly happier than we were several months ago, and we're glad we're working," David said. "We're also thankful that Nikki has been doing so well."

"I think we're happy," Nikki said, speaking up for the first time. "I'm going to have a brother. We're going to have a baby."

Bradley raised his eyebrows. "Is that true?"

"God willing," David said.

Angela just smiled.

ABOUT THE AUTHOR

"In a different life, I might have been an architect," says eye-surgeon-turned-novelist Robin Cook. In New York City recently to promote his latest book, Dr. Cook also made time to pursue his newest hobby: interior decorating—with a twist. He buys properties, fixes them up, and resells them. Though he admits it may sound like a ridiculous luxury to own properties all over the place, it's actually a hobby that pays for itself. His latest decorating project is an apartment in the Trump Tower on Fifth Avenue.

Robin Cook

Though he doesn't practice medicine anymore, Dr. Cook still considers himself very much a part of the medical profession. "I'm more of an advocate now," he says, in no way trying to skirt the most pressing issue at hand: health-care reform. "Most people in the U.S. are getting the best health care available in the world. The problem is, people have to take a more responsible role in their own health—exercise, eat right, get proper rest, quit smoking, moderate drinking. Those things will be more important to their health than any interaction they ever have with the medical profession."

Like the best advocates, Dr. Cook practices what he preaches. Along with skiing and tennis, a favorite workout is basketball. You might, in fact, run into him in a pickup game at Columbia University's medical school gym. It's recently been renovated and named for the alum who footed the bill: Robin Cook Gymnasium.

With seven appearances in Condensed Books and unqualified success on the best-seller lists, Dr. Cook has remained steadily focused on his goal: to teach readers about the medical world—while thrilling them with page-turning suspense. His favorite reading remains *The New England Journal of Medicine.* "And," he says with a smile, "if I had it all to do over, I'd study medicine again."

The Wrong House

Carol McD. Wallace

Frances Drummond has retirement all figured out. She and her husband will buy a quaint little cottage in Connecticut. She'll tend the garden. He'll restore the parquet floors. And they'll be close enough to New York so their grown children will be hard-pressed for excuses not to visit.

A rosy vision that unfortunately is not to be. For a monumental mishap, a case of unforgivable bumbling, is about to play a mean trick on Frances. And while the rest of the world might laugh it off, Frances, most assuredly, is not amused.

1

As Hart opened the back door and stepped onto the porch, Margaret Harwood's voice followed him. "It's been in the same family for generations," she was saying. "I adore that kind of old-fashioned continuity. You just know they've taken good care of the place. You say you live in a Victorian house now?" His wife's response was muffled. "Well, I always tell clients it's hard to settle for anything else after you're used to that kind of gracious living. Now, out here"—Margaret Harwood's high heels tapped their way onto the porch—"is the nicest rose garden in Weymouth. Are you much of a gardener?"

Hart turned away from his examination of the porch foundation to catch his wife's reaction. Frances' garden in Chester, New Jersey, was spellbinding, and she specialized in roses. Of course, she was too much of a lady to put Margaret Harwood in her place, but Hart, watching his wife's blue eyes scanning the forlorn-looking beds of roses in their little burlap tepees, could imagine what she would say about the real estate agent on the long drive back home.

He turned back to the porch, peering at a suspiciously powdery-looking spot where the steps reached the ground. Termites? Carpenter ants? There was so much to think about when you were buying a new house. This one was charming—a pretty little Victorian board-and-batten cottage with scrolled carving under the eaves. The rooms were nicely proportioned, with high ceilings, long windows, and a neat little fireplace in each one. What was more, two of the bedrooms had views of the harbor and Long Island Sound. Still, aesthetics were one thing, practicality another. Hart walked up onto the porch.

"What about the wiring?" he asked Margaret Harwood.

"Rewired in the '60s," she answered, all efficiency. "They put in a new furnace at the same time. To be perfectly honest," she said in a way Hart didn't much trust, "you may want a new hot-water heater."

Hart looked at Frances, who was now crouching and poking the frozen soil. "We don't use oceans of hot water," he said. "Can we get up to the roof?"

"We can probably get there through the attic," Margaret answered. Hart looked at her tight knee-length skirt and the stiletto heels. He couldn't quite envision her clambering up ladders or onto the steeply pitched roof in that getup.

"Okay. I'll tell Frances." Hart crossed the lawn, noticing that the grass, even in February, seemed strong and springy. "I'm going up to get a look at the roof," he said. "Check out the gutters and slates."

Frances straightened up and glanced at the house. "Right. Okay," she said with a little smile. "It's a nice house, isn't it?"

Hart followed her gaze and looked at it. "Yes," he agreed. "You said that about the last one, too."

Frances' smile broadened. "Yes. And the one this morning. It's going to be fun to pick."

Hart nodded and turned back to the house, then turned again with a little frown. "Could you live with that kitchen?" he asked. "Those fixtures looked familiar from my childhood."

Frances, who had crouched back down, looked at him. "A new stove would take care of the worst of it," she said.

"You wouldn't want to redo the whole thing?"

"Not right away," she answered, then smiled slightly again. "Not if the roof had to come first."

Margaret Harwood scented a sale. Frances and Hart Drummond were just the kind of people you could sell these old Victorians to. People who were older, probably retired, with the kind of money and time that it took to maintain a house like this. She'd taken a chance and shown them a modern house farther out Shore Road first thing in the morning, but it was not the kind of house that people like the Drummonds moved to Weymouth for.

Hart Drummond would have resisted the notion that moving to Weymouth was a predictable step, but in fact it was. The plan had been arrived at after several years of amicable discussion with Frances. When Hart retired from the New York law firm of which he was a partner, he and Frances would move out of the big Victorian house in Chester, New Jersey, where they had raised their two children. They had thought about Florida, but after a couple of unsatisfying winters in rented condos in Hobe Sound and Palm Beach, they decided instead to buy a year-round house in Weymouth, Connecticut.

Hart had discovered Weymouth when he was an undergraduate at Yale. In those days Weymouth had the architecture of a prosperous nineteenth-century port and almost no economy at all. Decades of neglect meant that although the Victorian houses were falling apart, there were relatively few twentieth-century eyesores. When the town was rediscovered in the 1960s by prosperous burghers from New Haven and Hartford, the gingerbreaded eaves and mansard roofs got tarted up. But there was enough working farmland nearby that Weymouth didn't become precious.

Weymouth, in fact, was a connoisseur's town. Most people rushed past on I-95 on their way to Madison or Old Lyme. There wasn't even a sign for it on the thruway; you had to hear about it by word of mouth. There were no shops to speak of; just a faintly dingy IGA store and a post office and one pathetic boutique that tried to sell sandals with shells on them. The only signs that the town was other than a simple New England village were the real estate office installed in a lovely house in the center of town and the large proportion of Mercedes parked by the post office. Yet lots of people still drove pickup trucks. That was probably the detail that had decided Hart, who, in spite of his patrician background, education, and career, cherished a romantic view of "the people." In Weymouth, although there would be plenty of citizens who read *The New Yorker* and *The Wall Street Journal,* there would also be plenty who watched the weather and fed their cows. Hart felt that gave the town a balance. He would have hated to know that Margaret Harwood considered him a typical client.

What Frances liked about Weymouth was the abundance of houses with what she thought of as potential. As she and Hart drove back to Chester, she mulled over the competing appeal of the houses on Shore Road, Elm Street, and Main Street.

"Which house do you like best?" she said to Hart, interrupting a long silence.

Hart looked straight ahead, thinking. "Of the Victorians? You know, I did kind of like that modern one we saw first."

"Oh, Hart." Frances sighed. "That house was impossible."

"I know," he conceded. "It was hideous. But I liked the views. Of the others, I think the one with the garden was in the best shape. Though I'm a little worried about that kitchen."

"Well," Frances said, "when we go back, I'll look extra hard at the kitchen."

THEY drove back up to Weymouth two weeks later with a measuring tape and notes on the dimensions of their furniture. It was a horribly busy day at Strong Harwood Realty. Margaret Harwood's partner was away, and her dim-witted assistant had called in sick. "Look," she said to Hart, cradling a phone on her shoulder, "I'm so swamped. Can I just give you the keys and you look around by yourself? I have a couple coming in an hour, and I don't want to rush you after you came all this way. I'll meet you here afterward, okay? Don't tell anyone." The Drummonds were rather relieved at the prospect of seeing the houses free of Margaret Harwood's strong personality, so they accepted three bunches of keys and gratefully left as two phones began ringing simultaneously.

The mansard-roofed house on Elm Street seemed just a little too rickety to Hart, and the house on Main Street was really too big. So they took measurements at Shore Road, and Frances took notes on the varieties of roses and scooped up soil to analyze.

When they got back to Strong Harwood Realty, there was no one there. A note from Margaret pasted to the door with a Band-Aid said, "Back 2 p.m.," but it was already three thirty.

"Should we wait?" Hart asked.

Frances looked at her watch. "She seems amazingly scatterbrained to be running this business. Do you think we can trust her to handle the closing?"

"It's the only game in town," Hart said. "We don't have to worry about the closing; I can keep her on track. Let's go have an early dinner in New Haven and wait out the traffic."

"Good idea," Frances said. "So you'll call in an offer next week?"

Hart nodded. "Right." They left the keys in the mail basket hung next to the front door, where they ended up staying all night, since Margaret Harwood had had a flat tire on I-95 and never did make it back to work that afternoon.

So Hart made an offer for the Shore Road house, which was accepted after the usual dickering. Meanwhile, they put the house in Chester on the market and a very gratifying offer was made. In fact, the Drummonds stood to make so much money on the sale that Hart astonished Frances by suggesting they take the *QE2* to England for a vacation before the move. It was so unlike Hart to be extravagant that Frances was shocked into agreeing.

A minor hitch came up as they got ready to leave: the owners of the Weymouth house wanted to move up the closing by a couple of weeks, which meant that they wanted to close while Hart and Frances would be away. Hart tried to put the closing off until their return, but the owners had to be in a new house and were intransigent. For a moment it looked as if the deal would fall apart, so Hart backed off. He would give his brother, Pete, power of attorney, and Pete would attend the closing. Frances said this made her a little nervous. Pete was the Drummond renegade, a bachelor inventor who made a lot of money designing electrical gadgets. But as Hart pointed out, what could go wrong? The worst of it was that they would own two houses for a couple of months.

So Frances and Hart steamed off to England on the *QE2*. They saw daffodils in the Cotswolds, lambs in the Lake District, and bought Hart a new tweed jacket in Edinburgh. When they got home, they owned the house in Weymouth.

Then one afternoon late in April, Hart had gone off to the city for a Yale Club dinner, and Frances, taking a break from measuring furniture, was leafing through some mail-order catalogues. There was some good-looking stationery in one of them, handsomely printed with just an address. She started to fill in the order blank. She wrote down the new address: "259 Shore Road, Weymouth, CT 06 . . ." What was the zip code? Frances put down her pen. Drat. She considered waiting until Hart got home—he would know. But she hated leaving anything unfinished. Anyway, it would be in Hart's file on the new house.

She found the file right on top of Hart's desk, and inside, a letter from their lawyer, "Re: Purchase of 751 Shore Road, Weymouth, Conn." That was odd. A letter from the attorney shouldn't have the wrong address on it. Frances flipped through a few more papers. There should be something else, maybe the engineer's report. The engineer's report, which Frances had never looked at before, was for 751 Shore Road.

She sat down in Hart's desk chair. This just wasn't possible. Maybe she'd had the address wrong. Maybe the Victorian cottage was 751 Shore Road. She started leafing through the rest of the file. At the very back she found the original listing sheet from the real estate broker, with a xeroxed photograph of the cottage—at 259 Shore Road.

At that point Frances was still calm. She called Strong Harwood Realty. Margaret Harwood was out, of course. So Frances asked the assistant very sweetly if she could look up the file for their purchase; could there be some confusion? No, there didn't seem to be. All the paperwork was for 751 Shore Road. And what did 751 Shore Road look like? Well, it was a two-story modern house with Swiss-style detailing, three bedrooms, three baths, maid's room, deck, waterfront property. . . . Frances felt a hollow sensation spreading from the pit of her stomach. She managed to get off the phone somewhat civilly and hung it up, staring at the receiver. The modern waterfront house on Shore Road. It just wasn't possible. She went through the file again, wondering with growing rage how her husband, the meticulous attorney, had overlooked the engineer's report on the soundness of the "new redwood deck." Shouldn't that have made him wonder? How could he have done it? How could he possibly have bought the wrong house?

This was the point when Frances tried calling her children. She dialed Harry first. She was of the generation that naturally turned to men in a crisis, and Harry, even though he wrote soap operas for a living, had developed into a substantial and responsible man. Of course, he probably wouldn't be at home, but he kept his answering machine on all the time anyway. The phone rang twice, and she heard his voice saying, "This is Harry Drummond's answering machine. You know what to do."

"Harry, are you there? If you are, I wish you'd pick up. It's your mother. Call me when you get in. It's very important."

But of course he didn't pick up. Frances glanced at her watch. Eleanor would still be in the office. She dialed that number and heard the secretary's voice: "Mrs. Gray's office."

"Is she there?"

"I'm sorry, Mrs. Gray is in a meeting," came the adenoidal response. Frances felt a spurt of irritation that some undereducated teenager was obstructing communication with her daughter.

"Could you ask her to call her mother, please?" requested Frances in her iciest, most intimidating tone, and hung up. She called Eleanor's apartment next.

"Hullo," said a very young voice in a rather muffled way. There was an audible swallow. "Sorry. Hullo," the voice repeated.

"Toby? It's your grandmother."

"Hi, Gran. Sorry. I was eating a muffin."

"At five thirty? Won't that ruin your appetite?" said Frances. Her children had never had snacks after four p.m.

"No," said Toby, chewing again. "Mom's not coming home until eight tonight, so we're having dinner late."

"Well, who's taking care of you?"

"Luz."

"Could I speak to her?"

"Sure. Bye, Gran." The phone clattered down, and Frances could hear Toby yelling, "Luz!" at the top of his lungs.

Footsteps shuffled toward the phone, and a soft voice said, "Yes?" with a strong Spanish accent.

"Luz, this is Mrs. Drummond. Could you have Mrs. Gray call me when she gets home?"

"Yes, of course, Mrs. Drummond. I tell her. Thank you." The phone was hung up before Frances could reply.

Frances found herself becoming increasingly annoyed. Having left messages with a machine, a semiliterate housekeeper, and Eleanor's novice secretary, she had no confidence that her offspring would call her back. Hart, of course, was incommunicado: that was the whole point of places like the Yale Club.

So Frances did what she always did in times of stress—she got busy. She pulled on her gardening gloves and put her pruning shears in a basket and set out to reform the privet hedge.

The house in Weymouth might not have been so wrong if the house in Chester hadn't been so right. And the house in Chester would certainly not have been so right if Frances hadn't spent forty years tending it like a child. It was a house of great charm, tall and elegant, with a mansard roof and a generous front porch. Over the years the house had grown more beautiful. Hand-me-down furniture from the '20s and '30s gave way to rather good American antiques. The butler's pantry filled with excellent porcelain, and the little tables in the parlor sprouted the odd Louis XV snuffbox. Frances got to be an expert gardener, and every year there was a seasonal parade of brilliantly arranged cut flowers: violets, lilacs, peonies, roses—especially roses.

This was all, unfortunately, lost on her husband. Hart loved Frances in his undemonstrative way and made a great effort to appreciate her handiwork. He had always been clever with his hands, so he took a course on restoring antiques and performed a number of clever repairs on injured chairs and tables. But the house, in the end, was her province.

It would have been very hard to leave except that Frances had felt that 259 Shore Road was a member of the same family of houses. Another house to be loved and burnished to perfection. She had already begun imagining the changes she would make: a wide-striped wallpaper in the hall, pretty swagged curtains in the parlor, and, in time, a completely new kitchen.

But now, Frances thought, clipping savagely, that wasn't going to happen. They were going to live in a horrible modern house. A ticky-tacky box. Frances entertained self-pitying visions of herself stuck in the kind of house she had always scorned. Shag carpet, TV aerials, shiny wallpaper in the bathroom, she thought. A rec room in the basement.

As darkness fell, she was still pruning away, angrier than ever.

ELEANOR Gray leafed through the pink message slips on her desk. She noticed the message from her mother and considered returning the call from her office, but it was seven thirty and her car was waiting, so she stuffed the message into her pocket on her way out the door.

Ordinarily Eleanor took the subway home. She always left the office after rush hour, so the clattering, jerking ride uptown represented half an hour of quiet time to her. But tonight she'd had a late meeting, so she took a radio car home to dinner with the boys. She leaned back and shut her eyes as the driver careered up West Street, and tried not to think about the documents due at the end of the week, the enormous assessment for rewiring her co-op building, or Toby's passionate desire for a skateboard.

Eleanor Gray's entire life was a closely fought war against entropy. Sometimes the war took the form of a major pitched battle, as it had in the year following her divorce. Faced with the task of raising the boys and running her large West End Avenue apartment single-handed, she had, like any canny general, turned to mercenaries. Luz, a grandmother from Ecuador, lovingly bullied the boys when their absurdly expensive private school let them out. Jadrancka, a Croatian electrical engineer with no English, cleaned and did the errands. A market delivered the weekly food order, a personal shopper from Saks helped Eleanor select two new suits each season, and every month the rather imposing salary paid her by a Wall Street law firm only just met the bills. After almost five years life had a routine, and Eleanor felt she had nothing substantial to complain about. Many women did just what she did, she would tell herself, with a lot less money and no support system.

Dark moments came when she felt overwhelmed, as she frequently did, by the little things—late subways, snagged stockings, a pregnant secretary, Simon's measles. There was always something about her life that was out of control.

Like the way she looked. She never managed to get her hair cut quite often enough, so she had a slightly unprofessional-looking mass of chestnut tendrils usually bundled into a knot. She was tall, which was a good thing, since she was also fifteen pounds overweight. There was often something not quite right about her clothes—a button missing from her silk blouse, a slip that was a sliver too long. Snagged stockings yet again.

It sometimes crossed her mind that her air of dishevelment might be a professional disadvantage. In fact, it was just the opposite. More than one fellow attorney had been completely disarmed by her distracted air and slightly mussed-up look.

"If she didn't look as if she'd just gotten out of bed," one of them had complained following a will contest that he'd lost, "one would be inclined to take her more seriously."

"Or stop thinking about getting her back there," sourly replied his colleague.

Which would have reassured Eleanor immensely. For all her busyness, all her resolute cheerfulness, she occasionally admitted to herself that she was lonely. What was missing was a man in her life. And what chance did she have, a plump thirty-eight-year-old mother of two, in a city where blond twigs of twenty-five were a dime a dozen? Ever since her divorce, friends had attempted to set her up with eligible men, but they always seemed to freeze when she mentioned her sons. Or they were intimidated. Or it was all too obvious why they were still single—or single again. As in the case of the plastic surgeon who within ten minutes of their meeting was discussing her need for an eyelift.

It shouldn't bother her, Eleanor thought as the driver pulled over in front of her building. Nobody had everything. She had been married once, she had two wonderful sons, whose voices she could hear the minute she got off the elevator.

"Catch her, quick!" Toby yelled.

"She went into the kitchen," Simon's higher voice piped up. "Quick—get her into the cupboards!"

Eleanor opened the door, put down her keys and briefcase, and picked up the mail from the hall table.

"Mom! Mom! Ramona's out again," Toby called. "Quick! She's coming your way." And the waters of family life closed over Eleanor's head.

In the fuss over getting Ramona, the guinea pig, back in her cage and then getting dinner on the table and the boys to bed, Eleanor forgot about calling her mother until she finally got around to hanging up her suit jacket. It was ten thirty. Eleanor weighed her filial duty against her fatigue and decided to go to bed and call her mother first thing in the morning.

Harry got home at midnight and went to bed without listening to his messages.

Hart caught the last train to Chester and crept into his bedroom at one a.m. By which time Frances' sense of injury had blossomed until she was filled with a sense of self-righteous resentment, and she lay there brooding in the dark while her husband quietly got ready for bed, not wanting to wake her. He fell asleep quickly, reflecting briefly what a fortunate man he was.

2

IT WAS a soft morning in early May. In Weymouth, Connecticut, the air from Long Island Sound still had a crisp edge. The tiny waves slapped and sucked at the pebbly shore. In the boatyard the seagulls strutted on the dock. From the water, the new leaves budding on the trees blended into a faint, mottled wash of yellow-green.

At the Vince Lombardi Service Station on Interstate 95 in New Jersey, the air smelled richly of burning rubber and diesel fuel, while the smooth roar of traffic on the highway made conversation impossible. Which was something of a relief to both Frances and Hart as they carefully locked the doors of their Mercedes.

Wordlessly they walked into the restaurant and separated—he to the men's room, she to the ladies'. In the ladies' room a pair of teenagers in black high-heeled boots and leather jackets were spraying their massive, disheveled locks into place. They eyed Frances in the mirror, taking in her tweed skirt and jacket, her Nantucket basket purse. Just as brazenly, she eyed them, and thought with relief that at least neither of her children had turned out like *that*.

When she came out of the ladies' room, she walked into the restaurant, where she was surprised to see her husband's tweed-clad back at the counter. He turned and came toward her, holding a paper bag.

"What did you get?" she asked. Hart had never eaten fast food that she knew of.

"Coffee. I'm a little groggy. And I thought I'd like to try one of those breakfast croissant things you hear about so much on the television." He patted the bag gently.

"Oh, Hart," Frances sighed. "They're so terrible for you."

"One won't hurt," he answered mildly. "Can I get you anything? Tea? Juice?"

"Not here," she said, turning to go back outside. "I'd rather keep going to avoid the traffic." She walked ahead of him to the car. He unlocked her door first and closed it after her. Frances sat still in the passenger seat while he unlocked his door and clambered in, holding his paper bag carefully.

"Could you punch that little hole in the lid for me?" he asked her, holding out the coffee cup with one hand as he pulled back onto I-95. Silently she accepted the cup and studied the plastic lid.

"There is no little hole."

"Well, could you *tear* a little hole?"

She studied the cup again. Then, holding it gingerly in one hand, she reached behind the seat and extracted a pair of gold stork-shaped sewing scissors from her needlepoint bag and carefully cut a hole in the lid. She handed it back to Hart, who sipped from it.

"Thank you. Perfect."

Frances didn't answer, but replaced the scissors in their bag and clasped her hands in her lap.

The traffic was already heavy, though it wasn't even seven. Soon, as the road narrowed to two northbound lanes, everyone halted. Hart put his coffee on the dashboard and, using one hand, began to unwrap his breakfast croissant. A smell of egg and bacon filled the car. Frances wrinkled her nose.

"Want a bite?" Hart offered it to her, and she shook her head.

"No, thank you," she said.

"It's actually quite good," Hart said judiciously. "I think maybe next time I'll try those potatoes they sell."

"Oh? Is this going to become a tradition?" Frances asked with a false mildness.

Hart didn't flinch. A honk behind him drew his attention to the ten-foot gap between him and the car in front, so he eased forward and took another bite of his breakfast.

Frances had not forgiven him, Hart thought. She'd been like this for days, ever since he'd come down for breakfast after the Yale Club dinner to find the real estate folder sitting on his plate.

Over and over he'd mentally rehearsed the steps of the deal, starting with his admittedly inexact offer on the "Shore Road house," telephoned to a distracted Margaret Harwood. Both houses had been on the market for the same price, but how could she *possibly* have thought he'd wanted the modern one? If Hart had been at the closing himself, he would probably have caught the error, but Pete could hardly be held responsible; he'd just been there to sign papers. Eleanor had offered to stand in for her parents at the closing. Looking back, Hart realized, he should have let her. Eleanor was a trusts-and-estates attorney; she often handled real estate. She would have been perfect. And if she had even laid eyes on the Wrong House before the closing, she would have known it was not what her parents meant to buy. But Hart knew how busy his daughter was and hadn't wanted her to sacrifice a day in the office. So now they had to be out of the Chester house on Memorial Day weekend.

Hart sneaked a glance at Frances, wondering how she would react to that. If the past ten days were anything to go by, it was going to be a pretty bleak summer.

It wasn't that she'd exploded. Frances didn't explode. In fact, she probably thought she was being a perfect trouper about the house. But Hart knew from the way her face froze when he told her they couldn't back out of the purchase of 751 that she was upset. She never reproached him—aloud. But in the cryptic language of their marriage, a dialect of expressions and sighs and gestures, she let him know exactly how little she thought of him.

What Hart didn't realize was that Frances was trying. She was trying to keep her temper and trying to put a brave face on things. But every now and then she lost control, and bitchy little remarks spurted out in spite of all her efforts. The fact was that she was miserable at the thought of living in a horrible modern house, and she had no way of explaining this to Hart.

The problem was that Hart didn't feel guilty. He had made a mistake. As a result of his mistake Frances was going to be inconvenienced for several months. But why couldn't she look on it as an adventure? After all, they weren't going to be pitched out on the street. The whole Connecticut coastline was for sale, and spending a summer in a modern house wasn't a matter of life and death. Frances was just being a little too rigid. Couldn't she relax and go along with things?

Of course she couldn't. Hart knew she couldn't. She didn't like adventures, and she never relaxed. But Hart was angry, too. He was tired of being reminded that he was an incompetent.

Hart glanced over at Frances again, stitching away on her needlepoint. This was one of a set of twelve seats for the mahogany dining-room chairs. She'd been working on them for three years and had only one left.

"What are you going to do when you've got those finished?" Hart asked.

"I don't know yet. I'll miss them," she said, holding the canvas away from her to see the whole design. "I was thinking about a rug, but I'm not sure I should get started on one. My eyes might not hold out."

"Are you having trouble with them?"

"No. But I'm getting to the age when people do."

"That's silly, Frances. Not to do something you want to do just because your eyes *might* give out."

"Well, I can't start on anything anyway until we get settled," Frances answered. "From what I remember, this isn't much of a needlepoint kind of house."

Hart felt his jaw tighten and drank some coffee. End of thaw. It was going to be a hell of a summer.

THE Drummonds' drive that morning was a long and nasty one. Even the bewitching air of a lovely May morning couldn't redeem the miles of truck exhaust, bone-jarring road surface, and shabby urban landscape. They hit Bridgeport at the peak of rush hour, and the congestion continued for another hour, until they were past Branford.

Branford was the last place where commerce fringed I-95. The highway narrowed to four lanes, cutting through a more rural landscape. They turned off the Weymouth exit at a quarter to eleven. On the way to the real estate agent's office they drove past 259 Shore Road. Hart noticed that Frances didn't even glance at it as they went past. Stiff upper lip, he thought, and admired her.

"I'll just run in and get the key," said Hart, leaving the car running. Frances, lost in silence, didn't even look up.

Margaret Harwood was on the phone but put her hand over the

receiver. "Listen, I'm expecting a couple of great things to come on the market soon. Then you can turn right around and sell 751. Listen, honey, in the end you'll get a free summer on the water out of this." She handed over the keys and waved her fuchsia fingertips. Hart, walking out the door, reflected how little a free summer on the water was going to console his wife.

The Wrong House was magnificently located. A short drive down Main Street brought you to Shore Road. Between the road and the Sound lay several acres of marsh and tufty grass, threaded with shallow tidal streams. Just beyond the swamp, marked by a bare aluminum mailbox, a driveway pierced a clump of eight-foot privet bushes. It dived straight through overgrown shrubs toward the water. When you came out of the bushes, you were alone on a little headland, with water all around.

Hart brought the car to a halt and got out. Without waiting for Frances, he strode across the coarse mustard-colored grass. The breeze off the water was stiff, cutting right through his old tweed jacket. No doubt it would whip up into quite a gale. But what a view! Hart stood at the very tip of the point, looking straight out to the misty blue line that was Long Island. Dotting the Sound artistically were a group of tiny islands. To the right the wetlands curved in a beige crescent toward the harbor.

On the left-hand side of the point where Hart stood, the rocks leveled out to sand. Treading carefully, he stepped off the lawn onto the highest rock and climbed down. It was warmer down on the sand, sheltered from the wind. As Hart walked along the little stretch of beach, dry, pebbly sand filled his shoes. Across this little cove he could see the town beach and, behind, another little point, with a much bigger house on it and a brick boathouse with a jetty.

Of course, we have our own little dock, thought Hart, and climbed up its ladder from the beach. He walked out to the end, admiring the sturdiness of the construction. There were several big cleats and another ladder leading down into the water, draped with sea lettuce.

He turned and surveyed the house. Through one of the big bay windows he could make out something moving—Frances, examining her new home. Hart sighed. Better go in and face the music. Maybe the house wouldn't be as bad inside as it was outside.

For in truth, it *was* ugly. It had apparently been inspired by a Swiss chalet, which, on this breeze-washed scrap of Connecticut, looked ridiculous. Painting the shutters pink hadn't helped. The famous deck thrust out from the house at an angle, with steps down to the lawn. Half of the house's seaward façade was covered with half-timbering, another third with weathered shingles. The rest, ludicrously enough, was brick. There were two long window boxes, both pink, beneath the big living-room windows.

Courage flagging, Hart walked across the deck and knocked on the Dutch door. The house would be better inside. It had to be. He could hear Frances' footsteps inside, echoing. It was only for a summer—just a few months. Latches on the inside of the door clicked. Maybe they should look in Old Lyme or Essex. The top half of the Dutch door swung inward. The westering sun, reflected off the water, flooded Frances' face in a beautiful golden light. She stood framed in the doorway like a Renaissance portrait, and fleetingly Hart admired the way the sun warmed her fair skin, brightening her clear blue eyes, gilding the silver hair that swept back from her temples. She was still, Hart realized, quite beautiful. And she was also, plainly, *enraged.*

"Can you get this damn door open?" she said, stepping out of the sunlight. "There's something the matter with the bottom half."

Hart leaned over and tried the knob, fiddling with the lock, but couldn't make it open. Reluctantly, he climbed stiffly over it, regretting as much as anything appearing elderly and ridiculous in front of his angry wife.

As Hart looked around, his heart sank. The room they were in was a big L, comprising both living and dining room. The living-room portion had a double-height ceiling and two huge bay windows overlooking the Sound. Beneath the windows, logs had been halved to form window seats. The previous owners had left the cushions, which matched the full-length curtains: a rust-and-olive large-scale plaid, rendered in shaggy wool. One wall was dominated by a large boulder-faced fireplace. From the ceiling hung an immense chandelier made of antlers.

In the dining area the decorative scheme lurched into another gear. The ceiling dropped to eight feet. On the wall, two large mirrors in pseudorococo frames hung against pale blue metallic paisley wallpaper. The chandelier was Venetian in style, festooned with pink, gold, and white blown-glass flowers.

Wordlessly Frances pushed through the swinging western-saloon-style half doors to the kitchen. Hart followed. "Oh, good heavens!" he exclaimed as Frances switched on the overhead fluorescent fixture. The floor was brick-patterned linoleum, the appliances turquoise, and the cabinets a deep, shiny cherry red.

Beyond the kitchen was a small powder room. Fuzzy gray kittens frolicked on the walls with balls of pink and blue yarn. There was also a little utility room, which, with its sedate orange-centered-daisy wallpaper and grass-green indoor-outdoor carpet, was a relief.

The banister at the edge of the stairs was fake wrought iron, while the staircase wall had been faced with what appeared to be barn siding. The three upstairs bedrooms were more conventionally laid out, but still a far cry from Frances' taste. The one at the top of the stairs sported pink wallpaper patterned in ballerina motifs—tutus, toe shoes, dancers en pointe.

"This can be the guest room," Frances said in an icy tone.

The bathroom, which Hart just peered into, was avocado green. The next bedroom had been given a hasty coat of white paint that didn't quite cover the black-and-white geometric pattern of the paper underneath.

"This will be my room," Frances announced, standing stiffly in the doorway. Hart glanced at her.

"But— The master bedroom?" he asked.

"*You* may want to sleep there. I will not."

Mystified, Hart crossed the hall into the third bedroom and understood instantly. There was an immense mirror on the ceiling over the bed. Frances Drummond would sleep bolt upright on a campstool before she lay down under that mirror. Tentatively Hart sat down and looked around. There was the water, on both sides of him; but there he was, too—a thin, freckled sixty-six-year-old in wire-framed glasses and an old tweed jacket. He was distracted for a moment by the view, new to him, of the top of his head. His hair was holding up pretty well, he thought.

His eyes turned back to the water, and he sat for a minute more, looking at the sunlight on the little waves. Sunrise would be beautiful from up here. The room wouldn't be bad without the mirror. It was big; plenty of space for his desk in here, and maybe his big club chair by the window. He went over and pressed the dimmer switch by the door. As he'd guessed, the spots were trained on the bed. Well, why not? Apparently the previous owners had a good time in the sack. What of it? There was probably a Jacuzzi in the bathtub.

There was, of course, along with a bidet and two sinks and yards of brownish marble. He went back into the bedroom for a last look at the water. To hell with Frances anyway. Of course the house was ugly, and it had been decorated in the worst possible taste. It wouldn't kill her to live in it for a few months. He turned off the spotlights and glanced around the room with a dawning fondness. In that moment, he and the house became allies.

Hart and Frances drove back to New Jersey in unbroken silence.

3

BY THE time she heard Harry's footsteps coming up the attic stairs, Eleanor had worked her way through about a quarter of the cardboard cartons that had accumulated in her portion of her parents' attic. It was a depressing experience. So far she had examined the contents of six boxes of old clothes and three boxes of books from college. She'd found nothing but drab, stretched-out turtlenecks and half-read English novels.

"How's it going?" Harry asked as he leaned down to kiss her. She looked at him and noted, for the thousandth time, his mysterious bandbox quality. Here she was, hair straggling down her neck, wearing a dusty old pair of sweatpants and her father's worn-out shirt. And there was Harry, impeccably handsome, his tawny hair sleek, yellow polo shirt and khakis creaseless, though he'd just driven down from New York.

"This is hell. Why can't I ever throw anything away?" she asked.

"That bad, huh?" Harry asked, sitting down. "Well, let me do some boxes. What's the system?"

"That pile is 'throw away,' " Eleanor said, gesturing at the largest stack of cartons. "That pile is 'keep,' and the pile in the middle is 'consider for tag sale.' "

Harry peered over at the tag sale pile, which so far consisted of a high chair and a pair of worn L. L. Bean boots. "You haven't

gotten to the wedding presents yet," he stated, standing up to select a box marked CRYSTAL. "Can I do that?"

"Fine," Eleanor said, slitting the tape of the CRYSTAL box with a kitchen knife. Resting on top of the crumpled newspaper was an index card listing the contents in her former husband's tiny, angular handwriting.

She handed the card to Harry, who studied it silently for a moment. Finally he asked, "Do you know any architects who aren't compulsively neat?"

Eleanor considered. "No. But even Jared's architect friends thought he was unusually . . . tidy. You realize all these cards were cross-referenced on a computerized list. I was so impressed. I thought my life might finally become organized."

Harry shot her a glance. "That should have been your first clue."

"Oh, come on, Harry," she answered, irritated. "I was madly in love. You know that stage when any characteristic of the other person seems incredibly wonderful, like the fact that he only uses Razor Point pens or never loses his temper?"

"Do I ever," Harry said ruefully. "My apartment is full of Razor Point pens, metaphorically speaking."

"Oh, I'm sorry," Eleanor said, full of compunction. "Have you heard from Gretchen?"

"Yes. She wants me to pack up her stuff and send it out. Apparently she found a great apartment in Iowa City, and everybody is so healthy and sincere out there, and she can't bear to pollute her lungs anymore with metropolitan carbon monoxide."

"Oh, Harry," Eleanor said. "I feel terrible."

Harry shrugged. "Yep. So do I. But she'll make lots of serious friends and walk around in her Birkenstock sandals and read Emily Dickinson and take up with some strapping bearded fellow in a lumberjack's shirt who's writing an epic novel." He looked at the card in his hand. " 'Six snowball candlesticks,' " he read. "No, thank you. 'One three-dimensional star ornament.' No. 'One modern vase.' What's that?"

Eleanor dug in the box, feeling for the largest bundle. She peeled off the newspaper, revealing a large free-form vase with a very rough surface, as if it had been carved from a block of ice with a hammer.

"It looks like something left over from the Dartmouth Winter Carnival," Harry said, turning it around in his hands. "Say, maybe we should give it to Mom for the new house. It's modern."

"You wouldn't dare. Believe me, it's not a laughing matter. Last night at dinner she was moaning and groaning about the sea air and her French furniture, and the minute Dad suggested putting her desk in storage, she got up and left the table."

"Really?" Harry put the vase down. "She might as well have slapped him in the face."

"Well, she did come back with a pitcher of mint sauce. But that was just to save face. Meanwhile, Dad sat peacefully eating his lamb, as if nothing had happened. I even wondered . . ."

"What? Go on," Harry urged.

"Well, I got this strange sense— I even wondered if he was baiting her. You know, he looked kind of smug."

Harry narrowed his eyes. "Things must have gotten really awful between them if he's egging her on." He looked down at his hands abstractedly. "It would be very unfunny if their marriage broke up over a stupid house."

"Yeah, well, it's more than a stupid house for Mom, you know that," Eleanor said, cutting the tape on a box marked RECORDS. "It's her persona or something."

"Maybe it'll do her good," Harry offered. "She was getting awfully tied up in all that house stuff."

Eleanor sat back with a pile of albums on her lap. "Yes, she was. But things are so ugly between the two of them right now. I mean, basically she's making a lot of fuss about something that isn't a big deal; so she'll have to live in this terrible house for a summer, maybe six months. It's not earthshaking. But she's so mad at Dad. As if he'd done it on purpose. When, if it was anyone's fault, it was that moronic Realtor's. And you know the way Mom and Dad are—they don't actually talk about stuff."

"Maybe they didn't want to discuss it in front of you," Harry suggested.

Eleanor shrugged. "Maybe."

As the morning wore on, it got hotter and hotter in the attic. Gradually the piles of boxes were shifted from one side of the attic to the other. The tag sale pile grew, increased by a Waring blender, a fondue pot, stacks of plates, cast-iron candlesticks, glass soufflé dishes, and an immense pewter platter in the shape of a fish.

When he'd sorted through all the wedding gifts, Harry said, "I want to look through my boxes before I put them in storage." He looked at his watch. "What time were you going back to the city?"

"I can pick the boys up at Jared's anytime before eight."

"I'll give you a ride back, then, if we can be done by five."

Eleanor looked at the remaining boxes on her side of the attic, which were labeled 12-24 MOS. SUMMER and 3T-4T, designating Simon's toddler period. "If I can't get this done by five, it'll be nervous breakdown time anyway."

Harry turned to the cartons he'd stacked under the window and opened the ones that said PAPERBACKS. Within seconds he had forgotten about Eleanor as he scanned the spines of the books: *Tristram Shandy, Tom Jones, Pamela.* Soon he had all the books out of the boxes in piles on the floor.

When he turned around to move the cartons to the tag sale pile, he noticed that Eleanor wasn't there. Some of the boxes of the boys' clothes had been opened and sorted through. Harry glanced at the stairs. She'd probably just gone down to the bathroom.

But ten minutes went by. He zipped through a box of old clothes. And a box of photo albums. He looked again at his watch and went down the stairs. He found her sitting disconsolately in what had been her bedroom, sniffling.

"It's okay, I'm just about done," she said in a strangled voice. "Done crying, I mean." She sniffed powerfully. "It was just . . ." Her voice trailed off, and she started to gulp. On her knee she spread out a baby's undershirt, yellowed at the neck. "They were so *little,*" she whispered. "And things turned out so wrong."

Harry sat down next to her and put an arm around her. "Look, let's get this finished," he said. "I'm just about done; I can help you with the clothes." He hesitated for an instant and added, "You know, El, you probably don't hear this from one month to the next, but you do a great job with the boys."

Eleanor turned to him, face crumpling. "Oh, Harry. You're awfully nice to say so." She stood up and straightened out the bedspread and the rumpled pillow. "Okay," she said, standing in the doorway. "I feel better." So Harry followed her upstairs.

"Now, look," he said when they got back up to the attic. "Do we really need to go through these at all?"

Eleanor heaved a sigh. "Yes. Some of the stuff I want to keep."

"What are you going to keep it for?" asked Harry, surprised. "Are you planning on having more children?"

"For my grandchildren," Eleanor said with exaggerated dignity. "Of course I'm not going to have any more children. I'm thirty-eight years old, and I haven't been on a date in five years. Let's get serious."

They worked in silence for a few minutes, then Harry said, "You really haven't been on a date since you got divorced?"

"Yep."

"But Ellie . . ."

"You know what the statistics are. Listen, I'm lucky that I've even *been* married."

"I guess," said Harry, unconvinced. "How long has it been since you had a vacation?" he asked, piling shoes on top of a ragged sweatshirt.

"We went to Disneyland last year, remember?"

"No, *you*. By yourself."

"Me? Oh, umm . . . well, it wasn't a vacation, but I spent a night in the Village with my friend Sophy last fall. It was great."

"Well, why don't you take some time off?"

"Oh, come on, Harry. How would I do that?"

"Doesn't your firm give you much time off?"

"Sure, but what about the boys? What would I do about them? Besides, I like to spend time with them."

"Yes, but surely you fantasize sometimes about going someplace alone." Harry persisted. "If you could go anywhere for a week by yourself, where would you go?"

Eleanor sat back on her heels, considering. "I think I'd have a week in Venice. I'd just wander around and look at pictures and eat and eat some more. And never wash a dish or make a bed or read anything more serious than a guidebook."

"Well then," said Harry more briskly. "Could the boys stay with Jared?"

"Not a chance. The carpets in that apartment are white," Eleanor said, as if concluding an argument.

Harry was silent for a minute, carefully folding a small raincoat. "I'll take them."

Eleanor just looked at him. "You're out of your mind."

"No. You'll have to work around my schedule, but I can take some time off in June or July. Mom and Dad will be in the new house. Maybe I'll take them up there."

Eleanor was silent for a moment. "I can't afford it," she said.

"You don't even know what it would cost," Harry countered. "You're trying to think of excuses not to go."

"No, I'm not." He looked straight at her, and her eyes fell. "Well, maybe I am. But I still can't see it."

"I just think a real vacation would be good for you," Harry said. "You deserve a treat."

"I'll think about it," she said, but that wasn't enough for Harry.

"No, Eleanor. I'll call you with the dates in a couple of days, and then if you don't get on the phone with your travel agent, I will."

Eleanor looked at him with eyes welling. "I guess I can't protest anymore."

"No."

"Well, what can I bring you as a present?"

"I could use some wineglasses," Harry said. "From Murano. With twisted, colored stems. You can carry them back on the plane and curse me every time you kick them."

"Hardly likely," Eleanor replied. "Venice, huh?" She smiled as she opened the next box.

A FEW hours later Harry was back in his apartment. Though he hadn't confessed as much to Eleanor, his heart sank whenever he walked in the door. The apartment didn't seem to belong to him anymore. It would probably be a good idea to get Gretchen's quilts and dried flower arrangements boxed up. Harry found them almost unbearable to look at.

It wasn't so much that he'd really thought he and Gretchen would marry. Maybe at first, when they'd only been going out for a few months and had spent a lot of time talking about movies and books; then, Harry might have been making vague assumptions about a rosy future. Gretchen had been an assistant at one of the Condé Nast magazines. She spent half of her salary on good shoes and two-hundred-dollar haircuts and lived in a dreary studio apartment in Queens. She devoted her weekends and nights to writing short stories. Harry had found the combination charming—the worldly life during the day, the life of art at night. After she moved in with him, Gretchen took fiction-writing classes after work. She was also promoted, having discovered a knack for writing fashion captions.

Looking back, Harry thought things had started to fall apart when Gretchen began wearing her long blond hair in braids. The silky plaits signaled her growing contempt for her milieu. Her entire style changed. She gave up caffeine and drank rose-hip tea. She bought a handmade mug to drink it from. She discovered Indian-print fabric, having been too young for it the first time around.

Then she applied to the Iowa Writers Workshop. By this time Harry was only sad. The thing about Gretchen was, she spoke his language. Their minds worked the same way. Harry had thought that was what you built a relationship on. And if it wasn't, what was?

But what made it worse was Gretchen's parting lecture about how Harry was wasting his talent writing for soap operas. He had sold out, she claimed. When she told him he was a cynical luxury-loving idler, it was a real betrayal. It revealed to him that she had misunderstood him all along.

He did like luxury; that he conceded. His apartment—before the quilts—was a serene renovated loft in the West Twenties, all Biedermeier and silver silk. He loved good clothes and ate out whenever he felt like it.

But he was not cynical. Gretchen had assumed that Harry was exploiting his talent in a form he despised, simply because he craved the money he could make. The truth was that he enjoyed his work. He loved manipulating the characters, and he had a priceless facility for inventing plots. In the industry, Harry was highly respected. He had won several Emmys and was, at thirty-two, one of the youngest head writers in the business.

But in the end Gretchen hadn't taken him seriously. It was bad enough that his mother was still waiting for him to settle down and get a "real" job. But when even your girlfriend considers you a lightweight, Harry thought, you have a problem.

He sighed as he looked around the living room. He unhooked a wreath of twigs from the wall nearest him and tossed it onto the kitchen counter. Maybe he shouldn't even wait until the weekend to purge his apartment of Gretchen's knickknacks. But he was due at dinner downtown. Leaving the wreath on the counter, Harry went off to take a shower.

George Sinclair was one of his newer friends. Harry had wandered into George's first one-man show at a Fifty-seventh Street gallery and had gone back, liking the huge historical paintings. He had finally bought one, and the dealer had taken Harry down to George's studio. The friendship had blossomed from there.

The two men had a great deal in common. They both read a lot, they liked the same kind of movies, and were interested in wine. Harry especially enjoyed the great pleasure George took in life—and George's love life was as hapless as his own.

For George, having reached the age of thirty-five, was ready to settle down. He was a man created for domesticity. He cooked, he cleaned, he ironed, he loved doing laundry. But in spite of his good looks, his charm, and his hunger for commitment, George had been unable to find a wife.

When Harry appeared at his door that evening, George, wearing an apron, let him in and said, "I'm basting. I'll be right with you," then disappeared into the kitchen. Harry followed him, looking around appreciatively, as he always did.

George also lived in a loft, but it was the very opposite of Harry's precious space with its bleached wood floors and matched settees. George had twenty-five hundred square feet of raw space that was still all but raw. At one end of the loft he had built a log cabin that he used as a bedroom. At the other end a plush Victorian sofa and a massive sideboard flanked an oak dining table, while a pegboarded wall, a butcher-block counter, and old restaurant fixtures comprised the kitchen. In between the two areas of civilization was the expanse George needed for his paintings.

The smell of garlic and roasting meat had met Harry at the door, and when he walked into the kitchen, George was just finishing basting four Cornish hens. Harry perched on a stool and watched George painstakingly drizzle fat onto a tiny drumstick. "There's a bottle of Stag's Leap chardonnay in the fridge," George said.

Harry looked speculatively at the hens. "Did you marinate them?"

"Yes. In soy sauce, with garlic and honey," George answered, closing the oven.

"How was your week?" Harry asked, opening the wine.

"Mixed," George said. "I got a job." He led the way to the sofa, carrying his wineglass and a plate of cheese and bread.

Harry followed, sitting in the wicker basket chair at an angle to the sofa. "So what's the job? You're not waiting tables?"

"Teaching," George said, leaning over to press a wedge of goat cheese onto some bread. "Teaching art at an extremely expensive, extremely stuffy boys' school on the Upper East Side. The boys call me sir. It's very odd."

"How will you have enough time for painting?" Harry said.

"No more movies. No dinners out. And no Edith." Edith was the current girlfriend—a tiny, humorless dancer who had pursued George ever since New Year's Eve.

"What school are you teaching at?" Harry asked.

"Place called Avalon. Right next to the river."

"Have you met a boy named Toby Gray?"

"I'm not sure. What does he look like?"

"Handsome, in a child-model way. Blue eyes."

"Oh, yes. Third grade. Precocious little kid."

Harry laughed. "Probably. He's my nephew."

George looked at him and laughed in turn. "No wonder. He looks just like you. Birds are done. Let's eat."

It wasn't until an hour later, when the birds had been reduced to bones, that Harry said, "You said the week had been mixed. Which part is good and which part bad?" He folded his hands to listen, eyes gleaming with interest.

George leaned back in his chair. "I don't really know. Edith . . ." He sighed and swallowed some wine. "She was a mistake, of course. But she was so aggressive, and I kept thinking I'd straighten things out with her next week, so . . . I guess having her out of my life is a good thing. Do you want coffee?"

Harry answered, "Sure."

George got up and took the plates with him into the kitchen. When he came back, he sat down again and said, "I'm very discouraged. The problem is, all the women I meet think I'm incredibly hip because I'm a painter, and they all expect me to stay up till four a.m. and dance at clubs. Meanwhile, all I want to do is have a good dinner, make love, and go to sleep at eleven so I can get up and paint in the morning."

"I know what you mean," Harry said bleakly. "I know there are lots of single women out there; all I have to do is listen to my sister talk about them. But why are the right ones so hard to find?"

"Why don't you have your sister set you up with someone?" George asked.

"She's seven years older than I am," Harry answered dismissively. "I don't think many of her friends would be all that interested in me."

"You'd be surprised," George countered. "I think people aren't as rigid about women being younger than their mates anymore. Is this Toby's mother, then? Wait a sec, I'll get the coffee."

Harry raised his voice as George clattered around in the kitchen. "Right. Eleanor. I spent the day helping her clean her stuff out of my parents' attic. She has a helpless streak. She's a lawyer, so she makes some money. She manages the kids and the job, but getting a bunch of boxes out of the attic was too much for her. I found her crying over a baby undershirt," Harry finished.

"I think that's sweet," said George, setting down the coffee cups.

"Well, it was pretty pathetic. Anyway, she's going to return the favor next weekend and help me send Gretchen's stuff to Iowa City. Maybe I'll buy another one of your pictures to put where her log-cabin quilt was."

George ruminated for a minute. "I don't think I have anything that shape, but why don't you let me do a fresco for you? A dealer is negotiating a commission for me to do a mural of Venice for a new Italian restaurant. I'd like to try fresco, and I can practice on your wall. Actually, I'm going to Venice for a research trip."

"First Eleanor, now you," Harry said. "Maybe I should go to Venice, too, to forget my sorrows."

"What do you mean?" George asked, pouring more coffee.

"El hasn't had a vacation from her kids—ever—so I talked her into going to Venice for a week while I take care of the boys. And now you. Where are you going to stay?"

"I don't know," George answered. "I was going to stay with a friend, but his wife just had a baby."

"I know a really nice place," Harry offered. "Right on the Giudecca Canal, so you can have a water view, but it's not too noisy or expensive. Let me write it down for you." Harry walked over to the desk and wrote down the address. "Actually, I gave the address to Eleanor, too. Pensione Inghilterra. You might be there at the same time. You should keep an eye out for her."

"I will," George said, nodding. "Will I recognize her? Does she look like you?"

"Not much," Harry answered, heading back to the table. "She's tall, big-boned. Like you. Lots of hair, kind of a mess, but some people might think it's attractive. It's brown, her hair. Green eyes. Sort of perpetually rumpled-looking."

"Well, I'll know her if I see her," George said. "Would I like your sister?"

"Oh, I think so," Harry answered. "But maybe it would be better if you didn't mention me. If you do meet her."

"Sure, fine," George said, shrugging. "But why?"

"Oh, it would be nice for her to get away from everything—her family, her kids. If she knows you're a friend of mine, she might, I don't know, feel less free."

"Well, we probably won't overlap anyway," George said. He looked at his watch. "You know, do you want to try to catch that new István Szabó movie? We can make it if we hustle."

So they hustled, and by the time Harry got home, he was too tired to be depressed about his love life.

4

THE next few weeks were hell for Frances. Getting ready for the move was not the problem. She had always found solace in being busy. But even the constant bustle—days filled with lists, measurements, and focus on detail—couldn't distract her for long from feeling miserable. The prospect of moving to what she privately thought of as that horrible house lay like a black cloud on every moment. As she moved around the Chester house being efficient, every decision she made saddened her. As the moving date neared, her conviction grew—the whole plan was a terrible mistake.

She dreaded the move and felt cut adrift. But at the same time she felt she was behaving badly. She should have been able to adapt, to simply accept a few months of life in a house she didn't care for. Frances knew she shouldn't be making such a fuss.

So she tried not to fuss. She didn't tell anyone about her disappointment or apprehension. In truth, she had become something of a loner since the children had grown. Though she had many friends, she had no real intimates. She had never been the kind of woman who sat over a glass of iced tea and complained about her husband.

Hart knew his wife was unhappy. But what was he supposed to do, beat his breast and tear his hair out? Every time he thought Frances had gotten over her snit, she would remind him, in the politest possible way, that he was a boor and an oaf and her life was in ruins. Or something to that effect. And he was tired of it.

What Hart didn't realize was that Frances was really trying. She believed that somehow, if she could remain civil, everything would work out. But all the time, anxiety and anger were simmering away, and sometimes they escaped in little bursts of nastiness that only made her feel worse afterward. She was tired of it, too.

THE move itself went as smoothly as these things ever do. The movers had been in the house for days, packing crystal and china, and taking the red-tagged things to long-term storage and the green-tagged things to a short-term warehouse. Frances moved among them with her clipboard, pitching in wherever she was needed, and Hart had to temporarily abandon resentment for admiration. Frances, for her part, felt more cheerful than she had in weeks.

As the two of them sat on the terrace on the last night eating chicken salad off paper plates, Hart said, "Well, I have to hand it to you. I've never seen such organization in my life." He paused. "You know, leaving here makes me very sad." He looked over at Frances. "They've been good years."

She nodded. "I know. Me, too." And when Hart reached out his hand, she put hers in it. It was an olive branch, and it made her feel a little better. They sat there for a few minutes looking out on the lawn where their children had learned to walk, where the tent had been pitched for Eleanor's wedding.

The next day the hostilities resumed over the matter of the master-bedroom ceiling.

While Frances had been organizing the move, it had been Hart's job to ready the new house. They had agreed to do a minimum of work, since they would put the house on the market immediately. Frances had certain requirements. The red kitchen must be painted white. (It took six coats.) The geometric and ballerina wallpapers upstairs must disappear; Frances wasn't fussy about how. The swinging saloon doors into the kitchen and the rococo mirrors in the dining room were also removed.

Though she didn't mention the mirror on the ceiling of the master bedroom, Hart knew that he'd have to get rid of it. Most of the work he had done himself, but he needed professional help to remove the mirror. As it happened, the contractor recommended by friends was at his Florida house and wouldn't be back in Weymouth until mid-June. Hart decided he would wait and be sure the job was done right. Meanwhile, he repainted the shutters and window boxes dark green, and as a goodwill gesture bought a flat of white impatiens and laboriously transplanted them into the window boxes, where they would wither—though he didn't know this—in the direct sun.

On the day of the move Frances left Chester early in the station wagon packed with clothes, bedding, pots and pans. Hart waited until the movers left, then drove the Mercedes up, reaching Weymouth late in the afternoon. The movers were already there, and Frances was directing the placement of the furniture.

What Hart noticed first when he walked in was the sofas. They were upholstered in a cheery pink-and-blue hydrangea print, and they looked, in that rustic living room with its antler chandelier and plaid curtains, like Barbara Cartland in the Wild West.

It was too bad about the barn siding, Hart thought, running his finger along it as he walked upstairs, but he pried back a little and discovered the studs beneath it. Damn! A splinter. Hearing voices from the former geometric-papered bedroom, he poked his head in.

"Yes, that lamp there, and there should be room for the night

table between the two beds," Frances was saying. She turned when he came in and looked at him as if her eyes were knives and she were filleting him for dinner. "So glad you could join us," she said. "When you've recovered from your drive, perhaps you could see to the things in the front bedroom. I've had your desk put in there."

Hart nodded. He walked across the hall, whistling "The British Grenadiers," and set to work shifting furniture around. He had noticed, as he was supposed to, that one of their bedside lamps was on the night table in the room with the painted-over geometric paper. And the other was in what he thought of unconsciously as his room. Where the offending mirror still hung from the ceiling, reflecting the king-size bed.

They had dinner that night at the pine table, surrounded by the ice-blue metallic paisley wallpaper of the dining area. Outside, the Sound had flattened to a glassy gray in the sunset calm. The sky had taken on a remote pearly tone, flushed with coral where it met the horizon. As Frances came out of the kitchen carrying two plates of Stouffer's chicken divan, Hart said, "Isn't it just beautiful?"

Frances put his plate in front of him. "I suppose so." She sat and began eating. There was a long pause.

"All in all, I thought the move went very well," Hart said. "You did a tremendous job organizing it all."

Frances raised her eyebrows, but didn't answer.

Hart put his fork on his plate with a little emphasis and it clattered onto the table. "Would you care to tell me what you are sulking about?"

"I am not sulking," she said, eyes blazing, jaw tight. "I am *tired.*"

"Nonsense, Frances. You're behaving like a child, so why don't you just spit it out. Why are you so angry?"

She hunched a shoulder and took a sip of wine. "If you can't figure it out for yourself, I could hardly tell you," she answered. "I think I'll go to bed now. Would you mind doing the dishes?"

"Not in the least," Hart answered, staring into the middle distance. He sat where he was, stoically forking in chicken and broccoli while Frances took her barely touched plate into the kitchen.

When Hart went upstairs, he noticed that the door of the geometric-papered room was shut. The master bedroom was empty, the enormous bed made up, spotlit and reflected in the ceiling mirror. Hart walked across the hall, knocking on the closed door.

"Come in."

His wife was sitting up in one of the twin beds, reading *Mapp and Lucia.* She looked up at him defiantly.

"What is going on here?" Hart asked wearily. "Why are you sleeping in this room?"

"I told you I would not sleep in that room while that mirror was on the ceiling," Frances answered. "It's still there. So I'm here."

"Would it help if I told you that the contractor who I want to help me with that mirror is in Florida and is going to come take it down in a couple of weeks?"

"Not particularly," said Frances.

"Oh," Hart answered, nodding as if she were being perfectly logical. "In other words, I sleep alone until the mirror's gone."

"That's right," agreed Frances. "I think I'm going to turn my light out now."

"Oh. Well. Sweet dreams," her husband said, and stalked across the hall.

In the middle of the night, when she woke up, Frances had no idea where she was. The square of light at the window was in the wrong place, and her husband's warm bulk was nowhere to be found. Then she remembered and settled herself to go back to sleep, still angry.

ELEANOR and Harry came to visit the next weekend. Jared was taking the boys to East Hampton, and Eleanor took the Friday afternoon off so she and Harry could leave New York early. As they drove up to the house, Harry said, "My, this house really is ugly." He sat for a moment looking at it through the windshield, then got out. "Can't wait to see inside."

Frances was out, so their father gave them an oddly neutral tour. Not "This is the living room, can you believe those curtains?" or "This is the living room, isn't it a swell view?" but "This is the living room. This is the dining room. This is the kitchen."

As they walked up the stairs, Eleanor's flowered skirt snagged on the barn siding. Everyone paused on the stairs, waiting silently as she bent down to detach it. Nobody mentioned the folly of paneling an interior wall in a high-traffic area with old, splintery wood. And nobody said anything as Hart showed them the master bedroom, with his desk and reading lamp, the guest room where Eleanor would sleep, or the geometric-papered room, where Frances' needlepoint and water glass by the bed trumpeted her occupancy.

Later, sitting on the end of the dock, Eleanor said, "It doesn't look good."

Harry, with his eyes shut and his face lifted to the last of the afternoon sun, answered soberly, "Nope. I was all ready to suggest a big party for their fortieth anniversary. I thought it might give Mom something fun to think about. But I'm not sure they'll feel much like celebrating." Out in the Sound, a Boston Whaler puttered by. Harry sat up and watched it, shading his eyes with one hand. "Listen." Harry suddenly turned to his sister. "Let's give them a Whaler for their anniversary."

"A what?" Eleanor asked, confused.

"A Boston Whaler. One of those motorboats." Harry pointed to the little boat. "They could have a lot of fun with it."

Eleanor looked at him sharply. "But—" She paused for a minute, trying to assess her objections. "It would be more of a present for Dad," she said. "Mom wouldn't enjoy it very much."

"She might, though," Harry answered. "Maybe she could be won over. And it would give them something in common."

Eleanor stared at him suspiciously. "You're plotting, Harry. Mom's not some character on your soap."

"I know, but it might work. Look, here she comes."

Harry and Eleanor both turned toward the house as their mother came out the Dutch door and walked across the dock. As she looked at them, her heart softened. They might have been teenagers sitting on someone's dock in Watch Hill, surreptitiously letting their cigarettes drop into the water at her approach. In fact, there was something about the way they stopped talking . . . Well, of course—they'd been talking about her. They'd seen the bedrooms. They'd figured out that she and Hart weren't sleeping together. She felt suddenly weary as she sat down next to them on the dock. For a moment she considered explaining, but the force of habit was too strong. It was unnatural to complain about Hart to anyone, let alone to his children. So she merely said with an attempt at a smile, "You two look like a Ralph Lauren ad, sitting here."

"Well, Harry does," Eleanor amended. "It's quite a house, Mom."

"Isn't it, though?" Frances answered with a tight little smile. "Your father thinks it's nifty."

"But you don't," Harry stated.

Frances glanced back at the roof. "Not exactly," she said, with creditable smoothness. "It's not quite what I had in mind."

Eleanor looked at her mother. "You know, this really is a beautiful spot. You guys should have a party while you're here. It's a perfect place for it."

"You must be joking," Frances said a bit coldly.

"Well," Eleanor plunged on, "the house is awful, but you could do something outside. Some kind of anniversary party."

"El's right," put in Harry helpfully. "Have everybody out on the deck. You could have a huge cocktail party."

"You can't ask people to drive three hours and just give them drinks," Frances protested, drawn into the scheme despite herself.

Harry shrugged. "Make it a buffet. Something simple. Chili. I can come up early and help."

"Oh, no." Frances frowned. "You'd have to do something a little more substantial. Maybe poached salmon."

"Okay," Harry said, catching Eleanor's eye. "We'll do poached salmon, dill sauce, maybe some cucumbers."

"And strawberry fool for dessert," Frances said, envisioning it all.

"Look, here comes Dad," Eleanor said, as Hart stepped onto the dock carrying a small tray with beer bottles and a glass of wine on it.

"Dad, we're planning your fortieth anniversary party," Harry announced. "A buffet on the deck for fifty of your very best friends."

Hart, handing Frances her wineglass, shot a startled glance at Harry. "Oh? And when is this going to be?"

"Late June," Harry answered smoothly. "Does that sound all right, Mom?"

In fact, it didn't. The whole idea was anathema to Frances. Why invite fifty people to see this ghastly place? "I don't know, Harry," she protested. "After all the work of the move."

"I'll be here to help," Harry said.

"It would be fun," Eleanor chimed in.
"I think it's a splendid idea," Hart added.
There didn't seem to be any graceful way out of it. "Well, why not?" Frances said with a sigh.

5

ENTERTAINING had never come easily to Frances. She did it often, she did it well, but it always entailed hours of planning and pages of lists. She was a hostess of the old school, insisting on lots of flowers, real glasses and china. In the new house, every detail that had been standard in the Chester house managed to look out of place. The silver candelabra, placed on the table in the dining area, demonstrated that the Venetian chandelier was tacky. In the living room the two chintz sofas huddled together against the tastelessness of the boulder-faced fireplace wall and the hideous curtains. The flowers, which Frances had arranged to look like a spontaneous gathering from a phenomenally well-stocked meadow, somehow looked like a funeral arrangement when she placed them in the living room.

"How I hate this house," she muttered to Eleanor as she put a stack of gold-rimmed plates on the table in the dining area. "Everything in it is wrong. Do you know that?"

"Oh, come on, Mom. It's a gorgeous night; everybody will spend the whole time on the deck."

"Until they're eaten alive by mosquitoes," Frances said bitterly.

"You've got the citronella candles. It'll be fine. And you look great."

Though she would have liked to object, Frances knew this was true. She had gone to New York and had bought an immensely expensive dress in periwinkle blue silk. With it she wore her grandmother's triple strand of pearls and her mother's matching pearl bracelets.

"Thank you, dear," Frances said, and leaned over to kiss her daughter on the cheek. "So do you."

Eleanor raised her eyebrows. She had never had the confidence in her looks that Frances and Harry shared. She had put on what she thought of as her party dress—bronze taffeta with a full skirt and a low neck. An unusually frank saleswoman had talked her into buying it by pointing out that it made the most of her shoulders and camouflaged her hips. The bronze color brought out the chestnut in her hair, and Harry had often admired the way the dress made her look like an expensive *Belle Époque* courtesan.

"Mom!" shouted Toby, skidding into the dining room. "Can you come help Simon with his tie?"

"Can you spare me?" Eleanor asked Frances.

"Yes, of course," Frances said, turning to her list.

"It's not Simon," Toby whispered as they reached the second floor. "Harry and Granddad can't get that mirror down." He knocked importantly on the master-bedroom door, and Hart peered out, then beckoned them in and shut the door behind them.

Inside the bedroom was a scene of barely suppressed chaos. A drop cloth on the bed was littered with chips of paint and plaster. Harry, in an immaculate white shirt and steel-gray linen pants, was up on a tall stepladder, squinting into the space between the mirror and the ceiling. Hart, in his party uniform of blue blazer and bow tie, went to the bottom of the ladder and peered up.

"As far as I can tell, it's *welded,*" Harry said.

"Oh, come on," Hart answered disgustedly.

Harry reached a hand in farther and tried to jiggle something. "Well, you can get up here and feel for yourself. It's like a giant hook and eye, welded shut."

"Why in hell would anybody do that?" Hart exclaimed.

"They wanted to be able to relax during their bedtime fun and games," Harry suggested, descending the ladder.

"So now what?" Harry asked, looking up at the mirror.

"It's probably sturdier than anything else in this whole house," Hart commented. "But we've got to get rid of it."

"Why?" Toby asked.

"Gran doesn't like the way it looks," Eleanor put in quickly. "Toby, the guests are going to be here any minute. Can you go make sure Simon is really getting dressed?"

"Oh, okay," Toby said, reluctant to leave what he sensed was a crisis, though his mother was clearly holding out on him about its true nature.

"Well, we can't get it down," Harry said flatly.

"Then we have to hide it," Hart said. "Your mother doesn't want her friends to see it, and the contractor who was supposed to take it down yesterday called this morning to say he was still in Florida."

Harry shot a glance at his father and said to Eleanor, "Mom's exact words were, 'If Clara Henschel sees that mirror, I will never live it down.' "

He looked at his watch. "Dad, you painted the kitchen, didn't you? Is there any paint left?"

"You're going to *paint* it?" Eleanor said. "It'll look ridiculous."

"I know. But what else can we do? It's a quarter to six."

Hart interrupted. "I think Harry's right. I have some white latex left over."

Harry unknotted his tie and handed it to his sister. "El, do you have something I can put over my hair? And Dad," he said as his father started to leave the room, "don't forget a small brush for the edges."

"I know, I know," Hart said, his voice receding as he went down the stairs.

AN HOUR and a half later the party was in full swing. The long driveway was lined with discreet foreign sedans. The noise of fifty confident, well-bred, well-fed pillars of the community drowned out the rhythmic hush of the waves and spilled out across the scrubby grass. Inside the house, a local teenager in a clip-on bow tie tended bar very competently. Toby and Simon, now wearing their school blazers and ties, squirmed through the crowd, shaking hands here and there where they couldn't evade grown-up attention and pestering the bartender for maraschino cherries. Pairs of men and women ambled across the lawn to the dock.

The deck was hugely popular. Retired stockbrokers propped their behinds and drinks on the broad railing, gesturing expansively at the Sound, talking about yacht clubs and property values. Meanwhile, their wives took tours of the house.

Frances had wondered, in the days before the party, exactly what line she should take about the house. Pretend it was all right? But her friends would know it wasn't. Permit herself to express irritation with Hart for having bought the wretched place? Not on her fortieth wedding anniversary. In the end, she settled on rueful relish: "Isn't it ghastly? Can you *believe* the taste?"

This tack involved special attention to the dining-room chandelier, the kitten wallpaper in the downstairs bath, the window seats and curtains, and the barn siding on the stairs. "Upstairs isn't as bad," she said over and over again. "Hart took down the ghastly wallpaper in the bedrooms. One of them made me absolutely dizzy, it was so bad!" It did occur to her to wonder what Hart had finally done about the mirror, but as she was on her way up to look, a fuse blew in the kitchen and she got sidetracked.

The guests who did go upstairs didn't find much to look at. Frances had moved her things back into the master bedroom, though anybody who looked in the closets—as some women, of course, did—would realize that all her clothes were in the bedroom across the hall. Really the only odd thing was the strong smell of paint in the master bedroom and that streaky slab over the bed.

"Do you think it's supposed to be some kind of modernist reference to a canopy bed?" said Lucy Whittall to Joan Failey, gesturing at the ceiling. Lucy was a docent at the Metropolitan Museum and never let anyone forget it.

"I don't think it knows what it's supposed to be," croaked Joan in her cigarettes-and-whiskey tenor. "Hope they don't suffocate in paint fumes tonight." She moved over to the window. "Still, it's a view to die for."

"Hmm. It looks like a late Kensett," mused Lucy. And she added on a more practical note, "I'd be a little frightened here in a storm."

"They'll be gone by hurricane season," predicted Joan.

"Oh, really?" Lucy asked, turning to go back downstairs. "Have they found something else?"

"Not that I know of," Joan answered, "but that was the original game plan. Once . . . you know, they realized," she said with a gesture that made her gold bangles clatter.

"Realized Hart had bought this monstrosity, you mean," Lucy said. "Honestly, how anybody could," she said, shaking her head as she went downstairs.

Frances had just sent another group upstairs when she glanced out the front door and saw an immense gleaming Bentley trundling up the drive. She put her glass of wine down on the bar and, smiling, went outside.

A short bowlegged man in a chauffeur's cap opened the back door of the Bentley. "Hello, Mr. Parker," Frances said to the little man. "How are you? Did you have a good winter?"

"Pretty good, thanks, Mrs. Drummond," the chauffeur answered. "You need some help in there, Mrs. Henschel?"

"Yes. Damn bracelet's hooked on my dress. Frances! Can you unhook this thing? Hate to snag the lace; it's real Chantilly."

"Here, scoot over into the light a bit," Frances said. "I've got it. Can you get out by yourself?"

"Well, now that you're halfway into the car, why don't you give me a good tug?" Clara said, holding out her hands.

Frances obliged, and Clara finally emerged from the car in a cloud of black lace and tulle.

"What a dress, Aunt Clara!" Frances said, kissing the older woman on the cheek.

"Chanel," Clara said succinctly. "Put on my best bib and tucker for you and Hart. My Lord, whoever built this ought to be shot," she said, taking a step toward the house. "Let me have my stick, Parker."

"Is your arthritis bad?" Frances asked, offering an arm for Clara to lean on.

"No, but it's a useful prop at a party," she answered, accepting the thin malacca cane with the carved ivory head. "Snag a waiter, trip a buffoon, pound the floor. In the unlikely event that I can't make myself heard," she added.

Clara Henschel had spent ninety-two years making sure that she was heard. She had been a great beauty and had married the son of a robber baron, who died; a French aristocrat, whom she divorced; an immensely successful songwriter, who divorced her; and a dry-cleaning millionaire who enjoyed ill health—and her occasional visits—in Palm Beach. She had been a great friend of Frances' mother's. When the mother died, she transferred her friendship to the daughter. The Drummond children adored her and visited her often at her splendid New York town house and her cottage at Fenwick, up the coast from Weymouth.

"My, my," Clara said as Frances helped her through the door. "Looks like a . . . You know, I don't know quite *what* it looks like," she said. "Why don't you settle me down here"—she pointed at a sofa with her cane—"and send me Harry with a strong martini?"

HARRY AND ELEANOR HAD ARGUED over exactly how to present the boat to their parents. Eleanor was all for driving it over early one morning and leaving it tied up on the dock. But Harry wanted a little more drama, so it was agreed that he would slip away from the party, drive to the marina where the boat was moored, and drive the boat back over to appear in front of the house with a flourish before the sun set. Toby and Simon, bored with the grown-ups' chatter, went with him to the marina.

Dinner had just been served, and the guests were all settled with their plates of salmon and asparagus. The roar of the conversation had died to a more polite don't-talk-with-your-mouth-full hum when Eleanor, standing on the deck, heard what she thought was an outboard motor. She stopped talking and cocked her ear.

"What?" asked her uncle Pete, who was, as he'd told Eleanor, loving the sight of "all these stuffy stockbrokers in a house built by an architect tripping on magic mushrooms."

Eleanor said, lowering her voice, "I thought I heard a motor. It's a surprise. We're giving Mom and Dad a Boston Whaler for an anniversary present so they can putter around on the water. Look! Here they come!"

And indeed, around the point came the little boat. Toby and Simon were standing in the stern, waving maniacally and jumping up and down, while Harry, looking incongruous in his Armani suit, steered in a graceful curve toward the dock.

"Umm, Mom?" Eleanor sidled through the crowd to her mother and beckoned to her father from across the deck. "Come on, Dad," she called. "It's a surprise!"

The guests all put their plates down and stepped out onto the deck. Clara Henschel, left in the living room with the teenage bartender, said imperiously, "Young man, please help me outside. I must see what's going on."

There, at the end of the dock, stood Frances and Hart, with Eleanor between them. Their voices could not be heard from the house, but their gestures were as clear as pantomime. Hart was grinning and turned to his wife with evident exhilaration. Frances, with a hand on her pearl necklace, was clearly dumbfounded. "She's wondering what the hell she's going to do with a boat," came Clara Henschel's voice, and several people watching the group chuckled. Hart bent down and held out his hand to Harry, who clambered a bit awkwardly onto the dock. For an instant the family group closed. Frances leaned forward and kissed her son. Her daughter moved closer, arm around her mother's waist. Then Hart took his wife by the shoulders and kissed her gently on each cheek.

As one, everyone on the deck and lawn started to clap. Clara Henschel said to the bartender, whose arm she was still clutching, "Is there any champagne?"

"Yes," he answered, "but I wasn't supposed to serve it until dessert."

"Never mind. Now's the moment. If you get in trouble, blame me," she said. So by the time Hart and Frances stepped back onto the deck, glasses of champagne were thrust into their hands and the Yale element was calling out, "Toast! Toast!"

Hart looked at Frances, who only shrugged her shoulders, so he climbed up onto the broad deck railing. He said in the silence, "I don't suppose you'd like to stand up here, too, Frances?" and added, when the laughter died down, "Never mind—she's got her own pedestal." He paused again, scanning the faces in front of him. "All I can say is thank you. Thank you to our friends, for coming here tonight. Thank you to our children, for this splendid surprise"—he waved in the direction of the boat—"and above all, thank you to Frances, for forty wonderful years." He jumped down from the railing and put his arm around Frances, who was blushing. He kissed her again on the cheek, and when her arm went around his waist, Hart felt satisfied. Surely that would placate her. After all, he'd just announced in front of fifty people that she was important to him. That he was fond of her. Whatever. He couldn't have put it more plainly, and she seemed to understand. Joan Failey, who had watched the whole thing with a sharp eye, raised an eyebrow and said to Lucy Whittall, "Well, maybe the closet space in the master bedroom is inadequate." Lucy Whittall only said, "Who knows?" and sat down again with her plate of salmon.

UP TO that moment the evening had been a sound success, a pleasant evening spent among friends. But after Hart's speech it took off into that memorable realm of really wonderful parties.

Every conversation seemed inspired. Frances, with a champagne glass in hand, finally relaxed, and when someone congratulated her on how comfortable she'd made the house, said, "I'm beginning to think we should have kept it just as it was, every horror in place, and charged admission!"

"Well, it's time for me to be going," Clara Henschel said, "so why don't you show me right now? Spare no details."

Frances helped Clara to her feet. "Stay away from that wall," Frances said as they started up the stairs. "The rustic touch won't do the Chantilly any good." She was beginning to wonder what Hart had done with the mirror. What if he hadn't been able to get it down? What if people had been looking into that room all night and seen that huge, obscene mirror hung over the bed?

"We've disguised the worst of it up here," Frances said, genuinely anxious now. "Hideous wallpaper." They peered into the bedroom she had been using, which was now strewn with Eleanor's clothes. "I don't know why I spent so many years yelling at Ellie to put her clothes away. It seems to have been a complete waste of breath," Frances said with undue irritation.

"Never mind," Clara said, crossing the hall. "She's a good girl. Got to find her another husband, though."

"Hush, Aunt Clara. The boys are still awake!" hissed Frances as they walked into the master bedroom.

"Oops. Sorry," said Clara unrepentantly. "I forgot. I need to sit for a moment," she said, perching on the side of bed. "Stairs were a bit ambitious. Grand view you get from here," she went on. "Do the waves keep you awake? Every time I come up here, I can't sleep for the first week or so. Sometimes I wonder why I bother keeping up the cottage, except that Gus loved it so much."

But Frances wasn't listening. She was looking at the mirror over the bed, which Hart hadn't removed.

It was the only thing she'd asked him to do. He knew how important it was to her. And all he'd done was slap a coat of paint on it.

Now all her friends had seen it. They'd probably known right away what it was. And suddenly Frances felt the tears start hot in her eyes. She tried to blink them back, but she couldn't control her face, and ignoring Clara's ongoing monologue, she ran into the brown marble bathroom. She pulled the door closed and sat on the edge of the bathtub with her head in her hands, weeping.

Once she'd begun, she couldn't stop. It wasn't just the mirror. It was the whole awful thing—the ghastly place they had to live in, Hart's callousness about how much she hated it, the frustration of trying to give a party there, having all her friends see that awful mirror. The tears welled up afresh with each new thought.

Clara tapped at the door. "May I come in?"

Frances sniffed. "Of course. I'm just blubbering away in here."

Clara stepped into the bathroom, closing and locking the door behind her. "My!" she exclaimed. "How unpleasant. Brown is such an odd choice for a bathroom." She leaned on her elegant stick and looked at Frances.

"Is Hart being odious?" she asked.

Frances dabbed at her eyelashes. "I don't know if Hart's being odious. I think he is, but apparently he doesn't see it that way."

Clara sat down on the lid of the toilet. "Do I gather the house is the problem?"

"You do," Frances said. "Aunt Clara, just how much nonsense do I have to put up with?"

Clara swung her cane. "You know, dear, much as I love to interfere, I don't think I can tell you that. You and Hart have always played your cards very close to the chest."

Outside, someone rattled the doorknob. "Just a moment," Clara sang out. "I'll only be a minute longer." She turned back to Frances. "You'd better powder your nose, dear, and get back to your guests."

Frances reached for her powder compact and sighed. "Oh, hell," she muttered, examining her pink nose. "I guess I'll have to stay outside in the dark for a while."

"You'll walk me to the car and have a nice long chat on the dock with Hart's brother, Pete," Clara recommended. "He's always thought the world of you, even if he does seem like a fool. Maybe he can cheer you up."

But even Pete's persiflage couldn't take away Frances' bleak, defeated feeling, and she was sure Harry noticed her red-rimmed eyes, but everyone else seemed oblivious as the party sparkled on. No one was more oblivious than Hart.

6

A WEEK later Eleanor flew off to Italy, and Harry brought the boys to Weymouth. On his first morning there, Toby came downstairs in his surfer shorts, poured himself a bowl of cereal, and planted himself at the table on the deck, where Frances was eating her toast. It was already a beautiful day. The air was perfectly clear and cool. "So, Gran," Toby said, "let's take the boat out to one of those islands today."

Frances looked at him over the pages of the paper. "What's your grandfather's game plan?"

"He's taking Harry and Simon to some museum," Toby said disgustedly.

Frances watched him, but didn't say anything. She did not, in fact, know how to drive the boat. She hadn't even been out in it, though several times when Hart wasn't at home she had walked out to the end of the dock to look at it.

She had been living in the house for a month now. Every now and then Frances mentally tested: Did she hate it any less? There were a few—a very few—good features. It had turned out that she and Hart ate most of their meals out on the deck. It was really quite pleasant, she conceded—the fresh air, the sound of the water, the magnificent view. It also meant she didn't have to look at the hideous wallpaper inside.

The master bedroom, too, had its advantages. The contractor had finally come and removed the wretched mirror. Frances noticed that it took a blowtorch, a hacksaw, and three burly men wearing wide leather weight-lifting belts to carry it, in a gingerly way, downstairs. When the contractor's truck drove away, Frances moved her things back into the master bedroom. Hart did not comment, but turned to her that night in bed and let her know he had missed her.

But there was nothing for her to do. She cooked the meals, naturally, and did the laundry and dishes. She had had lunch once or twice with friends and driven down to visit Clara Henschel, but time hung heavy on her hands. So why not explore the islands? she thought with a sudden rush of resolution.

"All right," she said to Toby. "I'll just get Granddad to show us how to drive the boat before he goes to the museum. And you'll have to wear a life preserver."

"Oh, Gran . . ." Toby objected.

Frances paid close attention to her driving lesson. She packed lunch and basted an unwilling Toby with sunscreen. She pored over one of Hart's charts. Just before eleven she and Toby drove away from the dock rather professionally and headed out into the Sound.

As she opened the throttle and the boat slapped over the waves, Frances' brow smoothed out. Feeling competent always cheered her up. The salty air rushed past, whipping the ends of the scarf she'd tied over her hair. She nudged the steering wheel an inch, and the boat responded, leaving a curve in the wake surging behind.

Farewell Island was their goal. It had picnic tables and a sandy beach where Toby and Frances could pull the boat ashore and have their picnic. Frances felt masterful as she cut the engine a few yards from shore, watching the sandy bottom loom up through the cloudy water.

She climbed cautiously overboard, landing in knee-deep water. "Come on. We're here."

She fixed the anchor and pulled the boat a bit farther out of the water. Toby threw his towel onto the sand and waded back into the water, intent on the tiny flickering fish.

Frances settled down in the sand to watch him. It was amazingly quiet. She leaned back on her elbows, closing her eyes. The sun baked into her, warming her very bones. It was peaceful. Hart would like this secluded little spot. He would be up on his feet, exploring the island, picking up remarkable pieces of dried seaweed or dingy pebbles striped with veins of pure quartz.

It was one of the things Frances had always liked about him—his energy and enthusiasm. But now that busyness was annoying. Hart adored life in the new house. He swam every day. He dug for clams at low tide—unsuccessfully, for the most part—and puttered around in the boat. He kept the birding glasses at hand and gloated over unusual sightings.

She didn't share his enthusiasm. She hated the narrow kitchen with its one silly window. They had moved the sofas three times without finding a really comfortable way to furnish the living room. It just wouldn't do.

They hadn't discussed moving. They'd been so busy getting ready for the party, and now with the boys here, Frances told herself. Somehow she felt she couldn't bring up looking for a new house.

"Gran, look!" Toby called. He scampered up to her holding out his sodden baseball cap, which contained three frantic minnows.

"Well done," Frances said. "And now what are you going to do with them?"

"I'm going to build them a water city," he said. "Want to help?"

"Yes, of course," said Frances, so they went down to the water's edge and started to dig.

ELEANOR, meanwhile, was reveling in the water city of Venice. From the moment her plane landed at Milan, she had been in a trance. All the way over on the plane she gloried in the fact that she could do exactly as she pleased. She read a novel for three hours straight. Didn't have to give her airline peanuts to one of her children. Monopolized the window.

Her dazed state lasted for hours, and afterward she could only remember odd details about her first day in Venice: her first glance of the city, hovering surrealistically on the surface of the lagoon; opening the window of her room in the Pensione Inghilterra, letting in the watery light reflected from the Giudecca Canal; the first taste of the risotto she had for lunch. She had spent most of the day just roaming, watching and listening and smelling and tasting, and feeling beneath her feet the old, worn paving stones of the Venetian alleys and bridges.

But by late afternoon the trance was wearing off. She became conscious of fatigue, and the ground felt unsteady, as if she'd just disembarked from an ocean voyage. She turned back to the *pensione* to take a nap.

It was easy enough to find, just a few doors down from the Church of the Gesuati on the Zattere. The café next door was busy, the tables full of tourists reviewing their days, comparing postcards, rewinding film. At the table closest to the door of the *pensione,* a man held a sketch pad on his lap and drew rapidly, looking not at the paper, but at the severe symmetrical lines of the Church of the Redentore across the water.

As Eleanor drew near, the artist put his pencil down and propped the sketch pad up straight to assess his work.

Eleanor paused, reaching into her bag for her room key, eyes on the sketch. Involuntarily she smiled. "It's lovely," she said, without even thinking to speak Italian.

The artist smiled up at her and looked back at the sketch in satisfaction. "Yes," he said contentedly. "It's very hard to make an ugly drawing in Venice. Do you think I should wash it? Color?"

Eleanor said seriously, "Only if you're sure you won't ruin it."

He reached absently for the wineglass on the table and studied his drawing. "That's always the risk. Still, I think just a blush. . . ." He bent down to open the box of paints on the ground beside him. Eleanor noticed suddenly that he was young and quite attractive.

"Well, good night," she said, grasping her key. "And good luck."

He glanced upward from his paint box. "Good night," he said. His gaze met hers, and he smiled again, a small, sweet smile. "Thanks."

Eleanor felt herself blushing as she went up to her room. And George Sinclair, following her with his eyes, wondered why Harry hadn't mentioned that his sister was incredibly alluring.

BY THE next morning the jet lag was gone, and Eleanor was ready for some serious sight-seeing. At college she had been an art history major, and some of her happiest moments with Jared had been the vacations in their early marriage, when they went from museum to art gallery to monument, discussing line and brushwork, iconography and composition. So over breakfast in the waterfront dining room she plotted her itinerary. Maybe St. Mark's first thing, then a quick spin through the Doges' Palace, then tea at Florian's.

As she looked up to see if her coffee was on the way, she saw the artist from yesterday standing in the doorway. He hesitated for a minute, scanning the tables, and she watched him. He was awfully attractive. Not really handsome; his features were a little too craggy for that. Too much nose, too much jaw. All a little larger than life. Thick, strong blond hair. Tall, too. Well over six feet, and sturdily built. She wondered how old he was; too young for her, that was sure. As she watched, the tall man's eye lit on an empty table for two, and he threaded his way between the tables to reach it. Hurriedly she turned her eyes to her Blue Guide as he walked past, conscious that she'd been staring. His girlfriend—he wore no wedding ring; she'd noticed that much the day before—was probably still getting dressed.

But he opened up a folder of papers, and by the time Eleanor had finished her rolls, no one had joined him. Which was odd because in Eleanor's experience, men who looked like that inevitably had mates. Thin girls in black with lots of hair and big earrings. Eleanor dismissed the thought of him and went upstairs.

It was a surprising day for Venice, clear and dry. Eleanor paused on the Accademia Bridge, looking up the Grand Canal, and watched the water of the canal sparkle where the morning sun sliced through the shadows.

Eleanor was an earnest tourist. Inside St. Mark's, she examined statues and paving stones. She admired the Pala d'Oro and, with waning enthusiasm, the reliquaries in the Treasury. Then she gave herself a rest at one of the tiny tables at Florian's before starting on the Accademia.

It was probably too much. By eleven thirty she was looking at a massive Tintoretto with a touch of irritation that had its roots, she recognized, in low blood sugar. There was no point in disliking paintings just because she was hungry, Eleanor thought. Better to come back when she was rested.

She turned abruptly for the door and bumped into the man from the *pensione.* He dropped the manila folder held under his arm, and the sketch pad and the pencil, and Eleanor felt her face flaming again as she stooped to pick things up.

"That was incredibly clumsy," she said in a resigned tone. "Here, do you have everything?" She held out the folder and the pad.

"Yes, I'm sure I do," he answered easily. "None of it's priceless anyway." He brushed a little dust off the sketch pad and turned it to show her. "See—your basic saint." He gestured up at a Vivarini polyptych. "Do you know who he is, by any chance?"

"Well, that one I think is Saint Peter," Eleanor offered. "Because of the keys."

"Of course, the keys," he agreed. "What about this one over

here?" He gestured to a freestanding panel in the middle of the room. "The one with that iron thing?"

Eleanor grinned. "That's Saint Lawrence, and that's his barbecue. That's how he was martyred. I think the story goes that halfway through he said to the men who were doing it, 'Gentlemen, I fear the other side is not yet well roasted.' Of course he's the patron saint of short-order cooks," she added, relishing the tale.

"Really?" His eyes slid over to look at her, unnoticed.

"Well." For Eleanor, that was often a sentence. It meant, Don't take me literally. She shrugged a shoulder.

He seemed to understand. "How do you know all this?"

"I was an art history major about a million years ago," she said, "and it stuck."

"So was I," he said ruefully, "and it didn't. My name's George Sinclair, by the way."

"Eleanor Gray," she said. There was an awkward little pause. George felt Eleanor starting to step back and mutter something about "see you later," or "must be going."

"I did ruin that sketch," he said to keep her standing there.

"You did? Oh, I'm so sorry. What did you do to it?" She was relaxing, distracted again.

"Spilled a glass of wine all over it," he said. He folded up his sketch pad and gestured toward the door. "Are you . . . ?"

"Yes," she said, falling into step with him, but still, he sensed, wary. "My eyes are pretty well stunned for the moment."

"Always a problem in Venice. It's very important to allow time for rest. I take a lot of naps when I'm here." They had reached the entrance of the museum. "Which way are you going?" he asked. "Would you have lunch with me?" The minute George had said it, he questioned his judgment. It had been an impulsive invitation, but now that he had started talking to Harry's sister, he didn't want to stop. There was something so beguiling about her. Something about intelligence she didn't mind showing, and a physical magnetism she seemed unconscious of. But now she looked startled. He went on, pretending that he hadn't noticed her alarm. "I know a very good little restaurant near here that does a wonderful fritto misto for two that I can't manage on my own. Of course, you may not like seafood," he finished.

They were standing outside the Accademia, in the little square in front of the bridge. Eleanor took a deep breath and felt annoyed at herself. Why was she so jumpy about a man asking her to have lunch with him?

"That sounds nice," she said temperately, and added, to make up for her lack of enthusiasm, "I love fish."

As THEY walked to the restaurant, Eleanor tried not to feel uncomfortable. Lunch. It was only lunch with a fellow tourist. An isolated incident. Everybody has to eat.

Even as she scolded herself, Eleanor recognized the source of her discomfort. They weren't having lunch to discuss the vagaries of a certain probate ruling or the complexities of the tax code. They were having lunch because—there was no way for Eleanor to avoid the thought—this man seemed to enjoy her company and want more of it. This was a situation that Eleanor had avoided ever since her divorce.

It hadn't been conscious. She had never set out to close herself off from romantic involvement. In fact, she sometimes wondered why it was that no one ever seemed to see her as anything besides an attorney or a mother. In truth, this was the defense she had unconsciously chosen.

But here she was in Venice, alone. Neither attorney nor mother. Faced with an attractive man who seemed attracted to her.

Of course, she was being ludicrous. Even to think that he had anything in mind . . . It was pathetic. She was at least five years older than he was. And she tuned in to his story about the time he'd been in Venice during a major flood.

George owed his great success with women to several factors. His looks, attractive but not intimidating, always helped with the initial approach. His open charm put everyone at ease. But his trump card was an almost uncanny sensitivity. More than one woman had accused him of reading her mind.

He was certainly reading Eleanor's. She walked along beside him, fading in and out of the conversation, focusing on some private argument she was having with herself. As they crossed a bridge, she was jostled by a flock of running boys. George put out an arm to steady her, and she all but flinched.

"It's just along here," he said to distract her, pointing to a tattered awning tangled with a flourishing grapevine. And he resolved, at that moment, to see if he couldn't get Eleanor Gray to unwind a little bit.

They both would have said lunch went well. There was a table in the courtyard, right next to a trickling fountain inhabited by a family of turtles. The waitress remembered George and asked him—fortunately in idiomatic Italian that Eleanor didn't catch—about the last woman he'd been there with. The wine, on an empty stomach, relaxed Eleanor. George managed to keep the conversation on interesting and completely impersonal topics. They ate the excellent fritto misto, and George noticed with approbation that Eleanor had no squeamishness about the little bits of calamari that looked like tentacles. (Edith had been a strict vegetarian.)

As they waited for coffee, George stretched out on the rickety folding chair and studied Eleanor. She was watching the turtles pursue their inscrutable turtle business in the moss of the fountain. The sun caught her bare arm, resting on the tablecloth. George looked at the freckles on her arm and the milky, private stretch above the elbow as it disappeared into her sleeve. He had a sudden strong urge to touch that skin, just the inside of her arm, with the back of his finger, the way a parent strokes a baby's cheek. He looked around for the waitress and drained his wineglass.

"We had turtles, growing up," Eleanor announced. "They were prettier than this. Green and yellow. I never liked to hold them, though, because of the way their little claws felt on my hands."

"I know the ones you mean. We'd find big brown turtles by the side of the road and make homes for them, but they always got boring after a few weeks, so we'd take them back to the lake." George glanced up at the waitress, who arrived with their coffee and the check, and looked back at Eleanor.

Eleanor stirred her coffee. "I think maybe it's the idea of being a turtle—you know, bask in the sun, take a little dip, bask some more." She yawned. "A little nap in the sun sounds so appealing. I haven't really adjusted to the time zone yet."

"You should go back and sleep a little now," George suggested. "Then by tonight you'll be on Italian time."

"Yes, I think I will," Eleanor said, bending down to get her wallet from her bag. She pulled out two ten-thousand-lira notes and put them on the tablecloth. "That looks about right," she said, and George could hear the echo of countless business lunches in dark restaurants near Wall Street. George didn't like it, but he let it pass. If splitting a lunch bill would calm Eleanor down, he'd split the bill.

They walked peacefully back to the *pensione.* Eleanor was rather pleased with herself. She'd had an enjoyable lunch. There'd been no fuss over paying, which eliminated any uncomfortable obligations. She was going to take a nap.

She and George got their keys at the desk and started up the wide staircase. On the second floor they turned along her hall. "My room's at the end," he said.

"This is me." Eleanor paused outside her door. "That was fun." She put the big old-fashioned key into the lock.

"Wait," George said. "I have a favor to ask. Do you think—" He paused and looked down. He felt awkward and was suddenly aware of the difference in their ages. "Could I draw you?" He looked back up and met her eyes.

Eleanor blushed. She could feel the color rising and flooding her cheeks. "Draw me? I don't think— What for?" she stammered.

Because I like the way your jaw meets your throat, George thought. Because the hair springs away from your temples. Because I think that under that gauzy skirt you have the body of a goddess. "Because," he finally said, "you have interesting features. And I'd like to see if I can catch the blue lights in your hair."

"Blue lights?" Eleanor said, pulling forward a lock of hair and frowning at it in puzzlement.

"Yes," he said. "You don't have to decide now. I'll be downstairs having a drink between six and seven. Just come and tell me. You're swaying on your feet. Go sleep." And he gently turned her around and urged her through her door.

7

ELEANOR slept. The sun crept around and turned yellow, then golden. George, returning sunburned and salty from the Lido, couldn't resist pressing his ear to her door. He heard her cough lightly and imagined opening the door and stepping in, but continued down the hall instead to take a lukewarm shower. By six o'clock he was back downstairs with his sketchbook. At six thirty Eleanor came and sat down opposite him.

She felt wonderful. She'd slept profoundly, the kind of deep, cushioned sleep she remembered from pregnancy. When she woke up, she simply stretched and lay in bed for a while, considering George Sinclair's proposition. When he'd made it, she had been taken aback. She hated thinking about her appearance, but she was powerfully curious. If he drew her, what would the drawing be like? Would he capture or reveal qualities she hadn't guessed at?

And so when she sat down opposite George in the café, her first words were, "Why not?"

"Why not what?" George asked, startled. Had she read *his* mind? For he had been sitting with his coffee, mapping out various avenues of approach. A dinner together, the Piazza San Marco at midnight, holding hands? A kiss during a Puccini aria? A drawing session that turned into love in the afternoon? Why not?

"I'll pose for you," Eleanor said, a little shyly now. "If you really want." But suddenly it seemed a little less simple. She had forgotten how compelling he was. Very male. She noticed for the first time the golden hair on the backs of his arms and glistening at his throat where he'd left the buttons of his shirt undone. And he was big, solid. He could probably pick her up and throw her over his shoulder. Not that she'd want him to, Eleanor told herself hurriedly. She said, "You don't want to do it now, do you?"

George, now in tune with her, held up his sketch pad. "Have a coffee and talk to me and don't think about what I'm doing."

"That's likely," Eleanor answered tartly. "When you're sitting there going scratch, scratch and telling me not to move my mouth."

George waved at the waiter. "I don't go scratch, scratch; I'm using pastels. And you can move your mouth as much as you want."

Eleanor nervously eyed the box of pastels George placed on the table. Even as he asked the waiter for another coffee, he was selecting his color—a russet brown. "Do you ever wear your hair up?" he asked abruptly.

Eleanor looked up, startled. It sounded creepy, like the kind of question an obscene caller would ask. "I thought it was my hair you wanted to draw," Eleanor said a bit sharply.

"That was before you bent over so gracefully," George responded, with half his mind on the paper before him.

It was the only kind of compliment Eleanor trusted. He wasn't even aware of what he'd said. He was concentrating on his drawing and the line of her neck. She bent down to her bag on the ground beside her, pulled out four of the fat tortoiseshell hairpins she bought at Caswell-Massey, and placed them on the table.

George took one and held it up to the light. "These are *wonderful!* Are they real tortoiseshell?"

"Probably not," Eleanor said, both her hands raised behind her as she twisted her hair. George hurriedly turned a page over and sketched the outline of her arms, thinking of Degas and Mary Cassatt. "Isn't real tortoiseshell illegal or cruel to endangered species or something?" Eleanor picked up another one and thrust it into the coil on the back of her head.

"It amazes me the way women can put their hair up without looking. It's all I can do to tie my sneakers."

"Men shave, though."

"Shaving's not an accomplishment; it's a chore," he said, happily tracing the line of her neck.

"Well," Eleanor said. "Tying a tie."

"Anyone can tie a tie. I bet you can tie a tie," George said.

"True."

"In fact," George said, looking up, "I'm willing to bet your mother always ties your father's tie when he wears a tuxedo."

Eleanor laughed, picturing her father and mother standing before the mirror over the fireplace in the Chester living room. Hart would stand in front with Frances behind, peering over his shoulder to make sure the ends of the black silk bow tie were even.

"Can you tie a bow tie?" she asked.

"I make a point of it," George answered. "But it's always crooked, and I end up tweaking it all night." What really happened was that women straightened it out for him, but he didn't feel it would be tactful to say this. "There. That's a start." He tore off the top sheet and showed it to her.

Eleanor took the page proffered across the table. It was not, somehow, what she had expected. It really was just a picture of the line of her neck, and her hair, swept up, and her ear. But she

recognized it the way you recognize yourself, with a start, in an oddly placed mirror. It was a beautiful little drawing but at the same time completely matter-of-fact. It said, This is what this woman's neck looks like. It happens to be beautiful, but if it were not, I would show that, too.

They sat there for about half an hour. George drew isolated parts of Eleanor and showed her each drawing as he finished. Her arm resting on the table, her feet in their sandals, her hand curled around her coffee cup. But they were brilliantly done. There was no clumsiness in any of them. Eleanor was quite sober when George shuffled them together and put all the pastels back in the box.

"You're very good, aren't you?" she asked. "Seriously."

George looked up, and his eyes met hers. "Yes. I'm a good draftsman," he said. "It's my great gift."

"I'm very impressed," she said, draining her cup.

"I'm glad," he answered simply, and tucked a few folded lira notes under his coffee cup. "I have to run; I just noticed the time." He stood up and paused. "Thank you very much," he said.

"You're welcome," she responded, and watched as he sprinted into the *pensione.* Eleanor stood up and shouldered her bag, heading off in search of some dinner, wondering about George Sinclair.

GEORGE's hasty departure hadn't been planned, but it was a masterstroke. Eleanor wondered over and over again, as she ate her pizza and listened to chamber music at the Palazzo Falier, what it all meant. When the concert was over, she strolled back to the *pensione* and wondered if she would see George Sinclair the next day. She watched for him at breakfast and mentally rehearsed the friendly but detached greeting she would give him. When he didn't appear, she went off to the Scuola di San Rocco and tried to appreciate Tintoretto properly, but failed.

By midday she had worked herself into a tizzy. She would catch herself imagining another encounter, maybe another sketching session, and tell herself brutally that he must have a girlfriend in New York. She would mull over bits of their conversation and remember that she was almost forty. Finally, sitting exhausted on a bench, Eleanor faced up to herself. She was developing a crush on George Sinclair. Her imagination, without any encouragement at all, was barging along inventing scenarios of lengthy kisses on arched bridges as the water lapped below. Those strong-looking hands— Never mind, Eleanor told herself. She stretched out her legs and rubbed her face.

It was all so depressing. George Sinclair had no doubt really wanted to eat fried fish for lunch. And draw her neck. "Grow up," Eleanor muttered, heaving herself to her feet. He hadn't even suggested another meeting, she told herself savagely. She was being ridiculous again.

IF ANOTHER day had gone by before she saw George, she would probably have had her feelings under control. She was, in fact, well on her way as she stood at the vaporetto station on the Grand Canal, scolding herself and making stern resolutions about blitzkrieg sight-seeing. She actually had her head in her Blue Guide when the next boat pulled up and a hand reached out to help her on board. A strong hand. Tanned, with golden hairs on the wrist and arm. She had a sinking feeling as she looked up and let the hand haul her onto the boat. It pulled her to a tiny space in the center of the boat's cabin, where George stopped, facing her.

"You look tired," George said. "You were standing there drooping on the dock, like a plant that needs water."

"Long day," Eleanor said, "and I thought I'd never get on a boat, they were all so full." Someone behind leaned steadily against her, pushing her forward. She tried to brace herself, but had to take a step toward George.

"I'm sorry," she said, trying to stand up straight. "Someone behind me is— Oh!" A foot had come down hard on her instep. She swayed and caught George's arm. "Damn!" she said, reaching down to assess the damage.

"Are you okay?" he asked, raising his voice over the din of the motor. The arm she'd been holding was around her shoulders.

She nodded, straightening up. People pressed against her on every side, swaying with the boat's slight roll. George's hand was at the back of her neck. The thumb moved softly upward until it met her hairline. All around them the chatter went on. The boat's motor chugged slower as it neared the next station. Eleanor didn't feel she could look George in the face.

As the boat came to a halt, he put his other arm down. It came to rest very naturally with a hand on her hip. Eleanor took a deep breath. The crowd shifted and jostled, squeezing her closer still to George; chest to chest, thigh to thigh, as if they were dancing. Then his hand brushed the hair aside from her ear, and she heard his voice say, "Excuse me, I need to kiss you." And before she had time to think, his mouth was on hers. Not urgently. It was a gentle, friendly kiss. With a hint of something else in reserve.

Then the boat pulled away from the dock. Eleanor's eyes flew open, and she looked up at George, astonished. "What was that all about?" she said without thinking.

George smiled a little sheepishly. "I'm sorry. I've been thinking about you all day and then to have you materialize like that and you were so close to me. . . ."

Eleanor couldn't think of what to say. She lifted his hand from where it rested on her hip. It was warm and dry. She touched the fingertips, where the nails were clipped short. There were a few hairs on the backs of the fingers. "At least you don't have sweaty palms," she thought, then realized she'd said it out loud.

"And if there were ever a time for sweaty palms . . ." George agreed, and leaned over to kiss her a bit briskly on the forehead.

They got off the boat together at the Accademia stop and turned toward the *pensione.* George waited for Eleanor to say something.

They had reached the little Campo Sant' Agnese before she turned to him and said, "I don't know what I'm supposed to say. Or do. Or anything."

"Well," George said, "I don't think you have to say or do anything. I mean, I find you enormously attractive, and I would like to go to bed with you right now, but . . ." He trailed off.

"It's not exactly the same as a friendly acquaintanceship," Eleanor pointed out mildly. "And we just met." They turned and walked toward the Church of the Gesuati. "Let's sit down for a minute," Eleanor said. She sat on the white marble steps of the church, and George settled down next to her. "This all seems so unusual."

"I think you could say it's unusual," George agreed.

Eleanor didn't answer. A pair of seagulls that they'd disturbed resumed patrolling the pavement.

"Look," said George finally. "I don't want to talk you into something you don't want to do. But could I urge you not to think too much about it? Look," he said again, and gestured. "Look at how beautiful this all is. It's a dream. Couldn't you just go along with it?"

Eleanor sighed. A damp little breeze lifted a curl from her forehead. What, she wondered, would she regret more afterward? Sleeping with him? Or saying no?

There was no question. Without a word she put her hand in his and leaned against him.

"It'll be okay," he said, kissing her on the temple. "I promise."

They walked hand in hand back to the *pensione,* Eleanor only faintly aware of the barges hooting on the canal, the recurring breeze that swirled her skirt around her legs. She didn't notice the carefully impassive face of the man behind the desk as they asked for their keys. She floated along up the stairs, George's hand against hers. But as they reached the landing, she felt herself hanging back.

So did George. "Cold feet?" he asked, turning toward her.

She nodded and dropped his hand. "I can't do this," she said, shaking her head. "I just can't."

George looked down at her. "Look," he said reasonably. "Could we talk about it? Not standing here in the hall?"

She looked up at him gratefully. He wasn't furious. He was at least willing to listen to her qualms. "Sure." She nodded, and turned to open the door to her room.

George stood while she put down her bag and opened the windows, then sat on the bed with her feet up.

"This is very awkward," she said with a sigh. "Sit. It makes it worse when you loom over me."

George hesitated. Sit where? Next to her on the bed? Or on the rickety-looking desk chair, to make it all seem cool and detached? He compromised, perching on the end of the bed, hands in his lap.

Eleanor leaned back against the pillows and closed her eyes. How could she possibly explain? There was no way to put all her doubts and fears into words. She hadn't slept with anyone since Jared left. She was unsure about her power to attract. She was acutely aware of her size-twelve hips.

"You know," remarked George, "I do understand that this is all a bit hasty." He paused, considering what to say. He looked over at

Eleanor and found her eyes on him, full of wary intelligence. And the instinct that so often guided him prompted a confession. "I want to go to bed with you. I was even planning how to go about it. But I hadn't planned to be so . . ." Words failed him, and he gestured helplessly. "I guess I jumped the gun," he finished.

He fell silent, annoyed at himself. His interest in Eleanor, piqued at the Accademia, had deepened into fascination. He was attracted to her in a way that was unfamiliar and a little unnerving.

By the end of their lunch together he wanted to take her to bed. And talk to her a lot. He wanted to spend his spare hours with her. So he worked out a little scenario of seduction—to put it bluntly. A dinner, an afternoon on the beach, a good-night kiss, and so on.

And then, standing next to her in the vaporetto, with her hand on his arm, a sheen of moisture on her collarbone—he'd lost it. Her proximity, the quasi-intimacy forced on them by the crowd had simply overwhelmed him. But he might have scared her away for good. George looked down and found he was cracking his knuckles.

"The best-laid plans?" said Eleanor. She put her head to one side and added, "You know, it is such a *relief* that you're being so honest. Can I make a suggestion? Could we just go back to plan A?" She fell silent and steeled herself for a confession of her own. "I would like to sleep with you." She looked at him steadily. "But not yet. I have nothing against the idea of a little Venetian idyll, but—"

George broke in, smiling. "I'm old enough to appreciate deferred gratification," he said. "Do you have plans for tonight?" She shook her head. "Good. We'll have dinner together. Shall we meet downstairs around seven?" She nodded again, with a smile of her own. George stood up. He bent down, with one hand on each of her shoulders. He kissed her gently and at some length. When he broke away, she was breathing faster, and she didn't move as he left the room, except to follow him with her eyes.

8

THE morning after the vaporetto incident Eleanor woke up with a feeling of immense anticipation. She couldn't help smiling. She would see George today. They were going to meet in the afternoon and go to Torcello, then spend the evening together.

Dinner had been "piquant," as George put it. Some of the time she actually forgot about the afternoon. George had gotten her to talk about why she loved the law, which was one aspect of her life Eleanor was uncharacteristically reticent about. Trading confidence for confidence, George talked about being an artist in New York, about his friends and college classmates making huge sums of money while he was still living in a rented loft with no assets beyond a three-month supply of blank canvases.

"Where is your loft?"

"Reade Street. Tribeca. Lonely at night, but safe."

"Oh, sure, I know where that is. My office is nearby. Isn't there a store that sells glass eyes for stuffed animals on Reade Street?"

"Right," George said, smiling. "With little trays in the window—brown and green and black—and a stuffed otter. I live right across the street from it. You should come and see me."

"I don't know," said Eleanor, suddenly somber. "I have a feeling this is just a shipboard romance."

George was silent for a moment. "I know. But it doesn't *have* to be." And he took her hand, and just the contact of his palm on hers made her throb.

WHEN they met on the Fondamente Nuove the afternoon after their dinner, Eleanor was wondering about the wisdom of the trip. The previous day's mist was consolidating into a brutally humid heat wave. The air was perfectly still, and Eleanor felt a tightness at the back of her neck that was going to creep upward and flower into a stunning headache. Still, she couldn't whine, Eleanor told herself. Here she was, about to get into a boat to cross the Venetian lagoon on a languid afternoon with an extremely attractive man. Who appeared on cue, hurrying toward her. Eleanor's heart lurched.

It might have been an awkward moment. Their relationship was so tenuous, yet so intense. How do you greet a man with whom, though you don't know him very well, you intend to sleep? Give him a peck on the cheek? A pat on the back? George seemed to feel no embarrassment. He put one arm around her and kissed her firmly on the mouth, then leaned back and said, "You look a little peaky. Did you sleep last night?" With his arm still around her.

Eleanor could only smile. "I did. It's just the heat. Did you?"

George grinned. "Nope. Restless dreams. Tossing and turning. All your fault."

They got onto the ferry and set off across the opaque blue water of the lagoon. The peach-colored walls of a cemetery, restraining the dense twisted zigzags of black-green cypress trees, slid past on the right.

When they got to the dock at Torcello, George suggested hanging back to let most of their fellow passengers go ahead. "Half of the charm of this place is its emptiness," he said.

Eleanor looked at the neat brick path leading through tufty grass and bushes. The spires of Venice floated on the horizon, a strip of filigree parting the great blue expanses of sky and water. The sun beat down from straight overhead, and she felt as if it were driving her into the ground. She turned to George, who was staring at the water. "Let's go. I need to get out of the sun."

He turned immediately, concerned. "Of course. Do you want to get a drink? I don't know how cool it would be—"

"No, let's go on," said Eleanor. What was a little unease or discomfort? Certainly no reason to skimp on sight-seeing. She was on the island of Torcello, and there was a cathedral to be inspected.

They took the path alongside a little canal. There were few real trees, just tall bushes with their lower branches dipping into the water. Amazingly, there was no one else in sight. A narrow arched bridge spanned the canal ahead of them. It had no handrails; anyone could trip and fall off it into the canal below. She didn't say anything, merely followed George to the cathedral, hoping it would be cool.

It wasn't. It was quite bright for a Romanesque cathedral. The Virgin and Child loomed high on the apse wall, with the mother's dark eyes staring out into space, and her elongated hands clasped around the Child. Eleanor looked around for somewhere to sit. The headache had moved forward, crushing against her temples. Her fingers found the throbbing artery in her left temple and rubbed it. Her left eye started to stream.

George had moved to the front of the church and was looking up at the saints and angels floating on the apse. As Eleanor stood rubbing her face blindly, a tall man with a video camera, walking backward as he filmed the *Last Judgment* mosaic, slammed into her. She closed her eyes against the wave of pain and, without hearing his halfhearted apology, walked out of the church to the porch, where she slid to the stony ground with her back against the wall, feeling ridiculous.

George found her sitting there ten minutes later, with her palms pressed to her eyes. "Are you all right?" he asked, squatting down next to her with a hand on her back.

"Not really," Eleanor said, controlling her voice, which was dangerously close to wobbling. "Can you look in my bag and see if there's any aspirin?"

He pulled her straw bag onto his lap and sifted through the contents. "No aspirin," he said, leaving his hands inside the bag for a moment, touching her wallet and camera and hairbrush—things she touched every day.

"Okay. I think I'd better go, then," Eleanor said from between her hands.

George smoothed the hair back from her forehead. "We shouldn't have come. I'll take you home."

"No, you stay," Eleanor said, but of course she really didn't want him to.

"No, no," George said soothingly. "You can't get home alone like this."

"Well, I don't think I can," Eleanor said, lowering her hands and turning to him. "I appreciate it."

George didn't move for a moment. He sat there looking at her pale face. There were faint purplish circles under her eyes. He couldn't know it, but this was as vulnerable as Eleanor Gray was ever going to get.

She let him lead her to the landing stage and didn't object when he hired a water taxi to skim across the lagoon directly to the Zattere. She sat leaning back against George's chest with her eyes shut. As they disembarked, she handed him her wallet, but he tucked it back into her bag, which he pulled onto his shoulder.

"That probably cost about two hundred dollars," Eleanor said.

"We'll settle it later," George said, handing her onto the quay. He hustled her upstairs and tucked her in bed with a cool washcloth over her eyes and a glass of orange juice wheedled from the café next door. He found some Tylenol with codeine in his shaving kit—left over from the recent extraction of his wisdom teeth—and gave her one of them, promising to come back in a few hours. But Eleanor barely heard him, having retreated to sleep.

WHEN she woke up, she felt as if she were floating. She lifted the washcloth from her eyes and saw the white sheet pulled over her body, the glass next to her, and George, sitting with a book on his lap in the room's one chair. She smiled at him. Her headache was gone. Instead, she felt light-headed, a little shaky, and euphoric. There was George, putting a marker in his book. The afternoon sunlight raked through the shutters. She could feel her hair, loose around her on the pillow, sliding over her shoulders. She stood up and went into the bathroom. She splashed some water on her face and collarbone and held her wrists under the faucet for a minute. Delaying tactics.

When she walked back into the room, George was still sitting in the chair, watchful and silent. She sat down on the corner of the bed nearest him and held out a hand.

George took her hand, smiling slightly, and put the book on the floor. Then he sat on the bed and kissed her.

They didn't talk. George let out a deep sigh when he lay down next to her. They tried to spin it out. They broke apart, panting, more than once. Eleanor sat up and ran a hand over his chest, tracing the hair where it grew inward toward his breastbone. Another time she pulled away to kiss him behind the ear. Finally urgency overcame them both in a tingling flood that expanded outward.

George stirred first, kissing her neck and then resting his head on her shoulder. Beneath her hands, she could feel his heartbeat gradually slowing. He breathed deeply. "I don't want to move. I want to stay here forever." He closed his eyes and burrowed his face into her neck. He ran his hand over her smooth skin. "I hope we'll be doing this again and again in the next few days. I started thinking about sleeping with you right after we had lunch that day."

"Do you sleep with every woman you have lunch with?" Eleanor asked, smiling.

"Only if she has special qualifications," George said, and went on to show her, explicitly, what a few of those qualifications were.

9

THAT was Tuesday. By Friday, Eleanor was getting alarmed. She awoke early, lying next to George, and instantly felt a thud of regret. Two more days. George was lying on his back, sleeping neatly with his mouth closed and his hands clasped over his chest. Eleanor turned onto her side to look at him and slid an arm over his rib cage. He felt warm and solid.

The night before, he had mentioned the future. "Why shouldn't we see each other in New York?" he had asked. And she hadn't really been able to tell him. The boys, of course; but the boys wouldn't mind that much. Time—simply fitting George into the schedule—was an issue; but Jared did take the boys every other weekend. Eleanor allowed herself to fantasize for a moment. She and George could meet at the Metropolitan Museum on a Friday night. Take Toby and Simon to South Street Seaport. They could even shop together.

But it didn't feel possible. She didn't have the time for it. She didn't have the strength for it. Lying next to the man who for the last four days had shown her kindness, consideration, humor, and lust, she began to panic.

Eleanor would not have been able to put it into words, but she realized that the fragile balance of her life was in danger. In the years since her divorce, her defenses had formed themselves, and one of the most important was her view of herself as sexually undesirable. But George had shattered that defense. Eleanor had abandoned herself to his unfeigned desire. Worse, she liked George. She had even—better to admit it, she thought bleakly—toyed with the idea of marrying him. She closed her eyes and tried to think clearly. There were really two problems. One was trying to integrate George into her life. The second was really a question. How far could they go together? She sighed and rolled onto her back.

"You don't have to decide everything at once," George remarked quietly.

Eleanor looked over at him, startled. Mind reading again?

"You're lying there huffing and puffing as if you were on a bed of nails. I know something's troubling you. What is the problem?"

"I don't know," Eleanor said, shaking her head. "It's just that shipboard-romance feeling. It's so easy here: it's a strange place, I have no responsibilities, nobody knows me."

"Ellie," George said in a voice that was close to a whisper, "I don't know exactly how you feel, but this is too important to me to be sloppy about. We have to be honest with each other. Okay?" She nodded. "Okay. First. Is there anything about me that is going to embarrass you in front of your friends or family?"

Eleanor looked down. At length she said, "Your age."

George nodded. "I wondered if that was worrying you. But you know, three years is not a big deal. It's not exactly cradle robbing."

Eleanor smiled. "No."

"What does that smile mean?" George asked suspiciously.

"It means that if my friends—particularly my unmarried friends—saw you, they'd be green with envy."

"Oh," George said, mollified. "Good."

"What would your friends say?" Eleanor asked him.

An image of Harry floated in front of George's eyes. "I think most of my friends would be . . ." He paused. "Delighted at my good fortune."

Eleanor, who had been picking at the hem of the sheet, looked up at George. There was something in his tone of voice, or maybe it was the stilted turn of phrase. It sounded as if he were being evasive. If not frankly lying.

But he was the one who'd asked for honesty, Eleanor told herself. How could she not take him at his word? George started to kiss her, and one thing led to another. After which it was time for breakfast, and as they dressed, George and Eleanor were both aware in the backs of their minds that they had left the biggest issue undiscussed—the delicate question of how serious they were about each other. Which was a pity. Because George had meant to tell Eleanor he wanted to marry her.

HART came slowly to the realization that Frances was still angry with him. Saturday morning, seeing that nobody else in the house seemed to be up, he took Toby to the marina in the next cove, where they had breakfast in a little hut that dispensed oily coffee and greasy doughnuts, along with bait and gasoline. When they got back, Hart found his wife in the kitchen, perched on a stool, with the yellow pages open in front of her and the phone cradled against her ear. Hart leaned over and saw the heading: REAL ESTATE.

"It's only eight thirty," Hart said. "You won't get any answer at this hour."

She shrugged and hung up. "I'm forced to believe you're right," she said. She picked up her coffee cup and slid off the stool, preparing to leave the room.

"Why are you calling Realtors?" Hart asked the back of her neck.

She turned around. "Hart," she said in an irritated voice, "I hate this house. You don't seem to be interested in finding a new place. Fine. I'll do it. But I wish you'd stop nagging me about it." Which was hardly fair, as he had simply asked once, politely.

"I see," Hart answered, stung. "I thought you were beginning to enjoy living here. But since you want to take things into your own hands, I won't stop you. Just don't expect me to help you." He put the bag of doughnuts down on the counter. "And don't expect me to like what you choose by yourself, either," he said with a viciousness that astonished him. He pushed past Frances and, grabbing the car keys from the hook by the front door, slammed out the door.

Driving rather too fast along the road that went north into the farmland, Hart ruminated. Living with Frances this summer had been like living with a cactus. Every time he backed into her he got stuck, Hart thought. And now, just when he thought she'd begun to cheer up, she started getting all excited again about a new house. Couldn't she relax and enjoy life, and they'd look for another house after Labor Day? No, she had to be a martyr and do the job herself. Well, fine. Let her. Let her find out that it was not all that easy to buy a house. Let her negotiate points and rates with a moronic bank officer. At this point Hart relented. Better not, perhaps. And so his plan formed. He'd keep an eye on Frances. When it came time for the difficult part, the financial part, he'd step in. Satisfied with this notion, Hart started looking for a place to turn the car around and drive back through the rolling green fields to the Wrong House.

ON SATURDAY, Eleanor and George went to a shop at the back of the Piazza San Marco to pick out Harry's wineglasses. George privately resolved that he would return and order an extra dozen, also for Harry, also in thanks.

It was a hushed, pretentious shop. The carpets were very thick; the mahogany counters glistened. A slender girl with blond hair and a black velvet headband offered her help in perfect English.

"I'm looking for wineglasses," Eleanor said, "with colored stems."

"We have these," the salesgirl said, setting a tall goblet on the counter. "Rhine-wine glasses. With the traditional green stem."

Eleanor picked up the glass. "Actually I was looking for twisted multicolored stems," she said.

The salesgirl nodded. "I'm sorry, we don't have anything like that. We have this—" and she turned away to lift a glass from the display case. The glass was quite spectacular. Its stem was formed out of a braid of glass, each strand a different pale color. Pink, lavender, coral, and yellow wove in and out, ending in a tiny knot at the bowl of the glass.

Eleanor hitched herself onto one of the chairs. "Oh, dear," she said. "This is going to be harder than I thought. Harry specifically asked for twisted stems, but . . ." She picked up the glass, gently stroking the braid of color. "This may be a bit much." She put it down and picked up the Rhine-wine glass. "Do you have these with twisted stems?"

George stepped closer. "He already has Rhine-wine glasses," he said without thinking, then shut his eyes, wincing at what he'd just said.

There was sudden silence. Eleanor heard a tiny clink as the salesgirl placed another glass on the counter. She turned around to look at George.

"He what?" she said blankly.

George's face was suddenly flushed under his Lido tan, but he looked straight at Eleanor. "Harry already has Rhine-wine glasses," he repeated. "Let's go. I'll explain." He seized her by the wrist and said to the salesgirl, "I'm sorry, we'll be back later," as they went out the door.

George and Eleanor stood in an arcade outside the shop. The sky was milky, covered with high clouds that held no threat of rain. George still grasped Eleanor's wrist as he then pulled her away from the glass shop into a doorway, where he leaned against the tall polished door and took a deep breath.

For a long time afterward, Eleanor would remember that door. It had a huge shiny brass knob right in the middle, at chest level. The wood was coffee-colored and highly varnished. George stood against it and clasped both of her hands.

"I know your brother," he said. "He's a good friend of mine."

Eleanor watched him, absorbing this information. George was a friend of Harry's. She thought immediately about his hesitation the morning before. "What would your friends say?" she had asked. No wonder he'd hesitated.

Eleanor's mind moved quickly. He was a friend of Harry's. If she'd known that when they met, she would not have gotten involved with him. Harry's friends always seemed young to her, just as Harry was inescapably her baby brother.

Looking at George now as he anxiously scanned her face, something struck her. "How do you know? I mean, how do you know your friend Harry is my brother Harry?"

For the first time since she'd met him, George seemed ill at ease. He looked across the piazza, as if the campanile were going to provide him with inspiration. Finally he looked back and said baldly, "Because he set us up. Sort of. He thought I would like you. I mean, it wasn't anything more than that."

"He set us up?" Eleanor was repeating. Something occurred to her. "Did he give you the name of the *pensione?*"

George nodded. "I tell you, it was just a casual thought on his part. And then he even said—" But he broke off, putting his hand to his mouth.

Eleanor grabbed his wrist. "He said what? I can't *believe* you two sat around talking about me! What did he say?"

"Stop," George said, trying to ease her fingers off his arm. "He just said I shouldn't mention him. He thought you might take me more seriously if we didn't meet through him. That was all."

"All!" Eleanor said with scorn, flinging his hand away and turning to face the piazza. "I'd like to strangle him. What a moron. What a naïve, sentimental moron I've been. What a credulous sucker." She turned around and started to stalk across the piazza. George went after her, easily catching up with his long stride.

"Look, El, I knew you'd be angry. Can you tell me one thing?"

"I don't know why I should," Eleanor snapped over her shoulder.

"Are you mad because I'm Harry's friend? Or because I didn't tell you I was Harry's friend?"

Eleanor wheeled around. The crowds milled about, buying, selling. "I'm not exactly sure. I'm too mad to think clearly. But I know that I am particularly offended by the fact that you and Harry sat around and discussed me and made plans for me and you acted on them as if I were some dumb doll. And I'm furious that I fell for it. *Furious!* And I don't want to see you again." Eleanor tried to turn and walk away, but her path was blocked by a man wearing a placard of Venetian masks. George grabbed her arm.

"I know you won't listen now, but maybe you'll remember this. I meant no harm. I like you, Eleanor. I'm fond of you; I mean well. I wanted to keep seeing you." Eleanor pulled her arm free and ran, dodging the vendors and tourists, toward the Piazzetta. "I'm starting to love you, damn it!" George called, running after her.

In response, Eleanor stopped. "Why on earth should I believe that?" she puffed. "Just leave me alone."

So George did. He stood there in the Piazzetta, watching Eleanor's back weaving through the crowd. And planning, already, how he could get her back.

10

BACK in New York, Eleanor felt a surge of anticipation as she walked into her apartment building. At least she would see the boys soon. Forget about George. A blip, that was all he was. Some kind of blip in the radar—an aberration. Something to put behind her and forget. As fast as possible. But as she put her key in the lock, she didn't hear the voices she expected, the quick footsteps running down the hall. The apartment was empty.

A note on the hall table in Harry's handwriting read, "Gone to the supermarket. Back soon." Eleanor kicked the door closed behind her and hauled her suitcase into her bedroom. A banner hanging over her bed said, WELCOME HOME MOM in unsteady lettering. Mail-order catalogues and bills lay in a slippery stack on her desk.

She wandered into the kitchen. The whole apartment was eerily quiet. Even the street below was empty when Eleanor peered out the kitchen window. It was unnerving. Where was everyone?

Eleanor yawned and looked at her watch. It was only four thirty. Ten thirty in Italy, she calculated. Her mind flinched away from the thought of George Sinclair, probably still awake in his bedroom at the *pensione.* She would not think about George. Better instead to make a pot of coffee and start to unpack. As the coffeepot began to gurgle and hiss, she went back into her bedroom and pressed the PLAY button on the answering machine. And just like that, George's voice filled the room. "Look, I'm sorry. It wasn't what it must have looked like to you. I wish you had let me explain." There was a pause. "Oh, hell," George's voice came back. "Here I am day-dreaming on a transatlantic phone line, wondering how I could have been more tactful. Or something. Oh, Eleanor, please don't give up. I won't give up." Then the beep sounded, and Eleanor stood there with tears pouring down her face.

It felt like a knife, hearing his voice like that, unexpectedly. Wounding. Eleanor stood rigid, willing her sobs to stop. It wouldn't do. This was not the way. The boys would be back in a moment; they mustn't find her crying. She went into the bathroom and blew her nose on a handful of toilet paper.

By the time Harry came back with the boys, Eleanor had herself under control. She burst into tears again when Toby and Simon threw themselves into her arms, but told them it was because she was so glad to see them. For her brother she had only a searing glance and the stiffest of thanks. Which might have puzzled him if George Sinclair hadn't wakened him in the middle of the night with an agonized phone call from Venice. So Harry vanished tactfully, wishing he had never uttered her name to George Sinclair.

Eleanor spent the next few days doing everything she could not to think about George. She threw herself into her work, mentally exaggerating the urgency of a few routine matters to keep her mind from wandering. She was so busy attempting to exorcise the pain that she gave little thought to its source. Without realizing it, she was mortally offended. Harry evidently thought she was so unattractive that she couldn't find a man unless he set her up with one.

She still felt such a sense of *shame* about it. She felt she'd been so eager, so pathetic in her willingness to fall for the guy.

Time, Eleanor knew, would dull the worst of what she felt. This was nothing compared to the divorce. She could weather it, but there were ways to make it easier. Keeping busy was important. Revisionist thinking helped, too, but this Eleanor was not able to manage. It would be simpler, she thought, walking home from the subway one evening, if she could only convince herself that it *had* just been a fling. If she could only pretend she hadn't fallen for George Sinclair like a ton of bricks.

Eleanor felt in the bottom of her purse for her keys, glad to be near home. She'd made it through the week. Nothing unseemly had happened. She hadn't burst into tears in a meeting or shrieked at her sons. She'd get over it—get over the embarrassment and the anger and the regret.

Eleanor stopped at her mailbox. As she pulled out the usual dispiriting assortment of things for sale that she didn't want to buy and bills for things she *had* bought, something fell to the floor. A postcard of Venice lay face up on the old circular tiles of the lobby, and Eleanor froze. She knew who had sent it even before her hand reached out very slowly to pick it up. On the reverse it said, "I think of you all the time," in a neat italic hand. It bore an Italian stamp and an illegible postmark. Eleanor drew a deep breath and slipped the card into her purse, aware that her hands were shaking. What the hell did it mean?

What it meant, although she had no way of knowing this, was that she had seriously shaken George Sinclair.

GEORGE had spent his three remaining days in Venice sketching, and thinking about Eleanor. He thought about her intelligence, her sense of humor, her courage. And he decided not to give up. There must be a way to win her over.

But he wasn't sure what it was. Flowers and a letter? Pleading on the telephone? She could ignore a letter, hang up the phone. George thought about this, leaving his studio the morning after he came back to New York. Could he bear it if Eleanor hung up on him? He flinched at the thought. No. He couldn't do it.

He closed the heavy front door and turned left toward Church Street. Across the street was the store that sold glass eyes, with the stuffed otter in the window. Dodging a delivery van, George crossed to take a closer look. The otter was lying on its back, clutching a dusty shell to its chest.

On impulse George went in. He came out five minutes later with a pair of green glass eyes on little steel loops, like fancy leather buttons. On the way uptown to meet his dealer, George bought a small padded envelope. He tore a corner of paper from his Venice sketch pad and wrote on it, "To keep an eye on you." Then he stopped by the post office and mailed the package to Eleanor. It never occurred to George that his gesture might be considered creepy or even threatening. It was a tribute to their innate compatibility that Eleanor took the oblique message in the spirit in which it was meant and slipped the eyes into the purse of her wallet.

THE oppressive heat held all that week, crushing the entire East Coast in humid misery. The beaches were almost too hot to bear. Movie theaters did stunning business.

Frances had begun the week with the best of intentions and a genuine resolve to avoid bitterness. Hart wasn't interested in finding a new house. Fine. She would take matters into her own hands. She certainly hadn't anything better to do. She would start by exploring. Getting to know the other towns on the coast. Then, with a better grasp of the surroundings, she would call real estate agents.

Or so Frances told herself. She would not acknowledge to herself that she was stalling. Somehow she just couldn't dial the telephone and announce to a real estate agent, "My name is Frances Drummond, and I am looking for a house."

So here she was roaming the outskirts of New London and searching for Gloucester Street, where an open house was being held at what the ad in the newspaper called a "spacious elegant 4BR Georgian" with "eat-in kitchen, marble baths, 3-car garage." It wasn't that she thought it would be the right house, but she did think it would be good practice.

Frances was relieved when she got to Folkestone Way and tiny quarter-acre lots gave way to a stretch of meadow. Her destination was obvious. There was only one house on Gloucester Street.

If Frances had more experience, she could have placed the house at a glance. It was the last hurrah of a contractor with delusions of grandeur. In the mid-1980s a young builder, dreaming of splendor, had bought the land on the cheap and put up a house he was prepared to build in multitudes for upwardly mobile young professionals. Who, alas, never turned up. The house had been on the market for a year. It was listed with every real estate agent in eastern Connecticut, and on that Saturday morning in July there was one young man with blow-dried hair standing languidly in front, squinting in the bright sunlight and smoking a cigarette.

As he spotted Frances in the car, he threw the cigarette into a weedy yew and hurried toward her. She sighed and cut the engine. It would have been just too rude to drive away.

"My name's Jim Fusco," he said eagerly as she got out of the car. "I'm with Shoreline Properties. How are you?"

Frances shook his hand and shaded her eyes to look up at the "Georgian" façade. It was a tall two-story house with a Palladian-style door that looked as if it might have come out of a mail-order catalogue. Four extremely thin pillars supported an extension of the roof over what might have been considered a veranda, though you couldn't even fit a camp chair on the flagstone beneath it, Frances thought as she walked inside.

"The owner is willing to sell furnished or unfurnished," the young man said as Frances gazed around the living room. There was an enormous pastel-hued silk screen of birds of paradise over a fake fireplace. A butterfly-patterned fabric swarmed over a vast sectional sofa. A big vase held fronds of pampas grass dyed coral and turquoise.

"Would you care to see the bedrooms," the young man asked, "or do you want to look over the downstairs first?"

Frances turned and looked at him. Poor boy, she thought. What an awful job. He must be so bored. The house was impossible, of course, but she might as well let the salesman do what he was supposed to.

They walked around, Frances glancing politely at the "gourmet kitchen" and the "gracious dining room" that was papered down to the outsized egg-and-dart chair rail in a startling maroon-and-yellow stripe. The upstairs rooms were notable only for the number of dead flies Frances noticed on their windowsills.

"It's awfully quiet, isn't it?" Frances said as she walked down the stairs.

"Oh, yes. Extremely quiet. And this isn't a through road, you know, so there's lots of privacy," the young man said earnestly.

"Mmm. Well, I don't think this is for me," Frances said, glancing at the asymmetrical modern chandelier in the hall. "Thank you."

Though she'd only been in the house for a few minutes, a surge of hot leather-scented air met her when she opened the car door. As she backed out of the driveway, the young man stood waving on the narrow veranda, and Frances wondered how soon he would be able to take off his suit and tie and take a cool shower.

When Hart asked Frances that night how she had spent the day, she made a vague answer about going for a drive. For some reason she didn't want Hart knowing what she was up to. But he had taken the boat out for a long trip and seemed more interested in telling her about the enormous jellyfish he'd seen that he thought was a Portuguese man-of-war.

11

IN THE middle of July came a day Eleanor had been dreading. She had to go to a meeting at the surrogate's court in Queens.

A pleasant old Viennese lady in Forest Hills, Mrs. Gast, had left a substantial estate to her three children. Unfortunately, the executor had neglected to file a federal estate-tax return when he should have, with the result that the estate had been obligated to pay thousands of dollars in penalties. Eleanor's clients, the Gast children, were objecting to the executor's characterization of the penalties as mere "miscellaneous expenses." A meeting had been arranged with the executor's lawyer and the clerk of the Queens County surrogate's court to discuss the executor's excuse for failing to file the tax return. It meant a morning that would be at once boring, confrontational, and supremely inconvenient.

So on a sweltering Wednesday morning Eleanor walked into her subway station and, with the misplaced confidence of the regular mass-transit passenger, assumed she knew how to get to Queens. It was only when she was sitting in an E train, leafing through her papers, that she realized she had gone too far. Muttering to herself, she moved down the subway car to find the map.

"You lost, miss?" The man sitting next to the map looked up at her and cracked his gum. He had on a beige pin-striped suit and a maroon tie. "You need some help?"

Eleanor stood up straight, trying to peer at the map without letting the man look down her blouse.

"I'm trying to get to the courthouse," she said.

"Oh, yeah? You an attorney?" he said. "Me, too. Howard Thaler," he added, sticking out a hand. "Nice to meet you."

"Oh, umm, Eleanor Gray," Eleanor said, distractedly shaking his hand and turning back to the map. Howard stood up and poked Forest Hills. "What you do is, next stop? You get out, cross the track, get on the inbound G train. It drops you off right at the courthouse.

"Now tell me, what's a lovely lady like you doing at the courthouse? C'mon, sit down." He sat and patted the seat next to his. "I'll bet you're some kind of fancy corporate lawyer, am I right?"

"No, actually, I usually handle trusts and estates," Eleanor said.

"No kidding!" he answered. "Say, listen, what time you going to be finished at the courthouse? We can have lunch. You want to meet on the steps around one?"

"I'm sorry," Eleanor said with huge relief. "I have to be back at my office for a meeting." The train was slowing down. She stood, picking up her briefcase. "Anyway, I'm married. Good-bye. Thank you." She nearly leaped onto the platform at Forest Hills. As she scurried up the stairs, she could hear a voice behind her calling out, "You oughta wear a ring, lady!" Then the train whooshed out of the station.

Ever since she'd come back from Venice, Eleanor felt besieged. It was the strangest thing, she thought, sitting on the inbound G train. People who had always seemed like the most polite and sexless of colleagues were . . . there was no other way to think of it—they were making passes at her.

Even the counterman who poured her coffee every morning tried to hold her hand when he gave her change. A young cabdriver with a Russian name had invited her to have dinner with him. A recently divorced partner had invited her to spend an afternoon on the yacht he kept moored at City Island, adding in a meaningful way, "It would be so nice to have some time alone with you."

Eleanor would have been horrified to know what was behind what she thought of as all those rampaging hormones, because it was actually a change in her. In what she was starting to think of as her previous life—before George—she had given off an aura of brisk capability. A firm handshake, a cheerful voice, and complete concentration on the matter at hand had served to repel masculine interest. That was Eleanor's disguise, and it went far to cloak the hint of vulnerability that sometimes made men curious about what Eleanor Gray was like without a suit on.

But she had changed; there was no getting around it. Since she'd come back from Italy, she had lost some of her focus. Her superprofessional demeanor had been slipping, and men, especially, noticed. She might have found this flattering. Instead, she was appalled. Life was complicated enough without having to fend off the Howard Thalers of this world. As the G train pulled into the station at Court Square, Eleanor felt a sense of relief. The Gast will business was going to be tricky, but at least it was purely business.

Alas, it wasn't Eleanor's day. When she opened the door to the clerk's office, he looked up from his desk with the expected expression of annoyance over her late arrival. And the other person in the office leaped to his feet. Eleanor felt her face go wooden. Professional conflict she could handle. Charlie Winter, very possibly, she could not. Before she could stop him, he rose and planted a kiss on her mouth, murmuring, "Nellie, what a surprise!"

Eleanor's past was anything but lurid. There had been a serious romance in college, a fling one summer on Nantucket, and Charlie Winter. Whom she preferred to forget. Charlie Winter, the rake of Yale Law, who had flirted with and flattered and wooed the studious Eleanor until on a warm May night just before graduation she finally gave in and let him seduce her. After which he had dropped her, as she'd anticipated. And here he was, in a clerk's office at the Queens County Courthouse, leering like the vampire in a grade B movie. Nellie, indeed!

Eleanor gave him a chilly little smile and dropped into the seat that was waiting for her. "Nice to see you again, Charlie," she said. "Have you been out west?"

For a moment he looked confused, then fingered the bolo tie around his neck and glared at her. "No, honey, I'm a slave to fashion," he said. "Surely you know that by now."

It was not a productive meeting. Charlie was representing the executor and seemed extremely ill acquainted with the facts of the account. He produced a string of halfhearted excuses for his client that were only a step better than the old the-dog-ate-my-homework line. Within ten minutes the clerk was as fed up as Eleanor. With a meaty harangue about incompetence, carelessness, and near criminal inefficiency, he demanded to see, within two weeks, cogent reasons why the executor shouldn't pay the IRS' penalty.

"You going back to the city?" Charlie asked later, striding down the hall next to her. "I'll give you a ride."

Eleanor looked at her watch, and sidelong at Charlie. She shrugged. "Yes, I'll come with you."

The sunlight on Queens Boulevard was searing. Charlie pulled a pair of black-lensed sunglasses from his jacket pocket and said, "I'm parked over here." His car turned out to be a black Jeep convertible. Charlie stuck a baseball cap on his head (Eleanor noticed it had a Y on it: trust Charlie to make sure everyone knew he'd gone to Yale) and pulled out of the parking lot with a squeal of rubber.

He was a terrible driver. That figured, too, Eleanor thought as he changed lanes in front of an oil truck without signaling, then gunned the engine through a changing light. Eleanor put a hand up to her hair and felt the wind pulling it loose from the knot.

"I see we have no fear of moving violations," Eleanor said in what she recognized as a prissy tone of voice.

"Hey, time is money, sweetie. Gotta get you back to the salt mines, right?"

"I guess so. What about you, Charlie? Where have you been for the last fifteen years?"

"Mmm, here and there," Charlie answered, turning around to assess the traffic behind him before cutting across three lanes. "Did some work in South America for a while. Then I came back here, and I'm angling to get into entertainment law. I'll probably end up on the Coast."

"That seems like a good place for you," Eleanor said mildly.

Charlie turned to grin at her. "So what have you been doing for the last fifteen years, Nellie? How come you're not married?"

"I was," Eleanor said in what she hoped would be a discouraging tone.

"Didn't take, huh? Yeah, I got married, too. Not a good idea. Let me tell you, the Argentine divorce laws . . . Boy, I thought I'd never get out of Buenos Aires alive! Here we are."

Eleanor looked around her. "Here" was not Wall Street. Instead, Charlie had pulled the Jeep up to the edge of a little strip of green facing a river. "Charlie, where are we?" she turned to ask him.

"Astoria, darlin'," he said, and put an arm around her shoulders. "We're taking the scenic route back." And then, to Eleanor's astonishment, he leaned over and kissed her.

"Charlie Winter!" she exclaimed, pulling away from the hand that had found its way into her hair. "What is this? What about your billable hours, Charlie?"

"I never let business interfere with pleasure," he said, pulling out a hairpin. "Relax, honey, it's just your old friend Charlie. You're so beautiful!" He leaned over to kiss her again.

"Oh, for goodness' sake!" yelled Eleanor. And before she knew it, her right hand—all by itself, with no prompting from her conscious mind—had slapped Charlie across the face.

"Ow!" he shouted, straightening up. He took his hand away from her neck. "Something tells me you mean business, honey." He rubbed his cheek thoughtfully. "You know, darlin', your life would be a lot more fun if you would just lighten up." He started the engine and reversed the Jeep in a wide arc.

Eleanor looked around. They were driving between rows of apartment buildings. There were tight lines of cars parked on either side of the street. Ahead she could see a stoplight and a busy commercial street.

"I'll get out here," she said as Charlie coasted through a stop sign.

"Don't be dumb," he said without looking at her. "I'll drive you back. We can still be friends."

"No," Eleanor said tersely, afraid she was going to cry. "I'll take the subway. Stop, Charlie!" The light turned red just as they reached it. She grabbed her briefcase, opened the door of the Jeep, and fled.

She paced along the street with tears pouring down her face. What an incomparable jerk! Was it possible that anybody could be so full of himself? Had she really hit him? Eleanor could feel, at the back of her head, her hair bobbing with each step. She pulled out the hairpins, combing her hair with her fingers.

After this hellish start to the day, what? She was standing on the corner of Astoria Boulevard. Ahead the elevated tracks of the subway spanned the horizon. Eleanor heaved a deep sigh and crossed the street. She could feel the dampness of her suit, and her hair hung like an unwanted blanket on her shoulders.

A few yards ahead a thin young woman wearing a skimpy shirt wrestled the iron shutter of a storefront upward until it retracted completely. Photographs of composed-looking models with extremely short hair were taped onto the shop window. Through the window Eleanor glimpsed three hairdressers' chairs facing a mirrored wall. Without an instant of hesitation she grasped the doorknob and entered.

"Can I help?" asked the girl with the skimpy shirt. Her dark brown hair was thick and stood out from her head in an artful tangle.

"Could you cut my hair?" Eleanor asked.

"Sure," the girl said with a grin. "That's what I'm here for."

In five minutes Eleanor was seated in a chair, wearing a leopard-print robe. "So how much do you want taken off?" asked the girl, pulling a pair of enormous shears from a drawer.

"I want it short," Eleanor said with determination.

"How short?"

"Short," Eleanor repeated, gesturing. "Like those pictures in the window. Really short."

"Oh, the androgynous look," the girl said, nodding. "You wanna watch or not?"

"I'd rather not," Eleanor answered, relieved at the option. So the girl spun her around with her back to the mirror. The first snip, at the lobe of her ear, sounded incredibly loud. Eleanor shuddered as the hair fell to the floor.

It took almost an hour. Eleanor sat there with her mind determinedly blank. She pushed out of her consciousness all thoughts of work, George, the children, Charlie Winter, Harry, how she was going to get back to her office.

"Done," the girl finally said. "I haven't cut so much hair off anyone since my sister went into the convent. You wanna see?"

Eleanor nodded, and the girl spun the chair around. Strange new breezes caressed her neck and ears. When she'd walked into the shop, she had assumed that with short hair like the girls in the photographs at the front of the shop, she would also acquire similar features. A straight nose, high cheekbones, and a firm jaw. Irrationally and unconsciously, Eleanor had assumed that the haircut would give her the confidence the models seemed to exude.

But as she looked at herself in the mirror, Eleanor realized that she had made an enormous mistake.

On top her hair was about two inches long. Above her ears it was shorter.

"You can style it different ways," the girl explained. "A little mousse, you can get some more height on top. Or comb it forward, you know, for a softer look." She brushed the hair forward into spiky Liza Minnelli bangs on Eleanor's forehead. "Whaddya think? You seem kind of shocked."

Eleanor raised her eyebrows at herself in the mirror. Yep, it was her face. Hell. She turned to the girl. "It's fine. It's just going to take some getting used to."

All the way home, Eleanor was sure people were staring at her. She practically sprinted from the subway station to her building. Mercifully, Eleanor managed to get into her apartment without being seen.

She dropped her briefcase on the bed and called her office. "Teresa, it's Eleanor. I'm at home," she said in a faint voice. "I've got a migraine. I'll call in when I'm better. Right. Bye." Then, standing in front of the mirror on the inside of the closet door, she dialed her brother's number.

"Harry? It's Eleanor. Can you come up here? Something awful has happened. I've cut off all my hair."

WHEN he got Eleanor's call, Harry thought she was just being melodramatic, but he was so glad to hear from her that he got in a cab and went right uptown. When his sister answered the door, he realized that the haircut was disastrous. Harry followed her down the hall, eyeing the back of her shorn head with pity.

"It's pretty bad, huh?" she said, sitting on the bed.

"It's a very . . . extreme cut," he said carefully. "Maybe a little young for you."

Eleanor looked up at him and made a noise. He couldn't tell if it was a sob or if she was laughing. "Oh, Harry, you are sweet. Thank you for coming up here. Especially when I've been so mean."

"You haven't been mean," Harry said, moving a pile of magazines off her desk chair and sitting down. "You've just been pretending I don't exist."

"Yeah. Well, if I'd seen you, I would have been mean. Harry, what am I going to do?"

"About what? About George, or about your hair?"

Eleanor leaned back on her pillows. "Let's start with the hair."

"With the hair, brazen it out. What else is there to do? I mean, wear a wig?"

"Jared will say he hates it."

"Right. Well, to hell with Jared anyway." He paused. "George will be heartbroken."

Eleanor turned over and lay with her face in her pillows. "Harry, I don't think I can talk to you about George," she said in a muffled voice. "Please."

Harry spun the desk chair around once and then spun it back. "Okay. But am I acquitted?"

"I don't blame you" came the response. "I'm not mad at you anymore. I can't afford to be."

Harry spun around again. "But what about George? He's crazy about you. I know you think I've interfered too much already. I won't say anything else. Listen, I have to get back to work. Now that I've seen you aren't actually suicidal, anyway."

"Yeah," Eleanor said, rolling over. "I'll live. I mean, I am beginning to see the humorous side of this." She got off the bed to walk Harry to the door. As they stood there in the dark hall, he said, "Why'd you do it, anyway? I mean, what inspired you?"

Eleanor thought about Charlie Winter and the man in the subway and didn't think she could explain. "I don't know, Harry. I was so hot."

He knew she wasn't telling him the whole truth, but he let it go at that.

ELEANOR got up enough nerve to return to her office that afternoon. The reaction was as bad as she'd feared. As she got off the elevator, a group of associates fell into stunned silence when she walked by. Teresa only said, "Mrs. Gray!" in a shocked tone of voice.

It was, in truth, a ridiculous haircut. First, it made Eleanor look more than usually pear-shaped. Her long hair had at least balanced the somewhat lush proportions of her figure, but now she seemed pinheaded. And in the businesslike world of pageboys and bobs, Eleanor now looked like a freak. At meetings, when she met people for the first time, Eleanor saw them carefully wipe the surprise off their faces when she introduced herself.

The only person who welcomed Eleanor's extravagant gesture was George Sinclair. He was jubilant when Harry told him. "Don't you see? It's a desperate measure!" he crowed. "Think of it, Harry. Widows who hack off their hair in ritual mourning. Nuns about to take the veil. How does she look?"

"Like a little shorn sheep," Harry said. "I have to get back to work now. Good-bye."

George hung up the phone and crossed to his desk, where he leafed through a sheaf of postcards, finally selecting a David portrait of Empress Josephine. "Where did you get your hair cut? I must have a lock to wear next to my heart," he wrote. It was a little ridiculous. Still, it hurt George to think of Eleanor's gorgeous mane being swept out to sit in some landfill on Long Island.

12

WHILE Eleanor moped and Harry fretted, while Frances drove aimlessly up and down eastern Connecticut, Hart was in heaven. In the months between retirement and moving to Weymouth, Hart had been more or less adrift, without a focus. But when he settled into the Wrong House, his focus presented itself. Hart began acquiring the lore of the sea. Or more precisely, the lore of eastern Long Island Sound. He bought nature guides and navigational charts. He ordered an immensely expensive pair of birding glasses and hid the bill from Frances. He crouched on the rocks at the town dock, communing in a taciturn way with the men seated on upturned buckets.

When Harry and the boys had appeared in the Whaler on the night of the anniversary party, Hart was overjoyed. Overnight his image of himself was transformed. He was no longer a retired corporate lawyer from New York. He became a waterman. He was gone from morning until dusk. He would bundle his charts and rod and bottle of sun goop into the boat and go chugging off right after breakfast, waving automatically to Frances without looking back. (He didn't realize that she rarely watched him.) He puttered up and down the coastline, putting into unfamiliar harbors, nosing up creeks, circling islands.

Hart's self-absorption during this period was almost complete. Frances, with her faculties sharpened by idleness and self-pity, often felt that a robot with good taste in clothes would satisfy Hart's needs as well as she could.

So Frances did the only thing left to her: she acted like one. She shut down completely. Well, not completely. She presented a calm face to her husband and did his laundry and cooked his meals. She listened—or pretended to listen, which Hart seemed to find equally satisfactory—to his tales of adventure and derring-do with the Whaler's seventy-horsepower engine. She read the real estate ads assiduously, and drove around.

She discovered how to read a neighborhood. What kinds of cars were parked in the driveways? Did the lawns look well cared for? Soon she could guess from the name of a street whether the house would be old or new. And she learned to decipher the real estate lingo: the grandiosities of "luxurious" and "spacious"; the euphemistic "cozy" and "needs work"; the cryptic initials like WBF for wood-burning fireplace and c/a/c for central air conditioning.

It wasn't exactly fun, but at least she was occupied. And one day she made a discovery that made her life more bearable. She had stopped for lunch in Old Lyme. Walking back to the car, she passed a drugstore and remembered that she and Hart needed toothpaste, so she went in. It was a big store, with a big display of books and magazines by the door. As Frances walked past, she stopped to pick up a book that had fallen from the rack. She glanced idly at the cover. An armor-clad woman with long auburn braids brandished a sword at a green dragon, while some kind of large spotted cat clung to the dragon's wings. The title, *Lironia's Deeds*, blocked out the sky in slightly bulbous golden type. Frances turned the book over curiously and read the copy on the back. "Reared from childhood by a band of querls (the holy cats of Sindon), Lironia seeks her heritage. Her startling powers of sword and sorcery, however, entangle her in a deadly struggle with the ice lords of Ranorth."

The redhead, with her feline sidekick and armor molded around her breasts, somehow looked like fun. Frances put the book on the counter, along with her tube of Crest. That night after dinner she sat down to read it while Hart attempted to tie a particularly complex fly.

She had never been much of a reader. She had plowed through selected classics in college and amassed quite a collection of cookbooks and gardening manuals over the years. But reading novels for entertainment had never appealed, and the White Flower Farm catalogue remained her favorite bedtime reading.

But *Lironia's Deeds* was something new. Lironia herself was refreshing. She stood no nonsense from anything she met, human or otherwise. Frances read half of the book in one sitting and came to a little stiffly when Hart announced he was heading off to bed.

She finished *Lironia* the next day and drove the forty minutes to Old Lyme to buy up the three other fantasy novels on their shelves. Two days later Frances drove down to New Haven and stocked up at Waldenbooks. She visited the Weymouth Library and discovered the ranks of Anne McCaffrey novels. The White Flower Farm catalogue fell under the bed and wasn't missed.

So life slipped into a pattern in the Wrong House. Each morning Hart and Frances separated. They met again for dinner, when Frances eluded Hart's perfunctory queries about her day, and Hart lectured his wife about the nesting habits of the stormy petrel. Then after dinner they sat in the hideous living room, facing each other on the chintz couches. Hart lost himself in his seaman's lore, and Frances escaped to another planet.

THE senior Drummonds could have gone on like this for the whole summer, but the schedule of their grandsons' day camp intervened. The administrators found it necessary to take four days off at the end of July, so Eleanor planned to bring the boys up to Weymouth. Frances seemed to have forgotten this when Eleanor mentioned the visit, which was unusual. But maybe, Eleanor thought, hanging up the phone, Frances had been concentrating on something else. (It was Tirranion's search for the scarlet rune stone, as a matter of fact.)

Eleanor sighed. She had been back in New York for nearly a month, and she was managing. In some respects life was back to normal. She was used to her schedule again, accustomed to the routine of work and children and household chores. She had partially regained her sense of humor, even if it had acquired a slightly bitter edge. Time was doing its job, and the memories of Venice were already less vivid. All in all, she was coping. But George Sinclair was screwing up her plans.

Dozens of times a day she heard Harry's voice say, "He's crazy about you." Insidiously, a little voice from her own psyche echoed Harry's words. He must still be attracted to you. Want you.

Eleanor didn't want to hope. She didn't want even to *want*. She wanted to forget about the terrifying, intoxicating possibilities of a love affair. Rescuing her from self-condemnation, the phone rang.

"What time are you going to Mom's?" asked Harry.

"Driving up Thursday night after work," Eleanor answered. "Renting a car. Are you going up?"

"Not sure. I think so. I may go spend a night with Clara," Harry said. "How are you doing?"

Eleanor paused. "Fine," she finally said. "I'm sort of dreading this weekend. Mom sounded odd on the phone."

"I wouldn't read too much into a phone call," Harry said. "I'll see you when I see you."

He hung up and glared at George Sinclair, who was standing right next to him trying to hear. "Okay?"

George shrugged. "It was better than nothing. I've heard her answering-machine message so often now that it doesn't even sound like her."

Harry went to the stove to make coffee. He looked across the room at his friend, on a chair with his chin against his chest, and noticed for the first time that George's face was looking a bit gaunt. "Are you pining away, George?" he asked lightly, scooping beans into the grinder.

"Pining," George answered, with a sigh and no hint of irony. "You know, I am. I can't work at all," he said, standing up and crossing to lean on the counter. "This fresco commission is going to melt away if I can't produce something soon, but every time I start, I keep thinking about your sister. I know I've been bugging you, calling every day, but believe me, it's not as often as I wish I could call." There was a salt shaker on the granite countertop. George slid it from his left hand to his right. "You know I call Eleanor every day."

Harry turned off the water, startled. "You what?"

"I call Eleanor every day. At home, when I know she won't be there. I've sent her a few things. A sketch. A postcard." He didn't feel up to explaining the glass eyes.

Harry shook his head and got two coffee cups out of the cupboard. "You've got it bad, pal."

"I know," George agreed somberly. He took a cup of coffee from Harry and sat on the sofa. "Harry," he said in a very soft voice, "I am getting desperate."

Harry looked at him carefully. This was interesting. This was what desperation looked like. "In what sense?" he asked.

"Well, I can't go on like this," George said. He shoved his hands through his hair. "I'm spending all my time running around the city thinking up clever ways to get messages to her. I am crazy about your sister, I have fantasies of marrying her." He fell silent. "But I don't dare call her. Harry, I'm afraid she'll tell me to go to hell. But I'm at the end of my rope. Pretty soon I'm going to have to give up and move on."

"No," Harry said, and was surprised to hear himself. "You can't do that."

"Why not?"

Harry thought. He stirred his coffee some more and tasted it. He knew he had a tendency to stand back from life, and he had never felt as intensely as George did now. But he knew true emotion when he saw it, and he respected it. "It's the real thing, George. I mean, if you think Eleanor is the woman to make you happy, you have to pursue her until you can't go any further."

"Well, what am I supposed to do—accost her on Broadway at eight a.m. and propose?"

"No." Harry paused. "I have a better idea. It's risky, but at this point I don't think you have much to lose."

"Nothing at all," George agreed. "What's your plan?" In spite of his experience with Harry's schemes, George listened, and asked a few questions. In the end he agreed. It was chancy. But things couldn't be worse than they were.

WHEN Eleanor woke up in the Weymouth house on the last Friday in July, she had trouble figuring out where she was. For the first night in weeks she had slept soundly and didn't remember any dreams, which lately had been of the trying-desperately-to-finish-an-impossible-task variety.

It was a glorious day. As Eleanor got out of bed and walked to the window, she felt a moment's sympathy with her father. Sure, the house was hideous, but what a view! Long Island Sound fanned out before her, brilliantly blue. Small dark green islands dotted its surface.

When she got downstairs, Hart was sitting at the table on the deck with a bowl of All-Bran, exuding the smugness of someone who has exercised before breakfast.

"Morning, Ellie," he said. "What are your plans for the day?"

"We're taking Mom out to Farewell Island," said Toby, standing in the doorway clutching a bowl, a gallon of milk, and a gigantic box of Cocoa Pebbles.

"Toby, where did you get those?" Eleanor said, grabbing the box.

"Out of the cupboard," Toby said, unconcerned.

"Did you buy these, Mom?" Eleanor asked her mother, who appeared in the door with a cup of coffee.

Frances sat down and took the box. "Goodness, I suppose I did," she said, examining the box as if it were the artifact of an unknown civilization. "Do you really want to eat these, Toby?"

In answer her grandson poured an enormous bowlful, then settled down to read the back with absolute concentration.

"Mom, you know I don't let them eat that stuff," Eleanor said. "Why did you buy it?"

"Oh, I don't know, dear. I just wasn't thinking," Frances said. "It won't kill them."

Eleanor looked at her mother, who was sliding a section of *The New York Times* out from under Hart's cereal bowl. "Just wasn't thinking" was unlike Frances. There hadn't been any sheets on the beds, either. And after dinner, Frances, instead of chatting with

Eleanor, had gone upstairs to read some weird sci-fi novel. It was bizarre: she was perfectly agreeable, but somehow *not there.*

Later Eleanor meditated on this as she steered the boat across the Sound. Simon stood next to her with a hand on the steering wheel, while Toby sat in the bow, the self-appointed lookout. Harry was due to arrive sometime in the afternoon. What would he say about the latest twist in their parents' relationship? Didn't Hart care that Frances seemed to be in a world of her own?

"Island off the port bow!" Toby yelled. Eleanor closed the throttle and let the boat drift to the beach.

"Okay," Eleanor said. "These are the rules. You stay where I can see you if you're going in the water. When we've beached the boat, I'm going to put some more sun stuff on you—"

"But you already did!" Simon yelled. "I hate that stuff!"

"Nevertheless," his mother went on implacably, "I'm going to put more on. And the food stays with me."

In twenty minutes the boat was securely moored, Eleanor was settled in a folding chair, and the boys had disappeared, though she could hear frequent crashing noises in the bushes. They were apparently building a fort. Eleanor looked down at the book she'd taken from the pile next to her mother's bed. *The Island Kingdom,* it was called. An hour later she had examined the fortress; helped Simon "swim"; rescued Toby, who couldn't turn around in the water and thought he was doomed to swim home; and then read ten pages.

When she glanced up, she noticed the sail of a small boat tacking toward the island. She thought she recognized the dinghy that Clara Henschel kept at the Fenwick house for her guests to use. It must be Harry, then. Typical of Harry to sail over from Clara's without worrying about how the boat was going to get back there. She wondered if he'd brought overnight things with him. She shaded her eyes to see if she could make out a duffel bag or something on board the boat. Then she froze. It wasn't Harry. There in Clara Henschel's dinghy, sailing toward her with an air of inevitability, was George Sinclair. She could barely make out his features, but she knew. That was George's hair. George's hand on the tiller. George's shoulders under the white T-shirt. Eleanor felt her mouth gaping open, and shut it.

In the instantaneous flood of emotions Eleanor could identify one overwhelming feeling: chagrin at being caught unawares. Here she was, with her hair clumped all over her head, wearing nothing more than a wet piece of Lycra. She was acutely aware of her hips and her thighs. And this feeling, half anticipation and half horror, clutched her stomach and made her shiver.

She waited, sitting in her chair, while George, with his customary tidiness, beached the boat and dropped the sail. He lifted an old wicker basket from the dinghy and walked toward her. He set it down carefully, then seated himself on the sand at her side. He gestured to it. "Peace offering. It's full of ritual sacrifices. I'm told that a young goat usually does the trick on these occasions."

Eleanor looked at him. He was pale and seemed thinner.

"You know, I'm going to skip over all the how-did-you-get-here stuff because I detect the interfering hand of my brother," said Eleanor. "Why are you here? And no more silliness about goats," she added sternly.

George noted a faint maternal tone in her voice. "I'm trying again, Ellie. All I do is think about you, and yes, Harry came up with this idea. I couldn't think how else to approach you."

Eleanor watched for a moment as he sifted the sand by his knees. Looking at his bowed head, just level with her shoulder, Eleanor felt a sudden rush of compunction. Maybe it was true. And if George was sincere, she was causing him a great deal of pain. Eleanor felt a new shame at the thought. She'd been so wrapped up in her own misery that she'd given no thought to George at all. Without thinking, she reached out to touch his hair. George leaned back against her hand slightly and turned to look at her.

"I'm sorry," Eleanor said quietly.

He turned his head further to kiss the palm of her hand.

"I am, too," he said, searching her face. "I can see now how it must have looked to you—"

"No," Eleanor interrupted, shifting in her chair so that she was facing him. "I was irrational. You know, it's just that for some reason I couldn't stand the idea of having been a dupe." She reached out to clasp his hands with her own.

"I understand," George answered. "Can I explain to you how it really happened? I promise, it was all so *innocent.* Harry probably

didn't imagine anything more than me helping you get your traveler's checks cashed or something."

Eleanor laughed, with a glorious feeling of relief. "I'm a pretty capable traveler, actually," she said, "and Harry probably believes I can cash my own traveler's checks."

Then, before George had time to reply, there was a crackle of twigs behind her. In a moment Toby emerged, scattering sand all over her legs. Before she had a chance to remonstrate, he was talking. "Hey! Mr. Sinclair! Mom, it's Mr. Sinclair. From school. Remember, I told you about him. I'm Toby Gray, remember me, sir? What are you doing here, sir?"

Eleanor froze. Her eyes widened, and she saw with horror the flush of embarrassment on George's face.

"This is true?" she said, in syntax deformed by stress.

George nodded hopelessly, "I was about to tell you."

In the following silence, Simon slid down next to his mother and put a hand on her shoulder. She closed her eyes and slid an arm around Simon's small waist, burying her face momentarily against his sandy stomach.

Simon spotted the basket George had brought. "Oh, good, lunch!" he said. "What did you bring? I'll trade you my tuna fish for whatever you've got," he offered.

"What if I have something you don't like? Like sardines?"

"Oh, Simon will eat anything," Toby said. "But maybe if you have sardines, we could use them for bait and try to catch something."

"I don't know if I'm staying," George protested, glancing at Eleanor. She was staring out at the water with an expression of grief in her eyes that he knew he had caused. He ached to put his arms around her, to explain everything, to try to kiss some color back into her face.

"But you have to stay," Simon said, looking up at George. "You brought lunch."

"It's up to your mother," George told the boys, watching Eleanor's frozen face.

"Why shouldn't he stay?" Toby asked.

They all looked at Eleanor. She looked back at them. If she sent George away now, she would have to spend the next twenty-four hours explaining herself to her sons. Better to let George stay for another hour or two, however painful. And that would be the end of it, Eleanor promised herself.

"No reason," Eleanor said with a fairly good imitation of a smile.

George looked at Eleanor, appreciating that she was making a heartbreaking choice for her children's sake. Then he crouched down to the basket and took out a sandwich, offering it to Simon. "It's pâté. Do you still want it?"

As George and the boys bustled around setting out their picnic, Eleanor was silent. She helped her children, attempted to eat half of an apple, and did not speak to George. When the boys walked down the beach to spit their melon seeds into the water, George sat down again next to Eleanor.

"I honestly was going to tell you," he said. "Only we didn't get that far."

She turned her head to look at him with a searing gaze. "Mr. Sinclair," she said in a quavering voice, "I am only barely in control of myself, so would you please *shut up?*" The last two words were little more than a hoarse whisper. Eleanor stood up and ran down the beach into the water, striking out in a fast crawl.

George reached into the picnic basket for his sketch pad and began to draw the boys, now intent on a sandcastle. In a few minutes Eleanor turned around and swam toward the shore. Quickly he turned over the page and drew her walking out of the water—Venus emerging from the waves. She lay down elaborately on a towel, as far away from George as she could get.

He sat there for a while longer, filling in his drawing of Eleanor coming out of the water. Then he joined the boys in the sand, where they dug an immense hole and filled it with hermit crabs, minnows, and an unlucky horseshoe crab.

The boys finally got thirsty, and since all the juice for the picnic had been consumed, Eleanor decided they would go home. Toby asked to go with George in the dinghy, and Eleanor gave her permission for both boys to sail home with him.

George watched Eleanor speeding off across the waves and wondered if she was even going home, but the Whaler was bobbing at the dock when he got there, and he could see, off to his right, someone—Eleanor—swimming away as if sharks were after her. Harry was on the dock when George maneuvered the dinghy alongside, and George said, "Harry, can you show the boys how to cleat the boat? I need to cool off." He slipped into the water and struck out after Eleanor.

She was a good swimmer, but she was out of shape, and George had been on his college swim team. Within a few minutes he was level with Eleanor, but she swam on. Maybe she didn't see him. He touched her heel, and she shrieked and sputtered to a stop.

She treaded water furiously, wiping water from her eyes. "How dare you!" she shouted. "How dare you tell me how miserable you've been! What the hell do I care, you . . . lout."

George reached toward her, trying to clasp her shoulders.

"Stop it!" she screamed. "Don't touch me. Have you considered at any point that I might feel I'd been made a fool of? Don't you understand, George? It's bad enough that you're a friend of Harry's. Can you really imagine that I'd have anything to do with one of the boys' *teachers?*"

"I'll quit. I'd rather have you than that dumb job," he said. "Eleanor, if you've been unhappy, too, why can't we be together?"

"Did you think," Eleanor said, flinging a piece of seaweed away from her, "that I was unhappy about you? No, George," she went on. "I felt used, and I felt stupid, but I did not miss you."

George stopped paddling. "You didn't?"

"No," said Eleanor with a hard tone in her voice. "And I wish you'd stop bothering me with your phone calls and weird postcards. I'm getting afraid to open the mailbox."

George looked at her. He couldn't read her expression. Did she mean it? Could he have been wrong?

"You really mean it?" he asked, grabbing her hand beneath the surface of the water. "You want me to go away?"

"Are you so conceited that you can't believe me?" she asked, pulling her hand from his. "Yes, I mean it, George Sinclair. I don't want anything more to do with you. Excuse me." She turned and began swimming toward the Drummonds' house.

George swam alongside, occasionally turning over for a few yards of backstroke. He knew she was tired, and the current was strong. He wanted to be sure she made it home. Once she got to the dock, though, he didn't go into the house, but stayed outside with the boys until Harry appeared and drove him back to Clara's.

13

A WEEK later Hart sat on an abandoned dock in Weymouth's harbor. It was hot. Haze shrouded the horizon and dulled the slanting gleam of the early sun. Hart gently pulled in his line and inspected the lure dripping at the end of it. It was the very latest thing from the tackle store: three hooks strung with shreds of opalescent Mylar. With what he considered to be admirable aplomb, Hart cast the lure out into the harbor and began reeling in again.

Hart had noticed the fishing activity on the old dock when he and Frances first moved to town. It appealed to him as an activity of "the people." The men who gathered there looked to him like crusty exemplars of old-fashioned Yankee virtues. He nosed around to find out how this game might be joined. He even underwent the embarrassing experience of being taught to cast, in public, by the owner of the tackle shop.

It was a little disappointing to find that most of the putative crusty old Yankees who gathered on the dock were actually retired professional men. Before long, Hart found himself gravitating to the end of the dock occupied by the retired brokers and college presidents. He was amused to find that one of them—a lean, dark-haired, spectacled man some twenty-five years younger than the rest who was introduced simply as Chip—turned out to be the other half of Strong Harwood Realty.

Hart looked with wonderment at the man who could stand sharing a business with Margaret Harwood. He led carefully up to the subject one day, adding that she was "quite a personality." Chip Strong said cheerfully to his new acquaintance, "She'd make a steamroller look subtle. But you've got to hand it to her—she moves property. Frankly, I try to see as little of her as possible."

Chip Strong became Hart Drummond's best friend in Weymouth. He was a bachelor who lived—as befitted a man in the real estate business—in a lovely house, but his domestic arrangements were eccentric. He slept on a futon in a ground-floor room and used another room as a closet, with his clothes hanging on racks. His kitchen counter was covered with appliances that each performed only one task: he had a waffle iron, an electric juicer, a popcorn popper, an ice-cream maker, and an immense black Italian coffee machine that dispensed espresso, cappuccino, and regular coffee, provided you pressed the correct buttons.

Hart was now preparing to cast again when he heard footsteps on the dock behind him. "Any luck?" said the unmistakable reedy voice of Chip Strong.

"No, it's too hot. Or too sunny," said Hart with all the expertise acquired in his month of fishing.

"Don't you believe it," answered Chip, setting down a large cooler. "Blues love hot weather. Where were you last weekend? I caught a four-pounder, but there weren't any witnesses."

"And you probably threw it back, too," Hart said. He had quickly adapted to the ritual banter about fishing.

"Nope. Took it home and filleted it."

"You filleted it yourself?" asked Hart. "The couple of fish I've caught, we've had them filleted at the fish market." It seemed paltry and unmanly somehow.

"Don't bother. You can do it yourself. And then—get this—you cook them in the dishwasher!"

"What? Frances always puts them under the broiler. I think," Hart added. "I don't think I could persuade her to cook in the dishwasher."

"Well, you should try. You put it on the top rack of the dishwasher, sealed up tight, and you run the dry cycle. Works like a charm, I promise you."

Hart was sure that Frances would never cook anything in the dishwasher. But filleting the fish—that was appealing. He saw himself skillfully wielding a razor-sharp knife, lifting away the backbone with a swift, sure motion. He almost forgot the reel in his hand until he felt some unmistakable resistance on the end of the line.

Three minutes later an eighteen-inch fish lay flapping in Chip Strong's cooler. Maybe Frances could be persuaded to try that dishwasher trick after all.

IGNORANT of her culinary fate, Frances was getting dressed. It was hard to find something in her closet that would be cool yet presentable. Flicking the neat row of hangers, she found a long, full skirt in a bandanna print and decided it would do. She was only going to look at another house, anyway.

Except that this time she was hopeful. Frances allowed herself to run through the ad again in her mind. "Mint Cond. Victorian," it said. "In same family for 80 years. Beautiful gardens, 3 br. 2 bath. For Sale by Owner." The house was in Madison, a town she'd grown to appreciate.

Frances tried to quell her anticipation as she drove down I-95. The house might be ghastly. What if the neighbors had a huge dog or played loud music? What if the owners had put up hideous wallpaper? But wouldn't "mint condition" rule that out?

As Frances pulled up to the designated address, she could see no immediate flaws. The house was a classic mansard-roofed Victorian with a front porch. A placard on the neatly trimmed lawn said, OPEN HOUSE TODAY in neat but amateurish writing. As Frances walked past it, the screen door opened.

Immediately Frances' heart sank. The woman standing there with a welcoming smile on her face was probably eighty. She was wearing a flowered blouse over teal-green knit pants, and comfortably squashy beige sandals. She held out her hand and smiled. "Are you here for the open house? I'm so glad you're our first visitor. Bill and I were so worried about this. I'm sure you'll love our house. I'm Virginia McCarthy."

Frances shook hands and smiled. "Frances Drummond. Thank you. Yes, I was so interested to read about your gardens."

"Would you like to see them first?"

"No, no, Virginia, we agreed—first the interior, then the gardens," boomed a voice from the dark hall. A very tall man in a white short-sleeved dress shirt and dark pants stepped onto the porch. "Virginia does most of the gardening, so she wants to show off her babies, don't you? I'm Bill McCarthy. Come on in, Mrs. Drummond."

"This is the hall," Virginia McCarthy said brightly.

Frances looked around. "Yes," she agreed. "I see." Her eye strayed to the fireplace in the living room. It had been filled in with what appeared to be plastic brick.

"We don't use the fireplace," Virginia said. "It got to be too much trouble to have it cleaned, so we just covered it over. Bill had some of that nice brick paneling left over from the kitchen." She advanced into the living room and gestured. "Now, you'll see, everywhere in the house, Bill has been making improvements."

He had obviously worked hard. The walls were covered with knotty pine paneling. The ceiling, which should have been some twelve feet from the floor, had been dropped to eight with acoustic tile. Shallow shelving made of the knotty pine displayed an extensive collection of china teacups, while a huge glass-fronted cabinet contained hundreds of commemorative teaspoons.

Frances' first glance into the living room had told her all she needed to know. Her hopes were dashed, and she felt stupid. Naïve. Harry and Eleanor had both, in tiresome stages of their youth, accused her of leading a sheltered life. She couldn't deny it. Most people she knew shared her values and tastes. What was wrong with that?

What was wrong with that, Frances realized as she looked at the rows of silvery spoons, was that she'd forgotten about other tastes. In a moment of unusual perception, Frances understood that Bill McCarthy had inherited a house he didn't much like. Its high ceilings and fireplaces made it hard to heat, the size of the rooms and the stairs were inconvenient, but it was the house he'd grown up in. For the first time, Frances grasped that maintaining a Victorian house—with its parquet floor polished and its slate roof restored—required a great deal that she took for granted: money, time, and the education to appreciate it.

"Come and see the dining room, Mrs. Drummond," Virginia said. "Bill put down a new linoleum floor in there. I was so tired of waxing the old wood, you know." Frances followed her and looked at the gold-flecked black and white tiles. She glanced around the walls, which had been paneled over with dark fake wood.

For a moment Frances wanted more than anything to simply flee, to drive as fast as she could back to— But the thought stopped there. To what? To the Wrong House? It wouldn't offer much comfort. Neither would Hart.

So she behaved heroically. She complimented Bill on his cleverness and practicality. When they went out to look at the gardens—a pair of oblong beds packed with zinnias and marigolds—she mentioned her own garden in Chester.

"But you don't live in New Jersey now," Bill said. "I thought your car had Connecticut plates."

"Yes," Frances said. "We moved up to Weymouth earlier this summer. We bought a modern house, but to tell you the truth, I don't like it. And it doesn't have a garden. I miss that terribly."

"Oh, you must," Virginia said sympathetically. "I always find such consolation in a garden. Mrs. Drummond, I feel so badly for you, I want to cut you some flowers. Just let me get my clippers off the porch," she said. And before Frances had a chance to protest, Virginia had clipped a tight little bunch of zinnias. "Here, dear. Good luck with the house, dear."

"Good luck to you," Frances said, and hesitantly patted Virginia on the arm. It wasn't the sort of thing she normally did, but she was so touched by this woman's warmth that something beyond the norm seemed required. "I'm sure you'll find a buyer who will appreciate all the work you've put into the house." And she managed to get to the car and drive away without blinking.

But the moment she was out of sight, Frances pulled over and turned off the engine, then buried her head in her arms.

Anger had carried her a long way that summer, and she had tried to keep self-pity at bay. But the unexpected sympathy from this nice, brave woman cracked Frances' composure.

She didn't cry. On the whole, Frances wasn't a weeper. After taking a few deep breaths, she sat with her head bowed until her hands, still gripping the steering wheel, grew numb. Then she sat up straight and rubbed her eyes. She touched the petals of one bright pink zinnia lying on the passenger seat. And she started the car to drive home.

Why, Frances wondered, had she been able to say so frankly to a perfect stranger what she could not express to Hart? Worrying about Hart's answer stopped her, she realized. What she would not get from Hart was the easy sympathy that Virginia McCarthy showed her.

She drove back in stony-faced glumness. When she got to the house, she noticed a square of paper fluttering on the front door. As she put the key into the lock, she read it: "Frances: sorry about mess. Back soon."

Incurious, she pulled it off the door and crumpled it up. Mess could hardly bother her now. Without putting down her purse, Frances went into the kitchen to get a glass of iced tea.

She stopped on the threshold, shocked out of her reverie and gasping. The kitchen was covered with blood.

There was a paper bag on the floor next to the sink. Leaking from its bottom was a sinister red ooze, which Hart had stepped in and tracked to the door. On the counter lay an immense fish. Its head had been hacked off roughly and lay with the huge bulbous eye staring at Frances. Entrails spilled from its stomach like jumbled-up knitting. A red-streaked butcher knife lay next to it. Two huge flies buzzed and fumbled over the fish.

As Frances stood there frozen in horror, an enormous gull landed on the windowsill with a clattering rush of wings. It pecked at the screen with its vast yellow beak and shrieked.

Frances bolted. It was too much. The gull, the flies, the fish, the blood, the day, the bunch of zinnias—it was all too much for her suddenly. Her self-control caved in. She ran upstairs and vomited in the brown marble bathroom.

Then, with shaky hands, she scrabbled some underwear and a nightgown into a bag, along with her reading glasses, Arden eye cream, and *The Hills of Maragon.* She ran down the stairs, threw her bag in the car, and sped away, leaving the house wide open. When Hart returned ten minutes later with the filleting knife borrowed from Chip Strong, he didn't even know she'd been there. Been, and left. It was only when she called him from New York later that afternoon that he found out she wouldn't be cooking his home-filleted bluefish for him, in the dishwasher or otherwise.

14

NEITHER of the Drummonds realized at first that Frances had left Hart. When she called him from a room at the Yale Club, Frances omitted to tell her husband precisely where she was or when she was coming home. Hart took advantage of her absence to cook the bluefish in the dishwasher and, furthermore, to throw it away after a few bites, since it turned out to be disgusting.

But after three days Hart opened his closet to find that he had no clean shirts. "Frances!" he bellowed, then checked himself, feeling silly. Right. Frances wasn't there. He sat down on the bed. His momentary curiosity about his wife's whereabouts was eclipsed by a more urgent dilemma. How could he get clean shirts? Hart looked at the phone by the bed. Frances was probably at the Yale Club. All it would take was a quick call. But maybe he could manage by himself. Show her. Why not? Anybody could do laundry.

So Hart gathered six dirty oxford-cloth shirts from his closet. He managed to load them into the washer successfully. Three kinds of laundry detergent stood on the shelf above the washer, and Hart, being systematic, read the labels of each one.

He measured out the prescribed capful of Tide and pressed the buttons on the washer, which started up with a gratifying whoosh. Feeling resourceful, he went off to eat breakfast.

The shirts came out of the washer looking fine. He loaded them into the dryer. This was a snap. Was this the kind of thing housewives complained about? And Frances had a cleaning lady, too! It hardly seemed necessary.

It was pleasant on the deck, since a cool front had moved in, pushing away the humidity. Hart read a long article in *The New York Times* about beach erosion and shoreline real estate values. He went upstairs to shave, and ran the dishwasher, when he remembered the shirts. So he set up the ironing board, plugged in the iron, and filled it with water from the plastic bottle, as he recalled having seen Mrs. Wilucki do. Then he opened the dryer and took out the first shirt.

It was wrinkled. That was to be expected. He spread it out on the ironing board. He touched the iron with the tips of his fingers, also as he'd seen Mrs. Wilucki do. The woman clearly had skin like a horse's hoof, he thought, shaking his burned fingers. Now the spray starch.

He lined up one of the sleeves straight on the ironing board. He sprayed. He ran the iron over the sleeve. It flattened a little. He turned it over. Oh. The iron had set some wrinkles on the other side of the sleeve. Iron again. Oops. No spray. He sprayed. Turned the sleeve over again. Hadn't he ironed that side once?

Hart stood the iron on end and picked up the shirt. He gave it a good hard flap. Maybe the sleeves were extra hard. He'd start on something easier, like the front. He laid the front panel of the shirt carefully on the ironing board and sprayed. He lowered the iron, which slid pleasantly along the fabric. He stood the iron on end again and held the shirt up.

What was this? It was all rumpled again. He checked the temperature on the iron. Probably wasn't hot enough. He goosed up the heat and ironed again. Better.

Hart flipped the shirt over and smoothed the back on the board. He sprayed, and enjoyed the hiss as the iron hit the foam of starch on the cotton. That pleat on the back was a little hard to manage, though. How were you supposed to make it line up? Hart lifted the shirt to see how the pleat hung. He turned it around again just to admire his handiwork on the front.

Somehow the front of the shirt, which had been submissively flat and fresh-looking only moments ago, had rumpled up again. What was it with this shirt? The damn thing was insubordinate. With irritation Hart laid it down again and reattacked the front panel. He knocked over the bottle of distilled water and knelt down carefully to get it. Wouldn't do to jostle the ironing board and get clobbered with a hot iron. Gingerly he straightened up, put down the water bottle, lifted the iron, which he had left resting on the shirt, and contemplated the neat ocher imprint left by the hot iron squarely on the front of his best white shirt. He shut his eyes and swore loud and long.

Hart put away the iron and collapsed the ironing board, and he drove into the village to take his shirts to the cleaner, where someone he'd never seen looked at an inscrutable mark on the collar and said, "Okay, Mr. Drummond, starched and boxed. We'll deliver them next week."

When he got home, the phone was ringing. It was Harry. "Hi, Dad, how are you?"

"Fine," Hart said. "Fine. We've got a nice breeze. And I caught a couple of huge blues the other day."

"What kind of lure?" Harry asked. He couldn't have cared less, but he was fond of his father.

"Something with little dangling pearly strips. Weird-looking, but the fish like it."

"That sounds good. Listen, is Mom there?"

"Ah, no. She's not."

"Oh. Okay. When will she be back?"

"Actually, she's in New York. Shopping, she said."

"Oh." Pause. "Okay. I'll try to reach her here. Is she at the Yale Club?"

"Umm, yes. I think so. Yes."

"But you're not sure?" Harry said, suddenly attentive to the shade of doubt in his father's voice.

"Well, I just assumed so. Listen, I have to go. Talk to you soon," Hart said, and hung up.

Harry raised his eyebrows at the phone. That was odd. Well, maybe not. Frances did come to New York to shop occasionally, and she did routinely stay at the Yale Club.

Harry dialed the Yale Club and asked for Mrs. Drummond's room. "I'm sorry, Mrs. Drummond isn't here anymore," answered a voice.

"She isn't?" Harry said, puzzled. "When did she leave?"

"Just a moment." Pages flipped audibly. "Yesterday," said the voice. "Can I help you with anything else?"

"No, thank you," Harry said, hanging up the phone. He dialed his father's number.

"Dad, she's not there," he said without preamble.

"Where? Who?" Hart answered, confused. He had been making a sandwich out of turkey bologna and dill-pickle chips, a delicate operation.

"Mom. She's not at the Yale Club. She left yesterday."

"Well, don't worry about it," Hart answered, sounding irritated. "She'll call in, and I'll have her call you. Bye."

This made Harry very suspicious. Neither of his parents was the type for open-ended plans. Harry got up from his desk and turned off his air conditioner. The hum suddenly seemed annoying.

TWENTY-FOUR hours earlier the object of all this discussion had been seated in the cafeteria at the Museum of Modern Art sipping tea and staring out the window, thinking how happy she was. Life, for the first time in several months, seemed, well, *attractive*. Fun. Frances drained her teacup and stood up, feeling remarkably alert. As she walked down Fifth Avenue, Frances could see her own silhouette dimly reflected in the plate-glass window of an airline office. She looked with approval at her new haircut. That was one thing you certainly couldn't get in Weymouth, she thought.

Really, some things about New York were marvelous, Frances went on thinking. Hart always fussed about the noise and the air and the crime. But if you cared about, well, civilization, Frances thought, nothing beat New York.

She wondered for a moment how Hart was getting on. He wasn't quite as helpless as many men of his age. She knew he wouldn't starve, but he probably wasn't very comfortable. She smiled momentarily. Hart had always claimed that he could live happily in army barracks. He always told her, when she complained about cooking, for instance, that she could just serve him tuna fish and he'd be happy. Well, his affection for tuna fish was probably being tested.

Frances headed downtown, walking just fast enough not to get jostled in the crowd. It was Tuesday afternoon. Maybe she'd head back to the Yale Club. Then maybe a nap. Or the movies. Or dinner at the Oyster Bar; that would be nice. It was such bliss to be free of housework for a change. Not that she found it so onerous. Not in Chester, anyway. Keeping the house running in Chester had been a real pleasure, an achievement. The Wrong House didn't need as much care, it was true. She hardly ever dusted, and Mrs. Wilucki did all the vacuuming. But there was no point in trying to make it into something it wasn't. The Wrong House was utilitarian. It wasn't civilized.

At the Yale Club she collected her key at the desk and was surprised to hear the telephone ringing as she opened the door to her room. She couldn't imagine how anyone had gotten her number, but it didn't seem to matter. In fact, the caller was Clara, who had apparently tracked her down by ESP.

"Silly to spend all that money at that club," Clara said. "If you want to stay in New York, go to my house. It's open. Beatriz is there; she can cook for you. Go ahead. It's a nicer neighborhood, anyway."

Frances hesitated. The house was on East Seventy-third Street. It *was* a nicer neighborhood. "Well, thank you, Aunt Clara," Frances said. "If you're sure I won't be bothering anyone."

"Not at all. I'd rather have someone in the house anyway. Go on up there tomorrow. I'll let Beatriz know. One more thing. Do you mind if they find out where you are?"

"They? You mean Hart and the children? Oh, no. I don't want them worrying. I suppose I should let them know."

"When they want you, they'll track you down. Tell me what's happening when you feel like it," Clara said, and hung up.

ELEANOR was busier than usual and rather grateful for this. She knew that if it did nothing else, hard work distracted you from your troubles. It also, if you were lucky, provided you with some tangible successes. The settlement of the Gast accounting had been one such triumph. Charlie Winter's client had evidently decided to play ball. At a deeply satisfying meeting, Charlie, without cowboy boots or bolo tie, had been obliged to tell Eleanor that his client recognized his responsibilities and would make restitution to the Gast estate. So Eleanor, trying not to smirk, laid out her requirements, which Charlie then had to accept. His expression of meekness almost made up to Eleanor for the rude crack he had made shortly before about her haircut. And as she took the E train back to the office, she was able to reflect with grim satisfaction that at least she could still manage her job. And the boys were fine. And her hair was growing out. If there was a certain joylessness to her demeanor, few people besides her family perceived it.

One of them, however, was her friend Sophy.

Sophy had known Eleanor since college. Sophy had memories of a girl whose earnestness was leavened by a sense of humor and an unexpected irreverent streak. She hadn't seen much of either characteristic in months. Something had to be done. She wanted Eleanor to visit a psychic. "He's just *helpful,* Ellie. I know you think I'm a crackpot, but honestly, Frank is very practical."

Eleanor didn't see how a practical psychic named Frank was going to make her life easier or more pleasant, so Sophy had resorted to force, emotionally speaking. For Eleanor's thirty-ninth birthday she gave her friend a session with Frank.

Eleanor knew she was beaten. So the day after Harry realized his mother had gone astray, Eleanor took the Lexington Avenue IRT to Eighty-sixth Street and walked a few blocks to a modern apartment building with a doorman. She wondered, as she asked for Frank Gerson, if the doorman knew the nature of his business. Did a stream of anxious-looking people come asking for him?

When Frank opened the door, Eleanor thought she had pressed the wrong doorbell. He was small and slim, with very short curly hair and horn-rimmed glasses. He wore khakis and an eggplant-colored polo shirt, and his feet were bare. Eleanor felt that, at least, was a psychic touch.

"Come in, come in," he said, a little irritably. "We don't all wear turbans and big earrings, you know."

Eleanor felt taken aback. Had he read her mind? She took a few steps into the bland beige living room.

"Come sit over here, please," Frank said. He was sitting at a square table, where two chairs faced each other.

Eleanor sat down. There were three packs of playing cards on the table. Frank picked up the pack closest to him and began to shuffle with startling dexterity.

"Sophy said you didn't want to come. You don't really believe I can see anything, do you?" Frank said. He had a slightly fussy manner, like a much older man.

"Well," said Eleanor apologetically, "no. I hope I won't waste your time."

"My time has been paid for," Frank said disconcertingly. "What you should worry about is yours. Here, choose three cards." He fanned out the pack. "You should give your brother a little more credit. He's not a child anymore, you know. He might be really helpful in this flap with your parents."

Eleanor sat still, eyes wide. "How do you know this stuff?" she blurted out.

"That's the gift, Eleanor," he said with a slight smile. "I know things about people. For instance, it doesn't take a lot of insight to see that you're a very unhappy woman right now." He laid out a single row of cards, face down. His hand hovered over them, pausing. Then he tapped one. "Turn it over, please."

Eleanor did. It was the king of hearts.

"But I knew right away," Frank said, satisfied. "No, I know you don't want to talk about him," Frank went on, shuffling again. Studying Eleanor's face, he fanned the cards. "You *know* you're making a terrible mistake," he said calmly. "There is nothing substantial standing in your way. He's a good man. He's honest and passionate. You'll have to learn to fight."

Eleanor said tightly, "What do you mean, learn to fight?"
"Well, fight to get him. Fight your pride. Determination can be a fault, you know. You're just being obstinate." He looked up at her. "I've lost you, haven't I? This is something you don't want to hear." He shrugged. "Let's look at something else."
Eleanor took a deep breath and tried to relax her shoulders. She rubbed her forehead and watched as Frank laid cards in a pyramid.
"What's going on with your parents? Someone's having a second childhood. Or both of them. The rift is not very deep," Frank said, frowning. "They may get back together and they may not."
"What do you mean, get back together?" Eleanor asked.
"She's left him," Frank said. "Didn't you know?"
"Well, she's in New York for a visit," Eleanor protested, "but she hasn't *left* him." She paused, disturbed. "At least that's not the story Dad's telling."
"Goodness, what a strange family," Frank responded. "Of course they're pretending it isn't what it looks like." He paused and looked at Eleanor again. "Don't be their go-between. Don't let your brother do it, either. They have to communicate directly."
By now Eleanor was relaxing, though her mind was reeling with Frank's advice. Her mother had left her father? What was she supposed to do about this?
"No, there's nothing for you to do," Frank's voice broke into her thoughts. "They're grown up. You and your brother can't manage their relationship. Manage yours instead. Listen, Eleanor. I know what you dream of. I do. I see all that yearning for a richer life. You tell yourself you can't be lonely because you're so busy. You've fooled yourself into thinking you're self-sufficient.
"Let me tell you a little more about this man. You are the woman of his dreams. He appreciates you. You're an unusual woman, Eleanor. You must know by now that you intimidate people. George is not afraid of you. He sees through you. He knows the tenderness inside. He would be loyal and protective." Frank suddenly looked down and picked up the cards. "That's all." He shuffled slowly, then laid out the cards in a circle. Meditatively he eased a card from the circle and placed it in the center.
"I sometimes have odd bits of images or information left over," he said in a voice that had lost its urgency. He paused.

"What?" she said, suddenly tired. "I don't think I can handle much more."

"I hesitate to tell you this," he said. "It may turn you against everything I've already said."

"Go ahead," Eleanor said. "I'll try not to let it weigh too heavily."

Frank sighed and flipped the card onto the table face up. It was a joker. "I don't know what it's doing here. I always take them out of the pack," he said. "I have a very strong and very strange image in my mind. Something you will see in the near future."

"What?" Eleanor said, a little irritated.

Frank took a deep breath. "I see a boat on the floor of a house," he said apologetically.

Eleanor looked at him incredulously. "Are you ever wrong about those things?"

"Not that I know of," Frank said. "It puzzles me, too." He looked at his watch. "I think you should go home. I don't think you are ready to hear more." He picked up the cards and laid them aside. "If you want to come back, I'd be glad to see you."

Eleanor dimly realized that he was being generous and thanked him, but she couldn't wait to get away.

Eleanor found Frank's news about her family disturbing enough to put George out of her mind completely. When she got home, she called her father, who was blandly obstructive. No, Frances wasn't there. No, he wasn't quite sure where she was staying or when she would be coming back. Oh, yes, he was doing fine. Good night.

It wasn't possible to press further. Eleanor couldn't ask her father, "Has Mom left you?" Even less could she tell him where she'd gotten that idea. She had a moment's amusement at the idea of his incredulous reaction and wondered, as she sat down to read the newspaper, about Frank's reliability. He had been very convincing until he got to the boat on the floor.

15

FROM the moment she stepped into Clara's house, Frances felt at home. Better than that. Soothed, somehow. Relaxed. As she sat in the living room on Thursday night, she let her eyes rove around the room. It had been decorated in the 1940s in a grand Francophile style, with gilded tables and brocade upholstery in a predominantly sea-green shade. There was potpourri in a big Chinese export porcelain bowl. The room was silent except for the ticking of the mantel clock. The taste was a bit more formal than what she would have chosen. But impeccable and comfortable and beautiful. That was it. It was simply beautiful. Maybe she needed to have beautiful things around her. Maybe that was why the Wrong House was so awful.

Hart would have pointed out that Long Island Sound was beautiful, and he was right. It was. But it wasn't the same thing, Frances thought. A forest was all very well in its way, but Frances preferred a garden.

Frances leaned back. She hadn't given much thought before to what she might need from life. Probably, she thought with a flash of insight, because she'd had it. Her life before the Wrong House had provided what she needed. Funny how you could never tell what that was until it was gone, she thought.

"We live and learn," she said aloud in the quiet room.

THE next day she called Harry.

"Good morning, Harry. I gather you've been trying to reach me," said his mother's voice, perfectly composed.

"Well, yes, Mom, I have," Harry said, walking with his cordless phone back to the dining-room table and his half-finished breakfast. "We've all been worried sick! What is going *on*?"

"What do you mean, what is going on?"

"Don't be obtuse, Mom. Have you left Dad?"

"Oh, no," said his mother's voice, surprised. "Where did you get that idea?"

Harry paused. Eleanor's psychic suddenly didn't seem to be a very credible source. "Well, Mom, you waltz out of the house with no warning, and you won't tell Dad when you're coming back. What are we supposed to conclude?"

"That I'm taking a spur-of-the-moment vacation," Frances said crisply.

"I see. And when is this vacation going to be over?" Harry asked.

"It's not clear," Frances said less confidently.

"Sounds like a trial separation to me," Harry said a little cruelly.

"Mom, Eleanor's already a zombie, and the idea that you and Dad might be splitting up is just too much for her. Dad is wandering around that house completely helpless."

Frances sighed. "I'm not worried about your father. He knows how to defrost. I'll give Ellie a call now."

"Okay," Harry said. When he hung up, he stared for a long time at his coffee cup, feeling rotten. Blunt as he'd been, he hadn't been able to tell his mother the most important thing—that he was worried and didn't want his parents to split up. The whole thing made him feel vulnerable as a child again.

AT FIRST Hart had looked on Frances' absence as an adventure. The debacle with the shirts was the first hint that it might be less than perfectly jolly. As the week went on, other clues intruded.

The impatiens in the window boxes died. He couldn't figure out how many scoops of coffee to put in the coffeepot. Laundry was an incredible bore. And making the meals got onerous. Hart got fed up with trying to really cook and fell back on cans and frozen meals.

Joan Failey called. Could he and Frances come for dinner next week? Hart said he thought so, and got off the phone fast.

The worst moment came when, on a gray Saturday morning, Margaret Harwood cornered Hart in the supermarket.

"Hart!" she cried, as if he were her long-lost brother. She had on a magenta velour jogging suit that was particularly unfortunate from behind. "I've been meaning to call you and Frances. How are you doing? You still interested in buying a Victorian? I've got something coming onto the market real soon if you are."

Hart surreptitiously tried to draw his shopping cart into a retreating position. The wheels, however, were hooked on the wheels of her cart, which contained mostly jugs of diet soda and Weight Watchers frozen meals. "I hadn't really given it much thought," he muttered without meeting her bold glance. "If you'll excuse me"—he gestured toward the checkout—"I need to . . ."

But she merely wheeled her cart around and followed him down the aisle. "I'm on my way out, too," she said. "Listen, I've been meaning to call to get you and Frances over for dinner. Maybe we could grill something you'd caught. Wouldn't that be fun?"

Frantically Hart scanned the checkout lines. Each one was obstructed by carts mounded high with food. Margaret Harwood was right behind Hart. Suddenly panic overcame him. What if she named a specific date, and he had to say Frances wouldn't be available? What if she started to pry information from him in that overpowering way she had? She'd probably extract the story of the mirror over the bed! "Sorry, I just realized—forgot—I need to get . . ." he babbled, and wheeled his cart around.

As he disappeared up the baby-food aisle, he heard Margaret's voice floating after him: "Don't forget about dinner. I'll call Frances."

Hart got home safely that day, but he was beginning to feel harassed. He didn't know how to handle this.

It was extremely awkward. What did Frances want him to say? Any day now her friends were going to start talking. Gossiping. He knew how it would go: "Have you heard about Hart and Frances? Oh, well . . ." with lots of lowered voices and raised eyebrows. Next the harpies would be calling him up.

He wanted to know what his wife had in mind. But there was more to it than that. He wanted her advice. Here he was, having wife troubles. He had to admit it. But the person he usually asked for advice in his troubles was—his wife. There wasn't anybody else.

He was out on the boat as this thought came to him. It was sunset, the time of day that somehow needed filling with Frances gone. The water was choppy, and the sky an unhelpful gray. On the shore, the house looked welcoming. The lights glowed yellow from the kitchen and the living room.

Hart sighed. He was really at a loss. Apparently he'd failed Frances in some way. Okay, he'd dragged his feet on finding a new house. There was no getting around that.

But could their marriage be breaking up over a house?

Hart sighed and turned the boat for home. He wished he could ask Frances. As he covered the boat, he felt a few drops of rain and ran inside before the storm broke.

IT WAS a sudden squall blowing up from the southeast, a dramatic end to a day of heavy dampness. In Fenwick, up the coast, the big old trees began to blow suddenly. Enthroned on her four-poster bed, Clara Henschel called down on the house intercom.

In the octagonal morning room, George Sinclair picked up the house phone. "George, dear, there's quite a squall blowing up. Would you get Sarge and check the windows?"

"No problem," George said, glancing out the window. "I'll do it right now." He put down his charcoal pencil and went to the kitchen to find Sarge.

This, George felt with some amusement, was typical Clara—a canny combination of prudence, generosity, and selfishness. While he and Sarge scurried around in the rain slamming windows and shutters, Clara would huddle up there in her boudoir reading the memoirs of Madame de Sévigné.

George had not paid much attention to Clara on the morning when he and Harry had borrowed her boat. He had been so tense about the upcoming meeting with Eleanor that he had completely missed Harry's whispered explanation to Clara. But when the two men came back dejected, Clara had virtually ordered them to stay the night and recount the Eleanor saga.

The story interested Clara. She watched George carefully and liked what she saw. It wasn't clear yet how she could intervene, but she intended to try.

Her opportunity came the next morning. George had left his sketchbook lying on the round front-hall table. Clara leafed through it, pausing at the picture of Toby and Simon on the beach. She glanced at the drawing of Eleanor emerging from the waves and felt suddenly as if she were prying.

When George came downstairs, Clara made a proposition. She had always hated the color of the morning-room walls. Would he consider doing a mural for her?

George agreed on the spot. He wasn't working well in New York; maybe the change of scene would do him good. At the very least, he might hear news of Eleanor through Clara.

George's idea was to paint an allegory of Clara Henschel's life. Each panel of the octagon could represent an important event. Clara's birth, debut, and three marriages would each occupy a wall. The two windows would be surrounded with foliage.

When he proposed this, Clara was delighted and entered happily into the planning. So George had become an established member of the Fenwick household. He had dinner each night with Clara and made free use of the dock, the boat, and the library. He gave his agent Clara's telephone number, and planned to stay in Fenwick for the remainder of the summer.

FRANCES had spent the summer trying to be something she wasn't: a relaxed person who could adapt to anything, who took life as it came.

She had failed. She had neither adapted to the Wrong House nor lived up to one of her cardinal rules, which was to put a pleasant face on things. All along, however, Frances felt that the Wrong House was a key. It had taken on a personality in her mind, the personality of a friendly but extremely unattractive dog. It wanted to please but was physically repulsive. She and Hart needed a house they could love. Winter would come and the "old man of the sea" would have to put the Whaler on blocks in the backyard, and then what was he going to do? Frances was determined that by the end of daylight saving time they would have a new home.

So she scanned the real estate ads, made a list, and picked up the phone to call. This time she had no hesitation placing these calls. Before noon she had scheduled three full days of house hunting and felt a glow of satisfaction. It occurred to her that part of her problem that summer had been that she simply hadn't had enough to do.

On Tuesday morning she took an early train to New Haven and reclaimed her car. Then she drove up to Stonington and spent the day looking at houses.

She stayed that night in Mystic at a motel with a fax machine. She made a few phone calls late in the afternoon and, before dinner, leafed through the faxes of listings that the next day's broker had sent her. As Harry would have said, she was on a roll.

There was something superb about Frances intent on a mission. She would ride smoothly over all obstacles with a small smile, never wavering from good manners and always closer to her goal. She was organized, thorough, and tireless—a courteous juggernaut.

On Wednesday she got as far south as Essex. In two days she had seen fifteen houses, and there were only four listing sheets left for consideration. Early on Thursday morning, from her room at the Griswold Inn, Frances called Chip Strong.

Chip was padding around in his knee-length plaid bathrobe,

tending to the coffee machine and the sandwich maker and the juicer (breakfast was a particularly machine-intensive meal), when the phone rang. He gulped when Frances identified herself.

"Listen, Chip," Frances went on, ignoring his audible consternation. "I need you to do something for me."

"Oh, of course, Frances," he said, aware that his voice was actually squeaking. "What can I do?"

"Well, it may not be easy. I think you know about the mix-up with the house we bought?"

Chip nodded, then realized she couldn't see him and said, "Yes." He noticed smoke coming from the sandwich maker and had to take the receiver away from his ear to flip the switch off.

As he listened again, he heard, "But not with Margaret Harwood. I just couldn't stand it, Chip. Do you understand?"

"Oh, I do," Chip said. "Only I didn't catch the beginning, I'm sorry. You want to do what without Margaret?"

"Look at houses, Chip," Frances' voice came patiently down the line. "You do have some for sale?"

"Oh, yes. Yes." Chip nodded.

"Well, look, Chip, could we do it Saturday morning, then? First thing? It won't cut into your fishing too much, will it?" Frances said, enjoying a flash of malice.

"No, no, of course not," Chip said. "But maybe we could meet at my house. If you want to keep away from Margaret."

"That's fine," Frances answered. "Oh, and don't tell Hart."

FRANCES Drummond on the phone was one thing, Chip found. Frances Drummond in the flesh was even more imposing.

Until that Saturday morning Chip had heard about Frances from Hart and had formed an image of her as a kind of middle-aged neurasthenic, drifting around with a book in her hand and refusing to cook bluefish in the dishwasher. So this crisp, opinionated woman came as something of a surprise.

She strode into his house and glanced around, taking in the futon on the floor of the parlor and the racks in the center of the other living room. Chip furtively inspected the baseboards for dust balls as he led Frances into the kitchen. She glanced at the array of machinery on the counter, but didn't comment.

"Would you like coffee?" Chip asked. "I've just made a pot."

"Thank you, that would be nice," Frances said, and sat down at the kitchen table.

Chip placed a handful of listings next to her and went over to the counter. Ignoring the mugs in the dish drainer, he reached into a cupboard. From the back he brought a pink lusterware cup and saucer, which he filled carefully with coffee and put in front of her.

Frances made short work of the listings. "No. No. No, we saw this one with Margaret—it's a dump. Hmm. This is interesting." She sipped the coffee. "This is very good coffee," she said, and he suddenly felt she might be human. "What about this one? Where is it?" she asked, holding out a listing.

Chip took it. "It's right on the corner of Main Street. You've probably never noticed it because of the trees."

Frances took the sheet back. "Why is it so cheap?"

"Needs work, as they say," Chip told her. "Cosmetic, mostly. Pair of old sisters lived there and went to a nursing home a few months ago. Can we go soon? Because if Margaret should happen to be driving by and sees you with me, she's going to create an unholy fuss. She thinks you and Hart are her personal property."

"I don't know how Hart feels about it," Frances said, "but I find the idea very disturbing. Let's go."

The first house was the carriage house for a big place that had been built by a very prosperous mill owner in the late nineteenth century.

Frances took one encompassing look around the living room and said slowly, "It's very charming, isn't it?" The low beamed ceiling was whitewashed, and the whole effect was cheerful and quirky. The kitchen and bathrooms were all brand-new. The bedrooms, however, were disappointing. "It stands to reason we'd have to sleep in the stalls, I suppose," was Frances' comment when she saw the first one. The lot, screened from the big house by a tall white fence, was virtually unlandscaped.

"Still," Frances said as they drove away, "it is very attractive. And the price is fair, I think, don't you?"

"Yes," Chip agreed. "For what you're getting, it's fair."

"What about the next place?" Frances continued. "It's the one with the hemlock trees? The price is just the same."

"Yes," Chip answered cautiously. "You'd get a lot more house for the same money."

"But . . ." Frances added for him.

He nodded. "You'll see."

She did see. They parked on the gravel driveway at the side of the lot. As Frances stepped out of the car, she noticed a patch of crabgrass thrusting its way up through the granite chips. She bent down to pull up a large clump and tossed it into the bushes that bordered the lot.

The porch sagged slightly, though an attempt had been made to shore it up with raw, unpainted two-by-fours. Frances looked at the peeling dark green paint and said, "Chip, this looks like a waste of time. The place is falling to wrack and ruin."

"No," he answered, a bit surprised at his temerity. "It's not as bad inside. I think you should see it, Frances." And he added cannily, "For comparison."

Of course. For comparison. She wouldn't actually consider living in a place that looked so ramshackle. Frances was reassured. "All right."

The door opened after a tussle with the lock, and Chip and Frances found themselves in a gloomy hall.

"Here's the kitchen," Chip said. They turned left into a big room that looked like a stage set for a movie about the Depression. An ancient gas stove dominated one side of the room, while a huge, deep double sink took up most of another wall. "I get the idea," she remarked.

Chip led her out through a swinging door into the dining room. The walls had been covered with a gold-on-white star-patterned paper, while the floor featured a lush purplish wall-to-wall carpet. But the ceilings were high and there was a handsome marble fireplace. Frances didn't say anything.

The hall had real elegance. The stairs, with turned balusters and a sinuous handrail, curved gracefully up to a landing where an arched niche looked out. Just the right place, Frances thought, for a big vase full of lilacs. But she wasn't really considering the house, she remembered. The floor was a handsome parquet, popping up in places.

She led the way upstairs. There were four bedrooms, all with marble fireplaces and twelve-foot ceilings. Two had bay windows with window seats. One had a built-in mirror over the fireplace. In all of them the paint was peeling, the windows were cloudy with dust, the doors stuck or hung crooked on their hinges.

In every corner of the house neglect had done its damage. Doors lacked doorknobs. Lights switched on with frayed pieces of string. Rust crept over medicine cabinets. Paint scaled off the tall old radiators. The two old women living there had hidden what could be hidden and added ugly conveniences like the plastic laundry rack standing in a corner of one of the bathrooms.

Frances gestured to this and said, "Chip, if you really want to sell this house, you should get rid of things like that."

"I can't," he said uncomfortably. "It's an estate sale, and I'm not allowed to move anything."

Frances shot him an impatient look and stalked into the bedroom. "Look," she said with irritation. "Do the heirs really want this?" She picked up a half-empty box of Kleenex from the bedside table. "Or *this?*" She waved a *TV Guide* in front of him. "Look, Chip, this has the date on it. Any sharp buyer is going to look at this *TV Guide,* see the date—December—and realize that the house has been empty and probably on the market for months. Your average buyer will deduce that the property is not moving and will make you a laughable offer. Or won't offer at all. The sooner the house sells, the happier the estate will be. In fact, you might *even* recoup the cost of that box of Kleenex for them if you can just spruce the place up a little and sell it sooner instead of later." Frances slapped the *TV Guide* down on the television, where it raised a cloud of dust.

Chip was looking around the room as if seeing it for the first time. "I suppose you're right. I never thought about it that way. I mean, the place does have potential."

"Of course it does," Frances said, turning to leave the room. "I'm sorry to fly off the handle like that, but really, you could be marketing this place much better." She started down the stairs.

She walked down the hall to the front door and paused for a minute under the crystal chandelier that hung from the ceiling, looking up at its balls and drops in the shadowy room. Chip waited for her by the back door.

"So are you interested?" he asked as he locked the door. Turning around, he discovered a softer look on her face than he'd seen yet.

"Yes," she said, meeting his gaze with a rueful smile. "Defying all common sense, I am."

16

FRANCES went back to New York trying not to yield to the feeling of exhilaration that kept welling up, an almost physical sensation around her heart. It was just a house. It needed a great deal of work.

But there was something there. Frances had felt it. That house had dignity. It held itself apart from the extension cords and the cracked linoleum and the exposed shanks of doorknobs. Frances could imagine how it had looked in 1880, and how it could look now, with the right care. Care she wanted to give it.

The difficulty was going to be selling this house to Hart. Because he could grow to love it, too; Frances felt sure of that. But he would have to be convinced.

Her first move, when she got back to Clara's house in New York, was to call an engineer, a contractor, and a landscape architect. Frances wanted ammunition. She wanted to be able to say to Hart, "It will take twenty-five thousand dollars to put in a new kitchen and ten thousand to do all the floors." And she wanted to be able to say to Chip Strong, "It will cost us seventy-five thousand to make the place livable. The price is much too high."

Since it was Saturday, Frances knew she was lucky to get the engineer at home. She had left messages for the others. When the phone rang later that evening, she thought it might be one of them returning her call.

"Frances, what is this about a house?" came Hart's voice, blustering down the phone cord.

"Oh," she said, "hello. You've been talking to Chip Strong. Did he tell you where I was, too?"

"Yes," snapped Hart. "I'm at his house now, talking on a pay phone, if you can believe such a thing. Chip says he showed you a house today!"

"Several, actually. I asked him not to tell you," Frances said, "because I wanted to surprise you." Some canny instinct prompted her to add, "I thought I could save you time by screening them."

"Oh," Hart said, sounding a bit mollified. "That's probably a good idea." The blustering tone came back into his voice. "But why are you even looking at houses?"

"Hart, you know I can't live in that house on the water," Frances said with the patience of a nursery school teacher.

"Well, can't you let it wait until the end of the summer?"

"Why?" asked his wife in a reasonable tone. There was a long pause as Hart examined this. Then a series of clicks came, punctuated by muffled swearing. "Damn. Running out of money—" The line went dead.

Three minutes later the phone rang again. Again Frances calmly reached for the receiver. Expecting to hear her husband's voice, she said sweetly, "Yes?"

"Mom? Is that you?" It was Harry, sounding confused.

"Oh, Harry! Goodness, such excitement tonight," his mother said.

"Mom, I want to talk to you about Eleanor. Do you remember George Sinclair? You met him this summer."

"No, Harry. Who is he?"

Harry sighed. "He is a friend of mine, and he was only there for a few minutes—remember, with Clara's boat? I may not have even introduced you. The thing is, Mom, Eleanor had an affair with him in Venice. And he's in love with her, and I swear she's in love with him, but she won't see him."

Frances put the book she had been leafing through on the floor. "What? What is all this? Eleanor in love? How did I miss this?"

Harry didn't answer right away. "It's a long story, Mom. Can I come and tell you in person?"

"I think you'd better," said Frances.

"I'll be there in fifteen minutes."

Frances hung up and went down to the kitchen to make a pot of decaf coffee. As she arranged a few almond cookies on a plate, the phone rang again. "You're running late?" she said.

"No," came Hart's exasperated voice, "I'm not running late. I had to borrow a roll of quarters from Chip, and then your phone was busy. What are you *up* to?"

"Up to?" Frances exclaimed in annoyance. "I'm not up to anything. I was talking to my son on the phone, which I suppose I am permitted to do."

"No, no, about the house," Hart said, sounding weary.

"I am trying to find a place to live," Frances answered.

"You have a place to live. Here, with me."

"No," Frances said very quietly. "I really am sorry, Hart. I just can't. Not in that horrible house."

There was a long pause. "I feel like you're railroading me," Hart said finally.

Frances stood in the quiet white kitchen, considering. She turned to get coffee cups from the cupboard. "Maybe I am," she answered. "But it seemed like the only way to get things moving."

"But what if I hate the house?" Hart answered.

"It does need a lot of work," Frances conceded. "But the price is reasonable and it has potential." The doorbell rang. "I have to go. Harry's here."

"Wait, Frances. When are you coming back?"

"I don't know," his wife said. "I'll talk to you during the week." And she hung up without saying good-bye.

Upstairs on the doorstep, Harry had turned his back to the house and was looking at the streetlight's yellowish glow filtering through the thick leaves of the plane trees. When Frances opened the door, she noticed that he looked tired. She kissed his cheek as he walked past her. The look of defeat on his face wrung her heart.

"I spoke to your father just now," she said.

"Oh?" Harry said as he followed Frances to the kitchen.

"We're looking at a house next week." She poured milk into Clara's little silver pitcher. "There, you can carry that up to the library.

"It's been quite a summer, hasn't it?" Frances said when she was settled on a loveseat in the library.

Harry sighed. "I'll be glad when it's over," he said. "I don't know why I mind so much about you and Dad. And Eleanor's got enough on her plate anyway. And I feel horrible about that, too. I feel incredibly responsible."

"How did I miss this?" Frances said. "Why didn't I know that Eleanor was so unhappy?"

Harry looked embarrassed. "Well, you've been . . . You were a little . . ." His eyes searched the bookshelves. "Distracted. Something. This summer."

Frances nodded. "True." She was silent for a few moments. "Yes. Well, that's over. So tell me about Ellie. If this man George is in love with her and she's in love with him, I don't see where the problem lies."

"Well, you know how stubborn she is," Harry began with relief. Frances settled back to listen.

WHEN Eleanor had flung herself away from him in the Piazza San Marco, George had been angry and disappointed. But he hadn't really felt that things were over. He wanted Eleanor to know that he wasn't giving up. He wanted her to have the sense that she was on his mind. He wanted to be on *her* mind. Ultimately, George wanted Eleanor to feel he was wooing her.

But the tactic had taken its toll. The price was complete preoccupation with Eleanor. He looked back on the month of July and remembered only thinking about her. At the time he had relished doing this; it had kept her image breathing in front of him. But now, walking home to his loft, where he was staying a few days, George felt he had made a terrible mistake. While he had become obsessed with this woman, she had only felt hounded. He had made himself miserable and had made her even more miserable.

The prudent, sober path now would probably be to try to forget her. But there was one more thing, one more gesture that he needed to make. Something else that he wanted her to have, regardless of what happened afterward.

His apartment had never been very appealing in the summer. The loft was stuffy, and a thin fog of dust lay everywhere. George opened the window onto the street, knowing it would not draw in a fresh breeze.

He had played his cards wrong; it was obvious now. There might have been a moment, if only he could have judged it, an interval when Eleanor would have listened to him. Before he blew everything by confronting her in Weymouth. After that, of course, it was hopeless.

George ambled over to the painting area and began packing brushes and sketch pads into a duffel bag. When the bag was nearly full, he threw in some clothes and books. As he crossed the loft with an armful of shirts, he glanced at his answering machine and flicked the switch to turn it off. If he was going to spend all of August in Fenwick, he might as well leave the machine off. He had given Clara's number to everyone who would need it. He wedged the shirts into the duffel bag, glanced at his watch, and realized that if he wanted to make his train, he'd have to leave. So neat, organized George Sinclair zipped his bags shut, picked up a brown-paper parcel that stood by his desk, and walked out of his loft, leaving an open window.

He took a cab up to the Upper West Side and had the driver wait while he left the parcel with Eleanor's doorman. Then the taxi took him to the train station at 125th Street. As the train swept through leafy suburbs to New Haven, he looked out the window numbly, with a pained expression on his face.

IT WAS an expression that would have been familiar to Eleanor, though it sat differently on her face. A certain tension between the eyebrows, an inability to smile. She wept easily, and her temper was shocking.

The worst of it was that the children had noticed. Toby taxed her with crabbiness and clowned around, trying to get her to smile. Simon, meanwhile, became heartbreakingly clingy. He whined and wrapped his arms around her as she put him on the bus for day camp in the morning. When she came home at night, he threw himself at her and nuzzled her neck like a baby.

Eleanor knew that if she could snap out of this depression, the boys would be back to normal in a week. But it wasn't the kind of depression you could snap out of, she thought bitterly as she walked past her doorman that Monday night. It was the kind of depression that you climbed out of an inch at a time, with a lot of backsliding.

"Mrs. Gray," the doorman said, "wait. I have a package for you." He disappeared into his little cubby and came back with a sizable brown-paper parcel. Eleanor's eyes flew to the familiar elegant handwriting on the front.

"Thank you, Eddie," she said, trying to sound composed. As she went up in the elevator, she studied her name, written in George's handwriting. It was a picture; she could feel the hard outline of the frame through the paper. She considered tearing the paper off, but caution conquered curiosity. Eleanor knew it was going to be upsetting. Better wait until the children were in bed.

It wasn't until three hours later that the children were asleep, the dishes done, the lunches made, the clothes laid out. Eleanor turned out the lights in the living room. Then she carried the package to her bedroom, loosening the tape as she went. She laid it down on her bed and took the paper off.

The tears welled up. She pressed a fist to her mouth as it pulled into a grimace. It was a pencil sketch of Toby and Simon at the beach. Toby knelt in a few inches of water, placing a shell on the battlement of his sandcastle. Simon stood watching, holding a forgotten bucket of water in his right hand.

It was just a pencil sketch, though George must have gone over the picture later, Eleanor thought, to refine the various textures: Toby's hair, sleek as a seal's fur, the little quivering leaves of the beach plum, the glassy water around Simon's ankles.

Eleanor inched backward on the bed until she was leaning against the pillows, with the picture propped up on her knees. What more could a woman want, she thought, than a man like George Sinclair? A man who knew the way to her heart. Thoughtful. Sensitive. A man who had been willing to *pursue* her. To let her know how much he wanted her.

There he was, hers if she would only reach out a hand. Why could she not reach out a hand? Eleanor asked herself with a sudden clarity. What is it I am afraid of?

Betrayal.

Nothing less. The answer came with a rush and a spurt of tears. Excruciating memories of loss and pain. Of Jared walking out the door as she held a screaming infant Simon, with Toby crying at her knees and her own tears pouring silently down her face. As she sat on her bed, Eleanor felt the tears again and remembered the desolation. More than a body could bear. She shook her head, still crying. More than anyone could bear twice.

She mopped her face and blew her nose. So that was it. She was simply afraid. She was afraid George would leave her. It didn't have anything to do with the minor deceptions he'd practiced. She remembered that moment in bed in Venice: "This is too important to me to be sloppy about." That was the real George, Eleanor believed. The subterfuges were an aberration. Had to be an aberration. Didn't they?

CHIP Strong was nervous. He had arrived at the Main Street house on his bicycle and had forgotten to take his bicycle clips off, so he stood on the sidewalk leafing through the engineer's report with his khakis bunched up around his ankles. Frances checked her watch. Hart, punctual to a fault, would be along in moments.

Frances admitted to herself that she was a little anxious, too. She had dithered over her clothes that morning and checked the train schedule three times. It had proved impossible to get estimates from a contractor or landscaper, but the engineer's report was good—better than she had expected. The important thing now was handling Hart. Frances told herself not to be emotional. A brisk, offhand attitude was the way to approach this.

So when Hart drove up, Frances was brisk and offhand. She offered her cheek for her husband to kiss and didn't tell him that he needed a haircut. They got right down to business.

The first thing Hart noticed was the propped-up porch. He knelt and knocked on the latticework. "Rotten," he said. "It's all rotten. Have to be replaced."

"Yes," Frances said. "I had an engineer look it over. There's quite a bit of work to be done."

Hart straightened up. "You got an engineer's report?" he said, surprised. "How did you know about that?"

"I've been doing my research," Frances said calmly.

And how, Chip Strong silently said to himself, and handed the report to Hart. Hart glanced at him. Unable to articulate his irritation, he merely glared.

Hart's eyes ran down the first page, and he flipped through the rest of it quickly. Frances gently took the key ring from Chip's hand, unlocked the side door, and went in. Glancing around at the flowered wallpaper and the dusty chandelier, she felt doubt. There was such a stifling old-lady aura about the whole house. Could it be eradicated? Did she and Hart have the energy for it?

"It's depressing, Frances," said Hart querulously as he came to stand by her in the front hall. "I can't imagine what you see in it."

"Possibilities, I suppose," she said. "I must see it as a diamond in the rough. Look," she said. "The proportions are wonderful."

Hart walked into the parlor and stood with his hands in his pockets, looking up at the ceiling, where a dusty cobweb floated gently in the corner. He didn't say a word, but walked back out into the hall, where he knelt and poked at a piece of the parquet that came right up in his hand.

"I know," Frances said. "It's probably not for us. What this house needs is really competent owners. Who are good with their hands and have a sense of history. We aren't the people to do it. Still, you might as well come see the rest while you're here."

Frances' little speech was not calculated. She had no subtle plan in mind. But what she had done instinctively, with all the skill of forty years of marriage, was appeal to Hart's personal myth. Hart believed *he* was competent, a can-do kind of guy. A man thoroughly at home with the more arcane elements of a workshop. So Frances' dismissive comment about what the house required was a direct challenge to his image of himself. After all, look at all the work he'd put into the Chester house. Had Frances forgotten that? He had an impulse to catch up to his wife as she climbed the stairs and remind her how he'd restored the mahogany pocket doors.

He noticed the niche at the head of the stairs and tapped the wall with his knuckles. Good sound plaster. All of the bathrooms would probably need complete tiling. In one of the bedrooms he stooped down to look up the fireplace, which was, predictably enough, a black cavern.

"Do they look clean?" Frances asked politely.

"I can't tell. It's all dark," her husband answered. They looked at each other. "Naturally," Hart said, and smiled wryly.

Frances smiled back. "Naturally," she agreed.

Chip Strong, who witnessed this exchange, began to get confused. If Frances had left Hart, why were they buying a house together? And if they were buying a house together, why weren't they living together? Chip knew that the refinements of married life were a closed book to him, but this situation seemed positively Oriental in its incomprehensibility.

Chip trailed along behind Frances and Hart as they went through the rest of the house. He didn't dare open his mouth to do his usual real estate agent spiel, since he felt that he would somehow be stepping on someone's toes. Anyway, Frances was doing just fine. Discreetly pointing out the best features. Frankly admitting to the drawbacks, a tactic that Chip had always thought made buyers trust you.

They were by now out in the yard. Hart turned his gaze on the hemlocks crowded around the house. "How much to get those trees out of here?" he asked his wife.

"I couldn't get a landscaper's estimate in time. Many thousands, I'd imagine. Well," she said, trying to be offhand, "let's go look at the other place. We can decide afterward what to do next."

"Let me just go look at the garage," Hart said. "Might as well be thorough while I'm here."

Frances watched him cross the lawn and come back a few minutes later with an expression of suppressed glee.

"There's a workshop in there," he told her as they walked to the car. "Beautifully laid out. Tons of space."

"That's nice," Frances said in a temperate tone. But inwardly she rejoiced. Behind Hart's back she winked at Chip, who was more confused than ever.

Hart hated the carriage house. He thought it was corny, and he objected strongly to sleeping in a former stall. He mistrusted the sleek Italian kitchen fixtures. The lighting, all artfully recessed next to the oak beams, drove him crazy, with all of its sliding dimmer switches.

Finally Frances interrupted one of his complaints and said, "Hart, I just don't understand you. This is a perfectly nice house, much nicer than that thing on Shore Road, and you can only find fault with it. What is the matter with you?"

Hart lifted his hands. "Darned if I know," he said. "This place just rubs me the wrong way."

"Well, now you know how I feel about Shore Road," Frances said tartly. "I'm going to have to catch a train back to the city, so maybe we can decide what to do next."

"Oh, fine," Hart said, abashed. "I don't need to see any more anyway." So they went outside to find Chip, who had given up on them completely and was sitting against a wall with his face lifted to the sun, thinking about fish.

When Eleanor woke up the morning after she'd received George's picture, she felt different. Both better and worse. She was calm, but there was a hollow, fearful feeling in the pit of her stomach. She knew she had to do something she dreaded. When her eyes opened, she remembered what it was. Today was the day she would talk to George Sinclair.

She chased the boys through their morning routine with a degree of absentmindedness that made Toby wilder than ever. All she could think about was what to say to George Sinclair. Hi. How are you? I got the picture. I really love it. Umm . . . Then what? By the time she marched into her office, Eleanor's stomach was sour with anxiety. Nevertheless, her first action was to look up his number in the phone book. She dialed, standing at her desk, looking out onto the sparkling water of New York harbor. It was only nine thirty. He would be there.

But he wasn't. The phone rang and rang. No answering machine picked up, and Eleanor was so puzzled by this (didn't everyone in Manhattan have an answering machine?) that she dialed again to be sure. Eight rings. She shrugged. No doubt he'd gone out.

At intervals for the rest of the day Eleanor called his number. Nothing changed. It just rang and rang.

Eleanor's family had spent the previous month reminding each other how stubborn she was, and they were right. Having decided that she needed to talk to George, she wanted to start right away. Get it over with. If you decide you must jump off a cliff, you don't want to hang around on the edge for days.

He wasn't there the next day. Or the next.

Still, Eleanor kept calling. By Thursday she no longer expected anyone to answer the phone, but doggedly, three times a day, Eleanor dialed George's number. Less than ever did she know what she would say to him. But talk to him she felt she must.

17

The laws of hospitality required that Hart invite Chip Strong over to dinner at the Wrong House. When the date had been set, Hart felt that it was comfortably distant, but sooner than he would have liked, it arrived.

There was one welcome aspect to this. Chip had seemed to be on the best of terms with Frances, and Hart intended to pump him about Frances' intentions, after plying his guest with food and wine. It was the plying part that was turning out to be harder than it looked.

By now Hart was aware of his housekeeping limitations. He ate a lot of boiled eggs and grilled Velveeta sandwiches, which formed a nice blistery skin under the broiler. This did not seem festive enough for Chip, so Hart had bought a chicken. Surely roasting a chicken was simple enough.

He washed the chicken as directed by *The Joy of Cooking,* hating the dank feel of the flesh and looking regretfully out the window at the sparkling waves. After a concentrated search did not produce the roasting pan, he called Frances at Clara's house in New York.

"Hi," he said tentatively when she answered the phone.

"Oh. Hi," she answered noncommittally, then waited.

"Listen," Hart said, "I'm cooking a chicken here. And I can't find the roasting pan."

"Oh," Frances said. "No, you wouldn't be able to. It's actually in the closet in that little bedroom down there. What are you planning on roasting?"

"I told you, I have this chicken. Here's another thing. How will I know it's done?"

"Make sure the meat isn't pink anywhere. Sometimes when the white meat is done, the dark meat is still bloody on the bone. Don't eat it that way." She paused. "Is that all?"

"Well . . ." Hart said, twirling the phone cord in his left hand. "What about next weekend? It's Labor Day weekend. I think Eleanor was planning on coming up."

"Oh," Frances said.

"It's only a weekend," Hart said.

"I know, but . . . remember the antler chandelier."

"Is it the antler chandelier, or is it me?" Hart found himself asking. "Because I miss you, Frances. And I need you. I wanted to ask you for advice about *us,*" he said. "It made me realize that I count on you."

There was silence from Frances' end of the phone. "Are you still there?"

"Yes." She paused. "I'll think about it," she said. "I'll call you tomorrow. We need to talk about that house. Do you want to have a contractor look at it? Or just keep looking?"

"I'll think about that," Hart said, untwisting himself from the phone cord.

"Okay. Good luck with the chicken," Frances said, and hung up.

Being a real belt-and-suspenders type, Hart managed to overcook the chicken into a desiccated state just short of incineration. Fortunately, he had bought a can of cranberry jelly, which made the stringy meat palatable.

Chip Strong didn't seem to notice much about the food, but he did take a strong interest in the six-pack of Miller in the refrigerator. They ate on the deck, and between chewing the tough chicken and swatting at gnats, they were kept pretty busy. Finally, as he plunked two bowls of ice cream on the table, Hart said, "What is all this with you and Frances anyway?"

"Oh, good, Heath Bar crunch," said Chip, looking at the bowl. He took a bite. "Frances is quite a woman, you know?"

"I know," Hart said dryly, looking out to sea.

Chip looked at Hart surreptitiously. "But you know what's weird?" he said. "The first time I took her to see that house on Main Street, I thought she really liked it. And then when the three of us saw it together, she . . . well, I thought she was pretending not to like it. To make you like it more. If you see what I mean."

Hart turned to Chip, who was excavating a chunk of toffee from the ice cream. "You mean you think she was pretending not to like it, thinking that I would be better disposed to the house if she made light of it?"

Chip swallowed and nodded. "She even winked at me."

"She *winked* at you?" It was a sprightly, waggish gesture, completely unlike Frances.

Chip watched Hart, curious to know how his friend would take this. Hart merely looked down at his bowl of melting ice cream, but Chip thought he could detect a smile. "You're not annoyed with her?" he asked.

Hart shook his head. He was definitely smiling. "She knows me pretty well," he said, and there was no mistaking the tone of pride in his voice.

Frances was sitting in the garden behind the house, where a glass table and four chairs sat beneath an old fruit tree. It was the kind of crisp, dry day that made Frances feel it was a crime to be indoors. She looked down at the newspaper in front of her and tried to focus on it, but her mind kept going back to Hart. He missed her. She could feel her mouth curving into a smile. Imagine being so pleased by such a little thing. It reminded her of the early months of their courtship, when she was in Philadelphia working at the art museum and he was in New York. He'd written her letters in those days, just a page or less in his spiky handwriting. And she remembered the thrill the first time he'd written that he missed her.

Frances sat back in the chair and contemplated the scrap of blue sky she could see between the buildings. When Hart told her, as an irritated aside, that he needed her and missed her, she understood what had made her so unhappy that summer. She had felt superfluous. Her flight to New York had been a spontaneous escape from an unbearable situation, but it had brought Hart to what Frances thought of as his senses. The recalcitrant shirts and the dry chicken and the many lonely evenings had ensured that henceforth he would appreciate his wife.

Frances had not been lonely in New York. She had managed just fine without her husband. But she realized that she was bored without him. Life was simply more interesting with Hart around. She missed him, too.

Of course, this all went unspoken. Frances called Hart the following day and told him that she would come to Weymouth for Labor Day weekend. He, in turn, told her that he was meeting three contractors at Main Street to get rough estimates. By the end of the conversation they were both quite pleased with themselves and with each other.

So was Harry, when he found out that his mother was going back to his father. Eleanor took the happy news in stride, however. Her mother's little sabbatical had always made sense to her. She could now stop worrying about them and devote more attention to her current preoccupation—the whereabouts of George Sinclair.

She was still calling George's number several times daily, but without hope of reaching him. She had even sent him a terse little note asking him to call her. No result.

She didn't know what to think or how to feel about this. What did she expect to achieve by talking to George now? Even that wasn't clear. The terrible tension of the week after his visit to Weymouth had diminished. You couldn't live at such an emotional pitch. Whatever she felt about George was in a state of suspended animation.

Nobody in the Drummond family watched Monday night's news, which featured a short segment about a tropical storm brewing up in the Caribbean. By Tuesday the storm—named Albertine—was twirling its way toward the Florida coast and got promoted to hurricane status. Poor little Bermuda was her first landfall, and suddenly the entire East Coast began to pay attention. By Friday morning she seemed to be aiming for New York.

New Yorkers pride themselves on their savvy and their coolness, yet there is nothing they enjoy more than a good crisis. A pleasant pre-panic energy filled the air. Rumors flew. You should fill your bathtub in case the water got cut off. Buy candles. Buy canned food. Put crosses of tape on your windows—nobody knew why. Get home while you can.

The wind had started blowing. Eleanor's office building was unmistakably swaying. The secretaries clutched each other in the hall with each gust, deliciously terrified. The wind made a keening noise that was somehow amplified by the steel bands framing the windows. People started fretting about their houses and their dogs. The managing partners consulted quickly and closed the firm.

During the morning flurry Eleanor's principal concern was Toby and Simon. Their day camp was sending them home, but there would be no one there. She called Jadrancka. She called Luz. Finally, in desperation, she called Harry, who agreed with alacrity to drive up to her apartment and meet the boys. But he said further, "I think we should go up to Weymouth. Dad is in that house."

"Oh, Lord," Eleanor said, aghast. "I guess you're right. But if he's in danger, won't they make him evacuate?"

"That's the point," Harry said. "We can help. Think of all the stuff. The silver. Books. Pictures."

"Right. Okay," Eleanor said, suddenly decisive. "I'll meet you at the apartment. If you have time, pack bags for the boys. A change of clothes, toothbrushes."

An hour and a half later, as Harry's Land Rover battled its way up

I-95 on the outskirts of New Haven, Eleanor's thoughts became alarmist. To her right lay the wide expanse of New Haven Harbor, usually a calm sheet of water. Now it was lashed with whitecaps, heaving with six-foot swells. The Land Rover quivered under an extra strong blast of wind.

"I wonder why this road isn't closed," Eleanor said rashly. "Aren't we in danger?"

"Danger! We're in danger!" yelped Simon in delight.

"No," Toby said disdainfully. "We aren't, are we, Uncle Harry?"

"No," said Harry. "Sorry, Simon. If we were, the road would be closed, but they're letting us drive on it."

The conditions were actually rather fierce, and Harry, though he knew enough not to tell Eleanor this, was surprised that the highway *was* still open. Rain was streaming down in a solid gray blanket, and the slashing windshield wipers gave Harry only a momentary view of the road ahead of him. When Harry saw New Haven Harbor, he suspected that the Wrong House would already be evacuated. He was correct.

Hart had been eagerly watching the storm develop. He had his birding glasses out to examine the growing waves. And he tried to ready the house for the storm. He unearthed the big flashlight and carefully tuned the transistor radio to the news. Then he climbed into his foul-weather gear and went out to haul the porch furniture into the garage.

He could barely open the door against the force of the wind, which made the air outside seem like a solid wall. The door slammed shut after him as if pushed by a gigantic invisible hand. Hart bent down to pick up the table. It was a fairly light affair, made of plastic-coated tubular metal. The wind got beneath it, and Hart could feel it tugging and shoving. Meanwhile, the rain was pelting down into his eyes and mouth and all over his hands, which were getting slippery. Hart struggled to the far edge of the deck and down the stairs. For the first time, he began to worry. Was it possible that this storm was going to do some damage?

He got the table into the garage. He floundered back up onto the deck, looked at the chaise, and reluctantly decided that he'd better go inside to rest before he tackled that. As he walked back into the house, he glanced at the boat, tossing on the waves at the end of the dock. When he went back out, he would have to be sure it was secured bow and stern.

Inside the house, he stripped off his streaming raincoat and pants. His shirtsleeves were drenched to the elbows, and his pants were wet to the knee. Pushing back a sense of defeat, Hart went upstairs to change his clothes.

He was in the master bedroom, pulling on a turtleneck and a dry pair of khakis, when the police car drove up. So he was unaware of the officer's presence until he heard the doorbell, instantly followed by a voice shouting up the stairs, "Hello? Anyone home?"

He came to the top of the stairs and saw, dripping onto his wood floor, a young man in a long, black, shiny wet raincoat.

"Sorry to bother you, sir. I'm Officer Malory of the state police. I have to ask you to leave your house," the young man said. "The storm is due to hit in a few hours, and we're expecting very high water. The Red Cross has set up a shelter in the high school auditorium. I need to ask you to go along there right away."

"Goodness," Hart said. "Evacuating! Can I secure a few things in the house first?"

"I'm afraid not, sir. I've got three other houses to get to, so I have to ask you to hurry."

Hart came down to the bottom of the stairs and looked around the living room. It had a certain coziness in the face of the storm. All the lights were on. There were magazines on the end tables, and a book lay open on the window seat.

"Sir . . ." said the policeman.

"I know," Hart said. "Just give me five minutes to pack a bag." Five minutes later he had packed a canvas holdall with his birding glasses, his favorite flies, a handful of family photographs in silver frames, and, at the last minute, a cribbage board and a couple of packs of cards. Ever methodical, he turned out the lights and locked the door as he left, recognizing the futility of the gesture.

Hart regretted that he hadn't been more careful about the house. The living room, he realized, was more or less doomed. Good-bye to the chintz sofas. And the plaid curtains and the antler chandelier. But maybe it was also good riddance. After all, there was that new house they were looking at. As he turned into the parking lot of the Weymouth High School, Hart was already thinking about insurance. Maybe Margaret Harwood was right. Maybe, after all of this, they would end up with "a free summer on the water." As he got out of his car, sheltering the cribbage board and cards beneath his raincoat, he wondered where his wife was.

18

HART had imagined Frances to be secure in Clara's New York house. He could picture her sitting serenely on one of Clara's silk sofas, reading something civilized and occasionally glancing out the window at the maelstrom.

But Hart did Frances an injustice. Ever since Albertine had been promoted to a hurricane, Frances had monitored the storm's progress. And when it began to look as if it would hit Connecticut, Frances made her plans. She awoke early Friday morning, drank a cup of coffee standing up, and took a cab to Penn Station, where she caught the Boston Amtrak train.

Frances had left her car in a small garage near the station in Old Saybrook, so she crammed her rain hat onto her head and clutched her long raincoat and walked the few blocks to the garage, wondering with each step how Hart was managing with the house.

The drive from Old Saybrook was terrifying. Frances kept to Route 1, reasoning that the road would be sheltered from the wind by the trees that lined it. But by the time she turned into Weymouth, she knew the trees were going to start falling and that she had been lucky to get so far.

Weymouth looked empty. The stores were all closed. No cars were on the street. As Frances drove slowly through the village, she began to wonder. Where was everyone? She had come to Weymouth to help Hart secure the house against the storm, but Weymouth seemed to be a ghost town. She turned down Main Street and saw, with a jolt, the police blockade at Shore Road.

Frances was not an imaginative woman, but when she saw the patrol cars with their roof lights flashing, horrible fantasies flooded her mind. Electrical lines down, Hart pinned beneath them. A massive tidal wave that had swept her husband out to sea. As she drew to a stop, a shaky, quivery current of alarm ran through her body. One of the police-car doors opened, and a young man ran over to her car window. When she rolled it down, the rain blew in all over her face and shoulders.

"Sorry, ma'am, I can't let you go down there," he said.

"But I live there," Frances said, aware she was talking too fast. "My husband is there. At seven fifty-one Shore Road."

"No, he isn't, ma'am," he said. "We evacuated the entire road an hour ago. They're all in the high school gym. I'm sure you'll find him there, ma'am."

She looked at him for a minute longer as the news sank in. He'd been evacuated. He was in the high school gym. Frances realized she was beaming at the officer and remembered to thank him as she rolled up her window.

Hart was all right. She wasn't going to spend the rest of her days regretting this stupid flap over the house. Suddenly Frances felt a flood of affection for Hart. Thinking of his warmth, his reliability, his patience, Frances drove slowly and carefully to Weymouth High School.

She was still alight with relief and rekindled fondness when she walked into the gym at Weymouth High. Children played under the basketball hoops, and along one wall there was a table covered with coffee percolators and trays of sandwiches. Frances stood in the doorway and scanned the room. There, sitting at a table with Chip Strong, was Hart. They were playing cards. As Chip looked at his hand, choosing his card, Hart glanced around the room. His eye caught Frances'.

She stood there at the end of the crowded room, innately elegant despite her dripping raincoat and sodden hat. Her composure was complete. Hart surprised Chip by putting down his cards and getting up from the table without a word.

She had come. He didn't know how, but she was there. For better, for worse, Hart thought. In sickness and in floods, or some such nonsense. Loyal and true. In that moment he loved his wife with a fierceness that surprised him. Would have surprised everyone, perhaps, but her.

He threaded through the crowd, reaching her in a moment. He reached out and clasped her in a bear hug, holding her tight. Then he reached down and took her hand after setting her wet rain hat at a rakish angle on his own head.

Chip looked up at the approaching apparition of Hart, ridiculous with his wife's hat on his head, and Frances, calm and collected as ever. Hart was beaming as if he had just caught a very large fish. It occurred to Chip that the look on Hart's face might somehow be connected with Frances' appearance on the scene, but that seemed far-fetched, especially when she sat down and casually said, "Who's winning?"

"Hart is," Chip said. "I never was any good at cards. I'd happily give you my hand," he said, holding out the cards.

"I brought my needlepoint," Frances said, slipping out of her coat, which Hart hung on the back of a nearby chair. "Since it looked as if we might be here for a while."

Half an hour later, when Harry's Land Rover pulled into the parking lot and its passengers struggled through the rain to the gymnasium door, Simon called out "There's Gran's car," pointing to a blue Mercedes.

"I don't think so," Eleanor said. "Gran's in New York. Now come *on*, Simon, I'm getting drenched!" she called.

They walked into the gym. "Look, I told you! There's Gran." And Simon was off, running across the gym floor to his grandparents, closely followed by Toby.

It was an unexpectedly pleasant afternoon. Somehow the coffee and sandwiches were supplemented with hot soup and baskets of fruit. Harry and Eleanor sat with their parents, unable to ask anything more than the most superficial questions. Hart told them the story of his evacuation, managing to make it sound as if he, an elderly cripple, had been forcibly ejected from his ancestral homestead by a sneering, goose-stepping officer. They played hearts and gin rummy and cribbage. Every now and then Eleanor got up to check on the boys.

When she came back to the table, Harry was laying out cards for clock solitaire. As his hand moved swiftly around the circle, Eleanor's eyes widened. "Oh, my goodness—the boat! The boat on the living-room floor!" Then she clapped a hand over her mouth.

"What are you talking about?" Harry asked, watching her as his hands went on laying out the cards. "What boat on what living-room floor?"

Eleanor glanced around at her mother, her father, and her brother. They were all staring at her.

"For my birthday Sophy made me go to a psychic," she explained. "He said he saw an image of a boat on the living-room floor. And when I saw Harry with the cards, I thought . . ." She looked up. "Dad, could the Whaler end up on the floor of the house?"

Hart shrugged. "It could. I guess a wave could fling it right through the bay window."

"So what else did the psychic tell you?" Harry asked. "Tall dark stranger in your future?"

Eleanor threw her brother a look of loathing and walked away from the table.

"Oh, Lord—George!" Harry said. He put the cards down. "Am I ever going to stop feeling like a heel about that?"

Frances only sighed.

Harry got up from the table and went to join his sister, who was standing at the door of the vestibule, looking out.

"Look, it's the eye of the storm," she said as Harry came to her side. The wind was slowing down and the rain visibly abating.

The quiet was eerie. For a few minutes the sun even came out.

"Is the hurricane over?" Simon asked, coming to his mother's side.

"No," she answered, putting a hand on his shoulder. "This is called the eye. It's a peaceful time in the middle of the storm. Soon the wind will start blowing again."

Toby joined them. "Mom, what about Aunt Clara? Do you think she had to evacuate?"

"I don't know," Eleanor said in the automatically soothing tone of a parent. "Maybe. But she has Sarge to help her. I'm sure she'll be all right."

"And George is there," Harry added to Toby in the same reassuring tone. "You know, Mr. Sinclair." Then, in a mirror image of the gesture Eleanor had just used inside, he clapped his hand over his mouth as he met Eleanor's gaze.

"What's Mr. Sinclair doing there?" came Simon's question in an unworried treble voice.

"He's painting a picture on Aunt Clara's walls," Harry said, watching Eleanor. "He's staying with her for most of the summer."

As Eleanor heard these words, she felt a flood of relief, a physical sensation, wash through her. He was at Clara's. He had been there all summer. He was not evading her calls, ignoring her letter. He didn't know. He didn't know.

Harry observed his sister as she took a deep breath and stood a little straighter. The lines in her face seemed to fade as he watched. And she looked him straight in the eye and said, "I've been trying to reach him."

She looked up at the sky, which was darkening. The sun had already faded and the leaves were rustling again in the trees. "It's starting up again. Let's get back."

By five o'clock the storm had blown itself out. The gym began to empty as evacuees were told they could go back to their homes. Shore Road, however, was not considered safe. "Not for at least twenty-four hours," said the state trooper who brought the news. "There's still a lot of extra water out there."

Hart and Frances took this news calmly and decided to spend the night at the Sound View Motel on Route 1. As they gathered up the cribbage board and the cards and Simon's bear and Frances' needlepoint, Harry took his sister aside. He pressed the key to his car into her hands.

"Just go," he said. "I know I've interfered too much, but you have to go. He'll be there. I'll take care of the boys." Eleanor looked at her brother with her eyes welling. She kissed him on the cheek and slipped out.

It was an eerie drive. The air was still wild, stirred up, as if currents had been set in motion that would not easily be stilled. The sky was white and opaque, but bright enough so that the trees cast shadows. There were trees down everywhere, elms and oaks and even a beech, flat on the pavement or dizzily angled against other tree trunks. Eleanor rolled down the windows of her brother's big car and listened to the birds begin again, tentatively, to chirp and sing.

There was half of an old elm down across Clara's drive. As Eleanor got out of the car, she glanced ahead to the house, suddenly worried. What if there had been damage there? What if they, too, had been evacuated? Would George even be there? And what would he say?

The ground was sodden. Water welled up in her footprints and squelched around her feet. Eleanor stepped over a branch that caught her sweater, and it took nearly a minute for her trembling hands to release the yarn from the splintered wood.

And all the time she was trying not to think. It was one of the hardest things she ever did, walking into Clara's house to see George. It took all of her courage to keep her feet moving. It was something that had to be done.

She got her sweater untangled and went onward. The light was brightening as the clouds cleared away, and turning a deep gold. Somewhere there should be a tremendous rainbow.

Eleanor walked up the steps, crossed the wide veranda, and reached out to the door. Should she ring? What if Clara was asleep? That was just an excuse, Eleanor realized. She wanted to get this over with. No, she wanted it to have happened already. Maybe George wasn't there anyway. The thought made her put her hand on the doorknob.

The door swung open silently. Eleanor stepped into the big front hall, clotted with gloomy shadows. The house felt empty. She walked silently forward, then stopped to listen again.

There. There was something. A tiny noise, a little click or something. Someone putting down a pencil. In the morning room, behind a closed door.

Eleanor walked forward again and stopped with her hand on the door. She closed her eyes. He was in there. Before she had time to race silently back out of the house, she opened the door.

There, with his back to her, was George. He was crouched on the floor, brush in hand. His T-shirt was covered with paint and his khakis seemed wet. He had tied a red bandanna over his hair.

Eleanor tried to speak. A rattling sound came from her throat. George turned around, startled, and dropped his brush. He stood up slowly. Eleanor thought irrelevantly how tall he was. She took a breath and tried again to speak. She stood in front of George like a ghost laboring to produce words. George stepped over to her and put a hand on each shoulder.

"What? You don't have bad news, do you? Is everyone all right?"

Eleanor gulped and shook her head. "No, no, we're all fine. Harry told me you were here."

"Uh-huh," George said, speaking in a soothing tone. "Clara's been in Lenox for a few days, so she missed the storm." He paused. "Here, sit down." He pulled a rag off a canvas-draped chair, and Eleanor sat. "And your parents are all right? Your father, I mean?"

Eleanor swallowed and coughed slightly. "He was evacuated this morning. They're at a motel in Weymouth." She fell silent and looked down at the floor. The room was so quiet, George thought he could hear her breathing. He stood there, hands at his side, trying not to acknowledge his dawning hope.

She took a deep breath and looked up. "I got your picture of Toby and Simon. It was beautiful." She straightened up. "I tried to call you. I wrote a note."

"To say what?" George asked in a voice that he managed to keep from shaking.

"That I needed to see you. I wanted to talk to you."

"Well, here I am," he said as lightly as he could.

"I know," Eleanor said. "Harry drove me up here with the children. He told me to come."

"Maybe this time Harry was right," George said.

"I think he was right before," Eleanor said to her lap.

George knelt on the floor next to her and sat back on his heels. "What do you mean?"

Eleanor's face was now level with his. "He was right, George. Harry was right. You were right. I've been trying to pretend this wasn't true, but I have fallen in love with you and if you don't want to have anything to do with me, I am completely sympathetic but I had to say this and get it out of my system." She looked at him squarely, with a kind of weary finality.

In reply, George lifted a hand to her cheek. He ran his thumb over her cheekbone, cupping her jaw with his palm. "Now neither of us has to," he murmured as she turned her head to kiss his palm.

"Has to what?" she asked.

"Get the other one out of his system." He reached forward to put his arms around her, chair and all. "It would have been such a waste." He pulled her up with him and backed away from the chair into a clear part of the room. "Eleanor, I am so *happy!* I want to waltz around with you. I feel like I should hire the largest brass band I can find to march down the Post Road in front of you and me, nodding and smiling graciously on an enormous heart-shaped float studded with roses. Oh, Eleanor, I do love you, too," he finally subsided, and kissed her.

EVENTUALLY George took Eleanor to the Sound View Motel, where the Drummond family was staying. Harry, seeing his sister incandescent with happiness, felt vindicated. He felt he had crafted a splendid happy ending for a real-life soap opera.

Frank Gerson's image of the boat on the living-room floor turned out to be perfectly accurate. When Hart and Frances opened the door, the Whaler lay beached between the two sofas, with the shards of the coffee table beneath it.

The damage wasn't profound, though. The house was unlivable, but once the windows were replaced and the walls repainted, the wiring renewed and the appliances repaired, it would be habitable. Only the barn siding was permanently damaged: the salt water had darkened it, so that there was a floodmark halfway up the stairs.

Hart managed to find a man from East Haddam to do the repairs. He expressed admiration for the house, and Hart offered facetiously to sell it. Soon they worked out a splendid deal that allowed the Drummonds to save several thousand dollars by not listing the house at all through Strong Harwood. Margaret Harwood was irate, but Chip was delighted for his friends and offered them his house to stay in while they renovated the Main Street house.

They turned him down, of course, and camped in successive rooms of the new house. Hart spent much of the fall and winter stripping the banister, hunting for antique doorknobs, and cleaning the marble fireplaces. Frances helped him as much as she could, but there were other demands on her time.

In the middle of September, Chip Strong astonished Frances by asking her to join his firm. He felt she had good taste, an intuitive grasp of real estate transactions, and a soothing sales personality. With some misgivings, Frances began going to the office to learn the business. She was, to her surprise, a brilliant saleswoman. When Margaret Harwood departed suddenly for Florida in pursuit of a retired concrete magnate, Chip and Frances ran the office very cozily together. Hart even became a kind of unofficial restoration consultant for them.

George and Eleanor were married at Christmas. Eleanor wore almond-colored velvet and George wore a blue blazer and a look of incredible pride. Toby and Simon behaved like princes. George quit teaching at Avalon and sold his loft to set up a much cheaper studio in Washington Heights. Eleanor didn't find that her life was any less complicated once she was remarried. It took several months for her hair to grow out to a graceful length. Toby still dawdled in the morning, and she still had trouble managing her wardrobe. George helped, though, by shopping with her, cooking, and keeping her warm at night. Among their wedding presents were an antique sleigh bed from George's parents, a little Van Dongen drawing from Clara Henschel, and an electric doughnut maker from Chip Strong.

Harry's confident management of his sister's love life went to his head a bit, and he gave a few friends unsolicited advice on romantic endeavors. George felt Harry should have a taste of his own medicine and invited him to dinner with a columnist from an art magazine, whom Harry afterward characterized as a "humorless bride of art." Everyone noticed how often he danced with Eleanor's friend Sophy at the wedding.

In time the summer of the Wrong House became a Drummond family story. It could be told to illustrate Frances' perfectionism or Hart's ability to ignore the unpleasant. Frances hated hearing the story. She hated being reminded how dreadful that summer had been and how badly she had behaved. But she never could imagine how else she might have gotten through it all.

ABOUT THE AUTHOR

After graduating from Princeton, Carol McD. Wallace did what many aspiring novelists do: she moved to New York and got a job in the publishing business. She spent two years polishing other people's books until somebody asked her to write one of her own. But there was a catch. It was a book about how to have beautiful fingernails. Despite the less-than-thrilling subject, Wallace grabbed the opportunity. "I said, 'Fine, why not?' I had always wanted to be a writer." Further offbeat projects followed, including *The Official Preppy Handbook,* a humorous look at fashions of the '70s, and the even more popular *20,001 Names for Baby.* But with *The Wrong House* she finally got to write the kind of book she's always dreamed of writing. The kind of book, she says, "that you pick up when the world seems like you can't deal with [it] anymore."

Carol McD. Wallace

Like her character Eleanor, Wallace lives in New York City and has two sons, ages four and seven. But that's where the resemblance ends. She does have a husband. He's an editor for *Guideposts* magazine as well as a professional musician who sings with the church choir. "He didn't have a job when I married him," she says. "An act of faith on my part."

Wallace grew up in a pretty Victorian house in Connecticut, with high ceilings and marble fireplaces. "It was a decorator showhouse last summer. I hadn't been back since my mother sold the house, when I was twenty-three. So I took my children and my husband . . . it was very strange . . . it felt the same. In some ways," she says, "you do live what you're writing about."

Readers will be glad to know that Wallace is already hard at work on another book and that it will be peopled with some of the same delightfully eccentric characters we got to know in *The Wrong House.*

RED

BY
GREG DINALLO

Skulduggery was so easy in the old Soviet Union. There were the corrupt party officials, the dissidents, the black marketeers. Working the angles, a streetwise newspaperman like Nikolai Katkov could get by nicely.

But now it's all changed. Ex-KGB assassins are looking over their own shoulders. A ruthless new criminal class is on the rise. Freedom and the profit motive have turned modern-day Moscow into a deadly free-for-all.

It's a dangerous time for anyone — even the best reporter—to go digging up a story.

CHAPTER ONE

It is winter, and it does not wait.

This thought wasn't penned by a Russian poet, but was uttered by Boris Yeltsin's chief economic adviser at a news conference I covered this morning. He also said that curbing inflation, stemming capital flight, and increasing private investment are crucial to stabilizing the Russian economy. Saving the worst for last, he warned that the coming months of subzero weather, when the demand for staples is highest and the supply meager, mean things will get much worse before they get better.

I've no idea why the line haunts me now as I enter a Moscow community center and make my way to a drafty meeting room where a handwritten sign proclaims MOSCOW BEGINNERS.

Everyone turns to look at me as I take my seat. Some with compassion, others with despair, all with a trace of apprehension. I study the tired faces: A housewife? A taxi driver? A seamstress? An engineer? I'm forced to guess because they're all strangers—strangers with whom I'm about to share one of the most painful moments of my life.

I'm seized by a compulsion to run, but I know from years of denial, the pain will be far worse tomorrow if I do.

My turn has come. I stub out my cigarette and stand. "My name is Nikolai K.," I begin. My throat is dry from anxiety, and I pause. "My name is Nikolai K., and I am an alcoholic."

Applause breaks out. My personal perestroika has begun. This once radical idea of rehabilitating oneself has become common since the new government identified alcoholism as a severe drag on the economy and started self-help clinics like Moscow Beginners.

"Why do you drink, Nikolai?" one of the strangers wonders.

"To get drunk," I quip nervously.

Silence. Not a chuckle, not a smile.

"Are you employed?" another asks.

"Sometimes. I mean, I write. Freelance."

"Maybe you're creatively frustrated?"

"No. I don't write fiction. I do investigative work."

"Investigative work," a woman muses suspiciously.

"For *Pravda*," a fellow cracks, eliciting a burst of laughter.

"Good riddance," the woman next to him chimes in, pleased that the once powerful propaganda rag of the Communist Party has been shut down.

"I disagree," I say. "I'm against censorship of any kind. Banning opposing views violates the right of free speech."

"Even banning the Communist Party?"

"Of course."

"Well, I'm still glad the bastards are gone. Is that what you write about, Nikolai? Politics?"

"I write about corruption and—"

"Ah, not politics. *Politicians.*"

More laughter.

"And injustice. I write about *Afganisty*, about striking coal miners, about Pamyat."

The room falls silent. The strangers know about the shabby treatment of veterans, about the epidemic of lung disease in mining regions, about the ultraright group that preaches anti-Semitism.

"Nikolai K.," a wizened man in a skullcap muses knowingly. "We have a famous dissident in our midst."

"Is he here to write about *us*?" the suspicious woman asks.

"Should I?" I ask, pretending I've sparked to the idea. "Have I stumbled upon a cell of subversives?"

Most of them laugh this time and settle back in their chairs, seeming to accept me.

I thank them and take my seat. I'm wondering who will be next when an attractive woman with pale skin stands.

"My name is Ludmilla T.," she says shyly; then brightening, she announces, "Today is my thirtieth birthday."

"Happy birthday, Ludmilla," several call out.

"So, Ludmilla," the suspicious woman prompts, "has this been a good week for you?"

"Well, yes; but I had to skip work today. I knew my co-workers would bring vodka to celebrate, and I was afraid I couldn't say no."

"You did the right thing," the woman says.

"No," the wizened man protests. "What's going to happen when she's offered vodka on someone else's birthday?"

"He's right, but I couldn't take the chance," Ludmilla protests timidly. "It's not just getting drunk. It's losing control, and then . . . other things happen."

"What other things?" the woman prompts knowingly.

Ludmilla lowers her eyes, working up the courage to reply. "I—I wake up next to men I don't remember meeting." She pauses, interrupted by an electronic chirping, and looks about for the source.

I'm having visions of Ludmilla waking up in *my* bed when I sense the strangers are all looking at me. Damn. It's my beeper.

I fumble for the switch and turn it off. I'm embarrassed, but bristling with curiosity and the need to get to a phone. "I'm sorry. Please don't be offended, but I have to go." I force a smile and hurry from the room, my commitment to sobriety already in question.

I make a beeline for a cinema on Taganskaya where there's a pay phone. I don't have to look at the beeper to know who called me. Vera Fedorenko is the only person who has the number. I thumb two kopeks into the slot and dial militia headquarters on Petrovka.

"Dispatcher seventeen," Vera answers over the din of the huge room through which all police communications are routed.

"It's Nikolai. You beeped me. What's going on?"

"Someone just reported finding a body on the grounds of the Embankment."

"The Embankment? Was it somebody important?"

"I've no idea. Just a minute. I've got another call." She clicks off and puts me on hold.

Vera had no doubt I'd be intrigued. The Embankment is an elite housing complex on the banks of the Moscow River where many members of the government reside. It's also where my parents were living forty-three years ago when I was born. I enjoyed all the privileges—played on the manicured grounds, swam in the indoor pools, dined in the gourmet food halls, and attended Special School Number 19—until the infamous spring of '68, when Brezhnev sent Soviet tanks rolling into Prague and my father's conscience overcame his fear of reprisal. An intellectual and a professor of political science, he was declared an enemy of the state.

"Sorry, Niko," Vera says, coming back on the line.

"What about cause of death? Anything on that?"

"No. That's all I have."

"Great. Heaven help you if it's a derelict who tripped over a curb. I have to go."

"Wait. Should I come by, later?"

"Sure."

"I'll bring some coffee in case this turns into something and you're writing all night."

I hang up, wondering how Vera is able to acquire coffee, and hurry to the corner for a taxi. Several years ago there wasn't a cabdriver in Moscow who wouldn't make a U-turn in a traffic jam for a pack of Marlboros. They still come in handy on occasion, and I usually carry a couple of packs with me, but American dollars are the coin of the realm now. Everyone haggles over the price.

I step off the curb, holding my rubles low to the ground. A few empty cabs roar past before one finally stops. "The Embankment," I say, leaning to the window.

"Six hundred rubles," the driver grunts.

"Three."

"Five."

"Outrageous," I protest as I clamber inside.

"I know; but I was just by there. The police have it cordoned off. That's going to cost me time."

Cordoned off? Because of a dead derelict? Not a chance. A smile tugs at the corners of my mouth. If someone important was murdered, I've got the jump on a big-ticket story.

THE Moscow River twists through the city like a nocturnal reptile, its wet skin shimmering in the moonlight. Centered between two bridges that link it to the Kremlin, the House on the Embankment has the look of an impenetrable fortress. Tonight its drab façade is ablaze with light from the flashers of militia vans.

The taxi deposits me at a wooden barricade where uniformed policemen stand. "Press," I announce over the crackle of radios.

A sergeant blinds me with his flashlight. "No press card?"

"I'm freelance."

"Sorry. No unauthorized personnel."

Before I can protest, a photographer's flash gives a fleeting glimpse of uniformed men gathered around a car.

"Who's in charge here?"

"Senior Investigator Shevchenko."

Valery Shevchenko is a senior homicide investigator. "Ah, we go way back. Tell him Nikolai Katkov's here, will you?"

Another flash erupts. This time from within the car. The passenger window looks like it's been hit by a rotten tomato. The grisly image sets crimson circles whirling in the darkness.

"Look, if I don't get this story, I'll write that the militia suppressed it," I say as headlights sweep the area and a Moskvitch sedan coasts to a stop. The door opens and Valery Shevchenko's narrow face thrusts upward into the cold air.

"What do you want, Katkov?" he growls impatiently.

"A little cooperation would be nice."

He scowls, then turns to the sergeant, who opens the barricade. "Good work. We can't have unaccredited reporters running loose at crime scenes, can we?" Shevchenko starts forward, then pauses. "Certainly not without supervision." He motions me to follow, then charges across the parking area, past the massive building where curious faces press against windows.

The militiamen guarding the car step aside as Shevchenko approaches and leans into the Volga with his flashlight. The beam moves from the open driver's door to the ignition, where the keys still dangle, then on to the windshield, passenger window, and roof liner, which are splattered with blood. He backs out slowly, pausing to sort through the items in a sack on the passenger seat—Western cigarettes, razor blades, blank audio cassettes among them—then crouches to examine a splotch of blood on the ground below the door, from which a reddish brown smear arcs across the pavement. It leads Shevchenko to the far side of a concrete wall, where the beam from his flashlight finds a man's corpse, on its back, head twisted sharply to the right.

The hole in the left cheek is cratered and scorched, indicating a large-caliber pistol fired at close range. The eyes are open, as if staring in shock at the pool of blood that comes from a gaping wound in the skull.

Shevchenko drifts back toward the car, puzzling something out. "The killer is waiting in the darkness, rushes forward, opens the door—and fires," he whispers. "Then instead of fleeing, pulls the body from the car and drags it behind the wall. Why?"

My heart sinks. The obvious answer isn't one rich in political intrigue. "Care to venture a guess?" I ask, pencil poised to jot down "motive: robbery."

"No. You?"

He knows what I want, and is getting some perverse pleasure out of making me sink my own ship. "Well, he probably didn't want to be spotted going through the guy's pockets."

We walk back to the body. Shevchenko smirks, then shifts his flashlight to the victim's left wrist. A metallic glint appears. "Sergeant."

The sergeant crouches down to the body and removes a gold wristwatch. He slips it into an envelope and follows it with a wedding band. From the victim's pockets he takes a billfold of rubles and a leather wallet, handing the latter to Shevchenko.

"Well, I guess robbery wasn't the motive," I say.

"Vladimir Vorontsov," Shevchenko says, scanning the victim's driver's license. He examines the wallet's contents, pausing at a plastic-laminated card, which he palms before I can get a look at it. "Who found him?"

"A neighbor," the sergeant answers. "She lives in the same wing as Vorontsov. Said he's a widower. His daughter and grandchildren moved in with him a few months ago."

Shevchenko nods and walks toward the building at a brisk pace. "Took in his daughter and grandchildren," he muses sarcastically. "Evidently, the new government hasn't solved the housing shortage or divorce rate yet."

"Evidently, you preferred the old system," I say.

He shrugs. "If the KGB was still in business, they'd be handling this and I'd be home with my wife and daughters." He mounts the steps to the entrance.

I haven't been in these buildings in over twenty-five years, but nothing's changed. The creak of hinges, the hiss of steam, the orange glow of chandeliers—I'm overwhelmed with familiar sensations as Shevchenko crosses the lobby to an elevator. The slow-moving elevator deposits us in a third-floor vestibule. He steps to a door and presses the buzzer. A petite woman in her early thirties appears. She seems gentle and refined: salon-styled hair, silk blouse, designer suit—clearly a woman of privilege.

"I'm Senior Investigator Shevchenko," he says, displaying his badge. "This is Mr. Katkov. He's a journalist. May we come in?"

"Why? Is something wrong?"

"Vladimir Vorontsov is your father?"

She nods, her eyes widening apprehensively.

"I'm afraid it's very bad news."

The color drains from her face as she leads the way to an elegant living room. My entire apartment could easily fit inside it, but it's very much like the one where I played as a child. I reach a sitting area at the far end of the room, where Shevchenko is briefing her.

"My God," she wails when he finishes. "Why would anyone do something like that?"

"I'm hoping you can help us find the answer, Mrs. . . ."

"Churkin. Tanya Churkin," she replies, overcome with grief. "He was late. I knew something was wrong. I just knew it."

Shevchenko nods. "He was late—on returning from where?"

"His lodge meeting. He gets together with his cronies. They drink, relive old times. You know."

"Did your father have any enemies you know of?"

"No. No, he was a good person."

"No ex-wife, no girlfriends or jilted mistresses?"

Her tear-filled eyes flare with indignation. "No. And I don't like what you're insinuating."

"I meant no offense, Mrs. Churkin. Someone shot your father in cold blood. The motive is crucial to tracking down his killer."

"The answer is still no. He was devoted to my mother. She died about a year ago. I don't want his good name sullied by you"—she shifts her glare to me—"or anyone else."

"That's not why we're here Mrs. Churkin, I assure you," Shevchenko replies.

She nods, her lips tightening into a thin line.

"Now, can you think of anyone who might want to hurt him? Anyone he didn't get along with?"

"No. He was well liked by everyone."

Shevchenko produces the laminated card he palmed earlier. "According to this he was employed at the Interior Ministry."

My brows twitch with intrigue. Mrs. Churkin nods sadly.

"In what capacity?"

"As a foreign-trade representative. He was usually posted abroad to one of our embassies, but lately he's been working out of Ministry offices here in Moscow."

"Did he ever take work home from the office?"

"Sometimes. His things are inside." She stands and leads the way to a study that overlooks the river. One wall is covered with citations and photographs—Vorontsov with various heads of state and world business leaders.

Shevchenko crosses to a desk, where several neat stacks of papers are aligned. After a perfunctory review he slips some official-looking documents into a briefcase that he finds there. "Someone will have to identify the body, Mrs. Churkin. You may do it now or when you come to headquarters to claim his personal effects."

She hesitates, chilled at the thought. "Yes. Yes, I think that would be better," she says, referring to the latter choice.

"Should you need to reach me in the meantime . . ." Shevchenko gives her one of his cards. Then, briefcase in hand, he leads the way from the apartment.

In the elevator, he pulls a flask from inside his trench coat and takes a swallow. "Long night," he says, offering me the flask.

"Thanks, no," I reply. "But I could use a ride."

"Sorry. I'm returning to headquarters."

"That's what I figured."

He glares at me as the elevator door opens, then charges through it into the lobby.

"Come on, Shevchenko," I protest as we cross the parking area. "You'll get home a lot sooner with some help; not to mention the time you'll save answering my questions now."

"Unfortunately, there *are* other reporters in Moscow, Katkov. I'll still have to answer theirs."

"No, you don't."

"You suggesting I deal with you exclusively?"

"I expected you would demand it. Of course, if what I've heard about your itch to make chief investigator is wrong . . ."

He opens the car door, tosses the briefcase inside, and whirls to face me. "I don't have time to play games. You'll clear every draft with me prior to publication and remove anything I find objectionable. Agreed?"

"Agreed."

"You're a terrible liar, Katkov." He slides behind the wheel, slams the door, and jerks his head, indicating I should get in.

About fifteen minutes later we're approaching militia headquarters, a crenellated fortress near the Hermitage Gardens. The uniformed sentry at the entrance to number 38 Petrovka recognizes Shevchenko and raises the gate arm, allowing the sedan to enter without stopping.

The senior investigator's office is on the fourth floor. Gray-green walls, poor lighting, and a scarred desk, on which Shevchenko drops Vorontsov's briefcase.

"No motive—no suspect," he announces, reciting the axiom glumly as he begins sorting the documents.

"You've eliminated thieves, mistresses, neighbors, which leaves what? Professionals. It would be fair to allege it was the *mafiya*. Some kind of a hit—" The phone rings, interrupting me.

"Shevchenko," he answers wearily. "Yes, I'm still here. . . . I'm sorry. I meant to. I didn't get a chance. . . . Yes, I know it's late. It's hard to— Katya? Katya?" He sighs and slowly lowers the phone.

"Old lady's mad at you, huh?"

He glares at me. "Stick to business, Katkov."

"I was about to say it's pretty obvious we're looking at a premeditated murder here."

"I didn't say that, and don't write that I did. I said cold-blooded murder. That's all I'm saying."

"Why?"

"Because there are pieces that still don't fit."

"Removing the body from the car . . ."

Shevchenko nods smugly before adding, "And the sack of sundries on the seat."

"What makes that a problem?"

"Time. He leaves the office and goes shopping at one of those trendy emporiums that sell Western goods. The end of the working day. Their busiest time. He'd have to take a number and queue for at least an hour, maybe two. Then time to drive all the way to his lodge, time to eat, drink, and be merry, and time to drive home. *All* in time to be killed sometime before eight forty-eight. I'm sure dispatcher"—he pauses and retrieves a report from his desk—"Vera Fedorenko recorded the time of the call accurately."

"I wouldn't know," I say offhandedly. "Far as the body being removed from the car is concerned, maybe Vorontsov dragged himself out."

"With half his cranium missing?"

"I still think somebody shut him up."

"No comment." He tosses a document aside, begins perusing another. "Not until I know exactly what he was up to at the Interior Ministry."

"Well, since you work for the Interior Ministry, I'm sure you have your ways of finding out."

He pauses in reaction to something in the documents. "I don't think we're going to need sources to find out what he's involved in."

"You found it?"

"Privatization," he says with disdain. "These reports were prepared by the Committee for State Property."

"The committee empowered to sell state property. The committee overrun by corrupt bureaucrats ripping off the industries they've been managing."

"Bloody hypocrites!" Shevchenko exclaims. "They buy them with money stolen from the party and make huge profits reselling them to Western corporations."

"For *dollars*—dollars that never enter the economy, as I understand it."

"It's called capital flight, Katkov. There are dozens of deals here. From high tech to agriculture."

"So, which one was Vorontsov trying to rip off?"

Shevchenko shrugs. "Maybe all of them. Maybe none." He kicks back in his chair with a prescient air and ticks facts off on his fingers. "A man of apparent stature and integrity. Rampant political corruption. Documents that cover a broad range of state industries."

"Your point?"

"It's possible he was reviewing the documents."

"A watchdog?"

Shevchenko nods. "It's also possible he died because he was about to blow the whistle on someone."

"But someone blew it on him first."

"Someone with a lot to lose." He looks off for a moment, then grins at a thought. "Why do Russians kill each other, Katkov? Love, hate, politics . . ."

"A bottle of vodka."

"Precisely. That's been about it up until now. Now we have greed. Money. That's a brand-new one."

CHAPTER TWO

THE Zhdanov-Krasny Metro line zigzags beneath the city from the suburbs in the northwest to the power corridors of central Moscow, and on to the industrial districts in the southeast. Lyublino, the drab, polluted area I call home, is at the end of the line in more ways than one, which means I can sleep on the train without missing my stop.

But I'm not sleeping tonight. Item by item I scribble down all I've learned about the privileged life and violent death of Vladimir Vorontsov, along with the endless questions that come to mind.

Was Vorontsov a watchdog or not? If so, which state assets did he suspect were being illegally sold?

Who were the buyers? The apparatchiks who managed those assets? Officials in the Interior Ministry? Foreign consortiums?

Who did Vorontsov report to? Who were his subordinates? Was he clean or dirty?

It will take weeks, maybe months to answer them all. The longer the better as far as I'm concerned. This is a major scandal. At the least, I'm looking at a lead story and series of follow-ups.

The train bends through a curve with a chilling screech and rumbles into the station. I slip out the door before it fully opens and charge up the escalator into early morning darkness. The baroque mansion where I live stands in gratifying defiance of the state's monolithic housing units; and the caretaker, whose family owned the house before the state divided it into dozens of cramped apartments, always allows me a few months' grace on the rent.

The harsh industrial odor outside gives way to the scent of perfume as I enter the vestibule. Vera's delicate fragrance draws me up the twisting staircase, gradually blending with the smell of coffee. "Hi," I say as I come through the door. "Sorry to be so late, but—"

That's strange. The sofa where I expect to find Vera curled up with a book is empty; the blanket she keeps tucked around her legs, tossed aside. Signs of Vera everywhere, but no Vera.

I call her apartment. No answer. Maybe she had to go back to work. I call the dispatcher's office at militia headquarters. The woman who answers informs me Vera finished her shift. I hang up and take stock of the apartment.

The pot of coffee on the stove smells earthy and tart. I pace anxiously as it heats, fighting to keep my imagination from getting the best of me. Vera probably got tired of waiting and went home; she's probably still on the Metro. I haven't had coffee in months, and I'm savoring the second cup when someone raps on the door.

Vera? Why wouldn't she use her key?

Another salvo of knocks rattles the latch. "Mr. Katkov, it's Mrs. Parfenov," an elderly voice calls out.

I open the door to find the old babushka who cares for the building clutching at her bathrobe in the unheated corridor. "It's three in the morning, Mrs. Parfenov. I know I'm a little behind in my rent, but—"

"They took her away, Nikasha," she says, and maneuvers past me into the apartment. She has the shaken look of those who have seen the secret police come in the night, though these things don't happen anymore.

"Took her away? Who?"

"Men. Who else? I watched from behind the curtains. They put her in a car." She cocks her head and sniffs at the air. "What's that?"

"Coffee."

"Ah," she whines with suspicion. "You have a source?"

"Vera does."

"Maybe that's why they arrested her."

"For buying coffee on the black market?"

"They're cracking down, Nikasha." She punctuates it with a chop of her bony hand, turns toward the door, then pauses and turns back. "There's something else I wanted to talk to you about. . . ." Her face twists with the confusion of age. "Aggghh, it escapes me."

"The rent."

"No. I know you're good for it. Don't worry, it'll come to me." She shuffles out the door.

Did Shevchenko say *if* the KGB was still in business? My gut is a knot of pain now. I know better, but I place calls to the militia and the KGB anyway. Anonymous calls. Neither has a record of Vera's arrest. That doesn't mean they don't have her. It's always been difficult to get information on citizens who've been arrested. I wrestle with the frustration for a while; then I roll a sheet of paper into the typewriter and get to work.

> V. I. Vorontsov, a longtime servant of the Motherland, was shot to death in his car last evening. This cold-blooded murder of a high-ranking Interior Ministry official raises many questions about the Committee for State Property. Thought to be rife with corruption, the CSP may be contributing to the rapid flight of capital that is stifling economic growth. Furthermore . . .

As Vera anticipated, the coffee keeps me sharp, and the pages continue to roll out of the typewriter until a ray of light that has found its way through the smog announces it's morning.

I try Vera again with the same result. The next call is to a friend at the Interior Ministry. A former dissident, Yuri Ternyak is now a respected economist engaged by the new government to draft market-oriented reforms. Our friendship began twenty-five years ago at Moscow State University, where he ran an underground literature exchange that has kept my library well stocked. Over the years, he's been a reliable source of information. We'd meet in parks or on public conveyances to avoid KGB surveillance. Now we talk more openly—but not today; not after what happened to Vera.

"You know the name Vorontsov?"

"Vaguely. I've heard it mentioned."

"Heard anything lately?"

"Not that I recall."

"Get me what you can on him, and meet me at GUM."

"I can't. My schedule's jammed. I'm crazed."

"Come on, Yuri. It's really important."

He lets out a long sigh. "All right. GUM. About noon?"

I'm not surprised that Yuri is pressed for time; he's been working round the clock of late. But the fact that the Ministry isn't buzzing with news of the murder piques my curiosity. Either something's wrong or Shevchenko is keeping the lid screwed on tight.

An hour later I'm fighting my way through the crowds in GUM, the massive department store opposite the Kremlin. The noise level is almost deafening. Yuri and I have had many meetings here without fear of being overheard. It's almost twelve thirty by the time he joins me on one of the pedestrian bridges that arch between the shopping arcades.

"Sorry. The phone rang just as I was leaving," he explains. Then, puzzled by my clandestine behavior, he lowers his voice and prompts, "So, what's going on?"

"They took Vera from my apartment last night."

Yuri's face pales. There's no need to ask who. His trimmed mustache, sharp cheekbones, and close-set eyes usually give him the look of a mischievous rodent; but he's deadly serious now. We walk to the opposite end of the bridge in silence.

I get Yuri to brief me on Vorontsov: sixty years old; born in an elite suburb of Moscow; studied economics at the Plekhanov Institute; attended the prestigious Institute for International Relations; a member of the nomenklatura, the privileged party hierarchy; served in embassies in London, Berlin, Tokyo, and Washington, D.C.; currently in charge of oversight for the Committee for State Property.

"Oversight? Vorontsov's a watchdog?"

Yuri nods. "One way of putting it."

"Clean or dirty?"

"I've no idea. Why?"

Yuri is clearly shaken when I brief him on the murder. "It threatens the development of a free economy. As it is, the G-Seven countries are hedging their bets and private investment is lagging, but this—this could destroy trust in the new government. Topple it, for that matter. We can kiss it all good-bye, and hard currency along with it." He pauses, stunned by his own assessment; then his eyes capture mine with concern. "I'd handle this very carefully if I were you."

I nod solemnly. We reach the end of the bridge and begin walking along the upper shopping level.

"Where are you taking it?" he asks. "The *News?*"

Moscow *News* was the breakthrough newspaper of glasnost—the first to exercise freedom of the press, to support political reform—but it has since become staid, lost its independence.

"Pravda."

"Pravda!" Yuri echoes with a derisive snort as we board the down escalator. "I thought *Pravda* was out of business."

"It's coming back as a political journal. Exposing the scandal would give it legitimacy. That alone would be news."

"Come on. No one takes that defunct communist rag seriously. You know better than I, the joke has always been that *pravda* means truth."

"The only way to stop the laughter is by proving it, by finally publishing truth. I'm going to offer them the best chance they'll ever have, and they're going to jump at it."

"*If* you're right. *If* this corruption can be proved. *If* you can—"

"Enough. I have a good feeling about this, Yuri. A very good feeling. It's going to change my life."

"Or end it."

"This is new? We've been dealing with thugs for years. Stalin's thugs, Khrushchev's thugs, Brezhnev's thugs. They're all gone, and we're still here."

"True," he says thoughtfully as the escalator deposits us in a crowd of shoppers. "But it's much more difficult to identify them now."

THE apartment is cold and empty. No perfume, no coffee, and no surprises this time. I spend several hours working Yuri's information into the story and fine-tuning clumsy paragraphs. A rush comes over me as I roll the last page from the typewriter. The sheet of carbon and the copy go into separate trays on my desk; the original, into a slim leather briefcase.

My wife gave it to me over twenty years ago when I sold my first story. Faded and scarred, it endured my career far better than our marriage, which ended when my activities endangered her promising medical practice. I snap the latch and hurry from the apartment.

There's a newspaper kiosk opposite the Metro station, and I spend the subway ride to *Pravda* checking afternoon editions for stories on the murder. Not a word in any of them. Shevchenko has kept his promise.

From the Belorussky station in north-central Moscow I walk through an icy drizzle to *Pravda*'s offices. I charge up the stairs to the newsroom. The furniture and manual typewriters are all right out of the '50s. Indeed, everything here is dated. Everything except the faces. Young and diligent, their eager eyes are riveted to the pages in their typewriters.

I snake between the desks to the row of offices at the far end of the newsroom. A chunky middle-aged man sits behind a glass partition labeled EDITOR. Round spectacles bridge his nose, giving him the look of a well-fed owl. This is a stroke of luck. Sergei Murashev is a highly respected journalist. Like many party intellectuals afraid of being shipped off to the gulag, he kept a low profile until the political climate changed, then came out swinging.

"What am I bid for a juicy political murder with a terrific scandal and an inside source?" I ask from the doorway.

"Nikolai!" he exclaims as he bolts from his chair to greet me.

"You're the last person I expected to find here, Sergei."

"Ah, it's a marriage of convenience. They couldn't find anyone to take the job, and I've grown unashamedly accustomed to food, clothing, and shelter. You really have something for me?"

I slip the pages from my briefcase. "Something special."

Sergei settles in his chair, pushes his glasses onto his forehead, and starts reading. His eyes widen, his jaw tightens, and he begins to fidget. Minutes seem like an eternity.

"Powerful," he finally pronounces. "Powerful, important, and shocking." His head cocks challengingly. "You're positive about this conspiracy to rip off state assets?"

"*Shevchenko*'s positive. Come on, Sergei. It's no secret the place is overrun with corruption."

"And you're also positive Vorontsov was killed because he was going to blow the whistle?"

"He was head of the CSP's oversight committee. Look, he was

either on to it or into it. We're talking political scandal no matter how you slice it."

Sergei nods and chortles at something that occurs to him. "I can see it in the Washington *Post* now: 'Former Communist Party newspaper exposes capitalist privatization scheme.' "

"We should be so lucky. I'm more interested in *Pravda*'s headline."

He hunches down in the chair, rocking back and forth thoughtfully; then, eyes twinkling with mischief, Sergei announces, "Murder for profit."

It's a stroke of genius. I laugh out loud with delight. "They've never seen that one in *Pravda.*"

He grins with satisfaction, then knocks his glasses down onto his nose. "Now for the hard part," he says awkwardly. "This is a great story, Nikolai, really, but the writing, it's—it's stilted."

"Stilted?"

"Yes. We don't use phrases like 'longtime servant of the Motherland' any longer. We don't *think* the CSP is rife with corruption, Nikolai. We *know* it. Correct?"

I nod, cursing decades spent cloaking the truth in order to slip it past KGB censors. "Old habits die hard."

"The syntax has to be more contemporary now. More conversational, more Westernized."

I'm crushed. "Well, Sergei, if you think it's beyond repair—"

"Beyond repair? This is a lead story—front page, above the fold."

"A series of follow-ups on Shevchenko go with it," I declare, pressing the advantage. "The investigator tracks down and apprehends suspects, files charges, testifies at trials—"

"A case history as seen through the eyes of a cop," Sergei says.

"An ambitious cop."

Sergei wiggles his hand. "I hear he's not enough of a bastard to make chief."

"Me too. Still, every exclusive has it's price. Speaking of which—"

"Hold it. You'll be well paid. I promise you."

"How well?"

"Four hundred thousand rubles."

"For the lead, and two follow-ups at two fifty each."

"No. No, two fifty for the *lead.* Seventy-five for each follow-up."

"Why don't we round it off to an even three for the lead and a hundred per follow-up?" I extend a hand.

A long moment passes before Sergei's meaty fist latches onto mine. "Fair enough. Five hundred thousand. Now all we have to do is get this Westernized in time for the morning edition."

"I'll do it here. Just give me a desk where I can—"

"Oh, no. No, not necessary." He reaches to the intercom box next to his phone. "Drevnya? Drevnya, get in here, will you."

On the other side of the glass partition a young reporter pushes back from a desk and makes his way through the newsroom. With his collar-length hair, blue jeans, T-shirt, and vest, the kid looks like he's just come from a rock concert.

Sergei introduces us. "Katkov has brought us a story," he explains. "An exclusive one. Something that will get this paper off the mark. But it needs your touch."

The young lion nods smugly and scans the pages. "Looks like an easy fix." He forces a smile and exits, then as an afterthought, calls back over his shoulder, "Hell of a piece."

"He's good. Very good," Sergei says, sensing my uneasiness. "If it makes you feel any better, he punches up my material too. He'll punch me right out the door if I'm not careful."

"Come on. You've got nothing to worry about, and I'm sure the kid'll do a fine job." I turn to leave, feeling as dated as the furniture.

"Wait!" Sergei beats me to the door and closes it. "Get that shade, will you?"

I'm reaching for the tasseled pull when my eyes dart to the kid in the newsroom. He's at his desk, but he's not typing. He's talking—animatedly—on the phone. I'm wondering what he's up to when I hear the clink of glassware behind me. Sergei has removed a bottle of vodka and two tumblers from a sideboard behind his desk.

"Na zdorovye," he says, handing me one of the glasses. He knocks back the vodka and looks at me, wondering what I'm waiting for.

So am I. I've been working my butt off. I have it coming. What *am* I waiting for? Vera's approval? Probably. This Moscow Beginners stuff was her idea. Where is she when I need her?

A couple of hours later I find out. I'm halfway up the stairs to my apartment when the scent hits me. "Vera?" I call out as I lunge through the door.

As I pictured last night, Vera is curled up on the sofa, reading. Her soft platinum hair is swept over one shoulder, the blanket tucked around her legs, the carbons of my article in her lap.

"What happened? You okay?"

"Pigs!" she exclaims bitterly as she sets the pages aside and runs into my arms.

"Who're you talking about?"

"Shevchenko. He didn't like me tipping you off. A couple of his goons busted in here and hauled me away."

"Are you kidding? He was thrilled. We made a deal. He's giving me an exclusive, and I'm giving him a promotion, so to speak."

"*Chief* Investigator Shevchenko," Vera intones knowingly. Then, gesturing to the pages on the sofa, she adds, "If that doesn't do it, nothing will." She shrugs, baffled. "I don't get it."

"The only thing that makes sense is Shevchenko wanted to make sure I know who's calling the shots."

"Well, you always said you were a liability I couldn't afford. I'm starting to think you're right."

"He fired you?"

"No. Docked me a couple of days' pay, though."

"Gosh, I'm sorry. I didn't know what to do. I called your apartment, I called the militia, I even called the damned KGB."

"Neither had a record of my arrest. Right?"

"Right."

"They stashed me in the drunk tank, the perfect place to confine citizens without any record of their being in custody. After spending the night watching the scum of the earth barf their brains out, I got a two-hour lecture from Shevchenko about not revealing information to outsiders."

"I'm still glad you did."

Her demeanor softens and she breaks into a satisfied smile. "This is the one, isn't it, Niko?"

"Uh-huh. I can live off it for a year."

"You already sold it?"

I nod emphatically. "A series of follow-ups too."

"Come on, come on. Who?"

"*Pravda.* Don't laugh. Sergei is there. They're paying five hundred thousand."

"Five hundred! That's fantastic." She giggles and kisses me. All of a sudden she breaks it off and glares at me accusingly.

Damn. The vodka. She's detected the vodka. "Sergei wanted to celebrate. I couldn't insult him. I only had one."

"That's one too many."

"Come on, Vera. I'm fine."

"Oh yeah?" she challenges seductively. "I'll be the judge of that." She spins me around and pushes me down on the bed, her mouth devouring mine, her hands tearing at my clothes. Thank God Sergei insisted the kid do the rewrite. Life has never been so good. Never.

Hours later I awaken to the strong smell of coffee and a rustling sound. I push up onto an elbow, squinting at the daylight coming through the curtains. "Vera?"

No reply.

I finally locate her in a chair by the window. She's fully dressed and is frantically turning the pages of a newspaper. "It's not here."

"What?"

"*Pravda.* I couldn't wait. I bought a copy at the newsstand. I can't find it. It's not on the front page, not even below the fold."

"It has to be." I tear the paper from her hands. But it's not on the front page, not opposite the editorial page, not anywhere that an important story would be found. Finally, near the bottom of the obituaries I find a small headline: V. I. VORONTSOV KILLED BY THIEF.

"Killed by thief?" I exclaim, my voice ringing with disbelief. " 'By M. I. Drevnya'!"

"Who?"

"The wise-guy kid who did the rewrite," I explode, throwing the newspaper across the room in disgust.

CHAPTER THREE

DREVNYA is at his desk, typing furiously, as I charge across the newsroom brandishing the paper. "What the hell is this?"

He recoils and swivels in his chair to face me. "Take it easy, Katkov, take it easy, okay?"

"Soon as you explain what happened to my story!"

He propels the chair backwards with his feet, then stands to confront me. "Look, I can understand why you're upset, but—"

"Upset? Upset is hardly—"

"Hey, hey," Sergei's voice booms. He weaves between the desks and pushes his way through the group that encircles us. "Let's do this in my office."

I'm seething, but I nod grudgingly and follow after him.

Sergei closes the door, then, like a teacher forced to reprimand a prize student, says, "I'm disappointed in you, Nikolai."

"The feeling's mutual. You should have called me."

"You expect me to wake you in the middle of the night? 'Hi, Nikolai, I have some bad news.' "

"What news? Vorontsov was murdered to keep the lid on a privatization scandal. Where'd this bull about a robbery come from?"

"Look, Niko, you're just going to have to accept that this story isn't what you thought."

"You didn't answer my question. What's all this robbery garbage?"

"It's not garbage. The kid has initiative. Yesterday afternoon he called Vorontsov's daughter to check some facts, but—"

"He wasn't supposed to check facts! He was going to 'Westernize' my syntax. Remember?"

"Yes, Nikolai, of course I do. Now hear me out, will you."

I drop into the chair opposite his desk with a sullen nod.

"When Drevnya called Mrs. Churkin, she was leaving for militia headquarters and couldn't talk. But the kid has some connections there or something, so he arranged to meet her. He just happened to be at her side when she claimed Vorontsov's personal effects and discovered something was missing."

"Come on. I was at the crime scene. Nothing was missing. His billfold, his watch, his—"

"I know, I know," Sergei interrupts. "But that was a cover."

"A cover!" I exclaim, jumping to my feet. "A cover for what?"

"For what was actually stolen."

"What is this, some sort of guessing game? Come on, dammit. If the kid was with her, he knows what was missing."

His head bobs sheepishly. "You're right. Shevchenko asked us to withhold it. You know, to weed out the nuts who always confess to these things."

"You can tell *me*, for pity's sake."

"Right now I wouldn't trust you with the time of day. You'll have to talk to Shevchenko."

"Oh, I plan to. But I'm talking to you now. We had an agreement, Sergei. It's my story, and—"

"No. No, Nikolai. We didn't run your story. The kid dug out the facts. It fell apart, and I spiked it."

"You should've consulted me."

"I didn't think you'd want your byline on an obit."

"Depends on whose it is."

"That a threat?"

"Take it any way you want."

I charge out of the office loaded for bear—a bear named Shevchenko. Yesterday's icy drizzle has turned into a freezing rain. There isn't a cab in sight. I hunch down into my parka and head toward militia headquarters about a mile away.

A half hour later I'm at number 38 Petrovka. A sergeant at the desk in the lobby explains Shevchenko isn't in yet and directs me to a waiting area.

I light a cigarette and begin pacing. The revolving door spits out a steady stream of soggy employees. I'm grinding my fifth Ducat into the terrazzo when Shevchenko arrives. He spots me and makes a beeline for the elevators.

"Investigator Shevchenko," I call out, vaulting a low partition to intercept him.

"Katkov, please."

"I thought we had a deal," I protest, purposely raising my voice. Everyone within earshot reacts. He stops and looks uncomfortable.

"*Had* is the operative word," he replies through clenched teeth, directing me into an anteroom just off the lobby. "I had something at stake too, remember?"

"Until somebody promised you more."

"Not true. I'm as angry as you are, Katkov. This was the best shot at chief I've ever had."

"Come on. Who got to you?"

"*Nobody.* This reporter from *Pravda* was here when Vorontsov's daughter showed up to I.D. her father. He—"

"I know. His name's Drevnya. You should have told him to take a hike."

"And violate his rights?" Shevchenko exclaims.

"*Pravda*'s obit said Vorontsov's valuables were stolen. You and I both know they weren't. Now, I want to know—what *was?*"

"Off the record?"

"Off the record," I say with an exasperated groan.

"His medals. He was killed for his medals."

"His medals?"

"Yes. They're solid gold, highly prestigious, and worth a small fortune on the black market—in the neighborhood of three hundred thousand rubles. The killer didn't want to tear them from Vorontsov's jacket and risk damaging them. So he dragged the body behind the wall, where, without risk of being seen, he could remove them with care. That piece fits rather neatly now, wouldn't you say?"

"What about the time discrepancy? That fit rather neatly now too?"

"Perfectly. Vorontsov didn't spend an hour or two shopping, because he didn't have to take a number and wait in a queue. He bypassed it completely because he was wearing the right medals."

"Are you saying that some thug just happened to see a guy with a chest covered with satin and brass leave his lodge hall? Followed him? Shot him? And stole his medals?"

"Yes, I am. A tipsy guy, by the way. Vorontsov's blood alcohol level was point one three. He was legally intoxicated, which made him an easy target."

"*If* he was wearing his medals. Just because his daughter said so doesn't mean he was."

Shevchenko beckons me to follow and blows out of the anteroom. He walks briskly to the end of the corridor and down a staircase to the basement, where evidence is stored.

Boxes, envelopes, folders, and large individually tagged items are stuffed onto rows of shelves behind wire-mesh fencing. Shevchenko fills out a requisition form and slips it to a clerk. The dour fellow fetches a large paper sack, from which Shevchenko removes Vorontsov's blood-spattered sport coat.

"I thought his daughter claimed his things."

"She did. That's how we know about the medals. She took one look at this and asked what we'd done with them. I'd no choice but to retain it."

"Because it proves he was wearing them."

Shevchenko pushes the coat toward me. "See for yourself."

I give the area next to the lapels a careful once-over. There are no impressions, no fading, no pinholes, tears, or marks—nothing to indicate there was ever one medal affixed to it, let alone a chestful. "Sorry. I don't get it."

"Try the lining."

I turn the jacket inside out, and there, puckering the fibers in neat rows, are dozens of pinholes.

"According to his daughter he was the proud holder of three Heroes of the Soviet Union, two Orders of the Red Banner, and the Order of Lenin, and enough secondary military and civilian decorations to adorn half the members of Parliament."

"Hold it. That still doesn't prove Vorontsov was wearing the medals when he was killed. They could've been removed ages ago."

"Good, Katkov. Very good. That was *my* question. Mrs. Churkin said it's a new coat. As a matter of fact, she helped her father transfer the medals from another the day before."

"What about those documents?"

"Vorontsov's?"

"Uh-huh. The Committee for State Property. What about your theory that he was hit because he was going to blow the whistle on someone?"

"I was wrong."

"You were right, dammit. You said you thought he was a watchdog, and he was."

"True, Katkov. But it's not relevant to my case. My report will state, 'Crime: homicide. Weapon: nine-millimeter Stechkin. Motive: robbery.' Have I made myself clear?"

"What's clear is, those documents should be turned over to the guys who handle this kind of stuff."

He burns me with a look and shoves the sport coat into the evidence bag. "Look, Katkov," he says, "I'm not going to be bringing charges against the ministry which employs me or against the CSP's privatization program, which just might—*might*—be the key to pulling our economic chestnuts out of the fire. Are you?"

"Yeah, if it's infested with corruption."

"And you have evidence of that?"

"No, but I know who might," I reply pointedly. "And I'd be more than happy to run with it if the documents just happened to fall into my hands."

Shevchenko's eyes flare. "Not a chance." He sweeps the bag off the table, pushes it through the window to the clerk, and charges out of the evidence room.

"Okay. Which section handles white-collar scams?"

"Economic Crimes."

"Why not give the documents to them?"

"Not how it works. CSP has a right to clean their own house. If they determine Vorontsov's suspicions are valid, they'll investigate."

"You don't really believe that."

"Sure I do. Maybe they already have." He starts up the staircase.

I'm right on his heels, thinking he knows better—knows that whatever Vorontsov uncovered probably goes from the top down, knows that the bureaucrats can't be trusted to investigate themselves. Furthermore, his evasiveness suggests he has an ulterior motive. And I know what it is. "Who's in charge of Economic Crimes, anyway?"

"Fellow named Gudonov."

"Would that be *Investigator* Gudonov?"

"Around here he's known as *Incinerator* Gudonov."

"Incinerator?"

"Yeah. Black market money transactions fall in his area. He hauls whatever he confiscates down to sanitation and burns it. Claims it's a deterrent."

We reach a landing and start up the next flight. "So, is that senior incinerator or chief incinerator?"

"Senior," Shevchenko replies apprehensively, sensing where I'm headed.

"Would you say he's an ambitious fellow?"

"A snake."

"Professionally frustrated?"

"Extremely."

"Just how many openings for chief are there?"

"Not enough."

"And if you gave Gudonov these documents, you'd be handing him the promotion, while you were stuck solving a two-bit homicide."

"I don't have to put up with this. Just get it into your head—the documents are CSP property and I'm returning them. Now, if you'll excuse me, I'm late for a seminar on how law-enforcement agencies can better share information." He forces a smile and makes a beeline for a set of double doors at the end of the corridor.

"No way, Niko. Not a chance," Vera replies when I bring up the subject of Vorontsov's documents.

We're in McDonald's on Pushkin Square, having lunch with Yuri. It's an extremely large place, with vast expanses of glass and brightly colored plastic, a short walk from militia headquarters and the Interior Ministry. A horde of middle-class locals are gorging themselves on cheeseburgers and french fries—inexpensive fast food most of them can't afford. For the three of us, the noise level is more than worth the price of admission.

"Come on, Vera," I protest. "You're in thirty-eight Petrovka every day. I've got to get my hands on those documents. You could at least try."

Her lips tighten defiantly. "I get caught this time, it'll cost me more than a couple of days' pay and a night in the drunk tank."

"Something I don't understand . . ." Yuri says. He pauses, savoring a spoonful of chocolate ice cream as he puzzles it out. He's as addicted to ice cream as I am to vodka. "If Vorontsov was killed to cover up a scandal, why take his medals?"

"To make it look like a robbery and for their value. How much you think a professional would get to take Vorontsov out?"

"I don't know," he muses. "Maybe a thousand rubles."

"If he's lucky. But in this case the shooter gets even luckier. He whacks Vorontsov, then spots the medals. Suddenly he's looking at two, maybe three *hundred* thousand. Not a bad bonus."

"Not a bad theory, either," Vera concedes. "Anything else?"

"No. Just that and the documents," I reply. "What about you, Yuri? If Shevchenko's returning the documents to the Interior Ministry, you should be able to get your hands on them."

"Impossible. Despite all the restructuring, access to documents is as restricted as ever. Besides, I don't have to tell you I'm a theoretician, not a salesman. Privatization deals aren't my area."

"Nothing like having friends come to your rescue."

Yuri scoops the last bit of ice cream from his cup, then seems to

БигМак

have a change of heart. "All right, I'll look into it. But don't hold your breath. Frankly, if I were you, I'd forget the whole thing."

"No," Vera pipes up. "No, I think he should forget the documents and focus on the medals."

"The medals? Why?"

"Well, if you can find them, there's a good chance you'll eventually find the killer. And he's going to turn out to be either a thief or a hired assassin."

"That *would* settle it one way or the other."

"And if he *is* a hired gun, once he's cornered, maybe he can be convinced to identify who paid him."

"Maybe. But I'm a writer, Vera, not a militia interrogator. Of course, I could do a piece on the black market in medals.

"Where would you take it?" Yuri prompts.

"*Independent Gazette.* They'd buy it in a minute."

"So would the wire services," Vera encourages. "They love all that Moscow subculture stuff."

"And I suppose you just happen to know where the black market medal dealers hang out?" Yuri remarks.

"No such luck," I say.

"What about that athlete you wrote about? Arkady . . ." Yuri prompts. "Arkady something, wasn't it?"

"Arkady Barkhin?"

"That's it. Barkhin. He might have a line on it."

Arkady Barkhin was a promising decathlete before a knee injury ended his career. He'd be in his mid-thirties now. I met him years ago while writing an article that exposed the government's practice of discarding athletes who are injured or past their prime. The famous ones find jobs as trainers and coaches, but the rest peddle their brawn to the *mafiya*, working as enforcers and loan collectors in the rackets that have spread like the plague to every Russian city.

When I last saw him, Arkady Barkhin was well on his way to becoming one of them.

MEDALS. A black market in medals. I've no doubt it exists, but I haven't the slightest idea where to find it. Moscow's underworld is hostile territory. Yuri was right. If anyone can give me an entrée and safe passage, it's Arkady Barkhin.

I dig his number out of my files and call him. The woman who answers has never heard of him. To make matters worse, Moscow still doesn't have a comprehensive telephone directory—which leaves me with my story notes. Hastily written years ago, they contain the names of restaurants and cafés where I'd met with Barkhin and other athletes who'd been junked by the government.

I take the Metro back to the city and spend the evening making the rounds of the Arbat District. A shopping mall by day, it turns into a freak show after dark. The pimps, prostitutes, and supporting cast of con artists are out in full force, feverishly hawking their wares. I'm being hustled by a rock groupie with purple hair selling back issues of *Rolling Stone* when I turn a corner and spot a weathered sign that whispers KAFE SKAZKA.

It's a grim cavern of cracked plaster that reeks of tobacco and stale beer. Loners hunch over a slab of stained marble that serves as a bar. The more gregarious commiserate at rickety tables on twisted-wire chairs. In a corner a group of athlete-enforcers stare blankly into their vodkas in search of past glories.

I'm dying for a drink but continue to resist the urge, and order a glass of mineral water.

The bartender slides it in my direction. "Get you anything else?"

I slip a pack of Marlboros from my pocket and place it on the bar. "Some information."

His eyes dart longingly to the cigarettes, then bristle along with his mustache. "See that?" He points to the warning that smoking can be hazardous to your health. "It goes double for guys like you."

"I'm not looking for trouble. Just a friend."

"There are a lot of cafés in Moscow, pal."

"Yeah, well, I'm hitting all his old haunts."

The bartender shrugs and wipes up a spill with a damp cloth.

"The last time we were in here," I continue as he works his way down the bar, "my friend sold the owner on the benefits of paying for protection."

That gets his attention. Ditto for the desultory characters in the far corner. There's a rumble of chair legs and a squeak of athletic shoes. The bartender hurries off to clear a distant table just as the pitted mirror behind him darkens with swaggering men.

A wall of leather closes around me. A gloved hand beats mine to the Marlboros. I turn on the barstool and find myself staring at the words ELECTRO SHOCK THERAPY. The name of the popular heavy metal band is printed on a skintight T-shirt that clings to the thug's chest. Neo-Nazi stubble covers his head. Sunglasses with the logo RAY-BAN on the lens bridge a broken nose.

"You're looking for a friend in the protection racket?" he demands, pushing his face to mine.

"Uh-huh. His name's Barkhin. Arkady Barkhin."

"Never heard of him," he says impassively, though his eyes could be wide with recognition behind those Ray-Bans.

"Well, thanks anyway. No harm in asking." I force a smile and turn back toward the bar.

"Don't count on it." Ray-Ban spins me around to face him.

My gut flutters and begins to tighten. "Pardon me?"

"You owe him money or something. Right?"

I'm getting the feeling he knows more about Arkady Barkhin than he's telling. If owing Barkhin money is what's on this thug's mind, I might as well go with it. "Yeah, matter of fact I do. I'm looking for him so I can settle my account."

"Shame." He pushes a Marlboro into the corner of his mouth and lights it. "I earn a living off people who welsh on debts."

"Nothing personal. I take mine seriously."

"Good. So do we. Come on, let's have it," he demands, motioning with his hand. "I'll make sure your friend gets it."

Damn. I should've seen that coming. "But you just said you didn't know him."

"I don't," he cackles, drawing raucous laughter from his colleagues. "But my time's worth more than a pack of Marlboros." He pockets the cigarettes and signals the others with a nod. Hands grip my arms like vises and pin me to the bar. Ray-Ban goes through my pockets and takes my wallet. He eyes the few rubles with disdain. "What d'you think you're paying back with this?"

"I don't have the money on me. I wasn't sure I'd find him. I didn't want to chance carrying it."

He snorts derisively. "Get him out of here." He stalks off with my wallet in the direction of the phone.

The thugs jerk me from the stool, then hustle me to the door and gleefully shove me into the street.

My arms break the fall, but the cobblestones are ungiving. I lie there a moment, then head for the Metro station on Kropotkinskaya. I've had all the electroshock therapy I can stand, and want out of the Arbat as fast as possible.

The evening was a total loss. Worse than total. I have less now than when I started: no Marlboros, no wallet, no I.D., no money, and no information on black market medal dealers.

It's almost midnight when the train pulls into Lyublino station. Vera's shift ends soon. I'm counting on her to tend to my bruised ego, aching muscles, and zero bank balance.

A slight breeze disperses the smog in wispy layers as I walk to my apartment. The streets are empty except for a few scavenging cats and a tradesman's van, its dim headlights glowing like balls of yellow cotton. I'm at the corner when I notice a Volvo sedan emerging from a darkened side street.

A Volvo! Volvos are favored by Moscow's mid-level gangsters. I quicken my pace. The sedan accelerates and cuts me off. For an instant I'm eyeball to eyeball with the driver. It's him—Ray-Ban.

"Katkov!" he calls out as the car shudders to a stop. "Katkov, wait!"

I sprint toward the intersection. Two thugs from Kafe Skazka pile out of the car and pursue. I turn into a street lined with boarded-up houses and storefronts. An alley flashes past. I reverse direction and duck into it before the thugs turn the corner. The alley is so narrow and dark I almost missed it. Maybe they will.

Ray-Ban's thugs dash past the alley. An instant later one returns, squinting into the darkness. I freeze against the gritty bricks. "Katkov?" he calls out. "Katkov, we just want to talk."

About what? Carrying me out of here feet first? No thanks.

He takes a few uncertain steps, leaning left and right to get an angle on the shadows; then, to my relief, he backs out of the alley and hurries off.

I've just begun searching for a way out when the thump of running shoes rises behind me. He's back. With his colleague. I run deeper into the alley. It zigzags wildly, but never intersects with the streets. I scan the darkness frantically. A pale red glow spills across the pavement just beyond the last building. All of a sudden it changes to green. A traffic light? I take the turn on the run and there, at the far end of the alley, is what looks like an intersection.

A car flashes past. It is an intersection! If I can make it into the streets, I've got a chance of losing them. But then what? They'll be all over my apartment. Ray-Ban is probably heading there right now. Vera's place! Her roommates will be annoyed, but I could stay there for a while. I'm sprinting down the narrow chasm when I sense something in the darkness. Vertical lines. I put on the brakes an instant before running into a wrought-iron fence, which keeps me from the street about thirty feet beyond.

The thugs keep coming. Walking rapidly now, not running, they advance confidently. I whirl and lunge between them, throwing a punch at the one nearest me. He blocks it, grasps my wrist, and snaps my arm up behind my back. The other puts a pistol to my head. "Didn't you hear what we said, Katkov? We want to talk."

The glint of the muzzle flickers in the corner of my eye. I'm terrified. Exhausted. I nod eagerly. "Sure. Whatever you say."

The thug lowers the pistol, and they march me from the alley in silence. Headlights bend around the corner as we reach the street. The Volvo screeches to a stop next to us. The thugs push me into the back seat and clamber in on either side. Ray-Ban floors the accelerator, and the Volvo heads west on the Outer Ring.

We finally turn off into the Frunze District. Ray-Ban maneuvers through desolate streets awash with litter, and stops in front of an abandoned building. Heavy bronze doors suggest the graffiti-scrawled edifice was once a bank.

Ray-Ban and his thugs escort me to the entrance. He presses a buzzer. A security slot opens, revealing wary eyes. Then with a portentous shudder the huge door swings back into a brilliantly lighted vestibule. Instead of the rat-infested hovel I expected, the well-dressed guard clears us into a tastefully decorated anteroom. The thugs remain behind as Ray-Ban leads the way through several more doors, where the rhythmic thump of music rises.

The last opens into a private club. They've been sprouting all over the city lately, offering everything from gourmet food and wine to erotic revues. But few Muscovites have ever imagined one like Paradise. Towering palms and lush floral arrangements are set against murals reminiscent of Gauguin's Tahitian landscapes. Colorful parrots stock a circular aviary. Indeed, it's a tropical paradise.

The dancers, exotic Latin women, are writhing suggestively to an infectious merengue beat. Seated on semicircular tiers are Moscow's well-heeled elite—members of government, diplomats, entrepreneurs—and an assortment of foreign business types. All are valiantly trying to guide food and beverages to their mouths without taking their eyes off the stage—all except those in the adjacent casino, who are captivated by the whiz of roulette wheels.

Ray-Ban leads the way to a corner booth where an elegantly dressed man with a phone pressed to his ear presides over the action. A magnum of champagne, a bowl of caviar, and my wallet are arranged on the table in front of him. Stunning young women are perched on either side. Rich, powerful, venerated—it's obvious he's a crime boss, but it takes a moment for me to realize that the handsome, deeply tanned fellow is Arkady Barkhin.

He finishes the call and glances up. "Nikolai Katkov. I hear you've been looking for me."

I nod apprehensively, my eyes darting about the dazzling interior. "In all the wrong places."

He smiles indulgently. "I also hear we have some unfinished business."

"No. No, that was his idea," I hear myself saying, indifferent to Ray-Ban's reaction. "Actually, Arkady, I was hoping you could—"

"Don't try to back out of it," he interrupts, locking his eyes onto mine. "I hate unpaid debts. It's time, Katkov. Time to settle up." Then his eyes soften with amusement. "But as I remember it, I don't hold the marker. You do."

My heart flutters with relief, then accelerates with intrigue. "Me?" I finally squeak.

"Yes. I'm the one in debt here," Barkhin replies. "See this club? I worked hard for it. But none of it would've happened without you, Katkov." He reaches inside his jacket for his wallet and plucks out a yellowed newspaper clipping, which he places in front of me. "Remember this?"

It's been almost ten years, and it takes a moment to recognize my own article. I light a cigarette, trying to recall what I said. The match fizzles. I'm about to strike another when Barkhin produces a butane lighter with PARADISE CLUB printed on the barrel. A stylized parrot serves as the P.

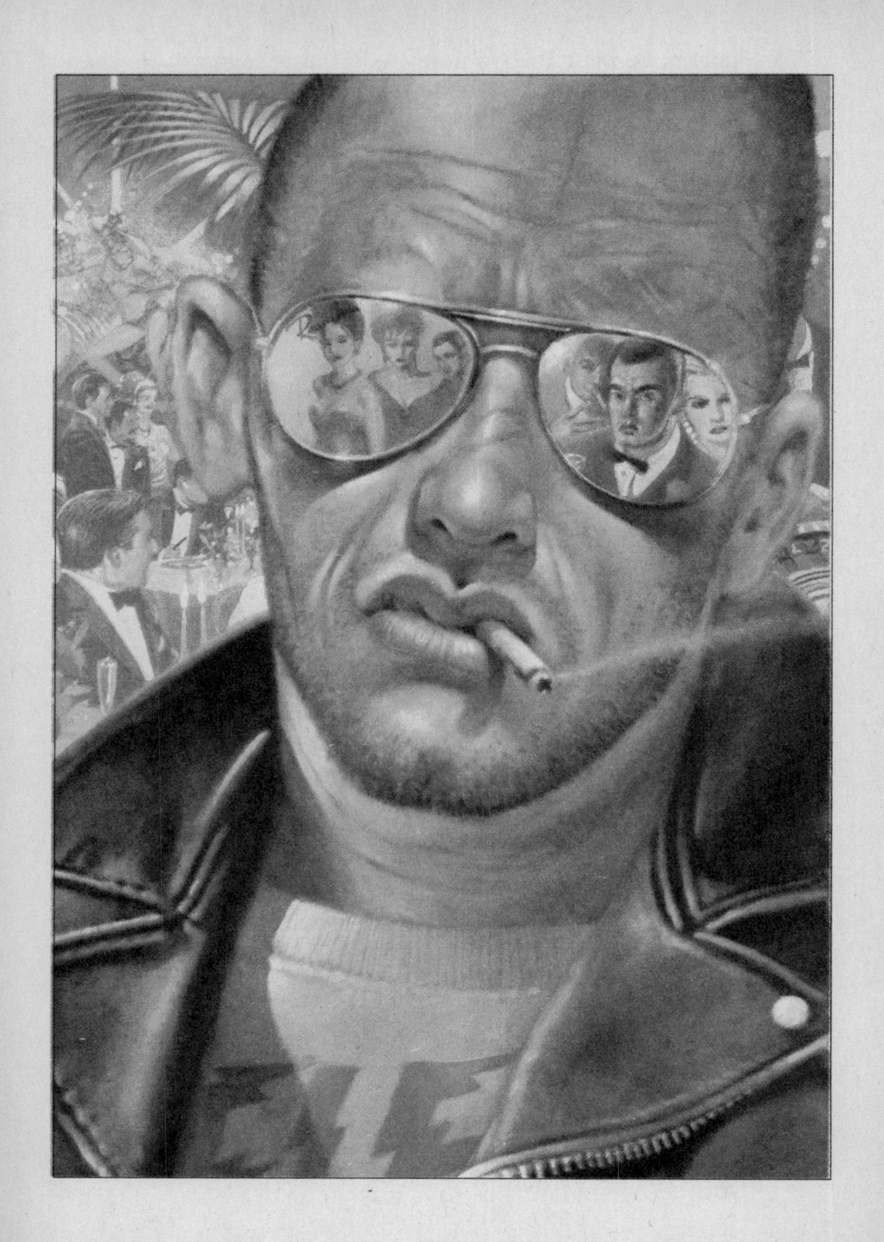

"I don't mean the part about being junked by the state," he explains. "The part I'm talking about is right here." He stabs a forefinger at a short paragraph bracketed in faded red marker. "I mean, when I read that retired athletes in the West were making it big in business—that their itch to compete, their work ethic, their let-the-best-man-win mentality were the keys to their success, it dawned on me that athletes have what it takes to make it in a free market. It changed my life."

His gratitude is such that after returning my wallet and apologizing for his thugs' behavior, he insists I join him. I spend the evening fending off glasses of champagne as he chronicles his rise from a one-man protection racket to an entrepreneur operating a string of what he refers to as service companies.

"How can I thank you? Money? A job? Name it."

"A source."

"A source?" he echoes with an incredulous cackle. "Who else but a journalist would trade such chances for information?" He cackles again; but when I reveal my intention to write a story about black market medal dealers, the levity ceases and his eyes narrow with concern. "Still taking risks, aren't you?"

I nod.

"You'll need an *inside* source."

"Preferably."

"Done," he says smartly, scooping up the phone. "It's not one of my operations, but I know someone who can take you in."

CHAPTER FOUR

Moscow always looks like a ghost town in the early morning hours—eerie, silent, unpopulated. It looks even gloomier through the tinted windows of Barkhin's Mercedes as it races west. We're on our way to the Lenin Hills and a meeting with his contact in the black market. Soon we're climbing into the heavily wooded terrain that surrounds Moscow State University. The area has a breathtaking view of the city as well as the distinction of being selected by black market dealers as the site for this week's get-together. According to Barkhin they set up shop at dawn, just prior to the militia shift change, when the officers are tired and anxious to get home. The Mercedes turns into a narrow service road and stops opposite a forest of evergreens.

Barkhin lowers the window. A moment later a short man in a pin-striped coat and tweed cap cocked forward on his head, giving him the look of a Bolshevik elf, emerges from the trees.

"That's him. His name's Rafik. Good luck."

"Thanks, Arkady. Thanks a lot."

"Thank you, Nikasha." He holds my eyes with his, then squeezes my hand. I slide out of the Mercedes and close the door. "Katkov?" Barkhin leans to the window and tosses me a butane lighter. "Keep in touch."

The Mercedes glides off into the dense mist that drifts between the hills. Rafik leads the way to a clearing in the evergreens where dozens of vehicles are parked. Bikes, motorcycles, cars, vans, pickup trucks. There's something instantly appealing about him, a serene confidence that gains my trust.

The dealers are surprisingly young, most in their twenties and late teens. Their merchandise sparkles in the early light, displayed on blankets that are spread across tailgates and hoods. Rafik leads the way to a small group gathered at the tailgate of a truck and introduces me.

"You want to write about us?" a young dealer with shoulder-length hair asks warily. "Why?"

"To earn a living."

An impromptu conclave, with much whispering and sagacious nodding of heads, follows. "Okay," the long-haired spokesman announces when they adjourn. "But no names. Agreed? We don't want any police harassment."

"Agreed. Where do you get your merchandise?"

"From people who need cash."

"Give me an example."

"Sure," one of the teenagers, with an IRON MAIDEN T-shirt and squeaky voice, pipes up. "My uncle had all kinds of medals from the war. When he died, my family sold them, took the cash, and went on a shopping spree. We got a new car, a TV, VCR. . . ."

"But that can't be your only source of supply. From what I hear, some medals are worth a lot of money. They could be stolen, couldn't they?"

"Stolen?" Long-hair snaps. The dealers move forward threateningly. "Are you accusing us of fencing stolen goods?"

"No. No, of course not. It was a poor choice of words. Why don't we say medals that were . . . lost, then found by an enterprising individual and sold to you?"

Uncertain looks dart between them. Several nod grudgingly. "It's possible," Long-hair concedes.

"Would there be a way to identify them?"

"It depends." He turns to one of the displays, selects several medals, and explains, "You can see right here—some are numbered, some have initials on the back, some even have names."

"Who are your buyers?" I ask.

"All kinds of people. Collectors, metal brokers, pensioners. A lot of them are just into special privileges, beating the long lines at markets, getting into shops closed to the average citizen. Not to mention scoring tickets to rock concerts and soccer finals."

"Sounds good. I wish I could afford some."

The group breaks into easy laughter. The tension evaporates. After a while the mood turns businesslike as the dealers notice customers hovering about. It's a perfect time to disengage.

"If some medals *were* stolen," I say to Rafik as we move off, "what are the chances of establishing a chain of custody?"

"You mean, find the dealer who bought them and work back to the thief?"

"Uh-huh."

Rafik's head cocks suspiciously. "There's more on your agenda than food and rent, isn't there, Katkov?"

I nod. "Look, I'm not out to make trouble. Frankly, this story began with a murder. I want to find out if it really was just a robbery, or a way to cover another reason for killing the victim."

"You have the poor guy's name?"

"Vladimir Vorontsov."

Rafik's brows rise and fall. He's mulling it over when the darkness is split by the sweeping headlights of acid-blue flashers of police vans. This sets off a frantic packing of cases and rolling of blankets, and sends dealers and buyers scattering to their vehicles.

"You have a car?" I call out to Rafik. There's no reply. I glance over my shoulder. He's gone, vanished as mysteriously as he'd appeared.

I'm running toward the evergreens when several of the scattering dealers up ahead reverse direction. A phalanx of uniformed officers with guns comes out of nowhere and fires a volley of warning shots. We freeze in our tracks, hands over our heads, as the officers advance. They frisk us and confiscate our I.D.s. Then a sergeant begins calling out names, checking them off, as each prisoner is handcuffed and put in a van.

"Here," I say when they reach mine. "Look, I'm a journalist. I'm not involved in anything illegal. I'm covering a story."

"Get in." He shoves me toward the door.

"You're making a big mistake. Senior Investigator Shevchenko's a friend of mine. Get him on the radio. Give him my name."

That does the trick. The sergeant takes my arm and leads me through the trees. The sun is creeping over the horizon as we emerge. It silhouettes a tall figure in a trench coat who's overseeing the operation. Son of a gun. It's the senior investigator himself. This is his show.

The sergeant prods me forward. "This one claims he knows you, sir."

"Up early today, Mr. Investigator?" I tease.

Shevchenko looks at me blankly for a long moment. "What's his name?" he asks, deadpan.

My eyes roll. "Come on, Shevchenko."

"Katkov, Nikolai," the sergeant growls.

Shevchenko's brow furrows. "Doesn't ring a bell." He whispers something to the sergeant, smiles thinly, and walks away.

The sergeant hustles me to a prisoner van, shoves me inside, and slams the door. Angry medal dealers crowd the two long benches. Their eyes burn with hatred, leaving no doubt who's to blame for what happened. Fortunately, their hands, like mine, are cuffed behind their backs.

The van shudders to life. It's gone a short distance when the long-haired dealer rears back and kicks me in the ribs, inciting the others, who leap from the benches and converge on me. I howl, racked with pain, and crumple to the floor. I'm convinced I'm going to die, when the van hurtles to a stop, sending the dealers tumbling forward in a tangled heap. The door opens, revealing the muzzles of two riot guns.

"Okay, that's enough! Settle down," the sergeant shouts. "You," he says pointing his weapon at me. "Out. Move it."

I extricate myself and crawl eagerly to the door. The cops help me to the ground and slam it shut. Then they hustle me around to the cab, shove me inside between them, and drive off.

"You okay?" the sergeant asks gruffly.

"Great. They damn near killed me. Thanks anyway."

"Don't thank us. It was Investigator Shevchenko's idea. He figured they'd take it out on you. He said to let it go on just long enough to teach you a lesson."

"Well, I'm a very fast learner."

"Good," the sergeant says with a malevolent sneer. "Your education's just begun."

I'M IN a cell in the bowels of 38 Petrovka. Fortunately, Shevchenko decided not to put me in with the dealers. I've got a cell all to myself.

I've been cooling my heels in this dank, wretched-smelling pigpen for over four hours when a familiar voice calls out, "Katkov?"

It's Shevchenko. He stands outside the cell with a smug grin, enjoying the sight of me behind bars.

"You just here to gloat, or what?"

"No. Someone vouched for you. I can't imagine why." He nods to a guard, who unlocks the cell, and we start down the corridor.

We pause while a security door rumbles open, and he leads the way past a massive out-processing area. A mesh fence contains the surly mob of prisoners, lawyers, friends, and relatives who are lined up at three windows where clerks work with listless detachment.

I recognize several medal dealers in the crowd. Unfortunately, the long-haired one recognizes me. "Informer!" he shouts, making the obvious assumption when he sees me with Shevchenko. "We're not finished with you yet, Katkov."

I ignore him. Shevchenko has reached the elevator and is impatiently thumbing the call button. What's on his mind is Vorontsov's murder, he says. "That's what's keeping me here till midnight and getting me out of bed at five in the morning to bust medal dealers."

"Your old lady still getting teed off?"

"None of your business," he says. "The bottom line is, this may not be a scandal, but it's still a homicide. And I've got to solve it."

"By locking up medal dealers? The poor bastards are just trying to earn a living."

"So am I. It sends a signal. They know they'll be harassed until someone comes up with information on Vorontsov's killer."

The elevator deposits us on the fourth floor. We navigate the labyrinth of depressing corridors to Shevchenko's office. He falls into his chair like a rag doll and pushes my paperwork across the desk. "Sign these." There are at least a half-dozen forms. Vera is listed as the person who vouched for me. I begin signing.

"She's moving out," Shevchenko says softly.

"Pardon me?"

"My wife. She's leaving me. She and the children."

I'm caught completely off guard by his surprising vulnerability and willingness to share it. "I'm sorry."

Shevchenko shrugs forlornly, then, shutting me out, swivels around and stares at a photograph of his family atop a file cabinet behind him. "You'll find Miss Fedorenko downstairs."

I whisper, "Thanks," and hurry from the office. I'm about to enter the elevator when I glimpse a familiar face through the window of a conference room. It's Drevnya, the kid from *Pravda*. He's writing furiously on his notepad while an obese man in a rumpled suit circles the table, slashing the air with emphatic gestures as he talks. He's a repulsive fellow with thick lips and a scarred complexion. I've no idea who he is, but Sergei said the kid has connections here. I guess he does.

Vera is waiting in the lobby. She frowns with concern when I join her. "You look awful."

"Long night."

"Why can't you just take a job like a normal person?"

"I can't be someone else. I thought you respected me for it."

"I did. I mean, I do. But I can't keep bailing you out of trouble."

"You wouldn't have to if you'd get me copies of those documents, like I asked."

Her eyes flare. "So that's all I am to you, isn't it? An inside source. A spy. Well, I'm sick and tired of it. Tired of taking chances. Tired of"—she pauses, eyes welling with emotion—"tired of being used." She turns and starts walking away.

"Vera? Vera, listen to me." I catch up and take her arm.

She jerks it loose, throws her head back defiantly, and strides across to the revolving door, which spins her into a gray haze.

It's past noon when I get to Lyublino. I walk from the Metro looking over my shoulder, a habit I acquired twenty-five years ago—the day the KGB arrested my father. A Saturday. The Jewish Sabbath. It was no accident. His outspokenness on the Prague issue is what landed him in the gulag, but his cultural heritage is what kept him there.

My apartment is like a meat locker, the radiator silent and cold, like Mrs. Parfenov's aging brain that can't remember to turn on the heat. I bang on the pipes with a wrench I keep handy, put up a pot of coffee, and roll a couple of sheets of paper into the typewriter with a worn carbon.

Countless cigarettes and cups of black coffee later, it's finished. Six double-spaced pages that bristle with energy—that are my best shot at getting a line on Vorontsov's killer. I slip them into my briefcase and head for *Pravda.*

Sergei is emerging from a meeting when I arrive.

"Sergei?" I call out, hurrying after him as he recognizes my voice and quickens his pace. "Sergei, wait. You were right."

That stops him. He turns to face me, head cocked challengingly.

"Look, I'm really sorry about what happened. I acted like a jerk."

"That's one word for it. Anything else?"

"Yes. I need a favor." I slip the pages from my briefcase.

Sergei snatches them, pushes up his glasses, and scowls. "The black market in medals? I thought I made it clear I'm not interested in street crime."

"I'm not asking you to buy it, Sergei; I'm asking you to read it. I need a critique."

He lumbers into his office, plucks a pencil from a mug as he rounds the desk, and goes to work. "Better, much better," he mutters. He's nearing the end when he looks up. "Where you going to submit this?"

"I was thinking about the *Independent Gazette.*"

"Good. You know Lydia?"

"Lydia?"

"Lydia Brelova," he says, dialing the phone as he talks. "Best metropolitan editor in the city— Lydia?" he says effusively when she answers. "Sergei here." After briefing her, he tells me I've got a shot at tomorrow's edition and offers me a typewriter to do the rewrite.

I'm about to get into it when something dawns on me. "By the way, Sergei, the piece on Vorontsov. I'd like it back, if it's handy."

"Oh? Oh yes, of course." He shuffles a stack of files on his desk and comes up empty. "Funny. I could swear it was here."

"You think maybe the kid has it?"

"Drevnya? It's possible. He's covering a story. I'll check when he gets back." Sergei chuckles. "He's a pip. Always out there digging. Relentless."

"Try ruthless."

"That too." Sergei points me to the newsroom. "Better get started. You'll miss the deadline."

I settle at a desk and make the changes. About an hour later I'm leaving the building when a taxi pulls to the curb and Drevnya jumps out, nose buried in the pages of his notebook. Like he's on to a story and can't wait to get to his typewriter. What story? I wonder. Where's he been? What's he up to?

"Hey! Hey, Drevnya. Got a minute?"

The kid pauses and eyes me apprehensively. "No. I'm on deadline," he replies, keeping his distance.

"Me too," I fire back, and ask about my Vorontsov article.

"Sergei has it," Drevnya replies, clearly puzzled.

"You're sure?"

"Uh-huh. He asked me for it."

Sergei is up to something, but I don't have time to go back upstairs and get into it now.

It's a short Metro ride to the *Independent Gazette,* the gutsy Western-style journal that took over where Moscow *News* left off. The *Gazette*'s efficient offices are alive with youthful energy and the hum of word processors.

Lydia Brelova is immediately taken by the article. She's a decisive woman who knows what she wants and drives a hard bargain to get it. I'm in no position to argue. Besides, after paying my rent, I'll still have enough left to bury the hatchet with Vera over dinner—if she doesn't bury one in me first. She's working tonight, so I head over to Yuri's instead. His tiny one-room flat is located in a rundown area of the city, though I expect his new status at the Interior Ministry will soon result in an upgrade.

He's on the phone with his mother when I arrive. She lives alone on a farm in Sudilova, two-plus hours north of the city by car, and every Saturday morning, without fail, Yuri drives out to see her. After hanging up, he mentions he's had no luck with Vorontsov's documents, but promises to keep trying. I've been so caught up in the medals, I'd almost forgotten about them. Besides, once this story hits the streets, I may not need them.

We celebrate with a few beers.

I've been up over thirty-six hours and on the wagon considerably longer. The alcohol hits me like a sledgehammer. I spend the night on the sofa and pick up a copy of the *Independent Gazette* in the morning on the way home. I've stopped counting how many times I've seen my byline in print, but I still get a little rush. This one is cut short by a man in a trench coat leaning against a Zhiguli parked across the street from my apartment.

Tall, slim, his angular face masked by sunglasses, he flicks a cigarette to the ground and steps on it as I approach, then follows me with his eyes—or so it seems. I'm climbing the steps of the old mansion when a shadow ripples across Mrs. Parfenov's curtain. Is she keeping an eye out for him or me?

"Nikasha," she says effusively, emerging from her apartment as I enter the foyer.

I know what she wants. "The rent," I announce, producing a wad of rubles before she can ask.

She stuffs them in the pocket of her apron without so much as a glance, then turns to the door behind her. "Come in for a minute, Nikasha. Please—it's important."

Important? Maybe she's finally recalled whatever it is she hasn't been able to remember. I follow her into her musty room as a truck lumbers to a stop outside, making the casements shudder. A moving van is backing into a space in front of the building.

I'm more interested in the Zhiguli across the street. It's still there, but the man in the trench coat isn't. "Someone moving in?" I ask, relieved.

"Out," she replies impassively. Then her posture straightens and she looks up at me. "Ah yes, I know now what I've wanted to tell you, Nikasha," she announces, pleased at having finally remembered. "At the end of this month—" A distant phone rings, interrupting her. It is coming from above us, from my apartment.

I excuse myself, dash up the stairs, and dive for the phone. "Vera?"

"No, Lydia" comes the reply, accompanied by an amused giggle.

"Oh? Oh, hi," I say, glad the "city's best metropolitan editor" can't see my sheepish expression.

"There's a Mrs. Churkin here looking for you. She wants to talk about your story."

"Churkin? Mrs. *Tanya* Churkin?"

"That's right. I told her I couldn't give out your number without permission. I'll put her on if you like."

"No. I want to do this in person. I'll be there in about an hour. Don't let her leave."

I've no doubt this is the break I've been looking for, no doubt that after reading my story, Vorontsov's daughter recalled something disturbing—something she doesn't want to take to the militia, whom she doesn't trust. Why else would she come to me?

I hurry from the apartment, stopping briefly at the Zhiguli. A half-dozen cigarette butts are crushed into the macadam. All Marlboros. The fellow in the trench coat is either a foreigner, or a Russian who's beating the system.

The escalator deposits me on the crowded Metro platform, where a man leans against a column reading a newspaper. A man in a trench coat. *The* man in a trench coat! I drift toward the opposite end of the platform. He watches me over the top of his newspaper, then does the same. I quicken my pace, weaving between the other passengers. As soon as I've put some distance between us, I step back into one of the arched seating alcoves and slip out of my parka, then turn it inside out, put it back on, put up the hood, and remove my glasses.

The station is a blur without them, but what looks like a woman with a rambunctious toddler hanging from one fist and shopping bags from the other comes toward me and takes a seat. I settle on the next bench and wave at the child. He screeches playfully in reply. My gut tightens as the soft-edged silhouette of a trench coat moves into view on the platform. The child screeches again and lunges at me, almost toppling off the bench. I catch him by the seat of the pants and swing him into my lap.

The man in the trench coat glances over at us. He's looking for unkempt hair, wire-rim glasses, and a beige parka; but I'm wearing a dark blue one with a hood now and have just acquired a lovely family. He anxiously sweeps his eyes over the other passengers as the train pulls into the station. The woman takes the squirming child from me and smiles in appreciation.

"Why don't I help you with those," I suggest, hefting her shopping bags. I casually escort my "wife" and "son" onto the train. The man in the trench coat moves off down the platform in search of me. There's no sign of him during the ride to Moscow or the walk to the *Independent Gazette.*

METROPOLITAN editor Lydia Brelova shows me to a small conference room where Vorontsov's daughter is waiting. Refined, well-dressed, and composed, she sits primly on the edge of a chair.

"So what do you have for me, Mrs. Churkin?" I ask, anxious to get down to business.

"Have for you?" she wonders with puzzled eyes.

"Uh-huh. As I understand it, you insisted on seeing me."

"Yes. I want you to help me find my father's medals."

"That's very disappointing."

"What do you mean?"

"Well, for one thing, I'm not sure that's why he was killed. It might've been related to his work."

She recoils slightly. "His work?"

"He ran oversight for the CSP. Surely you've heard of the corruption. The speculation is, he either was about to expose or was involved in a privatization scandal."

"Speculation!" she snaps, stiffening with anger.

"I was hoping you had some information that might settle it one way or the other."

"There's nothing to be settled, as far as I'm concerned. I'm interested in recovering his medals, nothing more. You wrote the story. You're the one with the connections."

"Yes, and if there's one thing I learned, it's that tracking down stolen medals is next to impossible."

"I don't see why. My father's name was on them."

"Then forget it. They've probably been sold to a private buyer."

"Fine. I'll buy them back from whoever has them." Her eyes capture mine with undeniable sincerity. "My father's medals are his legacy, Mr. Katkov. Their value is sentimental. Can't you understand that?"

I nod contritely. "Yes, I think I can. I'm sorry, Mrs. Churkin."

"Does that mean you'll find them for me?"

"I wouldn't stand a chance," I reply, though I'm suddenly aware it might give me another shot at finding out if Vorontsov's killer was a thief or assassin. "But I know someone who might. *Might.* And if he does, it will be expensive."

"I have money."

"Hard currency?"

She nods. "My father traveled extensively and lived abroad for many, many years."

"There's a chance the dealers will just take it and run."

"It's a chance I'll have to take," she says, her moist eyes hardening with resolve.

I cross to the phone and slip the butane lighter from my pocket—the number of the Paradise Club is printed on the barrel—and call Arkady Barkhin in search of Rafik. Barkhin hasn't seen him since that morning in the Lenin Hills, but suggests I try Kafe Graneetsa, a bar in Serebryany Bor. Its resident dockhands and rivermen work the ferries and cargo vessels that sail northern lakes. The desolate island is situated at the end of a canal that connects the Moscow River with the Volga.

Tanya Churkin offers to give me a lift. Her zeal and brand-new Lada make quick work of the journey, and we're soon crossing the Khoroshevsky Bridge onto the island. Dusk has fallen by the time we arrive at the Graneetsa, a typical waterfront dive.

I leave Mrs. Churkin in the car. The bar is alive with the clank of mugs and the dull thunk of darts. I spot a familiar cap bobbing in the midst of a raucous group of dart throwers.

"Katkov!" the diminutive Rafik exclaims when he sees me. "I read your article. Nice job."

"Thanks."

"I never thought of myself as 'the mysterious fellow in the evergreens,' but I'm glad you kept my name out of it."

"That was the deal."

A flick of his wrist sends his last dart at the board; then he directs me to a table away from the action, where I brief him. "*Valyuta,*" he replies, using slang for hard currency. "*Valyuta* is the key."

"Shevchenko seemed to think the medals are worth somewhere in the neighborhood of three hundred thousand rubles."

"That's damn near thirty thousand dollars. You're sure your client can come up with that much?"

"Yes. More if—" I pause, catching sight of a man who slips in a side door. It's the guy in the trench coat. He walks toward us calmly, pulls a handgun from a shoulder holster, and starts firing.

I dive beneath the table, turning it on its side like a shield. Rafik pulls a small revolver from a pocket and scurries to the end of the bar, returning the fire. Rivermen are running for cover as more blinding flashes erupt. Six, seven, eight sharp cracks in rapid succession. Then silence, smoke, and the sounds of people getting to their feet. I crawl out from behind the table slowly.

Several rivermen are crouching over the gunman's body sprawled on the floor. He's clearly dead. I push past and find Rafik slumped against the bar, clutching his abdomen. His shirt is drenched with blood. "Call an ambulance!" I shout at the crowd.

"No," Rafik growls through clenched teeth. "No hospital. They report gunshot wounds. They—"

"You want to die?"

He nods, struggling to get up. "Better than prison."

"You're not going to jail and you're not going to die either," I say, helping him to his feet and starting toward the door.

Despite the commotion, Tanya Churkin is still waiting when I emerge from the bar with Rafik. Her jaw drops as we stumble toward the car. She isn't thrilled at the idea of getting blood all over the upholstery of her new Lada, but she helps me settle Rafik in the back seat anyway.

"You know the Yushkov House?" I ask, referring to a famous building in Old Moscow.

"Of course," she snaps, wheeling the car around.

"Good. We're going right across the street. Sixty-three Myasnitskaya."

"Why?" Rafik rasps apprehensively. "What's there?"

"A doctor. One we can trust."

"You're sure?"

"No. But I was married to her once."

CHAPTER FIVE

"It's the last one on the right," I say as Tanya Churkin angles into Myasnitskaya. "Turn into the alley."

Like many buildings in this historic area that are being restored, Number 63 is sheathed in scaffolding. Mrs. Churkin maneuvers to a staircase that leads to the service entrance. She sets the hand brake and hurries up the steps ahead of me to open the door.

Rafik is ashen and barely conscious. I'm getting an arm under him when Mrs. Churkin returns on the run. "The door's locked."

"Damn. Stay with him." I dash up the stairs and try it, to no avail. Light spills across the scaffolding from nearby windows. I climb onto the rickety structure and peer into a doctor's waiting room. Every chair is occupied. Several patients queue at a desk where a harried nurse prioritizes files. My ex-wife was right. Getting rid of me and my political baggage paid off.

The shade on the next window is drawn, but a gap at the side affords a view of the examining room. Alexandra Sereva, the woman who promised to love, honor, and cherish me until death, sits at a desk jotting in a file. She's between patients. Alone.

I rap sharply on the window. She stands and advances to the window with caution.

"Alexandra?"

The shade suddenly goes up. We're face to face for the first time in years. She's startled, her eyes blinking in disbelief at the sight of me on the scaffold. The dusty pane that separates us frames her classic face like a painting. She's still attractive as ever.

"The door, Alexa. Open the door," I shout, gesturing toward it frantically.

"Come round front," she orders loudly.

"I can't. It's an emergency. Come on, Alexa. Open the door!"

She's momentarily taken aback, then nods and moves off. I jump to the ground and hurry to the Lada. Mrs. Churkin helps me remove Rafik; then without a word she drives off. I'm carrying Rafik up the stairs when the dead bolt retracts and the door opens.

"My God!" Alexa exclaims at the bloody sight cradled in my arms.

"Someone shot him. But I can't take him to a hospital."

Her brows go up.

"You don't want to know."

"In that case, I can't help him."

"Come on, he's going to die!" I push past her, down the corridor to the examining room. I lay Rafik on the table beneath the fluorescents. His face is the color of week-old snow.

"You're right," she concedes, taking his pulse. "He's barely alive." She takes the phone and stabs a finger at the intercom. "Nina? I think I'm coming down with something. . . . A nasty headache. . . . Yes, they'll have to be rescheduled. . . . No, you can leave when you're finished." She hangs up and glances to me. "Lock the door."

I do and step aside as she fetches an emergency kit from a cabinet, sets it on a cart, removes an IV unit, and plugs it into a bag of saline that she hangs on a mobile stand. She cuts one of Rafik's sleeves, searching anxiously for a vein. "Lost a lot of blood."

"Can you replace it?"

"If I had some. If I knew his type. This saline'll replete his intravascular volume, but it's no substitute for the red stuff."

Surgical gloves snap and squeak as she pulls them on, then douses Rafik's bloody shirt with disinfectant. "I don't know, Niko," she scolds as she begins cutting away the loosened fabric. "I haven't heard from you in years, and when I finally do, you're in trouble."

"Déjà vu. I know."

For an instant her eyes have the adoring affection they had when we first met, when she admired my outspokenness and shared my belief in a free society. Then they narrow in concentration and she peels away the last of the fabric, revealing a nasty wound.

"Cut this, will you, Nikolai?"

I take the scissors and snip the adhesive tape that she uses to secure a bandage beneath Rafik's rib cage. "He going to be okay?"

"If he gets to a hospital."

"There's no more you can do?"

"He needs blood, Nikolai. He needs surgery. He's got a couple of hours, maybe less. Don't waste them."

"I promised he wouldn't die and wouldn't go to jail. I might as well make good on one of 'em. Get an ambulance."

She crosses to her desk and calls for one. Then she fetches a blanket and covers Rafik. "He an old friend?"

"No. Poor guy was helping me with a story."

She nods knowingly. "It could've been you, couldn't it? You're going to run out of lives one of these days, Nikolai."

"I already did," I say, pausing before delivering the punch line: "I died the day you left me."

"A guilt trip. You haven't changed a bit, have you?"

"Sure I have. I don't drink anymore."

Her eyes latch onto mine, prying the truth out of me the way they used to.

"Well, not much, anyway."

"Alcoholics either drink or they don't," she says sharply. "There's no in-between."

"I'm trying."

She groans, exasperated.

A horn sounds in the alley.

I hurry down the corridor and open the door. Two emergency technicians are coming up the steps with a gurney. Soon Rafik—oxygen mask over his nose and mouth, IV bag swinging from a hook on the gurney—is on his way to the ambulance. Alexa and I follow.

"Take care of yourself, Nikolai," Alexa says as the E.M.T.s shove the gurney inside. "I mean it, Niko," she says poignantly. "I do."

I force a smile and climb into the ambulance after Rafik.

One of the E.M.T.s slams the door. The ambulance turns into the street and accelerates toward the Ring Road, siren screaming. A short time later Rafik's chest arches against the restraints and he expels a massive amount of blood into the oxygen mask. His head lolls to one side and stays there, blank eyes staring up at me.

The E.M.T. puts a finger to his neck, then shines a light in his eyes and closes them. "Save it," he calls out to the driver, who slows and changes direction, heading downtown. A short time later we clear the main gate at militia headquarters and circle around to the morgue. Attendants remove Rafik's body while the E.M.T.s turn over the paperwork to a clerk and leave.

"He was shot?" the clerk says after reviewing Alexa's transmittal form. "You don't know the circumstances?"

"No," I reply, wanting no part of a homicide.

"You his next of kin?"

"Good Samaritan."

"Put that down and explain it," he says, pushing a form across the desk. "You can't leave until I run it past the duty officer."

I cook up an innocuous story and scribble it on the report. He separates the copies, putting several into cylindrical carriers that vanish with a whoosh into a network of pneumatic tubes.

Ten minutes later Shevchenko appears. "Katkov," he calls out. "Saw your name. Thought I'd say hello." He produces a copy of my report. "It says here you found an injured stranger in the street."

"That's correct."

"And since you just happened to be in the vicinity of your wife's office, you took him there."

"Uh-huh. She did what she could for him. We were on the way to the hospital when—"

"I didn't know her office was in Serebryany Bor."

"It's not. It's in—" I bite it off, realizing he set me up.

"My people covered a shooting there today. In a bar. *Mafiya* style. One dead. One wounded. The latter, according to witnesses, was a short fellow named Rafik. He was with a third man, described as"—he pauses, making a show of checking his notes—"stocky, dark blue parka, unruly hair, wire-rim glasses."

"Get to the point, will you?"

"You're an accomplice to murder, Katkov."

"What? I was the target, dammit! The guy followed me around all day. Rafik saved my life. No thanks to you."

"What the hell does that mean?"

"The medal dealers—they thought I set them up. Rafik was my connection. They must've blamed him too."

Shevchenko nods thoughtfully, then studies me. I've a feeling he knows more than he's telling, and is deciding what to do about it. His eyes dart to his watch. "Sorry. I'm in the middle of something." He signs the report and leaves.

I wait while the clerk completes his work, then hurry outside, deciding to treat myself to a cab. I'm still waiting for one when headlights illuminate the courtyard and a car emerges. Shevchenko's car. It comes in my direction on the other side of Petrovka and stops at the employees' entrance, and a woman steps from the doorway. Her walk is familiar. Unfortunately, so is her face. Vera crosses to the car and gets in next to Shevchenko.

I feel as if I've been punched in the gut. He said he was in the middle of something! This sure explains it. I'm seized by an impulse to get roaring drunk, but if there was ever a time for a session at Moscow Beginners, it's now.

"Nikolai K.!" a heavyset fellow with wintry eyes enthuses as I enter the meeting room. "How've you been doing?"

"Lousy. Frankly, I'd rather be getting drunk."

"So would I," Ludmilla T. says with mischievous eyes that make brief contact with mine.

"So would we all," an old fellow chimes in. "Want to talk about it, Nikolai? You don't have to be afraid with us."

"I'm not afraid."

"Of course you are," the old fellow says gently. "The way to overcome fear is to meet it head on."

"Maybe he's not ready," Ludmilla says. "I hate confrontations. Especially with myself."

"It's like picking at a wound," another woman observes. "It never heals."

I couldn't agree more. It was a mistake to come here tonight. I've too many wounds, too much pain. "You'll have to excuse me," I say, and head for the door.

Heavy snow is falling as I leave the community center. I've gone about a block when I hear the crunch of footsteps behind me. A figure bundled in greatcoat, fur hat, and boots moves into view as I turn the corner. The snow obscures my view, but it looks like a woman. Is she tailing me? I'm tempted to duck into an alley until she passes, but I'm sick and tired of jumping at every shadow and sound. It's a few blocks to State Liquor Store Number 12. If she's there when I come out—if she *is* surveilling me—I just might confront one of my fears and offer to share my bottle of painkiller with her.

I'M RUNNING DOWN A LONG, narrow alley. It's dark and still except for the glint of steel and threatening movements of the person stalking me. The towering walls suddenly converge. There's no way out. I'm trapped. The assailant charges, shoves a pistol against my chest, and pulls the trigger. A deafening explosion!

Searing pain tears through my body. I stumble in the darkness. There's a door! My fists pound on it frantically. No one responds.

Another gunshot!

The pounding intensifies!

I scream and sit bolt upright, drenched in sweat. My tongue feels like it's made of wool, my head like it's being crushed in a slowly tightening vise. Someone's knocking on the door to my apartment. I crawl out of bed, stubbing my toe on an empty vodka bottle. I'm halfway there when I hear a key in the lock.

It's Vera. She recoils at the sight of me. Then her eyes flare with anger. "Who the hell is that?" she demands, stabbing a finger at the sleeping alcove.

I squint at the bed. Damn. There's a woman tangled in the sheets. A naked woman. One arm hanging over the side of the bed, the other bent at an angle over her face.

"I don't know," I rasp, shuddering at the sight of hastily removed clothing and another empty bottle. "Last night . . . Yes, yes, there was this woman. . . . She, she was following me. She—"

"You picked up a woman on the street!"

"Yes. Wait. No. I—I'm not sure," I stammer, leaning into the alcove for a closer look.

Ludmilla T. stirs, pushes up onto an elbow, then collapses with a groan. "No, she's not from the street, Vera," I say. "She's from Moscow Beginners."

"You go there to get rid of a vice, Nikolai!" Vera screeches, yanking the curtain to close off the alcove. "Not to pick one up!"

"Hey, people who live in glass dachas—"

"What the hell does that mean?"

"Come on, Vera. I saw you. He finally made chief—that it?"

"Chief? You can't mean Shevchenko!" Vera's about to launch a fusillade of indignant denials when someone knocks on the door. She opens it brusquely, revealing a tall, good-looking woman. Vera's eyes narrow and burn with anger—"another woman" written all over them. "It's over, Nikolai. I mean, over!" She takes a folded newspaper from under her arm and throws it at me. It whizzes past my head and hits the wall above the dresser. Vera turns on a heel and blows out of the apartment.

"Vera, wait!" I'm stumbling down the corridor after her when I realize I'm stark naked. I turn and slink back to my apartment.

The woman greets me with an amused smile. She is tall and zaftig, with large Mediterranean features. "Nikolai?" she says with uncertainty. "Nikolai Katkov?"

I nod numbly and slip into the apartment in search of my pants.

She gives me a moment to find them, then follows. "Gabriella Scotto, special agent, United States Treasury Department," she announces in heavily accented Russian, displaying her identification. "Could we talk for a few minutes?"

"If you insist," I reply in English. "But I'd rather we massacre your language than mine."

"Fair enough. My agency is interested in a story you wrote. They think it might tie in with something they're working on."

"Really?" I wonder, unable to imagine what the U.S. Treasury and black market medal dealers could possibly have in common. "You came all the way from Washington to talk to me?"

"Of course not. I happened to be here giving a seminar at militia headquarters, and my people asked me to—"

A loud moan comes from the sleeping alcove.

Agent Scotto's eyes sweep to the curtain. "Who's that?"

I shrug sheepishly. "I'm afraid we just met."

"I'm starting to understand. That was your girlfriend before?"

"*Was*," I reply glumly.

"We better talk someplace else," Scotto suggests. "Trouble is, where? This berg makes my old neighborhood in Brooklyn look like a country estate."

"You like country estates?"

"Not particularly."

"You'll fancy this one. Give me a few minutes." I slip behind the curtain and dress. I'm pulling on my boots when Ludmilla stirs.

"Hi," she whispers sleepy-eyed.

"Hi. You okay?"

She smiles weakly and nods.

"I'll be out for a while. Place is yours." I blow her a kiss and return to the parlor in search of my parka. Agent Scotto locates it behind an armchair and tosses it to me as we leave the apartment.

The air is cold and unusually clear thanks to a wind shift that took the smog south, along with the snow. "So, Agent Scotto," I begin as we walk north. "What does Moscow's black market in medals have to do with your Treasury Department?"

"Medals?" she wonders with a puzzled frown.

"My article. *Independent Gazette* published a story I wrote on black market medal dealers."

"Never saw it. The one they faxed me from D.C. is about a guy named Vorontsov. He was murdered to stop him from blowing the whistle on a privatization scandal."

My jaw drops. "How'd your people acquire it?"

"Picked it off your wire service."

"ITAR?"

"We call it RITA."

Either way, it's an acronym for the Russian Information Telegraph Agency, formerly Tass.

"That's rather puzzling. The story never ran. It was spiked—" The pieces suddenly fall into place. *"Sergei."*

"Who's he?"

"The editor who spiked it."

"And he never told you he sent it to RITA?"

"Maybe he didn't want to get my hopes up in case it didn't fly."

"We knew it'd been spiked, but we weren't sure why. So we weren't sure who to trust. That's why we came to you."

"Quite smart."

"I get paid to be smart. Those documents you mentioned in the story—you still have access to them?"

"No, but not for lack of trying."

"This Investigator . . ."

"Shevchenko."

"He still has them?"

"I doubt it. He said he was returning them to the Committee for State Property. The documents belong to them."

We turn a corner and come upon the Durasov Estate. Built on a wooded lakefront by a family of aristocrats, the eighteenth-century mansion now houses the Oceanographic Institute. Its spired, snow-dusted dome caps two intersecting wings that form a Greek cross, giving it churchlike scale and presence. "Wow!" Scotto exclaims. "You'd have to launder a hell of a lot of money to build that today."

I nod thoughtfully, reading between the lines. "That's what this is about, isn't it? Money laundering."

"Interdicting it. That's FinCEN's specialty."

"FinCEN?"

"Financial Crimes Enforcement Network—it's a federal task force that gathers financial intelligence. We have personnel from customs, IRS, Secret Service, postal inspection, FBI, BATF. . . . Right now we can access American commercial, financial, and law-enforcement databanks; but we're going global."

"Information-sharing expertise."

"And analysis. I'm deputy director."

"A bureaucrat. Russians abhor bureaucrats."

"So do I. I'm a cop by trade. Twenty years in the field. Undercover drug enforcement. I was running a network of informants when they put this operation together and bumped me upstairs."

"Sounds like you miss getting your hands dirty."

"Any agent pushing a desk who says otherwise is full of it." She stops walking and sits on a bench overlooking the frozen lake. "Anyway, some funds FinCEN's been tracking surfaced in a deal to build a pipeline from Siberia to Western Europe. The broker on the Russian side was a V. I. Vorontsov."

"That makes sense. He was an accomplished trade representative. This country is drowning in red ink. Hard dollars for oil is one of the keys to recovery."

"Yeah, but the pipeline deal's being put together with dirty money," she says. "If Vorontsov was responsible for oversight and brokering it at the same time, we have a classic case of the fox in the henhouse."

"Maybe. Then again, perhaps he was working undercover?"

"You have any proof he was murdered to stop him from blowing the whistle?"

"No. But I'm pretty sure he was."

"Why? Because it'll sell more newspapers?"

"No, dammit. Because somebody tried to kill me yesterday."

That stops Scotto cold. She's all ears now.

"I thought I knew why, but my story running on RITA changes things. If you lifted it off the wire, maybe other people did too."

"People threatened by it."

I nod.

"Then why did Vorontsov's obituary say it was a robbery?"

"The medals. Some are quite valuable. He was wearing them the night he was murdered. The police figured someone killed him for them, but now I'd wager that's not the case."

"Well, then maybe I should touch base with Shevchenko," she says. "See if he'll share some information."

"I wouldn't count on it if I were you. He said these matters are usually handled by Economic Crimes, anyway. Mentioned an investigator named Gudonov."

"Thanks, but no thanks."

"You know him?" I ask.

"Not really. We had a run-in at the seminar. He's an arrogant jerk. Anything else you can think of?"

"For what it's worth, Scotto, your people ever come across the name Barkhin? Arkady Barkhin?"

"No. I don't think so. Who is he?"

"The local mob boss. He operates a private club, among other things. All the high-level deal makers who come to town fancy it."

"You mean businessmen, bankers, government types?" she prompts, her eyes widening with intrigue.

"Yes. It's called the Paradise. Gambling, floor show, best cuisine in town."

"No kidding?"

"Uh-huh."

"Sounds like my kind of place."

CHAPTER SIX

"Six! The hard way!" the stickman calls out as the dice come to rest. Like most of the staff at the Paradise, he's a young Cuban.

"Yeah!" Agent Scotto exclaims in a husky growl that one of the caged parrots seconds with a piercing squawk.

It's midafternoon. We've been here an hour, and still no sign of Barkhin or his athlete-turned-enforcer types. Not that I'm sorry. The thug who tried to kill me was probably a discarded jock. If the medal dealers didn't hire him, who did? Barkhin put me on to Rafik, Barkhin sent me to Kafe Graneetsa, Barkhin and only Barkhin knew both Rafik and I would be there—but his motive, if he has one, escapes me. And why take out both of us? Why—

"Hey, Katkov!" Arkady Barkhin's voice rises over the din as the stickman pushes stack after stack of chips toward Scotto. The crowd parts. Ray-Ban is on point. Another thug brings up the rear. Barkhin shoulders his way toward me. "Katkov, what are you doing here?"

"Touring Moscow's hot spots with a friend," I reply, making the introductions.

"Gabriella Scotto," Barkhin repeats musically as he sweeps his eyes over her. "Italian?"

"On my father's side," she says in her New York–accented Russian. "My mother's family came from Kiev."

Barkhin's brows go up. "Really? So did mine," he offers in a puzzled tone. "No offense, but your accent, it doesn't sound like—"

"If you grew up in Brooklyn, you'd talk Russian like this too."

"So," Barkhin says with a laugh, "how do you two know each other?"

"Gabriella's a tourist. She—"

"Cash me out, will you, Nikolai?" Scotto interrupts. "I've got to make a pit stop." She scoops the chips into my cupped palms and hurries off.

Barkhin leads the way toward the cashier's cage but to my surprise continues past it and starts down a marble staircase. "Unfortunate about Rafik, wasn't it?" he says offhandedly.

Is he sincere? Or is he thinking, The shooter was supposed to get you too. Is that what's going to happen now?

"I shouldn't have sent you to the Graneetsa in the first place. The medals aren't out there."

"They aren't?" I'm not all that surprised, but he caught me off guard. "How do you know?"

"I offered to buy them. The dealers would've turned in their mothers for what I put on the table." The staircase takes us to a corridor sheathed in marble and lined with heavy wooden doors.

Barkhin stops at one of the doors and unlocks it with a key. We enter an elegant office that contrasts with the tropical decor of the club. Thick Persian rugs. Floor-to-ceiling hardwood paneling. A huge carved desk piled with papers. And—with the touch of a button that sends a section of wall panels sliding aside—a gleaming case-hardened stainless door to a bank vault.

Barkhin sets the tumblers, spins the wheel that retracts the dead bolts, and throws the opening lever. The door pivots smoothly on two immense hinges. We step through the circular opening into an enormous space. Deep bays of shelving units line the walls. Each hard-currency nation has it's own labeled section. The United States'—stocked with dollars of every denomination—is by far the largest. Counting machines are aligned on a table in the center.

Barkhin switches one on. "Five hundred sixty dollars," he announces seconds after I deposit the chips in the hopper; then he crosses to the appropriate bay, counts off a neat stack of bills, and slaps it into my palm with a grin. "Don't bring her back."

"Why not? You might get even."

He laughs, then closes up shop and escorts me back to the dining room, excusing himself to greet some new arrivals. Scotto is already seated in a booth near the stage. I slide in next to her and drop the money into her outstretched palm.

"Thanks. Not a bad haul, huh?"

"More than a year's wages for the average Russian."

"Enough. You're starting to sound like my husband."

"Your husband?"

"Yeah. I'm married. We've been separated for a while. I don't know where it's going." She pauses, then asks, "So, what'd your buddy Barkhin have to report?"

My respect for her acuity goes up another notch. She went to the ladies' room because she knew Barkhin wouldn't talk in front of her. "He said Vorontsov's medals aren't for sale on the black market."

"Then you're probably right about robbery not being the motive." She's nodding thoughtfully when champagne and caviar arrive. "Winner buys," she says, peeling off bills. The waiter explains that it's complimentary and fills our glasses. "By the way," she says offhandedly when he's gone. "You ever come across the name Michael Rubineau? R-u-b-i-n-e-a-u."

"No. Can't say that I have."

"Used to be Rubinowitz. That was a lot of years ago. He was working for Meyer Lansky at the time."

"Lansky? The one who ran the rackets in Cuba?"

"The one and only. Rubinowitz was being groomed to take over the operation, but Castro beat him to it, so to speak. He hung in there until Lansky retired, then went on his own. Done very well. Runs a chain of hotels now—Vegas, Atlantic City, Tahoe, Reno . . ."

"Something tells me *he* could teach Barkhin's people a thing or two."

"Something tells me he already has." She tilts her champagne glass in the direction of a large table. "He's sitting right over there."

I shift my position to see a group of Western businessmen, easily identified by their tailored suits. They're buzzing about a trim, aquiline man in his sixties who listens, responding with a decisive nod or shake of his head. Rimless glasses combine with graying, neatly parted hair and a deep tan to give him the look of a natty investment banker. "That fellow?"

"Uh-huh."

"You're watching *him* too?"

"Oh yeah." Agent Scotto locks her twinkling eyes onto mine. "FinCEN's watching lots of people."

DARKNESS has fallen and it's well below freezing when Scotto and I leave the Paradise. She wishes me luck, then hails a taxi to take her back to the U.S. embassy.

I'm walking to the Metro, wondering if FinCEN's watching me, when I start having second thoughts about returning to my apartment. Whoever hired the hit man might find someone else to finish the job. No, any place is better than mine. Even Vera's. I know I'm asking for trouble, but I call her at work anyway.

"Hi. It's me. I'm in trouble. I need a place to stay."

"Ask one of your other girlfriends to help you."

"They're not my girlfriends. Give me a chance to explain."

"I told you, Niko. It's finished." The line goes dead.

I jam my fists into my pockets and head off in the darkness. About a half hour later I find myself in front of Yuri's apartment. His window is dark. He's not back from work yet. I climb the three flights and camp out on the landing. Several hours pass before I hear footsteps.

"Why don't you just get it over with and move into your office?" I tease as his head rises into view.

"Believe me, I've thought about it." He holds up a mesh sack stuffed with canned goods. "I snuck out early tonight. My mother always gives me a list of things to bring on Saturday."

"How's she doing?"

He waggles a hand. "She's old. She's lived a long life." He shrugs philosophically and leads the way inside. "By the way, I'm sorry, but there's no way I can get them," he says, referring to Vorontsov's documents. "I wouldn't be surprised if they've been destroyed."

"Figures. Thanks for trying." I settle in a chair next to the radiator. "Actually, I dropped by because I need a place to stay."

"Oh? Why? What's going on?"

"Well, for openers, I fell off the wagon and into bed with another woman."

Yuri winces.

"Naturally, Vera caught me."

"Naturally. So you can't stay at Vera's place. You want to tell me why you can't stay at yours?"

"Someone's trying to kill me."

"Naturally." Yuri has the patient look of someone trying to raise a child who can't seem to stay out of trouble.

"I've no idea who."

Yuri nods. He fixes two bowls of vanilla ice cream drowned in peach brandy. "Might as well fill your veins with alcohol and save the embalmers the trouble." We spend the rest of the evening doing just that and discussing my encounter with Agent Scotto.

The next morning it's so cold, frost covers the windshield of Yuri's Lada. But by some miracle the engine starts, and he drops me near the Krimsky Bridge on his way to work, and I walk to the House on the Embankment.

At Tanya Churkin's apartment, a girl of about seven opens the door and leads me to Vorontsov's study. Mrs. Churkin is on a ladder, handing books to a somewhat older boy, who eyes me with suspicion.

"I'm sorry," I say as Mrs. Churkin climbs down to greet me. "I didn't know you were moving."

"We're not," she explains in a tone that suggests she wouldn't mind it. "I can't come in here without getting upset. And the children—they're in one small room. Now they can each have their own. You have some news for me?"

I nod solemnly. "Rafik died. I should've taken him to a hospital."

"Please," she protests. "I've enough misery. I'm interested in my father's medals. Nothing else."

"They're not for sale."

She pauses, her arms filled with books, and looks at me with a mixture of hope and uncertainty. "Does that mean you found them?"

"No. It means they're not on the black market. Never were."

"Why not? Why steal them otherwise?"

"To make your father's murder look like robbery."

"More speculation?" she flares. "Or have you proof he was involved in this—this scandal you mentioned?"

"No, but I'm betting he was, one way or another."

"Then we have nothing more to talk about," she says, turning her attention to the packing.

I'm about to leave when I notice a briefcase on the floor, next to the desk. "The police returned your father's briefcase?"

"Yes. When I picked up his things."

"Mind if I have a look?"

She shrugs in a suit-yourself gesture. I put it on the desk and discover a bulging manila envelope inside, the kind the police use to store evidence. It contains a watch, wallet, ring, currency, loose change, checkbook, keys, pens, and some business correspondence. Everything but the elusive documents.

I turn my attention to the briefcase. The file dividers and pockets are all empty, as are the four penholders. However, one of them feels rigid, as if a pen were inserted upside down in the leather sleeve, then removed, leaving the cap behind. I press my thumb against the bottom and force it out. It turns out to be a cigarette lighter—a butane cigarette lighter from the Paradise Club.

SHEVCHENKO sits behind his desk staring at the lighter. "Really—in his briefcase?" he says. "One of my men examined it."

"Don't be too hard on him. It was easy to miss."

"He doesn't get paid to miss," Shevchenko snaps. "What do you think it means?"

"That Vorontsov wasn't anywhere near his lodge hall the night he was killed. He was—"

"He wasn't," Shevchenko interrupts smugly. "As a matter of fact, several of his cronies told us he hadn't been there in months."

"No kidding? So Vorontsov lied to his daughter about where he was going. Why?"

"Because he didn't want her to know he liked to drink expensive champagne and watch naked women dance."

"I don't think he'd want her to know he was brokering a pipeline deal that was being put together with laundered money either."

Shevchenko leans back and studies me out of the corner of his eye. "Yes, Agent Scotto is a very impressive woman," he says with a little smirk. "She dropped by yesterday. She told me about the pipeline scam. She also mentioned her people picked your article off the wire service."

"And what did you tell her?"

"It's probably nothing, but one of the medal dealers we busted put us on to a shoe factory in Zuzino—a very productive one that's being privatized." He pauses, then sarcastically adds, "As a free-market advocate, I'm sure you know how these deals work."

"Of course. The employees have first crack at buying the business. If they vote no, the government can sell it to outsiders. Where does the medal dealer fit in?"

"His sister was the factory's bookkeeper. She was sleeping with the manager and doctoring the books for him."

"The factory would look like a loser, the workers would vote no, and the outsiders who paid off the manager would buy it."

"Precisely."

"But Vorontsov got wind of it, threatened to blow the whistle, and the manager killed him."

"No, your friend Rafik did that."

My jaw slackens. "How do you figure that?"

"I'll show you." He steps over to a file cabinet, then returns and slides the contents of an evidence envelope onto the blotter in front of me. "We searched Rafik's room. We didn't find anything to indicate who he was working for, but we did come across these."

There, glittering beneath the desk light in all their splendor, are Vladimir Vorontsov's medals.

I stare at them stupefied. "You sure they're Vorontsov's?"

Shevchenko nods, turns one over, and pushes it toward me. "Got his name on them."

"Look, Rafik knew I wanted them and he knew the market, right? Maybe he managed to acquire them and was playing a game to jack up the price. He was obviously a con man. And he—"

"A con man?" Shevchenko interrupts with a derisive cackle. "According to our records Rafik Obolensky was a trained assassin—did KGB wet work for years. We got his pistol from the bar. A nine-millimeter Stechkin. We fired some test rounds and compared them with the slug that killed Vorontsov." He slips a photograph in front of me. The two greatly enlarged slugs are side by side. "As you can see, the markings are identical."

I shake my head, feeling duped.

"They were keeping you close, Katkov. Probably figured killing a journalist who was crying scandal could give credence to the allegations; but when you wouldn't let go, they had no choice."

"Okay, but why kill us both? Why not have Rafik get rid of me?"

"Because he was the link to whoever hired him. They decided to sever it. It's an occupational hazard in his business."

"I can't believe it," I mutter as it dawns on me. "Arkady Barkhin. I played right into his hands."

"Perhaps, but I doubt this is all his doing. I mean, what's Barkhin's tie to it? Some meetings Vorontsov had at his club? Not enough. Besides, Barkhin has an army of thugs at his disposal"—he pauses and lights a cigarette with Vorontsov's butane, then resumes—"and therefore no need to import a hit man from Israel."

"The guy in the trench coat was an Israeli?"

Shevchenko nods. "A Russian emigré."

"The same people who hired Rafik must've hired him too."

Shevchenko exhales with a sarcastic snort. "Brilliant. We've just narrowed the suspect to everyone who saw your story on the wire."

"Did Agent Scotto mention the name Rubineau?"

"As a matter of fact, she did. I'd never heard of him. She had nothing to connect him to Vorontsov. I mean, other than that he hangs out at the Paradise when he's in Moscow. Have you?"

"No. Anything in those documents on him?"

He shakes his head no. "I went through them several times. Scotto wanted to see them anyway. But as I told her, they were returned a few days ago to the CSP over at the Interior Ministry."

"As of last night they hadn't shown up, according to my source. He's betting they've been destroyed. So am I."

"What if they were? It's out of my hands."

"You sound like you couldn't care less. What about your career? What happened to making—" I pause as the reason for his indifference dawns on me. "The promotion went to Gudonov, didn't it?"

Shevchenko nods resignedly.

"Sorry," I mutter, my compassion tempered by the memory of seeing him with Vera.

"Now, if you'll excuse me, I have an appointment," he says.

"You had one the last time I was here—you and Vera Fedorenko."

"What do you mean by that?"

"The night I brought Rafik to the morgue, you both left in your car. Ring a bell?"

His face tightens in disdain. "It was a purely professional matter. You may recall I'd taken some disciplinary action against her."

"Unwarranted action. Unnecessarily harsh action."

"That's what Miss Fedorenko thought too. She was in my office appealing it when you dropped by with Rafik's corpse. The office was cold, and we decided to continue elsewhere."

I challenge him with a stare.

"Believe what you like, Katkov," he says, putting the medals back in the envelope. He shoves a clipboard at me. "Sign right there."

"Why? What for?"

"These." He hands me the envelope. "I was planning to return them to Mrs. Churkin. But I have to pick up my daughters now, so thanks to you, there isn't enough time. It's the least you can do."

It takes a moment for his real motive to dawn on me. "It's true. You *aren't* enough of a bastard. Some people said that's why you wouldn't make chief."

"Perhaps; but I don't see the connection."

"Well, you could return the medals tomorrow, couldn't you?"

"Uh-huh. Guess I could. I just thought maybe you'd like to be the one to do it."

CHAPTER SEVEN

A HIGH-RANKING government official—dead.
A former KGB assassin—dead.
A hit man brought in from Israel—dead.
A Russian journalist—almost dead.
A Moscow *mafiya* chieftain.
A powerful unknown collaborator.
A U.S. Treasury agent.
A set of documents that vanished.
A ritzy gambling club.
A privatization scandal.
A pipeline being built with laundered money.

All are pieces to the same puzzle, the kind that front-page stories are made of. Mrs. Churkin will have to wait. Instead of returning the medals as planned, I return to Yuri's and begin writing.

Saturday morning Yuri's up at the crack of dawn to drive out to his mother's farm. I've written most of the night and have reached the point of diminishing returns.

"Mind if I tag along? Maybe the fresh air'll clear my head. Besides, I haven't seen your mother in ages."

"I know. She always asks about you," Yuri replies as he starts for the door. "By the way, chances are pretty good I'll be out there the whole weekend. I promised her I'd clean out the barn."

I slide the rough pages and writing materials into my briefcase, tuck Yuri's typewriter under an arm, and hurry after him. "Do me good to get out of the city for a couple of days."

We head north in Yuri's aging Lada. It's a two-hour drive to Sudilova, and then we swing west into the Ustye Valley. We've gone about ten kilometers when Yuri turns into a dirt road guarded by a wind-lashed tree. There's no name on the mailbox. Yuri's mother has lived here all her eighty-six years, and the postman needs no reminder. The road forks at a stand of frost-dusted pines. One leg meanders down a gentle slope to the barn and outbuildings, the other to the weathered stone farmhouse.

"Nikasha!" Mrs. Ternyak exclaims, embracing me. Stocky, with a deeply lined face, she's Mother Russia incarnated. She spends the weekend at a cast-iron stove, filling the house with incredible aromas. Yuri spends it cleaning out the barn, as promised—a curious task, since the fields haven't been plowed in decades. I spend it filling blank pages with words. I'm making some minor revisions when Yuri returns from an excursion to the local store.

"It's done!" I exclaim as I rip the last page from the typewriter. "Want to read it?"

"I already have," Yuri replies enigmatically. He tosses me a newspaper. It's yesterday's *Pravda.* I stare at the headline in disbelief. Set above the masthead, three all-too-familiar words proclaim MURDER FOR PROFIT. The byline reads "M. I. Drevnya."

I feel as if I've been disemboweled. It's all here: the information I gave to Shevchenko, the information he gave to me, and more—charges that apparatchiks in the Interior Ministry have been embezzling party funds to buy profitable businesses, and allegations that Vorontsov was killed because he found out about it and was blackmailing them. But it's Gudonov, hailed as the militia's canny new chief investigator, who's credited with breaking the case—not Shevchenko—and a leaked internal memorandum that's cited as the source.

"I'm really sorry," Yuri says. "It's beyond comprehension."

I shrug, too stunned to reply. How could Sergei let this kid steal my story? I grab the phone and dial *Pravda.* "Sergei Murashev," I bark when the switchboard operator answers. "He was what? . . . You're kidding. . . . Yeah, you can tell him Nikolai Katkov said he's an unethical s.o.b.!" I slam down the phone, fuming.

Yuri flinches and questions me with a look.

"Sergei was fired, and the kid got the job."

"What are you going to do?"

"Kill him with my bare hands."

Late Sunday afternoon we drive back to Yuri's apartment in gloomy silence. He settles in front of the television with his trademark bowl of ice cream. Moscow's evening news program is in progress. The anchorman reports, "Chief Investigator Yevgeny Gudonov held a news conference today to confirm that the CSP is under investigation. . . ."

My eyes bug at the image on the screen. The man holding court with reporters is the rumpled, repulsive-looking fellow I'd seen at militia headquarters with Drevnya. Sergei was right. The kid was connected—connected to Incinerator Gudonov.

"This is a serious, sensitive matter," Gudonov lectures in his gruff voice. "The person responsible for leaking a confidential militia memorandum will be identified and dealt with harshly."

"Sure he will," Yuri mutters.

"Conniving swine. Shevchenko filed the memo. Gudonov got his copy, revised it to suit his purposes, and used the kid to put out the story." I'm seized by a compulsion to wash my hands of the whole thing. Returning the medals to Mrs. Churkin would be a good start. I call her several times, but there's no answer.

I haven't been back to my apartment in almost a week. It's cold, depressing, and out of the way, but all of a sudden I miss it. I treat myself to a taxi.

A moving van is parked in front of my building when we arrive. Two men are coming down the steps, struggling to carry a chest of drawers. I get out of the taxi. "Wait a minute. That dresser—it's mine. There must be some mistake."

"No mistake, comrade," one of the movers growls. "I have orders to clean this place out and put everything in storage."

"You sure you have the right address?"

He lets go of his end of the dresser and trudges to the front of the truck. "Number eleven Kurskaya, second floor rear—Katkov?" he asks, brandishing a clipboard.

"That's me." I'm totally baffled. "I don't care what that says. Put that dresser back where it belongs. Put it all back," I demand, noticing they've already loaded most of my other furniture.

"Sure, soon as you pay the charges."

"Charges? Look, I don't know what's going on here, but—"

"Nikasha? Nikasha?" Mrs. Parfenov calls out. The old babushka is standing in the vestibule, waving a folded newspaper at me.

"Don't leave until I come back," I warn the movers as I hurry off.

"Someone was looking for you a few days ago," Mrs. Parfenov hisses when I join her.

"What did they look like?"

She shrugs. "There were two or three of them. Sunglasses. Sunglasses and a shaved head." She shuffles into her apartment. I hurry after her, wondering what Ray-Ban was up to. The place is empty except for a chair with a broken leg, and some packing crates.

"What the hell's going on around here?"

She tucks the newspaper under her arm and sits on a crate. "I told you. We all have to be out by today. The new owner—"

"New owner?" I interrupt, flabbergasted.

"The building's been sold. You know—"

"No. No, I don't know."

"Of course you do. I know I mentioned it."

"No. No, Mrs. Parfenov. Not to me. I have a feeling you may have been on the verge several times, but—"

"You're always so preoccupied, Nikasha. You probably just forgot. They're going to knock it down and put up a café to sell cheese-and-tomato pies to the refinery workers." She hands me a mailer that proudly proclaims this will be the site of Moscow's newest Pizza Hut.

I take a few moments to regain my composure, then charge outside. Mrs. Parfenov shuffles after me.

The movers have finished and are swinging the van's big door closed. I convince them to wait until I retrieve my typewriter and a suitcase that I quickly fill with clothing from the dresser.

Mrs. Parfenov and I watch as the van rumbles off. "You have a place to stay?" I ask.

"I have a sister in Leningrad," she replies. She can't bring herself to call it St. Petersburg.

"Well," I say after an awkward silence, "thanks for everything, Mrs. Parfenov. Take care of yourself." She smiles, wraps her bony arms around my torso and hugs me with surprising strength. I tuck the typewriter under one arm, grab the suitcase, and trudge off toward the Metro, my briefcase swinging from the other hand.

I've taken about a half-dozen steps when Mrs. Parfenov's voice cuts through the silence. "Nikasha? Nikasha? I almost forgot," she says, slipping the folded newspaper from within her shawl. "I found this behind the dresser when they moved it."

"It's a week-old newspaper, Mrs. Parfenov," I say, recalling Vera's rage when she threw it at me.

"Well, I thought maybe you'd put it there for safekeeping, in case those men who were looking for you searched your apartment and found this." She removes a rubber band from around the newspaper and reveals an envelope inside.

I set the typewriter atop the suitcase, then open the envelope and remove the contents. My eyes widen in total shock.

"Is it something important?"

I nod emphatically. "I got my wish, Mrs. Parfenov," I reply, unable to believe I'm actually holding Vorontsov's documents. "I just got my wish."

"MRS. Parfenov?" Yuri exclaims in disbelief as I slip the documents from my briefcase onto his desk in the Interior Ministry. "How did that old babushka get her hands on them?"

"Vera," I reply glumly, explaining about the newspaper.

Yuri tilts back in his chair and studies me curiously. "What's wrong? You should be thrilled."

"Half of me is; the other half feels awful. I mean, Vera took a big chance for me. Shevchenko'd lock her up and throw away the key if he knew. Then she finds me in the sack with Ludmilla. Think of how she must've felt. Besides, I really miss her."

"Well, call her and tell her that."

"I tried. She hung up on me."

"I'm sorry," he says solemnly.

We begin reviewing the documents. They confirm that Vorontsov was overseeing deals with companies wishing to invest in various Russian businesses and industries. The investors run the gamut from small businesses to multinational giants: IBM, ITT, ITZ, TWA, Amex, Exxon. But there's nothing to indicate that illegitimate money sources are involved, nothing that smells of capital flight or even hints at corruption. A crushing disappointment.

I'm about to put the documents back in my briefcase when something dawns on me. We identified all the companies except one—ITZ. The documents, dealing with privatizing state distribution systems—trucking, shipping, rail freight, air cargo, and warehousing—are filled with phrases like "ITZ will receive . . ." "ITZ will guarantee . . ." "ITZ will have access to . . ." But neither of us has any idea what ITZ stands for.

" 'I' probably stands for International," Yuri suggests, printing the three letters on a pad.

"Then again, it could be Institute, Inter, Intra, Independent—"

"Independent Television . . . something or other," Yuri suggests halfheartedly; then he notices the smile spreading across my face. "What? Come on, I know you have it."

I shake my head no, savoring the irony. "It doesn't stand for anything, Yuri." I take the pad and pencil and in front of the letters ITZ, I write the letters RUBINOW, so it now reads RUBINOWITZ.

"Rubinowitz?" Yuri wonders, baffled. "Who's he?"

"Michael Rubinowitz. That was thirty years ago. Now known as Michael Rubineau. Hangs out at the Paradise. Runs a chain of hotels in America. Connected to the Jewish mafia."

Yuri's brows arch with intrigue. "I get it now. You think he had Vorontsov killed?"

"I don't know. Shevchenko said he didn't think Barkhin was behind it."

"You realize how big this is if you're right? What're you going to do? Go to the cops?"

"Yeah," I hear myself say, "an American cop. You have the number for the U.S. embassy handy?"

Yuri fetches his little black book. He dials the number and hands me the phone.

"Yes. I'm trying to reach Special Agent Gabriella Scotto. . . . That's right, with your Treasury Department. A group called FinCEN. . . . Oh. . . . Yes, please. . . . Uh-huh. . . . Thank you."

Yuri questions me with a look. "She's gone?"

I nod glumly. "Back to Washington. They gave me her number."

"Good. Call. Be my guest." Then, picking up on my lack of enthusiasm, "You're not giving up?"

"No. No, just thinking. I'm out of work. I've got no place to live. People have been trying to kill me. Might be a good idea if I got away for a while."

Yuri recoils slightly. "You mean to America?"

"Why not? I've never been out of Russia. Maybe it's time."

"How? Airfare alone is hundreds of thousands of rubles. And in case you've forgotten, you're also broke."

"I don't need to be reminded, believe me. But you're forgetting about these." I remove Vorontsov's medals from my briefcase. "They just might be my ticket out of here."

Mrs. Churkin doesn't respond to the buzzer, so I settle in one of the big leather chairs in the lobby. Their musty odor conjures up distant memories, unpleasant ones—of my father being led away, of my mother crying, of being forced to move in with relatives, of the disgrace. I'm lost in my thoughts when the huge door creaks open and the children burst through it. Mrs. Churkin is right behind them. Her eyes flash at the sight of me, leaving no doubt she's seen the story in *Pravda*.

"I have some good news, Mrs. Churkin," I say.

"Blackmail? My father was a blackmailer?" she exclaims, shooing the children toward the elevator. "That's good news?"

"I didn't write that story. Any of it."

"You started it," she counters, thumbing the elevator button angrily. "You were supposed to get his medals for me. You—"

"I did," I fire back, holding up my briefcase. "I have them right here."

Her eyes flicker with hope that turns slowly to delight. "Oh. Oh, that's wonderful."

The elevator door rolls open and the four of us pile in. As soon as we enter the apartment, she sends the children off to their rooms, then takes the envelope from me, crosses to the dining-room table, and opens the flap, gently sliding the medals onto the white lace cloth. A colorful pile of satin and gold shimmers in the soft light.

"Did your father ever mention the name Rubineau?"

She shakes her head no, her attention riveted to the medals.

"What about Rubinowitz?"

"No, not that I recall," she replies. "Why?"

"Well, I'm betting that's who he was involved with—blackmailer, co-conspirator, whistle blower, I've no idea."

She sighs impatiently. "What do you want, Mr. Katkov? Money?"

"No, Mrs. Churkin. I want the truth."

"So do I. I've little hope of ever finding it."

"Depends on where you look."

"You know where?" she asks, picking up on the inference.

"U.S.A."

"America?" she says, a little awestruck. "Well, we're all free to travel now. Why don't you go there and find it?"

"I plan to; but first you must understand that instead of clearing your father's name, I may end up proving he was every bit the corrupt apparatchik they claim he is."

She nods. "I don't care. I have to know. What else?"

"I don't have a ruble to my name."

Her eyes shift from mine to the medals and back, softening. "I didn't know there were any honest men left in Moscow, Mr. Katkov."

"Thank you. Nikolai. Please."

"Nikolai," she repeats with a friendly smile. "Let me know how much you'll need."

CHAPTER EIGHT

FIRST thing in the morning I head over to the U.S. embassy to get a visa. It's not as easy as I thought, and I return to Yuri's apartment without it. It takes almost the entire afternoon to get a call through to Agent Scotto in Washington, D.C.

"Run that by me again," her New York accent crackles over the line. "You need a special letter from me to come here?"

"Your embassy does. No letter, no visa, I'm afraid."

"Mind telling me why you're coming?"

"I have Vladimir Vorontsov's documents."

"No kidding. What's in 'em? What do they say?"

"Not so fast. If I give you the documents when I arrive, you give me first crack at whomever and whatever they give you. Deal?"

"I don't make deals, Katkov. Especially with journalists."

"I'm quite certain you'll be more than delighted when you see the documents. Are you going to send me the letter or not?"

She emits an exasperated groan. "I'll pouch it to our embassy."

Next I turn my attention to getting a passport for foreign travel. Unfortunately, the Foreign Ministry is swamped with applications, and I spend several weeks standing in lines, filling out forms, and dealing with a succession of envious, mean-spirited passport officers before I finally have the ruby-red booklet in my hands.

The following evening Yuri drives me to Sheremetyevo Airport, twenty-five miles northwest of downtown Moscow. I suspect his generosity has as much to do with finally getting me out of that tiny apartment as saying bon voyage.

Just after midnight Aeroflot SU-317 takes off in a raging snowstorm and soars high above the clouds, taking my spirits with it. I've left the thugs in trench coats and Ray-Bans behind. I'm no longer lonely, homeless, and unemployed. For the first time in my life I feel free.

Forty-eight hundred miles after takeoff the wide-bodied jet descends over the Virginia countryside and touches down at Dulles International.

I'm coming off the boarding ramp, numbed by the long flight, when the public address system crackles to life. "Will arriving passenger Nikolai Katkov please proceed to inspection station number six," a soothing female voice requests in Russian.

I enter the brightly illuminated terminal, where a sign proclaims UNITED STATES DEPARTMENT OF IMMIGRATION AND NATURALIZATION. Long lines of weary passengers snake from stations one through five, but not from six. No, six is roped off and unused. A uniformed officer stands behind the counter. "Mr. Katkov?" he prompts with a friendly smile. "Welcome to the United States."

He directs me down a corridor and into an office where a fellow sits behind a desk. A nameplate identifies W. T. MACALISTER.

"Agent Scotto's meeting me here," I say.

MacAlister nods, then lifts the phone. He is asking for Scotto to be paged when someone knocks on the door.

Girdled in a leather sash and gun belt from which a sidearm hangs, festooned with decorations, hair tucked up into an officer's cap, a zaftig woman in a navy-blue uniform blows into the office.

"Scotto, Treasury," she says, showing her official I.D. to the two officers. "Sorry I'm late, Katkov. We got a break in the case."

Minutes later Scotto and I are marching across an airport parking lot with my things. She leads the way to a salt-spattered Buick sedan and opens the trunk. It's loaded with boxes of food, clothes, and various items of equipment. Stuffed between the boxes are a sleeping bag, blankets, and a shovel. We load my things and drive off, wipers chattering across the windshield.

"You do a lot of camping?" I ask.

"Camping?" she replies. "I'm from Brooklyn. I hate camping. You bring the documents?"

"Was Stalin a butcher?" I indicate my briefcase.

"Good. I want to go through them as soon as we get back to my office, but I've got some business to take care of first. You'll have to tag along."

"What kind of business? You wouldn't be making—what do you call it?—a bust, would you?"

"A bust?" she repeats derisively. "What would make you think that?"

"Well, that's not exactly a cocktail dress you're wearing."

She groans. "First, we call them takedowns, not busts. Second, FinCEN doesn't make them, per se. We support other law-enforcement agencies. Third, I haven't worn this zoot suit in years, and it's the last thing I'd ever wear to a takedown."

"Well, if you don't wear it to busts, what do you wear it for?"

"Funerals," she replies glumly.

SPECIAL Agent Scotto drives like a Moscow cabdriver. Despite traffic, she speeds, tailgates, and cuts off other vehicles.

"Hey, hey, easy does it," I protest. "They'll be burying us too."

"Not a chance," she says, turning off the highway into a tree-lined approach road. "You have to serve in the military to be buried at Arlington."

"Arlington . . . Your President Kennedy is there, isn't he?"

She nods solemnly. "I'm sorry to say he's about to be joined by Agent Edwin Woodruff—lovely wife, three great kids, one of the most decent people and dedicated cops I've ever known."

Iron gates hung from massive stone pillars flank the entrance to the cemetery. A marine sentry in dress blues glances at Scotto's I.D. and waves us on. The road winds through groves of bare trees that reach skyward in prayer. Beneath them, thousands of headstones march with military precision over the hillsides.

Scotto parks behind a line of cars. She gets out without a word and walks swiftly to a hearse, joining a group of uniformed pallbearers. On a signal from the minister, they remove the coffin and carry it at a solemn pace toward the gravesite where mourners wait.

Agent Woodruff's family emerges from a limousine and follows. They're African Americans. The possibility never occurred to me. There are few blacks in Russia. They stand with heads bowed as the honor guard sets the coffin on a platform adjacent to the grave.

I leave the car and make my way past a TV reporter whispering grimly into his microphone, until I'm close enough to see the widow's saddened eyes and hear the minister's words. My mind is drifting to the past, to another wintry day, to another cemetery and a weathered tombstone that proclaims KATKOV. The wail of a bugle pulls me out of it.

When the service ends, Woodruff's widow and Scotto hug like grieving sisters. The mourners quickly take their leave, sent to their cars by the numbing cold.

Scotto drives in silence, eyes welling with tears. She takes a hand from the wheel and pulls it across her eyes. "I still can't believe it. Two tours in Vietnam, he gets blown away by a fourteen-year-old in a junkyard in St. Louis."

"A fourteen-year-old," I echo incredulously.

"With an assault rifle. Woody was my partner before I took this job. I asked for him when I got into this case. If I hadn't, maybe—maybe he'd . . ." she groans and lets it trail off.

"Really. You can't blame yourself."

"Yes, I can. I sent him down there. As we say in this business, he was following the money."

"Whose money?"

"Drug cartel. We're talking big, real big. We figure the cartel's raking in somewhere in the neighborhood of a hundred K a minute—that's six million an hour, fifty *billion* a year. But before they can spend it or invest it, they have to launder it; and before they can do that, they have to collect it, count it, package it, and store it until they can move it. The question is, where? We keep looking for it. They keep moving it. We call it Operation Shell Game."

"How does this teenage gunman fit into that?"

"Woody and his partner were checking out a warehouse. The kid was riding shotgun for a drug deal going down in the junkyard across the alley. They just happened on it." She shakes her head in dismay. "We lost him over a couple of crummy vials of crack."

"And the warehouse?"

"Empty, unfortunately. We'd been informed it was being used by a certain corporation we've linked to the cartel."

"The company wouldn't be called ITZ, would it?"

"No. Why?"

"It has a nasty habit of turning up in Vorontsov's documents."

"Really? Never heard of it."

"I'm afraid you have. As a matter of fact, you're the one who put me on to it. Rubineau—Rubinowitz—ITZ. Follow?"

She whistles, clearly impressed, and makes short work of what's left of the drive to her office.

FinCEN is headquartered in Arlington, a few miles from the cemetery. As Scotto turns into the parking lot, a media horde surrounds the car, pushing TV and still cameras against the windows. She can barely get her door open. "Back off guys." She slips out and charges across the pavement.

The media pursue, shoving microphones into her face. "What was Agent Woodruff doing in that junkyard?"

"Giving his life for his country."

At the entrance, uniformed guards restrain the reporters from following us inside.

The lobby is a cramped space with few chairs and a gray steel reception desk. The guard has me sign the register, then clips a plastic visitor's badge to my parka.

"That was easy," I remark, following Scotto to the elevator. "No lie detector test, no background check, no strip search?"

"And no smoking," she says smartly, stabbing a finger at a sign. "As far as security goes, we already pulled your file—twice. Once when I looked you up in Moscow, and again after you called."

The elevator deposits us in an institutional-gray corridor on the fourth floor. Scotto parks me outside her office for a few moments and changes into street clothes, then leads the way to the director's office and introduces me to her boss.

Joseph Banzer is a heavyset fellow with thinning hair. He possesses a certain absentminded cunning and comes off more like a distracted law professor than a relentless investigator.

"This is very interesting, Mr. Katkov," he says softly as he peruses Vorontsov's documents. "We're familiar with the holding company for Rubineau's hotel operations, but—"

"Travis Enterprises," Scotto interrupts. "It's an acronym: Tahoe, Reno, Atlantic City, Vegas, Isabelle, and Sarah."

"Isabelle and Sarah?"

"His granddaughters," she replies.

"*But,*" Banzer repeats commandingly, "we haven't come across ITZ Corporation yet, have we, Agent Scotto?"

"No, it never turned up, let alone linked to Rubineau."

"I'm afraid you won't find a link in those either," I confess a little apprehensively. "It was just pure deduction on my part."

"Best kind," Banzer says smartly. "Anyway, it'll take some time to run these deals and determine whether or not they're legitimate. But ITZ is either Rubineau's company or it isn't. We can run that one right now." He slips the documents into a folder and heads for the door. "You see, Mr. Katkov," he explains as Scotto and I walk with him down a corridor, "FinCEN's primary mission is to identify national and international money-laundering schemes, mainly those involving the proceeds of narcotics trafficking."

He pushes through a set of doors into the operations center. The room is alive with the steady hum of computer processors, the zip-zip-zip of printer heads, and the questions of analysts who shoulder phones, freeing their hands to dance over keyboards.

Banzer turns Vorontsov's documents over to ops center section chief Tom Krauss, who spends a few minutes at his keyboard accessing a database before the printer next to his console comes to life.

Banzer tears off the printout. "ITZ Corporation," he announces, "president and C.E.O., Michael A. Rubineau."

"Way to go, Katkov," Scotto enthuses.

"Born Grodno, U.S.S.R., 1933; came to the U.S.A. with his parents at the outbreak of World War Two—"

"He's a Russian," I blurt. "A Russian Jew."

Banzer continues. "Magna cum laude Harvard Law, 1955, disbarred in '58 for consorting with known gamblers."

"Lansky."

"ITZ," Banzer concludes, "was recently spun off from a subsidiary of Travis Enterprises, a suspiciously complex network of companies with offices in New York, Miami, Los Angeles, and Tel Aviv."

"Did you say Tel Aviv?"

"Uh-huh," Banzer replies. "He lives there part of the year, according to his tax returns."

"You remember Shevchenko?" I ask Scotto. "According to him, the fellow who was hired to kill me was an Israeli."

"That doesn't mean Rubineau was behind it," she counters. "We need hard evidence, something specific, to even question him."

"Well, you folks may need hard evidence to question Rubineau, but I certainly don't."

Looks dart between the three of them.

"I'm a journalist writing a story on private investment in Russia. I'll interview him."

"Interview him?" Scotto echoes. She tears off a page from the printout and hands it to me. It lists over a dozen corporate and residential addresses. "That means you know where to find him?"

"No, but I'd wager one of your computers does."

"Maybe," she muses with a look to Krauss, who nods and takes the printout across the room to one of the intelligence analysts, a perky young woman with short-cropped hair, who goes to work on her computer terminal.

"You said Rubineau tried to kill you," Scotto goes on. "Why would he give you the time of day?"

"Because I'm a Russian, because I'm Jewish, because he missed."

"You sure it was him?"

"No. I don't have any proof, but—"

"Well, one thing you can be sure of," Scotto says. "If it was Rubineau, he won't miss twice."

I CATNAPPED on the plane and it's barely noon, but jet lag and the eight-hour time difference have taken their toll. I'm ready to fall face down on the nearest horizontal surface. I'd settle for the sofa in Scotto's office, but she suggests the Ramada Inn a couple of blocks away. I jump at the chance to get out of the building.

In the parking lot, Scotto opens the Buick's door, then pauses and removes a sheet of yellow paper from beneath the wiper. She's about to discard it when her eyes widen with intrigue. "The hotel's on hold, Katkov," she announces suddenly.

"On hold? Why?"

"Get in and button it, or you're walking." She slides behind the wheel and tosses the sheet of paper into my lap. Printed neatly are the letters J-P SE.

I'm closing the door when she starts the engine, backs out of her parking spot, and rockets into the street. We've gone about a mile when she slows at the intersection of Jackson and Pershing, and pulls to the curb on the southeast corner.

A fragile-looking man bundled in overcoat, scarf, and gloves exits a coffee shop carrying an attaché case. He sees me in the front seat and looks around nervously; then he opens the rear door and gets in. "Who's he?" the man asks warily as Scotto pulls away.

"It's okay. He's a friend. What do you have for me?"

"Nothing. I haven't been paid."

"We're working on it. You heard about Woody."

"That's not my problem."

"Hey, show a little compassion."

"Try telling that to the sharks sometime."

Scotto pulls to the curb, takes her wallet from her purse, removes a number of bills—I glimpse the numeral fifty—and hands them over the seat. "Here. This'll help hold 'em off."

"Thanks, Gabby," he says. "Thanks a lot."

"Get something for me, okay?"

"For *you,*" he replies pointedly, glaring at me. "Nobody else. No friends." He gets out and slams the door.

"As the man said, who's he?"

"Woody's informant," Scotto replies as she drives off. "Now he's mine. He's a traffic manager for a freight company—Coastline Commercial Carriers. Care to guess who owns 'em?"

"That corporation you linked to the drug cartel."

She nods emphatically.

"Why would he do business with you?"

"To keep the loan sharks from breaking his legs. He's a horse-player with a knack for picking losers, but his information's prime. We figure the cartel's using the freight company to transport the money. He's helping us figure out where." She pulls up to the Ramada's entrance. "I think this is your stop."

I open the door and start to get out when Scotto suddenly twists around and retrieves a white envelope that's been placed on the back seat. It contains a sheet of paper filled with neat printing. She reads it, then asks, "You in or out?"

I close the door quickly. She drives off, races two blocks, and swerves into the FinCEN parking lot. In an eyeblink she's out of the car and running toward the entrance, with me right on her heels. We enter the lobby. She charges right past the guard. By the time I catch up after signing in, Scotto's already in the elevator with the door closing. I scoot past it. "Come on, come on, dammit," she urges impatiently as it rattles and creaks upward.

We dash down the corridor toward Banzer's office. Scotto knocks on the door and blows through it, startling Banzer, Krauss, and several staff members who are in conference.

"Sorry, boss," Scotto says, a little out of breath. "We just got a break on Shell Game."

"Can it wait till we wrap this up?" Banzer pleads.

"No. We've got less than an hour to move."

"Okay. Give me the *TV Guide* version."

"Informant reveals a cartel-connected trucking company made hundreds of deliveries to east Baltimore factory last year."

"That's it?"

"The factory went belly-up three years ago."

That gets Banzer's attention. He dismisses the others. "No kidding. Three years ago?"

Scotto nods. "It's gotta be a stash house. Last delivery was in November."

"Where in east Baltimore? We have a name? An address?"

"That's what we're buying," Scotto replies with a glance to her watch. "I've got forty-eight minutes."

"How much?"

"Twenty-five thousand bucks."

Banzer winces. "Okay, but only if it pays off."

"He's checking out a phone booth on the corner of Wilson and Veitch at two thirty. If the money's taped beneath the coin shelf, he calls me with the info."

Banzer thinks it over, then nods grudgingly.

Scotto turns on a heel and heads for her office. In minutes she's into a three-way conference call and has several other lines on hold. It's almost two twenty when a field agent calls from the phone booth to report the money is in place.

Banzer joins us at two twenty-five. Two thirty comes and goes. Two thirty-five . . . thirty-six . . . seven . . . eight . . . nine. Scotto's pacing. Banzer's staring at his watch. We all jump when the phone finally rings. Scotto answers it, gives us a thumbs-up, and jots down the address, then presents it to Banzer.

He stares at it for a long moment. "Do we know who owns the building?"

Scotto groans. "No, but we know who owns the freight company."

"Yeah, but how do we know a perfectly legitimate company isn't using this building for perfectly legitimate storage?"

"You're right, Joe. I'll find out who owns it."

I follow Scotto to operations. An intelligence analyst accesses a database in the Baltimore city clerk's office and runs the address. "For openers," he says, scanning data on his monitor, "the building is currently *leased* by Coppelia Paper Products Limited."

Scotto's brows go up. "Limited? They Canadian?"

"Uh-huh."

Scotto shakes her head. "I don't recall coming across them."

"I have," I interject. "*Coppelia* is a rather famous ballet."

Scotto rolls her eyes. "Great. They're probably storing tutus in there." She asks the analyst, "Who owns this building?"

"Never heard of them either," he replies. "Somebody called ITZ Corporation."

Scotto's eyes dart to mine. "That's two for you, Katkov!" she exclaims, heading for Banzer's office. The look on his face when she tells him is all the approval she needs. She dashes back to her office and goes to work.

I'm ready to drop. I help myself to a cup of ops center coffee, and drift over to the perky analyst who's tracking down Rubineau. "How's it going?"

"Nothing yet," she replies with an exasperated sigh. "Called a number of places and asked for him. They all said he's not in."

"It sounds as if they've been instructed his whereabouts are nobody's business."

"I still have a few ideas. Hang in there."

I leave, wondering what I'll do if she finds him. Call and ask for an interview? I'm too tired for strategic thought. I flop on Scotto's sofa and make a few notes. The last thing I remember is thinking I should get a refill on the coffee.

"Katkov, you coming?" Scotto calls out, shaking me awake. "Come on, we're taking that factory down."

I push up onto an elbow and squint at the window. It's dark out. I grab my parka and stumble after Scotto. I don't know how long I napped, but in that time she obtained a search warrant, completely outlined the operation, and assembled a task force to carry it out. And now, like she said, that factory's going down.

ACCORDING to Scotto, Baltimore is about an hour's drive from Arlington. She makes it in just over forty minutes. En route she explains the task force includes: the Baltimore Police Department because it's in their jurisdiction, DEA because the money comes from illegal drug sales, and customs because the probability it would be smuggled out of the country is high.

Colgate Street, where the factory is located, has already been cordoned off and secured by the police. We park next to a boarded-up storefront that will serve as a command post.

Scotto reaches into her shoulder bag and removes an automatic pistol. She extracts the clip, examines it briefly, then slaps it back into the handgrip and jacks a round into the chamber. Her eyes are dispassionate, her hands steady. A cool professional conducting a precombat check on the equipment that keeps her alive. She slips the pistol into a shoulder holster, then grabs a black Windbreaker with TREASURY AGENT printed across the back, and heads inside.

Clusters of uniformed and plainclothes officers are sprinkled throughout the space. Banzer and officers from the other agencies involved are gathered around a long table reviewing the floor plan of the factory. A wiry black fellow, who seems to be in charge, introduces himself to Scotto as Captain Trask of the Baltimore PD, then glances at me curiously. "He one of yours?" he asks.

"Our guest," Scotto replies without batting an eye. "An investigator from Moscow."

Captain Trask nods warily, sweeping his eyes over me as he moves off. Moscow? A Russian?

I lean toward Scotto and ask, "An investigator?"

"Isn't that what journalists do?" she replies in a taut whisper.

A group of us move back outside to a vantage point from where we can see the factory. The single-story brick building has barred windows through which neither light nor occupants are visible.

Members of various law-enforcement groups move in and surround it. Some carry sidearms, others riot guns; all wear black Windbreakers identifying the respective agency: DEA, CUSTOMS, BPD. Each entrance is hit by brilliant spotlights.

"This is the police," Trask announces through a bullhorn. "You're surrounded. Come out in single file, hands on top of your heads."

No one responds. The announcement is repeated several times before members of a SWAT team, cloaked in black jumpsuits and body armor, advance on the main entrance. They're carrying a battering ram. The four officers swing it back and forth, building up momentum. The tremendous impact smashes the door to bits.

The SWAT team moves swiftly to secure the building. Scotto is the first one through the door when we get word the factory is unoccupied. Blue fluorescents are flickering to life as Banzer and other agents follow. We're stopped in our tracks by a devastating sight. The huge space is empty. Not a stick of furniture, not a box, packing crate, or piece of money-handling equipment is to be found, let alone huge amounts of illicit cash.

Scotto lets out a long breath and swings an apprehensive look to Banzer, who splays his hands resignedly and shrugs.

A routine search of offices and storage places gets under way. Scotto opens a door. A staircase leads down into the basement. She finds a light switch and throws it. Nothing happens. We begin our descent. Her flashlight reveals nothing but blank walls and a corridor lined with storage rooms. The first few turn out to be empty. We've just entered the next room when what sounds like the creak of a hinge comes from the corridor behind us.

Scotto freezes and crosses back toward the door. "Scotto, Treasury," she announces. "Who's that?"

There's no reply.

She slips the pistol from its holster and eases back into the corridor. A rat the size of a small dog scurries across the floor. Scotto shudders, then holsters the pistol, relieved.

We take a moment to let our heart rates return to normal, then resume our task. We're checking out the last few storage rooms when the circle of light moves across something in the distance that glimmers. "What's that?" I ask.

Scotto stops walking and shifts the beam back and forth. On a door with the word JANITOR stenciled across it is an impressive dead-bolt-lock assembly. "Must be some pretty high-priced mops in there," she says."

Scotto radios for assistance. Agents come clambering down the stairs. Banzer, Trask, and other command personnel follow, along with the battering-ram crew, which makes quick work of the door.

We move through onto an underground loading dock. There below, in the glare of the work lights—stacked on pallets, on tables, on the floor, almost to the ceiling—are bundles of cash, bags of cash, boxes of cash, crates of cash, an unimaginable amount of wet, blackened, crumbling, rotting cash standing in two feet of water, with rats crawling all over it.

We look in stunned silence—delighted, relieved. "How much you think is there?" I finally ask.

Banzer takes a moment to calculate. "I'd say we're looking at hundreds of millions."

Scotto grins broadly and nods. "This has gotta be four, maybe five times the size of that hundred we bagged in Detroit last year."

"Five hundred million?" I hear myself blurt in total disbelief. "That's a half billion dollars. They just abandoned it?"

"Sure as hell looks that way," Trask says.

"Probably decided it was too much trouble to mess with it," Scotto deduces. "What does that tell you?"

"It's pocket change," I say. "Is this what you needed to nail Rubineau?"

"Nail him?" Banzer challenges. "For what? Leasing his property to people of questionable character? He's not responsible for what they store here." Banzer pauses, savoring a thought, then looks over at Scotto and smiles. "Not yet, anyway."

CHAPTER NINE

IT's after nine by the time I check into the Ramada Inn. A red light on the phone is blinking when I enter the room. The message is from the perky computer tech at FinCEN's ops center.

"Got a fix on Rubineau for you," she reports when I return the call. "Picked him up in an FAA database. Turns out he's got a corporate jet. A Gulfstream. Last flight plan listed La Guardia as its destination, so the bird's still cooling its jets in New York."

"Do we know for certain he was on the flight?"

"Uh-huh. He has an apartment in the city. The address is Four thirty-five Sutton Place South. Odds are that's where he's bunking."

"Perfectly fine odds, if you ask me. Thanks."

After a few hours of fitful sleep, a steaming shower, and a change of clothes, I take the Metro to National Airport—one stop south of the Pentagon according to my guide—and board the morning's first shuttle to La Guardia.

In less than an hour the famous skyline appears off the right side of the aircraft, a stunning sight in the early morning darkness.

A dispatcher greets me as I exit the terminal and ushers me into a taxi. The driver proves he could go fender to fender with Moscow's best. We're soon crossing a spired bridge strung with necklaces of light, which takes us into New York's dark, empty streets.

At a sign reading SUTTON PLACE, we turn into the grounds of a residential high rise. A uniformed doorman escorts me to the security desk in the lobby. I give the guard my name and tell him I want to see Rubineau. He studies the pages of a register, then slowly shakes his head no. "Sorry, pal. Mr. Rubineau always notifies us when he's expecting someone. There's no Kirov here."

"It's *Katkov.* He isn't expecting me, but I—"

"Forget it. He ain't gonna see you."

"Well, maybe he 'ain't.' But knowing Mr. Rubineau, I'd let him make the decision, if I were you."

He mulls it over, then calls Rubineau's apartment and relays the information. He awaits the reply, then emits a cynical grunt. "Okay, Kirov. You're on." He shows me to an elevator.

The door opens, revealing a broad-shouldered young man who gestures for me to enter. As the elevator starts to rise, he frisks me without a word. My pulse quickens. The grave warning rings in my ears: "If it was Rubineau, he won't miss twice."

The elevator leaves us in the foyer of a penthouse apartment. A huge welded-bronze sculpture covers the entry wall. Floor-to-ceiling windows frame a panorama of twinkling lights. Pristine white walls display priceless art. I'm gawking at it all when a commanding voice calls out, "Mr. Katkov, welcome to New York."

Tanned, sartorially splendid in a finely cut dark blue suit, striped shirt, and boldly patterned tie, Michael Rubineau bounds down the steps with the vitality of a man half his age.

"Nice of you to drop by!" he exclaims with disarming sincerity as we shake hands. There's a combative sparkle in his eyes and traces of streetwise cunning beneath the polished veneer. He dismisses my escort with a nod, then leads the way to an intimate dining room. The table is set for two. "Why don't we have some breakfast and get to know each other."

"Sure," I reply warily as we take our seats. "It's only fair to warn you that people know I'm here. Federal law-enforcement people."

"Good. I was counting on it."

"You were?" I say, astonished. Other than Yuri, only Shevchenko knows about FinCEN. Are he and Rubineau connected?

He places a copy of *The New York Times* on the table next to me. At the bottom of the front page—beneath a caption that reads AGENT'S DEATH RELATED TO MONEY-LAUNDERING INVESTIGATION—is a picture of Scotto in the FinCEN parking lot. The puzzled-looking man next to her is me. "Have some orange juice," Rubineau urges with a wily smile. "It's freshly squeezed."

A uniformed maid fills our goblets, then serves blintzes, smoked salmon, and coffee from a cart.

"I'm rather confused, Mr. Rubineau," I say when she's finished. "How did you know that was me?"

"I make a habit of getting to know everyone who can hurt me or help me," he explains. "You straddle the line, Katkov. I'm still making up my mind about you."

"An assassin in Moscow gave me the impression you already had."

"Assassin?" he echoes, offended. "Where did you get that idea? *Mental* firepower is my weapon of choice. I select my targets carefully, and I rarely miss."

I'm thinking it'd be a perfect epitaph when he pushes back in his chair and crosses to a collection of family snapshots arranged on the mantel—adoring wife, giggling grandchildren, and the usual assortment of relatives. He hands one to me. "You know who that is?"

A man in his sixties holding a shaggy dog in his arms stares back at me from within the silver frame. "Your father?"

Rubineau shakes his head and smiles. "My rabbi. Eighty years ago when he came to this country, his name was Maier Suchowlijanski."

"Oh!" I exclaim, as it dawns on me. "Meyer Lansky."

Rubineau brightens. "He was a great man—an honest man in a dishonest business. His hotel, the Riviera, was the finest hotel and best-run casino in Havana. And he was a genius with numbers. Our families came from the same town in Russia."

"Grodno, near the Polish border."

Rubineau's eyes flicker and burn with curiosity.

"Perhaps you're forgetting I'm a journalist, Mr. Rubineau—an investigative journalist."

"We'll come back to that," he growls impatiently, returning Lansky's picture to its place of honor. "I was about to say Meyer knew all there was to know about business, and he taught it to me. Even the FBI said he could've run General Motors."

"From what I hear, he probably should have."

"He *would* have, had he chosen a different path." His expression darkening, he adds, "And been born a gentile."

"Is that why he changed his name?"

"That's two insults, Katkov. Meyer was proud of being a Jew—and so am I. It killed him when the Israelis denied him residency."

"I imagine they aren't interested in people who don't play by the rules."

"Play by the rules!" he explodes. "You know where Israel would be today if they played by the rules? But he advised me not to make the mistake he did, and I didn't. I've played by 'em from day one."

"Then what's a half billion dollars in drug money doing in the basement of one of your buildings, a factory in east Baltimore?"

"Baltimore? I've acquired a lot of real estate there. I can't rattle off every piece I own."

"I assume you *can* rattle off the names of your companies. The building in question is owned by ITZ Corporation. Ring a bell?"

"You're a cocky little guy, aren't you?"

"A necessary evil in my line of work. Is ITZ your company?"

"Of course it is. I put it together to do business in Russia. You realize the enormity of what's going on there? It took Margaret Thatcher twelve years to privatize fifteen percent of the British economy. Yeltsin's trying to do it all overnight. He doesn't stand a chance without private investment, but it's hard for investors to think long term with all this corruption going on. Banks that did business with the Soviet Union for years are backing away now."

"What does that have to do with me?"

"Your line of work. You've written some interesting things lately. You can do a lot of damage by making a big deal out of this so-called scandal. The Russian economy is like a house of cards. One push, one little bit of negative publicity, could bring it down. That would have a devastating impact on what I'm trying to do."

"Frequenting casinos run by mobsters might have the same effect."

"You mean Barkhin? His club is a good place to do business. That doesn't mean I like him. He's smart and selfish, building his own little empire. Believe me, he doesn't give a damn for Russia."

"That's not surprising. Russia didn't give a damn for him either. Nor for a lot of people. It's every man for himself now. And because any hustler can get much more selling his product outside the country, they're taking more out than they're bringing in."

"Not this hustler. I'm putting in plenty, and you can tell your friends at FinCEN that all my deals are bona fide."

"They'll find out on their own, believe me."

"Wasting their time. You and I care about our country. These law-enforcement types—Russians, Americans—they're cracking down too hard. Killing entrepreneurial spirit." He breaks into a satisfied smile. "Now, you didn't come here to listen to me pontificate. What are you after?"

"The name Vorontsov ring a bell?"

"It might."

"Really, Mr. Rubineau. You were doing business with him. ITZ documents were found in his briefcase. They put you square in the middle of the very scandal you're asking me to ignore."

"I don't like what you're implying. Vorontsov was a fine man and dedicated public servant. I enjoyed doing business with him."

"*Legitimate* business?"

"That's right. Why? What's it to you?"

"Nothing. It's of no concern to me. To his daughter. She thinks his reputation's been smeared rather unjustly."

"No thanks to guys like you. Look, Katkov," he glances again to the family snapshots, then locks his eyes onto mine. "I'd sure hate for my daughter to find herself in the same boat as Vorontsov's."

My return flight to Washington arrives well past noon. I loosen up Mrs. Churkin's purse strings and take a cab back to FinCEN. I'm crossing the parking lot to the main entrance when I notice a yellow sheet of paper fluttering against the windshield of Scotto's car. Printed in the same neat hand is another four-letter code for where her informant will meet her.

Scotto's on the phone when I reach her office. I lean against the doorjamb, taken by her eye-catching dress. The blue-purple wool hugs her generous figure alluringly. It's a marked change from her usual jacket and slacks. Furthermore, there's a cheerful, almost bubbly air about her.

Her eyes widen as I hold up her informant's message. She snatches it from my hand. "Hey, listen, something's come up." She finishes the call, then fetches her coat. "It was on my car?"

"The windshield. Like the last one."

"Thanks." She stabs an arm into a sleeve. "I thought you'd be in here first thing. I tried the hotel. Where you been?"

"I caught an early shuttle to New York."

Scotto stops in her tracks and questions me with a look.

"You know the little computer tech in ops who was tracking down Rubineau?" I ask.

"Jennifer."

"Jennifer. She found him in New York. We had breakfast."

"You're putting me on."

I shake my head no and grin smugly.

"What'd he have to say?"

"Quite a lot, actually. For openers—"

The phone twitters, and she spins back to her desk to answer it. "Scotto. . . . Uh-huh. . . . You're sure?" She groans unhappily at the reply. "Okay, thanks." She hangs up and frowns. "That was ops. They finished running those ITZ deals. They're all legit."

"That's what Rubineau told me. He said you were wasting your time."

"Guess so." She leads the way from the office, down the corridor toward the elevator. "What else he have to say?"

"He requested I refrain from doing anything that might hurt Russia. It seems Mr. Rubineau's developed a late-in-life passion for the land of his birth."

"What a pile of bull." She sighs, nervously thumbing the elevator button. "Where do we go from here?"

I sweep my eyes over her and smile. "Someplace quite special, I imagine."

She comes closer to blushing than I ever imagined possible. "Nothing like scoring a basement full of cash to warm an agent's heart. I felt so good when I got home last night, I called my husband and suggested we get away for the weekend, try and put our lives back together. We're flying down to Hilton Head tonight. That's a resort in South Carolina." The elevator door opens. Her forefinger stabs me square in the chest. "Far as you go," she says, hurrying off to meet with her informant. "Sorry."

"No friends," I call out as the door rolls closed. "I remember." I stand there for a long moment, thinking about Vera, and wonder if there's any chance to put *our* lives back together. I start drifting back toward Scotto's office, feeling a little empty, then detour to ops to see Jennifer, the computer tech.

"I want to thank you for tracking down Rubineau for me."

"My pleasure, Mr. Katkov. Put me on to something I wouldn't've found otherwise." She hands me a copy of the flight plan that Rubineau's crew filed with the FAA. "That flight to New York originated in Havana."

"What's so special about that?"

"Havana's off-limits to Americans. No diplomatic ties. No travel. No trade."

"Ah, yes, that's right!" I exclaim. "So what do you think Rubineau was doing down there?"

"Good question. The flight had FAA clearance. It's pretty unusual to get it. Maybe we can find out why Rubineau did." She returns to her work station and initiates a search.

A half hour later she's still at it when Scotto comes through the door. "Glad you're back. We may have something important here."

"That makes two of us," Scotto says, preoccupied. She tears a page from a small notepad and hands it to Jennifer. "Run that for me, will you? ASAP. I want to know who owns it."

Jennifer goes to work and soon announces, "Mid-Atlantic Trucking Depot, purchased two months ago by—ITZ Corporation."

Scotto swings a look in my direction. "Rubineau didn't just happen to mention anything about buying a trucking depot in Hagerstown, Maryland, did he?"

"Well, as long as we're on Rubineau, what would you say if I told you he made a trip to Havana recently."

"Havana? How the hell he manage that?"

"Good question. Jennifer's working on it."

"No. Jennifer just struck out," Jennifer says. She points to her monitor, to the phrase ACCESS DENIED. "Every time I cross-reference Cuba with Rubineau or his companies, that's what happens."

"Sounds like somebody's got something to hide. Good work. Keep trying." Scotto heads out the door and down the corridor.

I hurry after her. "What's all this about a trucking depot?"

"According to my informant, one of their shipping containers, number 95824 to be precise, is filled with cash—in the neighborhood of a couple of billion dollars."

"A couple of billion?" I exclaim, flabbergasted.

"Yeah. It rolls at midnight."

"Your guy isn't much for lead time, is he?"

"Tell me about it." She makes a beeline for the director's office.

"Way to go, Scotto," Banzer enthuses after she's briefed him. "I've got just one question."

"ITZ Corporation," Scotto chirps smartly, beating him to it. "I already checked."

"Okay, smarty. It may come as news to you, but Hagerstown just happens to be one of the hubs of this country's trucking industry. That container could be going just about anywhere."

"Try Atlanta," Scotto replies. "It's consigned to a recycling plant just west of downtown, near Fulton County Airport."

"Who's the shipper?"

"Coppelia Paper Products, and according to the bill of lading, the cargo is seven tons of scrap paper."

"Makes sense. Covers the cargo and weight." Banzer's eyes narrow. "I want both ends of this, Gabby. That means we set up surveillance at the trucking depot and the recycling plant; and tail the rig with the container between 'em. Krauss can fly ahead and handle the Atlanta end out of the local S.A.C. office."

"Special agent in charge," Scotto explains for me. She crosses to a wall map. "Looks like I-81 is the main drag south out of Hagerstown. Six, maybe seven hundred miles; four states—Maryland, Virginia, Tennessee, Georgia. I figure four units with a mix of customs and DEA oughtta do it. That way we can take turns—"

"*They*, Gabby," Banzer interrupts. "Not we. *They*. The only thing you're licensed to drive is a desk."

"I'm the agent in charge, Joe."

"You're the deputy director of FinCEN, dammit."

"Not if you stop me from doing this. Come on. It's my informant, Joe. That makes me the A.I.C."

"It's *Woody's* informant. Besides, I thought you and Marty were going away for the weekend?"

"Joe, I've had a pain in my gut ever since you called me in here and told me about Woody. Don't keep me from this. Please."

Banzer sighs. "Okay, Gabby," he says. "But DEA and customs are on point. You lay back and coordinate. Agreed?"

"Agreed."

"And get someone to ride shotgun with you."

"Done."

"What do you mean, done?"

"Don't ask."

Banzer's eyes widen with understanding and dart to mine. "No."

"I made a deal, Joe."

"No."

"It's a perfect cover. A couple of Russian tourists getting their first taste of—"

"No. He's not a professional."

"I take exception to that," I protest. "I venture to say you'd have no knowledge of ITZ whatsoever if it wasn't for me."

Banzer's posture slackens in capitulation. "I'm the boss. Why do I always lose these things?"

"Because you're a very smart boss, who always makes the right decision," Scotto says, and drags me out the door toward her office.

She leaves me outside it only long enough to change to jeans, running shoes, and a leather jacket. Then she wastes no time heating up the phone lines. Field strategy, operational briefings, interagency teamwork. "Right," she says, wrapping up a conference call with DEA and customs colleagues. "Four unmarked units counting mine. We'll rendezvous outside the depot at twenty-two hundred."

She hangs up, grabs her gear, and charges for the door. "Come on, Katkov. Move it. We've got to stop at my husband's office on the way. This isn't something I can do over the phone."

"Hard to check out of a hotel over it too."

She sighs, and hurries to the elevator. We blow through the lobby and across the darkened parking lot. We open the Buick's doors and jump inside. Neither of us gets to close them.

Scotto freezes in horror at what the dome light reveals. A man's body is sprawled across the hood. His anguished face presses grotesquely against the windshield. There's a bullet hole in his forehead. It's Scotto's informant.

CHAPTER TEN

Scotto is shaken but handles the aftermath with cool efficiency. I check out of the hotel in the meantime, and we're soon heading west toward Hagerstown. Scotto reaches for the cellular phone and dials her husband's office. "Hi. It's Gabby. Sorry about this. We got a last minute break in a case. . . . It's Woody's case. I'm taking it over. . . . I don't have any choice, honey. I can't go."

Scotto hangs up and drives in tight-lipped silence, leaving little doubt she'd prefer I not break it. About forty-five minutes later we're on a winding mountain road when she finally says, "He can't accept who I am. I can't be something I'm not."

"No one can, Scotto. It cost me a marriage ten years ago, not to mention someone else I care about."

"The woman at your apartment that morning?"

I nod glumly. "Vera. I try to put her first, but I get caught up in a story and . . ."

An hour later we cross the Hagerstown city line. Banzer was right—this is the center of the American trucking industry. Panel trucks, vans, tankers, and tractor-trailer rigs cruise the streets, line the curbs, and fill the massive parking lots that flank the highway.

We're more than an hour behind schedule when we approach the trucking depot. Beyond the high fence, trucks of every description are neatly aligned on acres of macadam. Scotto parks where we can observe the depot's entrance, then uses her radio to contact the other agents and confirm they're all in position.

"Affirmative," one agent replies, then, teasing, adds, "We've been waiting for you to check in, Scotto. We thought maybe you ran off with Dr. Zhivago."

"Eat your hearts out," Scotto taunts; then she slouches in her seat, keeping a low profile, and gestures I do the same.

About an hour later the hiss of air brakes puts an end to the boredom. A massive tractor-trailer thunders past the dispatcher's shack into the street. The cab's tinted windows obscure the driver and anyone who might be riding shotgun. But the trailing flatbed carries a container with large numerals identifying it as 95824.

"That's the one!" Scotto exclaims, starting the engine. She is inching toward the intersection when three identical rigs roll from the depot one after the other. Each carries a container on its flatbed. Each container has the number 95824 stenciled on it.

Scotto groans, hitting the brakes.

"How could they know?" I ask.

She shrugs, disgusted. "They're just being smart, making sure it doesn't get hijacked or anything. I should've foreseen it." She thinks for a moment. "Get my notepad. There's a license plate number. Come on, Katkov, find it. Fast."

I flip through the pages frantically. The convoy of eighteen-wheelers heads toward an I-81 on-ramp at the far end of the street. "It looks like 'Virginia four three nine LHT six six . . . five'? It's either a five or a three."

"Doesn't matter. That's it. That's the rig with the cash," Scotto growls, thumbing the transmit button on her radio. "This is Shell Game Leader to all units. The Virginia rig is mine," she announces, repeating the plate number. "Each of you take one of the others. Where it goes, you go. Good luck."

Engines roaring, exhaust stacks belching diesel smoke into the darkness, the four eighteen-wheelers accelerate onto the highway and fan out across the lanes.

"I'm rather puzzled, Scotto. Why didn't you tell them you know which one has the money?"

"Do I?" she says, slipping into the lane behind the truck. "You're positive my informant wasn't wrong? I mean, the poor guy didn't know zip about four containers with the same number, did he?"

"No, I'm afraid not," I reply. "And since those other agents are on point and you're laying back coordinating, its only fair to assign the decoys to them."

"You're too smart for your own good, Katkov."

"Thank you. While I'm at it, have you considered the possibility the money might not be in any of them?"

"Uh-huh. But my gut tells me it is. Sometimes you just have to go with it."

The Virginia rig merges into the galaxy of taillights streaking the darkness. We've gone a couple of miles when a delivery van slips in front of the Buick, blocking our view. When the van soon moves over, the Virginia rig is nowhere to be seen.

"Where'd he go, dammit?"

"I don't know. He was right there a moment ago."

"Use my binoculars," Scotto orders.

I scan the traffic up ahead, moving from one plate to the next. "Maryland, Washington . . . Ah, here we are—Virginia. Yes. Yes, it's Virginia. Four three nine LHT six six five."

"Good. Stay on him."

"Easier said than done. He keeps changing lanes."

"Yeah. We're going to have to do something about that. Open the glove compartment. There's an ice pick in there somewhere."

I rummage through the glove compartment. My fingers soon come upon the cold aluminum handle tucked between the scraps of paper and folded maps. Scotto glances over and nods. I stare at the ice pick, trying to imagine what it could possibly have to do with tailing a speeding eighteen-wheeler in the middle of the night.

Two hundred miles south of Hagerstown the concrete interstate zigzags through rugged terrain that Scotto explains is the heart of the Shenandoah Valley. A sign flashes past announcing CHARLOTTESVILLE/RICHMOND/NEWPORT NEWS–I-64–NEXT EXIT. Soon afterward the radio crackles into life. "Unit three to Leader. My guy's peeling off," an agent in one of the other pursuit units reports. "Heading east on 64."

"Copy that. Stay with him," Scotto replies. "Shell Game Leader to units two and four. What's your status?"

"Unchanged," agents from both units respond, confirming their targets are still proceeding south.

Scotto signs off. "Katkov, where's our boy?"

"Still in the fast lane," I reply, steadying the binoculars. "About a third of a mile ahead and pulling away."

Scotto glances at the speedometer, which is pushing eighty. "He's really moving." She darts into the adjacent lane, expertly weaves between several vehicles, but we lose him.

I spend the next several hours squinting through the binoculars, darting from one license plate to the next, but Virginia 439 LHT 665 isn't one of them.

We're approaching the Virginia-Tennessee border when a pink, yellow, and lime-green neon flashes BRISTOL TRUCK STOP. The main building is surrounded by a broad expanse of macadam where more than a hundred tractor-trailers are neatly aligned.

"He's in there," Scotto says, wheeling onto the grounds.

"What makes you so sure?"

"My fuel gauge and my bladder. The guy who built this place figured it's about as far south as you can go without filling one and emptying the other."

After dealing with the necessities, we begin cruising back and forth between the rows of eighteen-wheelers in search of our target. We soon spot a rig with container 95824 in it's flatbed, but the plate number reveals it's one of the two remaining decoys. Scotto raises the other agents on the radio. Both pursuit units and both decoys are here, and to our delight so is our target.

"There it is," she blurts out finally. She parks a distance away in a darkened area. "Ice pick," she commands like a surgeon.

I slap it smartly into her palm. "What do you want me to do?"

"Nothing. On second thought, get us some coffee. Anybody hassles you, play dumb, make believe you don't understand English."

I watch until she disappears behind the trailer, then head for the cafeteria. Laughter and loud voices rise as several drivers come through the door and lumber across the tarmac. A bearded one in a quilted vest and cowboy boots splits off and comes in my direction. He is headed right for our rig. He's checking the tires when Scotto emerges from behind the trailer.

"Hey, what you doin' back there?" the driver challenges.

Scotto takes her own advice, shrugs, and backs away, pretending she doesn't understand English.

"I asked what you were doing, lady!" He grabs Scotto's arm and shoves her toward the cab, then sees me hurrying over and pounds on the cab with his fist. "Harlan, we got us a problem here!"

I'm waiting for Scotto to go for her gun, waiting for the other agents to come to our rescue, but I wait in vain. "Excuse, please," I call out, purposely fracturing my syntax. "Excuse, please. She is not speaking the English yet."

The cab door opens, revealing Harlan to be a sleepy-eyed young fellow in a baseball cap cradling a shotgun. "What's going on?"

"Caught her nosing around the rig."

Harlan jumps to the ground and levels the weapon at us. My eyes widen at the double-barreled muzzle. "I couldn't stop him," I say in Russian. "What are we going to do now?"

"Lighten up," Scotto counsels coolly in her New York–accented Russian. "Give him some bull about me getting lost on the way back from the ladies' room."

"Sir? Sir, excuse, please, again? She is not nosing the rig; she is coming from the room for the ladies and . . . and her way became lost. Please, we are on the—how you say?—the honeyball."

"Honeyball?" the driver echoes with a cocky smirk. "You aren't speaking the English yet either, pal. The word's honeymoon."

Scotto forces an insipid smile and clings to me like a frightened waif. "Be affectionate, dammit," she orders sweetly in Russian.

"What's that?" the driver challenges as I wrap an arm around Scotto. "She make some crack about me?"

"No. She—she is asking if you know of the sights to be seeing?"

"Yeah," he smirks. "Ever been to Siberia?"

"C'mon, Curtis," Harlan says, lowering the shotgun. "They're just tourists. Leave 'em be." Curtis glares at us, then struts toward the cab.

The kid lingers. "I never met no Russians before. I don't want y'all getting the wrong idea. Americans are good people." He turns toward the cab, then brightens with a thought. "Disney World. Yeah, that's where y'all oughtta go."

"Diz-nee-vherl?" Scotto repeats.

"It's in Florida. Orlando. Me an' my girl went once."

"Come on, Harlan, let's roll," the driver calls out from the cab.

"Y'all go there," the kid concludes, hurrying off with his shotgun.

We force smiles and head for the Buick, arms around each other's waists.

At the husky roar of a diesel we clamber into the Buick. Scotto pulls the ice pick from inside her sleeve. "Stick this in there, will you?"

"Quite frankly, I was waiting for you to stick it in *him.* What did you do with it, anyway?"

She starts the engine and smiles. "You'll see."

Across the grounds, the eighteen-wheeler rolls onto the highway with a deafening blast from its air horns, followed by the other two rigs hauling containers numbered 95824.

Scotto gives them a head start, then pulls out and pursues. Traffic is heavy, but I've no trouble tailing our target now. Dead center in each of its red taillights, a blinding white point of light burns from the hole Scotto made with the ice pick.

We're well south of the Tennessee border when dawn breaks, silhouetting distant mountains. Outside Jefferson City, the second decoy peels off, taking one of the federal pursuit units with it. About an hour later, twenty miles south of Knoxville, agents in the last pursuit unit report their target has split off west. That leaves Scotto and me tailing the Virginia rig with the two billion in cash.

It's late morning when Atlanta appears on the horizon. Scotto reaches for her radio and thumbs the transmit button. "Hel-lo Atlan-ta," she says, singsonging it. "This is Shell Game Leader to Nutcracker One. Do you read?"

"This is Nutcracker," the agent in charge of the Atlanta task force replies. "Coming through loud and clear. Go ahead."

"Target is two miles north of the 285 turnoff. E.T.A. to your location, ten minutes."

"Copy that. All our units are in position."

"Sounds good," Scotto acknowledges. "I'll count it down for you: one mile . . . a half . . . a quarter. We got brake lights, we got a turn signal. Okay, we're rolling west on 285 now."

Highway 285 crosses the interstate about ten miles north of the city. Container 95824's ultimate destination is located near Fulton County Airport, just off a highway access road.

Nutcracker tells Scotto, "Back off when he makes the turn, and hold at the foot of the access road. We're hanging tight until the creeps take possession of the cargo."

"Copy that," Scotto replies as the sprawling recycling plant appears in the distance. "He's turning into the access road riiiiight . . ." She draws it out in anticipation of adding "now!" But she never gets to say it. Instead of slowing to make the turn, the eighteen-wheeler blows right past it. "Hold it, hold it. He kept going!"

"Damn," Nutcracker growls. "They're pulling a fast one. We better roll some units and take him."

"Negative!" Scotto barks sharply. "Negative. Is Tom Krauss there? . . . Tom?"

"Yeah."

"Pour some cold water on that guy, will you? I've been tailing this rig for over twelve hours. I don't want to blow this now. Let's lay back and see what he's up to."

"That's a read. I'll take care of it."

Scotto clicks off and swings me a concerned look. "He better do something soon." She points to the instrument panel. "Running on fumes again. Let's hope our boy is too."

"DAMMIT, Scotto," Banzer's voice crackles over the cellular. "I thought you were coordinating."

"Makes two of us," Scotto fires back. "But they pulled a couple of fast ones." She tells him about the decoy rigs.

"Heaven help you if we lost track of the cash."

"No way. We had the plate number of the rig that's carrying it. The recycling plant was a decoy too."

"Great. Any idea where the cash is headed?"

"For a train ride. Me and Katkov are sitting on it in the Atlanta yards right now. The eighteen-wheeler's crew dropped it off, trailer and all, and split."

"What's the drill?"

"Nutcracker's got a couple of units covering us. They're also putting a National Guard chopper on standby. Too chancy tailing a truck by air, but a freight shouldn't be a problem."

"Hold on a sec. I know a guy on the Amtrak PD. Maybe we can find out where it's going and when."

Scotto waits. We're parked on an overpass at one end of the yard, from which the entire network of track stretches out before us. She keeps the binoculars trained on our target. Container 95824 is

10931
0-9

one of hundreds in a section where long lines of flatcars wait to be loaded with containerized cargo. A gargantuan bridge crane straddles them, gliding back and forth on tracks of its own, transferring two of the forty-foot-long aluminum boxes to each flatcar.

"Still just sitting there, huh?"

Scotto squirms in her seat impatiently. She nods and lowers the binoculars as the cellular phone comes back to life.

"Gabby?" Banzer's voice crackles. "Good news and bad news. According to my guy, whoever's running this show is pretty sharp. Atlanta is the hub for the entire southeast. More than a dozen railroads run in and out of there."

"Great," Scotto groans sarcastically. "The target could be going anywhere, at any time. Now give me the bad news."

Banzer laughs. "It's a computerized yard. They use these scanners to read a code that's racked up on the side of each railcar. You get me the code, my guy can get into their database and find out date and time of departure, and destination."

"Way to go, Joe. But the container's not on a flatcar yet. We'll just have to hang in here until it is."

It's been at least thirty-six hours since either of us have had any sleep. We take turns napping and keeping an eye on the target. Container 95824 spends the afternoon sitting in the yard on its trailer. Before we know it, darkness is falling and our stomachs are growling. The Buick's trunk seems to have an inexhaustible supply of junk food and beverages, but we're both craving a hot meal. I volunteer to take the car and get us something.

"No, you stay here and mind the store." She gets out, digs a pager out of the trunk, and hands it to me. "That container starts moving, hit this button and I'll come running."

The Buick's taillights are soon red specks in the darkness. Down in the yard, containers come and go, but 95824 isn't one of them. About a half hour later headlights appear. It's Scotto. She gets out of the sedan with a flat, square box from Pizza Hut.

"I spotted this neat-looking Texas Chili joint across from where I gassed up, but decided against it."

"Doesn't agree with you?"

"I could live on the stuff. It was the thought of running into our favorite trucking crew that gave me a pain in my gut."

"You mean the two who were—"
"Uh-huh. Their tractor was parked right outside the place."
"Any chance they saw you?"
Scotto shrugs. "Hard to say. I didn't see *them.*" We settle on the tailgate of an abandoned pickup truck and dig into the pizza. She devours the first piece, then stares off into the darkness, ignoring the rest.
"Rather tasty. Come on, have another."
"Lost my appetite," she mutters, preoccupied. "I keep thinking about this thing with my husband. I don't know—
I interrupt. "The container, it's moving!"
Number 95824 hangs in a cross fire of work lights beneath the bridge crane's boom. The huge articulated structure rolls on its tracks, then stops, swivels, extends, and deftly deposits the forty-foot-long aluminum box in the bed of a flatcar.
"Can you see the code?" Scotto prompts anxiously.
"No. The angle's all wrong."
"Come on," she orders, jumping from the tailgate. "We better find one that's right."
I keep my eyes pressed to the binoculars for a moment. A diesel engine hooks up to the flatcar and moves the two-billion-dollar cargo through the yard. "Hold it. I'm afraid we're not going to have time."
Scotto fetches the radio and thumbs the transmit button. "Nutcracker, Nutcracker, this is Shell Game. It's moving. The target's moving. We need that chopper."
"Copy that. Bird is on standby as planned. E.T.A. your location, twenty minutes. Be advised max range for chopper is three hundred miles."
"Yeah, yeah, just make it fast." Scotto clicks off the radio with an angry scowl.
Moments later the flatcar is coupled to a long freight that's being assembled, and a half-dozen more railcars swiftly follow. The last one is a caboose. Within minutes the three-unit diesel at the head of the train unleashes its awesome power and lunges forward. Haunting blasts from air horns announce the fifty-plus-car freight's departure.
I dash to the Buick and climb in next to Scotto, and she takes off.

At the far end of the overpass, the cross street runs parallel to a concrete embankment that slopes sharply to the yard. Scotto puts the Buick into a high-speed slide and fishtails through the corner. The Buick is just settling down when an all-too-familiar tractor thunders into view and tries to cut us off. Scotto instinctively snaps the wheel right-left-right and slithers around it.

"What are *they* doing here?"

"Waiting for us. What else? One of 'em must've spotted me."

I look back. The tractor swerves to avoid going over the embankment, then comes out of it and pursues. The trainyard is dead ahead. Scotto rockets into a service road that parallels the tracks. She races the length of the yard in pursuit of the departing train.

I glance back again. The tractor is gaining. It's a hell of a lot faster without that forty-ton trailer behind it.

Scotto is radioing for backup units for help when another diesel approaches on an intersecting spur, pulling a long string of boxcars. The engineer leans on his air horn. Scotto flicks a glance to the mirror and curses. The tractor is still coming like a runaway freight. My heart's climbing into my mouth. My brain's screaming, Hit the brakes! Scotto steels herself and stands on the gas instead. The Buick zips across the tracks. The onrushing train misses us by millimeters and roars across the service road, blocking the tractor's way.

The freight carrying container 95824 is up ahead, traveling at the posted yard speed of five mph. We overtake it easily. Scotto keeps the pedal to the floor, racing along the service road that parallels the outbound spur. Railcar after railcar flashes past. The numbers on the target go by in a blur. She keeps going until we're so far ahead of the train, it's completely out of sight by the time she stops.

We jump out of the car. Scotto starts stuffing a nylon gym bag with things from the trunk. I'm pulling my typewriter from the back seat with one hand and a suitcase with the other when headlights sweep through a distant turn. If it's the train, it's moving so fast we'll never get aboard. But it's not the train; it's the tractor, coming at us at high speed.

We literally run for our lives, putting as much distance as possible between us and the Buick, which blocks the narrow service road. The speeding tractor closes the distance in an eyeblink. It's heading right for the sedan.

Scotto drops her bags, then pulls her pistol, steadies it with both hands, and coolly fires at the onrushing vehicle. The windshield shatters. The tractor swerves wildly out of control, narrowly missing the Buick. It rockets across a median and crashes into an embankment.

"Yes!" Scotto whoops, then advances on the tractor cautiously. The door cracks open and the shotgun emerges. She grasps the barrel and pulls hard, yanking Harlan from the cab. He gets a face full of gravel. "Police officer! Don't move," she commands sharply. She hands me the shotgun. "Shoot him if he moves." She swings the door open wide, leveling her pistol at the driver. "Police! Out. Now. Move it!" He stumbles from the cab. "Hit the deck," Scotto orders.

The wail of sirens rises as he flops face down next to his colleague. The backup units race along the service road and converge on the tractor. Krauss and Nutcracker are at the forefront of the agents who pile out, guns drawn.

"All yours, Tom," Scotto says coolly; then, noticing a single headlight streaking through the darkness, she breaks into a cocky grin. "Come on, Katkov. Don't want to miss our train."

The long freight seems to be picking up speed as it exits the yard. We scoop up our bags and start sprinting parallel to the tracks. The ground shudders violently as the throbbing diesel approaches. We're running clumsily with our cargo alongside an empty boxcar. I toss the typewriter and suitcase through the open door. Scotto does the same with the nylon sack and her shoulder bag. There's a boarding handle welded to the doorframe. It takes me several tries, but I finally get hold of it and belly flop aboard. Scotto makes a desperate, head-first lunge for the doorway. I manage to get hold of her wrist. She hooks a leg over the sill—half of her in, the other half hanging perilously out—and claws at the floor for a handhold. I grab the seat of her pants with my free hand and drag her inside. We stumble away from the door and fall against opposite walls of the boxcar, gasping for breath.

"You—you okay?" I finally ask.

She nods, unable to speak.

I smile. So does she. We're sitting there like rag dolls, watching the city go by, when it dawns on me we haven't the slightest idea where we're going.

CHAPTER ELEVEN

I'M JOLTED awake. My body is sore and stiff from the boxcar's hard floor. I let my head clear, then stagger to my feet and roll the corrugated steel door aside.

A shaft of daylight knifes into the darkness. Humid air with a sharp, salty bite follows. I inhale deeply, squinting at the glare. Beyond the lush tropical foliage that borders the right of way, a sparkling expanse of ocean stretches to a faint horizon. The climate and vegetation leave little doubt we're traveling south.

Scotto drifts over and stands next to me.

The train leans into a curve. The freight is soon stretched out over its entire length, and we can see container 95824 at the other end. I doubt anyone else is keeping an eye on it. I heard rotors several times during the night, but we must be well beyond the helicopter's three-hundred-mile range by now.

We're settled on the floor, going to work on the junk food and bottled water Scotto stuffed into the gym bag when, with several blasts on the air horn, the train thunders through a crossing on the outskirts of a town. A quaint steepled station with a sign that reads PORT ST. LUCIE flashes past.

"Florida," Scotto announces brightly. "Now I *can* tell you where we're going—Miami."

"Miami? How do you know that?"

"It's the fluff-and-fold capital of America. The creeps get that cash into the banking system down there, they can wire it anywhere in the world. I mean, there's more than a hundred international banks with branches in south Florida. Some collaborate outright, some are negligent, some are just plain stupid."

"I thought your banking system was highly regulated."

"Up to a point. Ten thou is the magic number. Anything over that has to be reported to the IRS. So they keep each transaction just under the limit, and we're none the wiser."

"But two billion dollars. It'd take forever to launder that much, wouldn't it?"

"Depends. Doesn't take more than a couple of seconds to run an electronic rinse."

"What's that?"

"A wire transfer. A trillion bucks a day is wired among the world's banks. But like I said, they have to get it into the system first."

"Despite all that technology, there's still no way to distinguish dirty money from clean?"

"Not once it's on the wire. Bankers have the best shot. Unfortunately, the very institutions that are in a position to do it have the least incentive."

"Because they're making money off it."

"Getting rich. Anywhere from seven to ten percent off the top."

It's late afternoon by the time Miami's beachfront hotels come into view across Biscayne Bay. Bathed in the glow of fading sunlight, the pastel façades appear as if they've been dusted with powdered sugar. Long, narrow bridges that Scotto calls causeways connect the overdeveloped strip of sand to the mainland.

The train begins slowing down, then enters a short tunnel that takes it into the railyards in northeast Miami.

Scotto and I gather our things and prepare to jump from the boxcar when it stops, but the train seems to be maintaining its speed. We exchange nervous glances as it becomes clear that it's going in one end of the yard and out the other.

"What the hell's going on now?" Scotto groans.

The long freight passes beneath a traffic interchange, where expressways, interstates, and causeways come together in a gigantic concrete knot. The tracks suddenly curve sharply eastward toward a short causeway that angles out across the water.

In the distance an immense man-made island of passenger terminals, warehouses, and piers hovers above the placid bay. A sign indicates PORT OF MIAMI—DODGE ISLAND TERMINUS. The superstructures of cruise ships and ocean-going freighters, beyond, make it painfully clear that the money isn't going into Miami's banking system to be laundered electronically. It's going out of the country in one of those cargo ships.

THE sun is below the rooftops when the long freight finally grinds to a stop somewhere in the middle of the immense island terminus. Scotto and I heft our bags and slip from the boxcar. We make our way through a maze of narrow corridors created by the hundreds of shipping containers on the wharf, then turn a corner and come upon a massive containerized freighter straining at its hawsers. Armed customs agents are posted at the entrances and along the perimeter of this section of the terminus. Signs point out RESTRICTED AREA at intervals along the high fence that encloses it.

"Hey, hold it right there," a man's voice calls out sharply.

We turn to see a customs agent leveling his sidearm at us. I expect Scotto to identify herself, but she raises her hands instead. The agent has us face one of the containers, hands raised and pressed against it, feet wide apart; then he radios for assistance.

Moments later a gray van screeches to a stop, and three more agents, one of them a sergeant, pile out and frisk us. One finds Scotto's pistol and hands it to the sergeant with an incriminating smirk.

"I've got I.D. to go with that, Sergeant," Scotto says in a taut whisper. "Inside-right jacket pocket."

The sergeant cautiously removes and examines her identification. "U.S. Treasury."

Scotto nods. "I don't want to advertise. Understand?"

"I'm listening," he says challengingly.

"We're working a money-laundering op. Make like we're a couple of rail-riding vagrants in case they're watching. Okay?"

The sergeant signals his men, who cuff us and shove us into the van. It heads for the customs building at the end of the terminus. Once inside, the handcuffs come off and we're ushered into an office.

The senior customs inspector is a round-faced man with captain's bars on his epaulets and a mustache as coarse as a hairbrush. His name tag reads AGUILAR. Scotto briefs him on the saga of container 95824.

"Two billion in cash!" he exclaims when she finishes, his eyes glowing. "That's quite a haul, Scotto. We'd be happy to inspect, interdict, whatever you need."

"Appreciate the offer, Inspector, but I can't take you up on it," she replies gently. "We want to take down the creeps at the other end. What I really need is a fix on where that container's going. Switzerland? Caymans? Panama? Gotta be one of your friendly neighborhood laundermats."

Aguilar leans back in his chair and smiles. In a mischievous whisper he replies, "Havana."

"But we don't ship anything to Cuba," Scotto argues, perplexed. "The way I hear it, the embargo was just extended. The screws are being tightened, not loosened."

Aguilar nods smugly. "Yes. It makes this shipment all the more sensitive."

"Shipment of what?" Scotto prompts.

Aguilar pulls himself from the chair and fetches a sheaf of computer printouts. "Dressers, chairs, mirrors, beds, artwork, linen, drapery, carpet, glassware, china, desks, lamps, televisions—"

"Sounds to me like furnishings for a hotel," I say.

"Close, but no cigar," Aguilar quips. "We also have containers full of slot machines, blackjack and roulette tables . . ."

Scotto whistles. "Cuba's back in the casino business? Who's the consignee?"

"Company called Turistica Internacional."

"Never heard of 'em."

"Me neither, but there've been dozens of shipments over the last couple of years. All signed, sealed, and sanctioned by the U.S."

Scotto's expression hardens. "Any idea when that freighter sails?"

Aguilar swivels to a computer, types a few keystrokes. "Let's see. *Halifax* puts to sea—"

"Halifax?" Scotto interrupts. "Canadian registry?"

Aguilar nods.

Scotto's eyes dart to mine. The puzzle's making a little more sense now. "You getting this, Katkov?"

"Canada has diplomatic ties to Cuba and the U.S.A."

"You're getting it. The shipper of container 95824 on that list, Inspector?"

Aguilar turns to his printouts. "Coppelia Paper Products Limited."

Another look from Scotto. "Okay. Now, when does she sail?"

"Wednesday—eighteen thirty hours."

"Three days." Scotto sighs, relieved. "Gives us some time to shower and catch our breaths."

An hour later Scotto and I are settled into adjoining rooms in the Best Western Hotel at the foot of the terminus causeway. I'm standing beneath a steaming shower in a bathroom Muscovites would kill for. It even has a telephone.

I've just finished shaving when Scotto knocks on the connecting door. "Hey, Katkov, open up." I pull on a pair of slacks and let her in. She's barefoot, dressed in white jeans and blue denim shirt. Her hair hangs around her face in a mass of wet tangles. "You have the boob tube on?" she asks. "There's something coming up on CNN you might want to catch." She saunters across the room, drying her hair with a towel, and turns on the television.

"Recapping today's top story," the anchorman says, "frustrated by Parliament's refusal to endorse his policies, Russian president Boris Yeltsin has declared emergency rule. Here with a live update from Moscow is CNN correspondent Jill Doherty."

This is shocking news. I'm trying to comprehend its meaning when an attractive woman appears on the screen. Bundled against the cold, she stands in Red Square with the illuminated onion-shaped domes of St. Basil's behind her and reports, "Angrily denouncing former supporters who have become archrivals, President Yeltsin said he will govern by decree if necessary and asked for a vote of confidence in a national referendum next month. . . ."

"What do you think?" Scotto prompts as the correspondent drones on.

"This could be quite a disaster for Russia."

"Why? You really think the Communists could take over again?"

I pause, loath to validate the thought by verbalizing it. "The danger is, people will remember things were better under Brezhnev—which they were—and decide freedom isn't worth the price."

"Come on. Under Brezhnev there's no way you'd be sitting here today. I mean, now you could even emigrate if you wanted to."

"If I wanted to."

"You saying you never thought of getting out? Start a new life somewhere? Israel, Brighton Beach . . ."

"All the time."

Scotto smiles and goes back to drying her hair as the television screen fills with demonstrators jammed into Red Square. The phone in her room rings, and she hurries to answer it.

I remain and stare numbly at the television. Less than a week has passed since I left, but it seems so much longer. I cross to the windows, feeling vulnerable and homesick. The lights across the bay twinkle hypnotically in the darkness.

"That was Banzer," Scotto announces brightly, pulling me out of it. "He's coming down tomorrow."

"That bad, huh?"

"I'd called and asked him to check on Turistica Internacional. For openers, it's an American company. It's been granted special permission to work with the Cuban government and redevelop their tourism and gaming industries."

"So much for the hard-nosed embargo. I imagine that explains why Jennifer couldn't get into their database."

"Sure does. It gets better. T.I. is a subsidiary of Travis Enterprises."

"Travis. That's Rubineau's holding company."

"Uh-huh. After talking with Joe, I had a brief chat with Jennifer. Guess where Rubineau's jet is cooling its turbines this week?"

"Miami International."

Scotto nods smartly.

"He's working out of his Miami office."

She nods again and breaks into a devilish smile. "I think it's time Mr. Rubinowitz and I got to know each other."

OVER breakfast Scotto and I discuss how to approach Rubineau. She sees the element of surprise as an advantage and decides against calling ahead for an appointment.

The Southeast Financial Center is a short walk from our hotel. Rubineau occupies a choice suite on the top of the fifty-five-story tower. On the wall behind the reception desk a compelling graphic diagrams the complex interlocking of his various companies. Travis Enterprises, ITZ, and Turistica Internacional are among the many names.

Rubineau handles our surprise visit with the aplomb and graciousness I anticipated, and receives us in a sleek corner office that overlooks downtown Miami. He wastes no time showing off his favorite toy—a scale model of a sprawling resort complex that sweeps majestically into the Caribbean on a finger of white sand. The detailed façades of literally dozens of beachfront hotels soar to eye level; charming bungalows cluster around Olympic-size swimming pools; chic condominiums line the fairways of championship golf courses.

"Varadero," he says, gesturing grandly as he walks around the gleaming model. "Less than two hours by car from Havana, an hour by plane from Miami." He whirls to a telescope and adds, "On a clear day you can almost see it from here."

"That's fascinating, Mr. Rubineau," Scotto says. "One of your companies, Turistica Internacional, is developing it. Correct?"

"Correct."

"Then perhaps I'm also correct in assuming you can tell us why a container with two billion dollars in illicit cash is part of a shipment consigned to Turistica Internacional in Cuba?"

"Two billion?" Rubineau echoes coolly. "In a container being shipped to T.I. in Cuba?"

"That's what I said."

"That's some pile of money."

"Drug money. One of several piles that've turned up on your doorstep lately."

Rubineau pauses and fires her an angry look. "That sounds like a threat, Agent Scotto."

"No, Mr. Rubineau. It's a fact."

"I thought this was going to be a friendly off-the-record chat. If I'm being accused of something, I'll call my lawyers now."

"Call whoever you like. Be sure to mention that you also own a building in Baltimore where close to five hundred million more turned up."

"I'll tell you what I told Katkov. I'm not responsible for what's stored in a building leased from me."

Scotto adds, "You also own a trucking depot in Maryland that dispatched the container with the two billion."

"The one in Hagerstown," he agrees.

Scotto nods incriminatingly.

"They don't inspect cargo, they ship it."

"It's your company."

"I'm not personally responsible for everything that goes through the place."

"Somebody is."

"Are you suggesting I'm being used?"

"Are you?"
"Anything's possible."
"Then I expect you'd want to do something about it."
"Who said I don't? Look, I checked my records. A company called Coppelia Paper Products leases the Baltimore building."
"That's not news."
"Did they also ship that container?"
"Sure did."
"Well, for the record," Rubineau says, indicating the architectural model, "this development is a co-venture with the Cuban government. My half is financed with profits from my other businesses."
"The State Department will verify that?"
"You can count on it."
"You can count on me checking with them. I also plan to ask why they're breaking their own embargo."
"I'll save you the time. It's the diplomatic version of good cop, bad cop. Smack 'em with one hand, massage 'em with the other, and let them decide which they prefer."
"No offense, but with your background why would the United States government—"
Rubineau's eyes glare with indignation. "Hold it right there. If you're referring to Mr. Lansky, I do take offense."
"Suit yourself, Mr. Rubineau. Now let's get back to my question. With all the people in the hotel and gaming business, why would the U.S. government come to you?"
"They didn't." A smug grin tugs at a corner of his mouth. "Castro did—*personally.*"
Scotto's jaw drops. So does mine.
"And the U.S. agreed to it?" she asks, stunned.
Rubineau smiles, pleased by her reaction. "Thirty years ago Castro destroyed Cuba's tourist industry and replaced the income with Soviet aid. Now it's gone. The economy's in the toilet, and he's desperate to turn it around. Reestablishing Cuba as a tourist mecca is the only move he's got. Legalized gambling is the key. And I'm the guy he hired to make it happen. Varadero's already in the black. It's becoming a playground for Canadians, Italians, Russians."
Scotto shakes her head incredulously. "I still can't believe the State Department agreed to do business with you."

"Why not? I'm an entrepreneur with experience in Cuba."

"A businessman Castro trusts."

"Very good, Katkov. Besides, compared to what some of our financial wizards have been up to lately, I'm Mr. Clean as far as the U.S. government is concerned."

"Don't blow that horn too loud, Mr. Rubineau," Scotto cautions. "You still have to deal with that two billion in drug money consigned to Turistica Internacional."

Rubineau nods thoughtfully. "You willing to give me the benefit of the doubt?"

"What do you mean?"

"Let that container go to Cuba. I mean, if somebody's using me, I want to find out who it is as badly as you do."

"Food for thought," Scotto muses; then she pointedly adds, "If somebody is using you, Mr. Rubineau, we'll find him. If not, we'll find that out too."

THE message light is flashing on Scotto's phone when we return to the hotel. Banzer and Krauss have checked in, and we waste no time heading down the corridor to Banzer's room. He listens intently as Scotto reviews our meeting with Rubineau. "Well," he says when she finishes, "if the man isn't clean, he's playing the game as well as it's ever been played."

"And he's gonna win big," Scotto adds smartly. She shifts her attention to Krauss. "Any news on Coppelia?"

"Nothing," the ops chief reports. "No connection to any of Rubineau's companies. Matter of fact, as you may suspect—"

"Coppelia Paper Products doesn't exist," Scotto finishes for him. "Except on paper."

Banzer grunts in disgust. "Just a name with a bank account to which funds are wired."

"From where?"

"We're still working on that."

"So, what're our options?" Krauss asks.

"One from column A and one from column A," Scotto replies sassily. "We either take Rubineau down or—we take him down."

"Why?" I wonder, baffled by her rashness. "Unless I missed something, he isn't culpable until he takes possession of the money."

"That's right," Krauss says. "And there's no way he's going to do that here."

Scotto frowns. "He may not do it anywhere. That's why I figure if we complicate his life a little, he might agree to cooperate."

"Correct me if I'm wrong, Agent Scotto," I say, "but less than an hour ago Rubineau offered to do just that."

"You mean that bull about letting the container go to Cuba?"

"Precisely. I thought the idea was to let the container take us to whoever's at the other end. You want the other end or not?"

"You bet I do."

"Well, then you can just as well bet it's Russia."

A look passes between Banzer and Krauss. "You're positive that's where it's going?" the latter prompts, taken by the theory.

"Positive. When I first got involved in this, I thought it had to do with moving money *out* of Russia. But I was wrong. It's about moving money *in.* Russia needs hard currency. The cartels and crime bosses have it; but thanks to you folks, the traditional laundering methods are becoming less and less viable. They need a new mechanism, and Rubineau's the key. He uses his U.S.-sanctioned deal in Cuba to set himself up as the pipeline, and all the dirty cash that's locked in the U.S.A. can be quite efficiently moved and invested in Russia."

"Quite cleverly too," Krauss says. "One container going directly to Russia stands a much greater chance of being nailed by customs than one of thousands going to Cuba under special sanction."

Banzer's eyes widen with intrigue. "All his deals in Russia are legit, but he's using mob money to pay for them."

"Rubineau actually told me he was bringing money in," I say. "He just didn't say whose."

"If Katkov's right," Banzer reasons, "if this money *is* going into Russia, there still has to be somebody on the inside."

"That'd be Arkady Barkhin," Krauss suggests.

"No way," Banzer declares. "He'll come away with a piece of the action, but the Russian government owns the industries ITZ is buying. And that means someone inside the government."

"I thought it might've been Vorontsov, early on," I venture. "But now I'm quite certain he was clean."

"Me too," Scotto chimes in. "They killed him because he was

about to blow the whistle on organized crime buying into Russian businesses."

"Yes, but someone had to finger him first," Banzer argues. "They had to know Vorontsov was going to blow the whistle. Which leaves us with an insider who blew it on *him.*"

"On the other hand," Scotto says, "the money could be going anywhere. Havana's—what?—about two hundred fifty miles from the Caymans, less than a thou from Bolivia or Panama . . ."

"You're forgetting it started in Moscow," I say, "and that's where it's ending. But you have to let that container go."

"What if you're wrong?" Scotto challenges. "Two billion slips through our fingers, and—"

"I'm not wrong."

"Hold it, hold it," Banzer interrupts. "You two chased that container for over fifteen hundred miles. Either of you get a look inside?"

We both shake our heads no.

"No one's actually seen the two billion?"

We both nod. From Scotto's expression I suspect her gut is getting that hollow feeling, like mine. "Katkov raised the issue when the decoy rigs showed up," she offers generously. "Two were empty. They were dropped off at depots for reuse. We lost track of the third."

"So," Krauss concludes, "we're fighting over whether or not we let a container of evidence go. And for all we know it could be filled with cat-box litter."

THE FinCEN gang spends the afternoon making arrangements with customs to inspect container 95824, and as darkness falls, the four of us pile into Banzer's rented sedan and cross the causeway to Dodge Island. Several cruise ships are about to sail. The passenger terminals are ablaze with light and buzzing with bon voyage festivities. Banzer parks in front of the customs building.

Inspector Aguilar is out of his chair the instant he sees us coming down the corridor. This could be the biggest money-laundering interdiction in history, and he wants to be part of it so badly he can taste it. He consults his computer for the location of container 95824. "Aisle thirty-four, slot twenty-one," he announces, leading the way outside.

The sergeant who took Scotto and me into custody packs the group into a gray customs van. It proceeds to the far end of the harbor, where cargo vessels are berthed. The massive pier is deserted.

The guard at the security gate salutes Aguilar and waves the van through. It crosses the restricted area, turns into a narrow aisle between the containers destined for the hold of the Havana-bound freighter, and stops.

The numerals 95824 are visible through the window next to me. My heart starts pounding. Aguilar rolls back the door, and the six of us pile out and gather around one end of the grimy container.

Aguilar nods. The sergeant breaks the customs seals and uses a master key to open the padlock, then retracts the dead bolts that secure the doors. He opens one, then the other, and turns on a flashlight. Krauss and Aguilar do the same, and there is an eight-foot-square wall of United States currency. Clear plastic bags stuffed with bundles of hundred-dollar bills are piled side to side and top to bottom, like tightly packed stones.

We're stunned by the sight of it. Even Scotto is at a loss for words. She tightens a fist in triumph.

"Yessss," Krauss hisses under his breath.

"Okay, button it up," Banzer says.

While the sergeant goes about slamming doors, setting dead bolts, and securing levers and locks, a thought occurs to me. I motion Scotto aside. "You have something sharp in there?"

"Uh-huh." She digs in her shoulder bag and, to my amazement, removes a hunting knife.

I use it to scratch my initials into the side of the container, next to the number. "There were four of these with the same number, but one is still unaccounted for—right?"

Scotto raises a brow in tribute.

A short time later we're packed into Aguilar's office in the customs building. Aguilar is beside himself, pacing the tiny space like a caged animal. "We let that container out of the country, we can kiss it good-bye."

"Be advised, Inspector," Banzer says, "that in the event we decide to let the container go on, my behind'll be on the line, not yours." He shifts his look to Krauss. "What's your take on this, Tom?"

"I don't know, boss. I mean, if it ends up in Cuba, we have no legal recourse—nothing."

"And if it doesn't, if it goes on," Scotto adds with a nod that acknowledges my theory, "we have no way to trace it."

"Yes, you do," I say mysteriously. "You have me."

"You?" Banzer prompts, baffled.

"That's right. Maybe none of you can go to Cuba, but I can."

"That's ridiculous," Aguilar scoffs.

"Why? I can book passage on that freighter as a tourist and be as close to that container when it gets to Cuba as we were tonight."

Banzer groans with exasperation. "Look, we got away with letting you hook up with Scotto, but I'm afraid that's as far as it goes."

"That's right," Krauss says. "No offense, Katkov, but you're not qualified to handle this."

Scotto has a strange look on her face. As if something of monumental significance just occurred to her. "I don't know about that. I mean, as partners go, he's sure held up his end so far. I mean, it never dawned on me Katkov could go to Cuba. All things considered, I think it's worth a shot."

"Give me one good reason," Banzer says.

"This." She points to the pit of her stomach. "My gut is telling me I think he's right about the container going to Russia."

"Not good enough."

"And you'll be getting me back," she adds brightly.

Banzer grins wryly and waggles a hand.

"Okay, Joe, but you're asking for both barrels," she says.

"Woody?" Banzer prompts warily. "Again? You want me to go along with this for Woody?"

Scotto nods solemnly.

"What do you think *he'd* say?"

"I'd give anything to be able to ask him, Joe."

Banzer removes his glasses, then holds them up to the light, scrutinizing the lenses as he thinks it through. "If I were you, Katkov, I'd spend the next couple of days working on my tan."

"You saying what I think you're saying?" Scotto asks.

"I'm saying that if he's going to Cuba as a tourist and Miami was his last stop, he better damn well look it. Get him some clothes, a camera, sunglasses, a T-shirt from Disney World—"

"Diz-nee-vherl?" Scotto says, breaking up.

I burst into laughter along with her.

Banzer puts the glasses back on. "Okay, where we going for dinner? I'm starving."

Scotto decides it should be a bon voyage party in my honor and tracks down a restaurant in Little Havana called Versailles. It's sweaty, raucous, and alive with rapid-fire Spanish and the thump of canned congas. The dishes of earthy Cuban food are massive. Banzer is absentmindedly stirring his café Cubano.

"What's bugging you, Joe?" Scotto asks. "You're drilling a hole in your cup. You always do that when something's on your mind."

He nods grimly. "This damned insider."

"The one we figure blew the whistle on Vorontsov," Krauss declares.

"Yeah. They cross paths, chances are he'll know Katkov, but Katkov won't know him."

Banzer's eyes search mine for a reaction.

"Well, it has to be someone in the Interior Ministry and I'm—I'm fairly certain I know who," I say. "It's a police officer. His name's Gudonov. He was in charge of Economic Crimes. Now, he's the new chief investigator."

Banzer winces. "And you're certain you still want to do this?"

"Try and stop me."

"Okay. We'll take care of the travel arrangements soon as we get back. Speaking of which"—Banzer glances at his watch, then flags the waiter for the check—"better move it. By the time we drop them at the hotel, we'll be lucky to make our flight."

"Go," Scotto says. "We'll grab a cab."

"Good luck then, Katkov," Banzer says.

They push back their chairs. Krauss shakes my hand, then slips between the tables. Banzer lingers to pay the check.

My eyes are drifting back toward Scotto when they catch sight of a man at the bar. Unremarkable features, gold neck chains, loose-fitting tropical shirt. I have an uneasy feeling I've seen him before.

"So," Scotto says after Banzer has left, "how you doing, Katkov?"

"Hey, this has been great fun. Thanks. How about you?"

"I'm doing okay." She lowers her eyes. "I called my husband last night. Invited him down for a couple of days."

"Good for you."

"Well, not really. He—he declined. Made up some excuse about having to be away on business."

"I'm sorry, Scotto."

"Yeah, well, I sort of figured he might, but . . ." She sighs wistfully, then stands and leads the way through the crowd. We're nearing the exit when I catch sight of the bar in a mirror. The man is gone.

WE'RE at a sidewalk stand on Calle Ocha, Little Havana's main shopping street. Scotto is looking at sunglasses. She has me try on nearly every pair before deciding on the Vuarnet knockoffs—heavy black plastic frame, dark wine-colored lenses. We spend the next hour or so on a minishopping spree amid the carts and stalls, then take a cab back to the hotel with our booty.

The next day is spent languishing about the pool in bone-warming sun. After dining at a beachfront restaurant, we return to the hotel to find a courier waiting with a prepaid ticket for my passage on the *Halifax.* Sailing time six thirty p.m. tonight.

A crescent moon hangs in the twilight as Scotto and I cross the pier in the customs van with Inspector Aguilar. It proceeds through the security gate to a boarding ramp near the freighter's stern, where the superstructure that houses the bridge, crew quarters, and passenger cabins is located. The *Halifax* sits low in the water now, her hold filled with containers.

I'm unloading my bags from the van when Scotto's eyes dart to my typewriter. She latches on to the handle possessively. "This is not exactly tourist gear, is it?"

"Never occurred to me," I reply, a little unsettled. "Just make sure you bring that when you come to Moscow."

"That's a promise."

"I'll call you as soon as I know what's going on."

"Don't wait that long. I want to know you're all right, Katkov. I *do.*" She grabs my shoulders and thinks about it for a moment, then hugs me. "Take care of yourself." A foghorn beckons, then again. I disengage, grab my bag, and hurry up the ramp onto the deck. A husky tug nudges the vessel away from the pier.

I'm standing at the rail watching Scotto recede into the darkness.

She's waving with one hand and hanging on to my typewriter with the other. I wave back until she's gone, then light a cigarette. I'm cupping the match when I notice the flashy gold script on the matchbook proclaims "Versailles." Suddenly I've no doubt that the man at the bar the other night was the man who frisked me in the elevator on the way up to Rubineau's apartment.

CHAPTER TWELVE

THE sun is well above the horizon when the *Halifax* glides past the crumbling castle at the entrance to Havana harbor. The brackish waters are alive with an armada of rusting freighters. The miles of battered seawall are lined with old tires, the level of decay equaling if not exceeding Moscow's.

After disembarking, I'm directed to a weathered two-story building where a customs official takes my passport. I speak no Spanish. He speaks neither Russian nor English. *"Intérprete, intérprete,"* he mutters. He escorts me to a room on the second floor that overlooks the pier. Then he forces a smile and leaves. It's going to be a long wait. I pass the time watching containers being unloaded from the freighter onto the flatbeds of eighteen-wheelers and keeping my eyes peeled for 95824.

Several hours later there's still no sign of the container when the customs official finally returns with the interpreter, a short, bony fellow with jaundiced eyes and a thin mustache.

He apologizes for the delay; then after several exchanges in rapid-fire Spanish with the customs officer, he turns to me and says, "He wants to know what you were doing in Miami."

"Sightseeing," I reply, indicating my Disney World T-shirt.

More bursts of Spanish. The interpreter smirks. "He's puzzled. He's says you're a Russian, an ally, yet you spend money in the United States when Cuba needs all it can get. Why?"

"Tell him it was a mistake. I didn't like it."

"You didn't like Disney World?"

"No," I reply with as much indignation as I can muster. "It's a false view of life. A capitalist-pig fantasy. That's why I came to Cuba."

After another exchange in Spanish, they leave the room to decide my fate. I return to the window. Several more containers are unloaded. I'm about to turn away when 95824 is lifted from the freighter's hold and deposited in the flatbed of an eighteen-wheeler.

Damn. I've got to get out of here and keep track of it. I'm beside myself when they finally return. The customs official hands me my passport. "You're free to go, Mr. Katkov," the interpreter says. "Enjoy your stay in Cuba."

"Thanks," I reply as calmly as possible. "Is there a place nearby where I can rent a car?"

"The next pier," he replies. "Where the cruise ships berth. Only tourists can afford them now," he goes on. "Fuel is very scarce. It's gotten so bad, we have power blackouts to conserve energy. Five to eight p.m. every day." He shakes his head, disgusted.

I slip past him and head downstairs to collect my bag. A tough-looking man exits an office clutching a sheaf of papers and comes toward me. I'm stunned by the sight of him. The flattened nose, designer sunglasses, and shaved head dotted with stubble are eerily familiar. It's Arkady Barkhin's thug Ray-Ban!

He charges straight down the center of the corridor. I cringe, anticipating the encounter. His shoulder brushes mine as he blows past without so much as a glance. Of course. He's not expecting to run into me here, let alone in Vuarnet knockoffs, Disney World T-shirt, Miami Beach tan, and camera hanging from my neck.

I hurry to a nearby window. Ray-Ban exits the building and crosses to the eighteen-wheeler with 95824 in its flatbed. He climbs into the cab. It belches black smoke and thunders off.

It's midmorning by the time I rent a car. The dusty Lada 1600 has eighty-five thousand kilometers on the odometer, worn tires, faded paint, but it has a full tank of gas, and a map of Cuba on the driver's seat. Container 95824 is long gone, but I know where it's going. Rubineau told me. Varadero, ninety miles east of Havana, where the Turistica Internacional resort complexes are being built. That's where all the rigs are going.

Via Blanca, the superhighway that connects Havana and Varadero, winds eastward along the coast. On one side, fields of sugarcane stretch to the horizon. On the other, miles of pristine beaches and picturesque villages go by. Except for the occasional car or motor scooter or decrepit bus, the container-laden eighteen-wheelers are the only motorized traffic. Each time the Lada overtakes one, I scrutinize the numbers; and each time, 95824 isn't one of them.

Rubineau wasn't lying about Varadero. Bathed in sunshine, dotted with swaying palms, cooled by gentle trade winds, it's a dream come true—actually, a dream under construction.

The narrow peninsula is barely a half mile at its widest point. Main Street, Avenida Primera, runs the entire length, joining intermittent short cross streets. I cruise the ten-mile strip of sand with my map, checking out construction sites, office buildings, and warehouses. Containers are everywhere—arriving, unloading—but to my profound dismay 95824 isn't one of them.

The sun is setting when I come upon a hotel that's nearing completion. Containers from the *Halifax* are aligned in the parking lot. Furniture, gaming tables, and slot machines are being unloaded and moved inside. I'm circling the lot in search of my target when I'm stunned to see Rubineau and Barkhin emerge from the hotel.

Rubineau said they had a business relationship. Banzer said he thought Barkhin would get a piece of the action. And from the looks of things, running the casinos in Varadero is it.

They have a brief exchange with a man supervising the operation, then get into a Russian Zil limousine and drive off. The clumsy vehicle lumbers down Avenida Primera, crosses the bridge that spans the narrow lagoon, and turns into Varadero Airport, where Rubineau's Gulfstream is parked. It buttons up and taxis the instant they're aboard.

I'm back to square one. No sign of the container, or Ray-Ban for that matter. I've no choice but to conclude that I was wrong; container 95824 wasn't taken to Varadero.

I head back to Havana. Darkness falls en route, deepening my mood. The power blackout follows. The coastal villages are lifeless, as if abandoned to an invading army. Every so often the distant flicker of a candle alleviates the monotony. Nothing alleviates my sense of failure. Scotto put her trust in me. I haven't been in Cuba a day and I've already blown it. How can I tell her I've lost track of the container? Dammit. It has to be here somewhere.

Havana is dark when I arrive. I'm proceeding cautiously through the pitch-black streets when the power suddenly comes back on. Every window in the city lights up at once. Signs flicker to life. Streetlights pop on with startling brilliance.

I'm slowing for a traffic light when I notice a wall in a small shopping plaza covered with posters. My eyes blink in weary disbelief. There, plastered across the sun-bleached stucco, dozens of posters with colorful typography advertise COPPELIA.

"Excuse me? Excuse me!" I'm out of the car and hurrying into the cobblestoned shopping plaza. A group of old men around a table outside a coffeehouse look up as I approach. "Coppelia?" I demand, pointing to the posters on the wall. "What's Coppelia?"

"Coppelia. Si, si, Coppelia." A barrage of rapid Spanish follows. They're pointing and gesturing, giving me directions. I hold up my hands to stop them, and fetch the map from the car. One of them screws his cigar into the corner of his mouth and takes the map from me. He stabs a gnarled finger at it; and there, smack in the middle of downtown Havana, is the word Coppelia.

"Gracias, gracias," I call back as I return to the Lada wondering about Coppelia. A wax doll. A factory that makes dolls? Coppelia. A ballet. The national ballet? Whatever it is, I've no doubt I'll find the cash-filled container there.

The lights are brighter in the Vedado District, the streets more crowded with pedestrians. I maneuver between them and turn into Avenida Rampa. Up ahead a large illuminated sign blazes COPPELIA. A long line of people snakes around the corner from the entrance. Ballet—it has to be the ballet. That's odd. The building doesn't resemble any theater I've ever seen. The two-story star-shaped structure looks more like something from outer space that landed in a park. I'm totally baffled now. Coppelia isn't a doll factory. It isn't a ballet. It isn't a paper company either. Coppelia is a gigantic ice-cream parlor.

A vague uneasiness begins gnawing at me. There's another connection here, but I can't put my finger on it. I leave the car and stroll through the park. It's like a festive picnic grounds filled with tables and chairs. Flirting teenagers. Couples holding hands. Children clutching melting cones, faces smeared with their favorite flavor.

The napkins that bulge from table dispensers do more than clean sticky hands and faces. They also explain in several languages that twenty-five years ago Fidel Castro decided his people would have quality ice cream. Named Coppelia, after the well-known ballet, it has since become a national institution.

By the time I finish reading, I've circled the building. There's no sign of container 95824 anywhere.

I'm reeling with disappointment when the vague connection snaps into focus. Chilling, insidious, too painful to contemplate, it points an ugly finger at the identity of the insider. The thought makes me shudder. I can't accept what it portends. No. No, it's Gudonov. I know it is. It has to be Gudonov who's on the inside.

I rack my brain for the whereabouts of the elusive container. I'm replaying the conversations I had with Rubineau, in search of a clue, when the pieces fall into place. There's only one other place in all of Havana it could be.

I'M BARRELING west on the Malecon, the six-lane boulevard that parallels the seawall. In the distance a modernistic Y-shaped building dominates the skyline. Sheathed in turquoise tile, the twenty-story hotel towers over the placid Caribbean. Next to it, Meyer Lansky's infamous casino turned convention center nestles like a gigantic Fabergé egg, its gilded shell shimmering in the darkness. A large sign flickers RIVIERA in green neon.

The service entrance is adjacent to the parking lot. A long driveway leads to a turnaround large enough to accommodate tractor-trailers. It's blocked by a wooden barricade, but I'm close enough to see the eighteen-wheeler backed up to one of the loading docks. Shafts of light stream from the opening, raking across the number on the container—number 95824!

My excitement is short lived. The area beyond the barricade is fenced. Razor wire spirals across the top of the chain-link. Armed guards are posted at the gate. One levels his rifle at me. Another advances and shines a flashlight in my face, then shifts it about the car's interior. The map, the tan, the T-shirt, the camera on the passenger seat do their job. *"Turista,"* he grunts.

The other nods sullenly. *"Parque de automóviles."* He points toward the guest parking lot and steps aside.

"Ah," I reply. *"Gracias."* I drive off. Okay, Katkov. You've just been officially declared a tourist, and it's time to act like one. Time to hang the camera around your neck and walk in the front door.

The Riviera's entrance is marked by a reflecting pool and a large sculpture of a mermaid and a sea horse. Like the rest of Havana, the once grand gaming palace is in desperate need of repair. The glass doors open into a shabby lobby where dusty chandeliers burn dimly. The carpeting, draperies, and furniture look threadbare. A few loiterers. A yawning bellman. An old man reading a newspaper.

The check-in desk is empty. I stroll past and come upon a marble atrium. The hotel elevators on one side, the main entrance to the convention center on the other. It's blocked now by a row of steel doors. Closed. Locked. Velvet ropes ward off straying guests with signs warning CLOSED TO THE PUBLIC in several languages.

There's no way I'm leaving without getting a look at the two-billion-dollar extravaganza going on inside. And if the casino's interior is still intact, I've got a pretty good idea how I can pull it off.

I slip behind the velvet ropes and past the steel doors into a corridor that turns left, then right, before reaching a door labeled ADMINISTRACIÓN. It opens into what looks like a converted backstage area. The dressing rooms where famous entertainers once held court serve as convention offices now, unoccupied at this hour. In one of them an old woman is vacuuming the worn carpet. I wait until her back is to the door and slip past it.

I finally come upon a curved section of corridor that rings the egg-shaped building. It leads to a makeshift storage area. Boxes of supplies are piled neatly in one corner. I'm about to move on when it dawns on me that they're rising in stepped tiers—like the disused staircase on which they're stored! This is what I've been looking for.

I pick my way between the cartons, climbing in darkness. The stairs lead to a landing that's strung with cobwebs. I claw them aside and feel my way along the wall. My hand finds a light switch. *Click-click*. Nothing happens. It's pitch-black up here. I strike a match. There's only one door. It's locked. The flame stings my fingers. I light another match and start back down.

The maid has moved on, her vacuum a distant hum now. I find the manager's office and rifle the desk, taking a flashlight and two rings of keys.

I return to the landing. The flashlight makes the task a little easier, but I'm down to the last few keys when one finally engages the tumblers with a crisp click and turns smoothly.

The door opens into the space above the convention center's ceiling. I *am* right. It's no longer a casino, but it's all still here.

Security office. Observation platforms. One-way mirrors through which the gaming tables below were once surveilled. A network of catwalks above the ceiling. I crouch to one of the mirrors. It's like being on a roof and looking down through a skylight. The massive hall below appears empty. Has the money already come and gone? I'm getting that hollow feeling when a muted shuffling sound rises. I trace it to a group of angled mirrors in the center, and there, directly below me, is a mountain of plastic bags filled with money.

Other one-way mirrors reveal an assembly-line operation cranking at full tilt. No dealers, no pit bosses, no feverish players; just diligent money handlers, their counting machines, and two armed watchdogs—Ray-Ban perched atop a stool, cradling a machine gun; and Rubineau's bodyguard, the one from the elevator, outfitted in an impressive shoulder holster. I slip the camera from my pocket and begin taking pictures through the mirrors.

Yet another mirror reveals equipment that packages the finished product. It combines twenty fifty-thousand-dollar bundles into a precise rectangular volume about the size of a large attaché case, then wraps it tightly in heat-sealed plastic. The million-dollar packages are stacked on the floor like concrete building blocks.

Though the crew and every piece of equipment are operating at breakneck speed, there's still a long way to go. I'm exhausted, hungry, and fearful of being discovered. I pocket the camera and follow the catwalks back to the security office. From here, eagle-eyed observers phoned reports about cheaters and complicit dealers to security personnel working the floor below. It's obvious no one's been up here in decades. I stretch out on a dusty sofa. The last thing I remember is hearing the muted shuffle of the counting machines below. I don't know how many hours I slept, but the machines are still going full tilt when I awaken and squint at my watch. Five in the morning. I pull myself together and make my way across the catwalks to the observation platforms. Bundles of cash still cover the tables, but the mountain of bags is gone and the operation is winding down.

The packages are separated into two stacks now, one much larger than the other. Something tells me I'm looking at a two-way split. The small stack contains two hundred packages. Assuming a two-billion-dollar total, that's a ten percent or two-hundred-million-dollar cut, probably for the Cuban government. That leaves ninety percent—eighteen hundred packages, or one point eight billion dollars—to be invested in Russia by Rubineau.

A few hours later a garage-size door in the wall rumbles open. People begin arriving in vehicles that are driven right onto the floor. Zil limousines. Official staff cars. Several spanking-new Mercedes sedans. With the camera I zoom in on their faces. Members of the Cuban government, resplendent in military uniforms. Crime bosses in baggy suits. Drug lords in gaudy jewelry and designer sunglasses. Then Arkady Barkhin, who gravitates toward Ray-Ban; and finally, Michael Rubineau.

Like high rollers cashing out after an incredible run of luck, they hover about the stacks of money, barely able to contain their delight. All appear to be waiting for someone; and suddenly, so am I. The representative from the Russian government—Banzer's dangerous insider, the official who can execute the industries-for-cash deal—has yet to arrive.

Another Zil pulls in. Several men get out. A face moves into the camera lens. Zoom. Focus. Red hair. Pockmarked complexion. Thick lips. Yes! I was right—it's Gudonov! He's the insider. My worst fears were unwarranted. Coppelia was a coincidence.

I'm sighing with relief when I notice the man who's with him. There's something familiar about his carriage as he steps forward, but my sight line is blocked. The Cubans and the others encircle him in a display of respect and deference. Then documents. Signatures. The deal is being consummated. Smiles all around.

I scurry across the catwalks to get a better angle. Eye pressed to camera. Waiting. The group parts. The man turns. Zoom. Focus. He's short. Thin-boned. I take a shot. And another. But nothing changes. The sharp cheekbones, the rodentlike countenance, the neatly razored mustache. The face centered in the lens is Yuri's.

YURI is preening like a peacock, below. Yuri? Quiet, unassuming, supportive Yuri! Half of me wants to crawl into a hole and die. The other half wants to go down there and beat him to a pulp.

Suddenly I understand why Yuri couldn't get me copies of the documents, why he suggested I look up Barkhin. He knew I'd track down the medal dealers sooner or later. Better to have control of

me. Yuri had Rafik killed to scare me off and, as Shevchenko said, sever the only link to who hired him. Lastly it explains how Rubineau knew I was working with FinCEN. It wasn't Shevchenko who tipped him off; it was Yuri.

But it raises as many questions as it answers. First, why let me go to Washington? He made an obligatory effort to dissuade me, but I've no doubt he could've easily had me stopped. Instead, he gives me carte blanche use of his phone, and drives me to the airport. And what's driving *him?* Was Yuri KGB all these years? Is that how he knew what Vorontsov was up to? Found out he was going to blow the whistle, and blew it on him first.

This is no time to lose my nerve. Nerve? Gall, stupidity, suicidal bent would be more like it. I'm in the ceiling of a defunct casino in Havana, up against ruthless thugs with machine guns and killer dogs—any one of whom would gladly hunt me down and kill me like a cockroach—and I'm armed with a camera and a flashlight.

My eyes drift back to the one-way mirror. The million-dollar packages of cash are being put into cartons labeled CUBAN CANE SUGAR. The cartons in the smaller stack are being loaded into a military van. The cartons from the large one, which I'm betting are going to Russia, are being loaded back into container 95824.

I notice Barkhin—who's standing directly below me—brushing something from his sleeve. It's as if dust is falling on it. Puzzled, he glances up at the ceiling, then back to his sleeve and brushes it again. Dust *is* falling on it! He waves Ray-Ban over, says something, and points to the ceiling. Ray-Ban storms off with his machine gun slung beneath his arm.

I know where he's going, and I know how he's getting there. I leave the observation platform, searching frantically for another way out. A sign on the opposite side of the ceiling indicates a fire exit. I scurry across the catwalks and slam my palms against the emergency bar. Nothing happens. The door is locked. I'm trapped. There's no way I can get across the catwalks and down the stairs before Ray-Ban reaches them and starts up.

If I can't get out, I've got to keep Ray-Ban from getting in. I run back across the catwalks. I'm a few steps from the door when I hear boots pounding up the staircase. I lunge for the door and throw the dead bolt an instant before Ray-Ban grabs the knob. It jiggles, then shakes, as he turns it left then right. Several dull thuds follow, as if he's slamming a shoulder into it. Then a burst from his machine gun rips through the metal around the dead bolt.

I'm on the verge of panicking when I notice that there's a space between the catwalks and the ceiling—enough space for a man to hide. I climb off the catwalk onto the ceiling and slide beneath the catwalk when another burst from the machine gun turns the dead-bolt assembly into a chunk of twisted metal.

The door opens and Ray-Ban thunders onto the catwalks. The entire structure creaks and sways. Decades-old dust falls on my face, dotting my glasses. He advances a few steps, then pauses. I can see the texture of his soles through the decking. He's standing directly above me. A sneeze, a cough, a sigh, and I'm a dead man. I have to get him to move off.

I work a hand into a pocket with painstaking care and get hold of a coin. My fingers are moist with sweat and slippery. The thought of dropping it makes me shudder. I squeeze it tightly, waiting until Ray-Ban's back is to me; then I extend my arm out from beneath the catwalk and fling the coin as hard as I can. It zips through the air, ricochets off the window of the security office with a loud ping, and clinks through the metal ceiling structure.

Ray-Ban dashes off in the direction of the sound. The entire catwalk structure begins bouncing up and down, slamming painfully against my chest. I wait until he works his way around to the far side of the security office, then ease my way out from beneath the catwalk and roll up onto it.

I'm getting to my feet when a shoelace snags and I stumble. My shoulder hits the door, which swings back against the railing with a loud slam. I run onto the landing and down the staircase, taking the steps two, three at a time, jumping over the boxes stored at the bottom. I'm dashing through the storage area when I hear Ray-Ban thundering down the stairs behind me.

The convention-center offices go by in a blur as I exit the administration area, continuing past the main entrance of the center and into the lobby. It's busier than it was last night. Guests are checking out, waiting in groups for tour buses. Better to slip in among the milling tourists than run for my life.

I take a moment to catch my breath and straighten my clothes, then walk casually past the check-in desk, toward the cashier's windows. The young woman smiles as I approach.

I put a twenty-dollar bill on the counter. "May I have pesos, please?" I ask in English.

"Certainly, sir," she replies. She opens the cash drawer. "I hope you're enjoying your stay at the Riviera?"

"Oh yes, very much." I force a smile and glance back over my shoulder in time to see Ray-Ban explode from the corridor. He freezes and scans the crowd. His eyes sweep right past me.

The cashier presents me with a neat stack of pesos. I scoop them up and turn from the window, ready to bolt.

Ray-Ban is poised to spring at anything that moves. A deliveryman emerges from the corridor behind him. Ray-Ban spots him out of the corner of his eye and is on him like an attack dog, slamming him against the wall. The poor fellow is terrified, sputtering in Spanish as Ray-Ban grills him unrelentingly in Russian.

The commotion attracts a small crowd. I stroll casually out of the lobby and across the parking lot toward the Lada.

WHATEVER its destination, container 95824 isn't going anywhere for a while. Not until all eighteen hundred packages are sealed into cardboard cartons, stacked on pallets, and loaded inside. I check into an inexpensive motel down the street from the Riviera. After a quick shower I get some breakfast and drive back there.

Opposite the hotel, on the ocean side of the Malecon, there's a clear view of the Riviera's service road. There's no way the eighteen-wheeler can leave without my seeing it.

I spend the better part of the day sitting on the seawall with some fishermen, and most of the night in the Lada drinking coffee to stay awake.

Very early the next morning the lumbering eighteen-wheeler emerges from behind the Riviera. A military van, a Cuban government staff car, and two Zil limousines follow.

The caravan exits the service road and turns into a main boulevard with towering palms that march down the median. I follow at a distance. The divided roadway cuts a triumphant path across the city to the Revolutionary Palace. The state treasury must be located here, because the cash-filled military van and government staff car turn into the grounds. The eighteen-wheeler and the two limousines continue south until they pass beneath a sign reading JOSÉ MARTÍ INTERNATIONAL AIRPORT.

The three vehicles continue past the passenger terminals and turn at a security kiosk manned by two uniformed guards. They evidently have their orders because the gate arm rises immediately, and the vehicles proceed onto the airport grounds.

I've no chance of getting past the guards, but I can see the caravan through the chain-link. I continue driving parallel to the fence. I've got one eye on the road, the other on the vehicles when they swing onto the tarmac where two jets are waiting.

One is Rubineau's Gulfstream. The other is a Russian-made Antonov-22 cargo plane. Massive, extremely slow, its wide-bodied, hundred-foot-long cargo hold can easily accommodate the eighteen-wheeler with room left over. Without coming to a stop, the rig accelerates up the loading ramp and vanishes inside the cavernous fuselage. Container 95824 is on its way to Russia.

The two limousines stop next to the Gulfstream. Barkhin, Ray-Ban, Rubineau, and his bodyguard get out of one, Gudonov and Yuri out of the other. They all board Rubineau's sleek corporate jet. The crew wastes no time buttoning up and taxiing. The Antonov's crew does the same.

I make a beeline for the passenger terminal. I drop off the Lada, proceed to the Aeroflot ticket counter, and book a seat on the day's only flight to Moscow. My next stop is a row of public phone booths marked for international calls, where I make a collect call to Scotto at home.

"Yeah, hello?" A sleepy voice answers—a sleepy *man's* voice.

He recognizes my name and accepts the call. "Gabby, it's for you. It's that guy Katkov."

A groan. The rustle of bedding. "Katkov?" Scotto rasps groggily, then more alertly, "Katkov? Katkov, you okay?"

"Yes. Yes, I'm fine. Listen, I'm sorry to wake you, Scotto, but—"

"No problem. Hang on, I want to change phones." She puts me on hold. "Hi," she says a little more brightly. "That was my husband, Marty. He was here when I got back from Florida."

"Sounds delightful. But I'm afraid I'm going to ruin it for you."

"The container's moving, right?"

"As we speak. They drove it, rig and all, into one of those big cargo jets."

"They? Who's 'they'?"

I knew she was going to ask. I've been wrestling with what to do about Yuri all night, and I still don't have the answer. "Barkhin, Rubineau, a couple of officious-looking Cubans, several repulsive thugs from the drug cartels, and my friend—Gudonov."

"Gudonov? No kidding. Then I guess he's the insider, isn't he?"

"Right," I reply, glad she can't see my eyes.

"Way to go, Katkov. You did good. Real good. That means we can trust Shevchenko."

"We have to trust someone. The flight out of here doesn't leave until late afternoon. I won't get to Moscow in time. What about you?"

"I don't know. There's one out of Dulles at nine."

"That cargo jet has the speed of a flying hippo. Add on a refueling stop, you just might pull it off."

"Good. Call Shevchenko and bring him up to speed in case I don't get there in time, and make sure he knows the idea is to tail it and take down the creeps at the other end."

"That's a given. He does it at the airport, I'll kill him. Safe flight."

"You too. Look, where can I reach you? You going to be staying at your friend Yuri's?"

"Yes. Yes, I'll be staying there," I reply as casually as I can. I'm still not sure why I didn't tell her. Maybe I'm just not up to facing the truth yet. Maybe knowing *who* is one thing and knowing *why* is a totally different matter. Only Yuri can tell me that.

I've got ten hours to kill before departure and then more in the air. I'm dialing Shevchenko's number when it hits me. I've risked my life, been betrayed by my best friend, chased this story all over the world, and now I'm going to miss the grand finale.

CHAPTER THIRTEEN

DARKNESS is falling as Aeroflot SU-416 touches down at Moscow's airport. The Antonov-22 with the eighteen-wheeler and cash-filled container arrived sometime this morning; Rubineau's swifter Gulfstream, at least several hours earlier, probably before dawn.

The instant I'm cleared through customs, I make a beeline for the taxi stand, anxious to hear about the takedown and what happened to Yuri. I'm passing the barrier when I hear my name.

"Katkov? Hey, Katkov, over here!" It's Scotto. She knifing sideways through the crowd to keep up with me. What's she doing here? And why isn't she smiling? Something's drastically wrong.

"What happened?" I ask as we meet at the end of the barrier. "Did Shevchenko move too soon? I warned him—"

"No," she interrupts sharply. "Gudonov did."

"Gudonov!" I echo, astonished.

She nods grimly. "The Gulfstream got in first, like you figured. Shevchenko had it under surveillance, but neither Gudonov nor the other passengers stuck around to claim their prize. My flight got in next. Shevchenko and I hung out until the Antonov showed, and tailed the eighteen-wheeler."

"Follow the money. Your favorite game."

"Not when I get beat. We were a couple miles south of the airport when all hell broke loose. I've never seen so many cops and reporters in my life. Like a Hollywood extravaganza."

"Starring Gudonov?"

Scotto grunts in the affirmative.

"It doesn't make sense. He was in the thick of things in Havana."

"He claims," Scotto says cynically, "he was working undercover."

"Bull."

"That's what Shevchenko said. He can't believe it." She leads the way to a rented Zhiguli in the parking lot. I toss my luggage into the back seat and settle next to her. "Shevchenko thought you'd want to see this." She drops a copy of *Pravda* in my lap and drives off.

The headline reads MILITIA MONEY-LAUNDERING STING. Beneath it is a photograph of the eighteen-wheeler pulled to the side of the highway. It's surrounded by police vehicles. Several sugar cartons have been opened, and the million-dollar packages of cash are prominently displayed. Gudonov poses next to them like a conquering invader. The byline on the article reads "M. I. Drevnya."

> This morning, while Muscovites slept, Chief Investigator Yevgeny Gudonov led a crack militia task force in a brilliantly executed operation which netted more than a billion and a half U.S. dollars.

> American crime czars were planning to use the profits from their illicit drug deals to buy Russian industries. Gudonov, who's been working on the case for months, risked his life to go undercover inside the smuggling operation. The scheme was—

"Risked his life to go undercover!" I exclaim, infuriated. "What a sham!" But it's the next to last paragraph that really gets my attention. I read it aloud in shock and disbelief. " 'Reliable sources have told *Pravda* that Investigator Gudonov plans to destroy the contraband at Moscow's garbage incinerating plant this evening.' I can't believe he's burning all that money."

"Burning the *evidence*. Shevchenko's trying to stop him. We're meeting him there."

We're soon spiraling down a road that winds through the marshlands. Thick smoke stretches in dense layers below the night sky. The Zhiguli climbs a steep hill, comes over the crest, and approaches the incineration plant. Like gigantic roman candles, its towering stacks send bursts of orange sparks shooting into the darkness.

The media are out in full force, all gathered around the huge incinerator, which roars with the intensity of a blast furnace. Container 95824 sits on the ground next to a work platform where Gudonov is supervising the operation.

Scotto and I push through the crowd in search of Shevchenko. She spots him off to one side, where a noisy forklift prowls in search of the next pallet. Evidently, most of the cartons have already been incinerated.

"Last one," Shevchenko says, clearly demoralized.

"Why the hell wouldn't he wait?"

"Wait?" Shevchenko snaps angrily. "The cocky little bastard won't even listen."

With a throaty rumble the forklift deposits the pallet on the platform. Workers manhandle it toward the incinerator.

Gudonov holds up a hand and instructs the workers to open several of the cartons. Then, with much fanfare, he removes one of the million-dollar packages and holds it high overhead before tossing it into the roaring inferno. Another soon follows, and then another. Sparks fly. Cameras whir. Strobes flash. The chief investigator struts triumphantly, then signals the workers, who roll the entire pallet into the roaring flames.

The media surge around Gudonov, firing off questions. "How high up in the Interior Ministry will your investigation reach? Do you know if—"

"Ask him why he's burning evidence," Shevchenko calls out.

"What about that?" one of the reporters prompts. "Care to comment, Chief?"

"Yes, but I'd prefer to introduce my colleague Senior Investigator Shevchenko first." The TV cameras and lights swing around and focus on Shevchenko. "This all began with a homicide—a homicide that Investigator Shevchenko solved with customary brilliance. In light of his firsthand knowledge of the case, I've no doubt he's aware that Comrade Vorontsov—the corrupt Interior Ministry official who masterminded this scheme—got involved with people who settle disputes in ways he wasn't accustomed to, and is deceased, as is the assassin who killed him. Nor do I doubt that the senior investigator also knows that the militia can't prosecute the dead—which makes his so-called evidence useless."

"What about the co-conspirators?" Shevchenko challenges. "What about prosecuting them?"

"Unfortunately, they've cleverly distanced themselves, and there's no way to connect them to the case."

"Thanks to you," Shevchenko counters angrily.

"However," Gudonov resumes, ignoring Shevchenko's barb, "just because we can't prosecute doesn't mean we can't prevent." He gestures dramatically to the conflagration behind him. "This serves strong notice that we're turning up the heat, that Russian justice is ruthless and swift, that neither this nation's economy nor her integrity can be bought by agents of the American underworld who traffic in filth."

Shevchenko scowls in disgust, then makes his way to his Moskvitch and drives off without a word.

Scotto and I are crossing to her car when a thought occurs to me. "Hold on. There's something I want to check." I circle the money container, examining it. Same number. Same color. Same cartons of sugar. Indeed, it has everything to identify it as the cash-filled target we've been tailing—except my initials scratched into the paint.

"A DECOY?" SHEVCHENKO exclaims, kicking back in his desk chair, astonished. "Did I see Gudonov tossing millions into that incinerator, or what?"

"Cost of doing business," Scotto replies. "They sacrificed a couple of mill for effect."

"Hold it. You and I saw the container come out of the plane. Katkov saw it go in." His eyes shift to mine. "Right?"

"Right. Unless the decoy was already aboard when I got there."

Scotto frowns skeptically. "Two eighteen-wheelers fit in that thing?"

"In an Antonov-twenty-two? Easy."

"Well, if you're right about that," Shevchenko muses, "maybe the one with the cash is still in the plane."

"It's been nearly fifteen hours," Scotto challenges. "No way they're letting two billion sit there that long."

Shevchenko lifts the phone and puts out an all-units alert for container 95824. He also dispatches a team to the airport to check out the Antonov. "Can't hurt. It's either still aboard or out there somewhere." Then he pushes up from his chair and crosses to a wall map of Moscow. "Where would they take it?"

"How about a former bank?" I stab a finger at the map, pointing to the Frunze District. "The Paradise Club. It used to be a bank. It's got a vault the size of an Antonov."

Shevchenko snatches up the phone. "I need three teams. The Paradise Club on Luzhniki. We'll rendezvous outside at twenty-three thirty." He heads for the door, slipping on his jacket. We hurry after him down the corridor.

Scotto and I leave the rented Zhiguli in the courtyard and pile into the Moskvitch with Shevchenko. It's almost midnight when we arrive at the Paradise Club. Shevchenko clicks on his radio and orders the other teams into position behind the columns that flank the huge bronze doors. "Okay, Katkov," he says. "You're on."

I take a deep breath and ring the buzzer. "It's Katkov," I announce to the thug who peers from the security slot. "Nikolai Katkov."

He grunts in acknowledgment and throws the latch. The door opens with a weighty shudder.

"Moscow militia," Shevchenko announces. He shoves his I.D. in the thug's face and leads the charge of detectives and uniformed officers past him into the club. Scotto and I follow.

Scantily clad dancers stop gyrating and hurry offstage. Gamblers stiffen apprehensively. Dealers freeze in midshuffle. The club is suddenly still and silent.

Shevchenko crosses to the corner table. I follow apprehensively, wondering if Yuri is here celebrating with his fellow conspirators. My eyes dart from Barkhin to Rubineau to the phalanx of bodyguards lurking in the background, but there's no sign of Yuri. No caviar, no champagne. Indeed, despite a week in sunny Havana, both men look pale and tense. They also look angry. Very angry. At me. I return their stares as Shevchenko identifies himself.

"Nice of you to drop in, Mr. Investigator," Barkhin says. "Unfortunately, we're all booked. With a party of this size, I suggest you call for a reservation next time."

"I'm making this one in person," Shevchenko counters. "For a tour of your vault. We're looking for two billion U.S. dollars."

Barkhin's brows arch. "Two billion. I have to admit the club is doing well, but I think that estimate's a little excessive."

"Two billion was smuggled into Moscow in a shipping container this morning," Scotto says. "Ring a bell now?"

"Ah, I vaguely recall seeing it in the newspaper."

"I distinctly recall you seeing it in Havana," I shoot back.

"Bad time to be away, Katkov." Barkhin fetches a copy of *Pravda* from the table. "Somebody beat you to the story."

"Yes, but he blew the ending. You're going to help me rewrite it."

"What about Mr. Clean here?" Scotto prompts, glaring at Rubineau. "Maybe he can help too?"

"My mission in life," Rubineau replies facetiously. "What do you need?"

"That container. The one you begged us to let go to Havana? The one that was going to lead us to whoever was using you?"

Rubineau grins. "I also remember telling Katkov that you were wasting your time, and you're still wasting it, believe me."

"The vault," Shevchenko prompts, losing patience.

"Of course," Barkhin says magnanimously. He's cocky, too cocky. They both are. Something's wrong. He leads the way downstairs to his elegant office. At the touch of a button the hardwood panels slide back, revealing the vault's gleaming door. He sets the tumblers, then spins the retracting wheel, swinging the enormous disc of case-hardened steel aside.

Shevchenko leads the charge inside and anxiously sweeps his eyes over the shelving bays filled with hard currency. His posture slackens. Not a single million-dollar package is to be found, let alone eighteen hundred of them.

Shevchenko mutters embarrassed apologies and leads the group of officers from the club. "Damn!" he exclaims angrily as the three of us pile into the Moskvitch and drive off.

"Back to square one," Scotto groans.

We're about a mile from militia headquarters when the radio comes alive. The team Shevchenko dispatched to check out the Antonov reports the container wasn't in the cargo hold, but something else was. The two detectives are waiting in Shevchenko's office when we enter. On the desk are several cans of spray paint and a numeral stencil.

"Great," Shevchenko groans. "They changed the number. We'll never find it now. Let alone nail whoever's at the other end!" He kicks a trash pail in frustration. "Anything more on the guy with Gudonov?" he asks.

The detective shakes his head no.

I'm rocked. They know someone was with Gudonov. But Yuri's name still hasn't surfaced. Nonchalantly I prompt, "What guy?"

"We ran the Gulfstream's manifest this morning," Shevchenko replies. "Rubineau, Barkhin, their flunkies, and two names we didn't recognize. The passport office had no record of them, so we know they were traveling on phony I.D.s. Obviously, one was Gudonov, but we've no fix on the other."

I know who it is, but I still can't get the pieces to fit. Yuri is the only one not mentioned in *Pravda;* he wasn't at the incinerating plant; he wasn't at the Paradise Club; and he's not on the Gulfstream's manifest. There has to be a reason. If Gudonov was undercover, is it possible Yuri was too?

"Why are we shifting our focus to people?" I ask. "Regardless of who the players are, we don't have a case without the money."

"He's right," Scotto says forcefully. "No money, no case. The world thinks it went up in smoke. We have to prove it didn't. We find that container, we'll have a shot at nailing the creeps. We don't, they're all gonna walk."

I hear myself say, "I know where it is." Two heads snap around as if reacting to a gunshot. "At least, I think I do."

"Come on, come on," Scotto urges, her eyes locked onto mine.

I hold them for a long moment, thinking. "No. No, this one's personal. I'm going to have to do it alone."

"No way," Shevchenko roars. "You tell us what you have, or I'm going to bust you for withholding evidence."

"I'm afraid I don't have evidence. It's little more than a vague hunch. You let me run with it, I just might get you some."

Shevchenko glares at me, deciding.

"You're the agent in charge, Shevchenko," Scotto says, "but I figure we've got nothing to lose."

Shevchenko scowls in thought, then nods grudgingly.

"I'm going to need your car, Scotto."

Scotto drops the keys in my palm. "Katkov?" She stops me as I head for the door. She takes the pistol from her holster and hands it to me. "I hope you don't need it."

CHAPTER FOURTEEN

THE trip to Sudilova takes well over two hours. After several wrong turns in the maze of ancient streets, I find the road that snakes west into the Ustye Valley. Dirt roads branch off in every direction. The wind-lashed tree that marks the one I want finally appears in the Zhiguli's headlights. I shut them off and make the turn past the mailbox without a name. Weathered farm buildings loom in the darkness. No lights. No vehicles. No sign of life save a curl of smoke from the chimney of the old house.

I park the Zhiguli behind the stand of pines where the road forks, and get out clutching Scotto's pistol. I take cover in the trees, scoop up a handful of rocks, and throw them at the barn's sagging door. No armed guards respond to the salvo.

Deep tire ruts lead right to the door. A tractor pulling a plow? Or an eighteen-wheeler pulling a cash-filled container? The hasp is thrown, but a rusty horseshoe nail, not a padlock, secures it. I open it just enough to slip inside.

A shaft of moonlight slices through the narrow opening and strikes the huge shipping container. There's no need to check for my initials or the restenciled number either. I've found what I'm after. I leave the barn and stride swiftly up the hill to the house.

A light burns dimly in one of the windows now. I peer inside. Wrapped in her coarse wool sweater, Yuri's mother is leaning into a massive stone fireplace, stoking the embers to life. I slip the pistol under my jacket and knock on the window. "Mrs. Ternyak?"

She straightens and turns. "Who's there?" she calls out.

"It's Nikolai, Mrs. Ternyak. Nikolai Katkov."

She shuffles to the door and opens it. "Nikolai?" she repeats, a little confused. She hugs me. "Is Yuri with you?"

"No. I'm sorry if I startled you."

"Well, he always comes on Saturday for breakfast. He shouldn't be long." Her brow furrows. "You know, I think he was here this week. Yesterday? The day before? He told me he put some equipment in the barn."

"Ah, he said he wanted to show me something. I guess that's it. Why don't I wait there for him?"

I return to the Zhiguli and drive it around to the side of the barn that's away from the road. I'm about to get out when a thought strikes me. I have something for Yuri, and this is the perfect time to give it to him. I rummage through my bags in the back seat until I find it, then hurry inside the barn.

Several hours pass before I hear the sound of Yuri's Lada. It lurches to a stop. I watch as Yuri gets out and looks curiously at the open barn door. Then I back away and crouch behind some hay bales.

A few footsteps. Yuri leans into the barn. "Mom?" he calls out warily. "You in there?" He enters, squinting at the darkness, and sweeps his eyes over the container. Satisfied that the locks are secure, he turns to leave, then stops suddenly and stiffens. His eyes are staring at the word Coppelia on the napkin that I've affixed inside the door. He fingers it curiously and removes it from the nail.

I step out behind him. "Hello, Yuri."

"Nikolai?" He stares at me for a long moment. My mind is racing. Is he armed? Will he go for his gun? Should I go for mine? Instead, he shrugs and smiles wanly in concession. "Did you have some when you were there?"

"No. I'm afraid I felt more like retching than eating when I realized what it meant."

"Shame. It's much better than anything we have here. One of the few things Castro did well, actually."

"So you needed a name for a dummy corporation, and naturally, Coppelia came to mind."

"Just a whim. Seemed like a good idea at the time."

"I thought privatization deals were outside your area. I mean, you've come a long way, but empowered to act on behalf of the government? I'd no idea."

"Well, I don't mean to be immodest, but my superiors were so taken by my ideas on reform, they eventually made me responsible for carrying them out." He pauses and looks at me. "That was you in the ceiling at the Riviera, wasn't it?"

"Yes. Took some rather interesting pictures too." Yuri's eyes show no reaction; he seems wholly unthreatened. "Why did you let me go in the first place?"

"You mean to Washington? As you recall, I tried to dissuade you at first; then it dawned on me that you couldn't hurt, you could only help. I figured if push came to shove, you'd be arguing to let the container go. I was right, wasn't I?"

"How—how could you be so sure?"

"You're not a cop, you're a journalist. That container doesn't get to Moscow, you don't get your story."

My eyes flare at the insult. "How could you do this? After all we've been through." I pull the pistol from inside my jacket and come at him in a rage. "All these years, you and the bloody KGB!"

"KGB? No! You're wrong," he shouts, hysterically, backing away. "Never! You don't understand. Listen, I—"

"Liar! I'm going to splatter your brains all over this barn." Yuri is backed up against the wall. I level the pistol at him and pull the trigger. A blue-orange flash. A loud crack. The bullet whistles past his head, punching a hole in the siding next to it.

Yuri emits a terrified yelp. I fire another shot, over his head. *Blam!* Wood chips fill the air. He's cowering, close to panic. "On second thought maybe I'll just beat the hell out of you." I raise the pistol and charge, threatening to smash him with the butt. He grasps my wrist and we tumble to the floor, struggling for control of the weapon. It slips from my grasp and skitters away. I lunge for it, but Yuri is quicker. As we scramble to our feet, he backs away, leveling the pistol at me.

"Now calm down and listen, dammit!" he shouts. "I'm a patriot, Nikolai. I care about Russia as much as you do. I spent my life trying to bring the Communists down. This is our chance to get rid of them forever. But it will take money; lots of it."

"You know where this comes from?"

"I couldn't care less!"

"You want American crime syndicates to take over our industries?"

"*They're* putting money into the country, Nikolai. The *Russian* mobsters are taking it out!"

"We don't need it, dammit! The United States just gave us a billion and a half dollars. The G-Seven countries will soon—"

"Aggghh! You're so naïve. Whether we have a communist or democratic government, it's still going to be a *Russian* government. A bottomless pit of bureaucratic quicksand that'll suck up everything in its path. None of that money'll ever get to the people."

"And this will?" I demand angrily.

"Yes. It's bypassing the system completely. Going directly to small businessmen, manufacturers, entrepreneurs. To buy equipment and raw materials; to create jobs and fill empty stomachs. It's going to ensure that the average Russian doesn't give up on democracy before this wretched economy gets turned around."

I'm stunned. "But I thought Rubineau was investing it in privatized industries."

Yuri breaks into that rodent's smile. "So did he."

The pieces have suddenly fallen into place with staggering impact. Barkhin and Rubineau weren't holding a celebration at the Paradise Club last night. They were holding a wake—a wake for a container of cash that never came. "You double-crossed him?"

Another smile. "*Used* him would be more accurate. He wanted to help Russia, and he has. A one-point-eight-billion-dollar donation. Of course, Rubineau can't very well invest money that's been incinerated by the police, now, can he?"

"Gudonov."

Yuri nods. "Couldn't have done it without him."

"I can't believe you're doing business with that creep."

"I'd deal with the devil himself if it'd buy us enough time. Do you know what today is?"

"Saturday, isn't it? Why?"

"It's also May Day, Nikolai."

"May Day!"

"How quickly we forget—the constant fear; the terror; the gulag; the KGB listening to every call, watching every move. You want the hard-liners back?"

"Fair enough." I study his eyes for a moment. "There's something else I have to know. You had Vorontsov killed?"

Yuri winces as if offended. "It wasn't quite that cold-blooded. Vorontsov was becoming a problem, and Barkhin was quick to—to take it on, for want of a better phrase."

"You're no better than him."

Yuri's face flushes with anger. "Vorontsov was a pompous fool, Nikolai. He didn't care about Russia. He was only interested in holding on to power. I begged him not to blow the whistle. I even told him what I was going to do. He wouldn't back down. I couldn't let one man stand in the way."

"Do you feel that way now?" I ask, taking a step toward him.

Yuri tightens his grip on the pistol. "Don't force me to make that choice, Nikolai."

"You're forcing *me* to make one."

He cocks his head and studies me, then his eyes soften. "I'm asking you to put your country before yourself. You've been doing it all your life. I can't imagine you're going to stop now."

"I'll think about it."

I push the muzzle of the gun aside and walk out of the barn into the morning sunlight. I've taken about a half-dozen steps when Yuri calls out, "Nikolai?" I keep walking, waiting for him to pull the trigger. "Dammit, Nikolai!" he calls out again as I reach the end of the barn. Nothing. I turn the corner, then get into the Zhiguli, start the engine, and circle back to Yuri. He's standing in front of the barn. The pistol is at his side.

I stop and roll down the window. "May I have that back, please? It's not mine."

Yuri nods curiously and hands me the weapon. "How did you know I wouldn't use it?"

"I didn't, but it was important to find out. You'd have had a hard time killing me without these." I open my hand, revealing the bullets I'd removed, drop them into his palm, and drive off.

THE willows along the river are dotted with fresh growth and bathed in sunlight that strikes the House on the Embankment at a flattering angle. The paths crowded with chatting strollers. The grounds alive with the playful shrieks of children. A bouncing ball. A soaring kite. I park the Zhiguli, put Scotto's pistol in the glove compartment, and make my way across the grounds to the entrance, taking the elevator to Mrs. Churkin's apartment.

"Nikolai!" she exclaims as she opens the door. "Please come in. I've been hoping to hear from you. I thought you might call from Washington."

"I wanted to be sure one way or the other first."

"And now you are?" she prompts apprehensively as we take seats in the grandly proportioned living room.

"Yes. You were right. He was wholly innocent."

She sighs, the pent-up anxiety released like air escaping from a balloon. "Oh. Thank God."

"He was murdered to prevent him from doing his job."

She smiles weakly, then looks off with a thought. "Then why are they still saying otherwise? First they called him a blackmailer. Now he's the mastermind."

"It's all part of the cover-up. He was neither, Mrs. Churkin, believe me. Your father was an honest man—honest to a fault."

"Will you write that?"

"Of course I will."

"Thank you, Nikolai," she says, beaming. "Thank you for . . . everything."

I leave the apartment and return to the Zhiguli. It seems to be giving off a faint electronic twitter when I open the door. The sound is coming from my briefcase. I pull it from the back seat and throw back the flap. It's my beeper. I'd forgotten all about it. I jog across to a phone kiosk and dial militia headquarters.

"Vera? Vera, it's Nikolai. You just beep me?"

"Of course. Several times in the last few weeks, I might add."

"I was away for a while. What's going on?"

"You're in trouble with the militia."

"Gudonov?"

"No, Shevchenko. He put out an alert for a rented Zhiguli and identified you as the driver, with a warning that you're armed."

"Great. Listen, Vera, I'm at the Embankment. Can you meet me?"

"No, I'm working."

"Get someone to cover for you. I need to talk."

"I can't. What about Yuri? Call him."

"It's *about* Yuri. Please—it's important."

"All right, Niko. I'm on my way."

My stomach flutters at the thought of seeing her. I settle on one of the benches, wondering if she's really going to come. Fifteen minutes. A half hour. I'm on the verge of giving up hope when I spot Vera's lithe figure weaving through the crowd.

She apologizes, explaining the May Day demonstration has snarled traffic. She's predictably impressed by my tale of adventure, and as confused by my dilemma as I am. "I can't tell you what to do, Nikolai," she replies with a comely shrug. "Besides, you never listened to me before. Why would you start now?"

"I'm desperate," I reply with a little smile. "And anyone who could come up with those documents is well worth listening to. I never thanked you. None of this could've happened without them."

She splays her hands and grins. "You still want advice from me?"

"What? Join a monastery?"

She chuckles and throws her hair back over her shoulder. "No. Trust your instincts. Just do what feels right. You'll be okay, Nikolai. I know you will." She glances at her watch. "I have to go." She pauses, then lunges into my arms. Her eyes are brimming with emotion. "I missed you. Will you call me?"

"If you really want me to."

"Of course I do." She kisses my cheek, then turns and hurries off.

I watch until she disappears in the crowd, then walk along the river lost in my thoughts. A half hour later I find myself back at the Zhiguli. I'm opening the door when four men come running toward me brandishing guns. "Police!" one of them shouts. "Turn around and put your hands on the car."

"I'm not armed," I call out, complying with the order. "The gun's in the glove compartment."

One of the officers fetches it. They frisk me anyway, confiscating my wallet and car keys, then spin me around to face them. "Nikolai Katkov?"

I nod wearily.

"Investigator Shevchenko wants to see you. You'll have to come with us."

Two of them hustle me into a patrol car. As we drive off, another gets behind the wheel of the Zhiguli and follows. Despite the May Day–clogged streets, the flashing red lights and screeching sirens make quick work of the drive to militia headquarters, and we're soon hurrying down the corridor to Shevchenko's office.

"Katkov, you okay?" Scotto asks anxiously as we enter.

"Yeah, I'm fine."

"Good, because I'm gonna kill you. Now, what the hell is going on?"

"Going on?" I stall. "What do you mean?"

"Twelve hours to check out a hunch," Shevchenko growls.

"Some take longer than others."

"Am I to assume you've completed your investigation into the container's whereabouts?" he asks sardonically.

I nod, buying every last second before deciding.

"And?" he groans exasperated.

A long moment passes before I shrug and hear myself say, "I was wrong."

"DROP you somewhere?" Scotto asks curtly as we leave militia headquarters and walk across the courtyard toward the Zhiguli. "Plenty of time before my flight."

"Okay. I'm going to Yuri's place, I guess. It's not far."

We drive in silence for a few blocks. She's still distant. We're stopped at a traffic light when she finally glances over. "You found it, didn't you, Katkov?"

"You sound like you already know the answer."

"Uh-huh," she says with a sassy nod. "You protecting someone?"

"Really, Scotto. You know I'd never do that."

"Then why? Why?"

"Because it's more complicated than I thought. It's not black and white."

"Look, I'm a fairly bright person. Why don't you run it past me? Who knows, I just might understand."

"I've a better idea. Make a left at the corner."

She turns and drives south to the Moskva Hotel. We park the car there and walk to Red Square. A barbarous roar echoes off the towering walls of brick. The die-hard Communists are out in full force. Hundreds of thousands of them, chanting, "Le-nin! Le-nin!" A sea of Soviet regalia, flags, banners, and posters surges through the square. The Hammer and Sickle. The glowering images of Lenin and Stalin. A mass of humanity eagerly protesting the fall of tyranny and the advent of freedom. It's a staggering sight.

"It'll be a long time before Russia is anything like the United States, Scotto."

"Hey, whether you agree with these clowns or not, it's a step in the right direction. Dissent is the cornerstone of a free society. If you want to be a democracy, you have to act like one. You can't have it both ways."

"We can't have it overnight either. The framework is barely in place. It's unsteady and very fragile. The slightest push could bring the whole thing down."

"And these clowns are pushing."

"Right. I don't want to stop them. I just want to buy enough time to reinforce the foundation."

"One point eight billion dollars' worth."

"I think you're starting to understand. At the moment, there are more important things in Russia than the letter of the law."

"More important than the truth?"

"I'm not sure."

"But you know what it is."

"Uh-huh. Just not sure what to do with it."

Scotto brightens with a thought. "Come on. I have something that might help." She leads the way back to the Zhiguli and opens the trunk. "Here," she says, presenting me with my typewriter.

I stare at it for a moment, struck by the realization that I've quite conveniently forgotten all about it. "I assure you, you've made your point."

"Just keeping a promise," she says, pulling the typewriter back with a giggle when I reach for it. "Trade you for the camera. With this budget crunch, I'm gonna have to account for it one way or the other."

I get the camera from my briefcase. "Come on. We better go," Scotto says, pocketing it. She's reaching for the door handle when she notices me removing my luggage from the back seat. "What're you doing?"

"Changing my mind. Something tells me I've worn out my welcome at Yuri's. I think I'll take a room here for a few days, then find a place of my own."

She studies me for a moment. "I've no doubt you'll know it when you find it," she says, poignantly.

"I just want to do the right thing, Scotto."

"Make sure you try real hard." She kisses my cheek, slides behind the wheel, and drives off with a tap of her horn.

The car winds down the hill past the Kremlin, past crenellated turrets and stands of towering pines that send long shadows across the expanse of centuries-old cobblestones. I watch until she's out of sight, then climb the steps to the hotel, wondering about Scotto, wondering if she really has to account for the camera or if the swap was a shrewdly veiled ploy to acquire its contents. I leave my bags with one of the Moskva's bellmen and go for a walk by the river. The early thaw has shattered the monolithic sheet of ice, and the current is sweeping the pieces away with unusual swiftness. I've no doubts now. No second thoughts. A flick of my wrist propels the canister of film into the air. It sails in a graceful arc, lands with a little splash, and vanishes beneath the raging torrent. On the opposite shore, the House on the Embankment cuts a jagged silhouette out of swiftly falling darkness.

ABOUT THE AUTHOR

Greg Dinallo was never much of a reader. As a "visually oriented kid," he says, "I was the one who'd always be down in the basement making little mountains and roads and villages for a model train set." And that's what writing a novel is like, he adds, "building a little universe."

Greg Dinallo

A native of Brooklyn, Dinallo studied design at the Pratt Institute and went to work creating large-scale exhibits for high-profile clients, such as Kodak's display at the 1970 Osaka World's Fair. "Naturally, every exhibit needed a film," he says. "So that's how the film thing started." Before long the "film thing," or writing for the screen, led Dinallo to Hollywood. There he pounded out scripts so well that he soon found himself the supervising producer of the TV series *Mike Hammer*. Calling the shots, being the chief in charge, suited him fine. "It has to be that way," he adds, "or you end up with a twenty-eight-humped camel."

Writing novels—where the author is master of all—was the logical next step in his drive toward ever greater independence. Unlike many authors, Dinallo does not write from personal experience. The fun of writing, for him, is the discovery of a whole new universe, finding things out at the same time as his characters.

Today Dinallo lives in a mission-style home a mile from the beach in Santa Monica, California, with his writer's bungalow on the property. He's been known to spend ten hours a day sequestered there whenever a new little universe is in the works. "I get into that world and I don't want to leave it." He does manage, however, to have lunch each day with his wife of thirty-two years, Gloria. And that makes it easy for him to avoid "the Hollywood lunch thing." As he says, "Why go out when I can have lunch with my wife every day?" It's nice to know that the world, for some, can still be what you make of it.

PHOTO: GLORIA DINALLO

HAVING

The Delany Sisters'

Sarah and A. Elizabeth Delan

OUR SAY

First 100 Years

with Amy Hill Hearth

Reaching the venerable age of a hundred plus is rare. But centenarian sisters Sadie and Bessie Delany are two rare individuals. Born into the poverty of the post–Civil War South, the Delany girls not only beat the odds, they made history.

Their story is inspiring. But be advised—when the Delany sisters speak out, the feathers fly. Seems that advanced years bring special privileges—among them, the right to have your say.

> "Bessie and Sadie Delany give themselves so completely to the reader it's as if you're in the home of these intelligent, humorous women listening to them talk over dinner."
>
> —*Los Angeles Times Book Review*

Part I

Sweet Sadie, Queen Bess

BOTH more than one hundred years old, Sarah "Sadie" Delany and her sister Annie Elizabeth "Bessie" Delany are among the oldest living witnesses to American history. They are also the oldest surviving members of one of the nation's preeminent black families that rose to prominence one generation after the Civil War.

Few families have ever achieved so much so quickly. Henry Beard Delany, the sisters' father, was born into slavery but eventually became the first elected "Negro" bishop of the Episcopal Church, U.S.A. All ten of his children were college-educated professionals at a time when few Americans—black or white—ever went beyond high school.

With the possible exception of Hubert, the sisters' younger brother who was a New York political leader, the Delanys were almost unknown in the white world. But in the black society of Raleigh, North Carolina, where they grew up, and later in Harlem, the Delanys were legendary.

The black press chronicled their remarkable achievements and held them up as role models. "The Delanys present a unique picture of family success," declared New York's *Amsterdam News* in 1951. "The saga of the Delany family emerges as a symbol of the Negro's struggle for survival, achievement and service," trumpeted *The People's Voice* in an editorial published in September 1942.

The Delany creed centered on self-improvement through education, civic-mindedness, and ethical living, along with a strong belief in God. The family motto was, Your job is to help somebody. According to Bessie and Sadie, this code applied to anyone who needed help, regardless of color. Their accomplishments could not shield them from discrimination and the pain of racism, but they held themselves to high standards of fair-minded idealism.

Today the Delanys are no longer concentrated in Raleigh or Harlem. As in most American families, the younger generation is scattered from coast to coast. At least once a year, however, everyone seems to find the time to journey to Mount Vernon, New York, to see the family matriarchs, Aunt Sadie and Aunt Bessie, the custodians of the Delany legacy.

Sadie

BESSIE and I have been together since time began, or so it seems. Bessie is my little sister, only she's not so little.

She is a hundred and one years old, and I am a hundred and three.

People always say they'd like to live to be one hundred, but no one really expects to, except Bessie. She always said she planned to be as old as Moses. Now, I think Moses lived to a hundred and twenty. So I told Bessie that if she lives to a hundred and twenty, then I'll just have to live to a hundred and twenty-two so I can take care of her.

Neither one of us ever married, and we've lived together most all of our lives and probably know each other better than any two human beings on this earth. In some ways we are like one person. If she were to die first, I'm not sure if I would want to go on living, because the reason I am living is to keep *her* living.

Bessie and I still keep house by ourselves. We still do our shopping and banking. We were in helping professions—Bessie was a dentist and I was a high school teacher—so we're not rich, but we get by.

We've buried so many people we've loved; that is the hard part of living this long. Most everyone we know has turned to dust. Well, there must be some reason we're still here. That's why we agreed to do this book; it gives us a sense of purpose. If it helps just one person, then it's worth doing. That's what Mama used to say.

Bessie and I have lived in New York for the last seventy-five years, but Raleigh will always be home. Raleigh is where Mama and Papa met, as students at Saint Augustine's School (now College). Mama and Papa got married in the campus chapel back in 1886 and raised all ten of us children right there at good old Saint Aug's. Papa became vice principal, and Mama was the matron.

In 1918 Papa became the first elected Negro bishop of the Episcopal Church, U.S.A. That's a long way for a man who was born a slave on a Georgia plantation. But if you had known Papa, you wouldn't be surprised. He was always improving himself, and he and Mama brought us up to reach high.

Papa was a smart, good-looking Negro man. Actually, his skin was a reddish brown, on account of his mother being part Indian. Mama, who was from Virginia, was an issue-free Negro. (An issue-free Negro was a person who had some black ancestry but whose mother was a free person, not a slave.) Mama looked white, but she never did try to "pass." She was proud to be a colored woman.

People would look at us Delany children and wonder where in the world this bunch came from. We were every different shade from nearly white to brown-sugar. I was one of the lighter children, and Bessie was browner. We were aware we were colored, but we never gave it a second thought. It's just the way it was.

I came into this world at seven thirty in the evening on the nineteenth day of September, 1889. It was a long day of hard labor for Mama. Everyone was nervous because I was Mama's second baby and the doctor had to be brought in after my older brother, Lemuel, was born two years earlier. This time Mama wanted her sister, Eliza, by her side. Eliza's presence was calming, and the doctor was not needed. As a matter of fact, after the midwife left, Mama sat up in bed and declared she was hungry. Eliza was just tickled to death at Mama's appetite and cooked up the biggest plate of fried apples and hot biscuits Mama ever saw. Mama said she ate every bite.

Mama got her confidence back with my birth and went on to have eight more healthy babies. Next in line was Annie Elizabeth, born two years after me and known as Bessie. I don't remember life without Bessie. Queen Bess, as Papa used to call her, was born on the third of September, 1891. Bessie was so alert at birth that Mama said she had a funny feeling that child would have a mind of her own.

Bessie was what we used to call a feeling child. She was sensitive and emotional; she was quick to anger and very outspoken. Now, I was a mama's child and followed my mama around like a shadow. I always did what I was told. I was calm and agreeable. The way I see it, there's room in the world for both me and Bessie. We kind of balance each other out.

Bessie

PAPA used to say, "You catch more flies with molasses than vinegar." He believed you could get further in life by being nice to people. Well, this is easy for Sadie to swallow. She can sweet-talk the world or play dumb or whatever it takes to get by without a fuss. But even as a tiny little child, I wasn't afraid of anything. I'd meet the devil before day and look him in the eye no matter what the price. If Sadie is molasses, then I am vinegar.

You know, Sadie doesn't approve of me sometimes. She frowns at me in her big-sister way and says it's a wonder I wasn't lynched. Well, it's true I almost was. But I'm still here. Yes, sir!

What worries me is that I know Sadie's going to get into heaven, but I'm not so sure about me. I'm working on it, but it sure is hard to change. I've been trying for one hundred years without success. That's not so good, is it? I'm afraid when I meet Saint Peter at the gate, he'll say, "Lord, child, you were *mean!*"

I have trouble with the idea of forgiving and forgetting. You see, I can forgive, but I can't seem to forget. I remember things that happened long long ago that still make me madder than a hornet. I wish they didn't. Most of the things that make me mad happened to me because I am colored. As a woman dentist, I faced sexual harassment, but racism was always a bigger problem.

Sometimes I am angry at all white people, until I stop and think of the nice white people I have known in my life. But the rebby boys tend to stand out, make themselves known. Rebby is what we used to call racist white men. I guess it's short for rebel. I'll tell you, the way those rebby types treated colored folks—well, it just makes me sick. If I had a pet buzzard, I'd treat him better than the way some white folks have treated me.

Now, Sadie doesn't get all agitated like this. She just shrugs it off.

It's been a little harder for me, partly because I'm darker than she is, and the darker you are, honey, the harder it is. But it's also been harder on me because I have a different personality than Sadie. She is a true Christian woman. I wish I were more like her.

Now, don't go thinking that I'm *all* mean. I am not so angry that I cannot laugh at myself. One thing most Negroes learn early is how to laugh at their situation.

If you asked me the secret to longevity, I would tell you that you have to work at taking care of your health. But a lot of it's attitude. I'm alive out of sheer determination, honey! Sometimes I think it's my *meanness* that keeps me going.

Sadie

EVERY morning I ask Bessie, "Are we going to have any visitors today?" And she will stop and get real quiet and think real hard and say, "No, we are not." Or she'll say, "Yes, so-and-so will be coming." And generally she is right.

You see, Bessie believes she is a little psychic. I try not to encourage this, because it's ungodly. But I have to admit, Bessie is a little, well, *intuitive.* And it often comes in handy. You see, we don't have a telephone. We have to rely on the mail and Bessie's intuition.

Everybody is always after us to get a phone. We hate phones! Of course, we had a phone years ago when Bessie was a practicing dentist. But ever since we moved to this house, in 1957, we have not had a phone. If we have an emergency, we have a light we put on in the house that we never use otherwise, and somebody always comes running over here right away.

The phone company came by and pestered us. Finally we told the man, "Mister, if the phone company installed a phone for free and paid for a man to stand there and answer it for us seven days a week, we *still* wouldn't want a phone." He got the message.

The world is a puzzling place today. All these banks sending us credit cards in the mail with our names on them. Well, we didn't order any credit cards. We don't spend what we don't have. So we just cut them in half and throw them out. Imagine a bank sending credit cards to two ladies over a hundred years old! What are those folks thinking?

One time I got this nasty letter from the New York City Board of Education. They wanted to cut off my pension. They demanded that I prove I am still alive. I guess they thought I was long dead and somebody was stealing my check. Well, we got it all straightened out, but that is the type of thing you have to deal with when you get to be our age.

Sometimes we get pestered by people who just show up at the door. The most persistent are these folks who go door to door evangelizing. I just look at them through the window and shake my head no. I won't even open the door. But sometimes Bessie will go upstairs and open the window, stick her head out, and call down to them. She'll say, "What do you want?"

And they'll say, "We just want to talk to you for a minute."

And Bessie'll say, "Oh, no, you don't. You don't want to *talk*. You want to *convert* me. And I'm more than a hundred years old, and I've been an Episcopalian all my life, and ain't nobody going to derail me or my sister now!"

I'll tell you something about Bessie. She has made a full-time job out of watching over the neighborhood. She's always looking out the window and reporting what so-and-so is doing. I say, "Now, Bessie, is that really your business?" And she says, "If it's going on in my neighborhood, it's my business." And I say, "Bessie, you are a nosy old gal." She says, "Sister Sadie, we bought a house with windows, those windows are here for a reason, and I'm going to use them."

Sometimes she gets really mad at me and says, "You wouldn't care if the whole neighborhood was burning down around us!" Of course that's not true, and she knows it. She just gets mad 'cause I'm not as nosy as she is.

Bessie

I'LL tell you a story. The house we own is a two-family house, and sometimes the neighbors can hear us through the wall. One time they had a guest who was up in arms. She heard these sounds, like laughter, coming from our side late at night, and she was convinced there were hants. Yes, sir, she thought we were ghosts.

Our neighbor came over the next day and quizzed us down. And I said, "Ain't no hants; it's just the two of us being silly." It hadn't occurred to them that these two old sisters, at our age, would be a-carrying on like that. I guess they think of old folks as people who sit around like old sourpusses. But not us. No, sir! When people ask me how we've lived past one hundred, I say, "Honey, we never married. We never had husbands to worry us to death!"

One thing Sadie and I do is stay away from doctors as much as possible. When they see how old you are, and that you still have a mind, they treat you like a curiosity—like, "Hey, nurse, come lookee here at this old woman. She's in such good shape. . . ."

One time some doctor asked Sadie to do a senility test. Of course she passed. A year later he asked her to do it again, and she said, "Don't waste your time, Doctor." And she answered all the questions from the year before, before he could ask them. And then she said to me, "Come on, Bess. Let's get on out of here."

People assume Sadie and I don't have any sense at our age. But we still have all our marbles. Yes, sir! I do get tired physically. But how can I complain about being tired? God don't ever get tired of putting his sun out every morning, does He? Who am I to complain about being weary?

Funny thing is, some days I feel like a young girl, and other days I'm feeling the grave, just a-feeling the grave. That's why it's important that we get all this stuff written down now, because you never know when you'll meet the Lord in the sky.

Part II

"I Am Free"

SADIE and Bessie's father, Henry Beard Delany, was born into slavery and came of age at a time of tremendous upheaval in the South. When the bloody Civil War came to a close, the South was left in ruins. The decade of Reconstruction that followed was a violent era, marked by power struggles between the North and South about how the postwar transition should proceed. Caught in the middle were four million freed slaves, who mostly lived in conditions not much improved from captivity.

Because they had been "house niggers," the Delanys had been forced to endure comparatively fewer privations than those who labored in the fields. More important, they could read and write and were better able than many former slaves to make a niche for themselves in the chaos of southern life.

The Delany sisters' maternal ancestors, the Logans of Virginia, held an even more ambiguous place in the social order. They were free Negroes—not enslaved, yet not accepted as citizens before the Civil War. In 1860 there were perhaps two hundred and fifty thousand free Negroes in the slaveholding states, mostly former slaves who had been freed. Their numbers were swollen by laws mandating that people of mixed race be classified as "colored," even if they appeared white.

Sadie and Bessie

ON FEBRUARY 5, 1858, our papa, Henry Beard Delany, was born into slavery on a plantation owned by the Mock family in Saint Marys, Georgia, on the coast near the Florida border. He was just seven years old when the Surrender came in 1865. The Surrender is the way Papa always referred to the end of the Civil War, when General Robert E. Lee surrendered at Appomattox Court House.

We used to ask Papa, "What do you remember about being a slave?" Well, like a lot of former slaves, he didn't say much about it. For most people, things had been so bad they didn't want to think about it, let alone talk about it.

Well, we persisted, and finally Papa told us of the day his people were freed. He remembered being in the kitchen and wearing a little apron, which little slave boys wore in those days. It had one button at the top, at the back of the neck, and the ends were loose. And when the news of the Surrender came, he said he ran about the house with that apron fluttering behind him, yelling, "Freedom. Freedom. I am free. I am free!"

Of course, being a little child, he did not know what this meant. Back in slavery days things were bad, but in some ways getting your freedom could be worse. To a small boy it meant leaving the only home you ever knew.

Now, Papa's family were house niggers, and the Mocks had been very good to them. We remember our papa saying the Mocks were as good as any people you could find anywhere in this world. That's a generous thing to say about the people who *owned* him, wouldn't you say? He said that not all the white people who owned slaves were evil. There was great variety in the way white people treated Negroes. That's what Papa told us about slavery days, and it's true now, too.

Mrs. Mock thought a heap of Papa's mother, Sarah, who was born on the plantation on the fifth of January, 1814. Why, Mrs. Mock even let Sarah have a wedding ceremony in the front parlor. Of course, this wasn't a legal marriage, since it was against the law for slaves to get married. But it was a ceremony, and Sarah was joined in matrimony to Thomas Sterling Delany. This was about 1831. Their first child, Julia, was born on the first of November, 1832. Altogether, Sarah and Thomas had eleven children, and our papa was the youngest.

Thomas was a handsome man. To what extent he was white we do not know. We were told he was mostly Negro. The family Bible says he was born in Saint Marys on the fifteenth of March, 1810.

Sarah was obviously part Indian; she had long, straight black hair but otherwise looked just like a Negro. When we were children, we always giggled about her photograph because her hair looked so peculiar to us. We never knew Papa's parents, because they died when we were tiny.

Thomas was part Scottish, which is where the Delany name came from. Now, of course, we haven't any idea what our original African name was. But it doesn't worry us none. We have been Delanys for a long time, and the name belongs to us.

The Mocks let the Delanys keep their name, and even broke Georgia law by teaching Papa and his brothers and sisters to read and write. Maybe the Mocks thought the Delanys wouldn't leave after the Surrender. But they did, and they each didn't have but the shirt on their backs. They crossed the Saint Marys River and set down roots in Fernandina Beach, Florida. Papa told us that each day they would wash their only shirt in the river and hang it up to dry, then put it on again after it had dried in the sun.

Those were hard times after slavery days. Much of the South was scarred by the Civil War, and there wasn't much food among the whites, let alone the Negroes. Most of the slaves, when they were freed, wandered about the countryside like shell-shocked soldiers. Papa said everywhere you went, it seemed you saw Negroes asking, begging for something. He said it was a pitiful sight.

The Delanys were among only a handful of former slaves in those parts who didn't end up begging. Papa was proud of this beyond words. They survived by eating fish they caught in the river and gathering up wild plants. They built a home—some kind of lean-to or log cabin. They were smart, but they were lucky, and they knew it. They could read and write, and their family was still together. That's a lot more than most former slaves had going for them.

Papa and his brothers all learned a trade. Following in the shoes of one of his older brothers, Papa became a mason. His brother was known in the South for being able to figure the number of bricks it would take to build a house. Another of Papa's brothers was said to be the first Negro harbor pilot in America, and his older sister Mary taught school, mostly at night to poor colored men who worked all day in the field.

The Delanys were Methodists through and through. Papa was already a grown man in his early twenties when one day the Reverend Owen Thackara, a white Episcopal priest, said to him, "Young man, you should go to college." Papa jumped at the chance, even though it meant giving up on being a Methodist. Reverend Thackara helped Papa go to Saint Augustine's School, way north in Raleigh, in the great state of North Carolina.

In college Papa did not disappoint anyone. He was as smart as he could be, and blessed with a personality that smoothed the waters. He soon met a fellow student named Nanny James Logan, the belle of the campus. She was a pretty gal and very popular despite the fact that she was smarter than all the boys.

Miss Nanny Logan, who would one day be our mama, was born in Virginia in a community called Yak, seven miles outside Danville. Today they call it Mountain Hill. Guess they think that sounds better than Yak.

Miss Logan was a feisty thing, a trait she could have gotten from either of her parents. Her father, James Miliam, was one hundred percent white and the meanest-looking man in Pittsylvania County, Virginia. Because he was white, he could not legally marry his ladylove—Nanny's mother—an issue-free Negro named Martha Logan.

This is what we were told by our mama: A fellow named John Logan, who was white, was an army officer called away to fight during the War of 1812. While he was gone, his wife took up with a Negro slave on their plantation. She was already the mother of seven daughters by her husband, and her romance with the slave produced two more daughters. When the husband returned, he forgave his wife—*forgave her*—and adopted the two mulatto girls as his own. No one remembers what happened to the slave, except he must've left town in a big hurry. This slave and this white woman were our great-great-grandparents.

The two little mulatto girls, Patricia and Eliza, were just part of the family. The only time anyone has heard tell of their older, white half sisters' mistreating them was when those white girls were old enough to start courting and they used to hide their little colored half sisters. One time they hid them in a hogshead barrel, and after their gentlemen callers left, they couldn't get them out! They had to use an axe to get Patricia out. Well, they slipped and cut Patricia's leg, and she carried that scar to the grave.

When Patricia grew up, she had ten children. One thing we remember about her was that one of her babies was born on the side of the road. She would walk to the mill to get her corn ground, carrying this big sack on her head. On the way back one day, she went into labor and had that baby on the side of the road by herself! And afterward she just put that baby under her arm and that sack of cornmeal back on her head and walked on home.

Patricia's sister, Eliza, meantime, had become involved with a white man named Jordan Motley. They had a child—Martha Louise Logan, our grandma, born in 1842. Eliza had three other daughters: Blanche, LaTisha, and Narcissa.

Those four girls were all only one-quarter Negro, but in the eyes of the world they were colored. It only took one drop of Negro blood for a person to be considered colored. So Martha Logan and her sisters were in a bind when it came to marrying. If they wanted to marry a colored man, well, most of them were slaves. And they couldn't marry white, because it was illegal for Negroes and whites to marry in Virginia at that time. Well, it didn't stop them from having love relationships. Martha Logan took up with James Miliam, who was as white as he could be. We remember our grandparents well because we used to go visit every summer and we were young women when they died.

Mr. Miliam built a log cabin for Grandma a few hundred feet from his clapboard house on the sixty-eight acres he owned in Yak.

He even built a walkway between the two houses so he could go see Grandma without getting his boots muddy. Now, this kind of arrangement was unusual between a white man and a colored woman. More common was when a white man had a white wife, and a colored mistress on the side. But James Miliam had no white wife and was entirely devoted to Grandma. They lived like man and wife for fifty years and didn't part until death.

If anyone was bothered by this relationship, they kept it to themselves. That's because Mr. Miliam was one tough fella. He was about six feet four at a time when most men were about a foot shorter. When he was very young, he had a job rolling huge hogsheads full of tobacco. Usually it took two men to roll a barrel. But James Miliam could roll one by himself. All of his adult life he carried a pistol in a shoulder holster for all the world to see. He was a mean-looking dude.

Mr. Miliam was a farmer and grew tobacco and everything else you can think of on his land. But he also served as a dentist. Of course he had no training. It's just that he owned the right tools and was willing to pull teeth. Mr. Miliam would get two big men to hold down the patient, and then he'd yank that old tooth right out.

Another thing—Mr. Miliam was a root doctor. He was always messing around with different herbs and roots and things, looking for cures. As an old man, he got a patent for a cure for scrofula, which was a skin problem that erupted on the necks of folks who had tuberculosis. Mr. Miliam got twenty-five hundred dollars for the patent.

Grandma was quite a businesswoman in her own right. She owned her own cow, and although she didn't know it, what she was doing was pasteurizing the milk and cheese. She had somehow discovered that if she scalded her pans with boiling water, the milk and cheese was healthier. Folks came from all over to buy Martha Logan's cheese because it tasted good and lasted longer.

Grandma and Mr. Miliam had two daughters: Eliza, born in 1859, and Nanny James, our mama, born on June 23, 1861. Mama was named after Mr. Miliam's mother (Nanny) and himself (James). Mr. Miliam's daughters could not carry his last name legally, but he was determined that his name be in there someplace.

Eliza got married young, but Nanny—our mama—was set on getting an education. She had been inspired at the little one-room schoolhouse by a teacher named Miss Fannie Coles. Nanny ad-

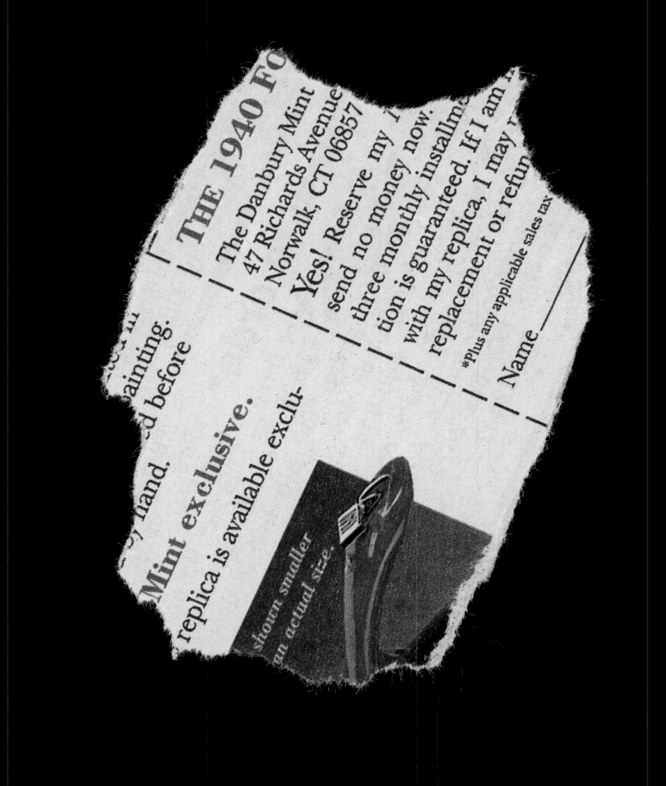

THE 1940 FO
The Danbury Mint
47 Richards Avenue
Norwalk, CT 06857
Yes! Reserve my
send no money now.
three monthly installm
tion is guaranteed. If I am
with my replica, I may
replacement or refun
*Plus any applicable sales tax
Name
painting.
d before
hand.
Mint exclusive.
replica is available exclu-
shown smaller
an actual size.

next one, rotating through the
three. The study subjects

How to order

A 30-day supply of three ThinPens costs $31.95, plus $4.95 shipping. To order using VISA or MasterCard, call: 1-800-844-6688. Or send check or money order to: L.A. Associates, P.O. Box 3672, Lantana, Fla. 33462.

the
— the
feel

"But so
more — up to
month.

"In fact, the aro
so well that some pe
ally had to drop
study because th
ing TOO MUCH

"In short, we
that aromas are
tool in achieving
ing weight loss,"

Psychologis
says he's re

mired Miss Coles so much that she would take her own lunch and give it to her teacher every day as a gift. Miss Coles had no idea that her student was sacrificing her own meal.

Mama always said she had a sweet childhood there in Yak, carefree and running around the farm, playing with her sister. She was sheltered from the world, though, and when she set her sights on going to Saint Augustine's School in Raleigh, North Carolina, Grandma declared she could not go alone. So when Mama packed her bags, so did Grandma. The whole time Mama was in college in Raleigh, Grandma was nearby. Grandma was an excellent cook and seamstress and was able to get as much work as she wanted.

Grandma suffered terribly from rheumatism. One day she told Mama, "Soon my time to die will be coming." She was sixty-six when she died in 1908, which was old in those days. Mama found all her clothes for the funeral pressed and ready, laid out in a drawer. Poor Mr. Miliam—he sat in Grandma's kitchen with his head in his big hands, and he said, "What I loved most in this world is lying in the other room."

Before Grandma died, she told Mama to have some of us grandchildren stay with Mr. Miliam when we could, because he would be lonely. So we went and cooked and kept him company. In the morning he would go out and shoot a squirrel for his breakfast. He always used to say those little ones were mighty tasty.

Grandma had predicted Mr. Miliam would not last long without her, and she was right. Despite our efforts to keep him happy, he died just two years later, in 1910. He was about seventy years old. He told us he had somehow lost track of his birth date, but he believed he was born in 1840.

They weren't supposed to be together in life, but Martha Logan and James Miliam are buried together side by side. Eliza, Mama's sister, had died, and so Mama was the only surviving child. Mr. Miliam left everything he had—his farm and his money from the patent—to her. The will was challenged by some white nephew of his who was just furious over the fact that this *colored* woman should get that land and that money, even if she was Mr. Miliam's daughter! Mama gave five hundred dollars to the nephew to keep the fellow happy. But she did what Mr. Miliam would have wanted: she hung on to that land. And to this day it is still in our family.

Part III
Saint Aug's

IN THE decades after the Civil War, education became the rallying cry of those seeking to improve the lot of former slaves, whose prospects were limited usually to hard labor in the fields or to domestic work in white people's homes. The few black students groomed for advancement during this era found colleges and universities unwelcoming. Indeed, most institutions frankly barred them from admittance. Black women faced even higher hurdles. At a time when most women were expected to marry and become mothers, higher education for them was deemed unnecessary.

Black colleges were the crucial stepping-stone to progress, and they flourished. Northern philanthropists had established, among others, Howard University in Washington, D.C.; Fisk University in Nashville, Tennessee; and Shaw University in Raleigh, North Carolina. Schools for Negroes stressing vocational training, such as the Tuskegee Institute in Alabama, were also founded with aid from private resources. At the same time, black colleges were started under the auspices of religious organizations such as the Episcopal Church. Such was the origin of Saint Augustine's School in Raleigh, founded in 1867. Growing up at Saint Augustine's School, the Delanys learned to "reach high."

Sadie and Bessie

OUR mama was always a bit embarrassed that her parents were not legally married. She was determined that she was going to have a legal marriage someday or not get married at all. Virginia was a much more conservative state about these things than North Carolina, and that may have figured into her decision to go to college at Saint Aug's in Raleigh and leave Virginia behind.

She got her pick of beaux at Saint Aug's, and it didn't matter to her in the least that her favorite was a lot darker than she was. She said he was the cream of the crop, a man of the highest quality. Oh, Mama was a smart woman. It takes a smart woman to fall in love with a good man.

Our papa felt the same way about her, but he was told at graduation time by his advisers that he should not marry—at least not yet. Now that he was educated, they hoped to see him devote himself to the ministry before starting a family. But Papa ignored this advice. He and Miss Logan were married at the chapel at Saint Aug's on the sixth of October, 1886.

Lemuel Thackara Delany, their firstborn, arrived the next year, on September 12, 1887. He was named after the white Episcopal priest who helped Papa go to college. Every two years after Lemuel's birth there was a new baby: Sadie in 1889, Bessie in 1891, Julia in 1893, Henry junior (Harry) in 1895, Lucius in 1897, William Manross in 1899, Hubert Thomas in 1901, Laura Edith in 1903, and Samuel Ray in 1906. All of our brothers and sisters have gone on to glory.

When Saint Aug's was founded after the Civil War, it was both a seminary and a school for teachers. Many fine young colored people graduated from Saint Aug's and went on to share what they learned with countless others. Since we grew up in this atmosphere, among students, reading and writing and thinking were as natural for us as sleeping and eating. We had a blessed childhood, which was unusual in those days for colored children. It was the rare child that got such schooling.

Our family lived right on the campus. We were not allowed to go off the campus without an escort. If it wasn't our mama or papa, the escort was one of the teachers or very often Papa's Cousin Laura from Florida. Papa called Cousin Laura "Cousin Lot." As children, we shortened that to Culot.

Poor Culot was a seamstress who had had a miserable job in Florida working for some white lady. The white lady made a lot of money, and Culot got next to nothing and did all the work. So Culot joined up with a convent in Baltimore, but left when she found out that the way those sisters raised money was to beg in the streets. She couldn't stand it. So our papa got her a job teaching sewing at Saint Aug's, where she stayed until she was a very old woman, when she went back to Fernandina Beach to die. She never worked for white folks again.

Culot was a maiden lady with no children of her own, and she liked to spoil us sometimes, so she would take us on the trolley car to Johnson's drugstore for a limeade or bring back some candy when she went downtown by herself. Funny thing about Culot is that she never could make a decision. She would tell us, Now clean out my dresser drawer and throw most of it out while I am downtown, but *don't ever tell me what you threw away*. And we'd do it. She just couldn't stand to throw anything away herself. A lot of former slaves were like that—they'd never owned anything, so they hung on to all kinds of junk they didn't know what to do with.

Of course, there were many people still alive then who had been slaves—including our papa. Most of these former slaves were down on their luck. Our parents thought it was their responsibility to treat these former slaves with courtesy and kindness, and with the dignity those folks had been denied by others.

At Thanksgiving, Papa made sure everybody in the neighborhood around Saint Aug's got a special meal. He would start weeks ahead making the baskets and finding out who might need one. Then Mama and the girls at the school made sweet potato pies and vegetables and chicken. On Thanksgiving morning it was our job to go out and distribute the baskets. One year a woman said to Bessie, "Honey child, there ain't a crumb in my house to eat, and I been on my knees praying for Thanksgiving for my chillun. When you got to my house, Thanksgiving surely got here."

Hunger was a big problem for the former slaves all year long. It always seemed like somebody was knocking on the door, looking for food. Mama never turned anyone away. She'd stop whatever she was doing and fix them a plate. Most of these folks went on their way, though one—a man named Jesse Edwards—stayed for ten years, until the day he died, living in an abandoned farmhouse on campus. We called him Uncle Jesse, and he became part of our family.

Uncle Jesse had been a slave in North Carolina. Papa felt sorry for him and gave him the job of carrying the mail. Uncle Jesse took this job so seriously that no matter how much we begged, he would not let us see the day's mail, and he'd say, "No, can't do it, cuz Mr. Delany said don't give no one dat mail. And dat's dat."

One day Uncle Jesse got sick, and Papa took him to the hospital. But there was nothing could be done, and poor Uncle Jesse died four days later. We had a potter's field on the campus, where Papa used to bury all the colored people in the area whose folks had no money, and Papa found an especially nice spot for Uncle Jesse.

We were the chief mourners, along with our little sister Julia. We picked wildflowers and wove them around a wooden cross. Mr. Hunter, the principal of the school, who was a very nice man, donated the coffin he was having made for himself at the school carpentry department. Papa presided over the service as if he was burying the King of England himself. All in all, Uncle Jesse had quite a send-off.

Sadie

MAMA and Papa were the two busiest people I ever knew, but they always had time for us. Once, our baby brother, Sam, shouted, "Mama, Mama! Come quick. Come quick!" Well, Mama thought some disaster had happened, and she dropped what she was doing in the kitchen and ran to him. And he said, "Mama, look at that sunset. Hasn't the Lord given us a pretty sunset today?" And the two of them watched the sun go down.

But Mama could also be a strict disciplinarian. My first memory is sitting on her lap, and someone gave me a little box of candy. I was eating a piece, and Mama said, "Now, share some with Lemuel." And I started whining and crying because I didn't want to. Finally Mama took it from me and just threw it right in the fire. She said, "That will teach you to share next time."

Maybe she had to be strict on account of there being ten of us. But she would always say to us, "Anything that happens, you can confide in Mama. Mama loves each child the way God loves his children. Nothing's too bad to tell Mama. Don't ever tell me a lie. It's not necessary, because Mama will understand."

She was really a working mother, with a job outside the home, making sure everything ran smoothly at Saint Aug's. After Mama had a baby, I would get a little chair and sit outside their bedroom and say, "You can't go in. Mama needs her rest." You'd be surprised at the people who would want to go in there. My younger brothers and sisters, of course, but also all these college students and various people who needed something. Mama was so loved by all the young folks on that campus that they called her Mother Delany, and they told her things they wouldn't tell a priest.

But I wouldn't let them in. So you see, I was a good little helper.

Still, I just don't know how Mama did it all. Her day always started long before dawn, and every night she bathed each one of us in a tin tub that she had to fill by hand. I used to get so tired waiting for my turn, because I was the second-oldest child and she would start with the youngest.

After each of us had our bath, we would go into Papa's study. After he read us Bible stories, Papa would see to it that any of us children who had had a fuss that day would make up. He didn't let us go to bed without resolving any conflicts.

Papa was the head of the house, though he always made sure that we treated Mama with great respect. All of us children had chores to do, and Papa saw to it that we did them. As a mama's child, I clung to my mother and was actually like her assistant. I would help Mama can fruits and vegetables, or anything she was doing at the moment. Since I was busy helping Mama, Bessie often would supervise the younger children in the family. Tell you the truth, I think she enjoyed bossing them around more than I would have. Bessie was a little dictator!

Each morning Papa would make us line up for inspection. He'd look us over to see if our shoes were polished, our ears were clean—things like that. He was proud of his children, and I think this was just a way for him to convey this. We carried the Delany name, and he wanted us to look respectable when we left the house.

After our inspection the bells would chime at the chapel, and Papa would scurry off to run the morning prayer service. We children would go to the service, then off to school on the campus. We attended classes taught by teachers in training at the college. Often there were people in the class who were grown men and women who lived nearby and wanted to learn to read and write. There were people of every age studying together.

Sometimes we Delany children felt the teachers were harder on us. Why, one teacher actually suspended me, but Mama marched down there and got me reinstated the very next morning. I remember the teacher had said that the children should come forward and warm their hands at the stove, and so I did, and I think she was angry because the other children were truly cold, having slept with no heat. I guess the teacher thought I was a little spoiled.

Funny thing is, we Delanys had no money at all. We were perceived as an elite family, since our parents were college-educated and had important jobs. But honestly, money was very tight. We bought all our clothes at the mission store, and only one time in my childhood do I recall having a new outfit. That was when some white missionaries in New England sent all the Delany children brand-new clothes one Christmas.

I remember once, Bessie and me and our little sister Julia made a circle around Papa and said, "Papa, we are going to squeeze a nickel out of you." And he laughed and said, "Go ahead and try, daughters, but there's no nickel here." But it is really true that you can get by without much money. We had love and respect and all those good things.

Papa was as good a man as you could find in America, or anywhere else for that matter. He was a good father, and we always listened to him. As far as we were concerned, that man knew everything.

He was highly intelligent, with many interests and hobbies. The one I remember best was astronomy. On a clear night he would take us all outside and teach us the names of the planets and star constellations. Papa knew them all. I remember that Papa was so excited when Halley's comet came by. He had us all outside that night, and it was a sight to see, flickering light across the landscape. Papa said, "I don't think any of us will be here to see Halley's comet the next time it comes around." Well, he was wrong about that, 'cause Bessie and I saw it again, and it wasn't as good the second time.

Papa whipped us once, and only once, when Bessie and I were children. He spotted us in a grove far from where we were supposed to go. Well, Papa was just very upset. He told us to get switches from the peach tree. While we were doing that, I whispered to Bessie, "Now, let's don't cry no matter how many times he hits us." Bessie agreed, and volunteered to go first with the whipping. Papa whipped her little shoulders and the backs of her legs, and of course she did not cry. Finally Papa quit and said, "Go on, you stubborn little mule."

Now it came my turn, and after seeing what Bessie had gone through, I changed my mind about not crying. So I howled at the very first lash, and one lash was all I got. I'm into surviving. What's the sense in getting licked if you don't have to?

Bessie

LORD, I am still mad at Sadie over that whipping incident. It was her idea not to cry in the first place. Well, I would rather die than back down, and that is the truth.

I take after Mama's people. Mama could be very feisty, and somehow, like me, she lived to tell about it. Papa tended to be gentle and calm. It was not in his nature to be mean or to make a fuss, so it was very difficult for him to whip us that day. And he had a lot of pride. He really believed in presenting yourself to the world in a dignified fashion. I think that's why he was unhappy about my pet pig, Retta.

You see, Retta was the runt of the litter, cast aside and left to die. Well, I took that little piglet, and I fed him with a bottle and fussed over him like a baby. Before I knew it, he weighed five hundred pounds, and he had these tusks that grew up around his nose. Wherever Sadie and I went, Retta wasn't far behind. I don't think Papa thought it was fitting for a Delany child to be wandering around the campus followed by a big grunting bull pig.

One day Retta bit a man, and that was the end of my poor pig. I imagine he was turned into bacon, and his fat used to make soap. It pains me to this day because I loved that old pig.

Papa and Mama always taught us to treat animals with respect. You never killed any of God's creatures unless you were going to eat them. Sometimes in the summer Papa and the boys would shoot bullbats, which I think people now call swallows. Those bullbats would swarm after the mosquitoes at dusk, just fill the sky, and Papa and the boys would shoot a dozen or two, and we'd eat them for supper. But Papa would never have let us kill them just for sport.

All of us knew a thing or two about guns. The boys were all taught to be expert hunters, and the girls at least knew the basics of gun safety. But one time our brother Lemuel was carrying a shotgun when a boy tripped him, and Lemuel was shot right through his hand. There were no antibiotics then, of course, and the wound was just full of lead shot, and all this corruption just came out of that hole in his hand. Poor Lemuel! Mama sat with him every day while the doctor soaked that hand in hot, hot water.

You could hear him scream all the way to the Capitol, a mile away.

Lemuel's hand healed finally, but the accident changed his life. He decided he wanted to be a doctor. One of the white doctors who had healed him took him under his wing. After graduating from Saint Aug's, he studied at Shaw University and then did his internship at the University of Pennsylvania. He returned to Raleigh and became a very well respected physician. In fact, not long ago a wing of one of the hospitals there was named in his honor.

We had other calamities besides Lemuel's hunting accident. The worst was a typhoid epidemic when I was about fifteen years old, which was nearly the end of me. A girl named Bessie Jackson, who had it first, died. Then everybody started getting sick. Sadie got typhoid fever and was not terribly ill, but I was hospitalized for about six weeks.

When I got out of the hospital, I looked like death. They had cut off my hair, real short, and I weighed next to nothing. Mama was so worried that she fixed a small basket of food each morning for me to carry with me all day so I could eat whenever I wanted. For a long time I was on crutches, and I was not expected to recover fully. They used to say that typhoid fever left its mark on people. Well, nothing has shown up yet, so I guess I'm in the clear.

Mama was real fussy about germs and also very careful about the foods we ate. She was ahead of her time about vitamins and minerals and things like that. Why, we used to say that Mama invented breakfast cereal. They would make bread in huge brick ovens at the school and cut the loaves with a large slicer. Mama would put a pan underneath to scoop up the crumbs, which she'd serve to us in a bowl with milk. People thought it was crazy.

We were very healthy compared to most children. In those days many babies and children died. They used to say, "There's more short graves in the cemetery than long ones." But Mama didn't lose any of us at birth, and none of us was born damaged.

Mama was very private about her pregnancies. When my younger brothers and sisters were born, she would say to me and Sadie, "Now, take the little ones to the grove by the spring and don't come back all day." Well, we'd just sit there quietly all day, and when we'd come back, there would be Miss Kenney, the midwife, and a new little darling colored baby. And we would say, "Mama, where did this baby come from?" And she would point to the midwife and say, "Why, Miss Kenney brought the baby." We thought she meant Miss Kenney brought the baby in her black leather bag.

Everyone expected a lot from the Delany children, but like all children, we could be mighty mean. Our little sister Julia was deathly afraid of bugs, and I used her fear to keep her in line. If there was a bug in our room at night, I could make Julia do things by threatening to throw that old bug in her bed. Wasn't I mean?

Julia followed us around and got in our way. Sadie and I, being older, preferred to play with each other. We were best friends from day one. Why, Sadie is in my earliest memory. We used to have these terrific thunderstorms in North Carolina that would scare the life out of you, and my first memory is Papa calling us all inside because a storm was coming. We all sat on the floor, and Papa said, "Just be quiet. Let God do his work." And the storm was crashing all around outside, and lightning was hitting the lightning rods Papa had put on the house. The whole house was just a-trembling. And so were we! When the storm was over, there was the most beautiful rainbow. Papa said, "Look, children, it is a gift from God." Sadie took my hand, and we ran outside to get a better look. We were certain God had hung it in the sky just for us.

We lived a clean life, but Lord, we had a good time. Every one of us children played an instrument, and you know, as a family we formed a band. We had a small organ, which Papa played beautifully. So did Julia, who had a perfect ear. We had all kinds of instruments, like a flute, a violin, a trombone, and a clarinet. Papa would lead us. We would play all kinds of music that was popular at the time.

Papa was extremely talented in music. I used to stand nearby and watch him play the piano. When he thought no one was around, he would play and sing these old Methodist hymns from his boyhood. He'd play "Amazing Grace"—things like that. I didn't realize it at the time, but I think he missed his people down in Florida. And when he'd play their Methodist hymns, he felt closer to them.

All of the values that made us strong came from the church. It was religious faith that formed the backbone of the Delany family. We were good Christians, and God never let us down.

I'll tell you something else. We were good citizens, good Americans. We loved our country even though it didn't love us back.

Part IV

Jim Crow Days

A GENERATION after the end of slavery, freedom for black Americans was still elusive. Strategies were being devised, such as poll taxes, to block black Americans from voting, and a flurry of racial restrictions was coming to be codified as Jim Crow laws.

Jim Crow became entrenched in southern society in 1896 with the Supreme Court ruling in *Plessy* v. *Ferguson*. The case stemmed from an incident in which a Louisiana citizen named Homer Plessy was arrested for refusing to sit in a "colored" railroad car. Mr. Plessy lost on his appeal to the Supreme Court, which sanctioned the establishment of "separate but equal" facilities for blacks and whites.

There had long been segregation by custom, but the Jim Crow laws, named for a minstrel-show character, made it legal and official. Under the new laws, black Americans faced separate—and inferior—facilities in every part of society, including schools, public transportation, and hospitals. Even public rest rooms and drinking fountains in the South were labeled COLORED and WHITES ONLY.

It would be decades before Jim Crow would begin to finally unravel. In 1954 the Supreme Court ruled in *Brown* v. *Board of Education of Topeka, Kansas,* that segregation in public schools was unconstitutional. The passage of the 1964 Civil Rights Act, the 1965 Voting Rights Act, and the 1968 Fair Housing Act were the final death knell for Jim Crow.

Sadie and Bessie

AMERICA has not ever been able to undo the mess created by those Jim Crow laws.

This is how we remember it: The reason they passed those Jim Crow laws is that powerful white people were getting more and more nervous with the way colored people after the Civil War were beginning to get their piece of the pie. Colored people were starting to accumulate some wealth, to vote, to make demands.

So this Jim Crow mess was started to keep the races apart and keep the Negroes down. Now, Mama and Papa knew these laws were coming, of course, but they didn't prepare us. I guess our parents could not find the words to explain it. They did not want to fill us with hatred. They wanted us to be children and not carry the troubles of the world on our shoulders.

We encountered Jim Crow laws for the first time on a summer Sunday afternoon. We were about five and seven years old at the time. Mama and Papa used to take us to Pullen Park in Raleigh for picnics, and that particular day the trolley driver told us to go to the back. We children objected loudly because we always liked to sit in front, where the breeze would blow your hair. That had been part of the fun for us. But Mama and Papa just gently told us to hush and took us to the back without making a fuss.

When we got to Pullen Park, we found changes there, too. The spring where you got water now had a big wooden sign across the middle. On one side the word "white" was painted, and on the other, the word "colored." We may have been little children, but honey, we got the message loud and clear. But when nobody was looking, Bessie took the dipper from the white side and drank from it.

On another day, soon afterward, a teacher from Saint Aug's took us to the drugstore for a limeade, which was something we had done hundreds of times. Well, this time the man behind the counter said, "I can't wait on you." The teacher got very upset. She said, "I can see you not waiting on me, but surely you are not going to deny these young children?" And he said, "Sorry. It's the law."

Jim Crow made any hope of equality between the races come to a grinding halt. Papa used to say that real equality would come as Negroes became more educated and owned their own land. Negroes had to support each other, he used to say.

So Papa would drag us all the way to Mr. Jones' store to buy groceries, since Mr. Jones was a Negro. It not only was inconvenient to shop at Mr. Jones', it was more expensive. We used to complain about it because we passed the A&P on the way. We would say, "Papa, why can't we shop at the A and P?" And Papa would say, "Mr. Jones needs our money to live on, and the A and P does not. We are buying our economic freedom."

Now, lest you think Papa was some kind of a saint, well, he did have a weakness. He did slip into the A&P now and then, and buy that Eight O'Clock coffee, which he was very partial to. So you see, he wasn't perfect. But Lord, he did try!

Sadie

JIM Crow was an ugly, complicated business. Fortunately for Bessie and me, our earliest experiences with whites predated Jim Crow. North Carolina was a fairly liberal state, and Raleigh was a center of education as well as the capital. Raleigh was a good place for a Negro to be living, compared to most places at that time.

So our first experience with whites was very positive. The white missionaries who came to Saint Aug's from New England were darling to us. They gave Bessie and me these beautiful china dolls that probably were very expensive. Those dolls were white, of course. You couldn't get a colored doll like that in those days. Well, I loved mine just the way it was, but do you know what Bessie did? She took an artist's palette they had also given us, and mixed the paints until she came up with a shade of brown that matched her skin. Then she painted that white doll's face! None of the missionaries ever said a word about it. Mama and Papa just smiled.

Those white missionaries and teachers at Saint Aug's were taking a great risk. They were outcasts for helping the Negro race. We so admired them that we thought they were perfect human beings.

There was one white woman in particular, Miss Grace Moseley, who was our favorite. She had come to Saint Aug's to teach, along with her mother, and those two were the cream of the crop. They were very fine, cultured women from a good family and with the best manners and education.

Now, every Wednesday evening Miss Moseley would invite Bessie and me and Julia to her quarters. We would all pile on her bed, and she would read us Shakespeare and all the classics. Julia would fall asleep, but Bessie and I would just snuggle up with Miss Moseley, and she would read to us. That is a lovely memory I carry with me, and it makes me smile to this day.

Jim Crow's not law anymore, but it's still in some people's hearts. I don't let it get to me, though. I just laugh it off. I have never let prejudice stop me from what I wanted to do in this life.

I'll tell you how I handled white people. There was a shoe store in Raleigh called Heller's. If you were colored, you had to go in the back to try on shoes, and the white people sat in the front. I would go in there and say, "Good morning, Mr. Heller. I would like to try on those shoes in the window." And he would say, "That's fine, Miss Delany. Go on and sit in the back." And I would say, "Where, Mr. Heller?" And he would gesture to the back and say, "Back there." And I would say, "Back *where?*"

Well, I'd just worry that man to death. Finally he'd say, "Just sit anywhere, Miss Delany." And so I would sit myself down in the white section and smile.

When I was a grown woman, after I got my master's degree from Columbia University, there was a white teacher who used to say this about me: "That Sarah Delany. You tell her to do something, she smiles at you, and then she just turns around and does what she wants anyway."

Just like Papa.

Bessie

THIS race business does get under my skin. I have suffered a lot in my life because of it. If you asked me how I endured it, I would have to say it was because I had a good upbringing. My parents did not encourage me to be bitter. If they had, I'd have been so mean it would have killed my spirit a long, long time ago.

As a child, every time I encountered prejudice, I would feel it down to my core. I was not a crying child except when it came to being treated badly because of my race, like when they wouldn't serve us at the drugstore counter. In those instances I would go home and sit on my bed and weep and weep and weep, the tears streaming down my face.

Now, Mama would come up and sit on the foot of my bed. She never said a word. She knew what I was feeling. She just did not want to encourage my rage. So my mama would just sit and look at me while I cried, and it comforted me. I knew that she understood, and that was the most soothing salve.

When I was a child, there was an attitude among some Negroes that to be lighter-skinned was more desirable. I doubt that was true among Negro people back when we were in Africa. It's probably just a cultural thing that Negroes picked up from white people in America. We saw in our own family that people treated the lighter-skinned children better. But it was not something that was even *discussed* in our household. We were different shades, and it didn't make a bit of difference among us. It didn't matter if you were white, black, grizzly, or gray. You were *you*.

I don't use the word black very often to describe myself and my sister. To us, black was a person who was, well, black; and honey, I mean *black as your shoe*. I'm not black; I'm brown. Actually, the best word to describe me, I think, is colored. I am a colored woman or a Negro woman. Either one is okay. People dislike those words now. Today they use this term *African American*. It wouldn't occur to me to use that. I prefer to think of myself as an American—that's all!

You see, I think I'm just as good as anyone. That's the way I was brought up. I remember being aware that colored people were supposed to feel inferior. I knew I was a smart little thing, a personality, an individual—a human being. I couldn't understand how people could look at me and not see that, because it sure was obvious to me.

You know, white people were always looking for good colored maids and mammies. Why, sometimes white people would visit the campus, and they would point to Sadie and me and ask Mama if they could take one or the other of us with them. Mama would bristle. "Those girls are my daughters, and they aren't going anywhere," she would say. Mama did not want us to be maids.

Mama and Papa tried to protect us, but the real world was out there, and they couldn't shelter us forever. Papa had his newspapers, and he wouldn't let us see them, but we were nosy children, especially me. My grandpa, Mr. Miliam, used to say to Mama, "Nanny, every one of your children could have been detectives, especially Bessie."

It wasn't long before we learned the worst news imaginable: Colored folks were being murdered. They were being lynched. We would hear the teachers talking about some poor Negro just walking down the road in the wrong place at the wrong time. These rebby boys would just grab him and hang him from a tree, just for fun. It was like entertainment to those fellas.

Pretty much, these rebby boys left us alone at Saint Aug's. But Papa still insisted that my brothers be home by dark, and he taught them how to keep out of trouble. You see, sometimes they'd lynch a colored man who objected to being called uncle, which was one of the put-down ways white people referred to colored people. If a white woman said a colored man had looked at her in a certain way, that was the end of him. The rebby boys would come in the middle of the night and get him out of his bed and hang him up in front of his wife and children.

Lord, have mercy! I do not understand any of this. And it doesn't make any more sense to me now than it did then.

Sadie

I SOMETIMES think maybe we were a little too sheltered. Why, I wasn't allowed to go downtown by myself until I was a grown girl, and then I was always kind of jittery.

You can imagine that when it came time for me to graduate from Saint Aug's, I didn't want to leave. That campus was the only home I'd ever known. Lemuel also did not want to go out into the world. When he finished medical school and was fixing to get married, he had this idea he'd move his bride right in with us. But Papa said, "I'm sorry, Lemuel, but you can't live at home once you have a wife. This is your mama's house. We can't have two queens in one hive."

Papa expected me to leave home, too. At the time I graduated, in 1910, a degree from Saint Aug's qualified you to teach school. Many students went on to four-year colleges from there. Now, on graduation day Papa said to me, "Daughter, you are college material. You owe it to your nation, your race, and yourself to go. And if you don't, then shame on you!"

Well, it seemed to me that I had no choice. But Papa said, "Daughter, I have no money. But you must not take a scholarship. If you take a scholarship, you will be beholden to the people who gave you the money. You must make your own way."

So I started looking for teaching jobs, and I found out there was an opening for Jeanes supervisor, which involved visiting schools all over Wake County, North Carolina. Now, I was not quite twenty-one years old in 1910, which was awfully young to be applying for the position, but I got the job.

Jeanes supervisors were called that after a white woman named Jeanes who had started a fund to introduce domestic science to colored schools in many parts of the South. The colored schools were far inferior to the white schools. There were usually no facilities to teach domestic science, so I would borrow someone's kitchen, and once I got a class started, I would hire a teacher to take up where I left off. Now, I was just supposed to be in charge of domestic science, but they made me do the county superintendent's work. So I ended up actually in charge of all the colored schools in Wake County, although they didn't pay me to do that or give me any credit.

I continued to live at home because I was able to visit many of these schools on day-trips. I would go by train or by horse and buggy. Then my brother Lemuel returned from Philadelphia, where he had done his medical internship, and he had a car—the first one in our family. I learned to drive Lemuel's car, and naturally, since I had learned to drive, Bessie decided she needed to learn, too. It seems to me she landed Lemuel's car in a ditch while she was learning. Lemuel wasn't too happy.

I got to be a good driver, and when Mr. Booker T. Washington would come to visit Raleigh, I would drive him all around the county and show him my schools. He was so appreciative of the work I was doing. He was a great American, a gentleman—a lovely man.

As Jeanes supervisor, I saw for the first time what life was really like for my people. I realized that I was a child of privilege and that I must share my good fortune. I kept remembering what my papa always said: "Your mission is to help somebody. Your job is to help people." Yes, those words kept me going.

This was forty-five years after the Surrender, and most of these Negroes were in bad shape, child. They didn't know how to cook, clean, eat properly, or anything. Oftentimes learning to read and write for the children was not the top priority. Teaching people about food preparation—like how to can food—was more important. Also, they didn't know much about sanitation or hygiene, and the women didn't know how to take care of their newborn babies.

I know that I helped many people as Jeanes supervisor, and I am very proud of that. I inspired many people to get an education, and quite a few went on to Saint Aug's. A lot of the time what those folks needed was inspiration, a little encouragement. They looked up to me, and I showed them it was possible to live a better life.

Well, here I was, traveling around the countryside, a grown woman with professional responsibilities. Yet Papa was still in charge of my social life. He didn't want me to go out with any fresh boys, so he selected my gentleman friends. When I had a caller, we would sit in the parlor to talk. Papa would sit in the other room with his newspaper, and I am quite sure he was listening to every word.

I had one beau named Frank, who was particularly fond of me. He was a fellow student of Lemuel's, studying medicine at Shaw University. Papa used to get kind of annoyed with Frank because he talked too much and would keep talking even when Papa thought it was time for him to leave. We used to have to practically shove Frank out the door.

Now, I liked Frank a lot, but then one day Papa told me, "Sadie, you won't be seeing any more of Frank for now." It seems Lemuel had reported to Papa that Frank had been linked to some scandal involving a young nurse. Well, Frank was never able to clear his name to Lemuel's and Papa's satisfaction. I guess he really was involved somehow, but I never learned the details. All I know is that I never saw Frank again.

Well, here I am an old maid. Oops, I shouldn't say old maid 'cause it makes Bessie mad. Bessie says we're maiden ladies. Well, whatever we are, I have no regrets. I think Frank would have worried me to death. I've had a good life, child.

Bessie

I SUPPOSE Lemuel and Papa thought they were doing the right thing by Sadie, forbidding her to see Frank anymore, but I don't think it was right. She was a grown woman. She should have had a say. It was her choice to make, not theirs.

Don't you go thinking because we are maidens that Sadie and I didn't have lots of beaux. We were popular, good-looking gals, but I think we were too smart, too independent for most men. This was especially true for me when I went to teach in Boardman, North Carolina. I kind of overwhelmed those boys back in 1911!

After I graduated from Saint Aug's, I got the same speech from Papa that Sadie got—the one about going on to college, paying my own way, and so on. So I got a job as a teacher, doing the same thing as Sadie: saving money and helping my people.

I was twenty years old, and it was the first time I was away from home by myself. Papa took me to the train station in Raleigh, and I put on a brave front. But when that train pulled away from the station and I looked back and saw my papa standing there watching me, I thought I was going to die. I started to sob. Well, I'm embarrassed to say I created quite a commotion. The conductor came along and said, "What's the matter? Did somebody die?" Now, what'd he have to go and say that for? It was my girlhood that was dying, and I knew it.

I just kept crying until I was all cried out. Then I wiped up my face and sat up straight for the rest of the trip. I tried to remember what my grandpa, Mr. Miliam, told me about holding your head up high. "Bessie, don't ever be afraid to look somebody in the eye. You're just as good as anybody."

When I got to Boardman, I was completely pulled together. But honey, I was appalled by the place. It was a nothing town. All the men worked in the lumbermill, and all the people shopped at the company store. I was to stay with the Atkinsons in their home.

It turned out I was the most exciting thing that had happened to Boardman in about a hundred years. Those poor colored folks thought I was *something,* which was a big surprise to me. My students loved me so much they would build a fire in the stove before I arrived at school, and they all fought to carry my lunch and my books, especially the little boys. I don't know why my students loved me so much, because I was a dictator. But the children would follow me home after school, and Mrs. Atkinson had to run them off.

Now, the menfolk in Boardman were just smitten with Miss Bessie Delany. I was pretty and had a nice figure, but looking back, I think they were impressed by my self-confidence and the way I carried myself. Papa didn't call me Queen Bess for nothing. I was an educated girl from Raleigh, the daughter of an Episcopal priest. Mrs. Atkinson said, "Child, they've never seen the likes of you."

I remember walking through that town, and the colored men would just stop and stare. They wouldn't say a word; they'd just take off their hats. One time I passed by several men, and I turned and said, *"Just what are you looking at?"* They didn't answer. Finally one of them said, "Why, Miss Delany, we can't help it; you look just like a slice of heaven." And I said, "Well, I ain't *your* slice of heaven, so put your eyes back in yo' *head.*" Honey, I meant business.

When it came to men, I never gave them an inch. But it could get mighty lonely. The whole time I was in Boardman—from 1911 to 1913—I had but a single caller. One day Mrs. Atkinson said to me, "Miss Delany, a young man from the mill would like to pay a call on you." And I said, "Well, that would be all right."

So he came by, and we sat in the little front room of the Atkinsons' house while the Atkinsons sat in their bedroom listening. We chatted for a while. I remember telling him that history was my favorite subject at Saint Aug's. This poor fella probably had a fourth-grade education at best, and there I was yammering about Raleigh and the Saint Aug's campus. Well, he never came by again.

Life was hard for me in Boardman. On my first night there I said to Mrs. Atkinson, "I would like to take my bath now, please." I figured I'd have to bathe in a tin tub in the kitchen. That's what most folks did—those who didn't have nice plumbing. Well, I went into my room to change, and she knocked on the door. I opened it, and she handed me a pitcher and a bowl of water. That was it. Well, I learned you can bathe pretty well that way. It was a bit of a shock for Miss Bessie Delany of Raleigh, though.

The food we ate in Boardman was about the worst diet I have ever been on. I have always been a slim thing, but honey, I got fat while I was there. When I came home at Christmas, I weighed a hundred and fifty-three pounds. But I lost that weight eventually and never gained it back. Sadie says it was from eating all that fatback and collards and sweet potatoes in Boardman.

Those people didn't know the first thing about vitamins or minerals. They were so poor and ignorant. It was the same thing Sadie was running into as Jeanes supervisor in Wake County. Mama was worried about me, and she would send me these little care packages. She would go to a store in Raleigh called the California Fruit Company and buy some grapefruits and ship them to me.

Well, Mr. Atkinson had never seen a grapefruit before. He said, "Miss Delany, what is that ugly-looking piece of fruit?" Now, I gave him a piece, and he just puckered up and spit it out and said it was the worst, most sour, miserable thing he'd ever put in his mouth. I said, "Mr. Atkinson, if you're going to waste my grapefruit, then please give it back to me." He gave me the rest back gladly.

After two years in Boardman it was time for me to move on to a new teaching assignment. The people didn't want to see me go, but I was ready for a new challenge. So in 1913 I went to Brunswick, Georgia, to teach at Saint Athanasius School, an Episcopal school for colored children. I wanted to see the world!

Brunswick was a sophisticated place compared to Boardman. But it was on my way to my job in Brunswick that I came close to being lynched. You see, I had to change trains in Waycross, Georgia. I was sitting in the little colored waiting room at the station, and I took my hair down and was combing it. I was fixing myself up. I was going to my new job, and I wanted to look nice.

Well, there I was with my long hair down, when this white man opened the door to the colored waiting room. There was no one in there except me and two colored teachers from New York, who were traveling with me to Brunswick. The white man stuck his head in and started, well, leering at me. He was drunk, and he started mumbling things. And I said, "Oh, why don't you shut up and go wait with your own kind in the white waiting room?"

What happened next was kind of like an explosion. He slammed the door, and I could hear him shouting at the top of his lungs outside, "The nigger bitch insulted me."

The two colored teachers traveling with me slipped out the back without a word and made a beeline for the woods. They hid in the woods. I guess I can't blame them. A colored porter came in and whispered to me, "Good for you!" But then he ran out on me, too. He left me there by myself.

Well, I could see a crowd begin to gather on the platform, and I knew I was in big trouble. Papa always said, "If you see a crowd, you go the other way. Don't even hang around long enough to find out what it's about." Now, this crowd was outside, gathering for *me.*

By now there were dozens of white people in the crowd, and the white man kept yelling. I was just waiting for somebody to get a rope. Thousands of Negroes had been lynched for far less than what I had just done. But I just continued to sit on the bench combing my hair. Two things saved me: That glorious, blessed train rounded the bend, breaking up the crowd and giving me my way to get on out of there. And it helped that the white man was drunk as a skunk, and that turned off some of the white people.

You know what Sadie says? Sadie says I was a fool to provoke that white man. As if I provoked *him.* Honey, he provoked *me.* Sadie says she would have *ignored* him. I say, how do you ignore some drunk treating you like trash? She says, child, it's better to put up with it and live to tell about it. She says at the very least I should have run off into the woods with those other two teachers. She says I am lucky to be alive. But I would rather die than back down.

Part V

Harlem-Town

HARLEM in its heyday of the 1920s and early 1930s was the spiritual center of black America and the birthplace of a vibrant culture that came to be celebrated as the Harlem Renaissance. Writers such as Langston Hughes and James Weldon Johnson were creating the first substantial body of literature to chart the current of black life. Jazz was in full flower, and Harlem was the showcase for such pioneering composers and performers as Ferdinand "Jelly Roll" Morton, Louis Armstrong, Bessie Smith, and Edward Kennedy "Duke" Ellington.

The creative ferment of the Jazz Age made Harlem the undisputed capital of nightlife not just in New York but for all of America. Among its famous night spots were the Lenox Club, the Plantation Club, and scores more. One of Bessie Delany's patients owned the famous Small's Paradise, known for waiters who danced the Charleston while balancing full trays of drinks.

The excitement spilled out of the nightclubs and into the community. But despite its carefree, high-living image, Harlem had a stable, churchgoing side. Political leadership often sprang from the pulpits. The Reverend Adam Clayton Powell and later his son, Congressman Adam Clayton Powell, Jr., led the powerful Abyssinian Baptist Church, the wealthiest Negro Baptist congregation in the world.

Harlem was a magnet for an entire generation of young black Americans with dreams of a better life. By the early 1930s, there were more than two hundred thousand black people living in Harlem. Among them were nine of the Delany children, who would soon make a niche for themselves in Harlem society.

Sadie and Bessie

WE MADE our first trip to New York City with our mama in 1915. We took the train from Raleigh to Norfolk, then took a boat to New York, which cost us eight dollars each. The boat left Norfolk in the afternoon. We slept on cots on the open deck, and woke up just as the boat pulled into New York harbor.

On that first visit we could not get over the size of New York. Papa had been there once and had tried to describe it, but it was beyond our imagination. The bridges and buildings were on a massive scale compared to anything we had ever seen.

And there were so many different *kinds* of people from all over the world. In North Carolina there were white people, Negroes, and Indians. That was it. In New York there were Irish people, German, Jewish, Italian, and so on. And they ate different foods, and you could smell strange things cooking when you walked by people's apartments and their windows were open. And you'd hear these voices speaking languages. Well, you could only guess what exotic place they were from and what they were saying.

On that first trip we stayed with friends for a few days; then we went home. But we wanted more. So when we returned to Raleigh, we talked to Papa about us moving to New York to attend college. Our brother Harry was already there, working as a Pullman porter, saving money to attend New York University. By then we were grown women, twenty-four and twenty-six years old. So when a Presbyterian minister asked Mama, "Aren't y'all afraid to let those girls go up to Harlem-town?" Mama said, "No, I'm not afraid to let my girls go anywhere. We've taught them right from wrong, and if they don't do what's right, there's nothing we can do about it."

So we had Mama and Papa's blessing—sort of. Of the two of us it was Sadie who made the move first, in 1916, followed by Bessie a year and a half later. Eventually all of us Delany children, except Lemuel, moved to New York City.

It was awfully hard to find an apartment in Harlem then. There were a lot of colored folks coming to Harlem at the same time, looking for a new life. You'd go from one place to the next, and the super would say, "There's no room now; come back next month." And you'd come back, but somebody had always beat you to the punch.

So it was common for people to take in boarders. Our brothers were boarding over at the Williamses' house, and we Delany girls boarded with the Scotts. The Scotts were a West Indian family, rather well-to-do. Mr. Scott worked in a white bank, which was absolutely unheard of for a colored man in those days.

Mrs. Scott had taken us in as a favor to Mrs. Russell, who lived across the street and ran a boardinghouse, only it was full. Mrs. Russell had been a pupil of Mama's. But Mr. Scott really didn't want us boarders living in his home, and so the whole time we lived at the Scotts', we never once ate in the dining room. They made us eat in the kitchen. It wasn't ideal, but it was the best we could do.

Our brother Lucius was the first one of us to get an apartment, and he let us all move in with him. So there we were—Sadie, Bessie, Julia, Hubert, and Lucius—living together in a three-room apartment at 2505 Seventh Avenue, at the corner of 145th Street. This was in about 1919. Our share of the rent was nine dollars each.

Poor Lucius! It was his apartment, but his sisters were the boss. Sadie was the oldest and, therefore, the head of the household. It worked like this: when a decision had to be made, Sadie had the last word, but Bessie kept everybody in line.

Still, it wasn't always easy living with our brothers. They would take our brand-new stockings and wear them on their heads at night to straighten their hair. Did that ever make us mad!

Now, the only brother who wouldn't mind us one bit when he'd come to visit was Manross. He was stubborn as a mule. He took after Mr. Miliam, our white grandpa. If you tried to tell Manross what to do, he'd just stare at you.

Manross had been in the R.O.T.C. at Shaw University in Raleigh, and the next thing we knew, he had gotten swept up into World War I. Funny thing about that war: it happened overseas, but it created bloodshed among us here at home. A lot of white people did not think colored men would serve our country with dignity. They thought they'd be cowards. Well, they didn't know Manross.

All the colored veterans came back just as proud as they could be, strutting around Harlem and everywhere else in the country in their uniforms. Manross and his buddies thought they had proved themselves. They thought they would surely come home and be treated like citizens. Manross was very disappointed because white folks sometimes gave him dirty looks or made nasty remarks when he'd wear his uniform. Manross said, "What more do I have to do to prove I'm an American, too?"

But a lot of white people were mad. They were saying, "Who do these colored boys think they are?" There were riots in Harlem and lynchings in the South because white people wanted to put us back in our place.

While this mess was going on, we just worked like dogs, trying to improve ourselves and counting our blessings that we had the chance. As far as we were concerned, Harlem was as close to heaven as we were going to find on this earth.

Sadie

HARLEM—and all of New York, for that matter—was a happier place then. It was much safer. I used to walk through the parks without any trouble, and you didn't have to worry about somebody shooting at you. Still, it was a meaner place than Raleigh. One day I was looking out the window of the house where we were boarding when a man stopped and waved to me. So I smiled and waved back. And the landlady said to me, "Sadie Delany, what on earth are you doing? This is not North Carolina."

You see, in Raleigh when you'd walk down the street, people nodded at each other and said, "Good morning" or "Good evening." Men would tip their hat at you and didn't mean anything other than a little sign of respect. In New York it meant they wanted something else entirely. You were foolish to be friendly to strangers in New York.

When I first came to New York, I was so green I don't know how I survived. I was shy, but I was determined. I set my sights high. I sure didn't pick the easy way when I chose Pratt Institute. Back then, in 1916, they used to say about Pratt, "They'll either make an excellent teacher out of you or flunk you."

One problem was that I was lonely. There were just two of us colored girls in the domestic science division at Pratt Institute when I enrolled, and the other girl dropped out.

I had a difficult time at first because I really had to scramble in courses like chemistry. At Saint Aug's there were no chemistry labs, so I was weak in that area. That was a problem for a lot of colored students. Often our early training was not as good as the white students', because colored schools had no money. Then you had to struggle to keep up if you got into a white college, and white people would label you dumb.

I remember that I got an A on the chemistry final exam, but then the teacher gave me a C for the course. He said it was because I wouldn't raise my hand and participate in class. He said I was lazy. But I was a little shy, and I found chemistry hard, and I was afraid I'd give the wrong answer. So I kept my mouth shut. I protested the grade, though, because I felt an A on the final exam spoke for itself. They compromised with me, and I got a B.

Back then Pratt was a two-year college. After graduating, I enrolled at Columbia University's Teachers College. I was set on getting a four-year degree.

I was very happy at Columbia. Bessie had a harder time there when she enrolled in the dental school in 1919. I did not encounter as much prejudice. Maybe it was easier to accept a colored woman studying to be a teacher than learning to be a dentist.

As much as possible I kept a low profile at Columbia. Once, when I gave a presentation, the teacher said, "Why, Miss Delany, you act like you've been in the classroom all your life." Well, I had been, growing up at Saint Aug's. But I had sense enough to keep my mouth shut.

I had saved enough money for tuition and rent in New York, but in the summer I'd go home to Raleigh to work to boost up my savings account. When I graduated from Columbia in 1920, I actually went back to my old Jeanes supervisor job. I had this foolish idea I would get paid more, now that I had graduated from Columbia. I guess I was making about forty-five dollars a month, and out of that I had to pay my own expenses. I worked up my nerve, and I went to the man in charge and asked—very politely, of course—for more money. And he said, "Why Miss Delany, we can't give you more than we give the white supervisor."

Even though my original intention was to graduate from college in New York and return to North Carolina and help my people, I knew I had to return to New York to live. I figured I'd just have to help my people up *there.*

I HAD always dreamed I would become a medical doctor, but I ran out of time and money. I was in my late twenties already, and I would have needed a few more credits to get into medical school. I was worried that by the time I earned the money and took those classes, I'd be too old.

So I picked up some science courses at Shaw University with the intention of enrolling in a dental degree program in New York. My brother Harry was a dentist, and he was going to see if I could enroll at New York University, where he had graduated. But N.Y.U. would not take women in its dentistry program.

Instead, I enrolled at Columbia University. This was in the fall of 1919. There were eleven women out of a class of about a hundred and seventy. There were about six colored men. And then there was me. I was the only colored woman.

Most of the students at the dental school were self-assured city folk, and their families were paying their tuition. I never had the luxury of focusing completely on my studies. I always had money on my mind. I needed more, honey! I had saved money from my teaching years in the South, but it wasn't enough. I remember that I always wore an old brown sweater to my classes because I couldn't even afford a coat. One day my brother Harry surprised me. He bought me a beautiful coat with a small fur collar. The first time I wore it to class, the students stood up and applauded. In a way it was mean, because they were sort of making fun of me. But I didn't care. No, sir!

My brothers were having the same difficulty with money, so they all worked their way through college as Pullman porters, which was one of the few jobs a Negro man could get. Hubert used to joke that he had earned an M.B.C. degree—master's of baggage carrying.

As a woman, you couldn't be a Pullman porter, and I refused to work as a maid. So in the summer I would go with my little sister Julia, who had come up from Raleigh to study at The Juilliard School, to look for factory jobs. And you know what? They would want to hire Julia because she was lighter than me. But we said it was both of us or neither of us, and sometimes we'd get the job.

Once, we had an assembly-line job where they made sewing needles, and our job was to package them in these little batches so they were ready for sale. Then for a while we worked as ushers at a movie house. The pay was twelve dollars a week, and we saw all these wonderful movies. My favorite star was Bing Crosby. Lord, we had fun. But I was always treated worse than Julia, and it was made clear that it was because I was darker-skinned.

It was probably a good thing that I was so determined or I never would have made it through dental school. I had a few girlfriends, but I never told any of them that I was about ten years older. I never talked about where I came from or my teaching years.

The reason I was so secretive is that I wanted to be taken seriously. Most of the women were not taken seriously. Truth is, it was just after World War I and a lot of men were still overseas or killed, so those girls were just looking for husbands. But not me. I was there to learn.

Before I enrolled in dental school, I had a long talk with my mama. She said, "You must decide whether you want to get married someday or have a career. Don't go putting all that time and effort into your education and career if you think you want to get married."

It didn't occur to anyone that you could be married *and* have a career. Well, I set my sights on the career. I thought, Why give up my freedom and independence to take care of some man? In those days a man expected you to be in charge of a perfect household, to look after his every need. Honey, I wasn't interested!

I studied very hard in dentistry school. My brother Harry—he was called Hap once he moved to New York—helped me out. He was a sweet brother. He loaned me some dental instruments, which were very expensive.

I remember like yesterday the first time our class had to do dissections. This was at the morgue at Bellevue Hospital in New York. The first two years of dental school at that time were identical to medical school, and we all had to do them. Well, all the girls in the class were just a-squealing and a-screaming and a-carrying on. And I strode in there like I was born to do it. They all said, "Look at that Bessie Delany. Why, she sure isn't scared." Truth is, I was a wreck. I had never touched a dead body before. It was pretty disgusting, but I was a great actress. I was determined to be the best dentist there ever was, and I knew I had to get through this.

I'd dissect a cadaver any day, rather than have to deal with some of those old white professors. To be fair, some of them treated me just fine, especially the dean of students. He was particularly supportive. But one instructor really had it out for me. There was an assignment where he failed me, yet I knew my work was good. One of my white girlfriends said, "Bessie, let me turn in your work as if it was mine, and see what grade he gives it."

I'll tell you what happened, honey. She passed with my failed work. That was the kind of thing that could make you crazy, as a Negro. It's no wonder some of us have stopped trying altogether. But as my papa used to say, "Don't ever give up. Remember, they can segregate you, but they can't control your mind. Your mind's still yours." Ain't it the truth.

Let me tell you something. Even on my graduation day at Columbia I ran into prejudice. It was the sixth of June, 1923. There I was, getting my doctor of dental surgery degree, and I was on top of the world. But you know what? The class selected me as the marshall, and I thought it was an honor. And then I found out it was because no one wanted to march beside me in front of their parents. It was a way to get rid of me. The class marshall carried the flag and marched out front, alone.

I suppose I should be grateful to Columbia that at that time they let in colored people. Well, I'm not. They let me in, but they beat me down for being there. I don't know how I got through that place, except when I was young, nothing could hold me back. No, sir! I thought I could change the world. It took me a hundred years to figure out I *can't* change the world. I can only change Bessie. And honey, that ain't easy, either.

Sadie

WHEN Papa became bishop in 1918, people were mighty impressed. His accomplishment was so extraordinary, I still wonder how he did it. He put up with a lot to get where he got. One time, not long after Papa was consecrated to the bishopric, he did a service at Christ Church in Raleigh. It was a white, segregated church. Our family attended, and do you know what happened? We had to sit in the balcony, which was built for slaves. And we were not given the privilege of Communion.

Left and below, the Delany sisters' paternal grandparents, Thomas Sterling Delany and his wife, Sarah. Bottom, the Henry Beard Delany family circa 1898. Bessie is seated on the floor at left, with Sadie standing behind her.

Maternal great-grandfather Jordan Motley, above, born around 1810

Maternal great-grandmother Eliza Logan, born around 1812

Above, maternal grandparents, Martha Logan, circa 1860, and James Miliam. Six feet four and always armed, he was said to be the "meanest-looking man in Pittsylvania County, Virginia."

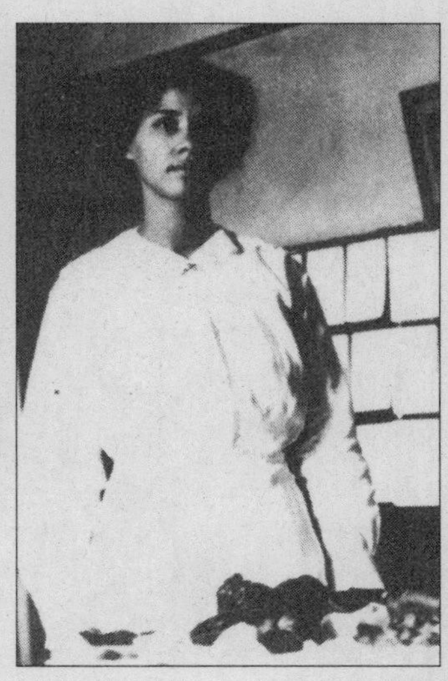

Sadie, above, in Greek class at Saint Aug's around 1908. Bessie, right, in her home economics classroom, Brunswick, Georgia, 1914.

Left, Sadie's graduation picture, Columbia University, 1920. Below, Bessie's yearbook photo, Columbia, 1923. Background shows the intersection of Seventh Avenue and 135th Street in Harlem, 1930. Dr. Bessie's dental office was in the first building at left, one flight up.

Above, Harlem, 1928. The last family portrait before Bishop Delany's death. Standing (from left): Manross, Lucius, Hubert, Hap, Sam, and Lemuel. Seated (from left): Julia, Sadie, Bishop Delany, Mrs. Delany, Bessie, and Laura.

Somehow Papa always endured this kind of degradation. He saw the hypocrisy, but he felt that gently, slowly, he was making true progress for himself and his people, and he was at peace with that. I learned a lot from my papa about coping with institutionalized racism. The way to succeed was simple: You had to be better at what you did than any of your white competition. But you couldn't be too smug about it, or white folks would feel threatened.

I got my first teaching job in New York in the fall of 1920. I think I was paid fifteen hundred dollars for the year. It was at P.S. 119 in Harlem, which was an elementary school—mostly colored. This was a typical assignment for a colored teacher. They certainly did not want us in schools where the children were white. The parents would object. One way the principals kept us out was to say they could not hire anyone with a southern accent, because it would be damaging to the children. Well, most of us colored teachers at the time had southern accents. So it was just a way of keeping us out.

When my southern accent was considered a problem, I found a way around that. I signed up with a speech coach—a white woman in Manhattan. I don't think she had too many colored clients. I remember that when I would go to her apartment for the lessons, the doorman made me take the freight elevator. I didn't make a fuss, because I wanted those speech lessons.

You had to decide: Am I going to change the world, or am I going to change me? Or maybe change the world a little bit, just by changing me? If I can get ahead, doesn't that help my people?

I was very ambitious. I wanted to teach at a high school because it was considered a promotion and it paid better. But I had to be a little clever—Bessie would say sneaky—to find ways to get around these brick walls they set up for colored folks. So I asked around quietly for some advice. A friend of my brother Hubert's who worked for the board of education suggested a plan, which I followed.

This is what I did: I applied for a high school position, and when I reached the top of the seniority list after three years, I received a letter in the mail saying they wished to meet with me in person. At the appointment they would have seen I was colored, and found some excuse to bounce me down the list. So I skipped the appointment and sent them a letter, acting like there was a mix-up. Then I just showed up on the first day of classes.

Child, when I showed up that day—at Theodore Roosevelt High School, a white high school—they just about died when they saw me. A colored woman! But my name was on the list to teach there, and it was too late for them to send me someplace else. The plan worked. Once I was in, they couldn't figure out how to get rid of me.

So I became the first colored teacher in the New York City system to teach domestic science on the high school level. I spent the rest of my career teaching at excellent high schools. Between 1930 and 1960, when I retired, I taught at Theodore Roosevelt High School, which is on Fordham Road in the Bronx; then at Girls' High School in Brooklyn; and finally at Evander Childs High School, which is on Gun Hill Road in the Bronx.

Plus I got a night job—at Washington Irving High School in lower Manhattan—teaching adults. This was something I really wanted to do. The way I got the job was that the girl who had it before me complained a lot, was late a lot, and would ask me to substitute for her. Eventually they just hired me instead of her.

Meanwhile, I was studying for my master's degree in education at Columbia, which I completed in 1925. I was a busy gal, but I was happy being busy. My classes were usually very demanding because as a colored teacher, I always got the meanest kids. Except once. That was the year they had me mixed up with a white woman whose name also was Delany. It was kind of funny. She was just furious because she got all these tough girls and I got the easy ones—college-bound and motivated. Tell you the truth, I did not mind the tough kids. I loved them all.

Bessie

I WAS known in the Negro community as Dr. Bessie, to distinguish me from my brother Hap, who was known as Dr. Delany. There was a time in Harlem, in the 1920s, '30s, and '40s, when just about every living soul knew of Dr. Bessie. My patients would go on vacation and send postcards addressed only to "Dr. Bessie, New York City," and I would get those cards.

Hap was four years younger than me, but he was already starting his practice by the time I got to dental school. When I graduated, he invited me to share an office with him and another dentist, Dr.

Chester Booth, at 2305 Seventh Avenue—that's at the corner of 135th Street. We were on the second floor, above the Corn Exchange Bank.

This was the center of Harlem. From the office window you could see everything that was going on. Harlem was like a beehive, with people running every which way, going to work, school, or entertainment. It was a positive place.

Hap and I loved having our offices in the middle of everything. After a while we moved next door—to 2303 Seventh Avenue—where we shared a suite of offices with our brother Lucius, who was an attorney, along with a Negro real estate agent, and Dr. MacDonald, a Negro dentist from Trinidad. We had our own X-ray lab, a technician, and two mechanics who made dentures and bridges. I was the only woman among the bunch of us, and I ran the show. On the day the rent was due, I'd say, "Okay, fellas, pay up." Somehow, among all those men, I ended up being the boss.

In those days many people simply would not go to a woman dentist. There were so very few women dentists at all, never mind colored women dentists. Why, I was only the second Negro woman licensed to practice in New York.

It was bad enough to be discriminated against by white people because I was colored. But then my own people would discriminate against me because I was a woman. Two times I remember that men patients of mine insisted that Hap come and pull their teeth. One man said to me, "Can you pull teeth with those little hands?" And I said, "Do you really want to find out?" That sexism was a nasty thing to deal with. But once a person had been my patient, they'd always come back. The word got out: that colored woman dentist has a gentle touch.

Even then, of course, there were many dentists who would not take colored patients. One time after graduation a white classmate of mine from Columbia called me up and said he was sending over a patient. At first I thought he was doing me a favor, but then he mentioned that it was his maid. And I realized he didn't want to work on her mouth, because she was colored. So I said to him, "You are not a doctor of dentistry. You are a doctor of segregation." I yelled at him so loud he hung up. Well, his maid came over, and of course I helped her. But I never spoke to him again.

And there were those who only wanted the money. Some dentists would even do poor quality work just to make the patient uncomfortable so that he'd have to come back. It would never have occurred to me to do that. No, sir! When I started my practice in 1923, I charged two dollars for a cleaning, two dollars for an extraction, five dollars for a silver filling, and ten dollars for a gold filling. When I retired in 1950, I was still charging the same rate. I never raised my rates, because I was getting by okay. I was always very proud of my work, and that was enough for me.

I never turned anyone away because they couldn't pay me. Back when I was a young dentist, a child could not enroll in New York City public schools without a dental exam. This was tricky for a lot of poor colored parents because they couldn't afford it. Honey, I must have done thousands of those dental exams without charge.

Not all the patients were poor. Hap and I had separate practices, and he had a large number of famous people, such as Walter White of the NAACP and entertainers like Bojangles Robinson and Alberta Hunter, who was one of the nicest women I ever knew. But some of Hap's jazz friends were annoying because they always wanted to use the phone. I still remember the number. It was the most well-used phone in Harlem. Once, the bill was one hundred dollars, and I nearly fainted dead on the floor. That was a lot of money in those days, and those jazz folks never did chip in to pay us back. So you know what I did? I went and had a pay phone put in.

I had a few famous patients of my own, including Ed Small, the nightclub owner. I also took care of James Weldon Johnson, and once he gave me a signed copy of a book of poetry he had just published. My patients were as nice to me as I was to them.

But there were people who couldn't stand the very idea of a colored woman being a dentist, and they weren't shy about letting me know. Once, about 1925, I went to a medical conference at the Hotel Pennsylvania in Manhattan. I went up to the front desk and identified myself as a dentist who was to attend the meeting, and this white fella looked at me like I was some little monkey that had just fallen out of a tree and landed in his soup and ruined his day. I asked him for directions to my meeting. Yes, he gave me directions—to the *men's toilet.*

When I found myself standing in front of the men's room instead of the conference room, I was so filled with rage that I couldn't move. Fortunately, one of my former classmates—he happened to be white—saved me from total humiliation. He saw me standing there and said, "Bessie Delany, what in the world are you doing *here?*" And he just took my arm and escorted me to the conference like I was the Queen of England.

That day was one of the lowest points of my life, but I didn't have time to dwell on it. I often worked about fifteen hours a day. Wednesday was supposed to be my day off, but often I spent it covering for Hap while he and Dr. Booth ran the Harlem Dental Clinic, which they founded with the help of the Urban League.

During the week I had no free time for myself. I had to get up at daybreak and go to the office and clean and disinfect it, since I was always too exhausted at the end of the day to sterilize things properly, and I couldn't afford a cleaning lady. To save money, I walked ten blocks to work rather than ride the trolley or the subway, which cost five cents. I'd walk home again after cleaning the office, then bathe and walk back to the office in time to open up at nine o'clock, looking fresh out of the bandbox.

I know it sounds like I *lived* at my office, but I did make room in my life for relaxation. If I hadn't, I wouldn't have lived this long. Saturday was often a day for fun, and sometimes I'd go shopping with Sadie or on a picnic with a beau. Occasionally I'd be real naughty and go to the horse races on Long Island. I would bet a little money—say, five dollars. But I always won. So did Sadie. We studied the horses carefully before the race, and since we grew up around animals, we knew which ones were winners.

I guess our most favorite pastime of all was baseball. We weren't too far away from the team that became the Yankees, but they were slow to integrate, so we weren't interested in them. We were really Giants fans. The day I heard they were moving out to San Francisco, well, I was beside myself with sorrow. I said, "How can they do this to me?" I was a-carrying on like somebody had up and died.

Another thing we used to do was go to the old Bronx opera house, where they used to preview Broadway plays. You could see the best musicals New York had to offer, and it only cost fifty cents if you sat in the balcony. I remember being there once with Papa, who must have come up from Raleigh with Mama to see us. Papa was nervous because it was Lent and he didn't think he should be at the old Bronx opera house. He said, "What if someone sees me?" Papa always did care about appearances. But I think it was because he had to; it was part of getting ahead. White people were watching you all the time, just waiting for you to make a mistake. So we not only *lived* a clean life, we wanted to be sure people *knew* that we did.

This is a burden that white people do not have, I think. It always seemed to me that white people were judged as individuals. But if a Negro did something stupid or wrong, it was held against *all* of us.

All I ever wanted in my life was to be treated as an individual. I have succeeded to some extent. At least I'm sure that in the Lord's eyes I am an individual. I am not a colored person or a Negro person in God's eyes. I am just me. The Lord won't hold it against me that I'm colored, because He made me that way. He thinks I am beautiful. And so do I, even with all my wrinkles. I am beautiful!

Sadie

ONE thing that happened to a lot of colored folks when they moved to Harlem was that they got a little too big for their britches. When they'd go back to visit their folks in the South, the men acted like dudes and the women acted like they thought they were the Queen of Ethiopia.

Well, I guess we thought we were a little special, too, but Mama and Papa kept us in line. The first time I went home, I said darn in front of my mama, and she gave me a piece of her mind. She said, "Is that what you've learned up there in New York? You've learned how to swear?" She shamed me good. I never swore again.

Well, we heard a few racy words in Harlem, child. Harlem was the playground for the rich. You couldn't help but run into flashy Negroes and high-living white folks. From 1920 to 1933 Prohibition was going on, and you couldn't drink legally, but that didn't stop anybody.

Being good girls, Bessie and I did not venture too far into the jazz scene. We didn't want to have anything to do with smooth-talking men and their fast women. If we went to a nightclub, it was always with a proper escort. Usually we went to places like Ed Small's. Once, Bessie went to the Cotton Club, which was hard to do because it was a white folks' club. Bessie got in because she had a beau who worked there.

Our brother Hubert became friendly with many famous entertainers. Eventually he bought a weekend house upstate, and people like Cab Calloway used to go up there to visit.

Over the years, through friends or through Hubert, we met entertainers like Ethel Waters, Duke Ellington, and Lena Horne. We were acquainted with these people, but our circle of close friends was the professional class. For example, one of the frequent guests at our home was Mr. William Kelly, the editor of the *Amsterdam News,* a very influential Negro newspaper that is still published in New York today.

Mr. Kelly never passed up an invitation for our cooking. He used to say he felt right at home except for one thing: he never saw anything like the way we Delanys always cleaned our plates. We used to laugh and tell him, "If you'd grown up in a family of ten children that had no money, you'd be in the habit of cleaning your plate, too."

We took great pride in preparing and serving meals for company. We had people over for dinner so often that for years we kept a journal of what we had served to whom, and when, so that we wouldn't accidentally cook the same thing twice in a row for a guest.

The whole time in Harlem, we lived the same way that we did in Raleigh. We didn't change our values or behavior one bit. Every Sunday was the Lord's day, and you could find us, sure as daylight, at Saint Martin's Episcopal Church.

Knowing that Mama and Papa were counting on us to behave like ladies put the pressure on us to be good. We were very proud of the Delany name, and because of our self-discipline it came to mean in Harlem what it had meant in North Carolina—that is, it stood for integrity.

We all relied on each other. Throughout the years we lived in Harlem—from World War I until Bessie and I moved to the Bronx after World War II—all the brothers and sisters saw each other at least once a day. Most often this was at the dental office. It was like a revolving door of Delanys.

We even continued to live together. Around 1926 we all chipped in money, and Hap took out a mortgage for some cooperatives on 121st Street. Bessie and I, along with our sisters Julia and Laura, lived in one apartment on the second floor. Our brother Sam lived next door, and our brother Hap and his family lived upstairs.

These were long, narrow apartments, like railroad flats. On holidays there wasn't room for a sit-down dinner for the whole family, so our younger brothers and sisters would have dinner in their own apartments and come by our place later. At Christmas we'd serve coffee, fruit, and waffles with whipped cream all day long, until no one could eat any more. One Christmas, Hap said he was going to come by and fix us some eggnog. I said, "Come on over, but don't bother with the eggnog, 'cause I hate the stuff." I remembered when Papa gave me a little way back when. Only, Papa gave me eggnog without any liquor in it, of course. Hap laughed and said, "Girl, you ain't never had no real eggnog." So he came over and made the real thing—with liquor—and yes, it was mighty good.

Bessie

BY THE mid-'20s my office had become a meeting place for Negro activists in Harlem, including E. Franklin Frazier. [E. Franklin Frazier (1894–1962) was a sociologist noted for his groundbreaking studies on the Negro family and race relations.] I met Frazier while we were both at Columbia. He later married Lemuel's wife's sister. I suppose I could have married him, but as I've said, I was not interested in marriage, so Frazier and I remained lifelong friends.

One time I encouraged a friend of Frazier's named Albert Robinson to fight back over a problem he was encountering in a sociology class at Columbia. He was a graduate student. There was this white professor who told the class that Negroes were inferior to white people, and he demonstrated this with IQ tests taken by children of different races. Robinson, who was colored but looked white, was just incensed. I suggested that he borrow two of Hap's little children to prove that professor wrong. So Robinson brought these two little Delanys to the class and challenged the professor to prove they were stupid. And the professor said fine, let them take the IQ test. And you know what? Those two little Delanys scored much higher than the white children.

Frazier and Robinson were real big on staging sit-ins at lunch counters of white restaurants in Harlem that wouldn't serve colored people. The whites resented the Negroes taking over Harlem, but eventually all of them had to serve Negroes or go out of business, because after a while there was nobody left but Negroes. White folks had run out of Harlem like fleas from a dead dog.

One time I got tired of listening to Frazier and his friends planning another sit-in. This was about 1925. They had just rereleased *The Birth of a Nation,* which was a very mean-spirited film which degraded Negroes. It was showing at the Capitol Theater in Manhattan.

So I said to Frazier, "How can y'all sit around here planning those silly sit-ins when they're showing *Birth of a Nation* at the Capitol? I don't know about you, but I'm going down there tonight and protest. And if you don't join me, well, shame on you!"

Well, I guess I inspired them. But what happened is kind of funny—at least to me. Hap had a patient with an emergency, and I stayed to help, so we were late. Well, we got there just in time to see the cops throwing poor Frazier and Robinson, along with a bunch of other protesters, into the police wagon.

The next day those boys chewed me out good. They came to my office and said, "You convinced us to protest, and then you didn't show up. You have a lot of nerve." And I said, "Well, Hap and I did show up. It's just that y'all were too busy getting yourselves arrested to notice." They didn't think it was too funny.

Honey, all you had to say was the word protest, and I was there. I marched in more protests in New York City than I care to remember. It's a wonder I didn't wear out my feet.

One time I participated in a protest march for Negro rights that went from Harlem down to Fifty-ninth Street. When I ran home from my office to change my clothes, I couldn't find any clean stockings in my drawer. So I did something we never ever did in our family: I helped myself to a pair of Sadie's stockings *without asking.* During the march I wore a hole in Sadie's stockings, and when I got back later, I explained what happened and she let it go, on the condition that I replace those stockings with a new pair. But I just realized after all this time that I never did buy her a new pair. She never said a word about it all this time. She is really a very sweet sister.

Sadie never did like marches and protests. She didn't like confrontations. So I told her, "Well, you gave *something* for the cause after all. Your stockings!"

There were a lot of colored people like Sadie. Really there were two extremes. On the one hand, you had Booker T. Washington, a smoother of the waters. Mr. Washington's goals were modest for his race. He wanted you to be literate, to own your forty acres and a mule. Sadie was more like Booker T. Washington.

And on the other hand, you had W.E.B. Du Bois, a militant. I can still see his face. He was a brown-skinned good-looking man, with a mustache and very intelligent-looking eyes. Dr. Du Bois was always speaking out against one thing or another, especially about lynchings in the South. Many people thought his approach was too fast, too threatening, and therefore dangerous for Negroes.

I believed in Dr. Du Bois's approach. I would have given life or limb to the cause. I wanted justice for my people or at least a better life. Sometimes colored women were not welcome in the movement, though. You got the message that some of the colored *men* thought the colored *women* should not be involved. Too bad. I was there whether they liked it or not. You couldn't keep me at home.

I was torn between two issues—colored rights and women's rights. But it seemed to me that no matter how much I had to put up with as a woman, the bigger problem was being colored. People looked at me, and the first thing they saw was *Negro,* not *woman.* So racial equality, as a cause, won in my heart.

But one of the happiest days of my life was back in 1920, when women got the right to vote. Sadie and I registered to vote immediately, and we have never missed a chance to vote since. Now the people at the polls have come to know us. They say, "Here come the Delany sisters. We knew you'd get here, one way or another."

Sadie

PEOPLE think of the 1920s as the good old days, but of course there were many of the same problems we have now—except then we didn't have this widespread drug problem or this thing called AIDS. Still, there was terrible poverty, even in our own family, mostly among our relatives down south.

Among my students in New York City there were plenty of children, white and colored, who had problems. There was one girl who comes to mind from P.S. 119. All the girls made fun of her because she had this mark, like a dark ring, around her neck. Well, it was obvious to me that it was just plain old *dirt*. When there were no other children around, I asked her about it, and she said, "My mama says it's a birthmark."

I said, "Child, I don't think it is. Would you like me to try and fix it?" So she stayed after school, and I took her into the girls' room and cleaned her neck. The next day she said, "Miss Delany, my mama said to thank you so much for cleaning up my neck."

Now, I think that's kind of funny. Imagine not knowing that your child's neck is dirty. Well, there are a lot of people who weren't raised properly themselves, so how can they teach their children right? Sometimes it's neglect; sometimes it's just ignorance. And what people don't know will really hold them back.

That's why you need home economics. Back in the '20s it was called domestic science. It was nutrition, cooking and canning, sewing, hygiene—anything you can think of that makes a home a proper, healthy environment.

It was domestic science that brought me the greatest accomplishment of my life: saving Cousin Daisy from dying. Cousin Daisy was Mama's cousin in Virginia. She was a granddaughter of Aunt Pat—the one who had her baby by the side of the road. Well, one day we got a letter that Cousin Daisy was sick. The white doctor in Danville said she had pellagra, and there was nothing could be done. Although she was still fairly young, she was going to die.

Pellagra was a disease that you got from not eating enough vegetables and fruit. First your hair fell out; then you'd get weak and not be able to walk, and eventually you had one foot in the grave.

Back then, people were just beginning to understand the importance of vitamins and minerals. As a teacher of domestic science, I kept up to date on the new developments in nutrition. One day I saw in the newspaper that Dr. Carlton Fredericks, a scientist who worked with the man who had discovered vitamin B-12, was going to visit New York City. So I invited him to speak at my school.

After his talk I took him aside and told him all about Cousin Daisy down in Virginia. I said, "Please, can you help me?" And he told me exactly what to do. So I went and bought these liquid vitamins at a store in New York. I shipped them to Daisy, along with a schedule for taking them. I also drew up menu plans for her of what I thought she should eat. She was eating too much fatback and corn bread—things like that.

Well, that old white doctor in Danville was wrong. There *was* something could be done for Cousin Daisy. With those vitamins and my meal plans she started to get a little better. Then she got a lot better. And her hair even grew back.

Once we realized that Cousin Daisy was going to live after all, Bessie and I had a little talk. Bessie said, "Sadie, now that you've saved Cousin Daisy, you are responsible for her life." So I sent those vitamins, plus twenty dollars a month for food, until Cousin Daisy died. I think she was eighty-three when she passed on.

It's only now that I'm telling anyone about how I helped Cousin Daisy. I never told anyone at the time except Bessie. The way we were brought up, it was only natural for Bessie and me to help other people. It was the example that was set by the good Lord Jesus. It was also the example set by Mama and Papa.

Bessie

IN APRIL 1928 Lemuel sent a telegram: COME HOME QUICK, PAPA'S VERY ILL. I thought, Lord, have mercy. We're going to lose him. It was a shock. None of us had died in a long, long time, and I guess we thought none of us ever would.

I did not get to Raleigh in time to see Papa. He died peacefully at home. I saw his body, and the only thing that looked like my papa was his hands. He had beautiful hands, and when I saw those hands, I realized it was true, that he was gone from this earth.

All my brothers came, and for a long time people remembered how those six Delany boys—three on each side—carried Papa's coffin to the chapel. They were tall good-looking boys, and it was quite a sight, the way they lifted Papa's coffin up on their shoulders.

Now that Papa was gone, Lemuel was the only one left in Raleigh, and so Mama wanted to be with the bunch of us in New York. I'm sure Mama had mixed feelings about leaving Raleigh because other than her hometown, outside Danville, Virginia, she had never lived anywhere else. She had been there for almost fifty years, living right on the campus of Saint Aug's, where she had been a college student back in the 1880s.

I stayed behind in Raleigh to help Mama pack her things, which was very hard, since she had so many belongings and memories to let go of. The worst part was the day she wanted to burn all of her love letters to Papa. He had tied them up with a ribbon in a neat little bundle. I didn't want her to burn those love letters, but Mama's like me. You can't talk her out of anything. So I watched from the window while she built a fire outside and then read each letter and put it in the fire. And these little black bits of ashes would blow around her. Lord, it was awful. I wouldn't relive that day for anything.

Fortunately, I had persuaded her to keep Papa's papers from his years as a teacher and clergyman. I packed them in suitcases and instructed my brother Hubert to carry them up to New York. But Hubert became so attached to those papers that Mama and I could not get them away from him. I would say to him, "Hubert, you give me those papers." And he would say, "Oh, Bessie, I can't give them up." This was an ongoing fuss that Hubert and I had until he died recently, when he was just shy of ninety years old.

There wasn't a soul in Harlem who didn't know my brother Hubert. He was very active in the NAACP. He was an assistant United States attorney for the Southern District of New York. He prosecuted five hundred cases and lost only two.

In 1929 Hubert ran for Congress in the Twenty-first Congressional District in Harlem. My dental office was his campaign headquarters, and they hung a banner, HUBERT DELANY FOR CONGRESS! in the big plate-glass window looking out over Seventh Avenue.

Hubert won the Republican primary, but he lost the general election. Still, he won the admiration of Fiorello La Guardia, who sort of took him under his wing. Mayor La Guardia appointed Hubert as tax commissioner for Manhattan in 1934, and justice of the domestic relations court in 1942. I remember during the 1935 race riot in Harlem that Hubert and Mayor La Guardia walked through the streets to try to quiet things down.

Hubert may have been the most famous of my brothers, but they all followed in my papa's footsteps, becoming good family men with successful careers—real leaders of the community. Papa was such an excellent role model for his children. I could understand Hubert's attachment to Papa's papers because all of us felt the same way. Why, I'd be nothing without my papa!

Sadie

PAPA'S death hit me hard; it hit us all hard. I didn't realize how safe I felt in this world because of Papa. But even as a grown woman, I was still something of a mama's child. I loved to be in the company of my mama, and I would just do anything for her.

While Papa was still alive, Mama had never seen much of the world at all. She had the whole world on her shoulders as the bishop's wife and being the matron at Saint Aug's. So after she moved up to New York, she was ready to go places. Even when she was very elderly, all you had to do was say, "Let's go," and she'd say, "Just let me get my hat."

Some of the happiest days of my life were going on trips with Mama—especially when we went abroad in the summer of 1930. We signed up for a tour that was run by a white man in Washington, D.C., who had a lot of colored clients. We took a ship out of New York and went to London, then on to Germany, Italy, France, Russia, Lithuania, Estonia, and Latvia.

The most memorable moment of the trip came in London, when we went to see Paul Robeson in *Othello.* Paul's performance in the play was legendary because he interpreted Othello from the perspective of a Negro man, which was a very important breakthrough in the history of theater. When Paul heard Mama and I were there, he was ecstatic. He had us brought backstage right away. He said it was so good to see some Delanys from Harlem. He seemed a little homesick.

When Mama and I were in Russia, after visiting London, we thought it was a most interesting country, but poor. I remember maids admiring our clothes at a hotel. And I remember that we were served cabbage soup at a hotel, and Mama and I laughed because in the South that is known as pot liquor. I wanted to go out and buy us some fruit, but it was so expensive—a ruble for a single pear.

Then in 1932 Mama and my little sister Laura and I went with Hubert and a man friend of his by car out to Los Angeles to see the Olympics. Los Angeles was sunny and clean, and you could hop in the car and go to the beach in no time. It took us a few days to understand the climate. We learned the hard way that it was cold in the morning but would get hot as a stove by midday. At first we were dressed all wrong, but we got the hang of it.

We would get up early in the morning and go to the Olympic events all day long. I especially loved the track-and-field meets. We were proud of the achievements of the Negro athletes, and it was very inspiring to see them represent America.

When we drove out to Los Angeles, we went the northern route across the United States—through the Great Plains—but on the way back we went the southern route. We wanted to see as much of our country as we possibly could. But in the South, Hubert was worried that a carload of well-dressed Negroes from New York in a big shiny car would attract the kind of attention we didn't need. He talked to people ahead of time about where to stay and where not to stop, so we didn't run into any problems.

A popular vacation resort in those days was Niagara Falls. Mama had her heart set on going up there, so of course I took her. To get a good view of the falls, we went up in a biplane—you know, one of those open-top little airplanes. We sent a postcard to Bessie, and she just blew her top. When we got back, she chewed me out good. She said to me, "What on earth were you thinking, letting Mama go up in that biplane? She's an old lady."

But you know, if Mama had her mind set on doing something, you couldn't stop her. And it sure was a beautiful view of Niagara Falls from up there. I will never forget it. It was like being a bird, flying through the sky. I turned around and looked back at Mama, and she was just sitting there smiling. She was having the time of her life, and that made me so very happy.

Bessie

LET me tell you a little story. Down south somebody asked an old Negro man why he wouldn't fly in an airplane. And this is what he said: "When you're in a train and it breaks down, well, there you is. But when you're in a plane and it breaks down, there you *ain't*."

That's exactly how I feel. I never did like to fly in airplanes. That's why I was so annoyed by Sadie taking Mama up in that biplane over those waterfalls. What on earth were they thinking? I think Sadie should have talked Mama out of it.

Mama and Sadie were always going off on these trips together. It worried me to death, getting these letters and postcards from those two from who knows where. But they were natural travelers. Now me, I like to sleep in my own bed at night, bathe in my own bathtub, eat my own food.

In 1932 I took the one big trip of my life. A patient of mine, Mary Watson, invited me to visit her homeland, Jamaica. We went by boat. One of my patients said before I left, "Dr. Bessie, you won't get seasick if you fold a newspaper across your stomach and tie a piece of string around your waist to hold it up." Now, I thought that was the silliest thing I ever heard. But when my patient said, "I'll pay for your trip if it doesn't work," I realized he meant business.

Well, we got in a terrible storm on that trip, and everybody on the boat got sick as a dog. Except me. I had a newspaper tied around my stomach. Me and the captain, we were the only two people who ate our dinner that night.

The boat stopped overnight in Cuba on the way to Jamaica. We got off and had dinner with an old beau of my mama's, a Cuban Negro who had attended Saint Aug's. I remember that the houses came right up to the street in Cuba. The homes did not have porches, which seemed a crime to me.

The next morning we went on to Jamaica, and oh, what a beautiful place that was. But you know, it was different racially from America. In Jamaica there were two official classes of Negroes: white Negroes and black Negroes. The white Negroes were higher class and had more privileges in society.

Now, my friend Mary was a very dark-skinned girl. And because I was lighter-skinned than Mary, I was treated like royalty by the higher-class Negroes. I wasn't *black*, and I was a dentist, from New York, and they all wanted to meet me. So all these invitations came to me from these elite Negroes, inviting me to dinner and to their clubs—invitations just for me.

I thought this was rude beyond belief. So I turned all those invitations down. I would write a note back and say, "No thank you, but I am a guest of Mary Watson, and I think it would be inappropriate for me to be your guest without her presence as well." My trip lasted several weeks, and finally they wore down and invited Mary, and so we went. So you see, I helped break some of these elite clubs in Jamaica.

Mary showed me the whole island from top to bottom. We walked, rode bicycles, drove these old rutted roads—just like North Carolina—all around the island. It was a beautiful place and very relaxing. They did everything the slow way.

I'll tell you another thing about Jamaica that I learned. It was a poor place, a very poor place. The poor folks were the poorest I'd ever seen. I remember when we pulled in the harbor, all these children were diving in the water. I thought they were just having a good time. And Mary said, "No, they're diving for pennies. They're looking for pennies that the tourists throw for them into the water." Now, that just about broke my heart.

Not long after I came back to the States, I had money problems of my own. The Depression was getting deeper and deeper, and money got tighter and tighter. Then one day I was walking down the street in Harlem, and I noticed something funny. I saw all these papers just blowing down the street. I reached down and grabbed one of those pieces of paper, and do you know what? They were *my papers*—records from my dental office. I had been dispossessed.

I ran all the way to my office and found that the landlord had put all my things in boxes and just left them on the sidewalk. And the wind was just a-carrying everything away. We were behind on the rent. Hap got thrown out, too.

One thing about us Delanys—we were the stubbornest things alive. We just kept a-going, no matter what. Well, as soon as Hap and me could scrape up the money for the rent, we moved right back in. Well, what do you think happened? The landlord threw us out again, about a year later, for the same reason. But we always got back on our own two feet. Yes, sir.

Sadie was not too affected by the Depression. You'd think everyone would be, and that was pretty much true. But Sadie was a teacher with the New York City Board of Education. She had a steady paycheck through the entire Depression.

Now me, I was in a different situation. My patients had no money to pay me. Things were bad enough for most colored folks before that Great Depression roared in like some old hurricane. When times are good for white people, things are tolerable for colored folks. But when times are *bad* for white people, well, look out!

When that old stock market crashed, the next thing you knew, the world was falling apart. The newspapers were full of stories of rich white men who had committed suicide, jumping out of buildings—things like that. I can't imagine having so little faith in the Lord and so much faith in money that you would end your life over a little thing like losing your fortune.

Well, a lot of these white folks were *lost* without their big money when that Great Depression hit. And they didn't have a clue how to live through hard times. Us Negroes, well, we knew what it was like to hit bottom, anyway. For my people hardship was a way of life. The Great Depression was just another crisis.

No matter how bad things got, I never actually went hungry. Sadie and Mama would cook a meal for almost nothing; that is the truth. You never saw people who can live cheaper than we can.

In fact, I *fed* people during the Depression. My patients would show up and say, "Dr. Bessie, I'm *hungry.*" And I'd always give them something—a piece of bread or whatever I had for myself.

Sadie was a little more practical about helping folks than I was. Sadie helped many, many people—one person at a time. But me—well, I always had everybody's problems on my shoulders, and honey, sometimes I got in over my head. Lord, I never knew when to draw the line.

One day one of my patients came to me in tears. And I said, "Why, what is the matter?" She told me she was pregnant and did not want the child. She had two other children. She said, "Oh, Dr. Bessie, I can't afford to feed another child. I am going to have an abortion." That was illegal then, of course, but you could still get it done.

She cried and cried. And I blurted out, "Don't do it. Why, I'll raise that child. If you carry that child, I will even pay the doctor. And then I will raise that child myself."

Whatever possessed me to say that, I don't know. I thought, Well, now I've really gone and gotten myself into a mess. Well, I would have stuck to what I said, but being a little psychic, I had a hunch that once this woman had the baby, she would not give it up. And what do you think happened? One day, just before she dropped that baby, she said, "Oh, Dr. Bessie, will you ever forgive me? I just can't give you this baby. I can't give it up." Lord, was I ever relieved!

It turned out to be a baby girl, and she was named Bessie after me. And when little Bessie grew up, her mama told her what had happened, and little Bessie has always been grateful to me. Once she told me that I was like a second mother to her.

Sometimes to this day my doorbell will ring, and there is Bessie with a pail and some rags, and she just shows up and cleans all my knickknacks, cleans up my house. I can't stop her. At Christmas she puts me and Sadie in her car and drives us around New York City to see the lights, takes us to Harlem to see all our old stomping grounds. So you can see why I call her my daughter. People who don't know nothing about my courting days—don't know I lived a clean life—they kind of raise their eyebrows when I talk about my "daughter." But I don't care.

I kept my practice going during the Depression, although now I wonder how I did. Then one day in the middle of the Depression one of my patients went to sign up for help from the government, and she asked me to go along to keep her company. They gave her some kind of little job. And I wasn't planning on this at all, but I said, "Say, do you have anything for me? I am a licensed dentist, and I'm not doing so well myself." Well, next thing I knew, the government agreed to set up a clinic near City Hall, with me running it. And so I worked there in the mornings, for the rest of the Depression, for a small salary. And in the afternoon I would go back to my office and work there. So the government helped, but it wasn't no handout. No, sir! Let me make that clear. It was work for hire. I have never taken a handout from the government in my life.

Part VI

Ties That Bind

THE stock market crash of October 1929 seemed remote to many residents of Harlem, like a foreign war being waged at the faraway tip of Manhattan Island. By the early 1930s, however, the Great Depression had devastated Harlem. There were four or five times more unemployed people in Harlem than in any other section of New York.

As the Depression deepened, evictions from offices and apartments occurred on every block with alarming regularity. It was not uncommon to see entire families digging through garbage for scraps of food. Government work programs brought some relief, but Harlem, along with the rest of the country, did not recover until America entered World War II, which spurred a manufacturing boom and stimulated the economy.

Harlemites embraced World War II with the same patriotic fervor as the rest of the nation. Women knitted socks and sweaters for the troops, volunteers worked as air-raid wardens, and just about everyone who could find a few yards of unpaved earth grew a victory garden.

It was an anxious time, and all eyes were on Europe, Africa, and Asia. For the Delany sisters, however, an unfolding personal tragedy kept their focus very much at home.

Sadie and Bessie

By this time we had a heap of nieces and nephews, and we loved them all dearly. But one of them, Little Hubie, had a special place in our hearts. He was a spastic child. He was damaged when he was born. Little Hubie was the greatest tragedy of our lives.

When we were growing up, there were a lot of children born sickly. Children who were damaged were not institutionalized the way they are today. At least among colored families that was the way it was. We don't know about white folks. But among colored folks you took care of your own.

We had never had anyone in our family that was damaged until Little Hubie was born. He was our sister Julia's only child. About ten years earlier Julia had followed Bessie and me to New York. She was a gifted musician and graduated from The Juilliard School. Her specialty was piano, which she taught when she graduated from college.

Julia always had an eye for very attractive men. We would say to her, "Now, Julia, you really must look for qualities beyond appearance." But she just couldn't help herself. Fortunately for her, she married a good-looking man who *also* happened to be nice. His name was Cecil Bourne, and he was a photographer.

Well, Julia and Cecil wanted a family, but Julia had a hard time. She became pregnant with twins, which they took from her because she nearly died. So when she became pregnant again, we were happy for her but scared. We all told the doctor that Julia was to come first. When the baby came, he was big, and the doctor used forceps. The baby, Hubert Delany Bourne, was born damaged.

At first Julia didn't see that the baby was damaged. But by the time he was one year of age, we knew he was not normal. Little Hubie couldn't walk, so Julia pushed him around in a carriage.

Still, he was a very beautiful child and easy to love; he was very charming in his own way. Why, people said they never saw a child with such beautiful, expressive eyes.

Since Julia was our sister, we tried to help her with Little Hubie. We tried to deal with the problem as we always did—as a family. We prayed a great deal, and we did not give up.

We had Little Hubie enrolled in a program that was probably the best in the world at that time for little spastic children. It was at Columbia—actually a school at the hospital for these children. The instructor gave us great hope because he himself was spastic but had managed to grow up and live a full life. We thought, If he can do it, then Little Hubie can, too. What we didn't grasp was that Hubie had problems that no one could diagnose or treat.

It just never occurred to us that Little Hubie would die. We all had this idea that he would be all right someday. We just thought that with enough prayer, enough love, and enough determination we would overcome this. But it wasn't part of God's plan. It was a shock to us.

It was pneumonia that finally took Little Hubie from us. He was ten years old when he died. The date was the seventh of March, 1943. To this day we always celebrate his birthday on June 10. Bessie still has his blanket on her bed and sleeps with it every night.

Little Hubie's death humbled us. We were sort of cocky before that. We thought we could do anything, fix any problem. We were not afraid of adversity. We were Delanys! After Little Hubie we realized you can't always get what you want in life.

You can get very close to God, tilling the soil. When the government asked people to grow victory gardens to help the war effort, we were only too happy to oblige. We knew it would help us get over Little Hubie.

During World War II we moved to 80 Edgecombe Avenue, a very fashionable section of Harlem, on a street with beautiful brownstones. It was a brick building, six stories high, with tile floors in all the hallways and hardwood floors in the apartments. There was no doorman, but the front door was kept locked, and there were mailboxes inside in the lobby. We felt lucky to get an apartment there. Ours was on the second floor.

But there really was no room to grow a substantial garden. So our cousins in the Bronx said it would be okay to use a vacant lot next to their property. We went up there as often as we could, and grew the best victory garden in the neighborhood.

Our brother Manross had made a career of the army, and so he was swept right up in World War II. He helped build the Burma Road. Now, Manross had an experience during World War II that made him very bitter, very angry. The army was still segregated then, but Manross's unit had been situated near a white unit, and somehow Manross saved some white fella's life. This white fella was also from North Carolina, and when Manross told him he was going home soon on leave, his new buddy told him to be sure to stop by and see his folks. Well, when poor Manross got there, he knocked on the door, but those white folks wouldn't let him in. They didn't want their neighbors to see a Negro coming to their front door. They told him to go around to the *back.* Manross was very deeply hurt by that experience.

When the war ended, people went wild in New York. We went to church and prayed. Thank the Lord, the war was finally done! It was a terrible, terrible thing, though, that they used that bomb. They said the war would have dragged on forever without it. But it was like man had lost his mind altogether that day.

After the war we didn't want to give up our victory garden. We started thinking about moving from Harlem to the Bronx. Why, wouldn't it be nice to live where Mama could have a garden?

Well, that's exactly what we did. We bought a little cottage in the North Bronx, next to our victory garden. There was lots of vacant land there then, and trees and shrubs. It was like the country.

The first thing we did was to hire a man to put a porch on our little cottage. He laughed at us. He said, "You're going to put a porch on that little old two-room cottage?" And we were very annoyed at him. We said, "Mister, we're from North Carolina, and we've been cooped up in apartments since the First World War.

Now we've got this cottage out in the country, and where we're from, a house ain't a home unless it has got itself a porch."

So we got ourselves a porch. And it meant that no matter how bad the weather, we were able to make sure Mama got her walk every day. Mama was getting very elderly, getting on ninety years old, and we wanted her to live forever. So we made sure she got her exercise every day. When the weather was nice, we would each take her by the arm, on either side, and we would walk around the neighborhood. By this time we were getting older ourselves. One little boy yelled at us, "Look. *Three* grandmas going for a walk." We thought it was funny, but it was true. We were getting old, too.

Soon we started having trouble keeping Mama in line. Our little cottage was equipped only with propane gas, and we were afraid Mama would burn herself up. When we left for our jobs in the morning, we would say, "Now, Mama, don't you go cooking a hot meal while we're away." And when we'd come home, she'd have a hot meal ready for us. She didn't listen to us one bit.

Mama also kept losing her pension check. She started hiding it, and then she couldn't find it. And she wouldn't like to admit that she had lost it. So she would wait until no one was around except Sadie. Then she would come up to Sadie and whisper, "I have misplaced my check. Can you help me find it?" Sometimes they'd have to take the whole house apart to locate that check.

It was getting so we couldn't count on Mama's judgment anymore, and we would rush home from our jobs in fear every day. Finally we decided that one of us was going to have to quit working and take care of Mama. What else could we do?

Bessie

WELL, it was obvious that I was the one who should quit my job, even though Sadie was a mama's child. We sat down and thought it through financially. If Sadie continued to work until 1960, she would get a hundred and fifty dollars a month from her pension with the New York City Board of Education. We figured that the three of us, living together, could do okay on a hundred and fifty dollars a month. And Mama got fifteen dollars a month from

Papa's pension. Mama was so funny about that fifteen dollars. She was so proud of it, you'd have thought it was fifteen *million.*

I was a dentist, working independently, and I had no pension plan. So it was settled. I was to close my practice. Truth is, I was only fifty-nine years old, and I had planned to work for many years yet. But once the decision was made, I accepted it.

I remember being at a dinner party just before I retired. There was a woman there, a very flashy, important Negro. She said to me in front of all these people, "You're going to give up your *career* to take care of your *mama?*" And I said, "Honey, let me tell you something. If you had my mama, you wouldn't think *twice.*"

I was never much of a housekeeper, but I set out to make that little cottage nicer than it had ever been. I polished the brass fixtures in the bathroom until they gleamed. Why, one of my little nieces told the whole neighborhood that we had gold fixtures. They were so bright, she thought they were gold.

Mama had been a perfect housekeeper, and I thought that's what she wanted. She would say, "Bessie, why don't you just sit down here next to me?" And I would say, "In a minute, Mama, when I'm done shaking out the rugs," or whatever. But she didn't want brass fixtures that gleamed like gold; she wanted *me.* She was an old lady, and she wanted her child to just sit with her, to be near her. Now that I am very old, I understand this. I say to Sadie, "What ever possessed me to try to make that little cottage perfect? Why didn't I just spend more time with Mama?"

Mama was still full of spunk right up to the end. Why, one time Hubert took Mama to the Statue of Liberty, and they raced each other down all those steps! I think Mama was ninety years old at the time. Well, when I heard about it, I really let Hubert have it. I said, "What in the world were you doing, letting Mama run like that? What if she had a heart attack or something?" I was really steaming. I don't know what got into those two, but it was awfully silly.

But Hubert also gave Mama her greatest moment as an old lady. He had been the attorney and adviser for the singer Marian Anderson. That was back in 1939, when the Daughters of the American Revolution kept her from singing in Constitution Hall in Washington, just because she was colored. And then Mrs. Roosevelt intervened and arranged for Marian to sing at the Lincoln Memorial.

Oh, that Mrs. Roosevelt was ahead of her time. To this day we admire her more than any other famous person.

So as a surprise for Mama, Hubert arranged for her to meet Eleanor Roosevelt. When we came into the room, there she was, and she jumped up like a jackrabbit to greet Mama, taking her hand. It was pretty wonderful to see the former First Lady jump up, so respectfullike, to greet Mama, an old colored lady.

Sadie and I were in charge of Mama's happiness, but all the children fussed over her. One time one of the brothers—I won't say who—was naughty and hadn't been seeing enough of Mama. She came right out and told him she felt neglected. He said, "Why, Mama, is that really the way you feel?" She said yes, it was. So from that day until the day she died, he visited her every single day, and if he was sick or away, he would send flowers or call her just to say hello. Mama was the queen bee.

But hard times were coming. First Manross died of a heart attack on November 3, 1955. When it happened, I called Lemuel on the telephone and said, "Lemuel, sit down. I have some bad news." He said, "Okay, I'm ready. It's Mama, isn't it?" He thought for sure I was going to tell him that Mama had gone. He said, "Manross? Manross?"

Losing Manross was a shock to all of us. He was the first of our generation to die, and we knew there would be more dying, because we Delanys tend to die in threes. Strange thing is, it was Lemuel who went to glory next. He died of a heart attack on January 9, 1956. Coming so soon after Manross had died, it was a terrible blow to poor Mama. She hadn't gotten over Manross yet, and I had to sit her down and tell her about Lemuel, and she cried and cried. She wasn't just sad; she was kind of angry. I don't think she ever expected to outlive any of her children. After she lost Manross and Lemuel, I guess it was only natural that Mama was ready to go. But to tell you what a silly old gal I am, I did not realize when Mama was leaving us. I did not realize my mama was dying.

We knew it would have to happen eventually because, after all, Mama was ninety-five years old. The day it happened was the second of June, 1956. Mama had been ailing and stayed in bed that day. My nephew Lloyd was there visiting, and he was sitting at the foot of the bed. Sadie was sitting at the head of the bed, and I was kind of hovering around. We noticed that Mama was breathing kind of heavy.

Sadie whispered to Lloyd, "Is she dying?" And he said, "I think so."

Now, I misunderstood what they said to each other. Even with all my medical training I didn't get what was going on. But Sadie knew; the mama's child could feel it in her bones. Silly me, I left the room and went out into the yard to feed my pet dogs and birds. Then Sadie came outside and said, "Bess, Mama's gone."

Well, in ten minutes' time all of the Delanys were swarming around our little cottage. The doctor came and pronounced Mama dead. Our brother Sam, an undertaker, drove up from Harlem and carried Mama away. Our sister Julia climbed into Mama's bed and stayed there all night. She wouldn't come out.

Bad as Mama's death was for me, it was ten times worse for Sadie. Poor Sadie just cried for weeks and weeks. Every time we sat down for a meal, with Mama's chair sitting there empty, the tears would come streaming down Sadie's face. Why, I wasn't sure she would make it. I thought she might die, too.

I don't think Mama would have been at all surprised that Sadie and I have kept living this long. We learned a lot from her about being old. Mama set a good example. She took care of herself, and she was surrounded by love.

I'll tell you something kind of funny. It had annoyed Mama that when Manross died, they made his wife return the pension check he had in his pocket. She thought that was mean. So she said, "If I die and I have a check in my pocket, Sadie, you must promise me that you will run to the bank and cash it and keep that money."

So while Mama was ailing, Sadie did just that. And do you know that the pension company sent a letter immediately? They had seen Mama's obituary in *The New York Times*—that Bishop Delany's widow had died—and they sent a letter that said, "Please return the last check." And Sadie wrote to them, "Sorry, but it was cashed."

We always did what Mama asked.

Sadie

Now, you might ask, what happens to a mama's child when her mama passes on? Well, it was worse than anything, except maybe when Little Hubie died. Little Hubie's death was a tragedy because he didn't get much of a chance at living. We knew Mama would have to go to glory sometime; she was a very old lady. Still, her passing hurt me something terrible.

I was so dependent on my mama. Why, as a young girl, I remember my mama had to go to see her parents for two weeks. I was a plump child, and Mr. Hunter, the white principal of the school, was trying to help me lose weight. Well, I lost eight pounds in those two weeks. And Mr. Hunter said to me, "Good heavens, child, what is wrong with you?" And I just burst into tears and said, "It's because my mama has gone away!"

Until the day she died, Mama called me her shadow. So when she died, I thought, Maybe I should die myself. I guess I was—what's that word people use today?—depressed.

But Mama was gone, and I had to think about the world in a completely different way. Bessie says that for the first time in my life I seemed to come into my own as an individual person. I was sixty-seven years old.

Bessie and I just figured we would keep living at the cottage in the Bronx. We didn't have any other plans. But the neighborhood there was not what it had been. Even before Mama had died, things had gone downhill.

You see, they put this housing project in. Why, the city had wanted to tear down our little cottage and put the housing project there. But Bessie and I filed a lawsuit. We asked that they salvage our little cottage, move it across the street.

On the day our case went to court, I was at school and couldn't get away. Bessie went to meet our lawyer at the courthouse, but he didn't show up. And you know what happened? Bessie just handled our side of things by herself. She told the judge that the cottage was all we had in this world and we wanted Mama to die there. And couldn't the city just move that old cottage across the street to a vacant lot?

I guess she was convincing, because she won the case. But when the day came for the city to move the house, they were very spiteful and mean. They moved it halfway. That's right. The workers left our little two-room cottage in the middle of the road overnight! They said, "You gals are going to have to find somewhere else to sleep tonight." Well, we slept there anyway out of sheer stubbornness. One end of the house was up on jacks, and the house was tilted at a weird angle, so our feet were above our heads when we went to sleep. Those men were astonished when they came the next day. It never occurred to them that we could be that stubborn.

Anyway, they went and built this housing project, with us living right across the street from it. Some of the children from the housing project got into trouble. You can't just take people who don't have anything, pack them in a bunch of buildings, and expect it's going to all work out somehow.

Now, Bessie and I did not have trouble from those children. Everybody on our side of the street would get upset because the children would do things like steal all the fruit from their fruit trees. And people would say, "Why don't those children bother *your* fruit trees?" The reason was that we were nicer to the children. We went out there and said to them, "The fruit on our peach trees isn't ripe yet, so please leave it alone. But when it is ripe, you come by and we'll share it with you." And we did. And those children never harmed us or our trees or anything we owned.

We loved the children in that neighborhood, but they were in our hair all the time. Part of it was our own fault. At Halloween, Bessie and I would make candied apples and homemade doughnuts, and the children went wild.

But we had no peace. We never had a meal at that cottage when we weren't interrupted. The doorbell would ring, and there would be a child wanting something. I remember once, it was a little boy holding a robin with a broken wing. And the child was crying and hoping Miss Sadie and Dr. Bessie could fix that bird. Bessie said to me, "It isn't the bird that needs attention as much as the *child.*" We never denied those children the attention they needed, but it just about wore us out.

Then one day Bessie went to visit our brother Hap at his new home in Mount Vernon, in the suburbs. While she was there, Hap's wife, Audrey, put this idea in Bessie's head that maybe the two of us ought to get out of the Bronx and move into their neighborhood in Westchester County.

Tell you the truth, we didn't think we could afford it. It was a white neighborhood. But then one day Audrey told Bessie that the house at the end of the street was for sale. Bessie sat down and figured out how much the taxes were, and so on, and realized that we could do it if we lived very very cheap. So we went ahead and bought the house.

Not only was our house at the end of a dead-end street but it faced away from the other houses, with a view of New York City. There was plenty of room for a great big garden, and since it was a two-family house, we moved into one side and rented out the other. For a long time we had our own kin living next door, including our sister Laura and her husband, Ed, before they moved to California. So it has been a safe and peaceful little haven for us.

Bessie says now that she had an ulterior motive in moving us out of the Bronx. She says she didn't think I would ever get over Mama's death and that maybe by moving away and starting over, it would help. I think she was right.

Part VII

Outliving the Rebby Boys

The decades following the end of World War II were an era of new hope for black Americans. In 1948 President Harry Truman desegregated the armed forces. Several years later—with the Supreme Court's ruling on *Brown* v. *Board of Education of Topeka, Kansas*—desegregation of schools became the law of the land.

Then, on December 1, 1955, a department store tailor named Rosa Parks single-handedly assailed the Jim Crow laws by not giving up her seat to a white man on a bus in Montgomery, Alabama. Her protest sparked a revolution, spearheaded by the Reverend Martin Luther King, Jr.—a decade of protests against racial discrimination at the voting booth and in schools, employment, and public accommodations. Those demonstrations would help secure passage of landmark civil rights legislation guaranteeing black Americans their full constitutional prerogatives.

But while the battle for integration was raging in the South, de facto segregation persisted in the North. Housing was one of the most visible arenas of struggle, as black people were frequently barred from moving into white neighborhoods. And now the Delanys—entering retirement and so sidelined during the years of civil rights demonstrations—joined the advance guard of a different integration movement.

TODAY all of Mount Vernon, it seems, is mostly Negro, but in 1957 it was mostly white. I don't think either Sadie or I had ever lived among so many white folks before, and it was a bit of a shock to us. Of course, we were a bit of a shock to *them.*

Hap had broken the neighborhood; he was the first colored person to move in there. They wouldn't let him buy a house. People blocked that. You know, the white real estate agents found excuses not to show him houses in certain neighborhoods—things like that. So do you know what Hap did? He *built* a house. He just went and bought a piece of land right smack in the middle of the nicest white neighborhood, and before the neighbors could figure out what was happening, they were pouring the foundation.

Hap had some trouble for a while after they moved in. More than once some white folks cut the tires on his Cadillac. But what those folks didn't understand was that Hap was a Delany, and the harder they tried to push him out, the more he dug in his heels. And his experience did not discourage Sadie and me from moving there. We figured, Why shouldn't we live where we want to?

There is only one white family left in our neighborhood now. And you know, they recently had a terrible blow: their son died tragically. He was about twenty years old. Now, that family had always been suspicious of us colored folks. I brought them some vegetables from my garden a long time ago, and they made it clear they didn't want to be friends. They never thanked me or anything. They were pretty rude.

Now, when that boy died, they sure were surprised at how the colored folks reacted on the block. We just went on over there quietly and brought food and flowers. Do you know what? That family sent every one of us a thank-you note. That surprised *us.*

Some white folks believe that Negroes bring down a neighborhood because they don't keep up their property. Well, in our case we had the neatest, spiffiest-looking yard on the block. Sadie and I set out to have the best garden you could find, and it has given us a great deal of pleasure. Of course, we had lots of flowers—roses, you name it—but we also grew vegetables, like Kentucky wonder-beans, which we would eat or can for the winter months.

Our biggest problem with that old house was that we did not have the money to furnish it. We didn't want to go spending all our savings on furniture. We didn't know how long we would live, and we thought if we took after Mama and lasted a long time, we would need that hard-time money in the bank. Yes, sir!

So I'll tell you what we did. We started buying furniture from the Salvation Army. Now, we didn't mind having things secondhand. After all, we grew up wearing secondhand clothes that Mama bought at the mission store. In those days rich people gave a lot of good furniture to the Salvation Army.

Next to the Salvation Army was a day-old-bread store. This became Sadie's job—to shop at the day-old-bread store. She knew what was good and what was not, just by looking at it. And honey, we saved a ton of money over the years, shopping at that bread store. We ain't too proud to eat day-old bread.

It was while we were shopping at the Salvation Army and the day-old-bread store that we heard that President Kennedy had been shot. They had a radio on in the Salvation Army, and when I heard the news, I ran to the bread store and told Sadie. It was such a shock that someone would kill our young President like that. It made my heart bleed.

After that it seemed like all the leaders were getting shot—Malcolm X, Martin Luther King, Robert Kennedy. Sadie and I were so distressed about it. I'm glad that Ted Kennedy didn't run for President, because I think he'd have gotten himself killed, too. Ted Kennedy has made some serious mistakes in his life, but Sadie and I decided he must be a nice boy, because we heard on the radio that he visits his mother all the time up in Massachusetts. And Sadie says, "If he's nice to his mama, then he's okay by me."

As far as Sadie and I are concerned, Martin Luther King was an angel. He just dropped from heaven. And there hasn't been anyone as special since then. Now, I know that Martin Luther King was not perfect. There are all these stories coming out about him now; they may not be true at all. And if they are? Well, I never expected him to be perfect. He was a man, after all.

One of the biggest regrets of my life was that Sadie and I didn't go to Washington for the big march in the summer of 1963. I would have loved to have heard Martin Luther King give his "I Have a

Dream" speech. We were already old ladies at the time—in our seventies—and some younger relatives talked us out of going. They thought we'd be overwhelmed in those crowds.

The civil rights movement was a time when we thought, Maybe now it will finally happen. Maybe now our country will finally grow up, come to terms with this race mess. But it seems like the momentum was lost when the Vietnam War happened. It was like all the energy of the young people and the focus of the country got shifted away from civil rights.

But it wasn't just Vietnam that slowed down the progress we made in the civil rights movement, in my opinion. It had a lot to do with lack of leadership after Martin Luther King died. Things have kind of slid downhill as far as equality is concerned. The 1980s were the worst. Yes, sir!

Sadie and I are registered Independents, and we usually favor the Democrats, like Mr. Clinton. We loved Jimmy Carter because he was an honest man and his heart was in the right place. And I liked Harry Truman; I surely liked that "Buck Stops Here" business.

I'll tell you something, honey. I would have made a very good President. That's right. *Me.* I would have done well. I'm honest and I'm tough and I could get the job done. Yes, sir!

The first thing I would do if I was President would be to say that people over one hundred years of age no longer have to pay taxes. Ha ha! Lord knows I've paid my share.

I guess it will be a thousand years before a colored person is elected President of the United States. Sadie disagrees with me. She says, "There will be a Negro President someday."

See, I think white people would rather die than vote for a Negro President. I predict there will be a white woman President before there is a Negro President. And if a Negro is elected President? That person will be a Negro *woman.*

Sadie

ONE thing I've noticed since I got this old is that I have started to dream in color. I'll remember that someone was wearing a red dress or a pink sweater—something like that. I also dream more than I used to, and when I wake up, I feel tired. I'll say to

Bessie, "I sure am tired this morning. I was teaching all night in my dreams!"

Bessie was always the big dreamer. She was always talking about what she dreamed the night before. She has this same dream over and over again, about a party she went to on Cotton Street in Raleigh way back when. Nothing special happens; she just keeps dreaming she's there. In our dreams we are always young.

Truth is, we both forget we're old. This happens all the time. I'll reach for something real quick, just like a young person, and realize my reflexes are not what they once were. It surprises me, but I can't complain. I still do what I want, pretty much.

These days I am usually the first one awake in the morning. And the first thing I do when I open my eyes is smile, and then I say, "Thank you, Lord, for another day."

If I don't hear Bessie get up, I'll go into her room and wake her. Sometimes I have to knock on her headboard. And she opens her eyes and says, "Oh Lord, another day?" I don't think Bessie would get up at all sometimes if it weren't for me. She stays up late in her room and listens to these talk-radio shows, and she doesn't get enough sleep.

In the mornings, Monday through Friday, we do our yoga exercises. I started doing yoga exercises with Mama about forty years ago. Mama was starting to shrink up and get bent down, and I started exercising with her to straighten her up again.

I kept doing my yoga exercises even after Mama died. Well, when Bessie turned eighty, she decided that I looked better than her. So she decided she would start doing yoga, too. So we've been doing our exercises together ever since.

Exercise is very important. A lot of older people don't exercise at all. Another thing that is terribly important is diet. About thirty years ago Bessie and I started eating much more healthy foods. We don't eat that fatty southern food very often. When we do, we feel like we can't move.

Every morning, after we do our yoga, we each take a clove of garlic, chop it up, and swallow it whole. If you swallow it all at once, there is no odor. We also take a teaspoon of cod-liver oil. Bessie thinks it's disgusting. But one day I said, "Now, dear little sister, if you want to keep up with me, you're going to have to start taking it every day and stop complainin'." And she's been good ever since.

These days I do most of the cooking, and Bessie does the serving. We eat our big meal of the day at noon. In the evening we usually have a milk shake for dinner, and then we go upstairs and watch *MacNeil/Lehrer* on the TV.

After that we say our prayers. We say prayers in the morning and before we go to bed. It takes a long time to pray for everyone because it's a very big family—we have fifteen nieces and nephews still living, plus all their children and grandchildren. We pray for each one, living and dead. The ones that Bessie doesn't approve of get extra prayers. Bessie can be very critical. I always have to say to her, "Everybody has to be themselves, Bessie. Live and let live."

Bessie can be very kind, though she usually saves her kind side for children and animals. She has a little dog, who belonged to someone in the neighborhood who didn't want him anymore. He's part Chihuahua and I don't know what else, and he has some nasty habits, but Bessie loves him.

Before Bessie got her little dog, we had a stray cat we named Mr. Delany. He had been run over by a car and had crawled up on our doorstep. So we brought the kitty in the house, rubbed salve into his cuts, and splinted him up. We fed him by hand and fussed over him day and night for two weeks. And you know what? He was just fine. But one day he ran off. Bessie's still grieving for that old cat. She says, "I know he must be dead, or he would have come back."

If only I could get Bessie to be as sweet to people as she is to her animals. Bessie can be a little bit nasty sometimes. She thinks it's her God-given duty to tell people the truth. I say to her, "Bessie, don't you realize people don't want to hear the truth?"

One time a priest was over here visiting us, and I noticed he'd put on a little weight. I thought to myself, Uh-oh, I bet she says something to him. Well, when he was leaving, Bessie said, "Now, Father, it seems to me you are getting fat. You've got to lose some weight." He laughed and said yes, he knew he needed to go on a diet. When he left, I said to Bessie, "What did you have to go and say that for?" And she said, "I care about people's health, and sometimes people need somebody to give it to 'em straight."

Bessie does not mince words, and when she has a strong opinion, she's not shy. Not long ago one of our nieces died, and somebody was over here describing the place where she died. It was called a hospice, and it sounded awfully nice. I said, "Well, maybe when my time comes, y'all should take me to a hospice." Bessie got real mad. She said, "You ain't dying in no hospice. You ain't dying nowhere but upstairs in yo' bed!"

Over the years we've buried a lot of people. Even the generation younger than us is starting to die off. I don't know why I'm still here, but I don't fret over it. It's in God's hands.

You know, when you are this old, you don't know if you're going to wake up in the morning. But I don't worry about dying, and neither does Bessie. We are at peace. You do kind of wonder, When's it going to happen? That's why you learn to love each and every day, child.

Truth is, I've gotten so old I'm starting to get a little *bold.* Not long ago some young men started hanging out in front of our house. They were part of a gang from the Bronx, and they just thought our dead-end street here was a good spot to play basketball and do drugs and I don't know what all.

Well, Bessie said to me, "I'll go out there and get rid of them." And I said, "No, Bess. For once I'm going to handle it. You stay in the house."

I went out the back door and around to the sidewalk, where they were hanging out. And I said, "You boys better get out of here."

They were kind of surprised. And then one of them said, "You can't make us leave. This is a public street."

And I said, "Yes, it's a public street, but it's not a *park,* so get moving."

And this fella said to me, "Just how do you think you're going to make us go?"

I pointed to my house. I said, "My sister is inside, and she has her hand on the phone to call the police." Of course, this was a little white lie, because we don't have a phone, but they didn't know that.

Well, they grumbled and complained, and finally they left. They came back about a week later, and our neighbor ran them off. And they never did come back.

Bessie was kind of surprised that I took those boys on like that. To tell you the truth, so was I.

Bessie

I WAS mighty proud of Sadie for taking on those no-good fellas and running them on out of there. It just goes to show she can be tough when she puts her mind to it. I said to her, "Sadie, our grandpa Miliam surely would have been proud."

I was just thinking about Mr. Miliam this morning. There was a cute little squirrel in my yard, and I said to it, "Oh, you better be glad Mr. Miliam and his gun ain't around, 'cause he'd shoot you and fry you up for his breakfast."

I wonder what Mr. Miliam would think of his granddaughters living this long. Why, I suppose he'd get a kick out of it. I know he'd have lived longer if Grandma hadn't died. Sometimes you need a reason to keep living.

Tell you the truth, I wouldn't be here without Sadie. We are companions. But I'll tell you something else. Sadie has taken on this business of getting old like it's a big *project*. She has it all figured out about diet and exercise. Sometimes I just don't want to do it, but she is my big sister, and I really don't want to disappoint her. Funny thing about Sadie is she rarely gets—what's the word?—depressed. She is an easygoing type.

Now, honey, I get the blues sometimes. It's a shock to me to be this old. Sometimes, when I realize I am a hundred and one years old, it hits me right between the eyes. I say, "Oh Lord, how did this happen?" Turning one hundred was the worst birthday of my life. I wouldn't wish it on my worst enemy. Turning a hundred and one was not so bad. Once you're past that century mark, it's just not as shocking.

There's a few things I have had to give up. I gave up driving a while back. I guess I was in my late eighties. That was terrible. Another thing I gave up on was cutting back my trees so we have a view of the New York City skyline to the south. Until I was ninety-eight years old, I would climb up on the ladder and saw those tree branches off so we had a view. I could do it perfectly well. Why pay somebody to do it? Then Sadie talked some sense into me, and I gave up doing it.

It's hard being old, because you can't always do everything you want, exactly as *you* want it done. When you get as old as we are, you have to struggle to hang on to your freedom, your independence. We try to pay people, even relatives, for whatever they buy for us, and gasoline for their car—things like that—so that we do not feel beholden to them.

Longevity runs in the family. I'm sure that's part of why we're still here. As a matter of fact, until recently there were still five of us, of the original ten children. Then Hubert went to glory on December 28, 1990, and Hap a few weeks later, in February 1991. Laura, our dear baby sister, passed on in August 1993. That leaves just me and Sadie.

You know what I've been thinking lately? All those people who were mean to me in my life—all those *rebby boys*—they have turned to dust, and this old gal is still here, along with sister Sadie.

We've outlived those old rebby boys.

That's justice!

They're turning in their graves while Sadie and me are getting the last word in this book. And honey, I surely do love getting the last word. I'm having my say, giving my opinion. Lord, ain't it good to be an *American*.

Truth is, I never thought I'd see the day when people would be interested in hearing what two old Negro women have to say. Life still surprises me. So maybe the last laugh's on *me*.

I'll tell you a little secret. I'm starting to get optimistic. I'm thinking, *Maybe I'll get into heaven after all.* Why, I've helped a lot of folks—even some white folks! I surely do have some redeeming qualities that must count for something. So I just might do it: I just might get into heaven. I may have to hang on to Sadie's heels, but I'll get there.

ABOUT THE AUTHORS

Amy Hill Hearth answers the door of the Delany sisters' house when a stranger knocks. Since their book made them celebrities, their co-author has become the Delanys' ad hoc agent, mail screener, confidante, door answerer—and friend. You have to promise to keep the address secret when you're granted an interview. It seems that every reporter in the country wants to beat a path to the sisters' door. Amy is also the palace guard.

Amy Hill Hearth with Dr. Bessie and Miss Sadie

Inside, the house is quiet, softly lit. Seated by the window, waiting, are Dr. Bessie, wearing a gray suit, her hair in a tight bun, and Miss Sadie, also wearing a gray suit but with a red baseball cap pulled down snug over her head.

There are piles of newspaper clippings, best-seller lists, fan mail heaped all around them. At first the Delanys may seem a bit overwhelmed by their success, which they never expected. But from the calm smiles and lively glint in their eyes, you can tell that they're not only safely above it all but they're getting a little kick out of it.

So how did they do it—three people writing a book together and still, apparently, talking to each other? "Mutual respect," Amy explains. "A good understanding of one another." As they worked, they got closer and closer. Something beyond friendship developed. They had similar values, the same approach to life. Something clicked. They meshed.

"She knows more about us than we do," says Dr. Bessie. "And *some* of the things, I'm glad I don't know."

And what about the rest of the Delany family? All told, the sisters have fifteen nieces and nephews. Extended family? "Oh, two or three hundred," Sadie estimates. Adds Bessie, "And they're coming out of the woodwork now."

You really can't blame them.

PHOTO: © BRIAN DOUGLAS

ILLUSTRATORS

Barbara Kiwak: *Fatal Cure*

Dahl Taylor: *The Wrong House*

Martin Hoffman: *Red Ink*

ACKNOWLEDGMENTS

Pages 490 (inset), 491 (inset), 534, 535, 536 (foreground), 537 (foreground): authors' collection.

Pages 490, 491: Brian Douglas.

Pages 536–537 (background): Photographs and Prints Division, Schomburg Center for Research in Black Culture, The New York Public Library Astor, Lenox and Tilden Foundations.

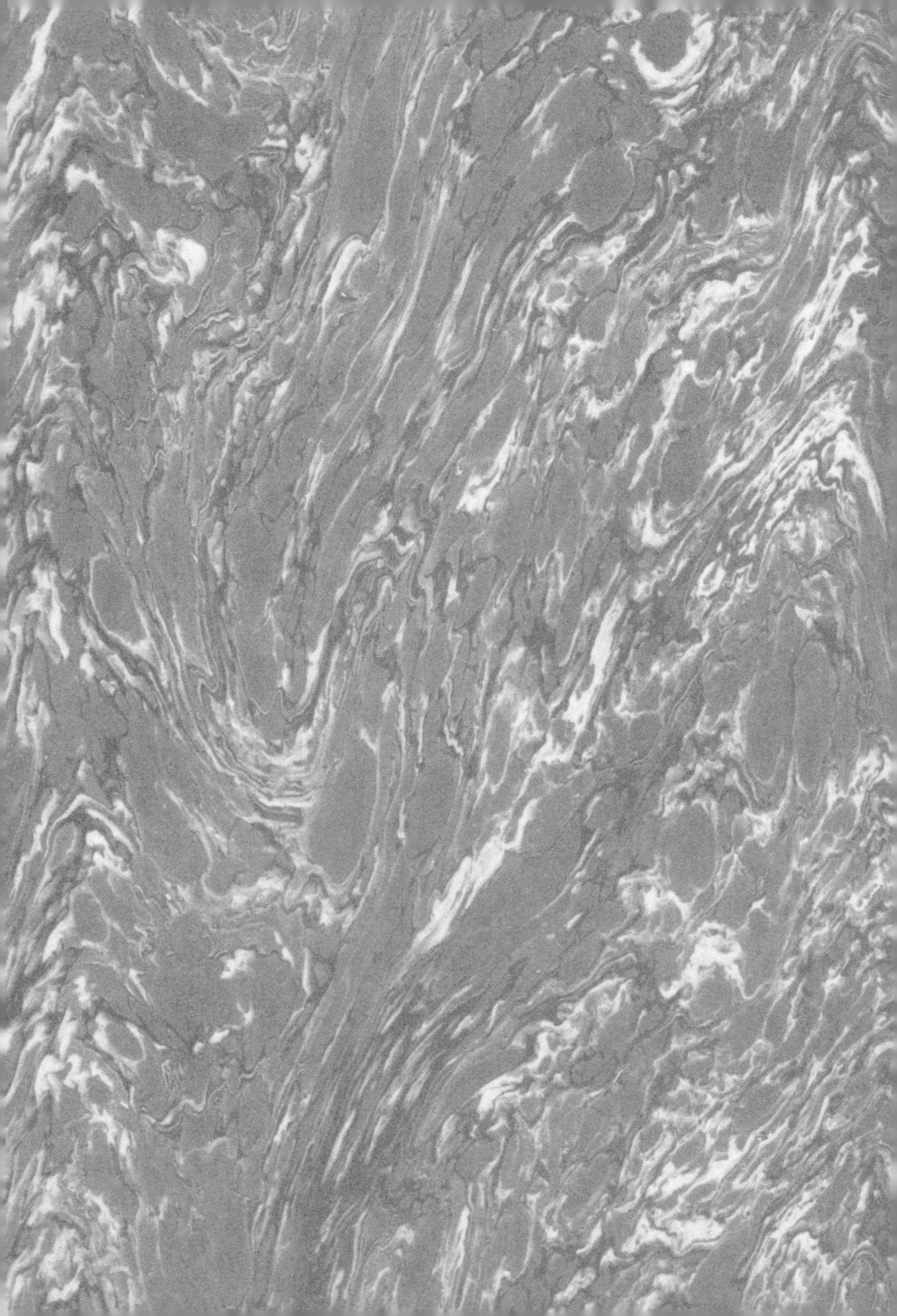